John D. MacDonald

FIVE COMPLETE TRAVIS McGEE NOVELS

❖

ABOUT THE AUTHOR

JOHN D. MACDONALD was born in 1916 in Sharon, Pennsylvania. He attended the University of Pennsylvania, received his B.S. from Syracuse University, and an M.B.A. in 1939 from Harvard. MacDonald served in the U.S. Army from 1940 to 1946, achieving the rank of Lt. Colonel.

MacDonald is the author of more than 60 volumes, including 18 books in the Travis McGee series, which are set in and around the Florida coast. His Travis McGee novel *The Green Ripper,* included in this volume, won the American Book Award for Best Mystery of 1979. John D. MacDonald lives in Sarasota, Florida.

John D. MacDonald

FIVE COMPLETE TRAVIS McGEE NOVELS

❖

A Tan and Sandy Silence

The Dreadful Lemon Sky

The Empty Copper Sea

The Green Ripper

Free Fall in Crimson

Avenel Books • New York

CONTENTS

❖

A Tan and Sandy Silence

❖

*To all the faithful readers
at the Northern Vancouver City Library*

*In northern Manitoba
a man saw a great bald eagle—
hanging from its neck,
teeth locked in skin and feathers,
the bleached skull of a weasel.*

JIM HARRISON
"A Year's Changes"

1

ON THE most beautiful day any April could be asked to come up with, I was kneeling in eight inches of oily water in the cramped bilge of Meyer's squatty little cabin cruiser, the *John Maynard Keynes,* taking his automatic bilge pump apart for the third time in an hour.

The socket wrench slipped, and I skinned yet another knuckle. Meyer stood blocking out a sizable piece of the deep blue sky. He stared down into the bilge and said, "Very inventive and very fluent. Nice mental images, Travis. Imagine one frail little bilge pump performing such an extraordinary act upon itself! But you began to repeat yourself toward the end."

"Would you like to crawl down in here and—"

He backed up a hasty half step. "I couldn't deprive you of the pleasure. You said you could fix it. Go ahead."

I got it apart again. I spun the little impeller blade and suddenly realized that maybe it turned too freely. Found the setscrew would take a full turn. Tightened it back down onto the shaft. Reassembled the crummy little monster, bolted it down underwater, heaved myself up out of the water, sat on the edge of the hatch, and had Meyer flip the switch. It started to make a nice steady *wheeeeeeng,* gouting dirty bilge water into the Bahia Mar yacht basin.

Mayer started to applaud, and I told him to save it until we found out if the adorable thing would turn itself the hell off like it says in the fine print. It took a good ten minutes to pump the water out. Then it went *weeeeeeng-guggle-chud.* Silence.

"Now cheer," I said.

"Hooray," he said mildly. "Thank you very much and hooray." I looked at him with exasperation and affection. My mild and bulky friend with the wise little blue eyes, bright and bemused, and with the bear hair, thatch black, curling out of the throat of his blue knit shirt.

"Another half inch of rain last night," I told him, "and you could have gone down like a stone."

He had stepped out of his bunk in the dark after the rain stopped and into ankle-deep water. He had sloshed over to my houseboat, *The Busted Flush,* and told me he had a small problem. At three in the morning we had toted my auxiliary pump over and set it on the dock and dropped the intake hose into his bilge. His home and refuge was very low in the water, the mooring lines taut enough to hum when plucked. By first light the *Keynes* was floating high again, and we could turn the pump off and carry it back. Now the repaired automatic bilge pump had taken out the last of the water, but he was going to live in dampness for quite a while.

"Perils of the sea," he said.

I stepped up onto the dock and squatted and began to rinse the grease and bilge water off my hands under the hose faucet. Meyer shaded his eyes and looked toward the *Flush*. "You've got a visitor, Travis. Isn't that what's-his-name?"

I stood up and stared. "It sure is. Good old what's-his-name. Harry Broll. Do you think that son of a bitch has come to try me again?"

"After the showing last time . . . was it two years ago?"

"At least."

"I think he's at least bright enough not to try again."

"Not the same way. But he did catch me with one very nice left. True, he broke his hand, but it was one to remember."

"Want company?"

"No, thanks."

Harry turned and saw me when I was about fifty feet away. He was big, and he had gotten bigger since I'd seen him last. More gut and more jowls. Not becoming. He wore a pale beige suit, a yellow shirt, and a chocolate-colored neckerchief with an ornate gold slip ring.

He raised his hands in the most primitive gesture of reassurance. Palms out. Sickly smile to go with it. As I came up to him, he said, "Hi, McGee." He put his hand out. I looked at it until he pulled it back. He tried to laugh. "Jesus, are you still sore?"

"I'm not sore, Harry. Why should we shake hands?"

"Look. I want to talk to you. Are you busy or anything?"

"What about?"

"About Mary. I know you've got no reason in the world to do me any favors. But this concerns . . . Mary's well-being."

"Is something wrong with her?"

"I don't know. I don't really know."

I studied him. He seemed concerned and upset. He had the pallor of desk work. His black hair had receded since I had seen him last. He said, "I couldn't think of anybody else to come to. I can say please if it'll help. Please?"

"Come on aboard."

"Thanks. Thanks a lot."

We went into the lounge. I had on an old pair of denim shorts and nothing else. The air conditioning cooled the sweat on my shoulders and chest. He looked around, nodding and beaming, and said, "Nice. Real nice. A nice way to live, huh?"

"Want a drink?"

"Bourbon, if you've got it."

"Got it."

"On the rocks."

I put out the bottle and the glass and said, glancing down at my soiled hands, "Ice is in the bin there. Help yourself while I clean up, Broll."

"Thanks. You sure keep yourself in shape, McGee. Wish I had the time. I guess I better make sure I have the time one of these days."

I shrugged and went forward, dropped the shorts into the hamper, and stepped into the oversized shower, thinking about Mary and wondering about her as I sudsed and scrubbed away the rest of the grime from the repair job. Miss Mary Dillon when I had known her. Then abruptly—maybe too abruptly—Mrs. Harry Broll. When I put my watch back on, I saw that it was nearly four o'clock. Meyer and I were invited for drinks at six aboard the *Jilly III*. I put on fresh slacks, an oyster-white sailcloth sport shirt, my ancient Mexican sandals. On the way back to the lounge I stopped in the galley and put some Plymouth on the rocks.

He was sitting on the yellow couch, and he had lit a small cigar with a white plastic mouthpiece. "It must really be something, being able to just take off any time you feel like it."

I slouched into a chair facing him, took a swallow of my drink, and put it on the coffee table. "You've got a problem, Harry?"

"About that time I made such a damn fool of myself . . ."

"Forget it."

"No. Please. Let me say something about that. Like they say, the first year of marriage is the hardest, right?"

"So they say."

"Well, I knew you and Mary were old friends. I couldn't help knowing that, right? I mean, you and Meyer came to the wedding and all. I wondered how good friends you had been. I couldn't help wondering, but I didn't want to really know. Do you understand?"

"Sure."

"The way it happened, we got into a hassle. It was the first real one we'd had. People shouldn't drink and fight when they're married. They say things they don't want to say. I started saying some pretty ugly things about her and you. You know Mary. She's got a lot of spirit. She took it and took it, and finally she let me have it right between the eyes. I deserved it. She blazed right up at me. She said she'd been cruising with you alone aboard this houseboat, down through the Keys and up the west coast to Tampa Bay, and she'd lived aboard for a month and cooked your food and washed your clothes and slept in your bed, and you were kind and decent and gentle and twice the man I am. So that Sunday afternoon I slammed out of the house and got in the car and came over here to beat on you. I could always handle myself pretty good. I wasn't drunk enough for that to be any excuse. Jesus, I never hit so many arms and elbows and shoulders in my life."

"And the top of my head."

"That's what popped the knuckles. Look. This knuckle is still sort of sunk in. How many times did you hit me? Do you know?"

"Sure I know. Twice."

"Twice," he said dolefully. "Oh, shit."

"I waited until you ran out of steam, Harry. I waited until you got arm weary."

He looked at me in an appraising way. "I wish I'd done more good."

"I had a pair of sore arms. You bruised me up, Harry. And a three-day headache."

"I guess I had to get it out of my system. Do you understand it's still pretty hard for me to come to you to ask for anything?"

"I suppose it might be."

"Mary kept telling me to grow up. Okay. I'm trying to grow up. I'm trying to be a mature, rational human being. Like they say, I've been examining my priorities and my options."

"Good for you. But where do I fit in?"

"Here's what I want you to tell Mary."

"But I—"

"Give me a chance. Okay? Tell her that as soon as the SeaGate project is all set up, I think we ought to get away, just the two of us. A cruise or fly over to Spain, whatever. And tell her that the Canadian girl didn't mean a damn thing to me, that I didn't bring her back down here or ask her down, that she came on her own. And tell her to please get in touch with me so we can talk."

"Hold it! I don't know where Mary is."

His face turned red. "Don't give me such crap. You willing to let me search this houseboat?"

"She isn't here, you damn fool."

"I'll find something of hers. Clothes, lipstick, something."

"Harry. Jesus. Look around all you want."

He settled back in the chair. "Okay. You and Mary knew I'd come here sooner or later. So you haven't been having your fun aboard this boat."

"That's called paranoia, old buddy. When did she leave you?"

"January fifth."

I stared at him in disbelief. "This is the fourteenth day of April. You have a slow reaction time."

"I've been hoping she'd come back or get in touch. Tell her how much I've been hoping. She caught me dead to rights. She went around the house with a face like a stone for nearly two weeks, then when I got home that Tuesday, she'd packed and left. No note, even. I went down the list of her friends and called them. It was humiliating for me."

"I bet."

"Now just one damn minute—"

"What makes you think she'd come to me?"

"I thought about it. I mean, back in January. It seemed the most likely thing for her to do. I spent a whole weekend hanging around here. You had . . . another friend. So I decided if Mary had come here, she'd found you were busy, gone someplace else."

"She didn't come here, Harry."

"Not right away."

"What is that supposed to mean?"

He leaned forward. "Okay. Where were you at ten o'clock on Friday morning, April second?"

"I haven't the faintest idea."

"You and Mary came off this houseboat at ten that morning, and you went out to the parking lot and got into a white Ford LTD convertible with rental plates. A friend of mine happened to be here and happened to see the two of you get in and drive off. This friend followed you. You went over to the Parkway and turned south toward Miami, and he came back, and he phoned me about it.''

"Are you willing to listen a minute? Are you willing to try to listen?"

"All I know is my wife left me and she's sleeping with you, McGee, and I'd like to see you dead.''

"The woman I was with is about Mary's height, and her figure is just as good, at least as good as Mary's used to be. Her hair is dark like Mary's. The woman is an old friend. That's her rental convertible, and it's still out there on the lot. With her hair in a scarf and dark glasses, she was all prepared for a trip in an open car. She's here aboard her boat. Her name is Jillian Brent-Archer. I haven't seen Mary since the wedding. Not once, Broll. And that was better than three years ago.''

He looked at me. "You're real cute, McGee. Jesus, you're cute. Most of the damn fools in this world would believe you. Are you going to tell Mary what I told you to tell her, what I've begged you to tell her?''

"How can I, when I don't even know . . . ?''

And the dumb little weapon came out from under his clothes somewhere, maybe from the waist area, wedged between the belt and the flab. A dumb little automatic pistol in blued steel, half-swallowed in his big, pale, meaty fist. His staring eyes were wet with tears, and his mouth was twisted downward at the corners. The muzzle was making a ragged little circle, and a remote part of my mind identified it as .25 or .32 caliber, there not being all that much difference between a quarter of an inch diameter and a third of an inch. There was a sour laugh back in another compartment of my skull. This could very possibly be the end of it, a long-odds chance of a mortal wound at the hand of a jealous husband wielding something just a little bit better than a cap gun. The ragged circle took in my heart, brain, and a certain essential viscera. And I was slouched deep in a chair facing him, just a little too far away to try to kick his wrist. He was going to talk or shoot. I saw his finger getting whiter, so I knew it was shoot.

I shoved with my heels and went over backward in the chair. The weapon made a noise like somebody slapping shingles together. My left heel went numb. I rolled to my right, knocked over a small table, fielded the chunky glass ashtray on the first bounce, rolled up onto my knees, and slung it underhand at his head as he came out of the depths of the yellow couch. I missed him shamefully and was caught there too close to him as he aimed at the middle of my face from five feet away and tried to pull the trigger. But the slide was all the way back, the clip empty.

I got slowly up onto very wobbly knees as Harry Broll lowered the gun to his side, relaxed his hand, let it fall. My heel tingled. A slug had grooved the hard leather on the bottom of the sandal. The lounge smelled like the Fourth of July.

Harry's big face wrinkled like a slapped baby, and he took a half step toward me, arms half reaching out for comfort and forgiveness, and then he plumped back down on the couch and bellowed once, a walrus on a lonely strand.

My drink was gone, spilling when the table went over. I moved cautiously, checking myself for any area that might feel dead and damp. This is the bullet feel, dead, damp, and strange, before the torn nerves and muscles catch up and begin screaming. No such areas. I made tall, careful steps into the galley, made a new drink. I went back in. Harry Broll sat with face in hands, snuffling drearily. The paper had kept me aware of him over the years. Broll plans new condominium complex. Broll given zoning board exception. Broll unveils shopping plaza concept. Chamber lauds Broll.

I sat opposite him again after putting the chair back on its legs. Looking around, I could count five ejected cartridge cases.

"How old are you, Harry?"

He sighed and mumbled it into his hands. "Thirty-five."

"You look fifty."

"Get off my back."

"You're too soft and too heavy. You sweat a lot, and you're short of breath, and your teeth need cleaning."

He lifted his mottled face and stared at me. "Why are you saying these things?"

"Maybe if you hadn't gotten so sloppy, Mary could have given you a second chance. Or maybe it was already a second chance."

"Oh, no. I don't play around. Jesus, I haven't had the time or the energy. This was the first time, I swear."

"You don't play around, and you don't go around killing people."

"You pushed me too far and—"

"You always carry that thing?"

"No, I—"

"You brought it along in case you felt like killing me?"

"Thank God I missed you. I'm not thinking right lately. Everything would have gone down the drain. Everything."

"It would sort of spoil my day, too."

"You know, when a man takes a good look at himself, he begins to wonder why. You know? I've been pushing myself hard. Drinking too much, smoking too much. Late nights. Conferences. For what? Damned if I know. For the sake of winning? How did that get to seem so important? But you shouldn't have tried to lie to me, McGee."

"Your friend is an idiot. Mary never came near me. She hasn't phoned me or written me. I didn't know she'd left you. Look, I knew her a long time ago. She was at one of those crisis points in her life. She'd never met you, Harry. Never seen you, never heard your name, never knew she'd marry you. We were friends. We took a cruise down through the Keys and up the west coast, and she got things sorted out. We made love. Not for the first two weeks of the cruise. That wasn't the purpose of it. Once all the knots and springs began to loosen up, then it seemed like a natural thing to have happen. It made pleasure. It was a way of saying hello. Nobody was a victim. She was a very sweet lady, and what I remember best is that we laughed a lot."

"I . . . I have to talk to her before the thirtieth."

"Why the deadline?"

"It's a business thing. Some things to sign. To protect my interest in SeaGate. Of course, if I'd shot you, what difference would it make whether I kept my share of SeaGate or not?"

"Will it make a lot of difference when I sign the complaint against you?"

"Complaint?"

"Assault with a deadly weapon? Attempted homicide?"

"You wouldn't!"

"What's to stop me? My undying affection for you?"

He pulled himself together visibly. He wrapped up the emotions and put them on a high shelf. I could almost see the nimble brain of the entrepreneur take over. "We'll both have versions of what happened here, McGee. I'm essentially a salesman. I think I can sell my version far easier than you can sell yours."

"What's your version?"

"I'll let that come as a surprise to you."

I could think of several variations that could leave him looking pretty good. And, of course, there was the usual problem of believability. Does one believe Harry Broll, pillar of the business community, or a certain Travis McGee, who seems to have no visible means of support, gentlemen?

"A man as shrewd as you, Harry, should realize that the guy who gave you the bad information made an honest mistake."

"I know Mary. She'd get in touch with you."

"Would that she had."

"What?"

"A troubled friend is a friend in trouble. I'm right here. She could have come around, but she didn't."

"She made you promise not to tell where she is."

I shook my head. "Broll, come with me. I will show you that rental convertible, and I will show you the lady who rented it and who went to Miami with me and came back with me."

"It's a nice try. You've got a lot of friends. They'd all lie for you. Every one. Think it over. Tell her what I said. She has to get in touch with me."

We stood up. I picked up his little automatic, released the catch and eased the slide forward, and handed it to him. He took it and looked at it, bounced it on his big hand, and slipped it into his side pocket. "I better get rid of it," he said.

"If you think you might get any more quaint ideas, you better."

"I was going to scare you. That's all."

I looked him over. "Harry. You did."

"Tell her to call the office. I'm not living at home. It was too empty there."

"If after all these years I should happen to see your wife, I'll tell her."

2

MEYER CAME aboard *The Busted Flush* at twenty minutes to six, five minutes after Harry Broll left. He was dressed for the small festival at six o'clock aboard Jillian's great big motor-sailer trimaran. He wore pants in a carnival awning pattern and a pink shirt that matched one of the myriad stripes in the awning.

"Goodness gracious," I said.

He put a hand on a bulky hip and made a slow 360-degree turn. "Plumage," he said. "And have you noticed it's spring?"

"If you'd carry a camera around your neck and walk fifty feet ahead of me, nobody would know we were together."

"Faw," he said. "And tush." He went toward the bottle department, saying, "About Mr. Harry Broll . . . ?"

"Who? Oh, yes. Of course. Mr. Broll."

"McGee, don't try me, please."

"You are supposed to walk in here, and instead of giving me a fashion show, you are supposed to snuff the air, look about with darting glances. Then you are supposed to find those six cartridge cases in that ashtray and snuff at them. Then you prowl around and find where all six hit, including the one that's hard to find. It hit right smack in the middle of my Model Eighteen Marantz and killed it as dead as Harry tried to kill me."

Meyer backed to the nearest chair and lowered himself into it. "Six shots?"

"Six."

"With serious intent?"

"Damn well told."

I explained the situation. Meyer listened, looking very troubled.

"Don't sit there looking like an old beagle," I told him. "Harry won't be back."

"Maybe somebody else will."

"What is that supposed to mean?"

"Travis, are you just a little slower than you were a few years ago? Half a step, maybe?"

"I don't know. Probably."

"Why should you get slower and get careless at the same time?"

"Careless?"

"Don't try to kid yourself. You would have stumbled against him or spilled something on him and brushed it off. You would have checked him out and located the gun and taken it away from him."

"This was just old Harry Broll."

"And you are just old T. McGee, trying to pretend you don't know what I'm saying. You could be on the floor with a leaking hole in your skull."

"I can't go around acting as if everybody was going to—"

"You used to. And you are alive. What has given you this illusion of immortality of late?"

"Lay off, Meyer."

"Staleness? People are very good at things they are very interested in. If you lose interest, you are dead. If a Harry Broll can damned near kill you, Travis, what about somebody with a more professional attitude and background?"

"Wouldn't I be more alert?"

"Don't some of them look and act as innocuous as Harry Broll?"

"What are you getting at?"

"If you just go through the motions, Travis, maybe it's time to give the whole thing up. What good is a way of life if it turns out to be fatal?"

"Are you going to support me?"

"Not a chance. Anyway, isn't Jillian first in line?"

"Come *on!*"

"There are worse ways to live."

"Several hundred thousand worse ways, Mayer, but just because Harry Broll . . . consider this. Six shots in a very confined space. What's the matter with my reaction time?"

"The trouble is that they were fired at all. He came here once to try to beat your face flat. So two years later he comes around again, and you invite him in to try his luck with a gun. What are you going to dodge next time? A satchel charge?"

"I have to depend on instinct. I did not sense any kind of murderous intent on his—"

"Then your instincts are stale. Listen. I don't want to lose a friend. Go where I can visit once in a while. Exchange Christmas cards. Better than putting a pebble on your gravestone."

"Just because—"

"Don't talk. Think a little. And we should be going."

I shrugged and sighed. When he gets into one of those moods, there is nothing one can do with him. He smells doom. I buttoned up the *Flush,* making certain my little security devices were in operation. The sun was low enough to make a yellow-orange glow across all the white gleam and brightwork of a vulgar multimillion dollars' worth of seagoing toys. Hundreds of millions, in truth. As we walked over I saw the sixty-plus feet of a big new Bertram, grumbling, bubbling, sliding elegantly into a slip. Six thousand dollars a foot. It doesn't take too many of those, too many Matthews, Burgers, Trumpys, Huckinses, Rybovitches, and Strikers, to make a row of zeros to stun the mind.

I stopped and leaned my crossed arm atop a cement piling and looked down at a rainbow sheen of oil on twilight waters.

"What's the matter now?" asked Meyer.

"Harry is right, you know."

"To try to kill you?"

"Very funny. He's right about Mary getting in touch. I get the feeling she would. Emotional logic. The last time her world ruptured, I helped her walk it off, talk it off, think it off."

"So maybe she had enough and said the hell with it."

"She is one stubborn lady. Harry is no prize. She married him a little too fast. But she would really bust a gut to make the marriage work. She wouldn't quit. She wouldn't run."

"Unless he did something that she just couldn't take. Maybe it got to her gag reflex. Wouldn't she run then?"

"Yes. I guess so. And maybe she's a stronger person than she was back when I knew her. All Harry said was that he had gotten mixed up with some Canadian girl, a first offense. I know that wouldn't make Mary give any ringing cheers. But I think she's human enough to know it wouldn't be the end of the world or the marriage. Well, he has to locate her before the end of April, or he has big business problems."

"Hmm?"

"Something about signing something so he can keep his interest in Sea-Gate, whatever the hell that is."

"It's a planned community up in the northeast corner of Martin County, above Hobe Sound where there's no A-1-A running along the beach. It's a syndicate thing, way too big for anybody like Broll to swing by himself."

"How do you know all that stuff?"

"There was a feature story about planned communities in the *Wall Street Journal* a month ago. The local papers have had articles about it for over a year. I believe *Newsweek* had a—"

"Truce. Could a guy like Broll do well in a deal like that?"

"Depends. The ownership structure would be the important consideration."

"Could you find out where he fits and how, and why Mary would have to sign something?"

"I imagine I could. But why?"

"Harry's nerves are bad. He looks bad. He has a money orientation. If he misses out on large money because Mary runs and hides and won't sign, it somehow doesn't sound like Mary. It would be a cheap shot and a dumb shot. She isn't dumb. Whether she stays with him or leaves him, it would be better for him to have money. She's been gone for three months. If he was so certain she'd run to me, where has he been for three months? Time is running out in two weeks. So he comes around with shaking hands and a sweaty shirt and a couple of places he missed while shaving. Time is running out not on the marriage, on the money. It makes me wonder."

"I'll look into it," he said as we walked.

End of discussion. We had arrived at the area where they park the show-boats, the ones too big to bring around inside, and thus have to leave them on the river, not far from the fuel pumps, where two out of every three Power Squadron types who cruise by can whap them against the cement with their curling wash. The *Jilly III* is a custom motor-sailer trimaran out of St. Kitts, owned by Jillian, the widow of Sir Henry Brent-Archer. It is seventy feet long with a beam that has to be close to fifty feet. It rides a bad sea with all the stability of a brick church. Minimal superstructure to emphasize an expanse of teak deck as big as a tennis court, with more than half of it shaded by the big colorful awning tarp her crew of three always strings up as soon as they are at dockside.

The bar table was positioned, draped in white damask. A piano tape was playing show tunes with muted discretion over the stereo system I'd helped her buy the last time she was in Lauderdale. There were a dozen guests assembled, three conversational groups of elegant folk sipping the very best booze from the most expensive glasses. Jilly saw us approaching the little gangplank and came a-striding, beaming, to welcome us aboard.

A lady of unguessable years, who made damned well certain she gave you no clues at all. If she turned up as a Jane Doe, DOA, traffic, a hasty coroner could not be blamed for penciling in the apparent age as plus or minus twenty-seven. Tall, slender brunette of such careful and elegant grooming, such exquisitely capped teeth, it seemed safe to assume she was in some area of entertainment. But she had such a much better tan and better physical condition than most show-business people, one might safely guess her to be, perhaps, a model for beachware? A lead in a commercial water ballet?

But a coroner less hasty, more sophisticated, who searched the scalp and elsewhere for the faintest of traces left by superb Swiss surgeons, who slipped the tinted plastic lenses off and studied her eyes closely, as well as the backs of the hands, base of the throat, ankles, wrists . . . he might add a quotient of years in direct ratio to his quality of observation and his experience.

Jilly had a lively and animated face peering out from the careless spill of black hair, all bright questing eyes, black brows, big nose, broad and generous mouth. Ever since I had known Jilly, her voice had cracked like that of a boy in early adolescence, changing from the piercing, songbird clarity of the Irish upperclass countryside to a burring baritone honk and back again. It was so effective it seemed contrived. But a small sailboat had foundered one night in a bad sea, and she had clung to a channel buoy, permanently spraining her vocal cords shouting at the boat traffic until finally she was heard and she and her injured friend were rescued.

"Meyer!" she cried. "My *word,* darling! You're of a surpassing radiance. Travis dear, what happened to him? Did he molt or something?" She linked her arms through ours and croaked, "Come on, dears. Meet the ones you don't know and get smashed soon as you can because I am gallons ahead of you."

The introductions were made. Jillian slipped away to greet more guests. We drank. The sun went down. The night breeze was gentle but cool, and ladies put their wraps back on. The party lights strung from the rigging were properly dim, flatteringly orange. The buffet materialized, as if the table had risen up out of the teak. The music tape was more lively, the volume louder than before.

I found myself inadvertently paired with a smallish, withered Englishwoman with a shrunken face the color of weak tea and hair dyed the color of raspberry ice. A Mrs. Ogleby. I had seen Meyer talking to her towering and cadaverous husband, pumping him about the latest Common Market difficulties. We carried our buffet plates forward where she could sit on a narrow shelflike bench built out from the bow where the rail was solid. I sat cross-legged on the deck with my plate atop the massive bow cleat.

"I understand that you are one of dear Jillian's very favorite Americans, Mr. McGee."

She managed to load the comment with sweetly venomous insinuation. I beamed up at her. "And she's one of my favorite foreigners."

"Really! How terribly nice for her. Actually, Geoffrey and I were old friends of poor Sir Henry long before he married Jillian."

"Then Jillian isn't one of your favorite people, eh?"

She clinked her fork against the plate and leaned forward and peered down at me. "Whatever gave you such an odd idea? She is *very* dear. Very dear to both of us."

"I knew Sir Henry, too."

"Really! I wouldn't have thought you would have known him."

"I was a houseguest at St. Kitts for a few weeks."

"But that would have been after he was quite ill, I take it." Her smile was thin and knowing in the light of the nearby party lantern. A truly poisonous little woman.

"No. As a matter of fact, Mrs. Ogleby, Henry and I swam our three miles every morning, went riding or sailing every afternoon, and played chess every evening."

She paused and regrouped. "Before he became ill, Sir Henry had really fantastic energies. How strange we all thought it that he would marry someone that young, after being a widower so long. It seemed odd. But, of course, that was so awfully long ago it is rather difficult to think of Jillian as—"

"Just think of me, dears, no matter how difficult it may be," said Jilly. "Hmmm. What is this you have, Lenore? I didn't see it at all. May I? Mmmm. Shrimp, and what a deliciously fiery sauce! Difficult to think of me as what, Lenore darling?"

When Mrs. Ogleby hesitated, I said, "She was about to pinpoint the date when you and Sir Henry were married."

"Were you, dear? It slips my mind, you know. Was it just before or just after that fuss with the Spanish Armada?"

"Don't be absurd! I was only—"

"You were only being Lenore, which is part of the trouble, isn't it? Travis, I was married to Henry long long ago. Matter of fact, I was but three years old at the time, and most of the people in the church thought it was some sort of delayed christening. There was talk that it was an unwholesome relationship, but by the time I was fourteen—eleven years later—I looked twenty, and everyone said that it had probably been all for the best. And it was, of course. Lenore, you seem to be finished. Dear, come with me and show me just where you found the shrimp, will you please?"

"But if there is any left, it should be quite obvi—"

"Lenore!"

"Quite. Of course. I shall be happy to show you, my dear Jillian."

"I knew it would make you happy to have a chance to be nice to me, Lenore."

Off they went. Old friends, smiling and chattering.

Twenty minutes later as I was moving away from the bar with some Wild Turkey straight, instead of brandy, Jilly intercepted me and moved me into relative shadow.

"Travis, if you are a truly thoughtful and understanding man, you have your toothbrush hidden away on your person."

"I had the idea the party girl would need her eight hours."

"Have a little mercy, dear. There's but one way to settle down from this sort of bash. You shall divert me."

"I can leave and then come back. You know. Like a house call."

"Is its tender little romantical pride bruised because the party girl thinks lovemaking is therapeutic? To say nothing of being a hell of a lot of fun. Just stay on, dear. Stay by me. Smile like a tomcat with a little yellow feather caught in his whiskers, and soon now we can smile them off and sing out our merry farewells."

"Giving Lenore more food for thought?"

"Thought? Christ, that poisonous bitch doesn't think. She slanders, because she has her own terrible hunger she can't ease in any way. She burns in fire, my darling, and hates and hates and hates. Poor thing. Brace yourself, pet. I want you horribly."

3

I DRIFTED in and out of a placid and amiable doze. Water slapped the triple hulls, whispering lies about how big the seas could really get. I cocked an eye at an upward angle at the battery digital clock fastened to the bulkhead over Jillian's bed. Watched 4:06 turn magically to 4:07. There was a single light on in her stateroom, a rose-colored globe of frosty glass, big as a cantaloupe, standing next to its twin reflection in the dressing table mirror.

It was warm in her stateroom, not unpleasantly so, just enough to leave a humid dew, rosy highlights on our entangled flesh, sprawled and spent, atop a wrinkled dampness of custom sheets in a pattern of green vines with yellow leaves against white.

Jilly lay oddly positioned, her upper torso diagonally across my chest, face in a pillow, cheek against my right shoulder, her slack right arm hooked around my neck. Her long tanned legs were sprawled down there, off to my left. My right arm was pinned, but my left arm was free, my hand resting on the small of her back.

I traced the velvet geographies of that small concave area of the country of Jilly and then made a coin-sized circle of fingernails and thumbnail and made a slow circling motion against her there, a circle as big as a teacup. In time the pattern of her breathing changed. She shifted. She exhaled through slack rubbery lips, making a sound like a small horse.

"Is someone mentioning my name?" she said in a sleepy voice.

"Pure telepathy."

She raised her head, clawed her hair out of the way, and peered up at the clock. "Gawd! What year is it? Don't tell me."

She heaved herself up, tugging her arm out from under my neck. She sat up and combed her hair back with the fingers of both hands, yawning widely as she did so. She shook and snapped her head back, settled her hair, then curled her limber legs under her and smiled down at me. "Been awake long, Travis?"

"Off and on."

"Thinking? About what?"

I hitched myself higher on the pillows. "Random things. This and that."

"Tell me about them."

"Let me think back. Oh, I was wondering how it's possible to make this bed up. It's shaped to fit perfectly into the curves of this middle hull right up at the bow and—"

"There are little lever things on the legs down there, and when you push them down, then you can roll the bed back and make it up. You certainly think about fascinating things."

"Then I heard a motor go on, and I was wondering if it was a bilge pump or a refrigeration compressor or—"

"You are trying to be tiresome. Didn't you think about what I asked you?"

"Maybe I did. A little bit. Like wondering why it has to be me."

"If one could know why a person settles upon a particular person, one would know one of the mysteries, wouldn't one? I think it was because of four years ago. I think it started then."

A friend of a friend had put Sir Henry Brent-Archer in touch with me. A

19

problem of simple extortion. I had gone down to the British Virgins and spent three weeks at their spacious and lovely home and found exactly the right way to pry the two-legged lamprey loose, file its sharp teeth off, and send it unhappily on its way. And during the three weeks I had become ever more sensuously aware of Sir Henry's handsome and lively wife. She made sure of the awareness.

"Because I kept it from starting?"

"Was I all that distasteful to you, my darling?"

"Not you. The situation. I liked Sir Henry. In spite of the fact I was working for him on a special problem, I was still a guest in his home. In a man's home you live by his code. It does not have to be typed out and glued to the guest suite door. He did not want me to kick his dogs, overwork his horses, bribe his servants, read his diary, filch his silverware, borrow his toothbrush, or lay his wife. I accepted the obligation when I moved in."

She snickered. "Would you believe that was the only time in the years I was his wife that I ever tried to be naughty?"

"There's no reason not to believe it."

"I was very grateful to Sir Henry. He came along at just the right time in my life. My whole dreadful family was sliding into the pit, and through him I could save them, so I snatched him up quickly. I liked him well enough for half the marriage, liked him a great deal for the rest of it, and started loving him after he was buried. Anyway, on that stupid night I lay and listened to my heart go *bump, bump, bump*. Then I got up and drenched myself with that lovely scent and put on the little froth of nightgown and crept through the night like a thief and slipped into your bed. And suddenly got lifted out bodily, carried to the door, given a great whack across my bare behind, and shoved out into the hall. I did not know whether to laugh or cry. I did both."

"It was closer than you'll ever know, Jilly."

"So it's you, dear man. The chosen. Relax and enjoy it. Why not? Am I trying to nail you down permanently? Of course, but through your own choice and decision. I give you full disclosure, dear. I have something over eight hundred thousand pounds, carefully managed by nice little Swiss elves. The income is about a hundred and fifth thousand of your dollars a year, and taxes take hardly any. There is the lovely house with the beach, the bay, and the view, and the boats and cars and horses. I am not exactly a junior miss, but I work very hard at myself, and I come from healthy stock. I suspect I shall go on about the same for years and years and years and suddenly one morning wake up as a shriveled, cackling little old witch. All I ask of you is that you come back home with me, darling. Be my houseguest. Be my love. We laugh at the same things. We enjoy the same things. Last trip and this trip we've certainly established . . . physical compatibility. Darling, please! We'll travel when you want to and go where you want to go. We'll be with people when you want to, and they will be the people you want to be with. Please!"

"Jilly, you are a dear and lovely lady—"

"But! I know, dammit. But! Why *not?* Do you even *know?*"

I knew but did not want to tell her. You see many such couples around the yacht clubs and bath clubs and tennis clubs of the Western world. The man, a little younger or a lot younger than the moneyed widow or divorcée he has either married or is traveling with. The man is usually brown and good at games, dresses youthfully, and talks amusingly. But he drinks a little too much. And completely trained and conditioned, he is ever alert for his cues. If his lady unsnaps her purse and frowns down into it, he at once presents his cigarettes, and they are always her brand. If she has her own cigarettes, he can cross twenty feet in a twelfth of a second to snap the unwavering flame to life, properly and conveniently positioned for her. It takes but the smallest sidelong look of query to send him in search of an ashtray to place close to her elbow. If at sundown she raises her elegant shoulders a half inch, he trots into the house or onto the boat or up to the suite to bring back her wrap. He knows just how to apply her suntan oil, knows which of her dresses have to be zipped up and snapped for her. He can draw her bath to the precise depth and temperature which please her. He can give her an acceptable message, brew a decent pot of coffee, take her phone messages accurately, keep her personal checkbook in balance, and remind her when to take her medications. Her litany is: Thank you, dearest. How nice, darling. You are so thoughtful, sweetheart.

It does not happen quickly, of course. It is an easy life. Other choices, once so numerous, disappear. Time is the random wind that blows down the long corridor, slamming all the doors. And finally, of course, it comes down to a very simple equation. Life is endurable when she is contented and difficult when she is displeased. It is a training process. Conditioned response.

"I'm used to the way I live," I told her.

"The way you live," she said. With brooding face she reached and ran gentle fingertips along the deep, gullied scar in my thigh, then leaned and touched the symmetrical dimple of the entrance wound of a bullet. She hunched closer to me, bent, and kissed the white welt of scar tissue that is nearly hidden by the scruffy, sun-faded hair at my temple. "The way you live, Travis. Trying to trick the tricky ones. Trying to make do with bluff and smiles and strange lies. Filching fresh meat right out of the jaws of the sharks. For how long, dear, before finally the odds go bad and the luck goes bad once and for all?"

"I'm sly."

"Not sly enough. Maybe not quick enough any more. I think you've been doing it for too long, darling. Too many years of getting things back for silly, careless people who should not have lost them in the first place. One day some dim little chap will come upon you suddenly and take out a gun and shoot you quite dead."

"Are you a witch? Do you so prophesy?"

She fell upon me, hugged me tight. "Ah, no, dear. No. You had all the years when that was the thing you had to do. Now the years belong to me. Is it such a sickening fate you can't endure the thought of it?"

"No, Jilly. No, honey. It's just that—"

"Give us a month. No. One week. One insignificant little week. Or else."

"Or else?"

She burrowed a bit, gently closed her teeth onto the upper third of my left ear, then released it. "I have splendid teeth and very strong jaw muscles. If you say no, I shall set my teeth into your ear and do my best to tear it right off your head, darling."

"You just might at that."

"You love to bluff people. Try me."

"No, thank you. One week."

She took a deep breath and let it out. "Lovely! Time in transit doesn't count, of course. Can we leave . . . day after tomorrow?"

"I don't know."

"Why don't you know?"

"I just found out that an old friend might be in trouble. It just seems to me that if she was in trouble, she'd come to me."

Jilly wiggled and thrust away from me and sat up. "She?"

"Frowning makes wrinkles."

"So it does. She?"

"A respectable married lady."

"If she's so respectable, how is it she knows *you?*"

"Before she was married."

"And I suppose you had an affair with her."

"Gee, honey. I'd have to look it up."

I caught her fist about five inches from my eye. "You bahstid," she said.

"Okay. An affair. A mad, wild, glorious liaison which kept us in an absolute frenzy of passion."

Her look was enigmatic. "You are perfectly right, of course, darling. It is none of my business. What's she like? I mean, what physical type?"

"In general, a lot like you, Jilly. Tall, slender brunette. Dark hair, takes a good tan. Long legs, short waisted. She would be . . . twenty-eight or -nine by now. Back when I knew her, she didn't race her motor the way you do. More of a placid, contented person. She really enjoyed cooking and scrubbing and bed-making. She could sleep ten or twelve hours a night."

"You damned well remember every detail, don't you?"

I smiled up into her leaning, earnest face—a small face but strong of feature in the black, bed-snarled dangle of hair. I looked at her limber, brown body in the rose glow of the lamp ten feet away, noting the way the deep tan above and below her breasts decreased in ever more pallid horizontal stripes and shadings down to that final band of pale and pure white which denoted her narrowest bikini top.

"Why are you laughing at me, you dull sod?"

"Not at you, Lady Jillian."

"I am *not* Lady Jillian. That usage is improper. If you are not laughing *at,* then you are laughing *with.* And if you are laughing *with,* why is it that I am not amused?"

"But you are, darling."

She tried to keep her mouth severe but lost the battle, gave a rusty honk of laughter, and flung herself upon me.

"I can't stay angry with you, Travis. You promised me a week. But I'll punish you for that dark-haired lady."

"How?"

"On our way to St. Kitts there will be at least one day or night when we'll spend hour after hour quartering into an ugly, irregular chop."

"I don't get seasick."

"Nor do I, my love. It would spoil it if either of us became ill."

"Spoil what?"

"Dear man, when the chop is effective, one cannot stay on this bed. You are lifted up, and then the bed and the hull drop away from you, and when you are on your way down, the bed comes up and smacks you and boosts you into the air again. It is like trying to post on a very bad horse. When that happens, dear, you and I are going to be right here, making love. We'll see how well you satisfy a lady in midair. I shall have you tottering about, wishing you'd never met Mrs. Whatever."

"Mrs. Broll. Mary Broll. Mary Dillon Broll."

"You think she should have come to you if she's in trouble? Isn't that a little patronizing and arrogant?"

"Possibly."

"What sort of trouble?"

"Marriage trouble. Her husband cheated, and she caught him at it and left him back in January."

"Good Lord, why should she come galloping to you?"

"It's an emotional problem, and when she had one sort of like it years ago, we got together, and she worked her way out of it."

"And fell in love with you?"

"I think that with Mary there would have to be some affection before there could be anything."

"You poor dumb beast. You're *so* obvious."

"What do you mean?"

"You can't for the life of you comprehend why she doesn't come scuttling back to Dr. McGee's free and famous clinic. Your pride is hurt, dear. I suspect she's found some other therapist."

"Even if she had, I think she'd have let me know the marriage had soured. I get the feeling something happened to her."

She yawned and stretched. "Let me make one thing abundantly clear, as one of your grubby little political types used to say. Once we have our design for living, if we have any doleful visits from one of your previous patients, my dear, I shall take a broom to her and beat her through the garden gate and down the drive."

"Don't you think you ought to type all these rules up and give me three copies?"

"You're so damned *defensive!* Good Christ, am I some sort of dog's dinner?"

"You are a lively, sexy, lovely, sexy, well-dressed, sexy, amusing, sexy, wealthy, sexy widow lady."

"And some *very* tidy and considerate men come flocking around. Men with all the social graces and very good at games. Not knuckly, scabrous, lazy, knobbly old ruins like you, McGee."

"So grab one of those tidy and considerate ones."

"Oh, sure. They are lovely men, and they are *so* anxious to please me. There's the money, and it makes them very jumpy and nervous. Their hands get cold and damp. If I frown, they look terrified. Couldn't you be more anxious to please me, dear? Just a little bit?"

"Like this, you mean?"

"Well . . . I didn't exactly mean that . . . I meant in a more general sense . . . but . . . now that you bring it up . . . God, I can't remember now what I did mean . . . I guess I meant this. Yes, darling. This."

*   *   *

The narrow horizontal ports above the custom bed led a cold and milky morning light into the stateroom at the bow of the center hull of the *Jilly III*.

As I looked up, 6:31 became 6:32. Jillian's small round rump, her flesh warmer than mine, was thrust with a domestic coziness into my belly. My chin rested against the crown of her head. Her tidy heft had turned my left arm numb. My right hand lay upon the sweet inward curve of her waist.

Worse fates, I thought. A life with Jilly Brent-Archer wouldn't be dull. Maybe it is time for the islands. In spite of all good intentions, all nervous concern, all political bombast, my dirty two-legged species is turning the lovely southeast coast into a sewer. On still days the stinking sky is bourbon brown, and in the sea there are only the dwindling runty fish that can survive in that poisoned brew.

It happens slowly, so you try not to notice it. You tell yourself it happens to be a bad day, that's all. The tides and the winds will scrub it all clean. But not clean enough any more. One life to live, so pop through the escape hatch, McGee. Try the islands. Damned few people can escape the smudge and sludge, the acids and stenches, the choking and weeping. You have to take care of yourself, man. Nobody else is going to. And this deft morsel, curled sleeping against you, is a first-class ticket for all the voyage you have left. Suppose you *do* have to do some bowing and scraping and fetching. Will it kill you? Think of what most people have to do for a living. You've been taking your retirement in small installments whenever you could afford it. So here's the rest of it in her lovely sleep. The ultimate social security.

I eased my dead arm out from under her and moved away. She made a sleep whine of discontent. I covered her with the big colorful sheet, dressed, turned out the rosy light, and made sure the main hatchway locked behind me when I left.

Back aboard the *Flush,* I put on swim trunks and a robe to keep me warm in the morning chill. The sun was coming up out of the sea when I walked across the pedestrian bridge over the highway and down onto the public beach. Morning birds were running along the wet sand, pecking and fleeing from the wash of the surf. An old man was jogging slowly by, his face in a clench of agony. A fat girl in a brown dress was looking for shells.

I went in, swam hard, and rested, again and again, using short bursts of total energy. I went back to the *Flush* and had a quart of orange juice, four scrambled eggs along with some rat cheese from Vermont, and a mug of black coffee.

I fell asleep seven and a half inches above my oversized bed in the master stateroom, falling toward the bed, long gone before I landed.

4

THURSDAY, WHEN I got up a little before noon, the remembered scene with Harry Broll and his little gun seemed unreal. Six loud whacks, not loud enough to attract the curious attention of people on the neighboring craft. The *Flush* had been buttoned up, the air conditioning on. No slug had gone through glass.

I found where five had hit. At last I spotted the sixth one in the overhead. It had hit tumbling and sideways and had not punched itself all the way out of sight, so by elimination it was the one that had grooved the leather sole of my sandal and numbed my heel.

I had rolled to my right after going over backward in the chair. It gave me the chance to kick a small table over, creating more distraction and confusion, and it also forced him, being right-handed, to bring his arm across his body to aim at me, which is more difficult than extending the arm out to the side. Two into the deck, one into the chair, one into the table, one into the overhead, and one into my stereo amplifier.

So maybe the clip held six, and he had not jacked one into the chamber until he got to the parking lot at the marina. If he'd put one in the chamber and filled the clip all the way, there would have been one left for the middle of my face.

Dead then or a long time in the institutional bed with the drains in place and the pain moving around under the sedatives like a snake under a blanket.

Don't give yourself any credit, Mr. Travis McGee. The fates could have counted to seven just as easily. You had an easy shot at him with the ashtray, but your hand was sweaty and the fingertips slipped. You missed badly.

Meyer could be right. I had depended on instinct. It had been my instinct that Harry Broll had not come to kill me. Then he had done his best, and I had lucked out. So was instinct becoming stale? When it stopped being a precision tool, when it ceased sending accurate messages up from the atavistic, animal level of the brain, I was as vulnerable as if sight or hearing had begun to fail. If soft, sloppy, nervous Harry Broll could almost do me in with a popgun, my next meeting with professional talent could be mortal.

There was another dimension to it. Once I started doubting my survival instinct, I would lose confidence in my own reactions. A loss of confidence creates hesitations. Hesitation is a fatal disease—for anyone in the salvage business.

There are worse careers than houseguest. Or pet gofer.

Too much solitary introspection started to depress me. I was ready for Geritol and cortisone. I pulled all the plugs and connections on the Marantz and lugged its considerable weight all the way to where I'd parked Miss Agnes, my ancient and amiable old blue Rolls pickup. I drove over to town to Al's Musicade. He is lean, sour, and knowledgeable. He does not say much. He took it out back himself and found bench space in his busy service department. I watched him finger the hole in the front of it. He quickly loosened the twelve Phillips screws that hold the top perforated plate down, lifted it off, found more damage, reached in with two fingers, and lifted out the deformed slug.

"Somebody didn't like the programming?"

"Bad lyrics."

"Week from today?"

"Loaner?"

"Got a Fisher you can use."

We walked out front, and he lifted it off the rack, a used one in apparently good condition. He made a note of the serial number and who was taking it out.

I put the borrowed amplifier on the passenger seat beside me and went looking for Harry Broll's place of business. I had seen it once and had a general idea where to find it. I had to ask at a gas station. It was west of Lauderdale, off Davie Road, over in an industrial park in pine and palmetto country. All of it except the office itself was circled by high hurricane fencing with slanted braces and three strands of barbed wire on top. There was a gate for the rail spur and a truck and equipment gate. I could see a central-mix concrete plant, a block plant, big piles of sand, gravel, and crushed stone. I could see warehouses, stacks of lumber, piles of prestressed concrete beams, and a vehicle park-and-repair area. This was a Thursday at one thirty in the afternoon, and I could count only ten cars. Four of those were in front of the office. The office was a long, low concrete-block building painted white with a flat roof. The landscaped grass was burned brown, and they had lost about half the small palm trees planted near the office.

There were too many trucks and pieces of equipment in the park. It looked neat enough but sleepy. BROLL ENTERPRISES, Inc. But some of the big plastic letters had blown off or fallen off. It said:

ROLL E TERP ISES, Inc.

I cruised slowly by. I was tempted to turn around and go back and go in and see if Harry was there and try once more to tell him I'd had no contact whatsoever with Mary for over three years. But he was going to believe what emotions told him to believe.

I wondered how Meyer was doing, using his friends in the banks, brokerage houses, and investment houses to find out just how sweaty Harry Broll might be. The tight-money times and the overbuilding of condominiums and the pyramiding costs had busted quite a few able fellows lately. Harry probably hadn't come through that bad period without some ugly bruises. I could tell Meyer how idle Broll's place of business looked, if he hadn't found out already.

When I got back to Bahia Mar, Meyer was still missing. I felt restless. I set up the Fisher, hooked up the tape decks, turntables, and the two sets of speakers. It checked out all right. I turned it off and paced. The itch you can't quite reach. Familiar feeling. Like the name you can't quite remember.

I looked up the number for Broll Enterprises and phoned. The girl answered by reciting the number I'd just dialed.

"Maybe you can help me, miss. I'm trying to get a home address for Mrs. Harry Broll."

"In what regard, please?"

"Well, this is the Shoe Mart, and it was way back in November we special-ordered a pair of shoes for Mrs. Broll. It took so long she's under no obligation to take them, but they're more a classic than a high-style item, so I figure she probably wants them, but I been drawing a blank on the home phone number, so I thought maybe they moved or something."

"Will you hold on a moment, please?"

I held. It took her about a minute and a half. "Mr. Broll says that you can deliver them here to the office. Do you know where we are?"

"Sure. Okay. Thanks. It'll probably be tomorrow."

I hung up, and once again, to make sure, I dialed the home phone number for Harry Broll, 21 Blue Heron Lane. "The number you have dialed is not in service at this time."

I scowled at my phone. Come on, McGee. The man is living somewhere. Information has no home number for him. The old home number is on temporary disconnect. The new number of wherever he's living must be unlisted. It probably doesn't matter a damn where he's living. It's the challenge.

Okay. Think a little. Possibly all his mail is directed to the business address. But some things have to be delivered. Booze, medicine, automobiles. Water, electricity . . . cablevision?

The lady had a lovely voice, gentle and musical and intriguingly breathy. "I could track it down more quickly, Mr. Broll, if you could give me your account number."

"I wish I could. I'm sorry, miss. I don't have the bill in front of me. But couldn't you check it by address? The last billing was sent to Twenty-one Blue Heron Lane. If it's too much trouble, I can phone you tomorrow. You see, the bill is at my home, and I'm at the office."

"Just a moment, please. Let me check the cross-index."

It took a good five minutes. "Sorry it took me so long," she said.

"It was my fault, not having my account number, miss."

"Broll. Bee-are-oh-el-el. Harry C.?"

"Correct."

"And you said the bill went where?"

"To Twenty-one Blue Heron Lane. That's where I used to live."

"Gee, Mr. Broll, I don't understand it at all. All billing is supposed to be mailed to Post Office Box Fifty-one fifty."

"I wonder if I've gotten a bill that belongs to someone else. The amount doesn't seem right either."

"You should be paying six twenty-four a month, sir. For the one outlet. You were paying more, of course, for the four outlets at Blue Heron Lane before you ordered the disconnect."

"Excuse me, but does your file show where I am getting the one-outlet service? Do you have the right address?"

"Oh, yes, sir. It's Eighty-five fifty-three Ocean Boulevard, Apartment sixty-one. I've got the installation order number. That *is* right, isn't it?"

"Yes. That's right. But I think the billing is for eleven dollars and something."

"Mr. Broll, please mail the bill back in the regular envelope we send out, but in the left bottom corner would you write *Customer Service, Miss Locklin?*"

"I will do that. I certainly appreciate your kindness and courtesy, Miss Locklin."

"No trouble, really. That's what we're here for."

*   *   *

Four o'clock and still no Meyer, so I went out and coaxed Miss Agnes back to life and went rolling on up Ocean Boulevard. I kept to the far right lane and went slowly because the yearly invasion of Easter bunnies was upon us, was beginning to dwindle, and there was too little time to enjoy them. They had been beaching long enough so that there were very few cases of lobster pink. The tans were nicely established, and the ones who still burned had a brown burn. There are seven lads to every Easter bunny, and the litheness and firmness of the young ladies gamboling on the beach, ambling across the highway, stretching out to take the sun, is something to stupefy the senses. It creates something which is beyond any of the erotic daydreams of traditional lust, even beyond that aesthetic pleasure of looking upon pleasing line and graceful move.

It is possible to stretch a generalized lust, or an aesthetic turn of mind, to encompass a hundred lassies—say five and a half tons of vibrant and youthful and sun-toned flesh clad in about enough fabric to half fill a bushel basket. The erotic imagination or the artistic temperament can assimilate these five and a half tons of flanks and thighs, nates and breasts, laughing mouths and bouncing hair and shining eyes, but neither lust nor art can deal with a few thousand of them. Perceptions go into stasis. You cannot compare one with another. They become a single silken and knowledgeable creature, unknowable, a thousand-legged contemptuous joy, armored by the total ignorance of the very young and by the total wisdom of body and instinct of the female kind. A single cell of the huge creature, a single entity, one girl, can be trapped and baffled, hurt and emptied, broken and abandoned. Or, to flip the coin, she can be isolated and cherished, wanted and needed, taken with contracts and ceremonies. In either case the great creature does not miss the single identity subtracted from the whole any more than the hive misses the single bee. It goes on in its glistening, giggling, leggy immortality, forever replenished from the equation of children plus time, existing every spring, unchangingly and challengingly invulnerable—an exquisite reservoir called Girl, aware of being admired and saying "Drink me!," knowing that no matter how deep the draughts, the level of sweetness in the reservoir remains the same forever.

There are miles of beach, and there were miles of bunnies along the tan Atlantic sand. When the public beach ended, I came to the great white wall of high-rise condominiums which conceal the sea and partition the sky. They are compartmented boxes stacked high in sterile sameness. The balconied ghetto. Soundproof, by the sea. So many conveniences and security measures and safety factors that life at last is reduced to an ultimate boredom, to the great decisions of the day—which channel to watch and whether to swim in the sea or the pool.

I found 8553. It was called Casa de Playa and was spray-creted as wedding-cake white as the rest of them. Twelve stories, in the shape of a shallow C, placed to give a maximum view of the sea to each apartment even though the lot was quite narrow. I had heard that raw land along there was going at four thousand a foot. It makes an architectural challenge to take a 200-foot lot which costs eight hundred thousand dollars and cram 360 apartments onto it, each with a view, and retain some elusive flavor of spaciousness and elegance.

Economics lesson. Pay eight hundred thou for the land. Put up two hundred thousand more for site preparation, improvement, landscaping, covered parking areas, swimming pool or pools. Put up a twelve-story building with thirty apartments on each of the floors from the second through the eleventh and fifteen penthouse apartments on top. You have 315 apartments. The building and the apartment equipment cost nine million. So you price them and move them on the basis that the higher in the air they are and the bigger they are, the more they cost. All you have to do is come out with about a thirty-three hundred net on each apartment on the average after all construction expenses, overhead expenses, and sales commissions, and you make one million dollars, and you are a sudden millionaire before taxes.

But if the apartments are retailing at an average forty thousand each and you sell off everything in the building except 10 percent of the apartments, then instead of being a million bucks ahead, you are two hundred thousand in the red.

It is deceptively simple and monstrously tricky. Meyer says that they should have a survey and find out how many condominium heart attacks have been admitted to Florida hospitals. A new syndrome. The first symptom is a secret urge to go up to an unsold penthouse and jump off your own building, counting vacancies all the way down.

As I did not care to be remembered because of Miss Agnes, I drove to a small shopping center on the left side of the highway, stashed her in the parking lot, and walked back to the Casa de Playa.

On foot I had time to read all of the sign in front.

NOW SHOWING. MODEL APARTMENTS. CASA DE PLAYA.
A NEW ADVENTURE IN LIVING. FROM $38,950 TO $98,950.
PRIVATE OCEAN BEACH. POOL. HOTEL SERVICES.
FIREPROOF AND SOUNDPROOF CONSTRUCTION.
SECURITY GUARD ON PREMISES.
NO PETS. NO CHILDREN UNDER FIFTEEN.
AUTOMATIC FIRE AND BURGULAR ALARM.
COMMUNITY LOUNGE AND GAME AREA.
ANOTHER ADVENTURE IN LIVING BY
BROLL ENTERPRISES, INC.

The big glass door swung shut behind me and closed out the perpetual sounds of the river of traffic, leaving me in a chilled hush on springy carpeting in a faint smell of fresh paint and antiseptic.

I walked by the elevators and saw a small desk in an alcove. The sign on the desk said: Jeannie Dolan, Sales Executive on Duty. A young lady sat behind the desk, hunched over, biting down on her underlip, scowling down at the heel of her left hand, and picking at the flesh with a pin or needle.

"Sliver?" I said.

She jumped about four inches off the desk chair. "Hey! Don't sneak up, huh?"

"I wasn't trying to."

"I know you weren't. I'm sorry. Yes, it's a sliver."

"Want some help?"

She looked up at me. Speculative and noncommittal. She couldn't decide whether I'd come to deliver something, repair something, serve legal papers, or buy all the unsold apartments in a package deal.

"Well . . . every time I take hold of something, it hurts."

I took her over to the daylight, to an upholstered bench near a big window which looked out at a wall made of pierced concrete blocks. I held her thin wrist and looked at her hand. There was red inflammation around the sliver and a drop of blood where she had been picking at it. I could see the dark narrow shape of the splinter under the pink and transparent skin. She had been working with a needle and a pair of tweezers. I sterilized the needle in her lighter flame, pinched up the skin so that I could pick a little edge of the splinter free. She sucked air through clenched teeth. I took the tweezers and got hold of the tiny end of it and pulled it out.

"Long," I said, holding it up. "Trophy size. You should get it mounted."

"Thank you very very much. It was driving me flippy," she said, standing up.

"Got anything to put on it?"

"Iodine in the first-aid kit."

I followed her back to the desk. She hissed again when the iodine touched the raw tissue. She asked my advice as to whether to put a little round Band-Aid patch on it, and I said I thought a splinter that big deserved a bandage and a sling, too.

She was lean, steamed-up, a quick-moving, fast-talking woman in her late twenties with a mobile face and a flexible, expressive voice. In repose she could have been quite ordinary. There was a vivacity, an air of enjoying life about her that made her attractive. Her hair was red-brown, her eyes a quick gray-green, her teeth too large, and her upper lip too short for her to comfortably pull her mouth shut, so it remained parted, making her look vital and breathless instead of vacuous. She used more eye makeup than I care for.

"Before I ask question one, Miss Dolan—"

"Mrs. Dolan. But Jeannie, please. And you are . . .?"

"John Q. Public until I find out something."

"John Q. Spy?"

"No. I want to know who you represent, Jeannie."

"Represent? I'm selling these condominium apartments as any fool can plainly—"

"For whom?"

"For Broll Enterprises."

"I happen to know Harry. Do the skies clear now?"

She tilted, frowned, then grinned. "Sure. If a realtor was handling this and you talked to me, then there'd have to be a commission paid, and you couldn't get a better price from Mr. Broll. There used to be a realtor handling it, but they didn't do so well, and I guess Mr. Broll decided this would be a better way. Can I sell you one of our penthouses today, sir? Mr. Public, sir?"

"McGee. Travis McGee. I don't know whether I'm a live one or not. I'm doing some scouting for a friend. I'd like to look at one with two bedrooms and two baths just to get an idea."

She took a sign out of her desk and propped it against the phone. *Back in ten minutes. Please be seated.* She locked her desk and went up to the eighth floor. She chattered all the way up and all the way down the eighth-floor corridor, telling me what a truly great place it was to live and how well constructed it was and how happy all the new residents were.

She unlocked the door and swung it open with a flourish. She kept on chattering, following a couple of steps behind me as I went from room to room. After quite a while she ran out of chatter. "Well . . . don't you want to ask *anything?*"

"The floor plan is efficient. The equipment looks pretty adequate. But the furniture and the carpeting and decorating make me feel sort of sick, Jeannie."

"A very expensive decorator did all our display apartments."

"Yeck."

"A lot of people are really turned on by it."

"Yeck."

"We've even sold some with all the decor intact, just as you see it. The buyers insisted."

"Still yeck."

"And I think it is absolutely hideous, and it makes me feel queasy, too. It looks too sweet. Cotton candy and candy cane and ribbon candy. Yeck."

"Got one just like this that hasn't been messed with?"

"Down on five. Come along."

We rode down three floors. The apartment was spotlessly clean and absolutely empty. She unlocked the sliding doors, and we went out onto the balcony and leaned against the railing.

"If the answers to the other questions make sense, Jeannie, my friend might be interested, provided you don't show her that one up on eight."

I asked the right questions. Was it long-term leasehold or actual ownership with undivided interest in the land? How much a year for taxes? How much for the maintenance contract? What were the escalation provisions in the maintenance contract? How much did utilities run? Would the apartment be managed, be rented if you wished when you were not using it?

"How many apartments are there all told?"

"Counting the penthouses—two hundred and ninety-eight."

"How many unsold?"

"Oh, very few, really."

"How many?"

"Well . . . Harry might cut my throat all the way around to the back if I told anybody. But after all, you are my surgeon, and I have the scar to prove it. We've got thirty-six to go. I've been here a month and a half, and I get free rent in one of the models and a fifty-buck-a-week draw against a thousand dollars a sale. Between the two of us, Betsy and me, we've sold two."

"So Harry Broll is hurting?"

"Would your friend live here alone, Travis?"

"It would be just more of a convenience for her than anything. She lives in the British Virgins. St. Kitts. She comes over here often, and she's thinking about getting an apartment. I imagine she'd use it four times a year probably, not over a week or two weeks at a time. She might loan it to friends. She doesn't have to worry about money."

Jeannie Dolan made a small rueful face. "How nice for her. Will you be bringing her around?"

"If I don't find anything she might like better."

"Remember, this floor plan is fifty-five thousand nine hundred and fifty. Complete with color-coded kitchen with—"

"I know, dear."

"Wind me up and I give my little spiel." She locked up, and we rode down in the elevator. She looked at her watch. "Hmmm. My long, exhausting day has been over for ten minutes. I read half a book, wrote four letters, and got operated on for a splinter.''

"There's some medication I want to prescribe, Mrs. Dolan. If there's an aid station nearby, I can take you there and buy the proper dosage and make sure you take it.''

She looked at me with the same expression as in the very beginning— speculative, noncommittal. "Well . . . there's Monty's Lounge up at the shopping center, behind the package store.''

5

MONTY'S WAS no shadowy cave. It was bright, sunny, and noisy. Terrazzo floor, orange tables, a din of laughter and talk, shouts of greeting, clink of ice. Hey, Jeannie. Hi, Jeannie, as we found our way to a table for two against the far wall. I could see that this was the place for a quick one after the business places in the shopping center closed. There were a savings and loan, insurance offices, a beauty parlor, specialty shops all nearby.

The waitress came over and said, "The usual, Jeannie? Okay. And what's for you, friend?'' Jeannie's turned out to be vodka tonic, and friend ordered a beer.

In those noisy and familiar surroundings Jeannie relaxed and talked freely. She and her friend Betsy had come down to Florida from Columbus, Ohio, in mid-January to arrange a couple of divorces. Their marriages had both gone sour. She had worked for an advertising agency, doing copy and layout, but couldn't find anything in her line in the Lauderdale area. Betsy Booker had been a dental hygienist in Columbus but hated it because, no matter what kind of shoes she bought, her feet hurt all the time. Betsy's husband was a city fireman, and Jeannie's husband was an accountant.

She seemed miffed at her friend Betsy. There was tension there, and it had something to do with Harry Broll. I tried to pry, but she sidestepped me, asked me what I did. I told her I was in marine salvage, and she said she knew it had to be some kind of outdoor work.

Finally I took a calculated risk and said, "If my friend likes the apartment, then I'll see what I can do with Harry Broll. Hope you don't mind hearing somebody bad-mouth him. Harry is such a pompous, obnoxious, self-important jackass, it will be a pleasure to see how far down he'll come on the price.''

"You said you were friends, McGee!''

"I said I knew him. Do I look like a man who needs friends like that?''

"Do I look like a girl who'd work for a man like that?''

We shook hands across the table, agreeing we both had better taste. Then she told me that Betsy Booker's taste was more questionable. Betsy had been having an affair with Harry Broll for two months.

"Betsy and I were in a two-bedroom on the fourth on the highway side, but she has gradually been moving her stuff up onto six into his one-bedroom, Apartment Sixty-one. I guess it hurt her sore feet, all that undressing and dressing and undressing and walking the length of the building.''

"Bitter about it?''

"I guess I sound bitter. It's more like hating to see her be so damned dumb. She's a real pretty blonde with a cute figure, and she just isn't used to being without a guy, I guess. It isn't a big sex thing going on. Betsy just has to have somebody beside her in the night, somebody she can hear breathing. She makes up these weird stories about how it's all going to work out. She says he's going to make a great big wad of money on some kind of land promotion stock and, because Mrs. Broll deserted her husband, he's going to be able to get a divorce and marry Betsy.''

"Couldn't it happen like that?''

"With him? Never!'' she said and explained how she hadn't liked Harry's looks and had checked him out. Her best source had been the housekeeper at the apartment building. Last November when the place had been finished, Harry Broll had taken over Apartment 61. He had an unlisted phone installed. He did not get any mail there.

"It's obvious what he was setting up,'' Jeannie said. "The world is full of Harry Broll-type husbands. The housekeeper said some Canadian broad moved into the apartment a week later. Harry would take long lunch hours. But he must have slipped up somehow, because Mrs. Broll arrived one day about Christmas-time and went busting in when Harry was leaving, and there was a lot of screaming going on. His wife left him, even though Harry had gotten rid of his girl friend. Then Harry moved out of his house and into the apartment. Betsy saw his house once. He took her there and showed it to her. She said it's big and beautiful. She won't ever get to live there. He'll dump her when he gets tired of her.''

She said two drinks would be plenty. I paid the check and took her out and introduced her to Miss Agnes. Jeannie was so delighted with my ancient Rolls that I had to drive her up to Pompano Beach and back. I let her out across from the Casa de Playa. I wondered if I should caution her about mentioning my name to Betsy, who might in turn mention it to Harry Broll and turn him more paranoid than ever. But it seemed to be too long a chance to worry about and too little damage from it even if it did happen.

She gave me an oblique, quick, half-shy look that said something about wondering if she would ever see me again. I discovered that I would like to see her again. We said cheerful and conspiratorial good-byes. She walked around the front of Miss Agnes, waited for a gap in traffic, and hastened across the highway. Her legs were not quite too thin, I decided. The brown-red hair had a lively bounce. From the far curb she turned and waved, her smile long-range but very visible.

*   *   *

It was dark when I parked Miss Agnes. I walked to F Dock and on out to Slip 18 and made a ritualistic check of the mooring line and spring lines, then checked to see how the *Muñequita* was riding, tucked in against the flank of *The Busted Flush,* fenders in proper placement to prevent thumps and gouges.

"Don't pretend you can't hear my foot tapping, you rude, tardy son of a bitch," Jilly said with acid sweetness. She was at the sun-deck rail, outlined against the misty stars with a pallor of dock lights against her face.

I went aboard, climbed up, and reached for her, but she ducked away. "What did I forget, woman?"

"The Townsends. I told you I accepted for both of us. Don't you remember at all?"

"What did we accept?"

"Drinks aboard the *Wastrel* and dinner ashore. They're over at Pier 66. Old friends, dear. She was the heavy little woman with the good diamonds."

"Oh."

"You're drawing a blank, aren't you?"

"I seem to be."

"Hurry and change and we can join them at dinner. And, dear, not quite as informal as you were at my little party, please?"

"Is she the woman who kept talking about her servant problem? No matter what anybody else was talking about?"

"Yes. That's Natalie. And Charles is hard of hearing, and he's too vain to admit it or buy one of those little electronic things. *Please* hurry, Travis." She eeled into my arms, pressed herself close to me. She smelled very good, and she felt springy and useful. "The sooner we go, dearest, the sooner we can leave their party and come back and have our own little party."

I gave her a good solid whack on the behind and said, "You go ahead and make excuses."

"Ouch! That was too rough, really. You'll be along soon?"

"Jilly honey, I don't know those people. I can't talk to them, and they can't talk to me. I could use up my life with people like that and never know where it went."

"They're my *friends!* I won't permit you to be rude to my friends. You accepted, you know."

"*You* accepted."

"But I expect you to have some consideration for—"

"Don't expect anything from me, Jillian. Sorry I forgot. Sorry you had to hang around waiting for me. Now go to your party and have a good time."

"Do you mean it?"

"Why shouldn't I want you to have a good time?"

"I have *had* it with you, you bahstid!"

"Sorry, Jilly. I just don't go to parties unless I like the people."

She went clicking down the outside ladderway and clacking her way aft and off the *Flush* and down the dock and away into the night. I went below, turned on a few lights, built a drink, ran a thumb down the stack of tapes, picked Eydie, and chunked her into the tape player and fixed volume.

Eydie has comforted me many times in periods of stress. She has the effortlessness of total professionalism. She is just so damned good that people have not been able to believe she is as good as she is. She's been handed a lot of dull material, some of it so bad that even her best hasn't been able to bring it to life. She's been mishandled, booked into the right places at the wrong time, the wrong places at the right time. But she can do every style and do it a little better than the people who can't do any other. Maybe a generation from now those old discs and tapes of Eydie will be the collectors' joy, because she does it all true, does it all with pride, does it all with heart.

So I settled back and listened to her open her throat and let go, backed by the Trio Los Panchos, Mexican love songs in flawless Mexican Spanish. She eased the little itch of remembering just how good my Irish lady had smelled, tasted, and felt.

A lot of the good ones get away. They want to impose structure upon my unstructured habits. It doesn't work. If I wanted structure, I'd live in a house with a Florida room, have 2.7 kids, a dog, a cat, a smiling wife, two cars, a viable retirement and profit-sharing plan, a seven handicap, and shortness of breath.

God only knows how many obligations there would have been once we were living in the British Virgins. Sing to me, Eydie. I just lost a pretty lady.

Through the music I heard the bong of my warning bell. I put on the aft floods and trapped Meyer in the white glare, blinking. I turned them off and let him in. I could not use Eydie for background music, so I ejected the tape and put a nothing tape on and dropped the sound down to the threshold of audibility.

Meyer said, "I was here an hour ago, and there was a beautiful, angry lady here, all dressed up, with someplace to go but nobody to go with."

"Fix yourself a knock. She decided to go alone."

"I bet."

"I am a crude, selfish bastard, and she is through with me."

He came back with a drink. He sat and said, "They tell me that a ring in the nose bothers you for the first week or so and then you never notice it again."

"Until somebody yanks on the rope."

"Oh, she wouldn't do that without good cause."

"Who the hell's side are you on?"

"She'll be back."

"Don't put any money on it."

"Speaking of money . . ."

"Harry Broll?"

"Yes, indeed. I had a long, tiring day. I talked to twenty people. I lied a lot. This is what I put together. It is all a fabric of assumption and supposition. Harry Broll is a small- to medium-sized cog in the machine called SeaGate, Inc. It is Canadian money, mostly from a Quebec financier named Dennis Waterbury, and New York money from a syndicate there which has been involved in other land deals. They needed Broll because of his knowledge of the local scene, the local contacts, legal short-cuts, and so on. It is a privately held corporation. They are going public. The offering price has not been set yet, but it will be about twenty-six or twenty-seven dollars a share. Most of the shares will be offered by the corporation, but about a third of the public offering will be by the present shareholders. Harry will be marketing a hundred thousand shares."

Cause for a long, low whistle. Old Harry with two and a half mil before taxes was a boggling picture for the mind to behold.

"How soon does he get rich?"

"Their fiscal year ends the last day of this month. The national accounting firm doing the audit is Jensen, Baker and Company. They will apparently get a guaranteed underwriting through Fairmont, Noyes. I hear that it is a pretty clean deal and that SEC approval should be pretty much cut and dried after they get the complete audit report, the draft of the red herring.''

I stared at him. ''Red herring?''

''Do you know what a prospectus is?''

''That thing that tells you more than you care to know about a new issue of stocks or bonds?''

''Yes. The red herring is the prospectus without the per share price of the stock on it or the date of issue. And it is a complete disclosure of *everything* to do with the company, background of executives and directors, how they got their stock, what stock options they may hold, what financial hanky-panky, if any, they've ever been involved in. Very interesting reading sometimes.''

''Nice to see an old acquaintance get rich enough to afford a hell of a lot of alimony.''

''When a company is in registration, they get very secretive, Travis. Loose lips can sink financial ships.''

''What would he want Mary to sign? He said it was to protect his interest in SeaGate.''

''I wouldn't have any idea.''

''Can you find out?''

''I can try to find out. I suppose the place to go would be West Palm. That's where the administrative offices of SeaGate are. That's where they are doing the audit, starting early so that they can close the books as of April thirtieth. It would be futile to try to pry anything out of the Jensen, Baker people. But maybe somebody in the SeaGate organization might talk. What did you do today?''

I told him. It was complicated and a lot of it was wasted time and effort, so I kept to the things that had worked.

Then I got to my big question. I had been bouncing it off the back of my mind for an hour, and it was going to be a pleasure to share the trauma with someone else.

''Here is this distrait husband, Meyer. He says he doesn't chase women. The Canadian girl was an exception, a big mistake. He wants me to tell Mary he wants her back. They'll go on a nice trip together. He is so rattled and upset he takes out his little gun and tries to kill me. Suppose he had. His two and a half mil would do him no good at all. And Mary could do him no good by coming back. Okay. He stashed his Canadian tail in Apartment Sixty-one at his Casa de Playa, and it was right there that Mary caught him. Harry got rid of the girl friend. Mary gloomed around for a time, and then she left him. He wants her back. He's sending messages through me, he thinks, to get her to come back to him. Let's say she decides to go back. She goes to their house and finds it closed up. She knows he has the apartment. So she'd go there next, and she'd find him all cozied up there with a blonde named Betsy Booker. Draw me some inferences, please.''

''Hmmm. We'll assume that the Booker woman is living in Broll's apartment with him, and the signs of her presence are too numerous to eliminate with short warning. Thus, when Broll came to see you, he either was very sure that Mary *would* not come back to him or that Mary *could* not come back to him. Or, possibly, if Mary could come back to him and decided to come back to him, he would have an early warning system to give him ample time to get the Booker woman out of the apartment and maybe even move back to Blue Heron Lane. This would imply that he knows where she is and has some pipeline to her. In either case, there would be considerable insincerity in his visit to you. Yet a man playing games does not pause in the middle of the game to murder someone out of jealousy. So we come to a final postulate which is not particularly satisfying. We assume that he is and was sincere but is too comfortable with his current living arrangement to want to think it through and see how easily it could spoil his second chance with Mary."

"He's not that dumb. Dumb, but not *that* dumb."

"Logic has to take into account all alternatives."

"Would you consider eating Hungarian tonight?" I asked him.

"Considered and approved."

"Poker dollar for the tab?"

"Food and drink, all on one."

6

THE WAY you find Mary is the same way you find anybody. Through friends and neighbors. And patience. Through shopping habits, money habits, doctor, dentist, bureaucratic forms and reports. And more patience.

You reconstruct the events of three and a half and four years ago and try to remember the names and places, the people who could be leads. You find out who Mary used to be, and from that maybe you find out where she is.

To start with, she was Tina Potter's friend. Came down to see Tina and Freddie. Came down from Rochester, New York. It was just a visit, and then she got her own place. Had some money, some kind of income. Didn't have to work. Came down because she had just been through a jolting and ugly divorce action. She's gotten her maiden name back by court order. Mary Dillon. Dillon and Dolan. I seemed to be working my way through the Ds. D for divorce.

A quiet young woman. We all got to like her. She had been putting the pieces of herself back together very very nicely. Then something happened. What the hell was it?

As last I remembered. Tina Potter had come over to the *Flush* late one afternoon and asked me if I could sort of keep an eye on Mary. Freddie had a special assignment in Bogotá, and Tina would go with him only if she was sure somebody would watch over Mary. The incident that had racked her up had been the accidental death of her divorced husband a few days before. A one-car accident on a rainy night somewhere near Rochester. Left the road and hit a tree.

I remembered Tina's earnest face as she said, "Two-bit psychology for whatever it's worth, McGee. I think Mary had the idea, hidden so deep she didn't even realize it, that one day her Wally would grow up and come back to her and then they'd have the kind of marriage she thought they were going to have the first time around. So with him dead, it can't ever be. She's trying to hang on, but it's very white-knuckle stuff. Would you mind too much? She trusts you. She can talk to you."

So I had spent a lot of time with Mary. Beach walking, driving around, listening to music. But if she laughed, she couldn't be sure it wouldn't turn into tears. She had no appetite. The weight loss was apparent. A drink would hit her too hard.

I suggested the aimless cruise. Get away. No destination. Mary knew by then it wasn't a shrewd way of hurrying her into the sack, because had that been the target, it would have happened one of the times when her guard was way down. She agreed without much enthusiasm, provided she could pay her share of the expenses and do her share of the chores aboard.

After two weeks she had really begun to come out of it. At first she had slept twelve and fourteen hours a night, as if her exhaustion was of the same kind that happens after an almost mortal wound. Then she had begun to eat. The listlessness had turned to a new energy. She could laugh without its turning to tears.

One day when we were anchored a dozen miles north of Marathon, among some unnamed islands, I took the little Sea Gull outboard apart, cleaned it, lubricated it, reassembled it, while she zipped around out there in the sailing dinghy, skidding and tacking in a brisk bright wind. When she came back aboard the *Flush,* she was windblown, sun glowing, salty, happy, and thirsty. Before she went off to take her very niggardly freshwater shower, she brought me a beer. She told me she hadn't felt so good in a long long time. We clinked bottles in a toast to a happy day. She looked, smiling, into my eyes, and then her eyes changed. Something went click. They widened in small shock and surprise, then looked soft and heavy. Her head was too heavy for her slender neck. Her mouth was softer. Her mouth said my name without making a sound. She got up and left me, her walk slow and swaying, and went below. It had been awareness, invitation, and acceptance all in a few moments, all without warning. I remember hastily fastening the last piece of the housing back onto the small motor and deciding that I could test it and stow it later. The lady was below, and there was a day to celebrate, a cruise to celebrate, a recovery to celebrate.

*   *   *

So try Tina and Freddie Potter. Long gone, of course. Scrabbled around in the locker where I throw cards and letters. Found one a year old. Address in Atlanta. Direct-dialed Atlanta information, then direct-dialed the Potter house. Squeals of delight, then desolation that I wasn't in Atlanta. Freddie had just gone off to work. She had to quiet the kids down, then she came back on the line.

"Mary? Gee, I guess the last I heard was Christmastime, Trav. She wrote kind of a short dreary note on the back of a New Year's card. She sounded pretty depressed, so I wrote her, but I didn't hear from her. What's the matter? Why are you looking for her?"

"She left Harry Broll early in January."

"That doesn't surprise me much. I never could understand why she married him. Or the first one, Wally, either. Some women seem to have to pick losers every time. Like some women pick alcoholics every time. But . . . I'd think she'd get in touch with you or with us. But you know Mary. Doesn't want to be a burden to anyone."

"How about family?"

"Well, there was just her mother up in Rochester, and she died two years ago. That was all she had, Trav. Gee, I can't think of who you could ask. But I'd think she'd have some friend she'd talk to. A neighbor or something."

She couldn't contribute anything more. She wanted me to let her know when I found out where Mary was, and she wanted me to come to Atlanta and stay with them and tell them all the news about everybody around the marina.

I couldn't use the Rolls pickup to visit the neighbors along Blue Heron Lane. There aren't any cover stories to fit that set of wheels. And housewives are very edgy these days. They have little peepholes set into the doors and outdoor intercom speakers and little panic buttons to push if they get too nervous. Respectability is essential. Nothing eccentric, please.

So I borrowed Johnny Dow's Plymouth sedan, and I wore pressed slacks, a sincere jacket, an earnest shirt, and a trustworthy necktie. I carried a black zipper portfolio and a dozen of my business cards. I am Travis McGee, Vice President of CDTA, Inc. It is no lie. Meyer incorporated the company a few years ago, and he keeps it active by paying the tiny annual tax. CDTA means nothing at all. Meyer picked the letters because they sound as if they have to mean something. Commercial Data Transmission Authority. Consolidated Division of Taxes and Audits. Contractors' Departmental Transit Acceptance.

In my sincere, earnest, trustworthy way I was going to hit the neighborhood on this hot Friday morning with a nice check which I had to deliver to Mrs. Harry Broll in settlement of her claim and get her to sign a release. I used one of the checks Meyer had ordered. It was on an actual account. Of course, the account was inactive and had about twelve dollars in it, but the blue checks were impressively imprinted with spaces for his signature and mine. He borrowed a checkwriter from a friend in one of the shops, and we debated the amount for some time before settling on a figure of $1,093.88.

"Good morning, ma'am. I hate to bother you like this, but I wonder if you can help me. My name is McGee. Here is my card. I've got out a check payable to Mrs. Harry Broll in full payment of her claim of last year, and I have a release here for her to sign, but the house looks as if they're off on a long trip or moved or something. Could you tell me how I could find Mrs. Broll?"

It was not a long street. Three short, curving blocks. Large lots, some of them vacant, so that the total was not over twenty-five homes right on Blue Heron Lane. The Broll house was in the middle of the middle block on the left. The canal ran behind the houses on the left-hand side, following the curves. Dig a canal and you have instant waterfront.

I made the logical moves. I parked the Plymouth in the Broll driveway, tried the doorbell, then tried the neighbors, the nearest ones first.

"I can't help you at all. We moved in here three weeks ago, all the way from Omaha, and that house has been empty since we moved in, and from any sign of neighborliness from anybody else around here, all the houses might as well be empty, if you ask me."

"Go away. I don't open the door to anyone. Go away."

"Mrs. Broll? Someone said they split up. No, we weren't friendly. I wouldn't have any idea where you could find her."

At the fourth front door—the fifth if you count the place where nobody answered—there was a slight tweak at the baited end of my line.

"I guess the one to ask would be Mrs. Dressner. Holly Dressner. She and Mrs. Broll were all the time visiting back and forth, morning coffee and so forth. That's the next house there, number twenty-nine, if she's home. She probably is. I didn't hear her backing out."

After the second try on the doorbell I was about to give up. I could hear the chimes inside. No answer. Then the intercom speaker fastened to the roughcut cypress board beside the front door clicked and said, "Who is it? And, for God's sake, just stand there and talk in a normal tone of voice. If you get close to the speaker and yell, I won't understand word one."

I gave my spiel, adding that the lady next door told me she would be the one to ask. She asked me if I had a card, and she had me poke it through the mail slot. I wondered why she sounded so out of breath.

I heard chains and locks, and she pulled the door open and said, "So come in." She wore a floor-length terry robe in wide yellow and white stripes, tightly belted. Her short, blond, water-dark hair was soaked. "I was in the pool. Daily discipline. Come on out onto the terrace. I'm too wet to sit in the living room."

She was a stocky woman with good shoulders and a slender waist. She had a tan, freckled face, broad and good humored, pale lashes and brows, pretty eyes. The terrace was screened, and the big pool took up most of the space. Sliding glass doors opened the terrace up into the living room. The yard beyond the screening and beyond the flower beds sloped down to a small concrete dock where a canopied Whaler was moored.

She invited me to sit across from her at a wrought iron table with a glass top.

"Try that on me again, Mr. McGee. Slowly. Is this the check?"

She picked it up and put it down and listened as I went through it again. "A claim for what?" she asked.

"Mrs. Dressner, it's company policy not to discuss casualty claims and settlements. I'm sure you can understand why."

"Mr. McGee, may I ask you a personal question?"

"Of course."

"How come you are so full of bullshit?"

I stared at her merry face and merry smile. But above the smile the hazel eyes were expressionless as poker chips.

"I . . . I don't quite understand."

"Go back to Harry and tell him that this didn't work, either. What does he think I am? Some kind of idiot, maybe? Good-bye, Mr. McGee."

"This isn't for Harry. This is for me."

"So who the hell are you?"

"How friendly are you with Mary anyway?"

"Very very very. Okay?"

"What happened to her when Wally got killed?"

She frowned at me. "She came apart. She flipped."

"And a man took her on a boat ride?"

"Right. And the way she talked about him, that's the one she should have played house with instead of Harry Broll."

"I almost thought about it seriously."

"You?"

"Travis McGee. *The Busted Flush*. Cruised the Keys and up the west coast to Tampa Bay. Taught her to sail. Taught her to read a chart. Taught her to navigate."

She put her determined chin on her fist and stared at me. "That *was* the name. You, huh? So what's with the funny games, coming here with your funny card and your funny check? If you knew we're close friends, why not start honest?"

"I have not seen her or talked to her in over three years, Holly. And don't jump on my knowing your first name and try to make anything out of it. The woman next door clued me."

"Hitting the whole neighborhood?"

"One at a time. Mary is . . . low-key intense. She hides a lot of herself. She doesn't make friends easily. But she needs people, so I thought she'd have to have a friend in the neighborhood. A friend, not an acquaintance. Right?"

"So right, McGee. Coffee and tears. Most women bug me. Mary doesn't. I . . . I still don't feel right about you. About taking you for granted. It *could* be some kind of a trick. I want to ask you things, but I can't think of anything to ask that you couldn't have gotten from Harry."

"He's trying to find her."

"You know it! I thought the silly son of a bitch was going to try to shake it out of me."

"When was this?"

"A couple of weeks ago. He'd had a couple. He got all weepy. He insisted I had to know where Mary is."

"Do you know where she is?"

"McGee, I know why Harry wants to find her. He wants her to come back to him and sign something and live happily ever after."

"It might be an ugly shock if she did come back."

"How?"

"She'd find the house empty, and she'd go look for Harry at the Casa de Playa, where he just so happens to be shacked with a divorcing blonde named Betsy Booker. In Apartment Sixty-one."

I couldn't read her expression. "So?"

"So isn't that where Mary found him with the Canadian?"

"Only two people could have told you that. Or three. Harry, Mary, or Lisa —the Canadian quiff."

"Wrong."

"The hell you say."

"I got it out of Betsy Booker's best friend, Jeannie Dolan, also from Columbus, who got part of it from Betsy and part of it from the housekeeper. Jeannie and Betsy take turns manning the sales desk at the Casa de Playa."

I saw her buy it and give a small nod. "So help me. That rotten Harry.

Jesus! The way I read it, Lisa was not the first. Just the first she caught him with. He really is one sorry bastard."

"How did she find out?"

"She thinks it was one of the girls in his office or a girl he'd fired, trying to make things rough for him. She got a phone call. The person on the other end whispered. Mary said it was spooky. Something very much to the point. 'Mrs. Broll, your husband has loaned Apartment Sixty-one in his new building to Lisa Dissat, and he'll be taking another long lunch hour today so he can drive out there and screw her.' So she drove out and hid somewhere until he arrived and went upstairs. Then she went up to the sixth floor and waited around until the door opened and he started to come out. She took a quick run at the door and knocked it open and charged past him and found the bare-ass Canadian getting ready to take a nice nap. I take it there was a certain amount of screaming going on for a while."

"Then Harry got rid of the girl friend?"

"She was packed and out of there the next day. Back to Canada. Harry told Mary. He confessed his sad story. He had gone to Quebec for business conferences with his Canadian partners. He had to dictate new agreements. They sent the secretary to the hotel. They worked very late. He was too tired to think clearly. She was pretty and available. It went on for the three days he was up there. He came back. Two days after he was back, she phoned him at his office from Miami. She had quit her job and followed him back to Florida. So he told Mary that while he was trying to talk Lisa into going back, he put her up at the apartment. I guess he was having a hard time convincing her. He talked from the end of November till two days before Christmas. That's a lot of long lunches and a lot of evening conferences."

"But Mary didn't leave him until January fifth."

"Harry told you that?"

I laughed. "I thought the silly son of a bitch was going to try to shake it out of me, too. This was just the other day. And he got weepy."

"So you're finding her for him?"

"May I ask you the same personal question you asked me?"

"Okay. Okay. I'm sorry. Why then?"

"For myself. Pride, I guess. Harry thought if she was really in trouble, she would come running to me. And the more I think about it, the more logical it seems. That she would. Besides—" I stopped suddenly.

"What's the matter?"

"When was Harry here, did you say?"

"Oh, two weeks ago."

"Can you pin it down to a day?"

"Let me go take a look at my kitchen calendar and see."

She came back and said, "Less than two weeks ago. It was a Monday morning. April fifth."

"He told me someone had seen Mary with me on April second. He was wrong, of course. Why would he come after you instead of me if she was seen with me?"

"Maybe he hadn't been told about it before he came to see me," she said.

"And maybe he was trying to get you to admit she'd moved in with me or some damn thing. What difference does it make anyway? He didn't act as if he was thinking very clearly."

"Mary was thinking about getting in touch with you. She was sitting in my kitchen wondering out loud if she should. That was after she'd decided to take off. Then she decided it would be better to have some breathing space in between, some time to herself first. I thought she would have written you long before now. It's over three months."

"She writes you?"

"Don't get too cute, McGee."

"Okay. Do you know where she is?"

"Yes."

"And she is okay?"

"I have no reason to think she isn't. If I was Mary, I would be relishing every damn moment. The farther from Harry, the better."

"That's all I wanted to know, Mrs. Dressner. That she is okay. I had to hear it from somebody I could believe."

"Hey! You're spoiling the fun. You're supposed to worm the whole story out of me. Or try to."

"It's Harry who has to know where she is. Not me."

"Friend McGee, I am not about to get you two men confused, one with the other."

"So she is a long distance from here. And should be relishing every moment. Right?"

"I've gotten some comedy postcards."

"I believe you. There are people you believe and people you don't. I don't need to know any more than I know right now."

She looked rueful. "Everybody believes me. Everything I'm thinking shows. I've got one of those faces. I'd make a rotten spy. Hey, sit down again. I haven't offered you anything. Coffee, tea, beer, booze? Even some lunch?"

"No, thanks."

"Believe me, I'm glad to have anybody show up there. This is one of the days when the house gets empty somehow. David—my husband—has been gone all week. He'll be home tomorrow, probably about noon. He's gone a week or more out of every month. Our two little gals are tennis freaks, so who sees them at all when the weather is like this? I miss hell out of Mary, I really do. You could choke down some terrible coffee at least. Pretend it's delicious, and I'll tell you where Mary is. Even if you don't have to know."

She brought coffee from the kitchen to the glass-top table on the screened terrace. Moving around had loosened the hitch in the terry belt, and when she bent to pour my coffee, the robe suddenly spilled open. She spilled coffee, clutched frantically, put the pot down, and gathered herself together and tied the robe firmly, her face dark red under the freckles. It was obvious she had not contrived it.

"Some people are solitary drinkers. I'm a solitary skinny-dipper."

"It's habit forming," I said.

She got paper towels and mopped up the spilled coffee and filled my cup the rest of the way. She sat and stared at me, lips pursed. Finally she said, "Thank you."

"For?"

"For not jumping to any conclusions, for which I could not exactly blame you. Good God, I tell you my husband is away, my kids are playing tennis,

I'm lonesome. I beg you to stay for coffee and then damn near drop my robe on the floor.''

"Some days are like that.''

"I like the way you can smile without hardly changing your mouth at all. It's kind of all in the eyes. Mary said you're a doll. She said big and brown and sort of beat-up looking. But you're bigger and browner than the idea I had of you. About Mary. That was a sordid scene at the Casa de Playa. It shook her. Friendship is friendship, but you don't tell your friends what to do when it comes to big emotional decisions. Through Christmas and the rest of December she spent a lot of time over here. I let her bounce it all off me. She was thinking aloud, arguing it out. Taking one side and then the other, while all I did was say 'um.' But I could tell which side was winning. Finally she said that if she hadn't already had one divorce, she would definitely decide to leave Harry. It was a lousy reason to stick around, just to avoid being divorced twice, which has a kind of ring of failure to it, failure as a person or as a woman. So she was going to leave him and go away and, to be real fair, think it all through. But the way she felt, she'd probably sue for divorce after the waiting period. I waited for her to really make her mind up, and then I questioned her to make certain she was sure, and finally I told her about a little problem I had once with her husband. There'd been a party down the street and the four of us, the Brolls and the Dressners, had walked back together, a little tight. They came over here for a nightcap. There were supposed to be falling stars. It was in the paper. I wanted to see them. We put out the lights on the terrace, and I stretched out on a sun mattress beside the pool, right over there, to watch up through the screening overhead. David went to the kitchen to fix drinks, and Mary changed her mind about what she wanted and went in the kitchen to tell him. Harry was on a sun mattress near mine. All of a sudden he rolled over and put his big old cigar mouth on mine and pressed me down with his big belly and ran his big paw up under my skirt and started groping me. I froze with shock for about one second, and then I gave a big snap of my back like a huge fishing shrimp and bucked him into the pool in all his clothes. It turned into a big joke. He said he'd gotten up and tripped and fallen in.

"When I told Mary about it, she was furious with me for not telling her sooner. I told her I hadn't told David, because he would have tried to beat Harry to death. I said that now she'd made her mind up, I could tell her about what Harry pulled that time. Frankly, what I was doing was trying to lock her into her decision to drop that jerk forever. Having her own money made it easy for her to get away. She got it from her trust officer at the Southern National Bank and Trust in Miami. Cash. A lot, I think. She didn't want Harry tracing her through credit cards or personal checks. She told me she didn't want to hear his voice or see his face once she left. Not for a long time anyway. We sat right out here one afternoon, a warm day for early January, and we looked at the travel folders she'd picked up from some little travel agency where she wasn't known. She wanted to go to the islands. Between the two of us we decided that Grenada looked the best, and it was certainly far enough, way down there at the bottom of the West Indies, almost as far as Trinidad. So the travel agency sent wires and cables and got her set up at what looked like a very plush place, the Spice Island Inn. She's sent me those joke greetings. Four or five, I guess. Airmail takes eight days! That place is a real hideaway.''

"Harry told me she left on January fifth. He said he came home from work and she was gone.''

"I think it was an impulse. She wasn't going to leave until Thursday or Friday. I was out most of that afternoon. Maybe she tried to say good-bye. I guess she probably drove down to Miami and stayed in a hotel or motel until her flight left.''

"I wonder what she did with her car?''

"I think she was going to leave it at Miami International.''

"Which is two fifty a day, no matter how many days, so she is up to a two-hundred-dollar parking charge.''

"McGee, the lady had decided to go first class all the way. That is what ladies do when they get mad enough.''

"What would Harry be wanting her to sign?''

"I haven't the faintest idea.''

"Good coffee.''

"Come on! It tastes like stewed tire patches.''

She walked me to the door. She got ahead of me and leaned back against the door and looked up quizzically. She stood a little taller than my elbow. "McGee, I just wondered. It seems like a hell of a lot of trouble you went to. The business cards and the funny check and the sales talk.''

"No big thing, Holly. The cards and the checks were in the cupboard. I have to hunt for people sometimes. You learn to use something that works.''

"Why do you hunt for people?''

"I do favors for friends.''

"Is that a line of work with you?''

"I really wouldn't know how to answer that question.''

She sighed. "Heck, I thought I could solve a problem for Mary. She never *was* able to figure out what it is that you do for a living.''

"Salvage consultant.''

"Sure. Sure.''

When I glanced back, she was standing on her shallow front steps, arms crossed. Her hair was beginning to dry and to curl a little. She smiled and waved. She was a sturdy, healthy woman with a very friendly smile.

7

I was on the beach by three o'clock that Friday afternoon and that was where Meyer found me at a few minutes to four. He dropped his towel, sat upon it, and sighed more loudly than the surf in front of us or the traffic behind us.

There were nine lithe maidens, miraculously unaccompanied by a flock of boys, playing some game of their own devising on the hard sand in the foamy wash of the waves. It involved an improvised club of driftwood, a small, yellow, inflated beach ball, one team out in the water, and one on the beach. Either you had to whack the ball out over the heads of the swimmers before they . . . or you had to hit it past a beach player who then . . . Anyway, it involved a lot of running, yelping, and team spirit.

"A gaggle of giggles?" Meyers said, trying that one on me.

My turn. "How about a prance of pussycats?"

"Not bad at all. Hmmm. A scramble of scrumptious?"

"Okay. You win. You always win."

He slowly scratched his pelted chest and smiled his brown-bear smile. "We both win. By being right here at this time. All the strain of a long, difficult, and futile day is evaporating quickly. Meyer is at peace. Play on, young ladies, because from here on out life will be a lot less fun for most of you."

"Grow up and be earnest and troubled?" I asked. "Why does it have to be that way?"

"It doesn't. It shouldn't be. Funny, though. They take all those high spirits, all that sense of fun and play, into a commune, and within a year they are doleful wenches indeed. Somber young versions of American Gothic, like young wagon-train mothers waiting for the Indians to ride over the ridge. And their men look like the pictures of the young ones slain at Shiloh. Idealism in our society is pretty damned funereal."

One of the players looked up the beach and gave a quick wave and then went churning into the water to capture the yellow ball.

"One of my constituents," Meyer said comfortably.

"You are a dirty old man."

"You have a dirty mind, McGee. I could not bring myself to ever touch the child. But in all fairness it does enter my mind. Lovely, isn't she?"

"Exquisite."

"Her last name is Kincaid, and I do not know her first name. She is known to everyone as Breadbox. She has an incredible appetite. She's an economics major at Yale. Quite a good mind. Her father grows tobacco in Connecticut. She drove down in a five-year-old Porsche with two other girls. This summer she is going to work in a boutique aboard a cruise ship. She has a dog at home named Rover, which seems to have come full circle and is now an 'in' name for a dog. She is getting over a romance which ended abruptly and does not want to become interested in another man for years and years, she says. Tennis used to be her sport, but now she prefers—"

"So all right already, Meyer. Damn it."

"I think she was waving at someone behind us."

"What?"

"I never saw the child before in my life. I was just putting together into one package some of the things some of the other young ladies have told me."

"Have you been drinking?"

"No. But you you'd like to . . ."

With as little warning as a flock of water birds, the nine maidens dropped the club and went jogging north along the beach, one of them clutching the yellow ball.

Meyer said, "I did not do well today, Travis. Just a few small items. Dennis

Waterbury is in his mid-thirties, bland, shrewd, tough, quick, merciless—and completely honest. He gives his word and keeps it.''

"Listen. I was able—''

"Let me deliver my few crumbs first. Harry Broll's cost on his one hundred thousand shares was ten dollars a share, and his money and the money the others put in was used to acquire the land, prepare sites, build roads, start the utility construction, water, waste processing, and so forth. A very golden opportunity for a man like Broll to get his foot in the door with people like Waterbury and friends. But in order to make it big, he had to pluck himself pretty clean, I imagine, and borrow to the hilt. Put up one million and drag down two million and a half. The odds are splendid, the risk low enough.''

"About Mary, I—''

"I can't seem to find out what she would have to sign. She wouldn't have to sign anything in connection with the stock. It's in his name. She isn't on his business paper.''

"Mary is alive and well and living in Grenada.''

"In Spain?''

"No. The island.''

"Dear chap, the one in Spain is Gran-AH-duh. The island is Gre-NAY-duh. The British corrupted it with their usual mispronunciation of all place names.''

"You've been there?''

"No.''

"But you know a lot about it?''

"No. I happen to know how to pronounce it. One has to start somewhere.''

"Let's swim.''

After about ten minutes Meyer intercepted me fifty yards from the beach, to ask, "How come you could find that out and Harry can't?''

"I found the only person who might really know for sure, aside from the travel agent. A neighbor lady, who shows her good taste by disliking the hell out of Harry Broll. She thought for a while Harry sent me. I softened her up. She makes terrible coffee.''

"Did Harry try to pry it out of her too?''

"Yes. Nearly two weeks ago. With tears. Without the gun. But rough. She said she thought he was going to try to shake it out of her.''

Meyer nodded and went gliding away, head up, in that powerful, slow, and tireless breaststroke that somehow makes me think of a seal when I see his head moving by.

When I came out of the water, he was sitting on his towel again, looking petulant, a rare mood for Meyer.

"Something bothering you?''

"Illogical actions and illogical emotions bother hell out of me, Travis. His wife has been gone over three months. How about checking accounts, credit cards?''

I explained about the trust account and her taking cash so that she couldn't be easily traced by her husband. He said he knew one friendly face in the trust department of Southern National, but of course it would be Monday before he could learn anything there.

"Why bother?" I asked him. "I'm satisfied. We know where she is. I don't give a damn how jittery Harry Broll gets."

We walked back across the bridge together, squinting toward the western sun setting into its usual broad band of whisky soup. "I guess it doesn't matter in any case," Meyer said.

"What doesn't matter?"

"What happens to anybody. Look at the cars, McGee. Look at the people in the cars, on the boats, on the beach, in the water. Everybody is heading toward their own obituary notice at precisely the same speed. Fat babies, and old women like lizards, and the beautiful young with long golden hair. And me and thee, McGee. A ticktock speed moving straight toward the grave, until all now living are as dead as if they had died in Ancient Rome. The only unknown, and that is a minor one, is how long will each individual travel at this unchanging, unchangeable pace?"

"Good God, Meyer! I was going to buy you dinner."

"Not today. This is not one of my good days. I think I'll open a can of something, go walking alone, fold up early. No need to poison somebody else's evening."

Away he trudged, not looking back. It happens sometimes. Not often. A curious gaiety, followed by bleak, black depression. It was a Meyer I seldom see and do not know at all.

Friday night. I took my time building a drink, showering, dressing, building a refill. Dark night by then, and a wind building up, so that the *Flush* moved uneasily, creaking and sighing against her lines, nudging at her fenders. I felt restless. I was wondering where to go, who to call, when Jillian came aboard.

She clung tightly and said she had been utterly miserable. She looked up at me with two perfect and effective tears caught in her lower lashes, her mouth quivering. The Townsend party had been desperately dull, really. She shouldn't have tried to force me to go. She shouldn't try to force me to do anything. She realized that now. She would not do it again, ever. Forgive me, Travis darling, please. I've been so lonely and so ashamed of myself, etc., etc., etc.

Once forgiven, all the lights came on behind her eyes, and the tears were flicked away. Mood of holiday. She had been confident of reconciliation; she had brought hairbrush and toothbrush. And all the urgencies a girl could muster.

*   *   *

In the morning a rare April rain was coming down hard, thrashing at the ports beside the half acre of the captain's wrinkled and rumpled bed, bathing us in gray ten-o'clock light.

"Is your friend in trouble?" she asked.

"Who?"

"That respectable married lady friend, of course."

"Oh. No, she's fine. It turns out she's hiding from her husband. She went down to Grenada."

She lifted her head. "Really? Henry and I went down there on the first really long cruise we took in the *Jilly III*. The Grenadines are one of the great sailing areas of the world. And the yacht basin at St. George's is really marvelous. You see people from everywhere, really. Yacht Services is very helpful.''

"She's staying at the Spice Island Inn.''

"Quite expensive. Is she alone down there?''

"Apparently.''

"She can get into all kinds of delicious mischief if she wants. If she's even half attractive, she won't be lonely. The air is full of spice and perfume down there, dear. It's a fabulously erotic island. Always so warm and lazy, with the hot hot sun and the hills and jungles and the beaches. Quite near the equator, you know.''

"I didn't know.''

"Well, it is. Don't you think we should go there one day?''

"I guess so.''

"You don't seem exactly overwhelmed with enthusiasm.''

"Sorry.''

"Are you going back to sleep, you wretch?''

"Not with you doing what you're doing.''

"This? Oh, it's just a sort of reflex thing, I guess. Darling, if you're no longer worried about your friend, could we be ready to aim the *Jilly* toward home on Tuesday? I can get her provisioned on Monday.''

"What? Oh, Tuesday. I guess so.''

"You don't seem to keep track of what I'm saying.''

"I guess I'm easily distracted.''

"You're easily something else, too.''

"What did you expect?''

"I expect, my dear, if we put our minds to it, we might make the *Guiness Book of Records*. Cozy? A nice rain always makes me very randy.'' After a moment she giggled.

"What's funny?''

"Oh, I was thinking I might decide we should go to Grenada during the rainy season, dear.''

"Ho ho ho.''

"Well . . . it amused *me*. When I feel this delicious, I laugh at practically anything. Sometimes at nothing at all.''

*   *   *

The unusual cold front that had brought the rain ahead of it moved through late on Saturday afternoon. She went back to the *Jilly III*. She said she had a thousand things to do before we sailed on Tuesday. She said to come over on Sunday, sometime in the afternoon. She said I could bring along some of my clothes and toys then if I wanted.

She left and I locked up again, hot-showered, and fell into a deep sleep. I woke at ten on Saturday night, drank a gallon of water, ate half a pound of rat cheese, and dropped right back down into the pit.

I woke with a hell of a start at four on Sunday morning and thought there was somebody coming aboard. Realized it had been something happening in a dream. Made a grab for what was left of the dream, but it was all gone too quickly. Almost a nightmare. It had pumped me so full of adrenaline there was no hope of going back to sleep. Heart bumped and banged. Legs felt shaky. I scrubbed a bad taste off my teeth, put on jeans and boat shoes and an old gray sweatshirt, and went out onto the deck.

A very silent night. No breeze. A fog so thick the nearer dock lights were haloed and the farther ones were a faint and milky pallor, beyond tangible gray. I could hear slow waves curl and thud against the sand. The craft on either side of the *Flush* were shrouded in the fog, half visible.

Meyer's gloomy message had been delivered none too soon. Everybody else had been ticktocked to the grave, leaving one more trip to complete—mine. Then, far away, I heard a long *screeeeee* of tormented rubber and a deep and ugly thud with a small accompanying orchestration of jangles and tinkles. The thud had been mortal, ticktocking some racing jackass into his satin-lined box, possibly along with the girl beside him or the surprised folk in the other car.

A few minutes later I heard the sirens, heard them stop at what seemed a plausible distance.

So stop thinking about this and that, McGee, and think about what you don't want to think about; namely, the lush future with the rich widow.

I climbed to the sun deck and went forward and slouched behind the wheel and propped my heels atop the instrument panel, ankles crossed.

That old honorary Cuban had simplified the question all to hell when he'd said that a moral act is something you feel good after. Conversely, you feel bad after an immoral act. But what about the act that is neither moral nor immoral, Papa? How are you supposed to feel then?

Look, we are very suited to each other. There is a lot of control either way on both sides, so timing is no problem at all. She pleases me. She knows how to intensify it. I like the textures and juices, spices and rhythms of her, all her tastes and tastings. We truly climb one hell of a hill, Papa, and when we fall off the far side together, it is truly one hell of a long fall, Papa, and we land truly and well and as zonked out as lovers can get. We laugh a lot. We like to hold each other afterward. We make bawdy jokes. She has a lot of body greed and finds me a satisfying stud. In her gratitude she takes a lot of extra effort to keep things varied and interesting. So?

There's this little problem. I go into the head, Papa, and look at this battered and skewed beach-bum countenance of mine, reflected in the mirror, and my eyes look dull, and my mouth looks slack, and I am wearing the remnants of a doggy little smirk. I know she is in there, a-sprawl on the bed, drifting in and out of her little love doze, and I look truly and well at myself in the mirror, and I do not feel good about anything or bad about anything. I just feel as if I had made one of those little diagonal lines you use to keep track. You know—four little vertical lines side by side and then the diagonal that crosses them out and ends the group.

In the mirror my nose looks too big and my skin looks grainy. I wear the doggy little grin. The smells of her cling to my body. There is the feeling of marking something off on a long score sheet. Something well and truly done that will have to be well and truly done for whatever years we both have left, because that is the bargain. Chop that cotton, tote that bale, plow that little acre of God.

What about it when you don't feel good and you don't feel bad? When you just feel that it's done for this time and done reasonably well, and later on the slack dangle of flesh will turn tumescent, and it will and can be done again, just as well as the last time? With proficiency, determination, patience, understanding, power, and skill. Isn't lovemaking as good a way as any to pass the time for the rest of your life? It tones the body, and it's acceptable exercise, and it makes two people feel good.

If I don't grasp the opportunity, somebody will find some quick and dirty way to let the sea air through my skull.

I'm overdue. That's what Meyer says, and that's what my gut says in a slow cold coil of tingling viscera. Overdue, and scared, and not ready for the end of it yet. The old bullfighters who have known the famous rings and famous breeds despise the little country corridas, because they know that if they do not quit, that is where they will die—and the bull that hooks their steaming guts out onto the sand will be a poor animal without class or distinction or style.

An animal as ordinary as Harry Broll.

I shifted position, dug the keys out of my pocket, and found the keyholes in the instrument panel. It is one of the tics of the boatman, turning on the juice without starting up, just to check fuel levels, battery charge. By leaning close, I could read the gauges in the pallid light.

Maybe it isn't just the woman. This woman. Or a passing of time. It is the awareness, perhaps, of the grasshopper years, of always pushing the pleasure buttons. The justification was a spavined sense of mission, galumphing out to face the dragon's fiery breath. It had been a focus upon the torment of individuals to my own profit. Along with a disinterest in doing anything at all about all those greater iniquities which affect most of us. Oh, I could note them and bitch about them and say somebody ought to do something. I could say it on my way to the beach or to the bed.

Who will know you were ever around, McGee? Or care?

Wait a minute! What am I supposed to be doing? Making up the slogan I shall paint on my placard and tote in the big parade? A parade is a group, and I'm not a group animal. I think a mob, no matter what it happens to be doing, is the lowest form of living thing, always steaming with potential murder. Several things I could write on my placard and then carry it all by myself down empty streets.

> UP WITH LIFE. STAMP OUT ALL SMALL AND LARGE INDIGNITIES. LEAVE EVERYONE ALONE TO MAKE IT WITHOUT PRESSURE. DOWN WITH HURTING. LOWER THE STANDARD OF LIVING. DO WITHOUT PLASTICS. SMASH THE SERVOMECHANISMS. STOP GRABBING. SNUFF THE BREEZE AND HUG THE KIDS. LOVE ALL LOVE. HATE ALL HATE.

Carry my placard and whistle between my teeth and wink and smirk at the girls on the sidewalk watching the nut with his sign.

Am I supposed to go out with my brush and yellow soap and scrub clean the wide grimy world?

If you can't change everything, why try to change any part of it, McGee?

The answer lit up in the foggy predawn morning, right over my head. A great big light bulb with glowing filaments, just like those old-timey ones over in Ft. Myers in the Edison place.

Because, you dumb-ass, when you stop scrubbing away at that tiny area you can reach, when you give up the illusion you are doing any good at all, then you start feeling like this. Jillian Brent-Archer is another name for giving up your fatuous, self-serving morality, and when you give it up, you feel grainy, stud-like, secure, and that doggy little smirk becomes ineradicable.

You are never going to like yourself a hell of a lot, T. McGee, so what little liking you have must be conserved. To become Jilly's amiable useful house-guest and bedguest would turn you into something which you are not—yet have an uncomfortable tendency to become.

You retain the fragile self-respect by giving Them the increasingly good chance of ventilating your skull or scragging you through the heart. There have been some rotten little scenes with Jilly, but the next one will be the most memorable of all.

So Mary Broll is okay. And there is a good lump of cash money stashed behind the fake hull in the forward bilge of the *Flush*. But it would be a good time, a very good time, to go steaming out and find the plucked pigeon and clean up its little corner of the world by getting its feathers back—half of them, anyway. Get out there on the range and go down to the pits and stand up for a moment and see if they can pot you between the eys. If they miss, maybe you'll get your nerve back, you tinhorn Gawain.

8

ON SUNDAY I did not feel up to facing the predictable fury of Lady Jillian. She wanted me aboard for drinks Monday evening. Time enough, I told myself.

Meyer came over to the *Flush* on Monday morning at about ten thirty. I was punishing myself for recent sensual excess by polishing some neglected brightwork on the instrument panel, using some new miracle goop that was no more miraculous than the old miracle goop.

Without preamble he said. "I phoned the trust department of the Southern National Bank and Trust Company and told the girl to put me through to somebody who could give me a trust account number. When another girl answered, I said that my name was Forrester and I was with Merrill Lynch. I said we had received a dividend which apparently should have been sent to Mrs. Harry Broll's trust account. I wanted to advise New York and mail the check along, and to prevent further confusion, I wanted the trust account number and the name of the trust officer handling that account. Mary Dillon Broll or Mrs. Harry Broll, Twenty-one Blue Heron Lane, and so forth. She told me to hold, and in a minute or two she came back and said the number was TA fifty-three ninety-one, and the trust officer was Mr. Woodrow Willow."

"Interesting, but—"

"I asked her to put me through to Mr. Willow. When he came on the line I introduced myself correctly and told him that I was a personal friend of Mrs. Broll, and she had told me before going away on a trip that he handled her account TA fifty-three ninety-one. He said that was correct. He sounded guarded. Properly so. I told him that Mrs. Broll had asked me to give her some advice regarding rephasing her accounts to provide a maximum income, as she anticipated some possible change in her personal status."

"You are getting very crafty lately, Meyer."

"Please stop rubbing those damned dials and look at me. Thank you. He sounded huffy then and said they were perfectly competent to give all necessary investment advice. I told him I knew that and that was why I had called him. I certainly didn't want to usurp their authority and responsibility. I said I seldom make portfolio recommendations any more, only for old friends and at no fee, of course. I said that women often become confused about the way a trust account is set up. I said I understood she had discretion over it, that she could determine what she wanted bought and sold and so direct them. He said that was indeed the case. He sounded wistful, as if he wished it weren't true. I said that I had been trying to get in touch with her in order to clear my ideas with her before coming in to discuss them with him. I said her husband had been unable to help me. I said her house was closed, and her neighbors did not know where she had gone. I asked if he could help me. He said she had phoned him early in January and had come in and drawn out all the accumulated interest and dividends, a sizable amount, and told him she was going away for a month or six weeks. She did not know where. He said he wished he could help me."

"A month or six weeks?'"

"Yes. Over three months ago."

"She could have decided to stay longer, you know."

"That's what Woodrow Willow said. He said she was quite upset when she came to see him. He said he could guess why she might be thinking in terms of independent income. So I said that, of course, maximizing income would enable her to live comfortably, but with a woman that young, inflation protection was important."

"Did it work?"

Meyer displayed an uncommonly wolflike smile. "He hesitated and I heard a desk calculator rattling and humming, and then he'd said that with her equities reinvested in income holdings, she'd have a pretax income of from twenty-five to twenty-seven thousand. So I told him that we should probably think in terms of eighteen to twenty or, in case of substantial alimony, consider tax exempts. He said he'd be delighted to talk to me about it, but of course he would have to have clearance from her to discuss her affairs. I said I realized that. He said he expected to hear from her very shortly, before the end of the month. Travis, I couldn't push him any further."

"I can see that. He was all set to snap shut at any moment. You got a hell of a lot out of him. Congratulations."

"I braced myself and took a risk. I said, 'Oh, yes, of course. To sign those things for Mr. Broll.' He hesitated and then said, 'It's inconvenient for her to come here in person. So she told me when she came in what Mr. Broll was asking of her. It's something that they did once before, and it was paid off. I had her sign the note. The loan was later approved by the loan committee and the board. A sizable loan, secured by the assets in her trust, with her signed authorization to me to deposit the loan proceeds in Mr. Broll's personal checking account. The effective date of the loan was to be April fifteenth, last Thursday. He requires the funds before the end of the month. She requested me to get it all set up but not to go ahead with it until she gets in touch with me and tells me to proceed or to destroy the signed documents and forget it. That's why I expect her to be in touch with me soon.' Travis, I remember you telling me to always press the luck when it is running your way. So I told him that I had heard that Broll was getting very agitated about getting the note and the authorization signed, so I imagined that Mr. Broll had been in touch with him. Mr. Willow has a very weary laugh. He said he hears from Mr. Broll almost constantly. He said he saw no reason to tell Mr. Broll everything was signed and ready to go, awaiting only authorization from her. I got the impression Harry tried to bulldoze him, and Mr. Willow got his back up. Then he began to realize he had told me more than he should. I could *feel* him pulling back. So I jumped in and said that actually the documents aren't signed until she says they are signed. Until then it is an approved line of credit, and if she doesn't care to use it, she doesn't have to. I told him he was quite correct, and I could feel him trying to persuade himself I was not working for Harry Broll. I hope he did.''

I put the cap on the miracle goop and swabbed up the few white places where it had dribbled on the varnish, miraculously removing the gloss. I spun the helmsman's seat around and looked at Meyer.

I said to him, "You are pretty damned intense about something I don't understand. We don't know whether Mary wants him to have that money or not. We know she's in Grenada, knowing he's sweating it out, and she's probably enjoying it every time she thinks about it. We know that Harry is getting so frantic he's losing control. He isn't thinking clearly. Are you?''

"She's been gone over three months now. Harry is living in a way that means he doesn't expect her to come back. You thought she'd get in touch with you if she was in trouble. She didn't. Who saw her leave? What travel agency did she use?''

I reached into the back of my mind and swatted something down. It had been buzzing in circles back there. I picked it up off the floor and looked at it. "Meyer, once on that cruise years ago we bought provisions and got a lot of green stamps. I think it was in Boca Grande. They got wet and got stuck together. Mary soaked them apart. It soaked all the glue off. She dried them between paper towels. Then she got a green stamp book and some Elmer's, and she glued them into the book. Meyer, she didn't even *save* green stamps. Another thing. We spent a lot of time anchored out, as far from marinas and boat traffic and shore sounds as we could get. So she kept turning off the generator, the air conditioning, even the little battery transistor radio. She made great things out of the leftovers from yesterday's leftovers. She's not stingy. If you asked for her last dime, she'd borrow two bits somewhere and give you thirty-five cents. But she has a waste-not, want-not twitch. I kidded her about it. She didn't mind. But it didn't change a thing. Holly Dressner told me Mary planned to leave her car at the Miami airport. Okay. Would Mary pay two and a half a day indefinitely? Ninety days is two hundred and twenty-five dollars. Not Mary. No matter how upset. She'd find out the rates and turn around, drive a few miles, make a deal with a gas station or parking lot, and take a cab back and catch her flight."

"If she had time."

"Unless she changed a lot, she'd get there two hours ahead when the ticket desk says one hour. She'd have time."

"So we should go look for her car?"

"Holly should be able to tell me what to look for?"

"Travis, I don't want to seem efficient, but why don't we phone Mary in Grenada? I would rather go below and drink one of your Tuborgs and listen to you fight with the island operators than drive to Miami."

I struck myself a heavy blow in the forehead with the heel of my hand, said a few one-, seven- and ten-syllable words, and we went below.

I started at eleven thirty, and by the time I got the desk at the Spice Island Inn, I was in a cold rage. It was a radio link, and nobody seemed to give a damn about completing it. I had mentally hung Alex Bell and Don Ameche in effigy several times.

At last I got the faint voice of a girl, saying, "Spice Island Inn. May I help you?" It was the singsong lilt of the West Indies, where the accented syllables seem to fall at random in strange places.

"Do you have a Mrs. Broll registered? A Mrs. Harry Broll?"

"Who? I am sorry. What last name, sir?"

"Broll. Bee-are-oh-el-el. Broll."

"Ah. Broll. There is no Mrs. Harry Broll."

"Was she there? Did she leave?"

"There is a Mrs. Mary Broll. She is here since many weeks."

"From Florida?"

"Yes. She is here from Florida."

"Can you put me through to her, please."

"I am sorry."

"Do you mean you can't?"

"There is the instruction, sir. Mrs. Broll does not take overseas calls. Not from anyone, sir."

"This is an emergency."

"I am sorry. I can write down for her your name and the number of your telephone. I cannot say if she returns the call. She does not wish to be disturbed by telephone calls from overseas. If you can give me your name?"

"Never mind. Thank you for your help."

"I am sorry." She said something else, but it faded away into an odd, humming silence. There were loud clicks. Somebody else said, "Code eighteen, route through Barbados, over."

I said, "Hey! Somebody."

The humming stopped and the line went dead as marble. I hung up. I stood up and stretched. "Mrs. Mary Broll has been there for a long time, but she doesn't take overseas calls."

"In case one might be from Harry, I suppose."

"That takes care of it. Right, Meyer?"

"I suppose so."

"It was your idea. I phoned. She's there."

"I know, but . . ."

"But?"

"The known facts now seem contradictory."

"Meyer, for God's sake!"

"Now listen to me. She wants to hide from her husband and think things out. She does not want to take any overseas calls. What would it cost her to get the operator and the desk clerk to deny that she's even registered? Ten Biwi dollars each, ten U.S. dollars total? No more, certainly. If she was sure her husband couldn't trace her, then the only call she *could* get would be from her friend Holly Dressner, and she would want to take a call from her I'd think. If she set it up so that he *can* find out where she is, then the refusal to take calls would mean she wants him to fly down, and the bait would be the loan he needs."

"First you simplify things, Meyer, and then you complicate the hell out of them. I don't know what to think now."

"Neither do I. That's my problem."

"So we drive to Miami anyway?"

*   *   *

Holly was home, and she was very helpful about the car. "It's one of those Volks with the fancy body. Oh, dear. What in the world are they called?"

"Karman Ghia."

"Right! Two years old. Dark red. Hardtop. Believe it or not, I can give you the license plate number even. We were shopping and we went to the place you get the plates together, and mine is about the same weight, so we were in the same series. Hers was one digit more than mine, so hers is One D three-one-oh-eight."

*   *   *

We drove down to Miami in Miss Agnes, and I jammed her through the confusions of the cloverleafs and put her in one of the new airport parking buildings, halfway up the long wide ramp leading to the third level, nosing her against the wall between two squatty Detroit products that made her look like a dowager queen at a rock fest. A mediocre hamburger, gobbled too hastily on the way down, lay like a stone on the floor of my stomach.

I pointed out to Meyer how our task was simplified. Apparently there was some kind of stone-crushing plant in operation not too far from the open parking garages. The longer any car had been parked there, sheltered from the rain, the more white powdered stone dust it had all over it. And Mary's would be one of the whitest of all.

There were more than enough ramps and levels and separate structures. Finally, on a top level on the side farthest from the entrance and exit ramp, I saw Karman Ghia lines, powdery white as a sugar doughnut. Even the plate was powder white, but the bas-relief of the digits made it readable as I neared it: 3108. Three months of sitting and accumulating stone dust and parking charges.

Meyer drew in the dust atop the trunk. It would have been a childish trick except for what he drew. A single large question mark. I wiped the windshield with the edge of my hand and bent and peered in. Nothing to see except a very empty automobile.

A police sedan drifted up and stopped close behind the Ghia. "Got a problem?" the driver asked. His partner got out.

"No problem, officer."

"Your car?"

"No. It belongs to a friend."

The driver got out. "And you can't quite remember the name of your friend, I suppose?"

I gave him my earnest, affable smile. "Now why'd you think that, officer? This belongs to Mrs. Mary Broll, Twenty-one Blue Heron Lane, Lauderdale, for sure."

"Girl friend?"

"Just a friend, officer."

"Doesn't your friend have anything to say?"

Meyer said, "I was not aware that you were addressing me with any of the prior questions, officer. I happen to have here—"

"Easy. Bring it out real slow."

"I happen to have here a page from a scratch pad which, if you will examine it, gives the name of the owner and the license number and description of the vehicle."

The nearest officer took the note and looked at it and handed it back. "Repo?"

"What?" Meyer asked. "Oh. Repossession. No. We happened to be parked here, and we knew Mrs. Broll has been gone for three months, and we wondered if she'd left her car here."

The other officer had gotten into their car. I heard his low voice as he used the hand mike. He waited, then got out again. "Isn't on the list, Al," he said.

"Parked here, you say. Now both of you, let me see some ID. Slow and easy. Take it out of the wallet. Keep the wallet. Hand me the ID. Okay. Now you. Okay. Now show me your parking ticket. What kind of a car?"

"Officer, it is a very old Rolls-Royce pickup truck. Bright blue. It's over there in that other—"

"I saw that, Al. Remember? That's the one I had you back up and see if it had the inspection sticker."

It stopped being confrontation and began to be conversation. "Nobody," said Al, "but nobody at all is going to arrive here in that freak truck to pull anything cute. Okay. For the hell of it, why were you wondering if this woman left her car here?"

"Not so much if she left it here, but to see if she was back yet. We were just wondering. If we didn't find it, maybe she left it someplace else, or she came back from her trip. But we found it, so that means she's still on her trip."

"She stays away too much longer, she can save money by forgetting the car." They got in and glided away without saying good-bye or looking back. I guessed they cruised the garages from time to time, checking their hot-car lists. It would make a good drop after a stolen car had been used for a felony. Leave it, walk across to the upper or lower level, leave the airport by cab or limousine. Or airplane. Or by private car previously stashed in the parking garage.

Meyer was quiet, and he did not speak until we were approaching Miss Agnes. He stopped, and I turned and looked back at him and strolled back to where he was standing.

"Are you going to break into tears?"

"Maybe. If you were as anxious to find your wife as Harry is, if it's financially important as well as emotionally important, wouldn't you report her missing and give her description and the description of her car with the tag number to the police?"

"I would think so."

"Then the number would be on their list, wouldn't it?"

"Yes. I mean, yes, dammit."

"And because you are thinking what I am thinking and because we happen to be right here, wouldn't it be a good time to find out about airline connections, McGee?"

"For two?"

"I have to finish my paper on the Eurocurrency which replaced the dollar. I promised the conference program chairman."

9

I SHOULD have boarded my early afternoon BWIA flight to Barbados with stops at Kingston and San Juan, thoroughly, if not visibly, bloodied by Jillian. This was Tuesday, and I should have been sailing the sea, not the air.

Cowardice is a very curious ailment. The attacks occur when you do not expect them. Instead of saying the rehearsed words, I heard myself say, "Jilly dear, the matter of the old friend has come up again. I wouldn't want to go cruising down to St. Kitts with that hanging over me. I wouldn't be able to stop thinking about it and wondering. It will take a few days . . ."

"Darling, I want you to be able to keep your mind on your work. Exclusively. Besides, the five-day forecast is foul. It might work out very nicely."

"No tantrum?"

"What sort of woman do you think I am, dear? That's hardly flattering, you know. All evidence to the contrary, I am not a spoiled bitch who goes about whining and screaming and drumming her heels. I'm grown up, you know. And more patient than you imagine. I have waited quite a while to have you all to myself."

"This shouldn't take very long."

"It'll be here when you return, dear Travis. Grenada?"

The habit of caution took over. It is an automatic reflex. Never tell anybody anything that they might in turn tell the wrong person. "No. That information is obsolete. San Juan."

"Of course. By this time Grenada must be well emptied out. She could have more fun in Puerto Rico. Are you and she going to have a lot of fun, Travis? Just like old times?"

"I'm not planning to. But you never can tell."

"Really! You are the most—"

"You keep asking the wrong questions. It's a bad habit."

"As bad as giving the wrong answers."

For a moment the tantrum was on the edge of happening, but she forced it back visibly, forgave me, kissed me a lingering farewell.

Now, five miles over Cuba, I wondered if it would have been better for both of us if I had made it clear I was never going to become her tame houseguest. I wondered if it had been cowardice or if I was really, underneath, the kind of miserable son of a bitch who likes to keep something in reserve in case he happens to change his mind.

Our captain, being a pleasantly enthusiastic host, invited us to look down at Cuba. I was following the McGee rule of international travel and was in first class, alone in the window seat, the bulkhead seat on the starboard side. It was British West Indian Airways, BWIA, and the leg room in the bulkhead seats on the 727 is good.

A clear and beautiful day. The tilled-field geometry of Cuba looked like the geometry of any other of the islands from five miles up. We moved across the southern coastline, and the shallow sea was a hundred shades, from the pale tan of shallow sand through lime and lavendar to cobalt.

"Sir?" the clear young voice said. She was a small, dusky stewardess with a high forehead, a blue-eyed stare of calculated innocence, a dark spill of glossy black hair. Her skin was a matte texture, and it was a half shade lighter than milk chocolate. She was the one with the absolutely great legs I had noticed when I had clambered onto their airplane. "You are going to . . ."

"Barbados."

"Ah, yes. Thank you, sir. Can I get you something to drink?"

"The last time I was on BWIA there was fresh orange juice. Do you still—"

"Oh, yes."

"With vodka then, please?"

"Oh, yes, right away, thank you." She twinkled at me and spun away, the short skirt flirting and snapping. It is changing in the islands, same as everywhere. The conservative island politicians and the white businessmen try to tell you that there is no racism, that black and white are treated alike and live amiably together in happy understanding and compassion.

But if you are observant, you notice that the more desirable the job, particularly the jobs women hold—stewardesses, cashiers in banks, clerks in specialty shops, hostesses in restaurants—the more likely they are to be bleached by past miscegenation. There are some true blacks in those positions, of course, but in the far lower ratio than exists in the general population. Look at the cleaning women, the cane-field workers, the laundry workers, to find the purest blacks in the islands. And the blackest blacks are, of course, probably 75 to 80 percent of the population of the West Indies, the Bahamas, the Windward and Leeward Islands. The other 20 percent is a perceptible lightening of color, shade by shade, all the way to unleavened white. Regardless of all protestations, the whiter you are the better you live. Blondes have the most fun. One of the most thoroughly ignored aspects of the Cuban revolution is how happily the black Cubans embraced the new order. Though the percentage is smaller in Cuba than elsewhere through the Caribbean, the pattern of discrimination was the same. Black Cuba was entirely ready for anything at all that promised equality in education, jobs, and health care. I didn't have to be Khrush or Mao. They would have built statues to a big green Martian if it could have delivered on the promises.

The curious and immediate and personal result of the color prejudice in the islands was that my pale chocolate stewardess with the great legs identified with me. We were both part of the ruling cabal. There could be an earnest friendliness in her unlikely blue eyes, an uninhibited flirtatiousness.

Another little girl of exactly the same color, but a citizen of the U.S. of A. and working, say, for Eastern on a domestic run, would have been working hard on an Afro hairdo, would have given me the precise number of millimeters of smile as prescribed by Eastern, would have been entirely correct, but her eyes would have been as empty as the ice of a long winter, concealing nothing more personal than a propagandized hostility, a prepackaged contempt, an ability to see me only as a symbol of oppression, not as a living creature walking two-legged on the same untidy world, trying to live through the weird years with a little bit of grace and care.

Too bad, somehow. The real guilt is in being a human being. That is the horrible reality which bugs us all. Wolves, as a class, are cleaner, more industrious, far less savage, and kinder to each other and their young.

When she came back with the screwdriver, she leaned one round, delicious knee on the empty seat beside me and reached and put the glass and napkin on the small built-in service area between the seats. I could read her name tag. Mia Cruikshank.

"Mia?" I said.

"Yes, sir?"

"I just meant . . . it's a pretty name."

She made a droll mouth. "Better than what it was, I think. Miriam. Mia is smashing compared to that."

"Smashing indeed."

*   *   *

So we went humming down across the blue seas under the blue skies of vacationland at approximately nine hundred feet per second, which is the muzzle velocity of the .45 caliber Colt automatic pistol, an ugly and cumbersome weapon. Our happy captain pointed out this and that. We stopped at Kingston and San Juan and points south. We lost more passengers than we took on. Each island had its quota of red tape, so that the stops were longer.

Mia kept me happily supplied with drinks and food, and we found it easy to smile at each other. We stood together when the sun was low, on the little platform at the top of the rolling stairs at the little airport on St. Lucia.

"You are remaining at Barbados, sir, or continuing?"

"To Grenada tomorrow morning."

"Oh, yes. That is so lovely an island. Of course, Barbados is very nice, too. Just one night is a short time to stay."

"I didn't want to stay there at all."

"I know. There is no way. You fly with us or Pan Am to Barbados or Trinidad, from Miami everyone arrives too late for the last flight to Grenada. It has to be daylight, of course, in the small aircraft. Where will you stay in Barbados?"

"I thought I would check it out after I get there."

"Oh, yes. The season is over. There is room everywhere. But really, there was room in most of the places during the season too this year. We did not carry so many people to Barbados this year."

"Why not?"

She glanced back over her shoulder and moved closer to me, lowered her voice. "I am not a rich, important person who owns a hotel, so perhaps they know what they are doing. But, sir, suppose this was in the season and you are traveling with a lady and you try to make a reservation for the two of you in Barbados, just to stay in a hotel room overnight to continue on in the morning. In your money, in U.S. dollars, to stay at the Barbados Hilton, it will be seventy dollars for one night, and there will be ten percent service charge added to that, so that it will be seventy-seven dollars. Even were you to stay at the Holiday Inn, sir, it will be fifty-five plus ten percent, or sixty dollars and fifty cents."

"Without meals? You have to be kidding."

"Oh, no. You see, sir, they will only make reservations for you on the Modified American Plan, which includes breakfast and dinner, even when it is clear you will have dinner aboard this flight and leave so early the next morning there is perhaps time for coffee and rolls. This is happening in all the islands, sir. It is perhaps the worst in Barbados, the worst of all. It is a fantastic greed. It is like some terrible animal out of control, so hungry it feeds upon itself and is killing itself. I should not say so much."

"I won't turn you over to the tourist board, Mia."

"Oh, thank you." She hesitated and scowled. "There is something I am trying to think how to say. It is really what is wrong now with the islands. It is why each year there will be fewer people coming to these lovely places."

"It's a shame."

She turned to face me directly and looked up at me. "Seventy-seven dollars is over a hundred and fifty dollars in our currency. In Biwi dollars. A house servant in Barbados *might* make fifty dollars, Biwi, a month. So how does a human person feel serving or cleaning up after another human person who pays two or three months' wages for one single night in a room? Sir, it is like such a terrible arrogance and thoughtlessness. It makes hate, sir. It makes contempt. So the cleaning is done badly, and the serving is done very slowly and badly, and there are no smiles. Then, sir, the person who is paying too much because the hotel owners are so greedy, he becomes very angry because, if he pays so much, the service should be of the very best, and everything should be very clean. When he is angry, then he seems to be more arrogant and rich and thoughtless, sir. Hate and anger back and forth, it is a terrible thing. There is no pleasure in work and no pleasure in vacationing here, and that is why each year, like this year, there will be fewer tourists, jobs, money. It is wicked. I keep thinking to myself, what can be done— what can be done? It is like the goose, sir."

"The goose?"

"The goose they killed to get at the golden eggs." She looked at her watch. An official was trotting up the stairs. "Now we will be going, sir."

After lift-off she gave me a final drink, and she and the other girls did their desk work and policed their area and changed to their ground uniforms. She had time to give me some advice. She told me that the nearest hotel to the airport was a five-dollar taxi ride, Biwi. The Crane Beach. She said the rooms were very small and primitive, but the beach was beautiful and the food was excellent. She said the management was surly and the waiters were insolent, but it was only for overnight, and it would be almost empty. Besides, the Barbados Hilton and the other hotels were a lot closer to Bridgetown, and so were ten to fifteen Biwi dollars one way from the airport. In most of the islands it appears that committees of taxi drivers determine airport locations.

"Just laugh at whatever they want to charge you at the Crane Beach, sir. The season is over. Put down ten dollars, Yankee, and tell them the service charge percentage is included, not extra. They will show you a rate schedule and tell you it is official and they cannot change it. Just laugh. They will take the money and give you a room. It is not so easy to get a taxi in the morning early from there. Just tear a Yankee dollar in two pieces and give half to the taxi driver and tell him when to come in the morning. He will be certain to return. Do not tip anyone at that hotel. They are shameless, and it is all included in the price of everything anyway."

I was genuinely grateful to Mia. I thanked her and said, "I hope I will get a chance to tell you how I made out."

"Perhaps, if you fly BWIA back to Miami, I will serve you again. How long shall you be in Grenada, sir?"

"A few days. Any idea where I should stay?"

"Oh, no. I do not know that island so well. This is not a vacation for you. Business, yes?"

"How do you know?"

"I think I can tell if a man is not one who would take a vacation alone, sir. Good luck, sir."

*   *   *

My taximan arrived the next day three minutes before the stipulated hour. He smiled broadly when he saw me standing in the early-morning light outside the hotel gates with my single piece of carryon luggage. He decided that it was a splendid idea, the half of the paper dollar. It left each of us with an investment to protect. He had brought some tape, and he put his dollar back together before we started off. His name was Oswald, and he was a thin man with several gold teeth. He drove his elderly white Plymouth with that kind of care which is more involved with not breaking anything than not hitting anybody.

I took LIAT, a BWIA subsidiary, to Grenada, a direct flight of about forty minutes. It was an old Avro with the rows shoved closer together to increase capacity, so that the little oval windows did not match the seat positions. Two big propjet Rolls-Royce brutes powered the small aircraft. The stewardess was about the same size and shape as Hubert Humphrey. The pilot had Walter Mitty dreams of being a fighter pilot. It was an interesting takeoff and an even more interesting landing.

At Grenada's grubby little airport I once again had to show my driver's license and turn over that card form which serves as embarkation and debarkation permit, depending on how you fill out the blanks.

And then came a fascinating ride in a taxi. The island is only twenty-one miles long and twelve miles wide. The airport is about as far as it could possibly be from the principal town, St. George's. The morning ride took one full hour, and I would not have wanted my man to have tried to shave five minutes off the elapsed time. I helped with the brakes so continuously that my right leg was nearly paralyzed when we finally came down out of the mountains to sea level. The driver—he gave me his card—was Albert Owen, and he had a Chevrolet assembled in Australia with a suspension system designed for the Outback of Australia. He had put fifty-three thousand incredible miles on it on that improbable road system, using up God only knows how many sets of brake linings. Drive on the left. Average width of road— one and a quarter lanes. No shoulders. Blind corners. Big lumps, deep potholes, children, dogs, pigs, donkeys, bicycles, trucks, buses, motorcycles. So honk the horn almost continuously, shift up and shift down, swerve, leap, squeal, slide, accelerate—and all the time Albert Owen was hollering back over his shoulder at me, pointing at bah-nah-nah tree, almond tree, sugarcane, sar. Over there mammy apple, coconut plahntation, sar, cocoa; also you are seeing nutmeg, sar. Many spices.

Once when a small insane truck came leaping at us on the wrong side around a bend, Albert swerved smartly. It missed us by the thickness of a coat of paint. Albert laughed and laughed. He said, "That is one foolish driver, sar. He nearly mosh us."

But nobody actually did mosh us. It was hard to believe they were not trying. Were the fates to put Albert down on any weekday morning on the Palmetto Turnpike heading into Miami with the inbound torrent, the terror of it might put him into a dead faint. A Miami cabdriver suddenly transported into Albert's mountains might conceivably run weeping into the jungle.

People certainly did go about moshing people. The dead cars amid the lush vines and wild shrubs were proof enough of that.

Albert asked me where my reservation was as we plummeted down toward the town and blue late-morning sea beyond. I said I had none but would look about a little. He said there were no problems this time of year. There had been trouble with the government water supply. When the hotel cisterns had run out, many people had left. Now the water was on again, but there were not so many tourists as on other Aprils. I found out that the Grenada Beach Hotel was the place most centrally located on Grande Anse, the two miles of crescent beach just south of the town, looking westward. I asked him if he would wait there for me. We made certain financial negotiations.

I left my single piece of luggage with him. He parked in the vehicle circle outside the main doors. I walked in and through an open lobby area and found a thatched bar off to the left, open to the outdoors, looking out across a long expanse of green lawn and tall, graceful coconut palms toward the garden of beach umbrellas, toward the bright colors of beach chairs and towels on the distant sand.

A bored bartender in a red coat appeared from some unknown hiding place, yawning. He made me a delicious rum punch with grated nutmeg afloat on it. He asked for my room number, and I paid cash for my drink, then gifted him with some of the Biwi I had picked up at the money-changer's booth in the temple of Miami International. He brightened visibly, and I asked him if he had a phone back there, and he said he did, and he said he would be glad to phone the Spice Island Inn for me. He did so and handed me the phone.

"What number is Mrs. Broll in, please? Mrs. Mary Broll?"

"Ah . . . yes, she is in Cottage Fifty, sir. Shall I ring her for you?"

"No, thank you," I said and hung up.

I finished my drink very very slowly. It is a very strange reluctance, a curious hesitation that can immobilize you at such a time. You are eager to prove to yourself that you've been quite wrong, that you've taken too many small things and built them up into a fantasy structure that cannot be true.

Yet, if by some chance the fantasy proves to be reality, most of the game is still left to play, and an ugly game it can be.

It could be a delicious surprise. I could see the shape of Mary's familiar mouth, the wide and startled eyes, and then the rush of pleasure, the embrace.

"The Spice Island Inn is close by?"

"That direction. Very close. A small walk, sir. Two minutes."

But in the hot tropical blaze of April a man in slacks and sport shirt, socks and shoes would be as conspicuous on that beach, I found, as in a Mother Hubbard at a nudist camp. I went back through the hotel and found Albert dozing in the shade. I woke him, and we got into the broiling taxi and rode south to the entrance to the Spice Island Inn.

Meyer and I had tried to cover all eventualities in the long planning session we'd had before I left. In the island there appeared to be so little interest in any verification of identity that the risk factor seemed very minor indeed. If we were wrong, I was going to feel a little foolish. But if we were right, there was a chance I could feel something beyond mere foolishness.

And so, in Albert Owen's back seat I switched the cash money, all of it, from one wallet to another and became Gavin Lee. Known as Gav. Known as Mr. Lee. This follows Meyer's theory that when you pick a new name, pick one that has the same basic vowel sounds. Then you will react if you hear somebody behind you say your assumed name.

I was going to carry my own suitcase in. Albert did not think that was appropriate. The desk was very cordial. Nothing creates such a flavor of genuine, heartfelt welcome as a nearly empty hotel. They showed me the rates. They told me I had a choice of plans. They showed me a map of the place with all manner of accommodations. What would please Mr. Lee, the ostensibly vacationing land developer from Miami, Scottsdale, Acapulco, Hawaii, Palm Springs, and Las Vegas? Well, I'm kind of curious about those with the private pool. These here on your map. Just this row of them, eh? How about this one right here on the end? Number . . . I can't read it upside down. Thank you, 50. Full. Are all these full then? Just 50, 57, and 58? I can see there are two bedrooms, but I don't see any one-bedroom ones with the walled garden and the pool, so . . . now what will it be on . . . a European Plan? After a few days I may change, depending on how the dining room is here. Of course. I'm sure it's marvelous. All right. Quote me on a per day . . . That's $28, single? That's U.S.? Hmmm. Plus ten percent service charge and five percent tax, which is . . . $32.34 per day. Look, I'm carrying a bit more cash than I intended. Would you mind taking this hundred-dollar bill for three days in advance? And I'll bring you an envelope to put in the safe.

I paid Albert off and told him I would keep his card and I would certainly get him to drive me back to the airport some day. A bellhop led me down a long long path to the newest line of attached bungalows, the ones with the pool in the garden. The row was a good 250 yards from the hotel proper. He demonstrated the air conditioning, the button to push for food service, the button to push for drink service.

Then he went away. I was left in silence, in the shadowed coolness of the tourist life.

Drive the clenched fist into the palm. *Pock!*

"Be here, baby, Just *be* here!"

10

THE ROW of tall attached cottages with a double peak on the roof of each one was set at a slight angle to the beach, so that architecturally they could be set back, one from the next, to provide total privacy for the individual walled gardens where the small swimming pools were.

The row of cottages were back a hundred feet and more from the beach. Between the front gates of the cottages and the beach itself was a private expanse of sand, landscaped palms, sea grapes, and almond trees, with sun chaises spotted about at intervals far enough apart for privacy.

I put on swim trunks and took up a position on a chaise fifty feet from my front gate, turning it in such a way that I could watch the gate of number 50. By then it was past noon. The tropic sun had such a hefty sting I knew even my deep and permanent tan would not be immune, not without a little oil and a little limitation on the exposure time.

At twenty minutes to one the gate opened and a young woman came out. She was of medium height, delicately and gracefully built. Her dark hair was quite long, and she had a white band above her forehead clipping it in place. She seemed to be somewhere in her twenties. I could not make a closer guess at that distance. She wore eccentric sunglasses with huge round lenses in dark amber. She wore a don't-swim-in-it bikini fashioned of white elasticized cord and swatches of watermelon-colored terry cloth. She was two shades darker than Mia Cruikshank, a perfect and even tan which could have come only from untold hours of total discipline and constant care.

A man came out with her. Youngish, lithe, laughing, and saying something that made her laugh. Awesomely muscled, moving well so that muscles bulged and slid under the red-bronze tan. A Riviera swimming outfit, little more than a white satin jock-strap. She walked a few steps and then turned in a proprietary way and went back and tested to see if the gate was locked. She looked in her small white Ratsey bag, apparently to make sure that her key was there. Then they walked toward the hotel.

My heart had turned heavy, and there was a taste of sickness in my throat. But you have to be certain, terribly certain. Like a biopsy. Make absolutely sure of the malignancy. Because the surgery is radical.

I gave them five minutes and then followed the same route. I found them in another of the ubiquitous thatched bars, having a drink at a shady table and still laughing. A cheerful pair. I went to the bar and ordered a drink. When I had a chance, I asked the bartender if the woman at the table was a certain Lois Jefferson. He looked troubled. He said he knew them by the numbers. Just a moment, please. He went to the other end of the bar and came back with a signed drink tab. Mary D. Broll. Number 50. He showed it to me. I thanked him, said I was wrong. I winked at him and said, "But that is not Mr. Broll?"

He had a knowing smile. "It is just a friend. He has been a friend for a week, I think. He works, I think, on a private boat. That is what I hear. It is easy to make friends here."

I picked my drink up and moved along the bar to a stool that was about a dozen feet from their table. I turned around on the stool, my back to the bar, and looked at her with obvious and amiable and very thorough apprecia-tion. She was worth appreciating, right from the brown, slender, tidy little ankles right on up—not too quickly—to a ripely cushioned little mouth, dark eyes set in an interesting tilt, a broad, immature, and vulgar little nose.

She put her glasses back on and leaned over and said something to her nautical friend. He put his drink down and turned around and stared back over his shoulder at me. I smiled and nodded at him. He had a Prince Valiant haircut, and his hair was the dark molten shade of some golden retrievers. His face had a tough, pinched, disadvantaged look which did not go with the Valiant hair or the beachboy body. I do not make any judgments about hair length, mine or anyone's. I own some Sears electric clippers with plastic gadgets of various shapes that fit on the clippers to keep you from acciden-tally peeling your hair off down to the skull. I find that long hair is a damned nuisance on boats, on the beach, and in the water. So when it gets long enough to start to make me aware of it, I clipper it off, doing the sides in the mirror and the back by feel. The sun bleaches my hair and burns it and dries it out. And the salt water makes it feel stiff and look like some kind of Dynel. Were I going to keep it long, I would have to take care of it. That would mean tonics and lotions and special shampoos. That would mean brushing it and combing it a lot more than I do and somehow fastening it out of the way in a stiff breeze. Life is so full of all those damned minor things you have to do anyway, it seems nonproductive to go looking for more. So I go hoe the hair down when it attracts my attention. The length is not an expression of any social, economic, emotional, political, or chronographic opinion. It is on account of being lazy and impatient. No reason why the male can't have long, lovely, dark-golden hair if he wants it. But it is a personal decision now, just as it was during the Crusades and the Civil War.

He kept staring right at me, and I kept smiling at him. So he got up fast and rolled his shoulders as he covered the twelve feet to stand in front of me, bare feet spread and braced.

"Chief, stop the bird-dog routine. You're annoying the lady."

"Me? Come *on* now! Don't let her kid you. Lois and I have known each other for a long time. She knows I like to look at her. Always have. And I know she likes being looked at. Right, dear?"

"You're out of your tree, chief. Knock it off. She isn't Lois."

I stood up. "She's Lois Jefferson. Believe me!" I edged by him as he tried to block me away from the table. "Lois, honey, it's Gav Lee, for God's sake. It was a good joke, but let's not run it into the ground."

She took the glasses off and looked up at me. "Really. I'm not Lois. I'm Mary Broll."

I boggled at her. "Not Lois Jefferson from Scarsdale? Not Tom's wife?"

It sucked in the fellow nicely. He was all alerted for games. When you roam in public with an item like that woman, you keep the guard way up. "Honey," he said, "how about this clown? You get it? Tom Jefferson. Thomas Jefferson. Stop annoying us, chief, or I'll call the—"

I turned on him. "Really. Would it put too much of a strain on you to have a little common courtesy? Her husband has always had the nickname Tom, for quite obvious reasons. His real name is . . ." I turned back to her. "What *is* Tom's real first name, dear?"

She laughed. "But I am really *not* your friend!"

I stared at her. "That can't be possible. It's the most fantastic look-alike . . . You wouldn't believe . . . Miss Broll, would you—"

"Mrs. Broll."

"I'm sorry. Mrs. Broll, would it be rude of me to ask you to stand up for just a moment."

"I guess not."

"Now just one goddamn—"

I turned on him again. "What harm can it do, Mr. Broll?"

She stood up beside her chair. I moved closer to her, and I stared into her eyes from close range. "By God, I *am* wrong. I would never have believed it. You are a little bit taller than Lois, and I think your eyes are a darker shade, Mrs. Broll."

"Now go away," the man said.

As she sat down she said, "Oh, shut up, Carl. You get so boring sometimes. The man made a mistake. All right? All right. Please forgive Carl, Mr. . . ."

"Lee. Gavin Lee. Gav to my friends."

"I don't see any friends of yours around here," the man said.

She gave me a pretty and well-practiced smile. "Gav, this rude animal is Carl Brego. Carl, shake hands nicely with Gav, or you can damned well take off."

I saw the little tightening around the eyes and knew the childish bit he was going to try. So when he put his hand out, I put my hand into his much too quickly for him to close his hand to get my knuckles. I got my hand all the way back, deep into the web between thumb and finger. Then I could just maintain a mild, firm clasp and smile at him as he nearly ruptured his shoulder muscles trying to squeeze my hand to broken pulp.

"Sorry about the little misunderstanding, Carl," I said. "I'd like to buy you two nice people a drink."

He let go of my hand and sat down. "Nobody invited you to join the party, chief."

He had fallen into that one, too. He was scoring very badly. I said, "I don't expect to sit down with you, Carl. Why should I? I was going to go to that table way over there and have my own drink over there and send two to this table. You act as if I'm trying to move in on you. How far would I get, Carl? As you are not Mr. Broll, then this lovely lady is a friend of yours. You are having lunch together. Just the two of you. If I were having lunch with her, I would be very ugly about anybody trying to move in. I just think you overreact, Carl. I made a little mistake. You keep getting rude for no reason.

But I'll still buy those drinks. I was thinking of it as an apology, not a ticket to the party."

So saying, I gave the lady a little bow and marched on over to my distant table and told the waiter to give them anything they might want. I sat with my back towards them.

It did not take her long. Four minutes, I think it was, before he appeared beside my chair, standing almost at attention.

"Excuse me. Mrs. Broll would be very happy if you would join us for lunch."

I smiled up at him. "Only if you are absolutely certain you don't mind, Brego."

It hurt his mouth to say it. It hurt his whole face. "Please join us, Mr. Lee."

*   *   *

All through lunch I knew Brego was waiting and planning. When I saw that he wasn't at all upset that I was living just a few doors—or a few gardens—away from his pretty friend, I could almost guess the kind of routine he had figured out.

And during lunch I had managed to steer the conversation in a direction that gave me a chance to awaken more than a flicker of interest in her eyes and at the same time gave her a chance to shove a little blade into Carl Brego and give it a twist.

I said, "I take little flyers in island property sometimes. Actually, that's why I'm here. Some associates said I ought to take a look at this one. Anyway, usually I like to pyramid, but quite a while ago I got into Freeport up in the Bahamas at the right time and got out at exactly the right time with much more than I'd expected, so I thought I'd give myself a little present. So I bought this great big, ridiculous brute of a schooner in Nassau and had the yard that sold it to me hire aboard a crew, and I actually set out for *this* island. But the guest I invited aboard for the trip became terribly seasick. We made it as far as Great Inagua and got off, both of us, at Matthew Town and arranged passage from there back to civilization. I had the crew take the boat back to Nassau. As I remember, my accountants told me the net loss was something like thirteen thousand dollars after I'd had the yard resell the schooner. But it would have been cruel and unusual punishment to have made the young lady sail one more mile."

Something behind her dark eyes went *ding,* and a cash drawer slid open in her skull. She counted the big bills and shut it again and smiled and said, "Carl knows all about yachts. He sails one around for a very fat rich lady, don't you, darling?"

"That must be very interesting," I said.

"He's waiting on Grenada until she arrives with friends," the woman said. "You know. Like a chauffeur, parked somewhere."

"Knock it off." Carl said in a small humble voice.

"Please?" she said.

"Please."

And that made it even more imperative. I decided I was reading her well enough to see that she knew the direction the tensions would take and would give the ceremony a chance to get under way at the first opportunity. And would want to watch.

When we got to her gate, there was no one in sight. The breeze had stopped. Sweat popped out immediately on all three of us. I felt it run down my back.

"Do come in, Gav," she said. "Do join us."

She was starting to unlock the gate. Carl said, "So it's enough already."

"Enough?" she said blankly. "Enough?"

"Honey, the guy is taking a cheap shot, and I'm going to run him off."

She licked her mouth. "Carl, sweetie, why do you have to be—"

"You can go in out of the heat, or you can stay and watch how it's done, Mary. Either way I run this smartass off."

"Any special direction?" I asked.

"Pick the one you like best, chief," he said with a jolly grin of anticipation. "Start now and save yourself grief."

"Take your best shot, Brego." He took it. I was worried that he might know too much about what he wanted to do. If he did, it was going to take a long time in the hot sun, and if he didn't, it could be reasonably quick.

He did a little bounce, a little prance. He pawed with the clumsy, measuring left and then came leaping in, following up on the right hook that he had brought up from about five feet behind him, practically at ground level. He did not know what he was doing. People who know do not go around taking the chance of hitting the solid bone of skull or jaw with the bare fist. A broken hand is incapacitating. It takes a long, tiresome time to heal. He wanted to pop me one and let the momentum carry him into me so he could get his hands and arms on me and put those muscles to work. He gave me lots of time for a decision. If I fell back away from it, he was going to tumble onto me. That way I might get a thumb in my eye before I could unwind and unravel him. The footing in the soft sand was a little uncertain for savate. So I moved forward, a little to my right. to take me inside that long, sweeping hook.

I felt it go around me, and I let his momentum then drive me back. I drove both hands, fingers spread, into his long hair, clenched hard, and went down, pulling him on top of me but getting my knees up against my chest in time. One shoe slipped off his sweaty body, but the sole of the other stayed in place against his belly, and momentum gave me enough leverage to push him up and over. It was a good, high kick, and he spun well. By then I was on my back with my hands straight up over my head.

He hit the soft sand flat on his back with one hell of a *whump*. It exploded the air out of his lungs. I was up first, and I moved into position, waiting for him. He got up slowly, gagging for air. As he pushed up, I cranked his arm around behind him and put my other hand on the nape of his neck and ran him into the weathered boards of the garden fence, quite close to the woman. He splintered a board with the top of his head. She squeaked and chewed her fist. I dragged him back by the ankles, face down. I picked him up and stood him on his noodle legs and slapped him until he started to come around. Then I bent him over and ran him into the fence again. I dragged him back again, and I turned his feet until he rolled over onto his back. I slapped him where he lay, and when he stirred and his eyes came into focus, I levered his mouth open by bracing the heel of my hand against his chin. I packed his mouth full of soft sand, from the back of his throat to his pretty white teeth. He came spluttering and gagging onto his hands and knees and coughed himself sick. I grabbed the hair and pulled his head up and back.

"Nod if you can understand me, Brego." He nodded. "Do you want me to break any bones? Do I have to do that?" He shook his head. "She isn't your woman any more. Understand?" He nodded. "Now I am going to start kicking your ass. You better head for the beach. If I ever see you back here, I'll break some bones."

I went around him and got a pretty good soccer kick into it, using the side of my foot. On the upswing. It slid him onto his face. He came scrambling up with more energy than I expected, but I got him again just as he got his feet under him and his hands free of the sand. Three running steps and he landed on his face again but didn't spend any time resting. He got up and went into a wobbly, scuffling run, fists against his chest, not daring or wanting to look back.

I watched him and then turned and looked at the woman. She gave me a very uncertain smile. There was an unhealthy skin tone under that deep lovely tan. "I . . . I thought you were going to kill him."

"Kill him? What in God's name for?"

"Well . . . it was so quick and so terrible."

"He won't be back, Mary. Are you going to miss him, particularly? You going to be lonesome?"

"That would depend, wouldn't it?"

"Is there any of his stuff in there?"

"Not much. A few things."

"Anything worth his coming back after?"

"I wouldn't think so. No."

"Now you can invite me in again."

Her color was back. "You take a hell of a lot for granted."

I put a knuckle under her chin and tilted her face up and looked at it inch by inch, a long and interested search. "If you want, girl, I can throw you back, like an undersized mackerel. The world is full of Carl Bregos. It's up to you."

She twisted her chin free. "I guess I wouldn't want to be thrown back. Gav. I guess it wouldn't fit my image. Was there really a Lois Jefferson?"

"If you think there was."

"I don't think so."

"Then there never was such a girl."

"Poor Carl. Do you always get what you want?"

"I usually get what I *think* I want."

She tilted her shoulders one way, her hips the other. Her look was challenge. "And sometimes you find out you didn't really want it after all. Me, too. Win a little, lose a little, huh?"

"If you wanted Brego, you'd still have him. I wouldn't have gotten to say more than two words to you."

"Like I was saying when we were so rudely interrupted, you want to come into my house? It's hot out here when the wind quits."

So we went in, and I wondered why I could find no trace of a Canadian accent. She had to be Lisa Dissat.

11

THOUGH THE plantings were different, the patio furniture of a different style and arrangement, the pool and the cold-water shower head were placed just as in my rented garden. I went to the shower and turned it on and sluiced off the sand that had caked thickly on my sweaty back and on my left side where I had rolled to get up quickly. The woman stood and watched me and then took a big, striped beach towel from a stone bench and brought it to me as I stepped out of the spray and turned the shower off.

As I dried myself, I realized how sexually aware of her I had become. Physical readiness. All her honey-brown curves and cushions were there, appropriate, ready for use.

It is such an old old thing, the pattern of male conflict that wins the female. It is deep in the blood and the secretions, a gut knowledge. We are mammals still caught up in all the midbrain mechanisms of survival. The bison female stood long ago and watched the males thud their brute heads together and tear up the sod with their hooves, watched the loser lope heavily away, and then she waited patiently to be mounted by the victor. The stronger the male, the stronger the calves, and the better protected the calves would be during the long months of helplessness. The victorious male, turning from battle to the prize of battle, would be physiologically ready to mate her and have no question about her readiness.

I knew the musky readiness of the woman. She told me in the way she stood, in the way she looked at me, in the shape of her placid mouth. Maybe 10 percent of what we can say to each other is with words, and words can conceal as easily as they can reveal. The rest of it is body language, our cants, tilts, postures, textures.

And who can prove there is not an actual telepathic signal being transmitted? Tiny electrical discharges occur in the living mind in great and complex profusion. Strong emotion, tautly focused, may send out an impulse so strong it can be read. Hate, fear, anger, joy, lust . . . these seem contagious beyond all objective reason. I knew she was so swollen, so moist, so ready that if I trotted her into the shadowy coolness of the apartment and into her bed, there would be no time or need for foreplay, that she would cling and grind and gasp and within a minute begin to go into a climax.

The violence had caught us up in the first act of the fleshy ceremony, and I wanted to take that quick, primitive jump so badly I felt hollowed out by the ache of it. Bed was her country. That was where, after the first great surge, she would take command. I would become what she was accustomed to and lose any chance of keeping her off balance. I shook myself like a big tired Labrador after a long swim, balled the damp towel, and flipped it at her face. She moved in her slow sensuous dream, getting her hand partway up before it hit her squarely in the face. It fluttered to the floor.

"Hey!" she said, frowning. "What's that for?"

"Pick it up!"

"Sure," she said. She picked the towel up. "What are you sore about? Why are you getting ugly and spoiling the fun?"

"He was supposed to hammer me to bloody ruin out there. That was supposed to be the fun. Thanks a lot."

She came toward me. "Darling, you've got it all wrong. I was getting *bored* with him! I was *so* glad you came along."

"Sure, Mary. Only I know the Bregos of this world. They don't start anything they don't think they can win. Their cheap women chouse them into it because they like the blood. You set me up by reacting to me. If you'd cooled it, there'd have been no fight. He was going to smash me around and that was going to turn you on for him, so you'd hustle him into your sack for a quick hump. A little midday entertainment. No thanks."

She leaned forward from the waist, face contorting, voice turning to a squalling fishwife. "*Goddamn* you! *You* moved in on us with all that crap about me looking like somebody else. *You* thought I was worth the chance of getting your ass whipped. Don't slam the gate on the way out, you son of a—"

Her lips started to say the obvious word, but I had fitted my big right hand to her slender throat, just firmly enough to cut off her wind, not firmly enough to crush any of the tender bones and cartilage. The ball of my thumb reached to the big artery in the side of her throat under the jaw hinge, and my fist and middle finger reached to the artery on the left side of her throat.

Her eyes went wide, and she dropped the towel and put her nails into the back of my hand and my wrist. I pinched the arteries gently, drastically reducing the flow of blood to the brain. It gave her a grayout to the edge of fainting. Her eyes went out of focus, and her mouth sagged. When I let up, she tried to kick me, so I pinched again. Her arms fell slack to her sides. When I released the pressure, adjusting my hand enough so that she could breathe, she raised her hands and then hung them upon my wrist.

I smiled at her, pulling her a half step closer, and said, "If you get loud and say nasty things, dear, if you get on my nerves, I can hold you like this, and I can take this free hand and make a big fist like this, and I can give you one little pop right here that will give you a nose three inches wide and a quarter inch high."

"Please," she said in a rusty little voice.

"You can get a job as a clown. Or you can see if you can find a surgeon willing to rebuild it."

"Please," she said again.

I let go of her and said, "Pick up the towel, love."

She coughed and bent and picked it up and backed away. I turned away from her and went into the cottage apartment and pulled the door open and went in. I went to the kitchen alcove and checked the bottle supply. I heard her slide the glass door shut again.

I fixed some Booth's with Rose's lime juice and a dash of bitters, humming softly but audibly. I took my glass over to the couch and sat and smiled at her and said, "Did I ever tell you I read minds?"

"You must be some kind of a crazy person." It was not said as an insult. It was said softly, wonderingly.

I pinched the bridge of my nose and closed my eyes. "Many messages are coming through. Ah, yes. You are wondering if you can get the hotel management to throw a net over me and get me out of here. No, dear. I think they would believe me instead of you. If they make life difficult, I could go down to the harbor and find your friend Brego and bounce him up and down until he agrees to write out a personal history of your touching romance and sign it. Then I could go find your husband and peddle it to him. It would cut the heart out of any alimony payments."

"I just want you to—"

"Where and when did you meet Brego?"

"On the beach. Over a week ago. My neck hurts."

"Of *course* it hurts a little! How could I do that without giving you a sore neck? Let me see. What else is in your mind? You're wondering if I'm going to lay you and if I'll be nicer to you afterward. The answer to both questions, dear, is: time will tell."

She went over to the kitchen bar. Ice clinked into a glass. She came back with a drink and sat on a hassock five feet away from me. Her eyes looked better. Her confidence was coming back. She squared her shoulders, tugged the bikini top and bottom into better adjustment, tilted her head, and risked a meager smile. "I guess all that lunch talk about land investments was a lot of crap, huh?"

"What makes you think so? It's what I do."

"You don't act like it's what you do. Like the way you were with Carl and with me, Gavin. I mean . . . well, it's like you enjoyed hurting."

"Well . . . let's suppose there's a man with a good idea where a new interstate is going or a new jetport, and suppose we teamed up, and had some nice long weekends with him, and he clued you about where to buy the raw land. Mary, I just couldn't stand having you get tricky with me about something like that. I wouldn't want to worry about you selling that information to somebody else. I'd have to have you so trained for the work that if I just stare at you for ten seconds, you start to have the cold sweats and the gags. Hurting is purely business. I guess I enjoy anything that helps make money."

She thought that over, sipping, frowning. "But it's not as if I was going to work with you, Mr. Lee."

"Time will tell."

"You keep saying that. Well, I'm not going to work with you or for you. For that kind of work you're talking about, what you want is some kind of a hooker, it seems to me."

"Does it seem like that to you? Really? I wouldn't say that. You're built for the work. You have just enough cheap invitation in the way you look and the way you handle yourself to keep a man from wasting a lot of time on unnecessary preliminaries."

"Now wait one goddamn minute—"

"Are you still with Brego? No. Then shut up."

"I'm sorry. Don't get sore."

"Fifty bucks makes you a hooker. For five hundred you're a call girl. Five thousand makes you a courtesan."

"What's that?"

"Never mind. But when we move the decimal point one more place, your end of the arrangement is fifty thousand. That makes you a career woman."

The pointed tongue moved slowly across the underlip. She swallowed and said, "I've got my own thing going, thanks."

"Alimony is a cheap hustle."

"It all depends."

"On how much he's got? On the evidence? On the law? It has to be a cheap hustle, because when there's enough money involved, there's more profit from going in some other direction."

I had wanted to test just how deep the hardness went. Her eyes changed. She slopped some of her drink onto her bare knees, wiped it off with her hand. "That's crazy talk."

"Not for careful people who've got the right contacts."

"For me, no thanks. I just wouldn't have the nerve, Gav."

I got up and moved around, carrying my drink. I did not know where to take it from there. I could guess that she had been ordered to keep to herself in Grenada, but had finally gotten so bored she had become reckless and picked up Brego. Now the Brego game had mushroomed into something a lot less comfortable for her. If she could live quietly at the inn for the length of time she was supposed to, she could get away with it. She wasn't too much shorter than Mary or too much younger. Dark hair. All American women look alike to the help.

I hadn't wanted to let myself think about Mary. From the physical description the housekeeper had given Jeannie Dolan, this woman was the Canadian, Lisa Dissat. If she was here, Mary was dead. I had the beginnings of an idea. I went back to the conversations at lunch. Neither the first name of her supposed husband nor her stateside residence had come up.

After mental rehearsal and rewrite I sat once again and looked placidly at her and said, "The way you spell that last name is bee-are-oh-el-el?"

"Yes."

"Kind of unusual. It rings a bell someplace. Mary Broll. Mary Broll. It's been bothering me ever since I met you in the bar."

"Why bother with it? Want me to fresh up your drink?"

"Got it!"

"Got what?"

"Where'd you register from? One buck will get you five it's the Fort Lauderdale area. Sure! We had a syndicate set up a couple of years back and we wanted a builder in the Lauderdale area who could put up a hotel and marina complex in a hurry. Heavyset fellow name of Broll. Big. Not old. Frank? Wally? Jerry? . . . Harry? Damn right. Harry Broll."

"Maybe there's more Brolls than you know, Gav."

"Bring me your purse, honey."

"What?"

"Go get your purse. Your pocketbook. Your handbag. Bring it to dear old Gavin Lee so he can look at your ID, dear."

She gave me a broad, bright smile, and her teeth chattered for a moment before she got herself under control. "Okay. My secret is out. You are speaking of the man I used to love."

"How long have you been married to him?"

"Nearly four years."

"Any kids? No? Lucky. Kids seem to get the rough end of the stick. Bring me the purse, honey."

"Why should I? I told you, didn't I?"

"Honey, if we stop getting along, we're going to have to hurt your neck a little until we get squared away."

"Please. It makes me sick to my stom—"

"Get the purse!"

She brought it to me. I found the billfold. I examined the identification. I looked at the signature on the driver's license. I knew my Mary had signed it, and I knew, looking at it, that she was dead.

"Honey, go over to that desk and take a piece of paper and sign your name on it. Mary D. Broll. And bring it back here to me."

"Who *are* you? What do you want?"

"I am the fellow who sat across the table from Mary D. Broll at Le Dome of the Four Seasons in Lauderdale two years ago last month. There were about ten of us at that dinner. Harry was making the big gesture, trying to sucker us into letting him build for us. I spent the evening trying to make his wife. She wouldn't give me a clue. I always have a better memory for the ones who get away. Here's her signature right here. Go over there and forge it for me, honey."

"Who *are* you?" she demanded, close to tears.

I gave her a broad, egg-sucking smile. "Me? I am the fellow who all of a sudden owns himself a whole woman, right from dandruff to bunions and everything in between. Broads like you don't play games like this unless there's money in it. And now it's *our* money, dear. I am the fellow who is going to get it all out of you, and I am going to beat on you until you convince me there's nothing left to tell. Me? Hell, baby, I am your new partner."

"Please. Please, I can't tell you—"

"The little lady in this corner is getting one chance, and one chance only, to go over to the desk and sign her real, true, legal name to a piece of paper and bring it back to the gentleman. And if it turns out that it is not her real true name, it is going to be one of those long afternoons. We're going to have to stuff a towel in the little lady's mouth so the screaming won't spoil anybody's vacation."

She walked to the desk, her back very straight. She wrote on a piece of paper and brought it back and handed it to me and began to weep. She covered her face and ran for the bedroom. Damned few women look well from the rear elevation, running away from you in a bikini. She was not one of them. She had written her name neatly. It was a schoolgirl neatness. Lisa Dissat.

I slowly crumpled the sheet of hotel paper. I felt tired. I got up and walked back to the bedroom, where she lay upon the unchanged sheets she and Brego had stained, sweated, and rumpled. She was on her side, knees hiked up, clenched fists tucked under her chin. She made sucking sounds, whining sounds. Fetal agony.

In the better interrogations there is always a good guy and a bad guy. I had been the bad guy. Time to change roles. I went into the bathroom and took a hand towel and soaked it in cold water. I wrung it out, took it to the bed, sat on the side of the bed, and cupped my hand on her shoulder and pulled her toward me. She resisted and made protest sounds, then let herself roll onto her back.

I hitched closer and gently swabbed her face and forehead. Her eyes went wide with astonishment. The last thing she had expected was gentleness. She snuffled. Her face looked touchingly young. Tears had washed away the challenge and the hardness.

"Have you got anything with you to prove your name is Lisa Dissat?"

"N-no."

"And you're pretending to be Mary Broll?"

"Yes. But I—"

"Does Broll know you're impersonating his wife?"

"Yes."

"Were you having an affair with him?"

"Yes."

"Where's the real Mary Broll?"

". . . I don't know."

"Lisa?"

"I didn't know what he was going to do! I *didn't!*"

"Lisa!"

"I couldn't have changed anything."

"Just say she's dead, Lisa. Go ahead."

"I didn't know he—"

"Lisa! Say it!"

"She's dead. Okay. She's dead."

"Harry killed her?"

She looked startled. "Oh, no!"

"Who killed her?"

"Please, Gavin. If he ever knew I told anybody—"

"You're in a real box, dear. You can worry about what's going to happen in the future, or you can worry about what's going to happen in the next ten minutes."

"I don't know if he really meant to."

"What's his name?"

". . . Paul. Paul Dissat. He is . . . my first cousin. We worked for the same man. In Quebec. Mr. Dennis Waterbury. Paul got me the job there. I'm a secretary. I was a secretary. Paul is an accountant. He is . . . very trusted. I think he might be crazy. Really crazy. Maybe he really planned to kill Harry's wife. I don't know. I don't even know if he knows."

"How much money is involved?"

"An awful lot. Really, an awful lot of money."

"Stop crying."

"I want to talk about it, and I don't want to talk about it. I've been scared for so long! I *want* you to make me tell you all of it, but I'm afraid to tell you."

12

IT WAS a very long afternoon for both of us. But longer for Lisa Dissat, because from time to time she tried to get cute. But the more she tried it, the more conditioned she became, and the more quickly she would correct herself.

At last I was able to bring the complex, wandering fragments of the story into reasonably sharp focus.

Paul Dissat had hungered for a long time to share in some of the large profits Dennis Waterbury made on his varied operations and investments in resort lands, oil and gas drilling programs, new urban office structures, tanker leasing, and so on. Paul Dissat was shrewd enough to realize that without investment capital he had no chance of participating in the profits and that if he used his skills to tinker with the records of the various corporations and their shifting, changing bank balances, sooner or later an audit would catch him.

He was single, she said, and did not look like anybody's idea of an accountant. Bachelor apartment, sports car. She said he was a superb skier, proficient at downhill racing and slalom. She said that three years ago, when she was working in Montreal, she had run up bills she was unable to pay. She was afraid of losing her job. She had gone up to Quebec to see Paul, whom she had not seen in several years. He had taken her to dinner and back to his apartment and made love to her. He had paid her bills and arranged for her to work for Waterbury. After they had been intimate many times, he had told her of his plan to share in some of the fat profits from Waterbury's operations. He would arrange the necessary leverage through her. He said he would let her know when the right opportunity came along.

He arranged for her to seduce the particularly unattractive minor partner in one of the Waterbury developments and to pretend infatuation. Paul prompted her during the affair, telling her what her lines should be. Eventually, in order to safely end the affair without Lisa's going to his wife, the man deposited a substantial amount of cash in her savings account. Paul told her that the cash was the proceeds from the stock in a Waterbury enterprise that the man had sold to get the money to buy her off. Paul had taken all the cash except a thousand dollars.

They had done it once again prior to her affair with Harry Broll and made a little more than the first time. Paul explained to her that a man who has suddenly made a substantial profit tends to be generous with a mistress who is becoming too demanding and possessive.

I wanted to know why she kept so little of the take and let her first cousin have all the rest. She said it was because she was in love with him. At first.

"The third one was Harry," she said. "I went to the hotel and took dictation. Just like the first two men. Ten minutes after I looked at him in a certain way and told him how real brilliant he was, I was helping him take off my bra, because his hands were shaking so bad. Then after Harry went back to the States, Paul made me quit my job and follow him. I didn't want to. He said this could be the big one, worth a big risk. So . . . I did what he said. Harry got jumpy when I phoned him last November from Miami. He was glad, but he was nervous, too. I told him I had followed him because I was so in love with him I couldn't live without him, and I was putting my future in his hands."

Harry had set her up in the apartment in the Casa de Playa. At about that time Paul Dissat had been transferred to the administrative office of SeaGate, Inc., in West Palm Beach, just as he had planned and expected. SeaGate was a large, complex situation with very complicated financing and special tax problems. Paul had been involved in it from the beginning.

"I called Paul once, but he got very angry. He told me to keep on following orders. The orders were to make myself just as agreeable as I possibly could, to make Harry as happy as possible, to really work on the sex part of it and do anything and everything to give him so much pleasure he'd never be able to get along without me. That wasn't easy, because Harry worked hard and he didn't keep in shape and didn't have much energy left for bed. But after I learned what turned him on the most, it got better for both of us. I had to pretend to be passionately in love with him. You know, it wasn't such a bad life. Go shopping, go out on the beach, get your hair done, watch your weight, do your nails, take naps. Not a bad life. Then a few days before Christmas, Paul wanted to know when Harry would be with me, definitely. I said I could make sure he'd come in the middle of the day on the twenty-third and spend an hour and a half with me. He told me not to be surprised if Mrs. Broll showed up. I couldn't understand what Paul was trying to do. He told me to shut up and do what I was told. She came barging in as Harry was leaving. Better looking than I'd thought from what Harry had told me about her. She called me some things, and I called her some things, and she went away crying."

Harry Broll had then become very upset. He had told Lisa Dissat that he needed her, that he wanted to get a divorce from Mary and marry her, but he couldn't do that yet. He had to make up with Mary, humble himself, promise never to see Lisa again. He said he had to do that because without Mary's financial backing he was going to miss out on his great opportunity at Sea-Gate. He said he had to move Lisa out of the apartment and be very careful about seeing her. He said it might last until May, but then he could leave Mary and marry her.

On the night of January 4, shortly before midnight, Harry came to Lisa's motel, where he had moved her after taking her out of the apartment. He was drunk. He said that he and Mary had had a terrible fight, and she was leaving him. As soon as Harry had passed out, Lisa phoned Paul to report, as required, any new development. Paul drove over to the motel, left his rented car there, borrowed Harry's car and house keys, and told Lisa to undress the unconscious Harry and keep him quiet for as long as she could manage.

"He wouldn't tell me what he was going to do. He acted all . . . keyed up, excited, on top of the world. He came back at daylight. He seemed very tired and very relaxed. He helped me get Harry up. Harry was confused. He knew Paul, of course, because of SeaGate and knew he was my cousin. But that was the first he realized that Paul knew about Harry and me. Paul pretended to be very upset about the affair, I guess to keep Harry off balance. The three of us went back in Harry's car to Harry's house on Blue Heron Lane. Paul kept telling Harry he was in trouble. Paul made me wait in the living room. He took Harry into the bedroom. Harry made a terrible sound. A kind of bellowing groan. I heard heavy footsteps running, and then I heard Harry throwing up. When Paul brought him back into the living room, all cleaned up, Harry was like a sleepwalker. Paul kept saying it was an accident, and Harry kept saying anything like that just couldn't be an accident, and Paul kept telling him that everything could be worked out for the best if Harry would just pull himself together. Paul had me make coffee, a lot of it."

Mary had, of course, been interrogated by Paul Dissat and murdered by Paul Dissat when he finally had everything he needed—the air reservations and tickets from the travel agency, the hotel reservation, the complete details of her arrangement with her trust officer, the fact that only one friend knew where she was going and why: Holly Dressner at 29 Blue Heron Lane, a few doors away. And he had the ninety-two hundred dollars in cash she had drawn from the income account of TA 5391. Mary was half packed for the trip. She had bought resort clothes. At Paul's order Lisa finished the packing, hunting through Mary's belongings for what she thought she would need.

"It was weird with her on the bed all covered up. I tried some of the stuff on in her dressing room. She was a little hippier than I am. I mean some of the things were a size ten when I'd be better off in an eight. Harry was like a very sick person. He couldn't seem to get himself out of it. Tears kept rolling down his face. Once he just sort of hung on me. He grabbed me and put so much weight on me he nearly rode me right down onto the floor. He was asking me something, mumbling about how could Paul do that, how could he? They had a terrible argument later on. I couldn't hear most of it. It was about what to do with her body. Harry said he couldn't stand having her buried on the place. There was something about the seawall and a transit-mix truck. Paul told Harry she was going to be buried right on the property; then Harry would not go back on any promises, ever."

She was given her orders, and Paul made her repeat them until there was no chance of her forgetting them. Drive to Miami International. Find accommodations for the night of the fifth and sixth. Stay in the room. Use Mary's ticket on the seventh. Use Mary's driver's license as proof of birthplace when needed. Use her immunization certificate if needed. Use her hairstyle. Wear big dark sunglasses. Travel in her new clothes. Go to Grenada. Register as Mary Broll. Live quietly. Keep to yourself. Send some postcards to Holly Dressner. Pick the kind that do not require a message. Sign with a little drawing of a smiling face.

"I *did* try to keep to myself. But, God, I've been here a long long time, Gav. I really have."

"What do you do next? What are Paul's orders?"

"On Monday, next Monday, I'm supposed to send a cable. Paul dictated it to me." I made her get it. It was to Woodrow Willow at Southern National in Miami.

PROCEED WITH LOAN AS ARRANGED EARLY JANUARY. HAVE ADVISED HARRY BY PHONE. HOME SOON. MARY BROLL.

Harry's part in it would be to phone Woodrow Willow that same day, Monday, April 26, and tell him that Mary had reached him by overseas phone call from Grenada to tell him she had cabled Willow to go ahead, tell him not to worry, tell him she would be home soon. He would inform Willow that Mary had given him the name of the travel agency she had used and had told him that her neighbor, Mrs. Dressner, had known all along where she was.

Very nice. If Willow felt like double-checking after he got the cable, he could call the travel agency and call Mrs. Dressner.

"Can't they check back on an overseas call?" I asked.

"Sure. That's why I call him at his office next Sunday afternoon. I've got the number. He'll have a secretary there. It will be person-to-person. Mrs.

Broll calling Mr. Broll. That's for afterward, in case they do a lot of check-ing.''

"Checking what?''

"I'm reserved to leave here on Monday, the third of May. Paul just didn't have time to work everything out before I left. But the way he wants it to happen, Mary Broll, will have some kind of accident. He's going to get a message to me telling me what to do. I just . . . leave everything of hers and arrive back home as myself somehow. Maybe a towel and a beach bag left on the beach, and nothing missing but a swimsuit and a cap.

"Where does the money come from?''

"The way I understand it, Gav, Harry invested seven hundred thousand in SeaGate. The letter of agreement said that on or before April thirtieth, he has to pay in another three hundred thousand to make one million dollars. There is a block of stock escrowed for him and a note escrowed, saying SeaGate owes him seven hundred thousand plus interest. It is an . . . indivisible block. He takes it all and wipes out the money SeaGate owes him and pays three hundred more. If he doesn't, he just gets his seven hundred back with interest, and the hundred thousand shares go to increase the number of shares the corporation is selling to the public and to reduce the number the stock-holders will offer. There is no way in the world Harry can get that money except from the bank on a loan on Mary's trust. He can't get an extension, and he can't cut down the number of shares he'll take. And he is borrowed to the hilt everywhere else.''

"So he had to keep Mary alive for about four months after she died?''

She shivered. "Or lose a big profit, a million and a half.''

"How much to your cousin?''

"He said a million. He didn't say that in front of Harry. I think he could get it all out of Harry.'' She frowned. "The thing about Paul, he stopped giving a damn *what* he does. It doesn't matter to him any more. It scares me. Once when I was little, a deaf boy took me to the movies, and he laughed when nobody else was laughing. Paul is like that now, sort of.''

"And I suppose Harry has been making a big fuss, storming around, shak-ing up Mary's friends, demanding they tell him where they're hiding her.''

"Maybe. I don't know. I guess it would make him look better later on if people could testify to that. I don't know how he is. I keep wondering how he'll sound on the phone.''

Her voice dragged. Her face looked puffy with fatigue. Her eyes were irritated because of the many times the tears had come. There wasn't much left of the day. She said, "Can we go for a walk on the beach? Would that be okay, Gavin?''

She got up and got a gaudy print dashiki and pulled it over her head, pushed her hair back into semiorder, put her big glasses on. "Gee, I feel emptied out, as if it's out of my hands somehow. I should be scared, but I'm too beaten down to be scared. You're in charge, Gav. You've taken over. I don't know where we're going, but you're running the ship.''

It was so nicely done I had my mouth all set for the bait and the hook. Poor little victim of a sordid conspiracy, clinging to the first man who'd give her the benefit of the doubt.

Sweet little immature face and a busy, nimble little butt and all the conscience and mercy of a leopard shark. Let me be your little pal, mister. Nobody else has ever understood me but you. She had slipped up on one little detail, but it was a bad slip. She let me see how she must have looked trying on Mary's new resort clothes while Mary lay dead. Probably Lisa turned this way and that. Looking in the mirror, smoothing her rear with the backs of her hands, wishing the damned dead woman had bought the cute clothes one size smaller. She tried on clothes while the men argued in the next room. "Look at it this way, Broll. You had a look at her an hour and a half ago. They'll want to know why you waited so long before reporting it. What do you tell them?" While Lisa hummed and bit her lip and frowned at herself and wondered if the colors were right for her.

13

WE WALKED up the beach in the orange and gold light of tropic sunset. The tide was moving out and the packed sand was damp and firm under our tread, a coarse, yellow-brown sand. The sun was behind us, setting into the sea just out beyond Long Point. Far ahead, beyond the rocks that marked the end of Grande Anse beach and beyond St. George's harbor, was the toy-town look of the town at evening, spilled up the green slopes, small formal shapes with windows looking toward the sea.

We walked past the Grande Anse Hotel, the Grenada Beach Hotel, the Holiday Inn. Cars had come down to the public areas to park under the sea grapes and the almond trees. People swam in the relative cool of twilight, and people walked the long broad promenade of packed sand. Sloops and ketches and multihull sailboats were anchored off the two-mile crescent of beach. A fast boat was pulling a limber black girl on water skis between the anchored sailboats. Behind us was the blinding dazzle of the sun's path on the quiet sea, and our shadows ahead of us were long in a slanting pattern against the damp sand.

"You were going to talk, I thought?"

"I am. I am." She moved closer, linked her arm through mine, hugged it against her body, and looked up at me. "I have to, I guess. Do you know how things can happen to your life that . . . don't fit it somehow? Then everything else isn't real. When you forget, then everything around you is real again, but what happened doesn't seem as if it could have ever happened. Do you know what I'm talking about?"

"Not yet, girl. Not yet."

"I guess in my own way I was as numb as Harry was. It seems like ten years ago, practically."

"Didn't you think it was pretty damned stupid for Paul to kill Mary Broll? Didn't you tell him it was stupid?"

She had to wait until we had passed a group of people strolling at a slower pace than ours. She indicated a stubby cement pier at the far border of the Holiday Inn property. It projected only to the surf line and seemed to have no purpose other than as some sort of groin to retain the sand. We went up the slope of beach, stepped up onto it, and walked out to sit near the end, our backs to the sunset.

She laced her fingers in mine, tugged at my hand, and rested it palm upward against the smooth, round brown of mid-thigh. She frowned toward the town.

"I've thought about it and thought about it, Gavin. I guess it got to be pretty obvious to Paul that an affair with me wasn't going to be enough leverage on Harry. Harry and his wife weren't getting along so great anyway. There wasn't anything real important to expose, you might say. So why did he tip off Mary Broll so she'd catch me and Harry together? Why did he make sure she *would* catch us? Why did he tell me to yell at Mrs. Broll and make a big scene out of it? Motive, right?"

The point was well taken. Mary would certainly confide her problem to someone. The scene at the apartment had attracted so much attention that even Jeannie Dolan heard about it later. Of late, Harry had been blustering around, threatening people, trying to locate his dead wife.

If the police were tipped, dug for Mary and found her, even the most inept state's attorney could put together a case F. Lee Bailey couldn't successfully defend.

"So, Lisa, you think Paul had decided to kill her when he made the phone call to her. Does that make sense? He didn't know then she'd decided to go away. He didn't know then what she'd arrange about the loan. She could have left without any warning at all. He'd have to be some kind of warlock, reading the future."

"I know. I think about it until my head starts to hurt, and then I give up."

"Did you think he'd ever kill anybody?"

"You don't go around wondering whether people you know can kill other people, do you? I knew he was mean. I knew how nasty he could get. I knew there was something kinky about him, the way he got something special out of sleeping with me and then making me sleep with those older guys. It was something to do with him never getting married, I think. We look alike, like brother and sister. His eyes are the same as mine, the same dark brown and long black lashes and—see?—the left one set straight and the right one slanty. His mouth is like mine, a lot of natural red to the lips, and the mouth small, and the lower lip heavy and curling out from the upper lip. We both look younger than we are, but that's always been true of the whole family. Aside from that, there isn't the least thing feminine about him. Even my eyes and mouth don't look girlish on Paul, somehow. Except when he's asleep. That's strange, isn't it? I'd watch him sleeping, and then his eyes and lips would look the most like mine and make me feel strange. He is big! He's almost as tall as you are and as big through the chest. But he moves a lot quicker. I guess I mean his normal way of moving is quicker. Nobody is quicker than you were with Carl. Jesus! You looked kind of dumb and sleepy, as if you couldn't believe he was really going to beat on you. Then you were something else."

"I want to know more about Paul. How old is he?"

"He'll be coming up onto thirty-seven, I think in July. Yes. Other companies have tried to hire him away from Mr. Waterbury. So I guess he's a good accountant. He stays in great shape all year. He does competition slalom in the winter and tennis in the summer. His legs are tremendously powerful, like fantastic springs.''

"An exercise nut?"

"With weights and springs and pulleys and things. And a sunlamp that travels by itself from one end of you to the other and turns itself off. He's real happy about those legs. One funny thing, he's dark as I am, and he has to shave twice a day when he goes out in the evening, but on his body, except for those places where everybody has hair, he hasn't any. His legs have a really great shape, and there isn't any hair on them or his chest or his arms. The muscles are long and smooth, not bunchy. When he tenses, his legs are like marble.''

"You called him kinky."

She frowned and thought for a little while. I saw the point of her tongue slowly moisten the curve of underlip. "No. That isn't the right word. The whole sex scene isn't a big thing with him. I mean it's there, all right. It was something we would do. You know, when he couldn't unwind and get to sleep, he'd phone me to come over to his place down in the city. We were five blocks apart. He makes me feel . . . I don't know . . . like one of his damn exercise machines, something with a motor and weights and springs, so that afterward he could put it in his exercise log. Ten minutes on the rowing machine. Eight minutes on the Lisa machine.''

"I can't really get the picture of you two."

"What's so difficult, honey?"

"You move to Quebec and change jobs because he tells you to. You come over whenever he phones you. He tells you to seduce Mr. X and then Mr. Y and tells you how to extort money from them, and he takes most of it. He tells you to secude Harry, quit your job, and follow Harry to Florida, and he tells you to come here and pretend to be Mary. You are awfully goddamn docile, Lisa.''

"I know. I know. Yes. It's funny about him. He's just so absolutely positive you're going to do what he tells you to do, it's a lot easier to do it than try to say you won't.''

"Did you ever try to say you wouldn't do something he asked you to do?"

"God, yes! In the very beginning, before he even got the job for me. I was at his place, and he asked me to get him something from across the room. I was sitting at the table, and I said something like 'You're not a cripple, are you?' He got up and went behind me and hit me on top of the head with his fist. I blacked out and fell off the chair and cut my chin. It did something funny to my neck, pinched a nerve or something, and I was in bed for three days with it, practically in agony. He was a darling. He waited on me hand and foot. He was so sweet and considerate. I guess . . . it's easier to do what he says, because you have the feeling that neither of you knows what he'll do if you say no. At work he's another person.''

"How do you feel about the way you're crossing him?"

"It keeps making me feel as if I'm going to throw up." She looked up at me with a piquant tilt of her dark head. "It's funny," she said. "I never saw you before today. Then you scared me so. You really did. Now you're so nice and understanding. I can really talk to you. About everything.''

Her fingers were laced in mine, and she pressed down on my hand, holding the back of my hand against the round, tan thigh, slowly swinging her dangling leg as she did so. I felt the smooth working of the thigh muscles against the back of my hand. It was a sensuous and persuasive feeling. She was a pretty piece, making her constant offer of herself in any way that she could.

"Why trust me?" I asked her.

She shrugged. "I don't know. I guess I'm trying to. I guess I can't go it alone, no matter what it is. I appreciate you didn't mark me up any. I mean I hate to get belted in the face where it shows. It cuts a person's mouth inside and there's a big puffy bruise, and maybe a mouse comes under a person's eye. It's a bad thing to do to a girl. She goes around ashamed."

"Paul belted you?"

"Sometimes."

"But you trust him?"

"He's a blood relative. Maybe I shouldn't trust him at all. He's strange. He really is. It doesn't show. You have to know him."

"I keep thinking of how boxed in you are."

"How do you mean?"

"Suppose after you go back, Harry is picked up for killing his wife. They have her body. It's certainly no big problem finding the girl friend and proving you were there. With that starting point, Lisa, how long before the state attorney's investigators learn about the impersonation? Would you want to explain on the stand why you took her money, her tickets, her reservations, her clothes, and her car?"

There was a sudden sallowness. "Come *on* now. Don't, honey! Jesus! I don't like jokes like that. We're in this together, aren't we?"

"Are we?"

"What do you *want* of me? What more do you want that I'm not ready and eager and willing to give, dear?"

"Do you think Cousin Paul is going to give you a short count of the money again?"

"If he gets the chance."

I pulled my hand away from her. "Now what would keep him from having the chance? Me?"

"Darling, please don't try to confuse me."

"How am I confusing you?"

"Well . . . you said you own me now, and you said there had to be money in it. So I guess you'll go after the money. I guess you'd have to have my help."

"Doing what?"

"That would be up to you, dear."

"To figure out how you can help me get rich?"

"That's the name of your game, I thought."

"Maybe Paul's game is over."

"How do you mean?"

"Harry Broll is not a complete idiot. Why couldn't he have gone quietly to the police and managed to tell them the truth? So they lay back and wait for you to return and for Paul to make his move, and scoop you both up."

"Damn! I forgot to tell you about the letter I wrote Paul. He was right there when I wrote it. He found Mary Broll's personal stationery for me to use. He told me what to write. I had to do it over because he said it was too neat the first time. I dated it January fifth. It said that Paul had been right and I never should have gotten involved with Harry. It said Harry had done something terrible while drunk and had gotten me to his house afterward to help him but I couldn't. I said I was frightened and I was going away and to wait until I got in touch with him. He held it in front of Harry and made him read it. Then he had me seal it in an envelope and put a stamp on it and address it to Paul's place in West Palm Beach. Paul put it in his pocket to mail as soon as he could."

The sun was gone. The world was darkening. The sky was a dying furnace, and the sea was slate. We walked back the way we had come, but more slowly.

"Gavin?"

"Shut up, Lisa. Please."

The beach was almost empty. The outdoor torches had been lighted at the Spice Island Inn. Birds were settling noisily to bed, arguing about the best places. Canned music was coming over all-weather speakers, a steel band playing carnival calypso.

When we reached her gate, she said, "Now can I say something? Like, please come in?"

"I want to sit out in the breeze, thanks. Over there."

"Join you?"

"Sure."

"Bring you a drink, maybe?"

"Thanks. Same as before."

I sat deep in a chaise, legs up, trying to work it out in every possible combination and permutation. With Mary Broll dead, Woodrow Willow was supposed to slam the lid on that trust account. Harry was probably the beneficiary under her will, possibly a coexecutor along with the bank. But had she died in early January, even in a traffic accident, the chances of processing the estate quickly enough for Harry to get his three hundred thousand before April thirtieth were very damned remote. She had to die later on.

So what if Meyer and I had not had all those vague feelings of uneasiness? What if we had accepted my phone call as being proof enough that she was alive and well and living in Grenada?

Then it would have worked like a railroad watch. The timely loan. The news of pending reconciliation. Enough supporting information for Willow to consider the cable legitimate authorization. Then the ironic tragedy. Estranged wife on the point of returning home to her contrite husband, missing in mysterious drowning incident. Search is on for body. However . . . .

"Here you go," she said. I thanked her for the drink. She had brought one for herself. She sat on the side of the chaise, facing me. I moved my legs over to make room. The stars were beginning to come out. I could see that she had brushed her hair, freshened her mouth. The bright, block-print dashiki had deep side slits, and she adjusted herself and it, either by accident or design, so that the side slit showed the outside of a bare thigh and a hip as high as the waist, a smoothness of flesh in the dying day that was not interrupted by the narrow encirclement of bikini I had seen there before.

"You certainly do an awful lot of thinking," she said.

"And here I am, dear, alive and well."

"But you have been terribly terribly hurt a few times, Gav."

"The times when I wasn't thinking clearly."

"Do I keep you from thinking clearly? I'd sure like a chance to try. Would you mind if I ask you politely to please make love to me?"

"What are we celebrating?"

"You're *such* a bastard! Gavin darling, I feel very very insecure about a lot of things. I've been alone a long time. Now I want somebody to hold me tight and make love to me and tell me I'm delicious. For morale, I guess. Why do you even make me ask? It doesn't have to be any big thing, you know. It doesn't have to take up a hell of a lot of your time. Hitch over just a little bit, darling, and let me . . ."

The way she started to manage it—to lie down beside me and hike her dashiki up and tug my swim trunks down and simultaneously hook one brown leg over me—certainly wasn't going to take up a great deal of anybody's time, the way she was going at it.

I pushed her erect and pulled the trunks back up. "Very flattering. Very generous. But no thanks."

She laughed harshly and picked her drink up off the sand near her feet. "Well, comparing you to Carl, I can say this. You've got a different kind of attitude. If I hadn't uncovered proof, I'd be wondering about you."

"I'm busy pretending I'm Paul, wondering how he has it all worked out."

"Different strokes for different folks."

"I hang back and make sure Harry Broll follows orders. I check with him about the Sunday afternoon phone call from you. On Tuesday morning, the twenty-seventh, I will get in touch with Mr. Willow, in my capacity as an employee of SeaGate, to verify that Mr. Broll will indeed have the funds to pick up his escrowed block of SeaGate shares. I am assured. The money comes through. And I am very very busy right through the thirtieth and through the weekend, because that is the end of the fiscal year for SeaGate. Right?"

"I guess so, dear."

"Then I have to do something about Cousin Lisa. She's expecting a message from me. I'll have to deliver it in person."

"To tell me what to do next?"

"Old Harry is twitchy about his dead wife. And Lisa is twitchy about Harry's dead wife. Harry and Lisa could testify against me if they ever join forces. Lisa is wearing the dead woman's rings. I just have to arrange a nice quick safe way to meet her in the islands and blow her face off and blow her dental work to paste. Then there's no mystery about a body. I can settle down and separate good old Harry from every cent of his gain and every cent he has left over when that's gone. When Harry is empty, it will be time to lay him to rest, too. By accident. Just in case."

I reached an idle hand and patted her on the shoulder. She remained quiveringly still, then was suddenly up and away, to come to rest five feet from the chaise, staring at me.

"No! No, Gavin. He's my first cousin. No."

"He couldn't do that?"

"Absolutely not. Not ever. Not any way."

"Then why are you so upset?"

"Anybody would be upset, hearing something so horrible."

"You know you are supposed to fake Mary Broll's death. There's less chance of a hitch if somebody plays the part of the body. You've been Mary Broll since January. Why switch now?"

"Don't be such a bastard!"

"It's the way I have to read him from everything you've told me. A quirky guy but very logical. A good improviser. If one logical plan doesn't develop the way he wants it to, he thinks up an alternative just as good or better. And . . . Lisa dear, just what the hell good are you to him? The end of usefulness. He knows there's a chance you'll make new friends who'll hear about how you died and get very upset about it and might run into you in an air terminal somewhere a year from now. All you are is a big risk, and an unnecessary risk."

"Shut *up*."

"Think about it."

"I *am* thinking about it."

"It wouldn't be *my* style, but I have to admire it in a way. It ties up the loose ends. No way out for Harry. Or you."

She found her drink had been kicked over. "Ready for another?"

"Not yet, thanks."

"Want to come in?"

"I'll stay here awhile."

"Be back soon, dear."

14

THOUGH LISA Dissat was not gone for more than ten minutes, it was full night when she came back, a velvet beach under a brilliance of stars. There were lights behind us from the Spice Island Inn cottages. The lights made a slanting yellow glow against the sand.

She sat beside me again. She had changed to tailored white shorts, a dark blouse with a Chinese collar and long sleeves. She smelled of perfume . . . and Off. The white fabric was snug on the round hip that pressed warm against the side of my knee.

"Took off your instant rape suit, eh?"

She pulled her shoulders up slightly, and her drink made the sounds of ice as she sipped. "I guess you made me lose interest."

"Are you a believer now?"

"Up to a point. I can't see any percentage in taking dumb risks. You are the loose end Paul doesn't know about. I guess I can be the bait in the trap. But we have to be awfully, awfully careful. He's very sensitive to ˙ . . . what people are thinking. We can't give him any chance at all."

"How do you mean that?"

"If it's like you say, if that's what he's going to try to do, then he'll have it all worked out so there won't be any risk in it, hardly any at all. So if he really wants to kill me, we have to kill him instead, darling."

"Your very own first cousin?"

"Don't be a stinker, please. What other choice is there?"

"Then what?"

"Then we have to get me back into the States in some safe way. I guess there's no reason why I couldn't go back in as Mary Broll, come to think of it. What harm would it do?"

"None, if you don't try to keep on being Mrs. Broll."

"If he isn't thinking about killing me like you say, then we'll have to play it by ear."

"All goes well, and you and I are back in the States. Then?"

"We just go and see Harry. That's all. I'll tell him that unless he gives us lots and lots of money, he's going to have lots and lots of trouble. And you can beat him up if he tries to bluff us."

"How much money?"

"I don't think we should make him really desperate or anything. I think we should leave him with enough so he'll think he came out of it pretty well. I think we could ask for half a million dollars."

"Each?"

"No, dear. He has to pay taxes on the whole thing, you know. I think with the holding period before the sale to the public, it will be long term. Yes, I know it will. He should get his money next December. Hmmm. His taxes will be a half million. That leaves him two million, and I know he owes four hundred thousand and he will have to pay back the three hundred thousand. So out of his million and three, we'll take five hundred thousand, darling, and he'll have eight hundred thousand left. It would be neater if we took six hundred and fifty and left him six hundred and fifty, don't you think?"

"A lot neater. And you want half?"

"What I want and what you'll let me have aren't the same, are they?"

"They could be with cooperation all the way."

"Moving money like that around without leaving traces that people can find later is very hard. Do you know anything about that kind of problem? I'd think you would."   (

"If Harry Broll will hold still for the bite, yes."

"There's no problem, Gav honey. None."

"Leaving only Paul."

She finished her drink, bunted me with her hip. "Scrooch over some, honey. Make room. No funny stuff this time, I promise."

She turned, lay back, and fitted her head to my shoulder, swinging her legs aboard.

After a while she said, "Want to order dinner in my place or yours, dear?"

"I don't know yet."

"I'm not hungry, either. Gee, look at all the damned stars. Like when I was a little kid, the night sky looked glittery like this."

"Where was that?"

"Way up in French Canada on the St. Lawrence, north of Rivière du Loup. A little town called Trois Pistoles. Ten thousand saints, ten thousand churches all over that country. Convent school, uniforms, vespers, acts of contrition, the whole scene. I ran away when I was fifteen. With my best friend, Diane Barbet. We got across the border and into the States. Things got kind of messy for us. You survive or you don't, I guess. I don't know what happened to Diane. I think about her sometimes. A guy in Detroit helped me really go to work on my hick Canuck accent. Movies, television, radio, and using a tape recorder. I think in English now, except if something startles the hell out of me or scares me. I get scared in French. Another man sent me to business school to learn to be an executive secretary. That was in Cincinnati. He was a real old guy. He picked me up. I was hitchhiking. He took me home. He lived alone—his wife had been dead two years. He wanted me to stay there with him and pretend I was his grandniece so the neighbors wouldn't turn him in. I wanted somebody to send me to school so I could be a secretary, so it worked out okay. He bought me pretty clothes. I was eighteen by then. He bought me a little car, even. He was retired. He cooked and kept the house clean and did the laundry and made the bed. He even ironed my things that needed it, and he rinsed out stuff. I was really pretty rotten to old Harv. He was forty years older than me. That is a lot of years. When he got on my nerves, I wouldn't let him touch me. I cut off the supply. He didn't really want me too often or give me much trouble. I finished school and got my certificate and got a job. The way I was living, I could put it all in the bank, and I did. I came home one evening, and he was on the floor in the utility room. His whole left side had gone dead. His eye drooped and spit ran out of the left side of his mouth, and he couldn't speak. He just made terrible noises when he tried. I packed all my things into the trunk of my car, and then I called the hospital. I parked in the next block and walked back to make sure they found him and put him in the ambulance. I went to a motel. I finished out the week after I gave notice. I got my money out of the bank. I left and went down to Mobile and sold the car there. You can sell cars easy in Alabama. Then I flew home to Canada and got a good job in Montreal. I kept missing old Harv. I still miss him, I guess. It was a pretty good way to live, you know? I wasn't very nice to him. If I had it to do over, I'd be a lot nicer. I'd never hold out on him the way I did. It never cost me a thing to make him feel good.

"Anyway. I had a wonderful life in Montreal. There was a great bunch of kids there. And then I fell really *really* in love. When my guy took off with a girl friend of mine, I did what I always do when I hurt. Buy, buy, buy. Shoes, clothes, wigs. I like money. I guess I spend it to hurt myself. You know? I knew I was in real trouble unless somebody bailed me out. So I went up to Quebec and saw Cousin Paul. I think I could have gone the rest of my life without the kind of help *he* gave me. Hey, look!"

"Shooting star."

"I know. But such a big, bright, slow one, huh? It lasted forever."

"Did you make a wish?"

"Was I supposed to? Would it work?"

"The way to make a wish come true is to wish for something you're going to get anyway."

"Is it okay to wish a little late?"

"Go ahead. It wasn't my shooting star."

"Okay. I wished." My arm was around her. She turned in a twisting motion that slipped her breast into my hand. Under the thin fabric of the blouse she wore no bra, and in seconds I felt the nipple growing and hardening. "Does that give you a clue, friend? Something I'm going to get anyway?"

I sat up, raising her with me, slid my hands onto her waist, picked her up, and dropped her onto the sand beside the chaise.

"Ow! That made me bite my tongue, you son of a bitch!"

"Just be a good girl and stop trying to hook me on the product. It's there any time I want it. Stop pushing it."

She stood up. "Don't be too damned sure it's going to be served up on a damn tray when you decide to ask for it, Gav. And I wasn't trying to hook you on anything. I just think it's friendly and nice to get laid. It isn't a big thing, is it? And it got me going, what I was talking about."

"Old Harv, for God's sake?"

"No, you dummy! The money. Big gobs of money. Just thinking about it makes me feel all hollow and crawly inside, and I guess it's so much like the feeling you get when you know you're going to get laid, it works the same way."

"Go take a cold shower."

"You're terribly nice to me. You're oceans of fun. I'm going to walk up and down the beach and think about blizzards and icicles and catheters and having my teeth drilled. That takes me off the edge fast."

"I should think it would."

So she went walking out there, clearly visible, scuffing barefoot through the foamy water that came running up the wet slope after the thud of each slow, small wave. A girl walking slowly, slow tilting swing of hips, legs shapely and dark below the white glow of the shorts.

She had deftly pushed a lot of my buttons. She had worked on proximity, touch, forthright invitation. She had talked in areas that accentuated sexual awareness. She smelled good, felt good, kept her voice furry and intimate. I knew she wasn't being made wanton and reckless by my fabulous magnetism. We were moving toward an association, possibly profitable. For maximum leverage within that association of two, she wanted to put that weapon to work which had profited her in the past, probably in every relationship except the one with her cousin.

I was another version of good old Harv, whom we last saw on the floor with spit running out of his mouth. She'd pushed Harv's buttons and got her secretarial training and a car and a lot of clothes. Her libido certainly wasn't out of control. It was just a useful thing for her to do, a nice little inexpensive favor for her to grant, and if it clouded the recipient's judgment, eventual profit from the relationship might improve.

Were I a great ape, a giant anthropoid, munching stalks torn from the jungle, and able to lead her to forgotten treasure, Lisa would take her best shot at making everything friendlier and nicer. As she said about Harv, it wouldn't cost a thing to make that big monkey feel good.

But knowing how and why the buttons are pushed doesn't diminish the physiological aftereffects of the button pushing. The tumescence is noticeable. The palm of the hand retains the shape of the breast—the precise size, warmth, and rate of erection. The eyes watch the slow walk, creating an increase in the heartbeat and rate of respiration and blood pressure and surface body temperature, as the conditioned mind anticipates the simple progression of events of calling to her, bringing her close, shucking her out of the shorts, pulling her astride, and settling her properly for that sweet, grinding task that would end so quickly the first time.

The buttons tripped certain relays. I had to go back into the mind, into central control, and reset those relays, compensate for the overload, switch the current back to those channels designed for it.

I went searching through the past for the right memory, the one that would most easily turn growing desire to indifference.

I thought a memory of Miss Mary Dillon long ago aboard *The Busted Flush* would do it. There were more than a few, but they would not come through vividly enough to achieve turnoff.

Lisa made it so damned easy, so completely available, there was no importance to it. And with no importance to an act, why did it matter whether or not it happened? Why did McGee need some cachet of importance in this world of wall-to-wall flesh in the weekend living room where the swingers courteously, diligently, skillfully, considerably hump one another to the big acid beat of the hi-fi installation, good from 20 to 20,000 cycles per second?

Is McGee still impaled upon some kind of weird Puritan dilemma, writhing and thrashing around, wrestling with an out-dated, old-time, inhibiting, and artificial sense of sin, guilt, and damnation? Is that why he couldn't accept the lifetime gift Lady Jillian offers? Is that why he has this sickly, sentimental idea that there has to be a productive and meaningful relationship first, or sex degrades? So bang the doxy, because easing the ball pressure is reason enough.

Who needs magic and mystery? Well, maybe it is magic and mystery that an Antarctic penguin will hunt all over hell and gone to find the right pebble to carry in his beak and lay between the funny feet of his intended, hoping for her favor. Maybe sex is a simple bodily function, akin to chewing, sneezing, and defecation. But bald eagles fly as high as they possibly can, up into the thinnest air, making the elegant flight patterns of intended mating all the way up, then cleave to each other and fall, fall, fall, mating as they fall fluttering, plummeting down toward the great rock mountains.

The way it is supposed to work nowadays, if you want to copulate with the lady, you politely suggest it to her, and you are not offended if she says no, and you are mannerly, considerate, and satisfying if she says yes.

But the Tibetan bar-headed goose and her gander have a very strange ceremony they perform *after* they have mated. They rise high in the water, wings spread wide, beaks aimed straight up at the sky, time and time again, making great bugle sounds of honking. The behaviorists think it is unprofessional to use subjective terms about animal patterns. So they don't call this ceremony joy. They don't know what to call it. These geese live for up to fifty years, and they mate for life. They celebrate the mating this same way year after year. If one dies, the other never mates again.

So penguins, eagles, geese, wolves, and many other creatures of land and sea and air are stuck with all this obsolete magic and mystery because they can't read and they can't listen to lectures. All they have is instinct. Man feels alienated from all feeling, so he sets up encounter groups to sensitize each member to human interrelationships. But the basic group of two, of male and female, is being desensitized as fast as we can manage it. . . .

"What the hell is there about me that turns you off?" Lisa demanded. She had walked up the slope to stand by the chaise, blotting out a Lisa-shaped abundance of stars as she looked down at me with a faint angle of pale yellow light lying across her cheekbone and lips.

"I was wondering what you'd do if I picked up a pebble in my beak and put it between your feet."

"I've heard of a lot of ways guys get kinky, but that is—"

"Why do you want reassurance from me? Take my word for it. You are a fantastic piece of ass. Ask practically anybody."

"I don't know. I haven't checked it."

She stood there for a few seconds in silence. Then she said, "If you ever do want some, friend, you're going to have to take it away from me, because that's the only damned way in this world you're ever going to get any."

"Good night, Lisa."

She walked away from the shoreline, a silhouette moving toward the yellow lights.

15

ON THURSDAY I was up early. Awakening in a new place makes the day of arrival seem unreal. There had been no Carl Brego, no Lisa Dissat trying to be Mary Broll, no Lisa Dissat striding angrily away from me in the hot, buggy night. I went to my cottage after she left, swam in my minipool, two strokes per lap, changed, and went to the open dining room. The food was good, the service indifferent. There were some beautiful people there. A fashion photography team. Some yacht people. Some twosome guests had tried to get as far as possible from wherever they didn't care to be seen together. Some guests were ritualistic sun worshipers who had been there for many many weeks, using the intense tropic sun to add each day's tiny increment of pigmentation at the cost of blinding, suffocating, dazed hours and quarts of whatever oil they happened to believe in: Johnson's or coconut or olive. They were working toward that heady goal of becoming a living legend in Bronxville or Scanton or Des Moines.

"Tan? You think that's a tan? So you didn't see Barbie and Ken when they got back from Grenada that time. Dark? I swear to Christ, in a dark room all you could see were white teeth. And Barbie's diamonds."

I took a cab into town, memorizing landmarks all the way. I negotiated the rental of an Austin Moke. A Moke is a shrunked jeep with a very attractive expression, if you look at the front of it and think of the headlights as eyes. It looks staunch, jaunty, and friendly. It is a simplified piece of machinery. Stick shift which, like the wheel on the right, you work with the left hand. The horn, a single-note, piercing *beeeeep,* is operated by pressing in on the turn indicator with the right hand. A quick whack with the heel of the hand is the approved method. Four speeds forward, small, air-cooled engine, pedals so tiny that if you try to operate one with your bare feet, it hurts like hell. Canvas top nobody ever folds down in the hot season, and all they have in Grenada are two hot seasons, one wet and one dry.

With the tourist season almost over, there were a lot of them in stock. I picked one with a lot of tread, and the rental man and I walked around it and tested lights, horn, directional signals, windshield wiper (singular). He wanted his total rental in advance, which is standard for the area. While we dickered, I practiced getting in and out of the damned thing. I'd learned in Grand Cayman and Jamaica that with the length of my legs there is only one possible way. Stand beside vehicle on right side. Bend over at waist. Reach across body and grasp steering wheel with right hand, while simultaneously lifting left leg and inserting it into vehicle so that foot comes to rest on floor well beyond pedal area. Swoop your behind onto the seat and pick up right leg and lift over high broad sill (which contains gas tank). In driving position both knees are bent sharply, spread wide apart. Steering wheel fits between knees, and lower part of legs must angle in to assure foot contact with pedals. Adjust to inevitability of frequently giving oneself a painful rap on the left leg while shifting.

We arrived at a mutually agreeable fee of five Yankee—ten Biwi—dollars a day for a one-week rental or any period of less than a week. I buy the gas. I will phone him when I leave and tell him to pick it up at the Spice Island Inn. I promise not to leave it at the airport. I tell him I would not drive it over that road to the airport for a hundred dollars a mile. Can I drive safely on the left side of the road? I suggest that perhaps no one in Grenada can drive safely on any side of the road. But yes. I have so driven on other islands of this British persuasion.

We accomplish the red tape, and he gives me a free map of St. George's and environs. I note that, as expected, there is at least half a pint of gas in the five-gallon gas tank. I edge carefully into the tourney and immediately am nearly bowled over and over by a small pale bus with a name across the front of it. The name is: I AM NOTHING.

After I have bought petrol and felt my way back into the center of town, avoiding too intimate a contact with a large gaudy city bus called LET IT BE ME, I park my Moke and wait until I am certain my legs will work. ("You will enjoy browsing in St. George's along the narrow, quaint streets.")

*　　*　　*

I changed another wad of Yankee dollars into Biwi at the Bank of Canada, picking that one from among all the shiny banks downtown, from Chase to Barclay's to the Bank of Nova Scotia, because there was a faint aroma of irony in the choice. The girl standing behind the money-changing counter was very dark, very thin, and totally antagonistic—so much so, there was no chance of ever making any kind of human contact with her unless you were her identical anthracite color.

I asked some questions and was directed to a big busy supermarket called EVERYBODY'S FOR EVERYTHING. As long as I had kitchen facilities and could make my own ice cubes, it seemed useful to set up shop. Gin, rum, fruit juices from Trinidad, mixes, and a couple of large substantial drink glasses. I am a fussy old party about glassware. Nothing takes the pleasure out of drinking like the tiny dim glasses supplied by hotels and motels. I always buy heavy glasses, always leave them behind. Tiny glasses turn drinking from a pleasure rite to a quasi-alcoholic twitch.

The final purchase was on impulse at a shop I saw on the Carenage on the way home: a great big planter's hat of straw with a batik band. Put a man in a rental Moke with advertising painted on the side of it and put a funny hat on him, and he is a tourist. All tourists look alike. Regardless of age, sex, or the number of extra lenses for their cameras, they all look alike.

I found my way back out to Grande Anse to hotel row, and I found an overland way to get the Moke close to my cottage. I carried my box of stuff in. From the moment I had awakened until the moment I finished putting the stuff away and sat down, I had not let myself think about Mary, Lisa, or the mechanics of impersonation.

It is a useful device. If you keep things in the front of your mind, you worry at them like a hound chomping a dead rabbit. Throw problems in the back cupboard and keep them there as long as you can. The act of stirring around seems to shuffle the elements of a problem into a new order, and when you take it out again, there are new ways to handle it.

I tossed my sweat-soaked shirt aside. The air conditioning felt good on my back and shoulders. Okay. Mary is dead. I want Paul Dissat. I want him very badly. The money is the bait, and Lisa is the bait in another sense. I want very badly to convince Paul and Lisa and Harry Broll that, if given a choice, they would elect retroactive birth control. I want them so eager to be out of it they'd dig their own graves with a bent spoon and their fingernails.

Secondly, as a professional, as a salvage consultant in areas of considerable difficulty, I want to come out of this with a little salvage for myself. If I walk away without a dime, with only expenses I can't reasonably afford, then I lose all respect for myself as a con artist. I would have kicked the hell out of their little wagon just to avenge one hell of a woman, Mary Dillon. Pure emotionalism is bush league.

So? So I do not advise Mr. Willow not to make the loan on Mary's securities. They go to Harry eventually anyway. That is, if Harry happens to be still around. The money has to be loaned to Harry, and Harry has to pick up his block of stock in time and get himself in position to make a great deal of money when the public issue comes out. But that is a long long time for me to wait for my money. I shall use the leverage to extract a reasonable chunk from Paul, maybe from Harry, maybe from both, before I set them to work with those bent spoons.

It may be enough to have Harry and Lisa dig their graves deep with the sides and ends properly squared off and stand in them without the slightest morsel of hope left. Then I walk away and leave them standing there. But Paul is something else.

Program: Lisa must perform exactly as instructed: make her phone call to Harry and send the cable to Mr. Willow at the bank. I want her to be desperately anxious to tell me all the details of any contact by Paul Dissat. Then I will prepare to greet him. Here. There. Somewhere.

I pulled on my salty swim trunks and put on my big tourist hat and went looking for the lady. She was not in Cottage 50. I trudged around, squinting into the hot glare, and found her on a sun cot at the top of the slope that led down to the beach proper. She was face down. The bikini was yellow today. The top was undone, and she had rolled the fabric of the bottom so that it was about as big around as a yellow lead pencil where it cut across the tanned cheeks of her behind. She was glossy with oil. Her towel was on the sand. I sat on it. Her face was turned away.

"You wanna buy nice coconut, Miss lady? Peanuts? Nice spices?"

She slowly turned her heat-stricken, slack-mouthed face toward me. "I don't want any—" She shaded her eyes, squinted. "Oh. It's you."

"Me. Absolutely correct. Me, himself."

"Who needs you?"

She lay with her face turned toward me, eyes closed. "You need me," I told her.

"Not any more. Thanks a lot. But not any more."

"I don't mean that kind of need, honey. I'm talking about financial need. Commercial necessities."

"Thanks loads. I think I'd better take my chances with Paul."

"That should be a lot of laughs for both of you. I wrote an interesting letter last night."

She forget her top wasn't latched. She sat up fast. "What kind of a letter? Who to?"

"What's the local policy about the tits on tourists?"

She picked up the top and put it on. "I know what *your* policy is, friend. You ignore them. What kind of a letter?"

"Double envelope. A sealed letter along, inside the sealed letter. If he doesn't hear from me on or before May tenth, he opens the second letter."

"Then what?"

"He takes action."

"*What* action?"

"Oh, he just gets in touch with the right people at the SEC and says that it looks as if one Mr. Harry Broll bought himself into SeaGate, Inc., with a final three hundred thou fraudulently obtained and that this fact might not be uncovered by the accounting firm preparing the material for the red herring and they should check with a Mr. Willow regarding evidence as to whether or not Mrs. Broll was alive at the time he released funds at her earlier request. My friend is an attorney. He knows all the steps in the new registration folk dance. Delicate, these new issues. They can die of a head cold."

"Oh, God! Why'd you think you couldn't trust me?"

"Who said anything about that?"

"Isn't that why you did it?"

"Lisa, Lisa, Lisa. What if we miss? Suppose your dear cousin nails us both, lays us to rest in a ceremonial boat, lights the pyre, and sends us out to sea. The last few moments would be a lot more enjoyable knowing Cousin Paul would never make a profit on the deal."

She swallowed hard and looked unhappy. "Don't talk about things like that." I knew that behind her sun squint her brain was ticking away, weighing and measuring advantages. I reached under the sun cot and retrieved her big sunglasses from the magazine on which they lay and handed them to her.

"Thanks, dear," she said, putting them on. "Sure. I see what you mean. And if he catches us sort of off base, it could maybe be handy to tell him about your lawyer friend."

"Yes. I think so. If he gives me a chance."

"Can't you see why I thought you did it on account of me?"

I thought it over. "Well, I suppose I can in a way. If you *did* decide he represents a better chance, you could tip him off about me and he could . . . tidy up the situation."

She turned over and put her feet down on the sand near my legs. Her hairline was sweaty. Trickles of sweat ran down her throat, and a little rivulet ran between her breasts and down across her belly to soak into the narrow yellow bikini. Her knees were apart, and the cot was so short-legged that her knees were on the same level as her breasts. Her eyes were even with the top of my head.

She leaned toward me, forearms on her knees, and said in a cooing voice, "You know, you act so weird about me, about us, that I'm afraid I'm going to keep on misinterpreting the things you say. We're going to keep on having misunderstandings. I waited a long time last night for you to come over to my place to say you were sorry."

I looked at her. Bright sunshine is as cruelly specific as lab lights and microscopes. There was a small double chin, caused by the angle of her head. There was a scar on her upper lip near the nostril. Her hands and feet were small, square and sturdy, nails carefully tended. Her posture made a narrow tan roll of fat across her trim belly. Her slender waist made a rich line that flowed in a double curve, concave, convex, into the ripe tan hip and thigh. She sat with her plump parts pouched into the yellow fabric, heavy and vital. Stray pubic hairs, longer than the others, curled over the top of the bikini and escaped with the sides of the crotch, hairs the color of dull copper.

Sweat, muscles, flesh, hair, closeness. So close the tightness of the yellow pouch revealed the cleavage of labia. This was the magic and mystery of a locker room, steam room, massage table, or of a coeducational volleyball game in a nudist colony. This was jockstrap sex, unadorned.

"Lisa, I guess we have to say things so carefully we won't have misunderstandings."

"Maybe I got the wrong impression yesterday. You wouldn't be queer, darling?"

"No more than any other true-blue American lad."

"Some kind of trouble? You can tell Lisa. Prostate, maybe? Or some kind of irritation?"

"I'm in glowing health."

"Honey, are you so strung out on some great broad that you just don't want to make it with another girl? I could understand that. I've been through that."

"Nobody I've met lately has gotten to me."

Her mouth firmed, and her throat turned darker. "Am I some kind of pig woman it would turn your stomach to—"

"Whoa! It's just a little rule of mine. Save the dessert until last."

Her mouth softened into a sudden smile. "Dessert? Darling, I am also homemade soup, meat and potatoes. hot rolls and butter, and your choice of beverages. I am mostly meat and potatoes."

"There's another reason for waiting, Lisa."

"Like?"

She was ready again, I decided. Like training a mule. A good solid blow between the eyes, and I should have her total attention.

"It's kind of a sad story, dear."

"I love sad stories. I love to cry and cry."

"Well, once upon a time there was this lovely, delicate little blonde lady, and she and I were partners in a complicated little business deal. We took our plans and problems to bed and talked them over during rest periods. I freaked over that little lady. She loved to make love. Then our business deal went sour. It fell apart. That was too damned bad because it was a nice piece of money for both of us. Well, one day a month later we romped all day together, happy as children, and that night I took her out in a boat, a nice runabout, out into the Atlantic. It was calm and beautiful, and I made her sit on the side rail, and I aimed a Colt forty-five with the muzzle an inch from her pretty brow and blew the top of her head off. I wired the spare anchor to her waist and let her go in a half mile of water, and the moon was so bright that night I could see her for a long way as she went down. Now you can cry."

Her mouth sagged open. She put a hand to her throat and in a husky whisper said, "Jesus H. Christ!"

"That idiot girl thought that by sleeping with me she was buying insurance, in case I ever found out she had gone behind my back and made her own deal for half again as much as she would have made as my partner. She was so convinced of it, she was starting to smile when I pulled the trigger. You're not crying."

"Jesus H. Christ!"

"You said that before, Lisa. After that I decided it's bad policy. I made the punishment fit the crime, but I hated myself. You know? I used to think of that little blonde a lot. It used to depress me. It seemed like a waste, all those goodies sinking to the bottom of the sea."

"What *are* you?"

"Me? I'm your partner, Lisa. And we trust each other, don't we? Nobody is going to try to be cute. But . . . just in case . . . let's save all the goodies until after we've made the money score?"

"Th-that suits me, Gavin," she said. She clapped her thighs together so smartly they made a damp slapping sound. "L-later. I . . . I got to go for a minute. I'll be back."

"I'll probably be swimming."

She went off toward her place, walking slightly knock-kneed, head bowed and shoulders hunched.

An imaginary letter and an imaginary blonde partner. I could imagine that dear imaginary girl sinking down, down through the black water, hair outspread, getting smaller and smaller and more indistinct until she was gone out of my imaginary life forever. Poor kid. Gavin Lee was a mean son of a bitch. It made me almost want to cry. Now the Lisa-McGee contest could be declared no contest. The lady wasn't going to come out for the third round. She was cowed. She was going to do as she was told. She was going to have as much sex drive from here on as a harem guard. And at the first word from her cousin she was going to come on the run to tell me all about it.

That evening she was so prim it was as if she had never left the convent school. We walked on the beach and got back to the cottages just after dark. We went to her place. She unlocked the gate. We went in, and she screamed as the two dark shapes jumped me. It got very interesting. They both knew a lot more about it than Carl Brego had. If they had been ready and willing to kill, they had me. But they weren't. And that gave me a better chance than I thought I was going to get.

I took punishment and gave it back. Whistling grunts of effort. Slap and thud of blows. Scuff of feet. I took one on the shoulder, off balance, and fell and rolled hard and came up near a yellow light bulb. A half-familiar voice said, "Hold it! I said *hold* it, Artie! I *know* this joker."

The voice was suddenly very familiar. "Rupe, your dreary bastard, what are you trying to do?"

"A favor for a friend. Lady, if you can get some Kleenex and some rubbing alcohol or some gin, I'd be obliged. And turn on some lights around here."

I told Lisa it was all right. She turned on the garden lights and the inside lights. She had some alcohol and a big roll of paper towels. All three of us were breathing hard. We were all marked, one way and another.

I said, "Mary, this is an old friend of mine. Rupert Darby, a sailing man. Rupe, Mary Broll."

"Pleased to meet you, Mary. And this here, Mary, is Artie Calivan. Artie is mate on the *Dulcinea,* and I'm hired captain. And this big rawboned bastard it's so hard to get a clean shot at, Artie, is an old friend of mine from way back. Trav McGee."

"McGee?" Lisa said blankly.

"It's a kind of joke name, honey," I said. "It comes from an old limerick. Trav rhymes with Gav for Gavin. And McGee rhymes with Lee."

If it had just hung there, I couldn't have brought it off. But Rupe came in very smoothly. "I'd like to recite you the limerick, Miz Mary, but it's just too dirty to repeat in front of a lady. I use that old name on Gav when I'm trying to get his goat. I think I've got one tooth here that isn't going to grow back tight again, dammit."

I looked at his mate. "You brought along a big one."

"Seems he was needed. I needed two like him."

"You were doing fine with just one of them. But *why?*"

"Oh, that damn Brego. What did you think? He whined all day about how us hired captains ought to help each other out, and he said this big fellow, quick and mean as a sneak, had filched his piece—excuse me, Miz Broll, his lady friend. So finally I said to Artie here, let's take the dinghy and run over there to the inn and bounce this tourist around some. Had no idea it was you, Tr—Gav. None at all. Sorry. But not too sorry. First time I haven't been half asleep in two weeks."

I dabbed at a long scratch on my jaw and moved over to Lisa and put my arm around her waist. "Honey, have you got any message you want these fine men to deliver to Mr. Brego?"

"Rupe? Artie? Would you tell him that Mrs. Broll suggests he stop by again and try his luck with Mr. Lee?"

Rupe laughed. "Sure."

"Would you mind taking some of his things back to him?"

"Not at all."

"Let me go gather them up. It won't take a second."

Rupe sent the young man down to keep an eye on the dinghy. Rupe and I sat in a shadowy corner of the garden.

"What happened to the *Marianne?*" I asked him.

"Two bad seasons and the bank finally grabbed her. I don't really mind a hell of a lot. I work for good people. Good wages."

"Thanks for the nice job of covering."

"That? Hell, that's what a good hired captain starts with or learns real fast. When somebody clues you, don't stand around saying 'Huh?' Run with the ball. No point in asking you what's going on. I certainly know something is going on, and that broad in there must be part of it. She looks good enough, but there's better on the island. Any time you have to scruff up a clown like Brego to grab yourself that kind of ass—"

"Like you said. There's more than meets the eye."

"By God, Trav, you know something? That was fun off and on."

"Glad you enjoyed it. How's Sally?"

"Fine, last I heard. She went back to her folks. She married a widower fellow with four kids. Our three plus his four makes a lot of family."

"Sorry to hear about that, Rupe. I really am."

"It hurt some. But I hate the land and everything on it. I hate a tree, and I hate a mountain. The only death worth dying is by drowning. With the licenses I've got I'll stay on the water all the rest of my time. When our oldest girl drowned, that did it for Sally. That finished her, up, down, and sideways. No more oceans. Next time I write the kids I'll put in a note to her saying I saw you. She always liked you, Trav."

Lisa came out with a brown paper bag and gave it to Rupe. "This won't be too much trouble?"

"Not one bit, Miz Mary."

"Thank you so much. Excuse me, but is that mate of yours a mute?"

"Artie just doesn't have very much to say."

We both walked Rupert down to the dinghy. He stowed the bag aboard, and then picked the little boat up and walked it out past the gentle surf, scrambled in, and started the little outboard and headed back toward the yacht basin.

"*Imagine* that Carl sending them to beat you up!"

"They gave it a good try."

"Did they hurt you, darling?"

"Hardly at all. A month in bed and I'll feel like new."

"I mean really."

"Honey, the adrenaline is still flowing. So the pain is suppressed. Tomorrow morning when I try to get out of bed I'll know how much damage they did."

"Rupe has really enormous hands, doesn't he?"

"And very hard, too."

"And that gigantic boy is *really* handsome, did you notice?"

"I wasn't thinking in those terms. Want to eat in the dining room?"

"Let's order it sent to my place. It's so much nicer, really. We can fix our own drinks and be comfortable. I won't make any passes, Gavin. None at all."

She kept her word. Long after we had dined, when the nightcap was down to the dregs, she came over to me and bent and peered at my face, teeth set into the softness of her underlip.

"You are going to have one great big mouse right on that cheekbone, friend."

"I can feel it."

She straightened up. "I can't read you, McGee."

"McGee? Who he?"

"Like the limerick. Tell me the limerick, huh?"

"Tell the truth, I can't remember it."

"Was it real dirty?"

"Not very, as I remember. But insulting."

"Funny, you knowing him. I would have thought he would have told Carl you were an old friend. Carl would have told him your name, Gavin Lee, and described you and all."

"Lee is a common name."

"Gavin Lee sure the hell isn't. And how many people are your size anyway?"

"Lisa honey, what are you trying to develop here?"

"I don't know. Is there anything you ought to tell me that you haven't?"

"Can't think of a thing."

"What are we going to do after we get rich, dear?"

"Live rich."

"Like this place?"

"And Las Brisas at Acapulco. And Cala de Volpe on Sardinia. The Reina Cristina in Algeciras."

"In where?"

"Spain, near Gibraltar."

She sat on the couch a couple of feet from me, eyes hooded, mouth pursed. "Will we travel well together when we're rich?"

"Get along?"

"Do you think we will?"

"We'll have to try it."

"Are you terribly dog-in-the-manger about things?"

"Like what?"

"If we had something going for us and I happened to see somebody like Artie Calivan. As long as I didn't overdo."

"Get the guests?"

She shrugged. "When they come in pairs, dear. And both exciting."

"I don't like to set policy. Take each situation on its merits. Okay?" I put my glass down and stood up. Winced. Flexed my leg. It was going to stiffen up very nicely during the night. She walked me out to the garden gate. I kissed her on the forehead and told her to dream about being rich. She said she had dreamed about that ever since she could remember.

16

I CAME bounding awake in the middle of the night from a dream so horrible I couldn't remember any part of it. I was drenched with icy sweat and trembling badly.

The dream made me recall lying to Lisa about sending a letter. A letter would be a comfort. I couldn't wait until morning. Leonard Sibelius, Esq., attorney-at-law.

The sealed letter inside was about the same, but the cover letter for the sealed letter varied. I asked him to read the sealed letter if he did not hear from me by the last day of May and then give it to some colleague wise in the ways of the SEC and the NASD.

After the lights were out again and the letter tucked away, I thought of how ironic it would be if Harry Broll ended up being defended by Lennie Sibelius on a charge of murder first. Lennie would get him off. He would extract every dime Harry had ever made and put a lock on every dime Harry might make in the future, but he would get him off.

I felt myself drifting off and wondered what the hell there had been in that nightmare that had so thoroughly chilled my blood.

I was up early again on Friday and made another exciting run into town. I stopped at the main post office and sent the letter to Lennie by air, special delivery, registered mail. I drove through the one-way tunnel that leads from the Carenage area under Hospital Hill to the Esplanade and the main part of downtown. The *Queen Elizabeth II* was in, and it was her last visit of the season. She had spewed about two thousand passengers into the town and onto the beaches. The ones in town were milling around, arguing with each other about the currency and looking for the nonexistent duty-free shops and being constantly importuned to hire a nice taxi and see the sights. The big single-stack ship was anchored out, with fast launches running back and forth like big white water beetles.

I ambled around and admired one out of every forty-three tourist ladies as being worth looking at and did some minor shopping of my own, then tested my skill and reflexes by driving back to the Spice Island Inn.

It was on that twenty-third day of April that I risked two lives instead of merely my own and drove Lisa out toward the Lance aux Epines area and had lunch at the Red Crab—burly sandwiches on long rolls, icy Tuborg beer, green salad—eaten outdoors at a white metal table by a green lawn in the shade of a graceful and gracious tree. After lunch we went exploring. We stopped and looked at the sailboats moored in Prickly Bay. I drove past large, lovely houses, and we got out of the Moke at Prickly Point and walked down the rocky slope and looked over the edge at the blue sea lifting and smashing at the rocks, working away on caves and stone sculpture, biting stubbornly and forever at the land. A curiously ugly species of black crab, big as teacups, foraged the dry sheer stone just above the reach of wave and tide, scrabbling in swift hundreds when we moved too near.

I studied my map and found, on the way back, a turn that led to a stretch of divided highway, probably the only bit of it on the little island. Weeds grew up through cracks. It was the grand entrance to the site of what had been the Grenada Expo of several years ago. I had heard that few visitors came. Many of the Expo buildings were never completed. The ones that had been finished lay under the midafternoon hum of sun's heat, warping plywood shedding thin scabs of bright holiday paint. Some faded, unraveling remnants of festive banners moved in a small sea breeze. We saw a VIP lounge where the doorsill brush grew as high as the unused and corroded doorknobs. Steel rods sprouted from cement foundation slabs where buildings had never stood.

We found a huge and elegant motel, totally empty, completely closed, yet with the lawns and gardens still maintained by the owners or the government.

I drove down crooked little dirt roads, creaking and swaying at two miles an hour over log-sized bumps and down into old rain gullies you could hide bodies in. She clung and laughed, and we made it down an angled slope to a pretty and private little stretch of beach where the almond trees and the coconuts and the sea grapes grew closer than usual to the high-tide mark because of the offshore protection of some small islands.

I parked in the shade. We walked on the beach and found one of the heavy local skiffs pulled well up between the trees, with red and blue and green paint peeling off the old weathered wood. She hiked a haunch onto the gunwale, near the hand-whittled tholepin, braced herself there with one knee locked, the other leg a-swing. The breeze moved the leaves overhead, changing the patterns of sun and shade on her face and hair, on her yellow-and-white-checkered sun top, her skimpy little yellow skirt. The big lenses of her sunglasses reflected the seascape behind me. She sucked at her cigarette, looked solemn, then tilted her head and smiled at me.

"I'm trying to figure out why it should be so much fun, just sort of churning around in the heat of the day," she said.

"Glad you're enjoying it."

"I guess it's because it's like a date. Like being a kid again in Trois Pistoles and going out on a date. It's a feeling I haven't had in a long long time. It's sort of sweet, somehow. Do you know what I mean, Gav?"

"Not exactly."

"Ever since I left when I was fifteen, I've been with guys I've either just been in bed with or am just about to get into bed with or both. And if it was a guy I'd already had or one I was going to have, if we were alone in a funny, private place like this, we'd be knocking off a stand-up piece right here. I was thinking I don't want you to try anything, because it would take away that feeling of being on a date. There's something funny and scary about it, like being a virgin again. Or maybe it's you that's scary to me, about the girl sinking in the ocean. I dreamed about her. Jesus! You really did that? Really?"

"It seemed like a good idea at the time."

She slid off the gunwale and snapped her cigarette into the surf line. She bent and picked up a coconut in the husk and threw it with a shot-put motion. She was wiry, and she got surprising distance with it.

"So this is just a little bit of time when nothing happens and we just wait, Gavin."

"For your cousin. After you make the phone call and send the cable."

I leaned on the boat. Some palm fronds had been tossed into it. I lifted them and saw the battered metal fuel tank for the missing outboard motor, and I saw a spade with a short handle, sawed off where it had broken, and decided it was a clumsy improvised paddle. Clumsy but better than none at all. With all that weight and freeboard she would be a bitch to try to paddle against wind or tide.

"Head back?" I asked.

"Can we keep on being tourists, dear? Let's look at that map again."

We went back to the Moke, studied the map, and decided to try the road out to Point Saline and look at the lighthouse. It was a road so wretched that by the time we were halfway I had decided only a jeeplike vehicle such as a Moke could make it. Then around the next hairpin corner I was shouldered into the shrubbery by three taxis coming back from the lighthouse, whamming and leaping over the ruts and broken paving, chock-full of tourists off the *QE2*.

My gratis map had little paragraphs on the back of it about local wonders, so just short of the lighthouse hill we stopped and dutifully got out to walk for a moment on the white sand beach of the Caribbean, then crossed the road and went down a path for about fifty yards to walk on the black sand beach of the Atlantic. Then I roared the Moke up the twenty-degree slope to the lighthouse.

The attendant was there, obviously eager to be a guide, obviously eager for bread. We climbed the several flights to the glass-enclosed top. The treads were very narrow, the steps very steep. Lisa was directly ahead of me, and I was staring at the backs of her knees as we climbed.

It was a view so breathtakingly, impossibly fabulous that it became meaningless. It was like being inserted into a living postcard. It does no good to stand and gawk at something like that. The mind goes blank as soon as you see it. Tourists take pictures and take them home and find out they have postcards. If they put Helen in front of the view, they have a postcard with Helen in it. The only way a person could accommodate himself to a place like that would be to live there until he ceased to see it and then slowly and at his own pace rediscover it for himself. When I found out what the attendant had to do to keep that fifty-mile light operating, I was happy to place some Biwi in his hand.

Lisa was quiet on the way back. When we were nearly back to the deserted Expo site, I glanced over at her and saw the tear running down her quiet cheek, coming out from under the sunglasses. I pulled over in a shady spot and said, "Hey!"

"Oh, God, I don't know, I don't know. Leave me alone."

"Sure."

Glasses off. Dab eyes, snuffle, sigh, blow nose. Fix mouth. Put glasses back on. Light cigarette. Sigh again, huffing smoke plume at windshield.

"Everything is supposed to be so great," she said. "Everything is some kind of a trick. Every time. Some kind of flaky trick, no matter what it is. Fifty-mile lighthouse! Good God! What the hell is a Fresnel lens?"

"A Frenchman invented it long ago. It focuses light into a beam."

"Nothing is ever what you expect. That's what got to me, Gav. A fifty-mile lighthouse and all there is up there is a mantle like off a Coleman lantern and not a hell of a lot bigger, and that poor scrawny black son of a bitch that has to get up every two hours all night long and run up there and pull on some goddamn weights like a big grandfather clock so his fucking light keeps turning round for another two hours. Fresnel! They fake everything in the world."

"What kind of a big deal did They promise you, Lisa?"

She pulled the glasses off and looked at me with reptilian venom and coldness. "They told me, friend, to sing in the choir, love Jesus, do unto others, pray to God, live a Christian life, and then live in heaven in eternal bliss forevermore. They forgot to explain that the choirmaster would give me free private voice lessons when I was fourteen and by the third lesson he'd have his finger up me. They didn't tell me that if I didn't report him, I'd lost out on all that eternal bliss. They didn't tell me that I wouldn't want to report him, because then he wouldn't have a chance to do it again. They didn't explain about it being the temptation of the flesh and how finally you get to the place where you either make a true confession or you run away. They were running their big lighthouse and making it look wonderful, shining its light all over the world to save souls. But it was just a gas mantle and weights and chains and a weird lens. The real thing they teach you without even knowing it is: do unto others before they do it unto you."

"My, my, my," I said in a gentle wonder, and the tears came again. She got them under control at last.

"Will you laugh at me if I tell you what I *really* want to do with the money, Gav?"

"I don't think I will."

"I want to join an order. I want to give the money to the order. I want to take a vow of silence. I want to kneel on stone floors and pray until my knees bleed and I faint. I don't ever want to be screwed again the rest of my life or be even touched by any man. I want to be a bride of Christ. Now laugh yourself sick."

"I don't hear anybody laughing."

"You think I'd go over the wall in a week, don't you?"

"Do you?"

"If I can find the guts to start, I'll never leave. Never. You're doing all this to me by making me feel the way I did a long long time ago. A lot of men ago. A lot of beds ago."

"I don't think people stick with projects they start because they think they should start them. That's image making. People stick to their truest, deepest gratifications, whether it's running banks, building temples out of beer cans, stuffing dead birds, or telling dirty jokes. Somewhere early you get marked."

"I got it early. Stations of the Cross. Easter. Christ is risen. At about twelve I felt so marvelously pure. Jesus loved me, that I know."

"So you fight it all your life or go back to it. Either way, it is a deep involvement."

She found her glasses on the floor, picked them up, and said wearily. "You know so goddamn much, don't you? You know something? You've got a big mouth. A great big mouth. Let's get back on the beach where I belong."

17

THAT RANDOM afternoon had turned Lisa Dissat off in a way she either couldn't explain or didn't care to explain. It amounted to the same thing. We became like neighbors in a new suburb, nodding and smiling when we met walking to or from the main hotel building or up and down the two-mile beach or back and forth from sun cot to cottage.

I saw some of the cruise-ship men, crew and passengers, take their try at her now and then when she walked the long wide beach alone. I saw male guests at our hotel and the other beach hotels make their approach, each one no doubt selecting the overworked line he thought might be most productive. They would fall in step with her, last about half a dozen steps before turning away. I followed her a couple of times and kept count. Prettier young women in bikinis just as revealing walked the beach unaccosted. It was difficult to identify those characteristics which made her such a frequent target. It was something about the tilt and position of her head in relation to the shape in which she held her mouth while walking. It was challenge, somehow. A contempt and an arrogance. Try me, you bastard. Try your luck and see how good you are. Do you think you're man enough to cope, you bastard? There were both invitation and rejection in the roll of her hip. To describe everything that happened to tilt, curve, and musculature in one complete stride from start to finish and into the next stride would have taken a seventeen-syllable word. Provocative, daring, and ineradicably cheap. That was what Rupe had seen so quickly, wondering why I risked even a bruised knuckle to take ass like that away from Carl Brego. It was what I had seen when she sat with Brego for a drink and lunch.

It was a compulsive cheapness. I could not believe that it was deliberate in the sense of being something she had thought out. It had to be something she could not help doing, yet did not do out of some physical warp or out of any flaw in intelligence or awareness.

She had been uncommonly determined to give herself to me. It had been too early an effort. She wanted to be used, not loved. She wanted to be quickly tumbled and plundered. It was what she expected and what she wanted, and it was that need which exuded the musky, murky challenge.

I have a need to try to put people together out of the pieces they show me. The McGee Construct-A-Lady Kit. For those on a budget we suggest our cheaper, simpler Build-A-Broad Kit.

Once you Build-A-Broad, it pleases you more than it did before you took it apart and examined the components.

She had ripened young. They had drilled virtue into her so mercilessly that, when she was seduced, she believed herself corrupt and evil. Purity could not be regained. So she ran away and had spent a dozen years corrupting because she believed herself corrupt, debauching because she had been debauched, defiling because she was the virgin defiled.

When you cannot like yourself or any part of yourself in mind or body, then you cannot love anyone else at all. If you spend the rest of your life on bleeding knees, maybe Jesus will have the compassion to love you a little bit. She had been destroyed twelve years ago. It was taking her a little while to stop breathing.

*   *   *

I kept in close touch with her. She heard nothing. I killed time restlessly. So on Saturday I got a clear connection and talked to Meyer. I told him to check out Paul Dissat in the SeaGate offices in West Palm. I had to spell the name in my own special kind of alphabet before he was sure of it. Detroit Indiana sugar sugar Alabama teacup.

"Dissat? Paul Dissat?"

"Yes. And be damned careful of him. Please. He bites."

"Is Mary there? Is she all right?"

"She's fine."

After all, what else could I say? Time to talk later.

*   *   *

Later on Saturday I drove until I finally found the way to Yacht Services. I parked the Moke and went out onto the long dock and found the *Dulcinea*. She was a custom motor sailer, broad of beam with sturdy, graceless lines. Rupe Darby and Artie kept her sparkling, and she looked competent.

Artie had gone over to the Carenage in the dinghy to do some shopping. Rupe asked me aboard and showed me the below-decks spaces, the brute diesels, all the electronics. He was fretting about the delivery of some highly necessary engine item. It was supposed to come in by air. They couldn't leave without it, and he didn't want to be late meeting his owners at Dominica. He hoped to be out by Wednesday.

I asked about Carl Brego, and he told me that Brego's rich lady had arrived with friends, and they had left early that morning for two weeks sailing the Grenadines.

A sunbrowned and brawny woman in blue denim shorts and a dirty white T-shirt came along the dock and waved and smiled. She had a collie ruff of coppery gold hair, a handsome weathered face. Rupe invited her to come aboard and have some coffee with us. She did, and we sat in the shade of the tarp rigged forward. She was Captain Mickey Laneer, owner and operator of the *Hell's Belle,* a big businesslike charter schooner I could see from where we sat. Mickey had a man's handshake and a State of Maine accent.

"Trav, Mickey here has the best damned charter business in the islands, bar none."

"Sure do," she said, and they both chuckled and chuckled.

"Could be out on charter all the time," Rupe said.

"But that would take all the fun out of it, too much of the same thing," Mickey said.

"She charges high, and she picks and chooses and doesn't have to advertise. Word of mouth," Rupe said, and they kept chuckling.

"Five hundred bucks a day, U.S., and I don't take the *Belle* out for less than five days, and I won't carry less than three or more than five passengers. Price stays the same."

"That's pretty high," I said.

"I keep telling her she ought to raise the rate again."

"Would you two mind telling me why you keep laughing?"

Mickey shoved her hair back, grinning. "Rupe and I just enjoy life, Mr. McGee."

"She does a good trade with business meetings. Three or four or five busy, successful executives usually fellows in their thirties or early forties, they come down to relax, get some fishing in, get a tan, do a little dickering and planning. You know."

"Why is everybody laughing but me?" I asked.

"She takes male passengers only, Trav."

I finally caught up. "I get it. Your crew is all female, Captain?"

"And," said Rupe, "all nimble and quick and beautiful and as strong as little bulls. They range from golden blond—a gal who has a master's in languages from the University of Dublin—to the color of coffee with hardly a dab of cream. Eight of them.''

"Seven, Rupe. Darn it. I had to dump Barbie. She was hustling a guest for extra the last time out. I've warned them and warned them. After I provision the *Belle*—the best booze and best food in the Windwards—I cut it down the middle, half for me and the boat, half for the gals. So on a five-day run, they make better than three hundred, Biwi. Everyone from golden Louise all the way to Hester, whose father is a bank official in Jamaica.''

"You need eight crew to work that thing, Mick?''

"I know. I know. We're going out Monday for ten days. Four fellows from a television network. Nice guys. It'll be their third cruise. Old friends. That means my gals will be topless before we clear Grand Mal Bay.''

"And bottomless before you get opposite Dragon Bay and Happy Hill.''

"Could be, dear. Louise flew up to Barbados today. She says she has a cute chum who loves sailing. It's a way for a certain kind of girl to combine her favorite hobbies and make a nice living. I don't take hard-case types. I like polite, happy girls from nice backgrounds. Then we have a happy ship.''

She got up and said, "A pleasure to meet any of Rupe's old friends, Travis. Hope you'll sail with us sometime. Rupe has.''

"Mickey invited four of us captains to a free five-day cruise last year.''

"I had a cancellation,'' Mickey said, "and we were all wondering what to give the other captains for a Christmas present. Well, nice to meet you.''

After she was on the dock, she turned and waved and said, "Tell him our motto, Rupe.''

He chuckled. She walked lithely away. He said, "Mickey likes you. In her line of work she gets to tell the men from the boys in a hurry.''

"What's the motto?''

"Oh. It's on her letterhead. 'Make a lot of lovely new chums every voyage.' ''

"Enjoy the cruise?''

"Oh, hell, yes. By God, it's different. There's rules, and Mickey enforces them. None of her gals get slopped. Any and all balling is done in the privacy of your own bunk in your own stateroom, curtains drawn. No pairing off with any special gal, even for a whole day. If a gal is wearing pants, long or short, it means hands off. Otherwise, grab whatever is passing by whenever you feel like it. The gals don't make the approach. The things you remember are like standing aft with a big rum punch in a fresh wind with Mickey at the wheel really *sailing* that thing, putting on all the sail it'll take, and those eight great bare-ass gals scampering around, hauling on those lines, trimming sail. And like being anchored in a cove in the moonlight, the evening meal done, and those gals singing harmony so sweet it would break your heart right in two. Great food and great drinks and good fishing. Everybody laughs a lot aboard the *Belle*. Between all they got to do, those gals put in a day full of work for a day's pay. I can't understand that damned stupid Barbie. Why'd she want to try some private hustling? Her old man must own half the state of South Carolina. Barbie's been a sailboat bum all her life. And she gets this chance to make a good living doing the two things in the world she does best and enjoys most, sailing and screwing, and she blows the whole deal. It's hard to understand. Anyway, we were out five days, and it was like being gone a month, I swear. It's . . . something different. If you ever see the *Belle* coming in here or leaving, you wouldn't figure it out. Those gals look like some kind of Olympic people trained for a race. Nimble and slender and tough and . . . fresh faced. Scrubbed. You know?''

*   *   *

On Sunday Lisa agreed without much argument to arrange her call so that I could hear both ends of the conversation. She placed it from the cottage. We had to wait a long time before the desk called back and said they had her party on the line. I sat close beside her, and she turned the phone slightly so we could both hear, my right ear and her left.

It was Harry's nervous, lying voice. ''Mary, honey? Is that you, Mary darling?''

''Yes, dear. Can you hear me?''

''Talk loud. You sound a million miles away, honey. Where are you? I've about gone out of my head with worry.''

I hope he sounded more convincing to his secretary than he did to me. Lisa followed her prepared script, telling Harry to let Holly Dressner know she was all right and that she had phoned. She said she was afraid he'd find the travel agency she'd used. The Seven Seas. Down in Hallandale. Mrs. De-Angela had been very nice and helpful.

''Are you going to come home? To stay?''

''I think so, Harry. I think that's best, really.''

''So do I. When, honey? When will you be home?''

''I've got reservations out of here May third. But don't try to meet me. I don't know when I'll get in. And I'll have my car. By the way, you don't have to worry about the money. Not any more. I'm going to cable Mr. Willow tomorrow to activate the loan and put the money in your account, dear.''

''I've been getting pretty nervous.''

''I can imagine. I guess I wanted you to sweat a little.''

And on and on, and finally it was over, and she hung up. She gave me a strange look and then wiped beads of sweat from her upper lip and throat.

''It spooked me.''

''I know.''

''If I'd been Mary, I certainly wouldn't arrange a loan for that son of a bitch. I don't see much point in that phone call, really. There's enough without that.''

''His secretary will make a good witness. Mary Broll is alive and well and in Grenada. She'll be home May third. She can say she was there when Mrs. Broll called her husband. Probably Harry will have his secretary get Mrs. Dressner on the phone to make sure his secretary hears him give her Mary's message.''

''I don't have to send her any more cards. If I was supposed to, Paul would have told me. He thinks everything out.''

''It's a good way to be, if you like to kill people.''

''It's weird. You know? I've thought and thought about what you said, Gav. The smart thing for him to do would be to kill me. Get word for me to meet him on the way back. Some other island. Arrange something. But I just can't believe he would. We're from the same town. We're family. I keep having this dream about him. He's standing watching me sleep, and I sneak my eyes open and find he isn't really looking at me. He's looking the other way, and he has a mask just like his face that he wears on the back of his head. He's pretending to watch me, but he's looking at something else I can't see. When the dream wakes me up, I'm cold all over."

"We won't have long to wait, Lisa. After you send the cable to Willow tomorrow, you're no use to him."

"Stay close to me, huh?"

I reassured her. I wouldn't let the bad man get her. She'd be safe. Sure.

18

I WAS up very early on Monday morning when the sun was still behind the green mountains. I swam. The tide was low and getting lower, still running out. I went back to take my shower before dressing for breakfast.

By then, of course, he had talked with Lisa long enough to discover I was one of his priorities. He had immobilized her and come after me. Usually I am pretty good at surprises. Some sense I cannot describe gives me a few microseconds of lead time, and when I get that kind of warning, the reaction time seems to be at its best. Perhaps it is hearing or the sense of smell at subliminal levels.

I don't know where he hid. There were good places in the garden. He could have crouched behind the bar in the service area or behind some of the bigger pieces of furniture in the living room. He worked it out well. He saw me go swimming, and he nipped over the wall unobserved. I'd locked the gate but not the sliding door. He could assume I would come inside to take my shower, and I would have no reason to close the bathroom door. Standard procedure is to reach in and turn the handles until you get the roaring water to the right temperature, and then you step in. It is a moment of helplessness, and there is a useful curtain of sound.

I remember that when I got the water temperature the way I wanted it, I straightened to strip the swim trunks off. The whole back of my head blew up, and I went spinning and fluttering down through torrents of white, blinding light.

I know what he probably used. I made things easy for him. I had picked up the piece of driftwood in the surf a few days before. It was iron hard, less than a yard long, a stick an inch and a half in diameter with a sea-polished clump of root structure at the end of it the size of a large clenched fist.

Because he did not give a particular damn whether he killed me or not, he waited for the water roar, then came prowling into the bathroom with the club cocked, poising like a laborer to sledge a stake into hard ground.

The brain is a tender gray jelly wrapped in membrane, threaded and fed with miles of blood tubes down to the diameter of thread. The gray jelly is a few billion cells which build up and discharge very small amounts of electric impulses. The whole wet, complex ball is encased in this bone, covered with a rubbery layer of scalp and a hair thatch which performs some small shock-absorbing service. Like the rest of the body, the brain is designed to include its own spare-parts system. Brain cells are always dying at a rate dependent on how you live but are never replaced. There are supposed to be enough to last you. If a stroke should kill all the cells in the right hemisphere involved with communication—hearing and speaking, reading and writing—there is a fair chance of dormant cells in the left hemisphere being awakened and trained and plugged into the other parts of the system. Research can run a very thin electrode into an animal brain and hit a pleasure center and offer a chimp two levers—push one, and he gets a little electrical charge that makes him feel intense pleasure; push the other, and he gets a banana. The chimp will happily starve to death, pushing the pleasure lever. They can make a rabbit dangerously savage, a cat afraid of mice. They can put electrodes against your skull and trace pictures of your brain waves. If you have nice big steep alpha waves, you learn quickly and well. People who smoke a lot have stunted alpha waves. People who live in an area with a high index of air pollution—New York, Los Angeles, Birmingham—have rotten alpha waves that are so tiny they are hard to find. No one knows yet why this is so. It may be a big fat waste of everybody's money, time, and energy sending kids to school in Los Angeles, Chicago, and lately Phoenix.

Anyway, if you take a club to all this miraculous gray tapioca with a good full swing and bash the back of the skull a little to the right of center where a right-hander is likely to hit, it is not going to function at all for a while, and then it is going to function in some partial manner for a varying period of time, which could be for as long as it lives. If you have any blood leaking in there and building pressure between the bone and the jelly, then it is not going to live very long at all.

Even if there is a perfect, unlikely, one hundred percent recovery, it is going to take a long time to gather up the scattered pieces of memory of the time just prior to the blow and the time just subsequent to the recovery of partial consciousness. The memories will never be complete and perfect. Drop one of those big Seeburg jukes off the back of a pickup truck and you are not going to get any music at all, and even if it can be fixed, the stereo might not ever work too well.

Forget the crap about the television-series hard guy who gets slugged and shoved out of a fast-moving car, wakes up in the ambulance, and immediately deduces that the kidnapper was a left-handed albino because Little Milly left her pill bottle on the second piling from the end of the pier. If hard case happens to wake up in the ambulance, he is going to be busy trying to remember his own name and wondering why he had double vision and what that loud noise is and why he keeps throwing up.

Assembling the bits of memory into some kind of proper order is a good trick, too.

Here's one fragment. On my left side, curled up in a cramped, tilting, bouncing place where things dug into me. Very hot. Some fabric pasted to me with sweat. Head in a small place full of blue light. Something abrasive under my left cheek. Arms immovable, hands dead. Motor grinding. A woman making a keening sound somewhere near, a thin long gassy cry, over and over, not in fear, in pain, in sorrow—but as if she were practicing, trying to imitate something, like a broken valve in a steam plant. Blackout.

Another: being jounced and joggled, hanging head down, bent over something hard digging into my belly. Thighs clasped. By an arm? One brute son of a bitch to carry me that way in a walk, but this one was jogging! Begin shallow coughing that announces imminent vomit. Immediately dropped heavily into sand. Gag, choke, and drift back into the gray void.

There were others, more vague. Some were real and some were dreams. The brain was trying to sort out the world, and it took bits of input and built dreams. On patrol, clenching myself motionless against stony ground while the flare floated down, swinging a little, moving over to burn out against the shoulder of the hill that closed off the end of the valley they were using. A brilliantly vivid fragment of old nightmare of Junior Allen surfacing behind the cruiser, tough jowls wedged into the gap of the Danforth anchor.

Then along came a more detailed one that continued so long the brain was able to go to work on it, sorting out evidences of reality, comparing them to evidences of fantasy. I awoke slowly. I was sitting on sand, leaning back against something that felt like the trunk of a tree. My arms were fasted around behind me, painfully cramped. I tried to move them and could not. I tried to move my hands, wiggle my fingers, and I could feel nothing.

I stared down at familiar swim trunks and down the brown length of my very own legs with the curled hair sun-bleached to pure white against the brown hide. A quarter-inch-in-diameter nylon cord had been tied to both ankles. It had been pulled so tight it bit into the skin. My feet are puffed. There was a two-foot length of cord from ankle to ankle. My legs spraddled. A sea-grape tree grew up out of the sand in the middle of the triangle formed by my spread legs and the ankle-to-ankle cord.

It took time to work it out. It was unlikely I had been there so long the tree had happened to grow there. Do trees grow slowly? Yes. Very slowly. Okay, could I have been fitted over the tree somehow? Long, careful thought. No. Too big. The ankles had been tied after they had been placed on either side of the tree. By me? No, the cord was too tight. My feet are swollen and blood dark. By somebody else then. Untie the cord? Not with arms I couldn't move and hands I couldn't feel. Remove tree? No way. I was supposed to stay there. No choice about it, I turned my head to the left, slowly, slowly. I was in shade. Out there the sand blazed under the high sun. Blue waves, small ones, moved in toward the sand and lifted, crested white, slapped, and ran up the sandslant and back into the next wave. I turned my head the other way as slowly and looked to my right.

A man was sitting there. He was sitting on a small, inflatable blue raft I had seen afloat in Lisa's pool. He had a weathered brown basket made of strips of woven palm frond, and he was pressing it back into shape and working new green strips of frond into it. He sat cross-legged, intent on his task. He had a trim cap of dark curls. He had dark eyes and long lashes. He had a plump red mouth. He wore white boxer shorts. He wore a gold cross on a chain around his neck. He wore a wristwatch with a stainless steel band and a complicated dial. That was all.

As he tugged and pulled at the stubborn fronds, a lot of useful-looking muscles bulged and writhed and slid around under the smooth skin of arms and shoulders. He rose effortlessly to a standing position and turned the basket this way and that. It was crude. Conical. Half-bushel size. His legs were slender, but the long muscles looked springy and powerful.

A name tugged at the edge of my mind until finally I could fit my sour mouth around it. An articulated croak. "Paul."

He looked at me. There is a way you look at people, and there is a way you look at objects. There is a difference in the way you look at objects. You do not look at your morning coffee cup, at a run-over toad in your driveway, or a flat tire the same way you look at people. This was the way a man might look at a flat tire that he was going to have to attend to in a little while. Not like the owner of the car but like the service station attendant. Damage appraisal, estimate of time required.

I managed another word. "Untie." I was becoming a chatterbox. He looked back down at his basket repair job. I couldn't understand why he wouldn't talk to me. Then gray mists came rolling in from some swamp in the back of my head, and the world faded away. . . .

*   *   *

I was being shaken awake. I was going to be late for school. I was picked up and placed on my feet. I squinted into a dazzling world and saw Paul looking at me. I was leaning back against a palm bole, weak and dizzy. I looked down and saw the familiar length of cord from ankle to ankle. Where could my sea-grape tree have gone? I could not imagine.

Paul pulled me away from the tree and turned me to face the sea. He walked me carefully, holding on to my upper arm with both hands, helping me with my balance. I had to take short steps. There was very little feeling in my feet. He guided me at an angle down the beach, the trees at my left, the sea at my right. We were out in the hot glare, away from the shade of the trees. He stopped me and said, "Sit." He helped me ease down onto the sea-damp brown sand, facing the basket I had seen him repairing. It was upside down on the sand, like a crude clown's hat. A wave slid up the sand and took a light lick at the edge of the basket and my right foot.

With the slow grace that accompanies ceremony, Paul reached and plucked the basket away. It was a magic trick. Lisa's head was balanced upright on the sand, facing the sea. Magicians can fool you with things like that. He stood easily in front of her and extended his right foot and put his bare sandy toes against her left temple and gently turned the head so that it faced me. As he did so, he spoke a rapid, guttural, unmusical French.

Lisa rolled mad and empty eyes toward me, eyes that looked through me at something on the other edge of the world beyond me and creaked her jaw wide and made a thin, gassy, aspirated scream, gagged for air, and screamed again.

He squatted, turned her head back, slid his palm under the chin to uptilt her face, spoke down at her, the French rapid but gentler, almost tender, chiding her.

A wave slid up and under him, and the edge of foam slapped the lower half of her face. She gagged and coughed. He stroked her dark, soaked hair back from her forehead with a tender and affectionate gesture, patted her cheek, said something else to her which ended with one word I understood. *Adieu.*

He moved toward me, and as he did so, I saw a bigger wave coming. She seemed to see it, too. She squeezed her eyes shut and clamped her mouth shut. It slapped against my hip. It washed completely over her head and reached six feet behind her and paused, then came sluicing back, leaving two small divergent ridges in the sand from the nape of her neck toward the sea, shaped like the wake of a boat. The sea had combed her hair forward, left it pasted down over her face.

He lifted me easily onto my feet, turned me to face up the slope of sand, urging me on. By dint of great mental effort I put three words together. "She can't see." Meaning, if she can't see, she can't see the wave coming the next time.

"Never mind," he said. His English was good, but there was a trace of the French-Canadian accent which Lisa had eliminated entirely. As we walked up the beach, I saw the old boat and remembered the day with Lisa. So she had guided Paul to this secluded spot. I saw the spade with the short handle stuck into the dry sand near the trees. Easy to dig a hole big enough for Lisa. With her knees against her chest, her ankles tied to her wrists, it wouldn't take much of a hole at all. I saw the Moke beyond the trees, on that rough little sand road, parked almost where I had parked it on that day of the lighthouse.

He helped me through the thick dry sand and eased me down in the shade with my back against a rough tree trunk. "Dig her out?" I said. I was getting pretty good with three-word sentences.

He sat on his heels, began picking up handfuls of dry sand and letting it trickle out of the bottom of his fist. "It's too late. Not that it would make any difference. I shouldn't have used the basket. She begged me not to use the basket. But I had to be sure she told every last thing. But something broke in her head. After she lost all her English. Something gave way. I thought seeing you might put her back together. I guess it was the basket. I'll be more careful with you."

I looked out at Lisa. I saw the biggest wave yet of the incoming tide. It did not curl and smash down at the packed sand until it reached her; then it bounced high off that dark roundness sparkling in the sun, the way a wave will bounce off a small boulder along the shore.

It was hard to believe it was Lisa. From the back only the dark hair showed. Her head looked like some large nut covered with a dark growth that had fallen from a tropical tree and rolled down, coming to rest in the incoming tide.

"If she holds her breath at the right time, she could last a long time, perhaps," he said. "But she is dead. Just as you are dead."

"And . . . Mary?"

There was a slight Gallic shrug. "That was bad luck. I went to her to try to convince her to leave Harry for good. Why should a woman like that have been loyal to a man like that? I wanted her to run because without her Harry would have to find three hundred thousand somewhere else. I have that much. I was going to squeeze Harry for half his stock. Waterbury should have let me buy in. Then nothing would have ever happened."

"Bad luck?"

"She tried to run. The house was dark. I caught her, and we fell badly. Very badly. It was an ugly situation. She knew who I was. I couldn't call an ambulance, could I? She knew how bad it was. I had to find out a lot from her while she could still talk. She was stubborn. I had to . . . amplify the pain to make her speak." He frowned. "I thought it would sicken me to do that.

But it was a strange pleasure in a little while. As if we were lovers. So that is bad luck too, I suppose, to learn that about oneself. Gratification is expensive and very dangerous, eh?''

He stood up, clapped his hands to remove the loose sand. ''And it was the same pleasure with Lisa, and we will discover if it is the same with a man, too. I should not care to dig a hole big enough for you, Mr. McGee.''

''McGee?''

''I am very good about details. Harry described you well enough. Mary is dead. Lisa is dead. McGee is dead. But we must find out who you sent the letter to and what it said. We shall improvise, eh? There is a tire pump and a jack in the tool compartment of that ugly little vehicle. Something will come to mind. There will be enough time to proceed slowly and carefully.''

He walked up toward the car, a hundred feet away. The equation was very simple. No unknowns. I could spend the afternoon on this hideaway beach as Paul Dissat whiled away the lazy hours with a question-and-answer game with the penalty for wrong answers and right answers precisely the same. Improvised agony.

Or I would try to stand up. That was the first step. If I couldn't there wasn't any point in wondering about step two. If I could stand, then I had to see if I could walk down the beach and into the sea. I had to hurry, but with short steps well within the range of my constraining nylon cord, and I had to keep my balance. The third part of it was getting into the water at just the right place. I had seen the place when I had been out there near Lisa's head in the hot sun.

There is no such thing as an undertow. Not anywhere in the world. All you ever find is a rip. To have a rip, you have to have a partial barrier parallel to the beach. It can be a sandbar or a reef. The barrier has to be underwater. There has to be a hole or channel through it. A great volume of water comes in on wind and waves and tide over the barrier, rushing toward the beach with waves marching right along behind each other, hurrying in. Then that big volume of water has to get out to make room for the water coming in. So it goes flowing out through the hole or channel. A big volume and a narrow, deep hole makes one hell of an outgoing current. It is sort of fan-shaped, wide at the beach end, narrowing toward the gap in the barrier, and going faster and stronger as it gets narrower.

You can read a rip on a sandy beach from the way it boils up the sand in a limited area and makes a foam line out toward the gap. If you get caught in one, you swim parallel to the beach until you are out of it, then turn toward the beach. Fight it and you can panic and drown, because they usually go faster than any man can swim.

I got up, scraping some hide off my back on the palm trunk. I went down the beach slope, stamping my feet wide for balance. The beach and the sea kept tilting, misting, merging, flowing. In nightmare slowness I passed the round, black, hairy thing, saw it vividly for just a moment. A wave had come in and covered it entirely. The top of it was a few inches under momentarily motionless water, at rest when a wave had come all the way in and gathered itself to run back out. Her black hair was fanned out, and in that instant of sharpened, memorable vision I saw the spume of sand drifting out of her open mouth, like s starnge cartoon balloon, a message without sand. A sandy, tan farewell.

Paul was shouting above the wave noises. I was off balance, leaning forward. A wave slepped my chest and straightened me up. I took a deep breath and lunged forward. I counted on the exceptional bouyancy of the water, the high salinity of the dry season. I had to know if I was in the rip. I managed to roll and float and look back at the beach and saw him and the trees and the raft and the Moke moving into the distance at six or eight miles an hour. It was a good rip, and I hoped it was a long gap in a barrier reef, that the reef was well offshore, and that it would move me out into a current that would take me away from there. Any direction at all. Out to sea and drown while laughing at how Lennie Sibelius was going to nail Paul Dissat, nail him and sweat him and find out how it happened. All of it.

The swell had built nicely, and it was going to play hell on him, trying to find me bobbing around in all that blue-and-white sparkle. If the hands are dead, it is less burdensome to drown, but you try not to drown if you can help it. I could arch my back and float high, my ears full of the drum sounds of the sea, a wave slapping me in the face now and then. Lift my head, pick a direction, and go kicking along. When all the luck has gone bad, do what you can.

19

It was a good rip that carried me way out and put me into a sea current that seemed to be taking me due north at a hell of a pace, increasing speed the farther out I got. The water was warm, and the sky was squinty bright, and I was gently lifted and dropped in the swell. It had been a good way to live, and given a choice of dying, it was as good as any that came to mind. I wanted to stay aware of the act of dying as long as I could. I wanted to touch it and taste it and feel it. When it is the last sensation left, there is a hunger to use all of it up, just to see what it is like at the very end, if it is peace or panic.

I kicked my bound legs slowly and easily. When I lifted up, I could no longer pick out the beach area where Lisa had died. I looked to the southwest and saw the checkerboard pattern of the town of Saint George's to the northeast growing more easterly as I floated farther. Finally, I began to see more and more of Grande Anse beach as I drifted farther out from shore and it came into view beyond Long Point. When all the beach was visible, I estimated that I was two miles from land. I saw the bright sails moving back and forth in the bay when a wave lifted me high. I could not guess how long I had been floating because I kept fading into a semidazed condition very much like sleep. The sun was so high I guess it was past noon.

There was a change in the direction of the current. I believed it had begun to carry me northwesterly, but I was too far from any reference points to be sure. I was opposite the town by then, and as near as I could estimate, I was just as far from the town as I was from Point Saline. When I could no longer see much of the town, see only the green mounded hills, I knew I was at least three miles offshore, possibly four.

I came out of a daze and saw a tall ship bearing down on me about a mile away. There was just enough angle so I could make her out as a three-masted schooner, and she had all the canvas on her, all the fore and aft sails flying tilting her on a long reach.

I knew it could be reality or fantasy, and the smart money would be on fantasy. I guessed she had come out of St. George's, and from my estimate of the wind, if she was headed north to the Grenadines, she would stay on that course until she was far enough out to come about and put her on the opposite tack for a single long run that would clear all of Grenada and head her for Carriacou.

I felt remote, as if working out a problem that had nothing to do with me. My arms had no feeling. I moved up and down on big, slow, blue swells. The crests were not breaking. I kept kicking myself back to an angle where I could watch her, see the boil of white water at her bows. My chance of being seen was one in thousand, even if she passed me fifty yards away.

But then I had an idea. I suppressed it because it was going to involve a lot of effort and any effort did not really seem worthwhile. There would be fishermen aboard, people who always scanned the sea even when there is no hope of stopping for a chance at whatever quarry they see. The big fish smash the water, whack it to foam, send the spray flying. Go to work. Make a fuss. Give them something to spot. Hard to do. Double up and snap. Get the bound legs up and whack them down. Get into a spin, writhing and turning the body, kicking. Duck under and come out and kick as high as you can. Dizziness then. Sickness. Vision going. A sound of sails slatting, lines creaking, a thin cry. Sound of an outboard nearby. Hands grasping, lifting me. Fall onto hardness, onto oil stink, fish smell, and vomit up quarts and quarts of seawater. . . .

Then came that burlesque of fantasy, an ironic parody of the seafarer's paradise. I was on a low, broad hatch cover, and I could feel the motion of a ship under me. I squinted up into brightness to see, clustered close around me—all their lovely faces somber, all their girl voices murmuring of concern —the sirens of all the legends, sea wind stirring their tresses, their lovely skin in shades from antique ivory to oiled walnut. They were close around me, a multitude of them, prodding and massaging calves, ankles, and puffy feet— forearms, wrists, and swollen hands.

One lifted my dead left hand, and I stared at it with remote interest. It was a dark purple rubber glove, overinflated, with deep dimples where the knuckles had been.

Suddenly I screamed. It astonished me. I am not the screaming type. There was a pain in my right hand equivalent to having all the fingernails yanked off simultaneously. Pain shoved me far enough into sudden darkness so that the raw scream seemed far away and I could think of it as an angry white bird, clawing and flapping its way out of my open throat.

I came out of blackness in time to get myself braced for the next pain. It was again in the right hand, and as it faded I got a big one in the left hand, which caught me off balance and so I roared. The enchantress moved back a little, looking down at me in worried speculation. They were all in little sleeveless blouses in bright colors, no two alike, all in little white shorts.

Captain Mickey Laneer came into view and perched a haunch on the hatch cover beside my hip. She wore a khaki shirt and a baseball cap. "What the hell have you been trying to do to yourself, McGee?"

"Hello, Mick. Lost an argument."

"Somebody throw you overboard?"

"Ran away, got into a rip, floated out from shore."

She stared at me. "From shore? Jesus! You could be a little bit hard to kill. Gals, this is an old and good friend of our old and dear friend, Rupert Darby, captain of the *Dulcinea*. Say hello to Travis McGee." They said hello in smiling musical chorus.

"McGee, clockwise around you, starting with Julia in the yellow shirt, meet Teddie, Louise, Hester, Janey, Joyce, Margot, and Valerie. Teddie, get to the helm on the double and tell Mr. Woodleigh he's falling off to port, for chrissake, and bring him back on. Janey, Mr. McGee needs a big mug of black coffee with four ounces of Fernandez rum in it. Margot, you help me get Mr. McGee onto his feet, and we'll put him in my cabin while we run back in."

I started to say something to her, then had to clamp down on the pains. Very savage pain but not as bad as the first ones.

"Speak to you privately, Mickey?"

"Move back, gals."

"Somebody is going to make very damned sure I drowned. It could revise their plans if I didn't. They'll keep a watch on the hospital. They could get to me there, I think. It's a bad risk."

"McGee, I like you. But I can't get involved in anything. The government pretends I don't exist. They like the money I bring in. The black-power types talk about me forcing blacks into prostitution. Bullshit! Hester is the only almost pure black, and there are three less than half. Every girl has freedom of choice, believe me. Any publicity of any kind, any infraction, they hit me with a heavy fine. Enough to hurt without driving me out of business. Don't kill the goose. But don't let her get fat. You need hospital attention for the head and the hands. So I'm going to come about and have a nice run back and turn you over to Rupe to put you in the hospital. I've got four good, regular customers aboard who've paid their money for a ten-day cruise. Sorry."

I started to fade out and couldn't have pulled myself back in time if a sudden pain hadn't hit my right foot, as if an electric icicle were being shoved through it.

"Mick. I'm . . . sorry, too. Rupe heading up to Dominica Wednesday. Take me up to Grenadines, set up a meet, transfer me. Reach him on radio?"

"Yes, but dammit—"

"Take me back, and I blow your tired businessman cruises right out of the water, captain. Sorry as hell. You probably fulfill a pressing need. No pun. Official complaint to your lady governor, if I have to. And the premier. And the *Miami Herald*."

"McGee, I like you less and less. You are a bastard!"

"Only when I have to be."

"But, damn you, you could *die* on me?"

"Sort of a risk for both of us."

"Valerie? *Val!* Get it on over here, girl. This big ugly son of a bitch going to die on me? She was a nurse, McGee."

Valerie was of that distinctive and very special mix you see in Honduras. Mayan, Chinese, and Spanish. She looked at my hands and she had me roll onto my belly while she checked the back of my head. Her touch was firm enough to hurt but gentle enough to let you know the hurt was necessary.

They helped me onto my back again, and she bent close and thumbed my eyelids up and looked gravely into one eye and then the other, back and forth, several times.

"Well?" Mickey said impatiently.

"Eet wass a terrible blow on the head. I don't know. The pupils are just the same size. Probably no fracture because the skull is solid and thick right there. Concussion. Could be bleeding in the brain, captain."

"How do we tell? What do we do?"

"One girl has to be with him every minute, and what she has to do all the time she is with him is count his pulse for one full minute and write it down. Count his respiration for one full minute. Write it down. Over and over. One hour is the most a girl can do that and be accurate. Half hour is better."

"So we set up half-hour shifts?"

"Then she must write down a column of figures. Suppose it is like . . . 71, 70, 72, 69, 71, 70, 69. Fine. Then it is 70, 69, 67, 68, 66, 67, 65 . . . right then the girl on duty finds me and finds you, and we get a seaplane alongside to take him to a hospital. They'll have to open his skull and see if the clot is shallow enough so they can take it out and keep him alive."

"My hands?" I asked.

"They'll hurt like hell," Valerie said. "Like living hell. But you'll be fine. No nerve damage. No dead tissue. Good circulation, so that even something that tight couldn't cut it all off."

The pain hit again as I was fading, but it just held me on the edge, and when it stopped I went the rest of the way down. Blurred memories of being carried, of choking on hot, pungent coffee, of hearing the hiss of water along the side of the hull. Then memories of it being nighttime, feeling that slow swing and turn of an anchored vessel, hearing faint music from topside, of moving in and out of sleep and seeing girls, sometimes the same one, sometimes a different one, solemnly and intently taking my pulse, lips moving writing on a pad, then staring back and forth from my chest to a watch, counting respirations, writing it down. A Coleman lantern was hung from the overhead with an improvised shade that left the bunk in relative shadow and filled the rest of the small cabin in harsh brightness.

I awoke to a gray morning light in the cabin. The lantern was out. A slender dark-haired girl sat taking my pulse. She had a narrow, pretty sallow skin. Her forehead and the end of her nose were sunburned.

"Where are we?"

"I'm counting."

"Sorry. Tell me when you're through."

"You made me get mixed up."

I let her count, write it down. "We're at anchor in a cove by some pretty little islands north of Grenada. They're called the Sisters. Now I have to count your breathing."

"Who are you?"

"Joyce. I'm new. Hush, please."

"From Barbados, eh?"

It startled her. "How'd you know that?"

"I can even remember the words. You are Louise's 'cute little chum.' She flew up and talked to you about the job."

She blushed. "Yes. Let me count, please."

"Dear girl, do your counting, and then I have to get up and use the head."

She wouldn't let me without going and bringing Valerie to check me over and give permission. I felt shaky and frail. When I came back from the nearby head, clutching at everything handy, Valerie was sitting on the bunk looking at the notebook tabulations, and Joyce was standing near her. They got out of my way, and I sighed as I got in and lay back.

"Now we can take you off the continuous count, I think," Valerie said. "Do you feel dizzy? Do your ears hum?"

"No."

"I think we'll take a count every fifteen minutes. Joyce, your hour will be up in . . . ten minutes. Stay another hour, okay? I'll have Margot take over from you at seven thirty, and you can go help with breakfast then."

"You're a good nurse," I told Valerie. "Isn't there a shortage of nurses around the islands?"

She was so still for a moment that her pretty face looked like a temple carving. Her Indian blood was more apparent. "Oh, yes. A shortage of nurses. And damn lots of patients. And not so many reasons for keeping them living, I think. The children die. The old ones come back, over and over, trying to die."

She spun and left quickly enough. I tried to smile at Joyce. Maybe I managed it convincingly enough. I think she smiled back as her face tilted and blurred and faded into gray-black. I had to say something to assure Joyce and myself I was not going sour on them.

"What did you do in Barbados, dear?" My voice seemed to come from the bottom of a brass barrel.

"Does it matter?" she said from the far end of a hundred-yard corridor.

"I'm interested. I'm curious. That's all."

She began to emerge out of the humming mists and the metallic distances. I saw her face again, shifting as if underwater, then firming up. "Are you all right?" she asked, frowning. I felt her fingertips moving on my wrists, seeking the pulse.

"I'm fine."

"You looked different. Your eyes were funny. I work in a boutique in Bridgetown. My husband worked at the desk in a couple of the good hotels. We could live on what we made if we were careful. Maybe he got tired of being careful. He left over a year ago, and I have no idea where he is. What else do you want to know? I'm English and Portuguese mostly with a bit of colored. I make about two hundred and seventy-five to three hundred, Biwi, a month in the season and a lot less when the tourists have gone. I can't quite live on it. I've sold the things Charles and I owned, like the music system we got on hire-purchase and was all paid for, and I let them come and take the things which weren't paid for. The last thing I let go, the last thing worth selling, was my little sailboat my father built for me before he died when I was twelve." Her words were coming faster and faster, and she had stopped searching for the pulse. Her thin fingers were wrapped around my lacerated wrist. "It was the only thing I could use to get away, to be someone else, and I took it out in a gale before I let it go, telling it to drown me, but it would not . . ."

"Hey, now," I said.

Her eyes had filled. "I mean there is no end to it, Mr. McGee. I've been a decent woman. I have no family at all. A fat political gentlemen wants to give me a cottage in a development he owns. There has been one girl every two years, I understand. He is quite old. They each end up with a cottage and some sort of small pension. I imagine a long street of them with the years marked on little signs in the little yards, with all of us sitting on our little porches. . . ."

"Joyce, honey. There, honey."

Kind words started the flood. She put her forehead down into the bend of my elbow, and the stifled sobs wracked her thin body. I stroked her hair and made soothing sounds. I identified my own feeling of guilt. I had not really wanted to know about her life and her problems. I had been talking in an effort to keep the brassy mists from sucking me under. But the words had opened her up, and it had come spilling out.

She pushed herself away, stood with her back to me, blew her nose. "Why should you give a damn?" she said in a choked voice. "Why should any-body."

"Is this cruise what your friend Louise described?"

She turned, snuffled, sat wearily in the chair. "Oh, yes. Louise didn't lie. She called a spade a spade. It's a ten-day trial, you might say. I will do deck duty, scut work, help with the food, drinks, laundry, scrubbing, and all that. But I don't have to be . . . available unless I decide to be and tell Captain Laneer first. The men really seem quite nice. I can keep my clothes on, thank God. Louise said it took her three days to get used to pottering about the deck and belowdecks entirely starko. I think it would take me forever and even then I couldn't adjust. The girls are so much nicer than I imagined. But an entirely naked woman is not really erotic, do you think? Of course, in a cold wind or offshore insects or one's time of the month or coming into port, clothes are definitely required." She had a brooding look, frowning down at her knuckles. "It's rather difficult for one to imagine being quite ready for it. I mean if one has taken a bucket of scraps aft after cleaning fish, it is so abrupt to be suddenly tweaked, then taken by the hand and led below." She roused herself and looked slightly startled. She had been voicing her internal monologue. "I go on, no?" She forced a wan smile. "At any rate, once the ten days are ended, I shall either go back to the boutique or stay or go back to quit my job and pack. I shall fret about it later, not now. Valerie told me it would be good for you to get as much sleep as you can now. Can you sleep, dear?"

I could. I slept and slept and slept. The dull ache in hands and feet and head did not inhibit it. In too many of the sleep periods Lisa was way down below the velvet black, waiting for me on the bright beach, the severed head propped on the delicate bones of the jaw, smiling at me.

*   *   *

It was another morning, and Mickey Laneer brought me a stone mug of coffee, nudged me awake, and put the coffee in my hand after I had hitched up, knuckled grainy eyes.

"You are some kind of a sleeper," she said.

"A long swim with your hands and feet tied will do it every time. We moved again, didn't we? Where are we, and what day is it?"

"Anchored in the lee of Frigate Island at eight o'clock on the morning of Thursday, April twenty-ninth."

"Thursday! But couldn't you get in touch with—"

"He'll be off to the west of here about opposite us at fourteen hundred. We'll make a radio check on him an hour beforehand. No sweat. We'll run out and intercept and put you aboard *Dulcinea*."

"I've been a lot of trouble to you and your crew, Mick."

Her smile was sour. "Better this kind than the kind you were going to lay on me if I ran you back in."

"Hard feelings, captain?"

She grinned, punched me on the side of the thigh. "My four passengers haven't made any complaints. Maybe because I run the only game in town. The gals have loved playing nurse. By doing it your way—with you having the grace not to die on me—I've kept my friendship with Rupe. And I put a high value on it. No, McGee. Except for having to give up my own cabin, no hard feelings. How do you feel, anyway? Strong?"

I checked and tested. "Better than I should."

"You look good. If you feel strong enough, I can send you down a little sample of our recreation program here aboard the *Hell's Belle*. Courtesy of the management. Name your favorite nurse, man."

"Joyce?"

The taut smile was gone. "Now you really are a smartass, you know that? I know damned well you know that girl's arrangement aboard, because she told me about talking to you."

"I thought maybe she'd made her decision."

"And you were curious? I wouldn't want you aboard long. You'd make too much mischief. Nobody puts any kind of pressure on that kid. She works it out for herself. She makes her own decisions."

"What will she decide?"

Mickey Laneer stood up, looking weary and cynical. "She'll decide that every other choice she has is worse. I'll send your breakfast."

Teddie brought my breakfast. She was the big, creamy, Minnesota Swede who had learned her sailing on Lake Superior. She was the one who giggled. Her hair was sea-weathered to a harsh spill of pure white hemp. From the bulge of bland forehead down to the clench of prehensible toes, she was tanned to the shade of macaroons. She giggled as she presented the tray with the menu she had devised. Two giant rum sours. A stack of toast. A platter of flying fish, perfectly sautéed and browned, crisp and sweet. A big enameled coffeepot and two of the stone mugs. She latched the door, giggling, and we had breakfast. She took the tray over to the table and came back, giggling. In the moist hollow of her throat, from earlobe to collarbone and across the socket in front, around to the other earlobe, she smelled exactly like fresh cinnamon and Pears' Soap.

*   *   *

The rendezvous was made about fifteen minutes past two, an estimated seven miles due west of Frigate Island. I convinced Mickey that there was no need to use the tender to transfer me. It was a freshening breeze, the sea running sparkling high. I said that though I didn't want to test my skull by diving, I could certainly swim a little. Rupe put the *Dulcinea* dead in the water, rocking in the trough, and hung the boarding ladder over. Mickey at the helm took the *Belle* across the *Dulcinea's* stern, laying her over so that as I sat on the lee rail and swung my legs around to the outboard side, my feet were but inches from the water.

I dropped and swam the fifty or sixty feet to the *Dulcinea,* bringing from the *Belle* no more than I had brought aboard—the swim trunks, leaving behind somewhere in the sea the scraps of nylon cord they had cut out of my flesh.

There was no hand extended to help me when I clambered aboard the *Dulcinea.* Rupe and Artie stood staring at the *Belle,* jaws slack, leathery paws dangling. Mickey saw no need to change the uniform regulations for an old friend like Rupe. Mickey showed off by taking the *Belle* fifty yards past us, coming about smartly, working hell out of her girls, and then coming back aslant, waving as she angled across our bows on a northeast course not over forty feet away. The girls shouted, grinned, laughed, and waved.

"Fool woman," Rupe said. "All sailor, that fool woman. Artie. Artie? *Artie!*"

"Huh? Me?"

"Bring in that boarding ladder and stow it right this time."

"Boarding ladder?"

"Artie!"

"Oh. Sure. Yessir, Rupe. Right away."

Rupe put the diesels back in gear, opened them up to full cruise, checked the chart and gave Artie the compass course, and left him at the wheel. We went below.

"Now what the *hell* is this all about, Trav?"

"It'll take some time."

"Time is what we've got the most of."

20

RUPE LOANED me the money to get home, and Artie loaned me the clothes, a set of fresh khakis that fit better than I would have guessed from looking at him. I had to buy straw sandals at Kingstown on St. Vincent. Customs and immigration clearance was at San Juan, and I had an interesting time there. People are supposed to have papers and luggage, a wallet and a toothbrush.

They wanted to take my citizenship away from me. I told them it was a little misfortune at sea. I told them we could make some collect phone calls. When I said a magic name they could call collect they came to attention. They almost smiled. That was on Sunday, the second day of May. I pulled the home number, unlisted, out of the damaged recesses of memory and got his wife, then got him. He talked to the boss immigration fellow, and when they were through, the boss immigration type felt a compulsion to pump my hand and call me sir and ask me if there was any little thing he could do, anything at all.

Before my flight left, I tried Meyer again, and this time he was aboard his boat, and when he heard and recognized my voice, he said in a shaky voice, "Thank God. Thank God." I told him what I needed and what to do and not to be so sentimental, anyway.

It was a bright, clear day to fly across the Bahamas and the incredible tones and shades of the Bahama flats. I wanted to think but not very much. I wasn't very sure about being able to think things through. I wanted to depend on Meyer. The weather across my internal landscape wasn't very good. Patches of gray, like drifting clouds, obscured things I wanted to see. And sometimes in a waking state I would have the same feeling, the same jolt as when you awaken from sleep. For a little while I would not know where I was or where the plane would land.

I got off that flight and walked through the lower level and out to vehicle pickup, and there was Meyer, bless him, standing beside a dark blue rental Ford as ordered. A very anonymous car. I told him he had better do the driving, as I was not entirely sure of the circuitry in my head. He drove. I talked. We selected a ma-and-pa motel on the way into Lauderdale on Route 1, and he got me a room in the back with an air conditioner that sounded like an air hammer breaking up paving. I finished the story in the room.

I unpacked the stuff Meyer had brought from the *Flush*, using that spare key I gave him, which he keeps hidden aboard the *Keynes*. He had packed some Plymouth, which seemed a kindly gesture. He went and got ice from the machine, and we drank from sleazy disposable glasses that looked as though they were about five room guests overdue for disposal.

I sat on the bed, sipping the clean, cool taste of juniper. Meyer paced and paced. He would stop in front of me to ask questions. "I'm not clear on one point. You *did* write the whole thing to Lennie Sibelius, telling him to get moving, open the inner envelope if you hadn't checked in by the end of May?"

"I did. But I told Lisa the tenth of May. I wrote to Lennie later. And I did not tell her who I wrote to, of course."

"She believed you?"

"She very definitely bought it. And she told Cousin Paul everything he wanted to know. Assumption: he believed her the way she believed me. But by the time he found out about the letter, he'd gone too far with both of us to start making deals. His next step was to make me talk to him. And he could have. I'm stubborn, Meyer. Need I mention it? The pain threshold is high, as measured on the dolorimeter. But I could have gotten so anxious to talk I would have fallen all over myself. He scares me. What was your reading on him?"

"Humble beginnings. Very bright, very reliable. Full scholarship to McGill. Went back to his village to work for the man who helped him. Worked for that man about three years, and then one of Waterbury's companies acquired the benefactor's business in a merger situation. Waterbury was impressed by Paul Dissat and took him into the Quebec headquarters. Dissat is thirty-six, single, conservative, devout Catholic. He doesn't drink or smoke. He's apparently managed his own savings very shrewdly. Handsome. Very fit. Superb skier and superior tennis player."

He paced and I sipped, and the air conditioner kept up its whangbang roaring, leaking condensation down the blue concrete-block wall.

He stopped in front of me, using his lectern mannerisms. "He functions very well in a highly pragmatic profession. He is perfectly aware of cause and effect. He can weigh the degree of risk he is willing to take. He will assume that the man who gets your letter will be competent. Can his whole plan stand determined investigation? No. Even without a link as weak as Harry Broll, enough could be learned to bring it before a grand jury. What would this sort of scandal do to the SeaGate stock offering? It would come out that a fraud had been committed to get funds from a bank to pay for a preoffering block of stock. Waterbury could not afford to proceed. Both Jensen, Baker, and Fairmont, Noyes would recommend the applications be withdrawn. This would all happen, if your letter exists, with or without Paul Dissat on stage. See where I'm going?"

"I think so."

"With no public issue to raise money through the sale of stock, SeaGate comes to a shuddering halt. Harry's indivisible block becomes worthless. I can think of a Dissat-like solution."

"Grab the three hundred thousand from Harry?"

"Yes. But don't burn the bridges. Not all the way. Kill Harry because he is the last useful witness left alive. Then take a leave of absence on an emergency basis, somewhere out of touch. Lie back and listen. If there is no letter at all, if it was a bluff, then come back after the deadline and pick up the project again."

I toasted him. "To you, Meyer. If he has left already, I get the letter back from Sibelius, and wait for him to reappear. If he's still here and working closer to the deadline of the tenth and if he hasn't gotten around to Harry, we pluck Harry away from him and take Harry to a private place and have a long chat about Mary and Lisa."

"If he has left, or is preparing to leave, and wants a door ajar so that he can get back just in case, then he'll have given Waterbury some sort of cover story, I imagine."

"Can we arrange a secret meeting with Waterbury?"

"Travis?"

"Why are you looking at me like that?"

"If we can't find Harry Broll anywhere and if Paul Dissat is still around and if Harry never did buy that block at SeaGate, even if Mary's body is dug up and identified, there's no way you can get Paul indicted. You probably can't even get him fired."

"He's got pretty legs."

"I don't want you to do some damned idiot thing."

"Long black eyelashes, Meyer. Red lips."

"Travis!"

"Maybe I want to dance with him. Maybe I want to whisper in his ear. But

I don't want to have him come to me. You see, he's a careful man. He knows I'll come back if I didn't drown. That's why I told you to be careful about being seen going aboard the *Flush*. Am I overreacting?''

"No. You are not overreacting.''

"Don't let him get to you, Meyer, when he starts looking for that letter.''

"I've never seen you like this.''

"He scrambled my brains. We should get away. I know a great cruise we could take.''

"A cruise! A cruise?''

"It's different. I'll tell you about it later.''

"Do that. There's been no report of Mary Broll's death from Grenada. It's taking a long time.''

"A guest is charged for the cottage whether she uses it or not and charged for the food whether she uses it or not. And in the absence of a body it is the kind of island where, if a lady gets invited aboard a yacht for cocktails or up into the hills to an estate for cocktails, a lady could decide to spend a week being entertained. It is, shall we say, an impulsive place. A carefree isle.''

"I phoned Mr. Willow last Wednesday. He got the cable from Mrs. Broll on Monday, and he talked with Harry Broll on Monday. On Tuesday morning he activated the loan papers and deposited the funds in Broll's personal account. I thought you'd like to know. That's when I started trying to get you on the phone. Wednesday, Thursday, Friday, Saturday. It was . . . pleasant to hear your voice.''

"Paul sent the cable in her name. No problem. I should have realized how easily he could do that.'' I looked at Meyer's watch after first staring at my empty wrist for the thousandth time. "Five o'clock on Sunday afternoon. About the only thing we can do is try to find Harry.''

"How?''

"There is a name in the back of this scrambled skull. All the file cards are spilled on the floor. Let me crawl around back there for a minute.''

I retrieved the red-brown hair, pale green eyes, the vital and expressive face, the lean, quick-moving body. I let her walk around and smile, and then I knew her. "Jeannie Dolan of Eighty-five fifty-three Ocean Boulevard.'' I hitched along the bed and got her number from information and called her.

"Who?'' she asked in a sleepy voice.

"McGee. The guy with the blue Rolls pickup.''

"Hey! It's you! I'd about decided I hadn't made any kind of dent on you at all. And that doesn't help a girl's pride. Where are you? Ask me out and then sweat out about three minutes of girlish reluctance and then come and get me, huh?''

"I am doing to do exactly that later on, but right now I can't do any stirring around.''

"Oh! Are you sick?''

"Not too sick to take you out, Jeannie. But I am trying to give the impression of being out of town. For good reasons.''

"Okay. I'm not even talking to you. I will go around saying, 'Whatever happened to good old whosis?' ''

"You are one nice lady.''

"Rrrr*right!*"

"For reasons I may tell you some day, right now I want to know how goes the course of true love and romance and convenience. Betsy and Harry."

"It isn't exactly a script Ali McGraw is going to want to star in. Right now Betsy is teed pretty good. He was real jumpy and mean last week, and Wednesday morning early, like five, he got a phone call. It woke her up, but she fell asleep, and then he's shaking her awake. It's just getting to be daylight, and he's dressed, and he's packed a suitcase. He tells her he's going away on business. By the time the front door slams, she has asked him where he's going and when he'll be back about three times—no answer. I told her I think she has been handed the personally engraved, natural-bristle brush and maybe she should move back down here onto four with me. She's been calling his office and getting brushed off there, too. She drove out there a couple of times, but there was no sign of his car. Maybe he is away on business. But it showed no consideration, the way he left."

"Sold any condominiums?"

"Not to that friend of yours. She never showed up. If she really exists."

"You are very suspicious of people."

"If you'd ever met my husband, you'd know why. He could walk into a phone booth and leave by a side door."

"I'm a sneaky type too, Jeannie."

"That's nice. It's what I'm used to."

"I'll be calling you soon."

"You do that, hon. Bye."

*   *   *

Meyer and I talked, establishing the new parameters. But it was like the game of guessing which fist contains the chess pawn. Harry had enough animal caution to know that if things went wrong for Paul Dissat, it was runaway time for Harry. So if it was Paul who phoned him, maybe Harry had started to run. Conversely, Paul would know Harry was shrewd enough to know when to run, and so if Paul gave Harry cause to run, he would make certain Harry wouldn't be able to.

"The money will be the clue," Meyer said. "The first thing in the morning, as soon as the bank is open. I don't think it was paid over to SeaGate. And I don't think it's still in the bank."

"How do you manage that?"

Meyer smiled an unexpectedly unkindly smile. "By almost giving Woodrow Willow a coronary. He deserves a jolt. One should not be able to con a trust officer out of any assets held in trust."

"I'm coming along."

"Do you think you—"

"In the disguise you're going to go out and buy me at Happy Sam's Giant Superstore Open Always Practically."

"And on the way back here I buy pizza and beer to go?"

*   *   *

The lobby of the Southern National Bank and Trust Company takes up half the ground floor of their new building on Biscayne. It is like three football fields. People at the far end are midgets, scurrying around in the cathedral lighting. The carpeting is soft and thick, dividing the lobby into function areas through the use of colors. Coral, lime, turquoise. The bank colors are pale blue and gold. The girls wear little blue-and-gold bank jackets with the initials *SNB* on the pocket, curled into a fanciful logo, the same logo that's stitched into the carpet, mosaicked into the walls, embossed on the stationery, and watermarked into the checks. The male employees and officers up to ambassadorial rank wear pale-blue-and-gold blazers. Everybody has been trained to smile at all times. The whole place looks like a huge, walk-in dental advertisement. There is probably also a bank song.

Meyer dropped me a block away, and while he found a parking space, I strolled back to the bank and went in. I wore a Hawaiian shirt, a straw ranch hat with a red band, a drugstore camera around my neck, sunglasses with big pale orange lenses.

A guard moved in from the side and asked if he could help me. I said I was meeting the little woman here because she had to cash a traveler's check, probably to buy some more of those damn silly leather boots, and where would she go to cash traveler's checks. He aimed me across the hundred yards of carpeting, under a forty-foot ceiling. Nobody else looked at me. Tourists are invisible, except to the man trying to sell them something. Otherwise, they are as alike as all the trees in the park. Only a botanist knows there is any difference between trees. Or an apple grower.

I kept moving, because if I stood still, one of the guards would come over and ask me if he could help me. I did not know how long it would take. Meyer said he would come in from the north side corridor after going up to the trust department and coming back down with Mr. Willow. Also, I kept moving because I wanted to make certain that by no ten-thousand-to-one chance was Cousin Paul doing a little banking business this hot, windy Monday morning. Sometimes his face would be completely gone from memory, and that would frighten me. Then it would pop back like a slide coming into automatic focus.

At long last I saw Meyer coming toward me, striding right along, and I guessed that was Mr. Woodrow Willow a half step to the rear. I watched Meyer. He was going to rub his nose if he wanted me to join the act. He looked through me and did not see me at all. Woodrow Willow was not what I expected. This was a young man, tall, fresh-faced, snub-nosed, round-headed, with the same mouth old Walt used to draw on his chipmunks. I sauntered after them and caught up when they talked to a man who had his own big blond desk in a solitary, private thirty-by-thirty area of coral carpet right out in the midst of everything. The man used a phone. Soon a rangy woman came over walking like one of those heel-and-toe competitors, elbows pointed outward. She listened. She picked up the phone. A far younger girl came, carrying a ledger card. She jogged. Every part of her jogged.

After she left, Meyer shook hands with the man at the desk, and Meyer, Willow, and the rangy woman walked all the way across to a line of teller's stations on the far side of the bank. The rangy woman spoke to a slender girl with brown hair. Then she spoke to a man patrolling behind the cages. The slender girl closed her window and came around and out onto the bank floor. Meyer turned toward me and rubbed his nose. The rangy woman was leaving.

I walked up, and Meyer said, "Mr. Willow, this is my associate, Mr. McGee. McGee, may I present Miss Kathy Marcus."

"Who *is* this person?" Willow said in a voice of despair. "Good God, I had no idea you were going to bring in—"

"A place where we can talk?" Meyer said. "Just to have Kathy tell us in her own words before we get into anything else. Then we won't be taking up so much of her time."

"Take a lot," she said. "I've got a three-dollar short that's driving me up the wall."

"We'd better use one of the small conference rooms upstairs," Willow said.

Upstairs was 1910 banking, as opposed to the 1984 version in the lobby. Oak paneling, green rugs, leather libraries. The computers were hidden off-stage. Park your Mercer under the elm trees and come in and talk about buying a block of Postal Telegraph.

There were six chairs around the table in the small conference room. There were two framed prints of clipper ships and a seventeen-pound glass ashtray on the polished walnut. As soon as the door was shut, I shed the ranch hat, shades and camera.

"Enjoying your stay?" Kathy asked me with a quick wink.

"Little gal, when I come across those Everglades in that big old air-conditioned Greyhound bus, I said to the little woman, I said, Mother, we shoulda —"

Kathy guffawed, stopping me. Willow rang the big glass ashtray with his pipe in authoritarian tempo, silencing everybody. "Please! This is a very serious matter. If I have your attention, Miss Marcus, we would like to find out to what extent you are involved—"

"Whoa, friend," she said sharply, no laughter in her voice or her level stare."

"Now you will *listen* to me, Miss Marcus! I was saying—"

She got up and went to the door and smiled and said, "When you go home to the wife and kiddies tonight, Woodie, tell her that nice Miss Marcus quit the bank and went right down the street to another bank. Some loyalty, huh?"

"Come back and—"

"Woodie dear, the banks are so hard up for anybody who is worth a damn, it's pathetic. They've been hiring people here if they're ambulatory and feel warm to the touch. And I am one very damned good teller, and I have been here four years, and I am not now, nor have I ever been, *involved* in anything hanky or panky."

"Please, come back and—"

"Woodie dear, you just can't have it both ways. You can't call me Kathy and fun around with me when we're alone in an elevator and give me a friendly little grab in the ass and a chummy little arm pressure on the tit and then expect me to sit meek and mild in front of these gentlemen and take some kind of accusatory shit from you. No thanks. I'll tell them downstairs who ran me out of this bank."

"Kathy," he said.

With her hand on the knob she looked at him with narrowed eyes and said, "That's a start at least. Say the rest of it."

"I'm sorry. I didn't mean to imply—"

"Do you want me to come back and sit down, Woodie?"

"Please. I would appreciate it very much."

She came slowly back to the chair, sat, and smiled and said. "If these men had been strangers, Woodie, I would have let you go on being a jackass, and I would have cooked you later. But I'm among friends. Friends who rescued an eerie blonde from the oldest floating house party in the world."

"I remember already," Meyer said.

I looked at her more closely. "Delmonica Pennypacker?"

"Just a little name I made up for my vacation. Anyway, as I understand it, Woodie, you want a play-by-play account of cashing the check for Mr. Harry Broll."

Woodrow Willow was coming out of shock. He cleared his throat and told how a Mr. Winkler, a vice-president of the bank, had received a telephone request last Wednesday at closing time from Harry Broll, stating that he would be in at about eleven on Thursday to cash a check for three hundred thousand on his personal account. He wanted to make certain the bank would have cash available in hundred-dollar bills. This is not an unusual request in an area where large real estate deals are made.

Kathy took over and said, "The way our system works, everything has to go through teller records or we're out of balance. The cashier is Herman Falck, and I suppose Mr. Winkler told Herm to have the cash on hand. Herm told me he would run it through my balance, and he said Mr. Broll would probably bring in a dispatch case for the money. That amount would fit with no trouble. We run a minimum cash balance in the drawers at all times to make the place less appealing to the knockover boys. We signal the vault for more cash or to come to make a pickup when we get too fat. They come zipping in a little electric money cart.

"So at ten after eleven Herm brings these two men over to me. I put out my closed sign so that a line won't build behind them. He takes the dispatch case from the man with Mr. Broll and hands it around to me. Mr. Broll gives me the check, and Herm initials it. Then Herm goes back and brings the cash cart behind the cage. It's just a matter of packing the sixty wrapped stacks of hundreds into the case. A black plastic case, imitation lizard. I counted them out as I packed them. Five, ten, fifteen, on up to three hundred. The case was below eye level, looking from the floor of the bank. I snapped the snaps, and slid it up onto the counter, and the other man took it, and they walked away."

"Had you ever seen Mr. Broll before?" I asked.

"I think so. He looked sort of familiar. Maybe I waited on him. The name seems familiar."

"How did he act?"

"Well, I guess he's really a pretty sick man. I don't think he could have managed without the other man helping him."

"In what way did he seem to you to be sick?"

"Well, he was very sweaty. His complexion was gray, and his face was wet. He kind of wheezed. Like asthma sometimes. He didn't have much to say. Usually, men joke about lots of money when they put it in or take it out. They joke with me because I'm all girl, I guess. His friend had to kind of support him walking to my window, I noticed. Mr. Broll walked slowly, a little bent over and taking small steps. His friend was very nice to him. Considerate."

"What did his friend look like?"

"Younger. Dark curly hair. Tall. Middle thirties, I'd guess. A very nice voice. Some kind of accent. Marvelous clothes. Conservative mod. But he was too pretty for my taste. Husky pretty. Great eyelashes. He called Mr. Broll 'Harry,' but Mr. Broll didn't call him anything. 'Let me help you, Harry. Here, let me take that, Harry. Come on, there's no hurry, Harry. Take your time, old man.' It took them a long time to walk to the main doors. The fellow helped Mr. Broll and carried the dispatch case. I watched them. They didn't go right out. I guess Mr. Broll felt faint, because they stopped and sat down in that lounge area left of the main doors. It made me uneasy. You like to see three hundred thousand get to where it has to go and get locked up again. They sat side by side on the couch. I could see the fellow leaning toward Mr. Broll and talking quietly and confidentially. I saw Mr. Broll put his hand over his eyes. The other man pulled it away and took his handkerchief and wiped Mr. Broll's face, wiping the sweat away, I guess." She frowned. "Maybe I shouldn't say this, but the whole scene had a funny flavor. It seemed faggoty to me, like a wife with a sick husband. . . . No. The other way around. A youngish husband with kind of a fat, sick old wife he doesn't really love but feels sort of affection and gratitude and . . . a sense of duty to, if I don't sound flippy."

"Not flippy at all."

"I was busy, and when I looked again, they were gone. I would guess it was about twenty minutes before noon when they left the bank together."

Willow said, "Would you say Mr. Broll was drunk or drugged?"

She thought it over. "No. He kept his eyes sort of squinted up. He knew what he was doing. He just seemed . . . fragile. As if he was in terrible pain. As if he had the world's worst bellyache and was wondering if he was going to pass out with it. And . . . he smelled sort of sour. He was wrinkled and he had beard stubble. I wondered if he'd been traveling all night or he'd slept in his clothes. I suppose it *could* have been the world's worst hangover."

"Thank you, Miss Marcus," Willow said. "Uh . . . Kathy."

"That means take off, huh?"

"With our thanks, Kathy," Meyer said. "You are a bright girl and a good observer. And if it ever becomes possible to tell you anything about this whole matter, we will."

"Thank *you*," Kathy said. She paused at the door and said, "McGee, do you still have that wild floating pad?"

"*The Busted Flush,* Slip F-Eighteen."

"I'll come visit. If you haven't gotten married up."

"Come visit, Kathy. Bring your swim pants."

"I'll bring a bowl of Greek salad. I make one hell of a Greek salad."

When the door shut, Willow said, "Good help is so terribly hard to find and keep that one has to . . . uh . . . put up with a degree of impertinence that . . . uh . . ."

"Like she said, Woodie," I told him, "it's a lot easier to get respect from the pretty ones if you don't keep grabbing them by the ass in the elevator. Right, Meyer?"

"Absolutely right. An executive can't have it both ways."

"Keep the pretty ones at a distance," I said. "Grab the dog-faced ones by the ass. Then you have a happy bank."

"A contented bank," Meyer said.

"Goddammit," Willow yelled. "Tell me what this is all about!"

Meyer said, "I'll ask you the same question I asked you before, Woodrow. Could you swear that you were absolutely, positively certain that Mary Broll was alive when you processed that loan?"

"The answer is still the same. But why are you asking the question?"

"I'll ask you another. What was Harry Broll going to use the money for?"

"To buy the SeaGate stock, to pay the balance due of three hundred thousand. Don't look at me like that. It's legal, you know. It is illegal to borrow money to buy *listed* securities."

"He'd lose a great opportunity if he didn't buy that block of stock?"

"Oh, yes! Really great."

"Would he have to have cash to buy that stock, Woodrow?"

"Of course not! A certified check would—"

"Do you think he bought it?"

"I don't know."

"Can you think of any way of finding out?"

"Don't go away."

We were left alone. Meyer sighed. I told him he was pushing Woodie around beautifully. All he did was sigh again. When Meyer gets the silents, he isn't very good company.

21

As MEYER drove conservatively back toward Lauderdale in fast traffic, he said, "We can summarize what we know, if you think it will help."

"You do it, and I'll tell you if it helps."

"We do not care whether Harry Broll was running from Dissat or hurrying to meet him. Immaterial. Dissat had him from some unknown hour early Wednesday morning until they walked into the bank Thursday at ten after eleven. By three o'clock Wednesday afternoon Harry Broll was forced to make the phone call to Mr. Winkler about the large cash withdrawal. Dissat had to then sustain Broll on that depressed level where he could make his appearance at the bank without creating suspicion, yet would have no interest in appealing for help. Total emotional and physical defeat. A person reduced to Harry Broll's condition is beyond feeling terror. Only despair. The only part left would be the details of disposal, or, if he'd already planned how to do it, to go ahead with it. If it required darkness, he would have to have a place to take Broll to wait for night or, better yet, a place to immobilize him safely so Dissat could put in an appearance elsewhere. If we are building the structure of limitation, the parameters of time and space, we need to know if

Dissat appeared at the West Palm office on Wednesday and, if he did, the time spent there.''

"And where he is right now," I said. "When I wonder where he is right now, I wonder if he's crouched on the floor behind us. That's what he does to me, Meyer. Sorry. He was so *pleased* with himself, so damned *delighted* when he reached out with his bare toes and turned her head so she looked at me with those empty, crazy eyes. It was a funny kind of innocent pleasure, as if he had no idea there was anything really wrong about it. He was like a little kid who'd built a kite that would fly, and he wanted me to tell him how great it was. He tried to talk tough. Movie tough. But it was like something that had to be said. An obligatory part of the ceremony. After that we were going to share something, he and I. Some special personal important relationship. Dammit. I can't say it so that you can understand how it was.''

"He fits the pattern of a certain kind of damaged personality I have read about, Travis. He could be called the activated sociopath sadist. Bright, healthy, energetic, competent. Excellent in areas requiring ritual. Mathematics, accounting, engineering. Quite cold inside. Tricky. Unable to concede the humanity of people around them because, having no basis of comparison, they think all of us have their same dry and barren soul. They are loners. They can charm when they choose. Sexually stunted, inhibited, often impotent. When Mary tried to escape from him and he caught her and they fell badly and injured her seriously, that activated him. Now he knows what he wants. He wants inventive episodes like the one with Lisa. The money will be meaningful only in how many such episodes it will buy. He isn't aware of evil. Only of being caught. You have to think of him as a bored child who suddenly discovers that it is wonderful fun to go to the pet store and buy a mouse and bring it home and do things to it until it is dead. Life is no longer boring. It is full of rich and wonderful excitement. The mouse shares the experience, so he feels fond of the mouse for as long as it lasts. You could say that the child loves the mouse to the extent he can feel love.''

"Jesus!"

"I know. Stroking Lisa's forehead, drying Harry's sweaty face, are imitations of emotion. We can imagine he spoke tender words to Mary because she was pleasing him, giving him release. He's not a madman in any traditional sense. He cannot feel guilt or shame. If caught, he would feel fury and indignation at the game's ending too soon. He'll go to great lengths to stay free, unsuspected. His career is a lot less important to him than it used to be. My guess is he'll be gone by the deadline, the tenth, a week from today.''

We rode in silence for a time. "Meyer? How did you get that Woodie Woodchuck to snap to attention?''

"By reminding him that he had informed me of the approximate value of the assets in one of his trust accounts without any authorization from the trust customer or the senior trust officer. Banks take all confidential relationships very seriously. He soon said he would be very happy to help me find out all about the three hundred thousand.''

"How did he find out Harry had forfeited his option?''

"I don't know. Probably phoned a contact at SeaGate and asked what value, as collateral, Harry's hundred-thousand-share block would have. The stuff is too closely held to have an OTC quote.''

"Couldn't he have borrowed against the stock he was going to get?"

"Not if he had already done so."

"Sick condominiums and a sick construction business. How about the seven hundred thousand he's supposed to get back from SeaGate?"

"If it went into land improvements at the site, then I guess he'd have to wait until the public issue money comes back to SeaGate."

"So that goes to pay off other debts, and then Harry's business quietly fades away and dies?"

"Reasonable guess."

"He had to take Harry somewhere and keep him there. Harry and Harry's car. Transportation problems, Meyer. Logistics and tactics. If he took him to wherever he lives—"

"A cluster apartment complex at West Palm on the bay shore. Rental apartments. Not likely."

"I suppose you have his phone number?"

"You asked me to check him out. Remember?"

"And your overall impression?"

"A very dull fellow, competent and humorless."

"You know the name of the cluster apartments?"

"I'd rather not say it. Palm Vista Gardens. D-Two."

"The first phone booth after we get off the pike, please."

*   *   *

He parked at a gas station by a shiny row of vending machines under a roof made of plastic thatch, incredibly green. I phoned from the hotbox provided by Gen Tel out on the cement wasteland. I hoped Palm Vista Gardens was big enough to have a rental and administration office on the premises. It was. The lady's voice came right from the resonant bridge of her Indiana nose.

"Yes, maybe you *can* help me. Have you got any furnished one-bedroom vacancies?"

She was not a well-organized lady. She tended to ramble. She gave information and then with cries of dismay retracted it and called herself names, mostly "old fool."

She finally discovered that one of their renters, "a nice young man" who had been on the special month-to-month basis with one month in advance (an arrangement they made with the "nice young people" from that new SeaGate company) had come in on the last day of April, just last Friday, and given his notice. He said he was vacating in a week. And that would make it . . . the eighth? No. The seventh. Yes. Next Friday. They could start showing it again the following Monday if there wasn't too much to be done. That was number D-2, which meant apartment 2 in cluster D. Just stop at the office. But don't wait too long. They go very quickly to nice young people, providing they don't have any pets. Or any babies, of course. I wondered how they felt about noisy goldfish, the kind that do a lot of leaping and splashing and churning about.

I tried to blot out all rational thought with a lot of peripheral items. Goldfish. Lead-free gasoline. Diminishing aquifer. I walked to the car, realizing I had left the cheap camera on the back seat. An essential part of my tourist costume. Meyer stood beside the rental car, drinking a can of orange pop, and it suddenly seemed insane that Meyer wore no tourist disguise. Paul

Dissat knew exactly who I was and where I lived. And if he had gone to Bahia Mar and poked around as such a thorough chap would, he would have learned that Meyer was associated with me in certain obscure, but apparently profitable ventures. Though believing me safely drowned off Grenada's lovely beaches, he might conclude that it was a very good chance my letter of self-insurance had been sent to Meyer to stow in a safe place. And so, as a percentage play . . .

It worked on me to the point that Meyer stared at me and said, "What the hell is wrong, Trav?"

My mouth wasn't going to work. Alarm is contagious. He trotted around and got behind the wheel, whipped us out into the traffic flow with a good imitation of teenage technique. At last I managed two words. "No hurry."

I saved the rest of it for my rackety motel unit. I tried to smile at Meyer. "Pure chicken. Sorry. I just don't know what the hell is . . ." Then I felt the sudden and humiliating sting of tears in my eyes and turned quickly to blink them away before Meyer could see them.

I stood with my back to him, staring out between the slats of the battered tin blinds at the side wall of a restaurant and a row of trash cans haloed with bluebottled buzzing. I spoke too fast and chuckled where there was no need, saying, "It's the old bit of the brave and noble hunter, gliding silently through the jungle, following the track of the big black panther and slowly beginning to realize that the panther is also a-hunting and maybe he's flattened out on top of that thick limb up ahead or behind that bush over there or in the shadow of that fallen tree, with just the tip of his thick glossy black tail moving and the shoulder muscles rippling and tightening under that black hide. I'm spooked because I kept telling myself the son of a bitch would be gone by now, but he isn't going until Friday, and—"

"Travis. Come on. Slow down."

Can't ever really fool ol' Meyer. I sat on the bed. We're all children. We invent the adult facade and don it and try to keep the buttons and the medals polished. We're all trying to give such a good imitation of being an adult that the real adults in the world won't catch on. Each of us takes up those shticks that compose the adult image we seek. I'd gone the route of lazy, ironic bravado, of amiable, unaffiliated insouciance. Tinhorn knights of a stumbling Rosinante from Rent-A-Steed, maybe with one little area of the heart so pinched, so parched. I never dared let anything really lasting happen to me. Or dared admit the flaw. Maybe in some crazy way Paul Dissat was a funhouse mirror image of me, a warped McGee with backspin, reverse English.

The adult you pretend to be convinces himself that the risk is worth the game, the game worth the risk. Tells himself the choice of life-style could get him killed—on the Daytona track, in the bullring, falling from the raw steel framework forty stories up, catching a rodeo hoof in the side of the head.

Adult pretenses are never a perfect fit for the child underneath, and when there is the presentiment of death, like a hard black light making panther eyes glow in the back of the cave, the cry is, "Mommy, mommy, mommy, it's so dark out there, so dark and so forever."

Cojones are such a cultural imperative, the man who feels suddenly deballed feels shame at reentering the childhood condition. Papa Hemingway will never take him fishing. George Patton will slap his face.

In all my approximately seventy-six inches of torn and mended flesh and hide, in all approximately fifteen-stone weight of meat, bone, and dismay, I sat on that damned bed and felt degraded. I was unmasked as a grotesque imitation of what I had believed myself to be.

Frowning, I tried to explain it in halting fashion to Meyer. "You talked about . . . the reflexes slowing, the warning system not working, the instincts inaccurate when . . . the only reason Harry Broll didn't kill me was because he lacked one more round in the clip. Then in Grenada I didn't even think of being careful . . . didn't sense his presence, got such a shot in the skullbone my head is still blurred. Meyer, people have been a few steps ahead of me other times. I've played pretty good catch-up. This time I have this feeling that there's no way. He's going to stay out in front, and if I get too close, he'll turn around and take care of the problem. Maybe I've gotten too close already, and I have ten more minutes or ten more hours."

"Travis."

"I know. I'm scared. It's like being very very cold. I can't move well, and I can't think at all."

"So I do the thinking?"

"I wish you would. Don't go back to your boat. I have a very ugly hunch about your boat."

"We have to talk to Dennis Waterbury in absolute privacy, and I have to make contact in such a way that he will trust us to the limited extent that rich and powerful people can trust anyone."

"Can you do it?"

"I don't know. I have to try to reach some people by phone. In Montreal and Toronto and Quebec."

"Start trying."

"If I can get through to someone he knows and trusts, who can tell him I am reputable, not a shakedown artist, then we are going to give him whatever lead time we can spare before I go to the law."

"With what?"

"With enough. Woodrow Willow's contact said Broll didn't buy the stock. So there's a missing three hudnred thousand and a missing Harry Broll. If they dig around the seawall at Blue Heron Lane, they'll find Mary's body. Kathy Marcus and the other bank people could pick Paul Dissat out of a lineup. Maybe it will sink the SeaGate public issue without a trace. Even if Dissat never took a penny from the Waterbury enterprises, a breath of scandal can make the accounting firm and the underwriters back off."

"So why don't we go to the law? Why do we screw around with Waterbury if we've got all this?"

"Think about it, Travis. Think about it."

I instinctively fingered the place on the back of my skull where I had been so soundly thumped. Meyer was right. SeaGate was a very large thing, and Dissat was an operating officer in the SeaGate power structure. The lower echelons of the law would never go cantering into battle on the say-so of an apparently unemployed beach bum and a semiretired and eccentric economist. It was a two-county operation with both state and federal implications. Lower echelons would take the eccentric pair into skeptical custody and sweat them both.

Suppose you go to the top level, such as approaching the United States attorney in the area and suggesting he refer the problem to the FBI for investigation because of possible violations of the criminal code insofar as banking regulations are concerned. Then the approach would be made so tentatively —due to the SeaGate clout and the dubious source of the tip—that Dissat would be alerted, and he would disappear into his large countryside or ours.

First, you sell Dennis Waterbury on the idea that his boy, Paul Dissat, has been a very very bad boy lately and any publicity given his activities can founder the SeaGate plans. You convince him and give him some facts he can quietly check. You speak to him in absolute privacy and secrecy. Then, when *he* picks up the phone and relays his unhappy suspicions to the highest level, Dissat will be pounced upon first and investigated later, giving Waterbury additional time to plug up the holes and protect the upcoming public issue from scandal.

I said, "Okay. Do you think I'll ever be able to think things out for myself any more? Or will you have to be on permanent standby?"

"I think they start you on baskets and work up to needlepoint."

"I am supposed to laugh. All right, Meyer. Ha ha ha. Make your phone calls. What if the bastard won't listen even if we can get him alone?"

"Men who are rich have times when they don't listen. Men who are quite bright have times when they don't listen. Men who are both bright and rich *always* listen. That is how they got the money, and that is how they keep it."

"Then do we go to Canada, or does he come here?"

"He's here now. I found that out when I was learning all I could about Paul Dissat. Waterbury is in a guest cottage on a Palm Beach estate. The owners are in Maine now, but they left enough staff to take care of Waterbury. Pool, tennis courts, security system, private beach."

He started making calls. He had to push the thermostat high enough to kill the compressor before he could hear. I lay a-doze, hearing his voice come from metallic distances, sounding like the voices of grown-ups when I had been a child half asleep in a moving car or train.

22

HE FOUND an old friend at last, a Professor Danielson in Toronto, who knew Waterbury well and was willing to try to set it up. Meyer gave Danielson the motel number and unit number and asked to have Waterbury phone him as soon as convenient. If Danielson found that Waterbury was unable or unwilling to phone Meyer for a secret meeting, Danielson would phone back.

Nothing to do but wait and try to digest a roast beef sandwich that lay in my stomach like a dead armadillo. The motel television was on the cable. We turned the sound off and watched the news on the electronic printer, going by at a pace for a retarded fifth grader, white-on-black printing with so many typos the spelling was more like third grade than fifth.

The woes of the world inched up the screen. Droughts and murders. Inflation and balance of payments. Drugs and demonstrations. Body counts and new juntas.

The trouble with the news is that everybody knows everything too fast and too often and too many times. News has always been bad. The tiger that lives in the forest just ate your wife and kids, Joe. There are no fat grubworms under the rotten logs this year, Al. Those sickies in the village on the other side of the mountain are training hairy mammoths to stomp us flat, Pete. They nailed up two thieves and one crackpot, Mary. So devote wire-service people and network people and syndication people to gathering up all the bad news they can possibly dredge and comb and scrape out of a news-tired world and have them spray it back at everybody in constant streams of electrons, and two things happen. First, we all stop listening, so they have to make it ever more horrendous to capture our attention. Second, we all become even more convinced that everything has gone rotten and there is no hope at all, no hope at all. In a world of no hope the motto is *semper fidelis,* which means in translation, "Every week is screw-your-buddy week and his wife too, if he's out of town."

The phone rang, and Meyer sprang up and cut off the compressor and took the call. He made a circle of thumb and finger to tell me we had gotten through the corporate curtain. He listened for several minutes, nodded, and said, "Yes, thank you, we'll be there." Hung up.

"A Miss Caroline Stoddard, Mr. Waterbury's private secretary. We're to meet with him out at the site of SeaGate. We go through the main entrance and follow little orange arrows on sticks that will lead us to the storage and warehouse area. There are two small contracts going on now out there. Earth moving and paving. They stop work at four, and the crews leave. The area is patrolled at night, and the guard shift starts at eight at this time of year. Mr. Waterbury will meet with us at an office out there in the end of one of the warehouses behind the hurricane fencing near the vehicle park and the asphalt plant. We can find the place by looking for his car. If we meet him out there at five, we should have plenty of time for uninterrupted talk."

*   *   *

We got to the area a little early, so we drove down A-1-A for a little way, and when we found a gap in the sour commercial honky-tonk, Meyer pulled over. Down the beach there was a cluster of fat-tire beach buggies, some people swimming. Meyer and I were walking and talking over our plans when a chunky trail bike came growling up behind us, passed us, and cut in and stopped, and a fellow with enough black beard to stuff a small pillow glowered at us and gunned the bike engine. He looked very fit and unfriendly.

"You've got a problem?" I asked.

"You are the guys with the problems. How come there are so many of you characters so cramped up you got to come creeping around to stare at naked people?"

"Where, where, where!" Meyer said, smiling. "If it's required, I'll stare. But as a rule, it's dull. If you have some graceful young girls cavorting, that is an aesthetic pleasure for a certain amount of time. Doesn't sand get into the working parts of that thing?"

Meyer is disarming. Maybe a completely frantic flip, stoned blind, could run a knife into him. Otherwise, the belligerent simmer down quickly.

"It's sealed so it doesn't happen too bad. But you can mess it up if you try. I thought you were more guys with binoculars, like the last pair. See, if you walk down this way far enough, then you can see around the end of the buggy and see the girls."

Meyer said, "Excuse me, but I was of the impression that the current belief is that the flaunting of the natural body cures the woes of society by blowing the minds of the repressed."

"A lot of people think that way. But we're opposed to the brazen display of the body and public sexuality. We're here on a pilgrimage mission for the church of Christ in the Highest. And we have permission to camp on this part of the beach while we're bringing the word of God to the young people in this area."

"Wouldn't it be a lot easier to cover those girls up?" I asked him.

"Four of our sisters have got the crabs, sir, and they are using the salt water and the sunshine to cure them. The drugstore stuff didn't work at all, hardly."

Meyer said, "I have worked and studied in primitive countries, and I have caught about every kind of body louse a bountiful nature provides. And I have yet to contract a case that did not respond immediately to plain old vinegar. Have your girls soak their heads, armpits, and their private parts in vinegar. It kills the crabs and kills the eggs, and the itching stops almost immediately."

"You wouldn't kid me?" the beard asked.

"It is the most useful and generally unknown information in the modern world."

"They've been going up the walls. Hey, thanks. And God bless you guys."

He roared away. I told Meyer he was fantastic. Meyer said that my continual adulation made him uncomfortable, and it was time to see The Man.

*   *   *

We turned around, and where A-1-A curved west, away from the Atlantic beach, Meyer drove straight, down a road that was all crushed shell, ruts, and potholes and marked private. Soon we came to the entrance pillars, a huge billboard telling of the fantastic city of the future that would rise upon the eleven square miles of sandy waste, where no child need cross a highway to get to school, where everything would be recycled (presumably vitiating the need for cemetery zoning), where clean industry would employ clean, smiling people, where nothing would rust, rot, or decay, where age would not wither nor custom stale the fixed, maniacal smiles on the palstic faces of the future multitude who here would dwell.

Once past the entrance pillars we were on a black velvet vehicle strip (trucks stay to right, off blacktop) which restored to the rental Ford the youth and ease it had lost during a few months, a few thousand miles of being warped, rocked, and crowded by the dozens of temporary owners.

We followed the small, plastic orange arrows and saw some yellow and green and blue arrows on yard-tall sticks marching in other directions, forming a routing code for workmen, planners, delivery people. A small sign in front of a wilderness of dwarf palmetto said starkly: SHOPPING PLAZA E 400,000 SQ. FT. ENCL. Yes, indeed. A multilevel, automated, air-controlled, musicated selling machine, where—to the violins of Mantovani and the chaingang shuffle of the housewife sandals—only those processed foods would be offered which the computer approved of as being salable in billion-unit production runs.

We turned away from the sea and against the glare of the high western sun saw the construction headquarters, the belly and stack and hoppers of a portable asphalt plant, saw the trucks and spreaders, piles of aggregate, loader, and loading ramp. That area outside the warehouse and office compound enclosed by hurricane fencing was deserted, as if a flock of Seabees had slapped blacktop on it and been airlifted out. There was a big vehicle gate in the hurricane fencing, and it stood wide open. In the fenced area were some above-ground fuel tanks and pumps for the vehicles, outdoor storage of some unidentifiable crated items, a generator building, and six small prefab steel warehouses backed up against a truck loading dock. A dark green Lincoln Continental limousine was parked by the next to the last warehouse.

Meyer parked nearby, and we got out. Meyer said in a low voice, "He'll be tempted to think it's some kind of a shakedown. Give us money, and we'll keep quiet about Dissat and let the public issue go through. But Danielson says Waterbury is honest by choice, not as a matter of necessity or operating policy."

There were three crude steps up to the cross-braced plywood door. It stood a few inches ajar, the hasp folded back, a thick padlock opened, hanging from the U-bolt in the door frame.

I gave the door a couple of thumps with the underside of my fist. It made a nice booming sound in the metal structure.

"Hello?" said a pleasantly feminine contralto voice, elusively familiar. "Are you the gentlemen who phoned? Come in, please."

It was dim inside. There were no windows at the end where we entered, only at the far end. We were on an elevated area with a floor made of decking with steps leading down to the slab floor of the warehouse proper. The office was at the far end. The air was very thick and still and hot in the warehouse portion, but I could hear the whine of air conditioning in the enclosed office at the far end.

"I'm Caroline Stoddard," she said. "So nice to see you again, Mr. McGee."

I located her off to the left, standing down on the lower level. At first I thought she was one very big secretary in some kind of slacks outfit, and I blinked again, and my eyes adjusted, and it was Paul Dissat. That odd feeling of having heard the voice before was because of the slight residual accent.

"Be very nice," he said in his normal voice, "and be *very* careful. This is a new automatic nailer. They must use it to knock the forms together for footings and pilings and so on. That hose goes over there to that pressure tank, and the compressor is automatic, and the generator is on.

It seemed heavy, the way he held it. He turned it to the side and triggered it. It made a hard, explosive, *phut*ting sound, and the nails zinged off the concrete and whanged the metal wall twenty feet away. He turned it toward us again.

"I'm a bad shot," he said. "But these things spray. At more than six inches they begin to turn. They'd make a ghastly hamburger of your legs, I think. I don't know why I've always been a poor shot. I'm well coordinated otherwise. Harry was a fantastic marksman. I guess it must be a natural gift."

"Fantastic marksman?" I asked numbly.

"Didn't you know? You could throw three cans in the air, and with that silly little popgun of his he could hit each one of them twice before they hit the ground without even seeming to aim, just pointing at them by some kind of instinct."

"When he came to see me—"

"He was coming apart. I was having trouble keeping him quiet. He had to make some mock show of being terribly concerned about Mary so that later people could testify he was almost out of his mind with worry. He said you moved so quickly and startled him so bad, he nearly hit you in the foot."

"Where is Mr. Waterbury?" Meyer asked in a tired and wistful tone.

"Playing tennis, I should imagine. This is his time of day for it. Cool of the evening. When word came this morning of the request for information from Mr. Willow, I called him back and after a little hesitation he told me one McGee and one Meyer had initiated the request. Don't keep edging sideways, McGee! It was really a shock. I thought you dead. From drowning or brain damage. You pranced like a sick, ugly stork, and you went floating out at an incredible speed. You are very lucky and very hard to kill."

"Where is Mr. Waterbury?" Meyer asked.

"You are a bore," Dissat said. "I went to his eminence and told him I had confidential information that two sharpshooters were going to try to get a private audience with him and try to frighten him into parting with money. I gave him the names. He told me to handle the problem. I handle a lot of problems for the man. When the information came in from Toronto, he had me take the call. Don't you think limousines allay all suspicions? They're so symbolic. Sit on the floor slowly and carefully, Travis. That's very good. Now, Meyer, make a wide circle around behind him and come down the steps. Fine. Walk over to that coil of wire on the floor next to the pliers and stretch out on your face with your head toward me. *Very* good. Now, Travis, you can come down and go around Meyer and kneel on the other side of him. Hold it. Now I want you to wire your friend's wrists together and then his ankles. The better job you do, the better all three of us will get along."

It was a heavy-gauge iron wire, quite soft and malleable. It was such dim light I felt I could do a fairly sloppy job. Dissat moved back to the wall, and an overhead bank of daylight fluorescent tubes winked on.

"You're doing a lot more talking, Paul," I said. "All keyed up, aren't you? All nerves?"

"Pull that strand tight. There. That's fine. Let's say I'm more talkative because you're more receptive. Would you like to know how the wave action affected Lisa's body?"

"I bet it was fascinating."

"It was. I sat and watched the whole thing. After the waves were breaking way in beyond where she was, the outgoing wash started to scoop the sand out from around her until she was almost uncovered. Finally she toppled over onto her left side. Then the waves began digging the sand out from under her, settling her lower and lower and flowing and forming around her as it began covering her. The very last thing I saw of her was her right shoulder, and it looked like a little, shiny brown bowl upside down on the smooth sand. And then that disappeared, too. I imagine that on all beaches the sea is a scavenger, burying the sad, dead things and the ugly litter every time the tide comes and goes. Now one more turn *under* the other wrist and then twist it and cut it. Good!''

I wished the pliers were heavier. I rehearsed the motions in my mind. Whip the arm up and hurl the pliers at his face, falling forward at the same time to give the throw more velocity and also shield Meyer from the expected hail of nails. I could scramble forward and take the nails in the back and get to his ankles and yank his feet out from under him, provided no nail went head-deep into the spine. And provided he didn't swing the muzzle down fast enough to drive a close pattern into my skull.

I hesitated, thinking how badly I had missed Harry with the ashtray, and while I hesitated, Dissat moved, making plier-throwing a much worse risk.

He shifted the heavy nailer, swinging the pneumatic hose out of the way, much as a singer manipulates the mike cable. In the bright fluorescence he looked almost theatrically handsome. He was like a color still shot for those strange ads Canadian Club used to use. ("I never knew how challenging it would be to hold two men captive with an automatic nailing device until I tried it.")

"Talkative?" he said. "Perhaps. Relief, I suppose. I've made a decision and simplified the future. Harry's money and mine make enough, you know. I've sent it to safe places. You two are the last loose ends. I'm taking sick leave. Actually, I'm retiring. Maintaining two identities compounds the risk factor. I told you in Grenada what I learned about myself from Mary Broll and poor Lisa. Now I shall have a chance to devote all my time to exploring it further. Very thoroughly. Very carefully. Mostly it's a matter of selecting people who might logically disappear of their own accord. I suppose the challenge excites me. So I talk a great deal, don't I? There's nothing I can reveal you can't guess, so it's not a help to you, is it? We shall explore the matter of the letter you sent from Grenada. As a matter of form. It isn't really important whether I learn about it or not, so I don't have to be awfully careful, do I? To keep everything tidy, I might leave with a traveling companion. A certain Mrs. Booker. Betsy. Would you know about her? Never mind. His ankles are finished? Walk backward on your knees. Further. Further. Right there. Sit down there, please, and wire your own ankles together, leaving a length of wire between them, the same length as the nylon cord that day on the little beach.''

One uses any small frail idea. From handling the thick soft wire I guessed that if one bent it back and forth enough times, it would snap. So I took a couple of turns around my ankles, tight enough to keep the wire from turning on my ankle. I made the binding turns, squeezed the wire knots with the pliers jaws, nipped away what was left. With luck, management, and timing the wire might part at the squeezed place after enough steps.

He moved to stand over Meyer. He bent over and held the business end of the nailer almost touching the base of Meyer's spine. "I have this on single fire, McGee. Or single nail. If you can wire your own wrists nicely, I'll be so pleased with you, I'll give up the pleasure of finding out just how he'd react to one nail right here. Use ingenuity, McGee. Do a nice job. After Grenada, I take no chances with you.''

I did a nice job. I was even able to nip off the extra wire by wedging the pliers between my forearm and the flooring. By holding my wrists together, exerting pressure, I could make it look as if there was no slack at all. Cheap little tricks never do any good at all, except to give the trickster false hope when he needs it.

Dissat came lithely over, bent, inspected, and kicked the pliers away with the edge of his foot. He grunted with satisfaction and walked over and put the nailer down beside the pressure tank, then swung and flexed his arms. "It got much too heavy," he said. He picked up a short, thick piece of metal. I thought it was steel pipe with a dull, gleaming finish, but as he walked toward Meyer, flipping it and catching it, I guessed from the way he handled it that it had to be very light metal, probably aluminum bar stock. It spun and smacked neatly into the palm of his hand each time.

"I don't even know what we use this for," he said. "There's a lot of it in the last warehouse. I've been taking an inventory personally, to check on pilferage of materials, small tools, and so on. That's where I kept Harry, in that warehouse. This piece just happens to have perfect weight and balance. I picked it up by accident the first time. After that, every time I picked it up, old Harry would start rolling his eyes like a horse in the bullring."

He bent suddenly and took a quick swing, very wristy, and hit Meyer on the back of the right leg, just above the knee. It made an impact sound halfway between smack and thud. Meyer bucked his heavy frame completely off the floor and roared.

"See?" said Paul, "Heavier stock would crush bone and tissue, and lighter stuff would merely sting. I experimented with Harry and went a little too far. I whacked him across his big belly once too often and possibly ruptured something in there. God knows what. For a time neither of us thought he could walk into the bank for the money."

"I'll trade Meyer for all you want to know about the letter."

He looked at me owlishly. "*All* of Meyer? Alive and free? That's naive, you know. Meyer is dead, and you are dead. There's no choice now. I *could* trade you, say, the last fifteen minutes of Meyer's life for information about the letter. He would approve a deal like that when the time comes. But what would be the point? I'm not that interested in your letter, really. I learned a little bit from Mary and more from Lisa and a little more from Harry. Now I can check what I learned and learn a little more. Why should I deprive myself?"

"Why indeed?" Meyer said in a husky boice.

"I like you both," Paul said. "I really do. That's part of it, of course. Remember, Travis, how Lisa became . . . just a thing, an object? It moved and made sounds, but Lisa was gone. I made the same mistake with Harry, but not until the very end. The problem is to keep the person's actual identity and awareness functioning right to the end. Now we have to get Meyer out of here. Get up and go bring that hand truck, Travis, please."

I got the truck, and at Paul's request I bent and clumsily wedged and tugged and lifted my old friend onto the bed of the truck. Meyer ended up on his right side. He squinted up at me and said, "I have this terrible pun I can't seem to get out of my head, like one of those songs you can't get rid of. Let's hope his craft is ebbing."

"How is your leg?" I asked him.

"Relatively shapely, I think, but considered too hairy by some."

"Are you trying to be amusing?" Paul asked.

Meyer said in his public-speaking voice, "We often notice in clinical studies that sado-sociopathic faggots have a very limited sense of humor."

Dissat moved to the side of the truck, took aim, and clubbed Meyer right
on the point of the shoulder and said, "Make more jokes, please."

Meyer, having exhaled explosively through clenched teeth, said, "I hope I
didn't give you the wrong impression, Dissat."

"Are you frightened, Meyer?" Paul asked politely.

"I have a lump of ice in my belly you wouldn't believe." Meyer said.

Instructed by Paul, I rolled the hand truck along the warehouse flooring,
turned it, and backed laboriously up a ramp, pulling it up. He unlatched a big
metal door with overhead wheels and rolled it aside. The white sunlight had
turned yellowish outside as the world moved toward evening, but it was still
bright enough to sting the eyes. I wheeled the truck along the loading dock
and down a steeper ramp where it almost got away from me.

I pushed the truck along the concrete roadway, the steel wheels grating
and clinking. I became aware that with each stride I could feel less resistance
to bending in the wire joining my ankles, and I was afraid it would snap
before I wanted it to. I took shorter steps and changed my stride, feet wider
apart to put less strain on the wire. We went through the big gates in the
fence and over toward the asphalt plant. Dissat told me to stop. He put a foot
against Meyer's back and rolled him off the hand truck. We were in a truck
loading area with a big overhead hopper. The concrete was scabbed thick,
black, and uneven with dried spills of asphalt tar. Paul motioned me away
from the hand truck and pushed it back out of the way. Above us were the
hopper and a square bulky tank that stood high on girder legs.

"Do you see that great big wad of wasted asphalt over there, Travis?
Meyer is faced the wrong way to see it. Vandalism is always a problem. Last
Thursday night some hippies apparently came over from the beach, and for
no reason at all they dropped at least two tons out of the holding tank. That's
the big square tank overhead. It's insulated. Just before the shift ends, they
run what's left in the plant into the holding tank. It's hot enough to stay liquid
all night in this climate, and in the morning while the plant is being fired up
and loaded, the trucks draw from the holding tank. But last Friday morning
they couldn't drive the trucks under the hopper until they got a small bull-
dozer over here to blade that solidified hunk of warm asphalt away from
where I'm standing. It's all cooled now, of course. And our old friend Harry
Broll is curled right in the middle of that black wad, snug as nutmeat in the
shell."

I remembered being taken on a hunt when I was a child and how my uncle
had packed partridge in clay, and put the crude balls into the hot coals until
they baked hard. When he had cracked them open, the feather and skin had
stuck to the clay, leaving the steaming meat. Acid came up into my throat
and stayed, then went slowly back down.

I swallowed and said, "And the patrol checks here tonight and finds more
vandalism?"

"You belabor the obvious, McGee. They'll have to blade your hydrocarbon tomb, big enough for two, over next to Harry's. It's hotter now, of
course, in the holding tank than it will be by morning." He moved over to

the side. "This is the lever the foreman uses. It's a manual system. If I move it to the side . . ."

He swung the lever over and pulled it back at once. A black glob about the size of your average Thanksgiving turkey came down the chute, banged the hanging baffle plate open, and fell—*swopp*—onto the stained concrete, making an ugly black pancake about four feet across, very thin at the perimeter, humped thick in the middle. A couple of dangling black strings fell into the pancake from overhead. A tendril of blue smoke arose from the pancake. Meyer had made a very weary sound. Pain, anger, resignation. The pancake had formed too close to him, splattering a hot black thread across his chin, cheek, and ear. In the silence I heard the faraway flute call of a meadowlark and then the thunder rumble of a jet. I smelled that sweet, thick, childhood scent of hot tar.

When Meyer spoke, his voice was so controlled it revealed how close he was to breaking. "I can certify. It comes out hot."

"Hardly any aggregate in it," Paul said. "It cools and hardens quickly. Travis, please turn Meyer around and put his feet in the middle of that circular spill, will you?"

I do not know what started the changes that were going on inside me. They had started before the meadowlark, but they seemed related somehow to the meadowlark. You used to be able to drive through Texas, and there would be meadowlarks so thick along the way, perched singing on so many fence posts, that at times you could drive through the constant sound of them like sweet and molten silver. Now the land has been silenced. The larks eat bugs, feed bugs to nestlings. The bugs are gone, and the meadowlarks are gone, and the world is strange, becoming more strange, a world spawning Paul Dissat instead of larks.

So somehow there is less risk, because losing such a world means losing less. I knew my head was still bad. It was like a car engine that badly needs tuning. Tromp the gas and it chokes, falters, and dies. It has to be babied up to speed. I had a remote curiosity about how my head would work with enough stress going on. Curiosity was changing to an odd prickling pleasure that seemed to grow high and hot, building and bulging itself up out of the belly into the shoulders and neck and chest.

I knew that feeling. I had almost forgotten it. It had happened before, but only when I had turned the last card and knew the hand was lost, the game was lost, the lights were fading. I had been working my wrists steadily within the small slack I had given myself, bending a tiny piece of connecting wire back and forth, and the bending was suddenly easier as the wire began to part.

The hard, anticipatory joy comes not from thinking there is any real chance but from knowing you can use it all without really giving that final damn about winning or losing. By happenstance, he'd made a bad choice of wire. And maybe the twisted child was so eager to squash his mice, he might give one of them a chance to bite him.

The wrist wire broke as I put my hands on Meyer to move him. "Can you roll?" I asked in a voice too low for Paul to hear. Meyer nodded. "Roll on signal to your left, fast and far."

"What are you saying!" Paul Dissat demanded. "Don't you *dare* say things I can't hear!"

"Careful, darling," I told him. "You're going into a towering snit. Let's not have any girlish tantrums."

He quieted immediately. He picked up his chunk of aluminum. "That won't do you any good, and it isn't very bright of you to even try it. You disappoint me when you misjudge me. You take some of the pleasure out of being with you again." I looked beyond him and then looked back at him very quickly. I couldn't be obvious about it.

The instant he turned I broke the ankle wire with the first swinging stride. He heard me and spun back, but by the time he raised the aluminum club I was inside the arc of it. I yelled to Meyer to roll clear.

My head went partly bad. I knew I had turned him back into a kind of corner where the girder legs of the holding tank were cross-braced. I was in a gray murk, expending huge efforts. It was a stage. Somebody was working the strings of the big doll, making it bounce and flap. At times its doll chin bounced on my shoulder. It flailed and flapped its sawdust arms. I stood flat-footed, knees slightly bent, swaying from left to right and back with the cadence of effort, getting calves, thighs, rump, back, and shoulder into each hook, trying to power the fist through the sawdust and into the gristle and membrane beyond.

Pretty doll with the graceful, powerful, hairless legs, with the long lashes, red mouth, and hero profile. Sawdust creaked out of its throat, and Raggedy Andy shoe-button eyes swung loose on the slackening threads.

Soon a blow would burst it, and it would die as only a doll can die, in torn fabric and disrepair. I had never killed a doll-thing with my hands before.

Somebody was shouting my name. There was urgency in the voice. I slowed and stopped, and the gray lifted the way a steamed windshield clears when the defroster is turned on. I backed away and saw Paul Dissat slumped against a cross brace, one arm hooked over it. There was not a mark on his face.

I backed away. I imagine that what happened next happened because he did not realize what punishment to the body will do to the legs. He was conscious. I imagine that from belly to heart he felt as if he had been twisted in half.

The shapely, powerful legs with their long muscle structure had carried him through the slalom gates down the long tricky slopes. They had kept their spring and bounce through the long sets of tennis. So perhaps he believed that all he had to do was force himself up onto those legs and run away on them.

He tried.

When his weight came onto them, they went slack and rubbery. He fought for balance. He was like a drunk in a comedy routine. He flailed with both arms and his left arm hit the load lever, and he staggered helplessly toward the thick, gouting torrent of asphalt from the overhead hopper. He tried to claw and fight back away from it, screaming as I once heard a horse scream, yet with an upward sliding note that went out of audible range, like a dog whistle. But it entrapped, ensnared those superb and nearly useless legs and brought him down in sticky agony. I ran to grab him, yank him out of that black, smoking jelly, but got a steaming smear of it across the back of my hand and forearm. I turned then and did what I should have done in the first place, went for the lever and swung it back to the closed position. The last sight I had before I turned was of Dissat buried halfway up his rib cage, hands braced against the concrete slab, elbows locked, head up, eyes half out of the sockets, mouth agape, cords standing out in his throat, as the black stuff piled higher behind him, higher than his head.

I yanked the lever back and spun, and he was gone. A part of the blackness seemed to bulge slightly and sag back. The last strings of it solidified and fell. It was heaped as high as my waist and as big as a grand piano.

I remembered Meyer and looked over and saw him. He had wiggled into a sitting position, his back against a girder. I took a staggering step and caught myself.

"Pliers," Meyer said. "Hang on, Travis. For God's sake, hang on."

Pliers. I knew there wasn't time for pliers. The gray was coming in from every side, misting the windshield as before. I found my way toward him, fell, then crawled and reached his wrists. I bent the wire, turning it, freeing it. I saw a sharp end bite into the ball of my thumb, saw blood run, felt nothing. Just one more turn and then he could . . .

23

I WAS not entirely asleep and not yet awake, and I could not remember ever having been so completely, perfectly, deliciously relaxed. The girl voices brought me further across the line into being awake.

Rupe said how very sweet their voices were, how touching, how heartbreaking, aboard the *Belle*. Their harmony was simple, their voices true and small.

"What a friend we have in Jeeeeee-zusss. All our sins and griefs to baaaaaaaare."

I wondered why the extraordinary crew of the *Hell's Belle* should select a number like that. Yet there was the tidy warmth of Teddie's thigh under the nape of my neck, a sweet, firm fit. Fabric over the thigh. I opened my eyes, and it was night. Light came slanting and touched the girl faces, touching their long, hanging hair. I realized I was on a blanket, and there was the unmistakable feel and consistency of dry sand under the blanket. Teddie's face was in shadow. I lifted a lazy, contented arm and put my hand over the young breast under thin fabric so close above my face. It had a sweet, rubbery firmness.

She took my wrist and pushed my hand down and said, "No, brother." They had stopped singing the words of the song. They were humming the melody. "He has awakened," the girl said. It was not Teddie's voice. They stopped singing.

A man's voice said, "How do you feel, brother?"

I raised my head. There were five or six of them in a glow of firelight. Bearded biblical men wrapped in coarse cloth. I had been hurled out of my historical time and place.

I sat up too quickly. I felt faint and bent forward to lower my head down between my knees.

A hand touched my shoulder. Meyer said, "I was trying to get you to a doctor and ran off into the sand. This one here is their healer, and he—"

"I was a third-year medical student when I heard the call. I'm the healer for the tribe on this pilgrimage mission."

I straightened and looked into a young bearded face. He nodded and took my pulse and nodded again. "We got that tar off your arm and hand with a solvent brother, and treated your burn and dressed it."

My arm was wrapped with gauze. There was a bandage on my thumb. I turned my head and saw the beach buggies and several campers. A baby was crying in one of the campers.

I lay back very carefully. The thigh was there, cozy as before. The face leaned over me and looked down. "I will comfort you, brother, but no more grabbing me, huh?"

"No more, sister. I thought I was somewhere else with someone else. A . . . different group of girls."

"On a pilgrimage, too?"

"In a certain sense of the word, yes."

"There is only one sense, brother, when you give your heart and your soul and your worldly goods and all the days of your years to the service of almighty God."

"Did your . . . healer put vinegar on my burns?"

She giggled. "That's me you smell, brother. Blessed providence sent you and your friend to us this afternoon before I flipped right out of my tree. If it isn't sacrilege, my sisters and I are enjoying a peace that passeth understanding ever since."

I tried sitting up again, and there was no dizziness. One of the sisters brought me a cup of hot clam broth. She wore a garment like an aba, made out of some kind of homespun. She too smelled of vinegar. There was a crude cross around her neck with green stones worked into it. The automatic slide projector in my head showed me a slide entitled The Last Known Sight of Paul Dissat in This World. A small gold cross hung free about his straining throat.

After I drank the broth, I tried standing, and it worked reasonably well. They were not paying any special attention to me or to Meyer. We were welcome to be with them. Feel free to ignore and be ignored. Listen to the sweet singing, taste the broth, and praise the Lord.

I found the vinegar girl and gave her back her cup with thanks. Meyer and I moved away from the fire and from the lights in the campers.

"I panicked," Meyer said. "I got the rest of the wire off me and threw you in the damned car and drove like a maniac."

"Where is the car?"

"Up there on the shoulder. It was in deep. They pulled it out with a beach buggy."

"What about that limousine?"

"Good question. Joshua and I went back in there on his trail bike. The keys to it were on the desk in the office. We put the trail bike into the trunk. I locked everything in sight, and we were out of there by seven thirty. I took the long way around, and we left it at the West Palm airport, keys in the ashtray. Call it a Dissat solution. By the way, I made a contribution to the pilgrimage mission collection plate in both our names.''

"That's nice."

"One of the wrapped stacks of hundreds from the Southern National. Initialed. Unbroken. There were four stacks in a brown paper bag on the desk in the warehouse office."

"What did Joshua say?''

"Thanks.''

"No questions about the kind of help you asked of him?''

"Just one. He said that before he took the name of Joshua, he had clouted cars to feed his habit. He said all he wanted to know was whether, if we had committed a sin, we repented of it. I said that even though I didn't think of it as a sin, I was going to pray for forgiveness. That's when he nodded and said thanks and riffled the stack with his thumb and shoved it into the saddlebag on the trail bike. I walked out of the airport parking lot, and he drove the bike out and waited for me down the road from the airport. Long way around coming back here, too. I had the idea you'd be dead when I got here.''

"Meyer?''

"Yes?''

"Get me home. Get me back to the *Flush*. Please.''

"Let's say good night to the tribe.''

* * *

I did a lot of sleeping. I was getting to be very good at it. I could get up at noon, shower, work up a big breakfast, and be ready for my nap at three. The gray fog rolled way back into the farthest corners of my mind. People left me alone. Meyer made certain of that. He passed the word. McGee has pulled the hole in after him. And he bites.

Meyer would come over during that part of each day when I was likely to be up and about.

We'd walk over and swim. We would come back and play chess. I did not want to be among people. Not yet. So he would cook, or I would cook, or he would go out and bring something back.

The longer we delayed the decision, the easier it was to make. The random parts fell together in a pattern we could find no reason to contradict. Harry Broll had grabbed his three-hundred-thousand loan in cash and fled with Lisa, the girl friend he had promised to give up. Except for some irate creditors, nobody was looking for him diligently. Harry's wife had been reported missing in the Windward Islands, presumed drowned while swimming alone. Paul Dissat was missing too, possibly by drowning, but in his case it would more likely be suicide, emotional depression, and anxiety over some kind of disease of the blood. He had requested sick leave.

Jillian had been astoundingly sweet and helpful and had even lived up to her promise to ask no questions. She had flown down to Grenada and stayed a few days and with the knowing assistance of an attorney friend had obtained my packet from the hotel safe and my other possessions from their storage room.

The favor was, of course, Jilly's concession to apology, to regret. When she and her new friend got back from Grenada, she came over with him to give me back my belongings. They had a drink with us, and they did not stay long. Meyer arrived before they left.

"I keep forgetting his name." Meyer said later.

"Foster Cramond. Still a close personal friend of both his ex-wives."

"Rich ex-wives."

"Of course."

"Likable," Meyer said judiciously. "Good manners. No harm in him. Good at games, what? Court tennis, polo, sailing. Splendid reflexes. Did you notice that fast draw with that solid gold lighter? Twelfth of a second. Interesting phenomenon when they looked at each other."

"What? Oh, you mean the visible steam that came out of her ears? And the way he went from a sixteen collar to an eighteen? Yes. I noticed."

"Travis, what was your reaction when you met her new friend?"

"Relief at not running into some big fuss about breaking my word to visit her for a week. And . . . some indignation, I guess. In all honesty, some indignation."

"And you wished you could change your mind again?"

I let his question hang in the air for a long time, for three moves, one involving tightening my defense against his queen's bishop. I found a response that created a new problem for him. While he was studying it, I leaned back.

"About changing my mind. No. My instincts hadn't turned bad when Harry came here. He had no intention of shooting me. So let's suppose I'm slower by half a step or a full step. Maybe I'm old enough and wise enough to move into positions where I don't need the speed. The only thing I know is that I am going to run out of luck in the future, just as I have in the past. And when I run out, I am going to have to make myself some luck. I know that what counts is the feeling I get when I make my own luck. The way I feel then is totally alive. In every dimension. In every possible way. It wouldn't have to be Jillian. I could lie back, watch the traffic, select a rich lady, and retire myself to stud. But that would be half-life. I have an addiction. I'm hooked on the smell, taste, and feel of the nearness of death and on the way I feel when I make my move to keep it from happening. If I *knew* I could keep it from happening, there'd be no taste to it at all."

Meyer gave that a lot of thought, and then he gave the game a lot of thought. Finally he said, "When in doubt, castle." He moved his king into the short corner, the rook standing guard. "Travis, I am very very glad that you were able to make us some luck. I am glad to be here. But . . ."

"But?"

"Something else is wrong with you."

"I dream some rotten things. I've got my memory almost all straightened out. Picked up nearly all the cards off the floor and put them back in the right order. But I have real rotten dreams. Last night I was buying a shirt. The girl said it was made in the islands, and they weren't sized correctly and I should try it on. When I put it on and came out, I realized that it was exactly the same print that Lisa had worn that first night I knew her. A dashiki. As I started to tell the girl that I didn't want it, she came up to me quickly, and she reached out, and she snapped something onto the front of the shirt. It made a clack. It was a big, round, white thing, too heavy for the front of a shirt. I turned it around, and I saw that the sound had been the lower jaw of a skull being closed with the fabric caught between the teeth. It was a very white, polished, delicate skull, and at first it looked feral, some predator's skull. Then I knew it was Lisa's skull. I tried to get the girl to take it off, but she said it went with that particular shirt. No other shirt. Just that one. And I woke up.''

"Good Christ," Meyer whispered softly.

"But usually I don't dream at all.''

"Be thankful, Travis. Is something else wrong?''

"Yes.''

"Do you have words for it yet?''

"I think it's getting to the point where there will be words for it. When there are words, I'll try them on you.''

"Are you going to check me with that knight? Go ahead. See what happens if you do.''

                    *   *   *

On the following Sunday afternoon, a Sunday late in May, Meyer and I were over on the beach. When the wind died, it got uncomfortably hot in the sun, so we moved to a bench in the shade. I watched two lovely ladies approaching along the beach, consciously keeping shoulders back and tummies in as they strode along, laughing and talking. Elegant lassies. Total strangers. They were walking across the edge of my life and right back out of it, and I would never know them or touch them, nor two million nor ten million of their graceful sisters.

"Maybe I can put that problem into words now. But it's just a try. Maybe you can be patient.''

"How often do you see me impatient?''

"This starts with a word Rupe Darby used down in Grenada. A phrase, not a word. It designates a condition. Womaned out. He meant it in the physical sense. Total sexual depletion to the point where you think you never want to see another woman. I think I'm womaned out in a different way. All my love life is pre-Grenada, and that was a lifetime ago.''

"So. Womaned out but not in a physical sense.''

"God, no. Those two who just went by created the intended reaction. And I keep remembering how neat and warm the thigh of the little Jesus singer felt under the nape of my neck. Physical capacity is just dandy. No, Meyer. I feel foundered and wind broke in some other dimension of myself. I feel sick of myself, as if the prospect of me in action would turn me off, way off.''

"How?''

"Everything I thought I believed about making love to a woman sounds very stale. I hear myself talking to too many of them. There has to be affection, dear. Respect for each other. We must not hurt each other or anyone else, darling. There has to be giving on both sides and taking on both sides, honeybunch. Oh, Meyer, God help me, it all sounds like a glossy sales talk. I was kidding them, and I was kidding myself. Look. I was holding out a package deal. And on the bottom of the package in small print was the guaran-goddamn-tee. Mary Dillon picked up the package. I didn't force it on her. I just left it around where she'd see it. She picked it up, enjoyed the product, and then married Harry Broll, and now she's buried in a washout behind a seawall under transit-mix concrete. So something is wrong with the small print or the service contract or the damned sales force, Meyer. I just can't . . . I can't stand the thought of ever again hearing my own sincere, manly, loving, crap-eating voice saying those stale words about how I won't ever hurt you, baby. I just want to screw you and make you a more sincere and emotionally healthy woman."

"Travis, Travis, Travis."

"I know. But that's what's wrong."

"Maybe there is some new kind of industrial waste in the air we breathe."

"Fractionated honesty?"

"Don't suffer all over me, McGee. You are a good man. There is no man alive who is not partially jackass. When we detect some area of jackassery within ourselves, we feel discontent. Our image suffers."

"What should I do?"

"How do I know what you should do? Don't make me an uncle. Go get lost in the Out Islands and fish for a couple months. Go hire onto a tug and work yourself into a stupor. Take five thousand of what was in that brown bag and lease the *Hell's Belle* all by yourself for ten days. Take cold showers. Study Hindustani."

"Why are you getting sore?"

He bounded off the bench, whirled, bent over, yelled into my face. "Who's getting sore? I'm not getting sore!" And he ran down to the water, bouncing hairily along, and plopped in and swam out.

Everyone was not acting like himself. Maybe there *was* some new kind of guck in the air lately.

By the time we had finished our swim, Meyer had gotten over his unusual tizzy. We walked slowly back across the bridge, and as we neared the *Flush* I could see a figure aboard her in the shade of the sun-deck overhang, sitting on the shallow little afterdeck.

I did not recognize her until we were within thirty feet. She lay asleep in the deck chair with the tidy, boneless look of a resting cat. There was a big red suitcase beside the chair and a matching red train case, both well scuffed by travel. She wore a little denim dress with white stitching. Her white sandals were on the deck under the chair. Her sleeping arm clamped her white purse against her.

Suddenly her eyes opened wide. There was no sleep-stunned transition. She leapt back into life and up onto her feet in the same instant, all smiling vitality. "Hey! McGee! It's me. Jeannie. Jeannie Dolan. I should have looked over on the beach, huh?"

I introduced them. Meyer said he had heard nice things about her. He seemed to approve of the lively mop of red-brown hair and the quick glinting of the gray-green eyes.

I unlocked the *Flush,* and we went in. She said, "Leave my stuff right there, unless you've got thieves. Hey, can I look around? Say, this is a great kind of boat, Trav! Look, is the timing bad? Am I in the way or anything? If you guys have something all lined up . . ."

"Nothing," Meyer said. "Nothing at all."

"Wow, what a great kitchen."

"Galley," I said.

She looked at me blankly. "Galley? They row those with big oars. And a man walking around with a whip. Do you row this thing, for God's sake?"

"Okay, Jeannie. It's a kitchen," I said.

"Does it have engines in it? I mean, it will cruise around and so forth?"

"And so forth," Meyer said, looking happier.

"Wow, would I ever like to go someplace on a boat like this."

"Where's your friend?" I asked her.

"Betsy? We got tossed out of that Casa de Playa by the bank that took over. Not we, just me. Because she was gone by then. She went back to cleaning teeth. For a widower dentist in North Miami."

"Vodka tonic for you?" I asked her.

"Exactly right! It's wonderful when people remember things, isn't it? What I'm going to do, I'm on my way back to Columbus. No, not back to Charlie, that creep. But I called my old job, and I can make enough money so I can save enough to fly to the Dominican Republic and get a quickie divorce, instead of beating my brains out down here."

"Won't you sit down, Jeannie?" I asked her.

"I'm too nervous and jumpy, dear. Whenever I impose on people I get like this. I've got the bus schedule and all, and then I thought, Oh, what the hell, I wanted to see that McGee guy again and never did. A girl sometimes has to be brassy or settle for nothing, right?"

I looked at Meyer. He was wearing a very strange expression. I handed Jeannie her drink and said, "Sometimes a girl gets brassy at just exactly the right time, and she gets invited on a private cruise. What would you say to that?"

"Aboard this wonderful ship? Wow! I'd say yes so fast—"

"*Hold it!*" Meyer roared, startling her. He trotted over to her and with raised finger backed her over to a chair. She sat down on command, staring up at him with her mouth open.

"I am going to ask you some very personal questions, Mrs. Dolan."

"What's the *matter* with you, huh?"

"Have you been in a lot of emotional turmoil lately?"

"Me? Turmoil? Like what?"

"Are you at a crisis point in your life?"

"Crisis? I'm just trying to get myself a plain, ordinary, divorce-type divorce."

"Mrs. Dolan, do you feel like a pathetic little bird with a busted wing who has fluttered aboard, looking for patience, understanding, and gentleness and love which will make you well and whole again?"

She looked at me with wide, round eyes. "Does he get like this a lot, Travis?"

"Pay attention!" Meyer ordered. "How do you relate to your analyst?"

"Analyst? Shrink? What do I need one for? Chee! You need one, maybe."

"Are you in love?" he asked.

"This minute? Hmmm. I guess not. But I sort of usually am. And pretty often, I guess. I'm not a real serious kind of person. I'm just sort of dumb and happy."

"One more question, and I must ask you both this one."

"You answer him, honey," Jeannie said to me.

"Would either of you two happy people mind too much if I spend the next few weeks in Seneca Falls, New York?"

"Speaking for the two of us, Meyer, I can't think of a serious objection, really."

He trotted to the doorway to the rear deck and opened it. He picked up the two pieces of red luggage and set them inside the door, gave us a maniacal smile, and slammed the door and was gone.

Jeannie stood up and sipped frowningly at her drink. Then she looked at me. "McGee?"

"Yes, dear."

"Everybody I know is acting weirder all the time. Have you noticed that too?"

"Yes, I have. Meyer isn't often like that."

"It's pretty weird and pushy for me to barge in on you like this. I'm not like this, really."

"It does have engines."

"That's nice. But do you feel you've been maneuvered into something you'd just as soon not do, huh?"

"The more I think about it, the better I like it."

She put her drink down and came over and gave me one quick, thorough, and enthusiastic kiss. "There! Now it's just a case of getting acquainted, huh? Want to start by helping me unpack?"

We carried the luggage back to the master stateroom. She asked me what Meyer had meant about her having a broken wing. I said he was one of the last of the great romantics. I said there used to be two. But now there was just the one left. The hairy one.

The Dreadful Lemon Sky

❖

For each true friend of Travis McGee

Life is not a spectacle or a feast:
it is a predicament.

SANTAYANA

1

I was in a deep sleep, alone aboard my houseboat, alone in the half acre of bed, alone in a sweaty dream of chase, fear, and monstrous predators. A shot rang off steel bars. Another. I came bursting up out of sleep to hear the secretive sound of the little bell which rings at my bedside when anyone steps aboard *The Busted Flush*. It was almost four in the morning.

It could be some kid prowling the decks for a forgotten camera, portable radio, or bottle of Scotch. Or a friendly drunk. Or a drunken friend. Or trouble. I could not know how long I had slept past the first ting of the bell. I pulled on a pair of shorts and went padding through the blackness, past the head and the galley, through into the lounge to the locked doorway that opens onto the sheltered deck aft. The handgun which I had slipped from its handy recess before I was totally awake felt cold in my grasp.

I heard a small knocking sound, secret and tentative. "Trav?" A husky, half-whispering girl voice. "Trav McGee? Trav, honey?"

I moved over to where I could see through glass at an angle, just enough to make out the girl shape of the small figure huddled close to the door, out of the brightness of the dock lights. She seemed to be quite alone.

I called through the closed door. "Who are you?"

"Trav? Don't turn on any lights, huh? Please!"

"Who is it?"

"It's me! It's Carrie. Carrie Milligan."

I hesitated, then sheathed the revolver under the waistband of the shorts, cold against belly flesh. I unlocked and let her in and locked the door again.

She hooked one arm around me and hugged her small self tightly against me and let out a long breath. "Hey, hello," she said. "No lights. Okay? I don't want to get you involved."

"Lights will get me involved?"

"You know what I mean. If somebody was close, if they knew I came over toward this way and they watched and saw lights go on here, then they'd want to find out."

"So I can black out the captain's quarters."

"Sure. It'll be easier to talk."

I took her by the hand and led her back through the darkness. Just enough light came in so that the lounge furniture made bulky shapes to left and right. When we reached my stateroom I released her and pulled both thicknesses

161

of draperies across the ports. Then I turned on a light, the reading lamp over the bed which makes a bright round pattern on a book and leaves the rest of the room in darkness. It shone on the wrinkled sheets of recent dreams and bounced off, illuminating her in soft light.

She had hugged with one arm because she held a package and her purse in the other. The package was the shape of a shoe box, wrapped in brown paper, tied with cord.

"I know, I know," she said, backing away from the light. "I'm not wearing very damn well. I'm not lasting so good. What's it been? Six years. So I was twenty-four, right? And now I look forty."

"How's Ben?"

"I wouldn't have the faintest idea."

"Oh."

"Yes, it's like that. I haven't lived with him in . . . over three years. I threw him the hell out."

"Oh."

"Stop saying 'Oh.' You know, I felt a little pinch when I saw this great old boat. I really did. I didn't know I could feel anything like that, related to Ben. I thought it was all gone. But we were happy aboard this crock. It was the only really happy time, I think. Shiny new marriage, and not a dime in the world, but a great boat to have a honeymoon aboard." She sat in the chair in the corner by the locker, out of the light. In a different voice she said, "I should have settled for you."

"You figured I wouldn't marry anybody," I said. I sat on the bed, facing her.

"I know, I know. What I don't know is why I was so red hot to get married. So I married Ben Milligan. Jesus! Know what he was, really? He was a child bride. His mother spent twenty-five years picking up after him, waiting on him, telling him how great he was, and then she turned him over to me. Whine, whine, whine. He couldn't hold a job. Nobody appreciated him. Bitch, bitch, bitch. He had like fourteen jobs in two years, and the last part of that two years, he didn't even *look*. He stayed home and watched the soaps on TV. He did all that body-building stuff all the time. Muscles on muscles. When I came home from work, I was supposed to cook, or at least stop on the way home and buy pizza or hamburgers. Trav, couldn't you tell what he was like?"

"Sure."

"Couldn't you have said something?"

"And lose an eye?"

"Okay, so I was in love. Thank God for no kids. I think it was him, not me. But he wouldn't go see a doctor about it. He got very grumpy that I could say anything might be wrong with the perfect body. Look, McGee, it was all a long time ago. All forgotten. I didn't come here to talk about my great married life. I was thinking on the way here, I don't *really* know Travis McGee. But you made me feel close to you, way back. I had to find somebody I could trust. I went through an awful lot of names. I came up with you. Then I started thinking, Maybe he's got somebody aboard with him, or somebody lives aboard, or he's away, or he's married. My God, it's six *years*. You know? I stepped aboard and six years were gone. You look great. You know it? Absolutely great. You haven't changed at all. It isn't fair. Look at me!"

It happens to people. They get up to the point of explaining the mission and can't make it, so they go into a talking jag. She needed help. There was a thin edge of anxiety in her tone, and the words came too fast.

So I gave her some help. "What have you got in the box?" I asked.

She exhaled harshly. Almost a gasp. "You get right to it, don't you? What have I got in the box? In this here box, you mean? Once you said you had a safe place for things. Do you still?"

"Yes."

She came over and put the package on the bed beside where I was sitting. She grasped the cord and popped it with a swift sure motion. She stripped the brown paper off. Meyer says whole tracts could be written about character revealed in opening a package.

"What I've got in this box," she said, "is money."

She lifted the lid. It was money. It was packed in tightly. Used bills, some loose, most tied into tidy bricks with string, with adding-machine tape tucked under the string. "I've got here ninety-four thousand two hundred dollars. Plus ten thousand for you, for keeping it until I want it."

"No need for that."

"It's worth that to me. And I'd feel better."

"Can I ask any questions?"

"Hardly any. That's part of the fee."

"Stolen?"

"Like from a bank or payroll or something? No."

"And if you don't come back?"

"I'll be back before . . . what's today?"

"Early early in the morning of May the sixteenth, a Thursday."

"Okay, if I don't come get it before the fifteenth of June, or get some kind of word to you before the fifteenth of June, then I'm not coming at all. So it should go to my sister, Susie. Do you remember my maiden name?"

"Dee. Carrie Dee."

"That was short for Dobrovsky. She uses the whole name. Susie . . . Susan Dobrovsky. You get it to her. That's part of the fee. And not telling anybody at all about me being here. That's the rest of the way you earn ten."

"Where is your sister?"

"Oh. Sorry. She's in Nutley, New Jersey. She's younger. She teaches nursery school. She's now like about the age I was when I knew you before. Twenty-three? Yes. Two months ago. She's nice, but . . . dumb about things. She doesn't know how things are yet. Wouldn't it be nice if she didn't have to find out? Look, will you put this in a safe place and keep it for me?"

"Yes, of course."

She swayed, took one dizzy step, and turned around abruptly and sat down on my bed beside the box, bouncing it, spilling the bricks of money. She shook her head. "I'm dead for sleep. And I'm dirty, Trav. I've been in these same clothes too long. I can smell myself. These clothes, they ought to be buried. For the ten thousand, dear, could I ask for three more things?"

"Like a bath, a place to sleep, and a change of clothes?"

"I'm a size ten."

After she was throat deep in the big tub, sploshing and sudsing, scrubbing her cropped pale hair along with the rest of her, I located an old surplus ammo box, the kind with the rubber gasket and the flat metal lever that fastens it safely tight. I moved the money, all except the ten thousand, into the ammo box and put that forward in the flooded area between the double hull. I added the ten to my own cache, mentally adding another four or five months to my retirement. I retire whenever I can afford it. When the money is gone, I go back to work. Salvage work. Retirement comes when you are too old to enjoy it completely, so I take some of mine whenever I can. What good are beaches without beach bums. What would the little vacationing lady urchins do for their holiday pleasures were not some of us out there wastreling away? After the large money was all stowed and quite safe, I went digging into the big locker drawer under the bed in the guest stateroom. It is always packed with girl clothes. They get left aboard. They are purchased in the ports I can reach with my old houseboat, and they are left aboard for another time. No trouble to have them cleaned and put away. And having the supply facilitates spur-of-the-moment decisions.

I found her some navy flairs and a pink sleeveless turtleneck shirt. And I found her the kind of terry robe which fits anyone. It fit her and dragged on the floor behind her. She helped me make up the guest bed. She was yawning with every second breath. Her eyes were glazed with fatigue. When I went in not more than three minutes later to ask her if she'd like some hot chocolate or a drink, she interrupted the question with a long, gentle, purring snore.

I stood for a few minutes leaning against the doorframe, looking at her in the semidarkness, remembering her. I remembered the pre-Ben Carrie Dee, a pretty girl who worked at Peerless Marine and was seen now and again at some of the parties in and around Bahia Mar. We are never the best judges of what is meaningful and what is trivial in our lives, I guess. The accidents of time and place change the script, and later we say it happened on purpose.

Carrie didn't happen to me on purpose. Or I to her. There was a TV crew at Bahia Mar making a commercial. The Alabama Tiger had them at his permanent floating house party every night of the week they were there. The boss fellow was squat and hairy and very loud. Mod clothes and a glossy wig and a conviction that his profession and personality made him irresistible. I went topside at midnight on the *'Bama Gal* to get some air and see if there were any stars to look at. Boss Fellow had a girl down on the deck by the overturned dinghy and was mauling her around, riding her clothes up over her hips as she kicked and bleated and yelped, her protests lost in the Tiger's two hundred amps of speakers.

I plucked him off her and, while he flailed and cursed, I carried him to a place along the rail where I could get a clear drop into the boat basin. He made a mighty splash after the twelve-foot drop. When I was sure he could swim, I let him fend for himself. It was Carrie, and she was not in great shape. She was ripped and scuffed and close to hysterics. She was certainly in no shape to rejoin the party, so I walked her back to *The Busted Flush* and found some clothes that would fit her. She spent a half hour alone in the head, getting herself back together.

It had shaken her badly. He had come all too close to taking her. She looked spooked and sallow. By all the accepted rules of human behavior, she should have been so turned off by the near rape she would have felt neuter for quite a while. And I should have been reluctant to give her any new reason for alarm. But in some strange way the episode became a stimulant. We sat and talked, moved closer and talked, moved closer yet and kissed, and I took her to bed. It was a very gentle time, and very sweet in a strange way. In body language she was saying, *This* is the way it should be. And I was saying, Replace that memory with *this* one.

It was an isolated episode. Except perhaps by glance or by fleeting expression, we did not mention it again. Knowing her in that biblical sense changed my status with her to that of benign uncle. She sought me out to ask my advice about how she should live her life. She was so determined, months later, that I should approve of Ben Milligan, I think she convinced herself that I had approved. She wanted a good life. It is not an unusual hope, but a very unusual attainment.

*   *   *

I pulled the door shut. I made myself the drink and dressed while I worked at it. After the drink it was time for juice and coffee. After coffee, it was time to go find her purse. False dawn let a little light into the stateroom. I moved silently on bare feet and found the purse at the pillow end, shoved between mattress and box springs. I eased it out and took it to the galley and opened it at the table in the breakfast booth, under the light.

And hello to you, Carolyn Milligan. Florida registration receipt on a two-year-old Datsun, tag number 24D-1313. I found the car keys and put them in my shirt pocket. The occupation, which used to be given on the driving license, no longer appears there. Assume she is still a secretarial type. I copied down the tag number of the car and the address as given: 1500 Seaway Boulevard, Apt. 38B, Bayside, Florida. Comb, lipstick, dental floss, matchbooks, payroll stub, airplane tickets, used. Misc. intimacies. So Mrs. Milligan worked for Superior Building Supplies in Junction Park in Bayside, Florida, and she made $171.54 per week after deducts. She had been in Jamaica, at a Montego Bay hotel, in April. She had six hundred and some dollars in the purse. And a Master Charge card. And three kinds of pills. Everybody has three kinds as a minimum allowance. It is the creature adjustment to a rapidly changing world.

By then real dawn had arrived, and I locked up the *Flush* and walked through the deceptive coolness and the varying shades of gray, looking in the lots for her car. I found it. Bright orange. Imitation leather. Thirty-one thousand miles on it. Nothing significant in the glove compartment. A case of twelve bottles of an industrial abrasive in the trunk. Tru-Kut, it was called. I opened one, wet my fingers, rubbed and snuffed. Industrial abrasive. A milky white solution that smelled like men's rooms, overly sanitized, and contained a gritty cutting agent. So secretary makes deliveries for the boss fellow of Superior Building Supplies.

Nothing else of any moment. The tires were new, doubtless recently replaced. Windshield starred by a kicked-up pebble. Half a tank of gas. I relocked the car. Nobody seemed to be paying any attention to me. Over on charter-boat row they were getting ready to go rumbling out of the basin and roar out to the edge of the Stream. Early birds were beginning to arrive to get the shops ready to open. The early maid shift was reporting to the motel housekeeper. The early bird who gets the worm works for somebody who comes in late and owns the worm farm.

I sauntered back to the *Flush* by a different route. I unlocked it, slipped keys in purse, slipped purse under mattress while she still snored on and on into this new day. By morning light she did indeed look as if she had not weathered the years too well. New deep lines bracketed her mouth. Her eyes were pouched, her chin slightly doubled, her skin grainy. She frowned in her sleep. By my count, she was thirty. The body was younger, the face older than thirty. Some great-looking couple, those two. Ben and Carrie. Travel-poster people. Photograph them on red bikes in Bermuda, and you would sell tickets on the airplanes. Too much boyish petulance in Ben's face. Too much pseudomasculine heartiness in his manner. His momma had loved him, all too well.

2

CARRIE SLEPT through the morning and into the afternoon. At three I went in and put my hand on her shoulder and shook her gently. She made a blurred noise of complaint and then gave a great start and snapped her eyes open. She looked terrified. Then she knew me and the lids got heavy again and she put a fist in front of a creaking yawn.

"Whassamarra?" she said. "Whatimezit?"

"Three P.M. on Thursday, love. Keep sleeping. You seem to need it. I'm going to lock you in and go over to the beach for a while."

"Look. When you come back. Wake me up again? Okay?"

"Sure."

It had taken such a great effort of will and so much pain to get back in good shape, I had vowed never to let myself get sloppy again. And that meant hot sun and sweat and exercise every day, no tobacco ever again, and easy on the booze, heavy on the protein. Meyer was involved in writing a long and complicated dissertation on the lasting effect on international currencies of the Arab oil production disputes, and he quit each day at three and joined me on the beach to get in his daily stint. Meyer never looks fat and he never never looks slender. He is merely broad and durable in a rubbery way, and hairy as an Adirondack black bear.

He believes in exercise in moderation. He says that he is not interested in celebrations of masochism, and so, aside from a part of the swimming, we do not see much of each other until the exercise hour is over.

He was already sitting on his towel at the high-tide line when I finished sprinting the last hundred yards of my one-mile run. When I stopped puffing and panting and groaning, I took a final dip and then stretched out close by.

"You ought to run a little," I told him.

"Would that I could. When the beach people see you running, they know at a glance that it is exercise. There you are, all sinew and brown hide, and you wear that earnest, dumb, strained expression of the old jock keeping in shape. You have the style. Knees high, arms swinging just right, head up. But suppose I came running down this beach? They would look at me, and then look again. I look so little like a runner or a jock that the only possible guess as to what would make me run is terror. So they look way down the beach to see what is chasing me. They can't see anything, but to be on the safe side, they start walking swiftly in the same direction I'm running. First just a few, then a dozen, then a score. All going faster and faster. Looking back. Breaking into a run. And soon you would have two or three thousand people thundering along the beach, eyes popping out of the sockets, cords in their necks standing out. A huge stampede, stomping everything and everybody in their path into the sand. You wouldn't want me to cause a catastrophe like that, would you?''

"Oh, boy."

"It might not happen, but I can't take the chance."

"Meyer."

"Once it started, I could drop out and they would keep on going. The contagion of panic. Once you see it, you never forget it."

"Meyer, do you remember Carrie Milligan?"

"A thundering herd of . . . what? Who?"

"About six years ago. I loaned Carrie and Ben *The Busted Flush*. Not to take on a cruise. Just to live aboard, during a honeymoon.''

"And told me to keep an eye on them. Very funny. I think I saw them come out into the daylight once. Let me see. She worked in the office over at Peerless Marine. Pretty little thing. I forget why you loaned them the *Flush*.''

"I owed Dake Heath a favor and that's what he asked for. He was her half brother and he wanted things nice for her. Carrie and Ben were broke and so was Dake. So I broke a rule and said okay."

"To answer your question, yes, I remember her. Why?"

So I told all. I had promised Carrie not to tell anyone. But all rules are off when it comes to Meyer. Also, it was a form of protection. When somebody comes up and gives you that much money to tuck away for safekeeping, special precautions are in order. Checking the purse and the car, for example. And telling Meyer everything, including my checking the purse and the car. If the law moved in, I wanted to be able to give some plausible answers, with somebody to verify them if need be. Also, if somebody grabbed Carrie and bent her until she told them where to look for money, it would be nice to have Meyer know exactly why my luck had, at last, run out. And it will run out. Maybe not this time, or the next time. Sometime, though. And like everybody else, I will go down with that universal plea blazing in the back of my mind. "Not me! Not yet! Wait!"

Meyer was curious about the money, so I described the stacks to him, each neatly tied with white cotton string, each of mixed denominations, each totaling ten thousand, And, of course there were the loose bills, probably from a broken stack, which could mean that she had spent fifty-eight hundred. Each stack had an adding-machine tape stuffed under the string. Yes, all apparently from the same machine, but I hadn't examined them closely. It was used money, but reasonably clean and tidy. Under black light, it might fluoresce. Or somebody might have a list of serial numbers. Or it could all be funny, printed in a small room by night.

"You know her better than I do," Meyer said.

"I don't know her well."

"Have you formed any opinions about her and about the money?"

"Like what? Like did she steal it? I don't know. She's not a bum. She's a worker. Something happened that makes her feel she's got some sort of a right to the money. She arrived physically and emotionally exhausted. She didn't know if she was being followed. She thought she might be. Anyway, I'll hold it for her. If she comes and gets it, no fuss, it's a very easy ten, so easy I'll have an uneasy conscience."

A late-afternoon breeze riffled the water out beyond the lazy breakers and hustled some candy wrappers down the wet brown beach. Two tall young ladies came sauntering by, brown, brawny, and bikinied, as confident and at home in their bodies as a pair of young lionesses, their hair sun-streaked and salt-tangled, their hips rolling and canting to the slow cadence of their long walk in the sunshine.

Meyer smiled his smile and sighed his audible sigh. It is both a pleasure and a sadness to watch the very young ones walk by. They know so very little, and so frighteningly much. They are on the edge of life, thinking they are in the midst of it. Pretty soon we got up and snapped the sand off the towels and went trudging back across the pedestrian bridge. We parted, and as I stepped aboard the *Flush* I had the sudden strong feeling that harm had come to Carrie, that harm had come aboard, a feral, crouching, bone-gnawing creature.

But all was well. Such hunches happen all the time, for every one of us. We forget them all—except when one turns out to be right. Then we say, I knew! I knew!

She waited to be awakened, waited there with brushed hair, touch of lipstick, new smudge of eye shadow. She faked a sweet awakening from her drowse to pull me down into the mint taste of my own toothpaste, murmuring, "Hello, hello."

It was supposed to be very easy. No need for talk, for claiming and disclaiming. All inevitable because she had made it so through contrivance and through the directness of invitation. Worm my way out of the swim pants and glide sweetly into the lady. Thank you, ma'am. The good-boatkeeping seal of approval. Only a total fink person would decline an offer so frankly made. But the problem of her motive got in my way. Was this supposed to be in addition to the ten? Was it supposed to cloud my mind and make me less curious? Was she setting up some justification or rationalization of her own? The problem of playing somebody else's game is the problem of finding yourself stuck in a role you can't play. You can't say your lines.

So I disentangled her and sat up from the steamy kiss and smiled down at her and thumbed a strand of hair back from her round forehead. "You certainly needed a lot of sleep."

"I guess I did," she said, looking sullen.

"While you were sleeping, I was thinking."

"Goody!"

"Let's say it gets to be June fifteenth and Carrie doesn't come for her money. Don't you want me to try to find out why you couldn't make it? Or who kept you from making it?"

"It wouldn't matter a damn to me by then, would it?"

"That's what I'm asking."

"The answer is no. Just get the money to my sister. That's all."

"And she'll want to know where it came from."

"Tell her it's from me."

"Maybe she's so straight she might not take it. Then what?"

She bit her lip and looked thoughtful. "I could write her, I guess. Phone her. Something to clue her a little."

"Want to clue me too?"

"No. I don't want to talk about it and I don't want to think about it, okay? It's my personal problem."

"You're paying me enough so you can ask for help."

"I better not try asking for anything else, huh? A girl shouldn't make it too obvious. Not and get turned down."

"I just get suspicious of free gifts."

"Some gift. From a fire sale. We had us one night, a long time ago. Remember? I was okay for you then, but not now. Not the way I am now. It was a dumb idea. Sorry, fellow."

I took her hand and then despised myself for checking to find those little fingertip calluses acquired from operating office equipment. McGee checks everything, as do all paranoids.

I kissed her slack, cool, unresponsive mouth, and as I straightened up she said, "No charity, thanks. The impulse has come and gone."

"Suit yourself."

"Am I doing something to spoil your day?"

"You don't leave me any options. Any move I make is wrong."

"That's the way it goes. Check with an expert."

"At least I can tell you that you are still very attractive to me, Carrie."

"Sure, sure, sure."

"I mean it."

"Six years ago you meant it, but that was a different girl, six years ago."

"You confuse two things. Okay, I didn't react the way I was supposed to. My guard is up. What do you expect? After six years you show up with a bundle of money and want me to keep it for you. You claim you've shed Ben. I stay alive by keeping my inputs open. Is it gambling money? Is it street money? Is it ransom money? I know some people who are hungry enough to nail me, they'd unearth a girl from six years ago and use her to get to me, to set me up. Marked money. Counterfeit money. Nearly everybody can be manipulated. McGee is alive and well because he is very very careful about a lot of things. Carrie, if you had been Miss Universe stretched out here waving your eyelashes at me, the word would have been the same word. Whoa! Look out for free gifts. I check everything I can check. What I found in your purse about working in an office matches the fingertip calluses on your hands. The industrial goop in the trunk of your car tastes and smells like legitimate industrial abrasive solution."

She spun quickly and stuffed her hand under the mattress, looking for the purse.

"It's there," I said. "I put it back."

She sat up, hauling the sheet up under her chin. She stared at me. "Jesus! You *are* jumpy."

"And alive. Be glad you are leaving your money at the right place, if you still want to leave it here."

"I still want to leave it. It could have been more."

"It's a tidy sum. You are overpaying me."

"I'll decide that. Look, don't worry about the money. Okay? It isn't marked or anything. It's sort of . . . my share of some action. But somebody might grab it." Suddenly she grinned. "Hey! Thanks for giving me back my pride."

"Any time. Want some steak and eggs?"

She looked wistful but refused. She wanted to be on her way. She wore the borrowed clothes and carried her soiled ones in a brown paper bag. She waited for full dark before she left. She marched away under the dock lights, taking a roundabout route to her car. I expected her to look back, but she didn't.

There was a residual affection for her. The six years had aged her more than she could reasonably expect and had tested and toughened her. Her eyes were watchful, her merriment sardonic. There are too many of them in the world lately, the hopeful ladies who married grown-up boy children and soon lost all hope. They are the secretaries and nurses and switchboard people, the store clerks, schoolteachers, cab drivers, and Avon ladies. They lead the singles life. Lots of laughs and lots of barren mornings. Skilled sex, mod conversation, and all heartaches carefully concealed. They are not ardent libbers, yet at the same time they are not looking for some man to "take care." God knows they are expert in taking care of themselves. They just want a grown-up man to share their life with, each of them taking care. But there are one hell of a lot more grown-up ladies than grown-up men.

I wished her well. Lonely ladies can get into damned fool capers. I wished her very well indeed.

3

So two weeks went by. A pair of lovely weeks in May. A steady breeze off the Atlantic kept the bright tacky strip of Florida seacoast reasonably free of smodge, fugg, and schlutch. Old parties tottered out of their condominiums and baked themselves black in the white high glare of the beaches, pleased that their eyes didn't water and they could breathe without coughing.

On the tube the local advertising for condominiums always shows the nifty communal features, such as swimming pool, putting green, sandy beach, being enjoyed by jolly hearty folk in their very early thirties. These are the same folk you see dancing in the moonlight aboard ship in the tour ads. These are the people who keep saying that if you've got your health, you don't need anything else. But when the condominiums are finished and peopled, and the speculator has taken his maximum slice of the tax-related profits and moved on to crud up somebody else's skyline, the inhabitants all seem to be on the frangible side of seventy, sitting in the sunlight, blinking like lizards, and wondering if these are indeed the golden years or if it is all a big sell, an inflation game that you have to play, wondering which you are going to run out of first, your money or your life. The developers leave enough to go wrong in each condominium apartment that it becomes an odds-on bet the money runs out first. Nursing homes are a big industry in sunny Florida.

Anyway, it was Meyer who picked it up, a minor item on a back page, and brought it over to the *Flush* on the thirtieth day of May. It was early afternoon and I was topside, wrestling with too many yards of white nylon canvas, and with a borrowed gadget which, when properly operated, puts brass grommets into the fabric. I was irritated at how slowly my self-imposed chore was going. I was dripping sweat onto the grommet machine and the clean white nylon and the vinyl imitation-teak decking.

"Now what?" I asked sourly.

"This is what," said Meyer, and handed me the clip he had torn out of the paper.

PEDESTRIAN FATALITY

The City of Bayside registered its fourth traffic fatality of the year when Mrs. Carolyn Milligan was struck and killed at 10:30 Wednesday night while walking on County Road 858 just inside the city limits. Roderick Webbel, driver of the farm truck which struck and killed the Milligan woman, claimed that he did not see her until the moment of impact when she apparently stepped from the shoulder of the road into the path of the vehicle. Mrs. Milligan, who lived alone at 1500 Seaway Boulevard, was employed by Superior Building Supplies, Junction Park, Bayside. Police are investigating the accident and no charges have been filed as yet.

A fat drop of sweat fell from the tip of my nose and made a dark pattern of a sloppy star on the newsprint, the same color as the sweat smudge from my fingers. Meyer followed me into the shade of the canopy over the topside controls.

I leaned my rear against the instrument panel and propped one bare foot on the pilot's chair. The breeze began to cool me off.

"Accident?" Meyer asked. When I stared at him he said hastily. "Rhetorical question, of course."

"Of course. And who the hell knows? Damn it, anyway!"

I am cursed by an imagination which turns vivid when I wish it would turn itself off. She had been sturdy bone and sinew, sweet flesh and quick blood. She had been scents and secrets. Then a great bewildering bash, a tiny light in the back of the brain flickering out, as spoiled flesh, crushed bone, ripped connective tissue went slamming off into the roadside brush, spraying blood as it spun.

"Meyer, she gave me the orders. Just get the money to my sister, she said. That's all, she said. She said that if she couldn't come back and get the money, she wouldn't give much of a damn who kept her from it."

"And," Meyer said, "she paid you to do just what she said."

"I know."

"But?"

"I look at it this way. Two thousand would have been more than fair. It would have paid my way to Nutley and back, with a nice hunk left over. So she's got eight thousand worth of service coming."

"Posthumous service?"

"Which she didn't want." I doubled my right fist and gave myself a heavy thump on the top of the thigh. Painful. "It is the merry month of May, Meyer, and the lady is going to be dead for a very long time. I would be doing what she wanted. Giving the money to the sister. And making certain there are no strings attached, nobody following the scent, nobody mashing the sister too."

"I admire your talent for instant rationalization."

"This is *not* romanticism, dammit."

"Did I say it was?"

"By the expression on your face. Patronizing, amused, superior."

"You are reading it wrong. The face is just some skin and fat and muscle stretched over bone. I was actually looking apprehensive."

"About what?"

"About what you might be getting me into."

"You can stay right here and work on your treatise."

"I'm at a stopping point, waiting for translations of some Swedish journals to arrive. I could struggle through them myself, but . . ." He shrugged and went over and picked up some of the canvas, inspected a grommet. "Is this crooked?"

"Very."

"Then it won't look very good, will it?"

"No. It won't."

"Travis, do we know anybody at all in Bayside?"

"I keep thinking there was somebody."

So we went below, and while I checked out the book in the desk, Meyer opened a pair of cold Tuborgs. No friends in Bayside. None. Meyer blew across the top of the Tuborg bottle, a foghorn note far away. "So why are we up there fussing around?" he asked.

"A question which will be asked."

"Insurance?"

"Possibly, but it doesn't feel right."

"Good old United Beneficent Casualty and Life. Those are such beautiful blank policies. I can type in all the—"

"I know. I know. But it could be in a dead end. Accidental death, fellows. And these days you get checked out too often. It just doesn't feel right. I think that when she was here two weeks ago I borrowed some money from her. Maybe I gave her a promissory note. I'm in shape to pay it back, but I'd just as soon not pay it back to her heirs and assigns, not if I can get my hands on the note I signed."

"And you take some cash along. For credibility."

"Right! Maybe we both borrowed it and both signed. We're a pair of real-estate gunslingers trying to cheat the little dead lady's estate. We'll pay up if we have to. But we'd rather not."

Meyer closed his eyes and thought long and hard, taking a deep draft on the Tuborg as he did so. He nodded. "I like it."

"We'll take all the cash along," I said.

He looked startled. "All?"

"We'll operate from this gallant watercraft. In comfort. Even in certain vulgar luxury. Go pack your toothbrush, my friend."

After he left I checked my Waterway Guide and picked out what looked like the best of Bayside's several marinas. It was called Westway Harbor, operated by Cal and Cindy Birdsong. I phoned and got a young man in the office named Oliver. Yes, he had a nice slot for *The Busted Flush,* one that would take up to a sixty-footer, one with water, electric, and phone hookup and about a hundred feet from the facilities. I said we'd check in on Friday, probably around noon. The fee sounded a little bit on the high side. Oliver wanted to know how long we would be with them, and I said it was hard to say, very hard to say. He told me to look for a high round water tower north of the center of town, and when I was opposite it, I was to look for their private channel markers and they would lead me right in, and he would be there to direct me to the slip. "You can't miss it," he said.

By the time I'd notified the office we were taking off, exchanged a few lies with Irv Diebert, picked up the laundry, arranged with Johnny Dow to take the mail out of the box and hold it, unplugged the shoreside connections, topped the tanks, and tied the *Muñequita* well off in the slip, tarped and snug, it was after four o'clock. We chugged out to the channel and turned north.

At drinking time I left Meyer at the wheel and went below and broke out the very last bottle of the Plymouth gin which had been bottled in the United Kingdom. All the others were bottled in the U.S. Gin People, it isn't the same. It's still a pretty good gin but it is not a superb, stingingly dry, and lovely gin. The sailor on the label no longer looks staunch and forthright, but merely hokey. There is something self-destructive about Western technology and distribution. Whenever any consumer object is so excellent that it attracts a devoted following, some of the slide rule and computer types come in on their twinkle toes and take over the store, and in a trice they figure out just how far they can cut quality and still increase the market penetration. Their reasoning is that it is idiotic to make and sell a hundred thousand units of something and make a profit of thirty cents a unit, when you can increase the advertising, sell five million units, and make a nickel profit a unit. Thus the very good things of the world go down the drain, from honest turkey to honest eggs to honest tomatoes. And gin.

I put cracked ice in two sturdy glass mugs, dumped in some sherry and dumped it out again, filled with Plymouth gin, rubbed peel around the rims of mugs, squeezed oil onto surface of gin, threw peel away, and carried mugs up to the topside controls, where Meyer was using his best twelve-syllable words on a yuk who had pounded by us, lifting a nine-foot wash behind him. I saw it coming and had time to prepare. I did some twinkle toes myself: three to port, three to starboard, never spilling a drop.

We clinked glasses, took the testing sip, then the deep single swallow. Delicious. The birds were circling, the sun needles were dancing off the water, and the *Flush* was lumbering along, slowed imperceptibly by a fouled bottom. It is unseemly to feel festive about checking out the death of a dead friend. But there is something heartening about having a sense of mission. A clean purpose. A noble intent, no matter how foolish. Behind us, a couple of slow hours back of us, the 17,000 resident boats and the thirteen big marinas of Lauderdale, where 150,000 people grow ever more furious in the traffic tangles. Ahead, some murky mystery locked in the broken skull of a dead lady. The knight errant, earning his own self-esteem, holding the palms cupped to make a dragon trap. Peer inside. S'right, by God, a dragon! But what color, fella?

Before nightfall I found the anchorage I had used before, a sheltered slot between two small mangrove islands. Fortunately nobody had yet built a causeway to either island, or erected thereon one of those glassy monuments to the herd instinct. I nestled the houseboat into the slot and went over the side and made four lines fast to the tough twisted trunks of mangroves, at ten, two, four, and eight o'clock. The night air was full of bugs homing on my earlobes, screaming their hunger, so we buttoned the *Flush* up, testing night breezes and screens until it was comfortable in the lounge.

While Meyer was broiling a very large number of very small lamb chops, a skiff went churning across the flats, heading out toward the channel. The people aboard were yelping like maniacs, making wolf yelps, panther screams, rebel yells. I heard the crazed laughter of a woman. And then there was a sharp authoritative barking. Thrice. *Bam, bam, bam.* Tinkle of glass inside the lounge. Sharp knock against paneling. The skiff picked up speed. The woman laughed in that same crazy way. I stopped rolling and got up onto one knee, then raced topside and yanked the shark rifle out of its greasy nest. No point in firing at one small light far away, the sound fading.

"Why?" Meyer said, beside me.

I didn't answer until we were below again, out of the bugs' hungry clasp. "For kicks. For nothing. For self-expression. Good ol' Charlie shows those rich bastards they don't own the whole goddamn world. It was a handgun and it was a long way off, and having one hit us was pure luck."

"It could have been between the eyes. Pure luck."

"Stoned and smashed. Beer and booze and too much sun. Uppers and downers, hash and smack, all spaced out. Take any guess."

Meyer went quietly back to his broiling. He seemed moody during the meal, working things out his own way inside that gentle, thoughtful skull. The misshapen slug had dented the paneling but had penetrated so shallowly I had been able to pry it loose with a thumbnail. It was on the table beside my cup, a small metallic turd dropped by a dwarf robot. I had stuck Saran Wrap across the starred hole in the glass port.

"Let me give it a try," he said.

"You think you can explain why? Come *on!*"

"When I was twelve years old I received on my birthday a single-shot twenty-two rifle chambered for shorts. It was a magical adventure to have a gun. It made a thin and wicked cracking sound, and an exotic smell of burned powder and oil. A tin can would leap into the air at some distance when I had merely moved my index finger a fraction of an inch."

"Meyer, the killer."

He smiled. "You anticipate me. There were good birds and bad birds. One of the bad birds was a grackle. Of the family *Icteridae,* genus *Quiscalus.* I do not recall why it was in such bad repute. Possibly it eats the eggs of other birds. At any rate, it seemed to be acceptable to shoot one, whereas shooting a robin would have been unthinkable. I had watched grackles through my mother's binoculars. A fantastic color scheme, an iridescence over black, as if there were a thin sheen of oil atop a pool of india ink. I had shown enough reliability with the rifle to be allowed to take it into the woodlands behind our place, provided I followed all the rules. There was no rule about grackles. I went out one Saturday afternoon after a rain. A grackle took a busy splashing bath in a puddle and flew up to a limb. I aimed and fired, and it fell right back down into the same puddle and did some frantic thrashing and then was still. I went and looked at it. Its beak was opening and closing, just under the surface of the water. I picked it up with some vague idea of keeping it from drowning. It made a terminal tremorous spasm in my hand and then it was still. Unforgettably, unbearably still. As still as a stone, as a dead branch, as a fence post. I want to say all of this very carefully, Travis. See this scar on the edge of my thumb? I was using a jackknife to make a hole in a shingle boat for a mast, and the blade of the knife closed. This bled a good deal, and because it sliced into the thumbnail, it hurt. It hurt as much as anything had ever hurt me up until that time. And that had happened about two months before I murdered the grackle. The grackle lay in my hand, and all that fabulous iridescence was gone. It had a dirty look, the feathers all scruffed and wet. I put it down hastily on the damp grass. I could not have endured dropping it. I put it down gently, and there was blood left on my hand. Bird blood. As red as mine. And the pain had been like mine, I knew. Bright and hot and savage."

He was silent so long I said, "You mean that . . ."

"I'm looking for the right way to express the relationships. Travis, the gun was an abstraction, the bullet an abstraction. Death was an abstraction. A tiny movement of a finger. A crackling sound. A smell. I could not comprehend a gun, a bullet, and a death until the bird died. It became all too specific and too concrete. I had engineered this death, and it was dirty. I had given pain. I had blood on my hand. I did not know what to do with myself. I did not know how to escape from myself, to go back to what I had been before I had slain the bird. I wanted to get outside the new experience of being me. I was, in all truth, in all solemnity, filled with horror at the nature of reality. I have never killed another bird, nor will I ever, unless I should come upon one in some kind of hopeless agony. Now here is the meat of my analogy. Those young people in that boat have never killed their grackle. They have not been bloodied by reality. They have shed the make-believe blood of a West that never existed. They have gawped at the gore of the Godfather. They have seen the slow terminal dance of Bonnie and Clyde. They have seen the stain on the front of the shirt of the man who has fallen gracefully into the dust of Marshal Dillon's main street. It is as if . . . I had walked into those woods and seen a picture of a dead grackle. They do not yet know the nature of reality. They do not yet know, and may never learn, what a death is like. What an ugly thing it is. The sphincters let go and there is a rich sickening stink of fecal matter and urine. There is that ugly stillness, black blood caking and clotting and stinking. To them, that gun somebody took out of his fish box is an abstraction. They find no relationship between the movement of the index finger and the first stinking step into eternity. It is emotional poverty with cause and effect in a state of disassociation. And they . . ."

He had become hesitant, the words coming more slowly, with less certainty. He smiled with strange shyness and shrugged and said, "But that doesn't work, does it?"

"I think it works pretty well."

"No. Because then they could only kill once. But some of them go on and on. Pointlessly."

"Some of them. Weird ones. Whippy ones."

"Theorizing is my disease, Travis. A friend of mine, Albert Eide Parr, has written, 'Whether you get an idea from looking into a sunset or into a beehive has nothing to do with its merits and possibilities.' I seem to get too many of my ideas by looking into my childhood."

"They didn't nail either of us between the eyes this time."

"Ever the realist."

We cleaned up and sacked out early. I lay wakeful in the big bed, resentful of Meyer nearby in the guest stateroom, placidly asleep. When he had been involved in a government study in India, he had learned how to take his mind out of gear and go immediately to sleep. I had known how, without thinking about it, when I had been in the army, but in time I had lost the knack.

Meyer had explained very carefully how he did it. "You imagine a black circle about two inches behind your eyes, and big enough to fill your skull from ear to ear, from crown to jaw hinges. You know that each intrusion of thought is going to make a pattern on that perfect blackness. So you merely concentrate on keeping the blackness perfect, unmarked, and mathematically round. As you do that, you breathe slowly and steadily, and with each exhalation, you feel yourself sinking a tiny bit further into the mattress. And in moments you are asleep."

He was, but I wasn't. Once I had explained Meyer's system to a very jumpy restless lady, telling her it wouldn't work for me and it wouldn't work for her. I said, "Go ahead. Try it. It's just a lot of nonsense, Judy. Right, Judy! Hey! Judy? Judy?"

Tonight I was too aware of all the world around me. I was a dot on the Waterway chart between the small islands. Above me starlight hit the deck after traveling for years and for trillions of miles. Under the hull, in the ooze and sand and grass of the bottom, small creatures were gagging and strangling on the excreta of civilization. The farthest stars had moved so much since the starlight left them that the long path of light was curved. After the planet was cindered, totally barren of life, that cold starlight would still be taking the long curved path down to bound off black frozen stone. Ripples slapped the hull. I heard a big cruiser go barreling down the Waterway, piloted by some idiot racing to keep his inevitable appointment with floating palm bole or oil drum. Long minutes after the sound had faded, his wash tipped the *Flush,* creaked the lines, clinked something or other in the galley. It disturbed a night bird, which rose from one of the islands, making a single horrid strangled croak. Far off on the north-south highways there was the insect sound of the fast-moving trucks, whining toward warehouses, laden with emergency rush orders of plastic animals, roach tablets, eye shadow, ash- trays, toilet brushes, pottery crocodiles, and all the other items essential to a constantly increasing GNP.

My heart made a slow, solemn ka-thudding sound, and the busy blood raced around, nourishing, repairing, slaying invaders, and carrying secretions. My unruly memory went stumbling and tumbling down the black corridors, through the doors I try to keep closed. A trickle of sweat ran along my throat, and I pushed the single sheet off.

Where had Carrie Milligan gotten the money?

Had she told anyone I had it?

What had the money to do with being in the same clothes too long?

Kidnap?

Smuggling?

Casino?

Robbery?

Let's take it to Nutley and give it all to the little sister and then go fishing, preferably down off Isla de las Mujeres.

But first, friend, let us try to get the hell to sleep. Please? Please? Keep the black circle absolutely round. Sink deeper with each exhalation. Absolutely round . . .

4

A GOOD marina—and rare they are indeed—is a comfort and a joy. The private channel to Westway Harbor was about six hundred yards long. It was a seminatural basin, dredged to depth, with the entrance narrowed for protection from wash, storm waves, and chop. The gas dock was inside the entrance, tucked over to the south side. Small-boat dockage was on the southern perimeter of the basin. There were an estimated eighty berths for bigger craft dead ahead and to my right as I came through their entrance.

A brown young man in khaki shorts came out of the dockmaster's office, gave me a follow-me wave of his arm, and hopped onto an electric service cart. I eased to starboard and followed him to the indicated slip, then swung out and backed in between the finger piers as Meyer went forward and put loops over the pilings as we eased past. When the young man sliced the edge of his hand across his throat, Meyer made both bow lines fast to the bow cleat, and I killed my little diesels. The young man was polite. He helped with the lines. He asked permission to come aboard. He handed me a neatly printed sheet of rules, rates, and regulations, services available, and hours of availability. I asked him if he was Oliver, and he said Oliver had gone to lunch. He was Jason. Jason had a jock body, Jesus head, and gold-wire Franklin glasses.

The instructions were clear and precise. I helped him plug me into the dockside electricity. He took a meter reading. I said we'd like phone service, and he said he'd go bring an instrument. I tasted the hose water and told Meyer to top off the water tank while I went to the dockmaster's office to make arrangements.

As I walked, I admired the construction of the docks. Concrete piers and big timbers and oversized galvanized bolts holding them together. The trash cans were in big fiberglass bins. There were safety stations, with life rings and fire extinguishers. The water lines and power lines were slung under the docks, out of sight. They had about thirty empty berths. The fifty boats in sight looked substantial and well kept, especially a row of a half dozen big motor sailers. A calico cat sitting on the bow of a big Chris stopped washing to stare at me as I walked by.

There was a big tall lady behind the counter in the office. She had very short black hair and strong features. She was barelegged and barefooted and wore yellow shorts and a white T-shirt and a gold wedding ring. She stood about six feet high, and though the face was strong enough to look just a little bit masculine, there was nothing masculine about the legs or the way she filled the T-shirt. And she was almost as tan as I am. It made her cool blue eyes look very vivid, and it made her teeth look very very white.

"Mr. McGee?"

"Yes. You've got a fine-looking marina here."

"Thank you. I'm Mrs. Birdsong. We've been open exactly two years today."

"Congratulations."

"Thank you." Her smile was small and formal. This was an arm's-length girl. With a long arm. Twenty-eight? Hard to guess her age because her face had that Indian shape which doesn't show much erosion from eighteen to forty.

We made the arrangements. I paid cash for three days in advance, saying we might stay longer. I asked about a rental car, and she walked me over to a side window and pointed to a Texaco sign visible above the roof of the next-door motel and said I could get a car there.

Just as we turned away from the window there was a roar, a yelp of rubber, and a heavy thud as someone drove a dusty blue sedan into the side of the building.

A big man struggled out from behind the wheel and walked unsteadily to the doorway and paused there, staring at her and then at me.

"Where have you been? Where—have—you—been?" she asked. Her eyes looked sick.

He was six and a half feet tall, and almost as broad as the doorway. He had a thick tangle of gray-blond hair, a mottled and puffy red face. He wore soiled khakis, with what looked like dried vomit on the front of the shirt. There was a bruise on his forehead and his knuckles were swollen. He wafted a stink of the unwashed into the small office.

He gave her a stupid glaring look and mumbled, "Peddle your ass anybody comes along, eh. Cindy? Bangin' dock boys, bangin' customers. I know what you are, you cheap hooker."

"Cal! You don't know what you're saying?"

He turned ponderously toward me. "Show you not to fool around with somebody's wife, you bas'ard, you rotten suhva bish."

She came trotting toward him from the side, reaching for him, saying, "No, Cal. No, honey. Please."

He swung a backhand blow at her face, a full swing of his left arm. She saw it coming and tried to duck under it, but it caught her high on the head, over the ear. It felled her. She hit and rolled loose, with a thudding of joints and bones and skull against the vinyl tile floor. ending up a-sprawl, face down.

Cal didn't look at her. He came shuffling toward me, big fists waving gently, shoulder hiked up to shield the jaw. If he'd left enough room for me to slide past him and bolt out the doorway, I would have. Dog drunk as he was, he was immense and seemed to know how to move. I did not want to be in the middle of any family quarrel. Or any wife-killing. She was totally out, unmoving.

One thing I was not going to do, and that was stand up and play fisticuffs. Not with this one. I was getting a good flow of adrenaline. I felt edgy and fast and tricky. I put my hands out, palms toward him, as though pleading with him not to hit me. He looked very happy, in a bleary way, and launched a big right fist at the middle of my face. I snapped my open palms onto that thick right wrist and turned it violently clockwise, yanking downward at the same time. The leverage spun him around, and his wrist and fist went up between his shoulder blades. I got him started and, with increasing momentum, ran him into the cement block wall. He smacked it, dropped to his knees, and then spilled sideways and sat up, blood running down into his eye and down his cheek from a new split in his forehead. He smiled in a thoughtful way and struggled up and came hunching toward me again. This time I moved inside a pawing left hand and hit him as fast and as hard as I could, left-right, left-right, to throat and belly. I knew it damaged him, but as I tried to slide past him, once more thinking of the doorway, he hit me squarely in the forehead. It creaked my neck, turned the bright day to a cloudy vagueness, and put me into slow motion. As I was going down, my head cleared. I hooked my left foot around the back of his right ankle and kicked his kneecap with my right foot. He grunted and tried to stomp me as I rolled away.

As I came to my feet I saw he was having trouble making his right leg hold him up. And the blood obscured his vision. And he was gagging and wheezing. But he was coming on, and I wanted no part of him. I had lost the edge of my reflexes. I was halfway aware of the whirling blue lights of the cop car outside, and of men moving smartly through the doorway.

"Cal!" some man yelled. "Cal, damn you!"

Then they walloped the back of his head with a hickory stick. They rang the hard wood off the skull bone. He tottered and turned and pawed at them, and they moved aside and hit him again. He puddled down, slowly, still smiling, with the unbloodied eye turning upward until only the white showed.

One of the officers rolled the limp hulk face down, brought the hands around behind, and pressed the cuffs onto the wrists. He said, "Hoo-wee, Ralph. He do have a stink onto him. We want him riding in with us?"

"Not after the last time we don't."

Jason, who had helped us dock, was kneeling on the floor. He had lifted Mrs. Birdsong into a sitting position. Her head was a little loose on her neck, and her eyes were vacant. He was gentle with her, murmuring comfort to her.

"She okay, Jason?" an officer asked.

"I . . . I guess I'm all right," she said.

"How about you?" he asked me.

I worked my arms, massaged the back of my neck. My head was clearing the rest of the way, taking me out of slow motion. I felt of my forehead. It was beginning to puff. "He hit me one good lick."

"Why?"

"I haven't the faintest idea. I was checking in."

"He brought his boat in a little while ago," Jason said. He helped Cindy Birdsong to her feet. She pulled free of him and walked over to a canvas chair and sat down, looking gray-green under her heavy tan.

"Want to prefer charges?" the officer asked.

I looked at Cindy. She lifted her head and gave a little negative shake.

"I guess not."

The cop named Ralph sighed. He was young and heavy, with a Csonka mustache. "Arthur and me figured he might head back here. We've been trying to catch up with him for two hours, Cindy. We got all the charges we need. He run two cars off the road. He busted up Dewey's Pizza Shack and broke Dewey's arm for him."

"Oh, God."

"Earlier he was out to the Gateway Bar on Route Seven-Eighty-Seven, and he pure beat the living hell out of three truck drivers. They're in the hospital. I'm sorry, Cindy. It's since he got on the sauce so bad. And being on probation from the last time . . . look, he's going to have to spend some time in the county jail. I'm sorry, but that's the way it is."

She closed her eyes. She shuddered. Suddenly Cal Birdsong began to snore. There was a little puddle of blood under his face. The ambulance arrived. The cuffs were removed. The attendants handled him with less difficulty than I expected. Cindy got a sweater and her purse and rode along with the snoring gigantic drunk, after asking Jason to take care of things.

Jason leaned on the counter and said, "He was okay. You know? A nice guy up to about a year ago. I've worked here since they opened. He drank, but like anybody else. Then he started drinking more and more. Now it makes him crazy. She's really a very great person. It's really breaking her heart, you know?"

"Booze sneaks up on people."

"It's made him crazy. The things he yells at her."

"I heard some of them."

The part of his face not covered by the Jesus beard turned redder. "She's not like that at all. I don't know what it is with him."

"Where do they live?"

"Oh, right over there, in this end unit in the motel. They built the motel the same time as the marina, and leased it out, and in the lease they get to use the unit at this end, a little bigger than the others. Cal inherited some money and they bought this piece of waterfront and put up the marina and the motel. But they could lose it if it keeps up this way."

He went and got a mop and a pail and swabbed up the blood. While he was at it he mopped the rest of the floor. A good man.

I stepped around the wet parts and went back to the *Flush*. Meyer was annoyed. Where had I been? What had happened to my forehead? What were we going to do about lunch?

I told him how I'd happened to meet the Birdsongs. Lovely couple.

When we went to get a car and get lunch, I saw a different fellow in the office. This one was beardless and smaller and rounder, but just as muscular.

"Jason here?"

"He went to lunch. Can I help you?"

"I'm McGee. We're in Slip Sixty."

"Oh, sure. We talked on the phone. I'm Oliver Tarbeck. I understand you and Cal went around and around."

"Sort of. If I can get a rental car, where should I park it?"

"In that row over there where it says Marina Only. If it's full, come here to the office and we'll work something out."

"Place to eat?"

"A block to the left, on this side. Gil's Kitchen. It's okay for lunch."

We had lunch first. The place wasn't okay for lunch. Gil had a dirty kitchen. A fried egg sandwich was probably safe. We went from there to Texaco, which had some sort of budget rental deal, and I tested to see if I could get my knees under the wheel of the yellow Gremlin before giving him the Diners Card. Nobody will take a cash deposit on a car any more. It forces everybody into cards. As the world gets bigger, it gets a lot duller.

I asked him if he could tell me how to find Junction Park. He gave me a city map and marked the route.

The Gremlin did not have air, but it had some big vents. Meyer read the map and called the turns. It was easy to see the shape and history of Bayside, Florida. There had been a little town on the bay shore, a few hundred people, a sleepy downtown with live oaks and Spanish moss. Then International Amalgamated Development had moved in, bought a couple of thousand acres, and put in shopping centers, town houses, condominiums, and rental apartments, just south of town. Next had arrived Consolidated Construction Enterprises and done the same thing north of town. Smaller operators had done the same things on a smaller scale west of town. When downtown decayed, the town fathers widened the streets and cut down the shade trees in an attempt to look just like a shopping center. It didn't work. It never does. This was instant Florida, tacky and stifling and full of ugly and spurious energies. They had every chain food-service outfit known to man, interspersed with used-car lots and furniture stores.

Junction Park was inland and not far from a turnpike interchange. It had been laid out with some thought to system and symmetry. Big steel buildings were placed in herringbone pattern, with big truck docks and parking areas. The tall sign at the entrance said that Superior Building Supplies was the fourth building on the right.

I parked and told Meyer to see what he could pick up at the neighbor establishments, a heating and air-conditioning outfit, a ladder plant, and a boatbuilder.

I went into the front office of Superior Building Supplies. A slender and pretty girl in a dress made of ticking was taking file folders out of a metal file and putting them into a cardboard storage file. She straightened and looked at me and said in a nasal little voice, "It isn't until Monday."

"What isn't?"

"The special sale of everything. They're taking inventory over the weekend. And right now."

"Going out of business?"

She went over to her desk and picked up a can of Coke and drank several swallows. She gave me a long look of appraisal.

"We sure the hell are," she said finally. She shook her gingery hair back and wiped her pretty mouth with the back of her hand, then belched like any boy in the fifth grade.

A man came through the open door that led back to the warehouse portion. He had a clipboard in his hand. He was sweaty and he had a smudge of grease on his forehead. Lots of red-brown hair, carefully sprayed into position. Early thirties. Outdoor look. Western shirt with a lot of snaps and zippers. Whipcord pants. Boots. A nervous harried look and manner.

"We're not open for business, friend. Sorry. Joanna, find me the invoices on that redwood fencing, precut, huh?"

"Cheez, I keep telling you and telling you, it was Carrie who knew where all that—"

"Carrie isn't here to help us, goddammit. So shake your ass and start looking."

"Listen, Harry, I don't even know if I'm going to get paid for this time I'm putting in, right?"

"Joanna, honey, of course you'll get your pay. Come on dear. *Please* find the invoices for me?"

She gave him a long dark stare, underlip protruding. "Buster, you've been talking just a little too much pore-mouth. Just a little too much. And you've been getting evil with me too often, hear? I think you better go doodle in your hat. I'm going to go get my hair done. I might come back and I might retire. Who knows?"

She slung her big leather purse over her shoulder. He tried to block her way to the door. He was begging, pleading, insisting. She paid no attention to him. There was no expression on her face. When he took hold of her arm she wrenched away and left, and the glass door swung shut.

Harry went over to a big desk and sat in the large red leather chair. He closed his eyes and pinched the bridge of his nose. He sighed and looked at me and frowned. "Friend, we are still not open for business. We are even less open than we were. Let me give you some sound advice. Never hump the help. They get uppity. They take advantage."

"I came by to ask about Carrie Milligan."

"She used to work here. She's dead. What's your interest?"

"I heard she was killed. I'm a friend of hers from Fort Lauderdale."

"Didn't she used to live there?"

A bare-chested young man in jeans came out of the warehouse area and held up two big bolts. "Mr. Hascomb, you want I should count every damn one of these things? There's thousands!"

"Hundreds. Count how many in five pounds and then weigh all we got. That'll be close enough."

The boy left, and Harry Hascomb shook his head and said, "It's hard to believe she's dead. She worked day before yesterday. That's her desk over there. It happened so sudden. She really held this place together. She was a good worker, Carrie was. What did you say you want?"

"She came to see me two weeks ago. In Fort Lauderdale."

He was so still I wondered if he was holding his breath. He licked his lips and swallowed and said, "Two weeks ago?"

"Does that mean anything?"

"Why should it mean anything?"

I did not know where to go from here. The loan of money seemed all at once frail and implausible. I needed to find a better direction. "She came to see me because she was in trouble."

"Trouble? What kind of trouble?"

"She wanted to leave something with me for safekeeping. It happened it wasn't the best time for me to try to take care of anything for anybody. There are times you can, and times you shouldn't. I hated to say I couldn't. I was very fond of Carrie Milligan."

"Everybody was. What did she want you to keep?"

"Some money."

"How much?"

"She didn't say. She said it was a lot. When I heard about her being killed in that accident, I began to wonder if she'd found anybody to hold the money. Would you know anything about anything like that?"

Once again Harry went into his motionless trance, looking over my shoulder and into the faraway distance. It took him a long time. I wondered what he was sorting, weighing, appraising.

At last he shook his head slowly. "My God, I wouldn't have believed it. She must have been in on it."

"In on what?"

He undid a snap and a zipper and fingered a cigarette out of his Western pocket, popped it against a thumbnail, lit it and blew out a long plume of smoke. "Oh, shit, it's an old story. It happens all the time. You never expect it to happen to you."

"What happened?"

"What's your name again?"

"McGee. Travis McGee."

"Don't ever go partners with anybody, McGee. That's my second piece of advice for you today. Jack and I had a good thing going here. My good old partner, Jack Omaha. It wasn't exactly a fantastic gold mine, but we lived very well for quite a few years. And then the ass fell right off the construction business. We had to cut way back. Way way back. Trying to hold out until conditions improve. I think we might have made it. Things were looking a little bit better. I've always been the sales guy and Jack was the office guy. Anyway, he took off two weeks ago last Tuesday. On May fourteenth. Know what he was doing before he took off? Selling off warehouse stock at less than cost. Letting the bills pile up. Turning every damned thing into money. The auditors are trying to come up with the total figure. I'm a bankrupt. Good old Jack. Come to think of it, I guess he had to have Carrie's help to clean the place out. She only worked two days that week. Monday and Friday. Went out sick Monday afternoon. Came back in Friday. That was the day I finally decided Jack hadn't just gone fishing, that maybe he was gone for good. When did you see Carrie?"

"Thursday."

"It figures. I never figured her for anything like that. Even though she and Jack did have something going. No great big thing. It was going on for maybe three years, like ever since she started working for us. Just a little something on the side now and then. An overnighter. What we used to do, we'd send the girls, Carrie and Joanna, on another flight up to Atlanta, and then Jack and me would go up to catch the Falcons and stay in the HJ's next to the stadium. Just some laughs."

"And you think that was the money Carrie wanted me to keep for her?"

"Where else would she get it? Maybe Jack wanted her to run away with him. He was more hooked than she was, you know. Think of it this way. She helps him and gets a nice piece of change, and everybody thinks Jack took it all. When the dust settles, she can get the money and who'd know the difference?"

"Except she's dead."

"Yes, there's that. I want to make one thing clear, McGee. If you come across that money it belongs right here in this business. It was stolen from this business. It was stolen from me, and if you find it, it belongs right here."

"I'll keep that in mind."

He squashed his cigarette out. "None of this had to happen," he said softly. "I wake up in the night and think about it. If I'd had the sense when the money was rolling in, I would have put it in a safe place. Instead I farted it away on boats and cars and houses. If I'd kept it, I could have bought Jack out when things got slow. I could have squeaked through. In the night I think about it and I get sweaty and I feel like my gut was full of sharp rocks."

"What will happen?"

"I have to sell off what we've got left and throw it in the pot. It gets divided up among the creditors. I guess I'll lose the house too, maybe the cars. Then I'll start hitting my friends for a job. That son of a bitch said he was going fishing Tuesday and he'd be in Wednesday, and he said he had some money lined up to tide us over. I wanted to believe him. By Friday I got worried. I got some phone calls about bills I thought were paid. I called Chris. Jack's wife. She didn't know where the hell he was. She thought he was off in the boat somewhere. I phoned the marina and the boat was tied up there, nobody aboard. You know what? I just remembered. I had Carrie check out the bank accounts. She acted like she hated to tell me he had cleaned them out. He'd left ten bucks in each of them. He's a wanted man. I brought charges. I signed papers. It was on the news. I hope they find the son of a bitch, and I hope he has a lot of money left when they find him."

"You never thought Carrie was involved?"

"Not until you told me about her being in Lauderdale when I thought she was sick in bed. Not until you told me she wanted you to hold a lot of money for her. I swear. I mean I thought Jack was smarter than let some girl in on a thing like that. I wouldn't ever give Joanna any kind of leverage. I guess it was just that she kept a close enough eye on the books, he couldn't work it without her help. And, knowing that, she cut herself in pretty good. Maybe she was afraid Jack might come back to her for the money."

"Did you case her as a thief?"

"Her! I thought I was surrounded by friends. I guess they decided that since the business was going to fold no matter what anybody did, the thing to do was grab the goodies and run. Like maybe running into a burning motel and grabbing a wallet. Shit, maybe I would have cleaned the place out first if I'd thought of it before Jack did. And if I knew how. I wonder where Jack is now. Brazil?"

For once Meyer followed my standing instructions. He came in and folded his arms and leaned against the wall beside the door. He didn't say a word.

"We're closed," Harry told him.

I said, "He's with me."

Harry stared at him. Meyer stared back, letting his underlip and his eyelids sag. With all that hair and with that inch of simian forehead he looked so baleful as to be almost subhuman. Of course the effect is ruined if he opens his professorial mouth.

Harry swallowed and said, "Oh. Uh . . . what kind of work are you in, Mr. McGee?"

He rolled a yellow pencil under his palm, the flat sides clicking against the top of the desk. I let him roll it four times before I said, "Oh, I guess you could call it investments."

He smiled too brightly. "Want to buy a nice building supply business?"

I gave it a slow four count while the smile faded.

"No."

The kid came out of the warehouse again. "For Chrissake, there's supposed to be almost two dozen wheelbarras and I can't find a good goddamn one out there."

"Wait a second," Harry said. He took a sheet of letterhead, turned it over. and with a marking pen printed C L O S E D on it, and put pieces of Scotch tape on the corners. He stood up and said to me, "Nice to have met you, Mr. McGee."

"I'll stay in touch," I said. It didn't seem to make him happy.

After we left I looked back and saw him tape the sign to the inside of the glass door.

Meyer said, "What kind of fantasy were you selling him in there?"

"I was making it up as I went along. I was throwing in stuff to keep him talking. I dropped the loan idea."

As I drove slowly back toward town, I briefed Meyer on what I had learned. Then it was his turn. He gave it such a long dramatic pause, I knew he had done well. Why shouldn't he do well? I have busted my gut to learn how to make people open up. Meyer was born with it. A loving empathy shines out of those little bright-blue eyes. Strangers tell him things they have never told their husband or their priest.

He said that the secretary to the president of the Bayside Ladder Company, Inc., was one Betty Joller and, being Carrie Milligan's best friend, Betty was all racked up over the accident. Once upon a time Betty and Carrie and girls named Flossie Speck and Joanna Freeler had shared a little old frame house on the waterfront, at 28 Mangrove Lane. When Carrie moved out, they had gotten another girl to share rent and expenses. Meyer couldn't recall the new girl's name.

Anyway, Carrie Milligan was at the Rucker Funeral Home on Florida Boulevard, and there was to be a memorial service for her tomorrow, Saturday morning, at eleven o'clock. The sister, Susan Dobrovsky, was down from Nutley. She had arrived late last night. Betty Joller had picked her up at the airport and taken her to the Holiday Inn.

"You did well!" I told him. "Very very well."

It made him beam with pleasure.

I found 1500 Seaway Boulevard. I reminded him that Carrie had lived in 38B. I dropped him off and told him to see what he could get from the neighbors, and then work his own way back to Westway Harbor, and wait for me there if I wasn't back yet.

5

THE OMAHA house was in a fairly new subdivision called Carolridge. The developer had bulldozed it clean in his attempt to turn it from flatlands to slightly rolling contours. The new trees were all growing as fast as they could. In twenty years, when the block houses were moldering away, the shade would be pleasant and inviting. But in the mid-afternoon heat, all the houses sat baking white in the sun, and the spray heads made rainbows against immature gardenia bushes.

There were two cars in the carport at the Omaha place, and a fairly new cream-colored Oldsmobile in the driveway. A little wrought-iron sign was stuck into the parched grass, spelling out THE OMAHAS.

They give the development houses names. This was probably called The Executive or The Diplomat. It looked like eighty to ninety thousand, the top of the line for the neighbourhood. Purchase would guarantee membership in the Carolridge Golf and Country Club. You could read the house from the outside. Three bedrooms, three and a half baths, colonial kitchen, game room, cathedral ceilings, patio pool, fiberglass screening.

I pushed the button and heard the distant chimes inside. Bugs keened in the heat. Some little girls went creaking and grinding past on their Sears ten-speeds, giggling. Somebody was running some kind of lawn machinery three houses away. A cardinal was sitting on a wire, saying *T-bird, T-bird, T-bird-cool, cool, cool.* I pushed the button again. And finally again. Just as I was about to give up, a woman opened the door. She had a broad, coarse, pretty face. She wore fresh lipstick, a sculptured blond wig, tie-dye jeans, and a white sunback blouse with no sleeves.

"Mrs. Omaha?"

"Yes. We were out in the back. I hope you haven't been ringing the doorbell long?"

"Not very long."

"I didn't know you'd come so soon. What happens is I keep getting a dial tone all the time, even when I'm trying to talk to somebody." She had a thin little-girl voice. She had the dazed glazed manner of someone awakened from deep sleep. Her mouth was puffy, her eyes heavy. The fresh lipstick missed its mark at one corner of her mouth. The sculptured wig was slightly off center. There was a red suck mark on the side of her throat, slowly disappearing as I looked at it.

"I'm not from the phone company," I said.

Her gaze sharpened. "Oh, boy, you better not try telling me you're selling something. You just better not try that."

"My name is McGee. Travis McGee from Fort Lauderdale. A friend of Carrie Milligan."

She was puzzled. "So what? What do you want here?"

"Did I come at a bad time?"

"Brother!"

"Suppose I come back later?"

"What for? Carrie is dead, right? Jack took off. Let's say they were very very good friends and I couldn't care less."

"I was talking to Harry over at Junction Park. He says Jack cleaned out the partnership accounts on May fourteenth. Carrie came down to Lauderdale to see me on the sixteenth. She was jumpy. She thought she was being followed. She gave me some money to keep for her."

"How much?"

"Maybe some other time would be . . . ."

"Come on in, Mr. Gee. It's real hot this afternoon, isn't it?"

I followed her through the foyer to the long living room. She filled the rear of the stretch jeans abundantly. As she walked she reached up and patted the wig. The draperies were pulled shut. The subdued daylight came from the outdoor terrace area where, through the mesh of the drapery fabric, I could see a screened swimming pool as motionless as lime Jell-O in the white glare.

A tall and slender man stood in front of a mirror, combing his dark hair down with spread fingers. He wore a pair of quiet plaid slacks and a white shirt. His necktie hung untied. Over the back of a nearby chair I saw a dark blazer with silver buttons.

He said, "Honey, I'll get in touch again about the . . ." He spotted me in the mirror. He whirled and said, "Who the hell are you?"

"This is Mr. Gee, Freddy."

"McGee," I said. "Travis McGee."

"This here is Fred Van Harn, my lawyer," Chris explained.

I put my hand out. He hesitated and then shook hands and gave me a very pleasant smile. "How do you do?"

"Honey, I asked him in because he says he's got some of the money. Maybe he's got all of it. Tell him he has to give it to me, dear. Mr. McGee, it's my money."

I looked at her in astonishment. "I haven't got any money!"

"You said Carrie gave it to you to keep for her!"

"She did, but I gave it right back. I couldn't accept the responsibility."

"How much was it?" Chris Omaha demanded.

"I'm sure I wouldn't have the slightest idea. She said it was a lot. She didn't say how much. What is a lot to one person is not a lot to another person."

Chris said, "Oh, God damn everything." She plumped herself down on a fat hassock which hissed as she sat on it.

Freddy said, "Do you know who did agree to keep the money for her?"

"She didn't say who she was going to try next."

"Where did this happen? And when?"

"On Thursday, May sixteenth, at about three or four in the morning aboard my houseboat moored at Bahia Mar in Fort Lauderdale."

"Why would she come to you?"

"Perhaps because she trusted me. We were old and good friends. I loaned her my houseboat for her honeymoon."

Freddy had long lashes, rather delicate features, olive skin. His eyes were a gentle brown, his manner ingratiating.

"Why did you come here, Mr. McGee?"

"I had a long talk with Mr. Hascomb. I just thought Mrs. Omaha would like to know about Mrs. Milligan coming to me. I thought it might answer some questions about her husband."

"You wouldn't listen to me, would you?" the woman said to Freddy in a whiny and irritating voice. "I told you that Milligan slut had to be in on it somehow, but you wouldn't listen to me. I happen to know as a fact that Jack was screwing her for years, even though he didn't know I knew, and—"

"Be quiet, Chris."

"You can't tell me to be quiet! You know what I think? He cleaned out the business and mortgaged everything in sight, this house and even the boat, and she was going to run off with him, but she probably had some boy friend and they decided it was safer and easier to chunk my husband on the head and throw him into—"

He moved close to her. "Shut *up*, Chris!"

"I can put two and two together even if you can't, Freddy, and let me tell you one thing—"

She didn't tell him one thing. He was one very fast fellow. He had a sinewy hand and a long whippy arm and a very nice clean pivot. He slapped her so fast and so hard I thought for one crazy moment he had shot her with a small-caliber handgun. It knocked her completely off the hassock. She landed on her hip and rolled over onto her shoulder and ended up face down on the carpeting. He got to her quickly, turned her, and pulled her up to a sitting position. Her eyes were crossed. The impact area was white as milk. I knew it would turn pink, then red, and finally purple. She was going to be lopsided for quite a few days. A little trickle of blood ran from the corner of her mouth down her chin.

He sat on his heels, holding her hand, and said, "Darling, when your attorney tells you to be quiet, there might be a very good reason for it. So you have to learn to be still when he tells you to."

"Freddy," she said in a broken voice.

He pulled her up to her feet and turned her toward a doorway and gave her a little push. "Go in and lie down, darling. I'll come in and say good-bye in a few minutes. Close the door, please."

She did as ordered. He turned mildly toward me and said, "Now let's understand where you fit, Mr. McGee. You just wanted to get involved?"

"Doing my duty as a citizen."

"I'm familiar with your type. The smell of money brings people like you out of the woodwork. I can't think of a way you can work any kind of a con in this situation. So give up and go home."

"You're a familiar type too. I saw the way you tied that tie. Very quick and neat. Ready Freddy, servicing another client. I bet you're in and out of those clothes as often as a fashion model."

I saw the little flare behind his eyes and hoped he would try me. I tried to look smaller and slower than I am. Finally he smiled and looked at a microthin gold watch gold-clamped to a lean and hairy wrist.

"With a deposition at four o'clock, there's no time for schoolyard games, my friend."

"Nor will there ever be, eh?"

A sudden flush made him look healthier, and then pallor turned him gray-green. "I think you'd better leave, McGee. Now!"

So I left that enchanting place. Pale shag, silk lampshades, velvet wing chairs, brocade, imitation Tiffany stained glass, Japanese lacquer, gilt mirror frames. Somehow like a matinee in a department store. Van Harn looked about thirty, or a shade under. The lady looked well over. They were consenting adults, consenting to afternoon games in the tangly bed under the long exhalation of the air conditioning.

As I backed out a phone truck pulled up. I smiled and waved at him and wondered what kind of reception he'd get. Good luck, fella. Must be an interesting line of work.

It was quarter to four. The yellow Gremlin was hot enough to bake glaze on pottery.The steering wheel was almost, not quite, too hot to touch. I stopped wondering what to do next and ran around for a mile or two trying to get cool in a hot wind.

I found a shopping center and discovered that they had left some giant oaks in the parking lot. This runs counter to the sworn oath of all shopping center developers. One must never deprive thy project of even one parking slot. And, wonder of wonders, there was an empty slot under one tree, in the shade. As I got out of the Gremlin, a cruising granny glowered at me from the air-conditioned, tinted-blue depths of her white Continental.

I found pay phones in a big Eckerd Drug, the phone stations half hidden by huge piles of pitchman's merchandise.

At the Holiday Inn they had a Miss Dobrovsky registered in Room 30, but she did not answer the phone. I looked up Webbel, who had driven the truck. There were about fifteen of them, but no Roderick. I wondered why Susan Dobrovsky would stay in the Holiday Inn instead of in Carrie's apartment. Squeamish, maybe. But sooner or later she would have to decide what to do with Carrie's personal belongings. That made me think of personal arrangements, and so I looked up the number for the Rucker Funeral Home and asked for Miss Susan Dobrovsky. After a long wait the man came back on the line and said that Miss Dobrovsky was busy with Mr. Rucker, Senior. I told him to tell her to wait there for me. Wait for McGee. Right there.

*   *   *

Rucker's Funeral Home was from the orange plaster and glass brick era. It had arches and some fake Moorish curlicues along the edge of the flat room. A small black man was listlessly rubbing a black hearse parked at the side entrance. There was a large cemented area at the side and in back where doubtless they shaped up the corteges. I saw Carrie's bright orange Datsun in the parking lot on the other side of the building. On one side of the home there was a savings and loan branch, and on the other side a defunct car wash. I stuck my yellow Gremlin beside the orange Datsun, wondering if the industrial abrasive was still in the trunk. The bright colors screamed at each other.

She was sitting on a marble bench in the hallway just inside the front door. She looked enough like Carrie so that I was able to recognize her at once. She was a taller, younger, softer version of Carrie. She had on a dark gray tailored suit, a small round hat. She carried a purse and white gloves. Her eyes were swollen and red. She looked dejected and exhausted. But she was a marvelously handsome lady.

"I'm pleased to meet you, Mr. McGee."

"Did Carrie write you about me?"

"No. It was just . . . she phoned me long distance over a week ago, one night about ten. I was getting ready for bed. She talked a whole hour. It must have cost a fortune. She was funny. She kept laughing and saying silly things. Maybe she was drinking. Anyway, she made me get a pencil and paper and write down how to get in touch with you. She said that if anything happened to her, it was important I should get in touch with you. She said I could trust you. She said you're a nice person."

"She was in a loyal minority, Miss Susan."

"I . . . I don't know what to do about this," she said. She took a sheet of letterhead paper, folded once, out of her dark plastic purse and handed it to me. It was a heavy, creamy bond, and the statement of account had been typed with a carbon-ribbon electric, flawlessly. It added up to $1677.90. It contained all manner of processing charges and service charges and mortuary overhead charges. It contained a coffin for $416 including tax, and it included an embalming fee, crematorium fee, death certification fee.

"She wanted to be cremated. It's in her will even. I can't pay all that. He has some kind of installment note he wants me to sign. He seems very nice . . . but . . ."

By being very firm with a chubby sallow fellow I gained an audience with Mr. Rucker, Senior. If you shaved Abe Lincoln and gave him a thick white Caesar hairpiece, and left the eyebrows black, you would have a reasonable duplicate of Rucker, sitting there in perpetual twilight behind his big walnut desk.

His voice was hushed, gentle, personal.

"I should be pleased to go over the billing with you, sir, item by item. Let me say I am glad the little lady has someone to help her in this time of need."

"Shall we discuss the coffin first?"

"Why not, if you wish? It is very inexpensive, as you can see."

"The decedent is to be, or has been, cremated."

"Cremation will take place this evening, I think. I can determine for sure."

"So there's no need for a coffin."

He smiled sweetly and sadly. "Ah, so many people have that misconception. It is a regulation, sir."

"Whose regulation?"

"The State of Florida, sir."

"Then you will be willing to show me the statutes which pertain?"

"Believe me, sir, it is standard practice and . . ."

"The statutes?"

"It may not be specifically spelled out in the law, but . . ."

I reached out and took the pen from his desk set and drew a thick black line through the coffin and said, "Now we're down to twelve sixty-one ninety. I see you've charged for embalming."

"Of course. And a great deal of cosmetic attention was required. There were severe facial lacerations which—"

"It wasn't ordered and is not required by law prior to cremation."

He gave me a saintly smile. "I am afraid I cannot accept your judgments on these matters, sir. I must refer them to the sister of the deceased. We must bring her in on this. I must caution you that this is a very difficult situation for her, all this petty squabbling about the account as rendered."

"It's easier on her to just go ahead and pay it?"

"This is very sad occasion for her."

"Wait right here," I said.

I went and found Susan on the bench in the hallway. I sat beside her and said, "We can cut that bill by a thousand dollars, but he thinks it will be such a rough experience for you to haggle over price, we should go ahead and pay it. What do you think?"

For a moment she was blank. Then I saw the tender jaw clamp into firmness and saw her eyes narrow. "I know what Carrie would say."

Mr. Rucker, Senior stood up behind his desk when I walked in with Susan Dobrovsky. "Do sit down, my dear. We'll try to make this as painless as we possibly—"

"What's this crap about you overcharging me a thousand dollars?" she said in a high, strident, demanding voice.

He was taken aback but he recovered quickly. "You don't quite understand. For example, it may not be absolutely legally necessary for you to purchase a casket, my dear, but I think it would be a gross disrespect to your poor sister to have her . . . tumbled into the burning chamber like some kind of . . . debris."

She braced her fists on his desk and leaned closer to him. "That is not my sister! That is a body! That *is* debris! My sister is not in there any more and there is no reason for you to . . . to try to get me to worship the empty body, damn you, you greedy old man!"

He moved around the side of the desk, his face quiet as any death mask, and said, "Excuse me. I'll have this account recomputed. It will take just a few minutes."

He went out a side door. When it was open I could hear an electric typewriter rattling away. When he closed it behind him, she turned blindly into my arms. She rolled her head against my shoulder and gave three big gulping sobs and then pulled herself together, pushed away from me, honked into a Kleenex, and tried to smile.

"Was I okay?" she asked.

"You were beautiful."

"I was pretending I was Carrie and it was me who was dead. She'd never let him take advantage. I was just so confused when he gave me the bill before."

"Is the memorial service to be here?"

"Oh, no. Betty Joller sort of arranged it. It's going to be on the beach there at Mangrove Lane where she used to live."

Rucker Senior came back into the room and tried to hand her the new billing. I reached across her and took it. It was far more specific. It came to $686.50. I noticed he had included a sixty-dollar urn, sixty-two forty with tax. I was tempted to strike it but decided it was best to let him have a minor victory.

"Here are the rings from the deceased," he said, holding out a small manila envelope. She hesitated, and I took that also and slipped it into my shirt pocket.

"Satisfactory arrangements for payment will have to be made," the man said.

I took out my money clip, slipped the currency out of it, and counted out seven one-hundred-dollar bills on the front edge of his desk. "We'll need thirteen fifty in change and your certification on this bill, Mr. Rucker."

He expressed his opinion by looking most carefully at each bill, back and front. He made change from his own pocket and receipted the bill. *Paid in Full. B. J. Rucker, Sr.*

"You may pick up the urn here between one and two tomorrow afternoon," he said.

I nodded. There were no good-byes. We walked out.

Out in the afternoon sunshine of the parking lot, she swayed against me, leaned heavily on my arm as we walked. She shook her head and straightened up and lengthened her stride.

"He had me go back in there and see her," she said. "I thought there was some mistake. Her face wasn't the right shape even. She looked like she was made of wax. He showed me how the inside of the casket is all quilted, the kind he was selling me. Would he have really had it burned up, or would he have saved it for the next person?"

"I think B.J. would have had it burned up."

The lower angle of the sun had stretched casuarina shadows across our two bright little cars. Before she unlocked the Datsun she turned to face me and said, "About that money in there, I'll be able to . . ."

"It was your money."

"What do you mean?"

"I owed it to Carrie."

"Is that true? Is that really true?"

"Really true."

"How much did you owe her?"

"It's a long story."

"Well, I'd like to know."

"She told you to trust me."

"Yes . . .?"

"Trust me not to tell you now, and trust me to have good reasons not to tell you. Okay?"

She looked at me for a long moment and then slowly nodded. "Okay, Mr. McGee." Her hair was long, and a couple of shades darker than Carrie's cropped silvery mop. The face was as round as Carrie's, the cheekbones high and heavy, but her eyes had more of a Slavic tilt, and their color was a seagreen-gray.

I made her try calling me Trav, and after three times it came easier and she smiled.

"How long are you going to stay?"

"Well, I guess until the lawyer says it's okay to go back to New Jersey. I've got to sort out all her stuff in that apartment. It's in a terrible mess. Somebody broke in and tore up the furniture and rugs and emptied everything out on the floor."

"When did this happen?"

"So much is happening, I'm getting confused on the dates. She was killed Wednesday night. Betty Joller was in bed and heard it on the eleven o'clock news. Betty, being her best friend, got dressed and drove to the apartment figuring my phone number would be in Carrie's phone index someplace, and I should be told. Betty has a key to the apartment that Carrie gave her. Betty got to the apartment about midnight and found it all in such a mess it took her a half hour to find my phone number. She was crying to hard I couldn't understand what she was trying to tell me. And when she did . . . wow, it was like the sky falling down. Carrie was seven years older, and I saw her just once in the last six years, when she came back to Nutley five years ago for our mother's funeral. I had no idea it would hit me so hard. I guess it's because she was the only close family I had left. There's some cousins I've never seen since I was a baby."

"Did Betty Joller report it to the police?"

"I don't really know. I guess she would have. I mean it would be a normal thing to tell the police about it. I told the lawyer about it, and he asked me if there was any specific thing we could report as being taken in the robbery, and I said maybe Betty could figure out what was missing, that I wouldn't know."

"Who's your lawyer?"

"He's a good friend of a girl that lives at 28 Mangrove Lane. I keep forgetting his name. But I've got his card here. Here. Frederick Van Harn. He just has to straighten out about the will and the car and all that. I guess it will be okay because he is the one who drew up the will for her. After she broke up with Ben she wanted to be sure he didn't get a dime that was hers if anything happened to her. Ben was at the funeral too, five years ago, but I can't remember him at all." She looked at her watch. "Hey, I've got to get going. Betty is coming over to the Inn, and we're going to work it all out about tomorrow. You're coming, aren't you?"

"Of course."

She drove away and I drove back to Westway Harbor.

6

I PARKED my rental in one of the reserved slots. As I walked past the office toward the docks, Cindy Birdsong came to the door and said, "Can I speak to you a moment, Mr. McGee?"

"Of course."

She had changed to a white sunback dress, and she wore heels, which put her over the six-foot line. A big brown lady with great shoulders and other solid and heavy accessories. And a mighty cool blue eye, and a lot of composure and pride.

"I want to apologize to you for the trouble my husband gave you this noon. I am very sorry it happened."

"It's perfectly all right, Mrs. Birdsong."

"It's not all right. It was a very ugly scene. If they release him on bail, I am sure he will want to apologize personally. I'm going to visit him this evening in the hospital, and I know he will be very ashamed of himself."

"He had a few over the limit."

"A few! He was pig drunk. He never used to get like . . . well, I shouldn't burden you with our personal history. Thank you for giving me the time. If there is anything you need we are . . . always anxious to serve our customers. Oh, and I meant to thank you for not signing a complaint." Her smile was inverted and bitter. "There are enough of those to go around as it is."

"If there's any way I can help . . ."

She blinked rapidly. "Thank you very much. Very much."

*   *   *

Meyer was aboard *The Busted Flush*, dressing after having just gotten back from taking a shoreside shower. I broke open a pair of cold beers and took him one and sat on the guest stateroom bed and watched him put on a fresh white guayabera.

"Fifteen Hundred Seaway's one of those bachelor boys and girls places," Meyer said. "Everybody seems to laugh a lot. It's very depressing. Eighty small apartments. There's a kind of . . . watchful anxiety about those people. It's as if they're all in spring training, trying out for the team, all trying to hit the long ball, trying to be a star. And in a sense, they're all in training. They're pretty trim and brown. Very mod in the clothes and hair departments. They're all delighted that there's a long waiting list for Fifteen Hundred. Pools and saunas and a gym. Four-channel sound systems. Health fads. Copper bracelets. *The Joy of Sex* on each and every coffee table, I would guess. Water beds, biofeedback machines. There doesn't seem to be any kind of murky kinky flavor about them. No group perversion scenes. Just a terrible urgency about finding and maintaining an orgasm batting average acceptable to the peer group. Their environment is making terrible demands upon them. I bet their consumption of vitamins and health foods is extraordinary."

We went up onto the sun deck and sat in the shade of the big canopy over the topside controls. "It doesn't sound like the kind of place where Carrie would want to live."

"No. It doesn't. It isn't. I didn't say why I was asking about her. I imagine they assumed I'm some kind of relative of hers. There was a coolness toward her. They thought she was standoffish, too much of a private person. She didn't get into the swing of things. I guess the pun is intentional."

"An outcast in Swingleville, eh?"

"Not exactly. More like a special friend of the management. The management is Walter J. Demos. He owns it and manages it and is sort of a den mother to all. He lives there, in the biggest apartment. He personally approves or disapproves of every applicant. He won't accept tenants who are too young or too old. He settles quarrels and disputes. He collects the rents, repairs plumbing, plants flowers, and he laughs a lot."

"How old a man?"

"I wouldn't want to guess. He looks like a broader, browner version of Kojak. He has a deep voice and a huge laugh. He is a very charming and likable man. He is very popular with his tenants. He is Uncle Walter. I think Uncle Walter is a smart businessman. The rents start at three hundred and seventy-five a month, and his occupancy rate is one hundred percent. By the way, he told me about Carrie's apartment being burglarized the same night she—"

"I heard about it. Was the door forced?"

"No. The layout is arranged for maximum privacy. If you go from your apartment to visit somebody, there's very little chance of your being seen. And it seems to be local custom to have a batch of keys made and hand them out to your friends."

"How long had she lived there?"

"Four months only. I picked up the rumor that Uncle Walter had moved her to the top of the list. They all seemed miffed about it. Jealous, almost. They don't want Uncle Walter to have a special girl."

"Did you get the feeling from him that she was special to him?"

"He seemed very upset about it, about her being killed. He said all the usual things. She had the best years of her life ahead of her. A pointless tragedy. And so forth."

"Seems like high rent for Carrie to pay."

"That's something that kept cropping up in conversation. Those tenants seem to feel they have to give a continual sales talk about the joys of living in Fifteen Hundred. They claim that because they don't have any urge to go out at night or away for vacations, it really saves money to live there. The little shopping center is so close you can walk over and wheel the stuff home. The ones who work close, some of them at least, have given up cars and use bikes. It's fascinating, in a way. A village culture. Maybe it's part of the shape of the world to come, Travis."

"Let us hope not."

"You seem a bit sour."

I stretched and sighed. "Carrie is in an upholstered box at Rucker's, her face reassembled with wax and invisible stitching. Tonight they will tote her off to the electric furnace and turn her into a very small pile of dry gray powder. So I am depressed."

"I don't think I can add anything of interest. Carrie didn't make any close friends there."

"Pun intended?"

"Not that time. Maybe you're not as sour as you act?"

"I'll tell you my adventures," I said. And did.

When I had finished he said, "I suppose we'll learn that young Mr. Van Harn is the attorney for Superior Building Supplies, which would account for his doing Carrie's will and being recommended to the sister, and being with Mrs. Omaha."

"I had the same feeling."

"What next?"

"We have a drink with a little more authority, and then we find a place to eat."

"Please don't give Gil's Kitchen another chance."

"And you call yourself fair?"

"You wouldn't!"

"You are right. I wouldn't. But between the drinking and the eating, let's go see where Carrie was killed."

*   *   *

By seven o'clock we had found the approximate place where it had happened. County Road 858 was called Avenida de Flores. It was an old concrete road, the slabs cracked and canted. Weeds stood tall on the shoulders. The shoulders slanted down into overgrown drainage ditches. There were a few old frame houses, spaced far apart, on the west side of the road. On the east side was a grove, with high rusty hurricane fencing installed on the other side of the drainage ditch. I went on out past the city limits sign and turned around in the parking area of a new shopping plaza and came back, driving slowly.

I pulled off into the weeds of the shoulder, car at a big list to starboard, and stopped.

"For what?" Meyer asked.

I nodded toward the house two hundred feet ahead. An old man was riding a little blue power mower back and forth across the big expanse of front yard. "We just get out and start looking up and down the shoulder, and he'll come over and tell us all."

That is one of the few bonuses when looking into a fatal accident. People do love to talk about it.

In a few minutes I heard the mower cough, sputter, and die. Cars whooshed by, whipping the weeds around, blasting the hot wind against us. I looked up and saw the old man fifteen feet away, walking smartly, his face aglow with the terrible delight of someone loaded down with ghastly details.

"Hey, you wouldn't be looking for the spot where that there Mulligan woman got killed Wednesday night, would you?"

I straightened up and said, "Milligan. The name was Milligan, Carolyn Dobrovsky Milligan, Fifteen Hundred Seaway Boulevard, Bayside, tag number Twenty-four D, thirteen thirteen. Her name was not Mulligan, it was Milligan."

I used the voice and manner of the small-bore bureaucrat, petulant, precise, and patronizing. I needed no further identification as far as he was concerned. I was one of Them.

"Milligan, Mulligan, Malligan. Shoot, you're looking on the wrong side of the road is what you're doing."

"I doubt that," I said. "I doubt that very much."

He peered up at me. "Well, by Jesus H. Sufferin' Christ, you are something, you are! You may know her name right, but you don't know the first goddamn thing about the rest of it."

"I think he might be able to give us a little help," Meyer said, right on cue.

"Your partner here has got a little bit of sense," the old man said. "My name is Sherman Howe, and I've lived in that house there twelve years now, and you wouldn't believe the number of idiots get smashed up and killed on this straight piece of road in the nighttime. One drunk son of a bitch about six months ago—see over there where that fence by the grove is fixed up new?—he come off the road and went through that fence, and he went into that grove a hundred and ten feet—I paced it off—went weaving amongst the trees until he zigged instead of zagged and hit one dead center and mushed his skull on the windshield, dead as a fried mule, I keep my clothes on a chair by my bed and I keep a big flashlight handy, and when I hear that crunching in the night, I dress fast and come see what help I can give because that's the Christian thing to do. If it's bad, I blink the light back at the house here, and Mabel is watching for it, and she phones for the ambulance, and that's exactly what happened Wednesday night, and I was down here before that poor boy had even found the body, so don't tell me what side of the road it was on, mister. I know what side. Come with me. Watch out, now, you don't get yourself killed. Nobody slows down. Nobody gives a shit any more what happens to anybody else in the world. Let me see now . . . Sure. Here's where her car was. She was heading north, out of town, when she ran out of gas and pulled over onto the shoulder right here. See where she drove in? See the tracks? And the grass is still matted where the wheels set. It happened at twelve minutes after ten by my digital clock on my bed stand, and I'd just turned out the light to go to sleep. Mabel was in the living room watching the teevee. She still likes it, but it's got to the point where all that slop looks alike to me. I think the dead woman was . . . wait, follow me and I'll show you where the body was. I'm the one found it. That Webbel kid didn't have a flashlight at all. It was right about here I seen her arm kind of laying up against the side of the ditch in the grass, and the grass sort of hid the rest of her. She was right here, down in this dry ditch, her head aimed that way and her feet this way, neat as you please. Would have played hell finding her if that arm hadn't been up like it was and bare, so it caught the light from my flashlight. Sixty-five feet from the point of impact. I paced it off. Lordy, she was a mess. That whole left side of her face and head . . . Anyway, I put the light on her and that boy fainted dead away. He fell like his spine had give way on him. I put my fingers on that girl's neck and thought I felt something, but I couldn't be sure. I ran and flashed my light three times at the window where Mabel was waiting, and she phoned it in. Then there was a terrible screeching and nearly another accident on account of that Webbel kid had parked half on the road and half off, being so shocked by hitting her the way he did. His motor was still running, so I run the truck off all the way onto the shoulder and turned it off. He was sitting up by then, moaning to himself. Pretty soon I heard the sirens coming from way off. The cops got here first. Those blue lights tamed traffic down. They took flash pictures of the two cars and the body, and they measured the skid marks, which didn't start until he was right at or a little past the point where he hit her. Any fool could see it wasn't the kid's fault.''

"Would you care to explain your . . . theory, Mister Howe?''

"Theory! Goddammit, it's fact! Now you look and see that she was parked real close, too close, to the pavement. Maybe it was as far as she could get, running out of gas like that. The car lights were off. That's supposed to be what you ought to do if you are over on the grass at night, because, you leave taillights on, some dumb stupid drunken son of a bitch is going to aim right for those taillights thinking he's following you. Now the Webbel boy was driving one of those big Dodge pickups that's built like a van in the front, where the driver sits high, right over the wheels. You can see that this road is two lane and pretty narrow lanes at that. They talk about widening it, but all they do is talk. I heard them question the boy. There was a car coming the other way. He couldn't swing out around that girl's car. No room. He had to cut it pretty close. Now she must have slid across and got out the passenger side so as not to open her car door into traffic. Then she walked around the front of the car and stepped right in front of that farm truck. It sort of dented in the front right corner of that truck. Busted the right headlight, dented the metal, and so on. You could see where the post hit her head. She didn't realize a car would be so close. He said he saw her out of the corner of his eye just as he hit her. He said there wasn't anything he could have done about it, and that kid is absolutely right. He was on his way home, and my guess is she was on her way to that gas station up across from the plaza, that stays open way late. When the ambulance came the medical fellow said she was dead. Massive skull fractures, he said. But he said it would be declared a DOA and the certificate would be made out at the hospital. Let me see. They took her away, no need for sirens. They'd got her ID from her purse in the car. The keys were in the ignition. It wouldn't start. When the wrecker came, the fellow looked at the gas gauge on the woman's car, and he had a can of gas on the back of the wrecker. He put some in and it started right up. I forget who drove it away. They took it down to the City Police Station. By that time the television truck was here, but there was nothing to take pictures of. So they just got the facts and used their radio to call them in. There was no cause to hold the Webbel boy. He was too shook to drive, but by then his father and his brother had arrived, and the brother drove the truck on back home. Their place is in the northwest part of the county. I guess that's all of it. You got any other . . . theory, mister?"

"When all the facts are in, all the *pertinent* facts, Mister Howe. I'll be able to summarize."

He turned toward Meyer. "Summarize, winterize, I feel sorry for you, friend, having to work with this sorry son of a bitch." He marched away without a backward glance. When I heard the mower start up again, I looked and saw him riding solemnly back and forth in the fading light of day.

Meyer said, "You couldn't have gotten any more under hypnotherapy. What are you looking at?"

I was down on one knee in the weeds, between the matted places where the rear wheels had rested. I pointed to the place where the weeds and grass were withered and blackened. It began at a point midway between the wheels and slightly behind them. There was an area six inches in diameter and a random line half that width leading down the slope into the dry ditch, getting narrower and less evident as it approached the ditch.

"Gasoline spill will do this," I said. I dug down into the dirt with thumb and finger and pinched some of it up and sniffed it. It had a faint odor of gasoline. "I think her car fills on the left corner, aft of the wheel. But if it fills there or in the rear center, no matter how clumsy the man was who dumped gas into it, he could hardly manage to spill this much way under here without getting a lot right under where he was pouring."

"It soaked in before it got to the ditch," Meyer said.

"There had to be a lot of spill for it to run down the slope at all. It's been dry lately."

Meyer nodded. "And so she didn't stop because she ran out of gas. But it had to look as if she had a good reason for stopping. Is there some kind of drain under there, on the underside of the gas tank?"

"We'll be able to check that out. For now let's say yes."

"Am I following your scenario, Travis? X is in the car with Carrie. X is driving, let's say. He pulls off the road and stops. He picks a place a long way from any house. No street lights. He strikes her on the head with the traditional blunt object. He leans across her and opens the door. He pushes her out. The weeds are tall enough so that she would not be picked up in the lights of any passing car. He wiggles under the car with a wrench and a flashlight and opens the drain valve. When all the gas has run out, he closes the valve. He pulls her around to the front of the car, waits until he gets the right traffic situation and the right kind of oncoming vehicle, then boosts her up and walks her into the front corner of it. Then he takes off. Isn't that a little bit too much to get out of some weeds and grasses killed by gasoline? Isn't that too much of a dreadful risk?"

"Maybe it's too much. If X wears dark clothing, that would diminish the risk. He could stretch out flat beside her just ahead of the front bumper. He could look under the car for oncoming traffic heading the same way."

We went to where the front of the Datsun had been and looked at the weeds. It is too easy to let your imagination interpret the patterns.

"If so," Meyer said, "he didn't have much time to get out of sight. Too risky to go across the highway. Over the fence?"

I studied the fence line. "Under it. Where it's washed out. I think this was one very cool cat who checked his escape route first."

"Would your scenario include some telltale dark threads caught on the wire at the bottom?"

"There could have been, until you mentioned it."

I slid under the fence, on my back. Meyer stayed outside. There were inches to spare. I searched a quarter-acre area and came up with the startling conclusion that it was a very well-maintained grove. Nothing more. He could heave her into the front of the Webbel truck and spin and hit the hole before the truck could stop. Then, in dark clothing, he could melt back into the black shadows of the night and walk parallel to the fence line until it was safe to go over or under the fence.

Or, I thought as I went back under the fence, another vehicle had stopped there. Maybe a wife got nervous about a can of gas in the trunk of the family car. Dump it out this minute, dearest. Or maybe a can started leaking and somebody abandoned it there, and later somebody picked up the can, thinking it usable. Many false structures have been built from the flawed assumption of the simultaneity of seemingly related events.

As we got into the rental car, Meyer said, "We have no way of knowing that the gasoline was spilled—"

"At the same time. I just went through that."

"There are certain concepts which offend emotional logic. You have stopped beside a two-lane road at night. Traffic is light but fast. You walk to the front of your car, after sliding out on the passenger side. What are you going to do? Cross the road? Hitchhike? Open the door on the driver's side? Assume there is a good reason, do you step out, or do you look first?"

"If you are smashed, maybe you step out."

"If you are drunk, you would have opened the door on the driver's side, wouldn't you?"

"I don't know. But what the hell was she trying to do? Walk to one of those houses and phone? If so, Meyer, would she leave her purse and car keys?"

"Nice point. Now what?"

*   *   *

The wrecker stood beside the large gas station across from the entrance to the shopping center. It was a very muscular beast. It was painted bright red. It had warning lights, emergency lights, floodlights, and blinkers affixed to all available surfaces. The big tires stood chest high. The array of winches and cables and reels on the back end of it looked capable of hoisting a small tank up the side of an office building.

"Something I can do for you?" the bald sunburned man said.

"I didn't know they were making them so big."

"Mister, when you get a tractor trailer rig totaled across three lanes of an Interstate, you need something big to get it out of the way fast."

"Did that go out Wednesday night when that woman got killed just down the road there?"

His face twisted in pain. He spat and sighed. "Oh, Jesus, yes, it went out. Ray took it out. I had two guys out with flu. That goddamn Ray. You know what the payments run on this brute son of a bitch?" He kicked a high tire.

"No idea."

"Four hundred a month. A *month*. And Ray, the dummy, has to diagnose. Is he some kind of mechanic already? Hey, he says, no gas. So he puts some in. So what does that cost me? Thirty bucks' tow charge, Jesus!"

"Is he around?"

"Look, what's your interest in this thing, mister?"

"It's a case study project for the Traffic Advisory Council for the State Department of Transportation."

"Oh. Well, that's him in the far island there, checking the oil on the green Cadillac. Just don't hold him up on working the island, okay? It's money out of my pocket."

Ray was a stumpy nineteen with blue eyes empty of guile and with a face ravaged by acne.

"Gassy smell? Well, yeah. The way it was, see, I leaned inside to check the gear it was in and the brake. I was glad to see the keys there because it was in park, you know, and I was moving it to N when on account of the gassy smell inside it I looked at the gauge and seen it was empty. I turned the lights on. It's best at night, a short tow, keep the lights on, all the lights you got. I put gas in, figuring if it would run what's the sense towing it. I didn't know the boss would get his ass in such a big uproar about it, see. And I didn't even think who is going to pay for the couple gallons I put in, or the service call. That made it worse. Jesus, he's been all over me all the time since Wednesday. I'm about ready to tell him to shove his job."

I went to the boss and thanked him and said, "I have to interview the dead woman's sister. I can give her the bill for the gas and service, if you want."

He brightened up. We went into the office. He made out the bill. I looked at it and shook my head and handed it back. "Not like that, friend. Two gallons, not five. Five dollars' charge, not ten."

"So what are you, her brother? Look, the dead lady is in no shape to care what the bills are."

"Do you want to take a dead loss or fix the bill?"

"Everybody is all of a sudden getting weird," he muttered, and made out a new bill.

*   *   *

At ten o'clock we were back aboard the *Flush*, up on the sun deck under hazy stars, in two unfolded deck chairs like old tourists on a cruise ship. The events of the long day had been more abrasive than I had realized while they were happening. I felt a leaden weariness of bone and spirit.

I whapped a mosquito which tasted the side of my neck and rolled him into a tiny moist gobbet of meat and dropped him out of his life onto the deck. In many ways the Hindu is right. All life in all forms is so terribly transient there is an innocence about all acts and functions of life. Death, icy and irrevocable, is the genuine definition of reality. In my unthinking reflex I was doubtless improving the mosquito breed. If, over a millennium, man whapped every side-of-the-neck biter, maybe the mosquito race would bite only neck napes.

"Mr. McGee?" the polite voice said from the dock. I got up and walked aft to look down. There was Jason with the Jesus face and wire glasses standing under the dock light in a T-shirt with the short sleeves torn off, ragged blue-jean shorts, and a pair of boat shoes so exquisitely and totally worn out it looked as though he had wrapped his feet neatly in rags.

"Hi, Jason."

"Permission to come aboard?"

"Come on."

He came up the side ladderway like a big swift cat. He accepted a can of beer from the cooler. He had something to say, but he seemed to be puzzling out how to say it. He sat on his heels, on those brown legs bulging with big muscles.

I finally had to give him some help. "Something bothering you?"

"Sort of. I mean maybe it isn't any of my business. What I wouldn't want is her having a worse time than she's having already. Okay?"

"Her being Mrs. Birdsong."

"She's really a great person. If I could have got to the office quicker, maybe the two of us, you and me, we could have grabbed onto Cal and quieted him down. I know how he could get. Did you hit him with anything? Did you pick up anything and hit him on the head?"

"I sort of hurried him into the wall once. Ralph or Arthur rapped him on the head with a hickory stick, a couple of good licks."

"Hey! That's *right*. I forget that part. Then maybe it was from them. Look, can you tell—not you but medical doctors—can they tell which knock on the head did the most damage?"

Meyer answered. "I don't think so. Provided, of course, there's no depressed fracture or anything like that. The brain is a jelly suspended in a lot of protection, and oftentimes the greatest damage happens in the area directly opposite the point of impact. This could be in the form of a subdural hematoma, a bleeding which gradually creates enough pressure inside the brain to suppress the vital functions.''

"Well, she visited him and then went out and got something to eat and went back and found a half dozen people working on him, but he was dead. There's going to be an autopsy. She came back in terrible shape. They gave her some pills. She's asleep now. A girl friend of Oliver's is sitting with her. Bet you it was a heart attack, or maybe a stroke that didn't have anything to do with getting hit on the head.''

My neck was still sprained from being popped on the forehead. I hadn't enjoyed meeting the fellow, but had not wished him dead.

"Thanks for letting me know," I said.

"It's okay. I've been here the whole two years, you know. He was a pretty great person until he got to boozing real bad. And until just a little while ago, even though he got too drunk when he got drunk, he wouldn't drink when there was something he had to do that was best done sober. Like when Jack Omaha would hire him to captain.''

"Jack Omaha!''

He turned toward me. He was slowly and carefully folding his empty beer can the way somebody might fold a Dixie cup, turning it into a smaller and smaller wad. "You knew Jack?" he said.

"No. But I heard he took off with a lot of money.''

"That's what they say.''

"You don't believe he did it?''

"No. But that's because somebody told me he didn't.''

"Who would that be?''

"Somebody that knew him better than I did.''

"Carrie?" I said.

I heard the air whoosh out of him. He stood up. "Who the hell *are* you?''

"Carrie's friend. When she married Ben Milligan she honeymooned aboard this old barge.''

"Hey! I remember something about that. Sure. Have you got a great big shower stall aboard, and a big tub? And . . . uh . . .''

"A big bed? All three.''

He leaned his rear against the rail and stood with ankles crossed and arms folded.

"Cheez. That Ben came by a year ago. She was still living at the cottage then. She and Betty Joller and Joanna Freeler and some bird name of Flossie. How come she ever married him, I wouldn't know.''

"Nor anybody else. It happens.''

"Mister America. Mister Biceps. He was in some kind of movie deal they were making up in Jax, probably an X movie. He came down to con some money off of Carrie. He'd done it before. She didn't have any. He said he would hang around until she got some. Betty came over and got me. It was a Sunday afternoon. Mangrove Lane is right down the shoreline to the south of us. I got there and he was sprawled out in the living room. I told him it was time for him to get on his Yamaha and into his helmet and head north. So we went out into the side yard and he began jumping back and forth and yelling 'Hah! Hah!' and making chopping motions. He came toward me and I kept moving back. I picked up the rhythm of the way he was hopping, and when he was up in the air, or starting up, I stepped into him and hit him in the mouth so hard it pushed this middle knuckle back in, and the first thing that hit the sod was the nape of his neck. He jumped up with both hands on his mouth, yelling, 'Not in the mouth. My God, not my mouth. Oh, God, my career!' So the girls babied him a little and I stood around until he got on his bike and roared away. I haven't seen him since. I don't think Carrie saw him either before she got killed. Are you coming to the service tomorrow morning?"

"At eleven? Yes. The sister asked me."

"She seems nice, that Susan. Carrie was too old for me. Maybe she wasn't, but she thought she was, which is the same thing. We had some laughs. She was making it with Jack Omaha. I told her that was dead end, and she said, What the hell, everything is. And there's not much answer to that, I guess."

"Where did Omaha keep his boat?"

"Right here. There it is, tied up to that shoreline dock at the end there, past the office, over beyond the lights."

I stood up. It was hard to see. "Bertram?"

"Right. Forty-six-foot with all the high-speed diesel you can use. All the extras. One hell of a lot of boat."

"I can believe it. It's one hell of a lot of price too."

"You can get that one at a pretty good price now. The bank wants off the hook on it. I understand they'll take ninety-five cash."

"They ought to get that with no trouble if it's been maintained."

"Two years old and clean."

"Do you mean Omaha couldn't run it himself?"

"No. He could run it. But you can't fish and run it at the same time. When he got an urge to go billfishing, he'd get Cal lined up. He liked the edge of the Stream up beyond Grand Bahama. That's a good run, so they'd take off way before daylight and come back in by midnight or later. It makes a long day. Sometimes Carrie would go along."

"When was the last time?" Meyer asked. "Do you remember?"

"Only on account of the cops being here asking us. It was on a Tuesday, the fourteenth of . . . this month? Is it still May? Yes, the thirty-first. May is one of the months I always think should have thirty days. Yes, Jack Omaha took off with Cal about three in the morning, and they didn't come back in until after midnight. They questioned Cal about it. Just the two of them alone? Where had they fished? How had Jack acted? What time did they get back? How was Jack dressed? What was he driving? And so on and so on."

He stood up, shrugged, moved toward the ladderway.

"What time is it?" he asked. "I've got to go help Oliver lock the place. Anything you want, just ask either one of us."

After he was gone I strolled over and looked at the Bertram. It was called *Christina III*. It looked very fit and very husky. When I went back, Meyer was in the lounge. He was tilted back in a chair, hands laced behind his thick neck, staring at the overhead and frowning.

"Now what?" I asked.

"Do you know how they locate invisible planets?"

"No. How do they do that, Professor?"

"Because the visible ones act in erratic and inexplicable fashion. Their orbits are . . . warped. So you apply gravitational theory and a little geometry of moving spheres and you say, Aha, if there is a planetary body right *there* of such and such a mass and such and such an orbit, then all the random movements of the other planets become logical, even imperative."

I sat on the yellow couch. "So what kind of mass and orbit are we looking for?"

"Something large, important, illegal, and profitable."

"Involving a fast cruiser?"

"Possibly."

"Okay. Sunken treasure or Jamaican grass, routed via the Bahamas."

"Isn't there a lot of cannabis coming into Florida?"

"All the way from Jax around to Fort Walton Beach. Yes. Based on what they've intercepted and what they think they've probably missed, it would be at least ten tons a week. From Colombia, Mexico, Jamaica, and maybe some other BIWI islands."

"Big money?"

"Not as big as you read in the papers. Street value doesn't mean a hell of a lot. It passes through a lot of hands. The biggest bite is in getting it into the country and into the hands of a distributor. That's where you double your money, or a little better. Five thousand worth of good-quality, nicely cured Jamaican marijuana will go here for possibly twelve thousand. But if it is intercepted, they'll call it a quarter-million street value. It has to go from distributor to big dealer to little dealer to pusher-user to user. Everybody bites."

"How do you know all this?"

"What I don't know, I make up."

"Seriously, Travis."

"Boo Brodey wanted me to come in with him on a run last year. He laid it all out, including the comparison with Prohibition and so on. I said, Thanks but no thanks."

"Didn't he get picked up?"

"He's out again."

"Did you disapprove?"

"Can't you read me on that?"

Meyer chuckled. "I guess I can. You don't like partnership ventures and middleman status. You don't like large investments. You don't like coming to the notice and attention of the law. You wouldn't want anybody to have the kind of hold over you that Boo would have had. It's not your idea of high adventure. It's what the British would call a hole-and-corner affair. Tawdry. A gesture of defiance for the very young."

"So why ask questions you can answer?"

"I guess I meant, Do you disapprove of a person using the weed?"

"Me? I think people should do whatever they want to do, provided they go to the trouble of informing themselves first of any possible problems. Once they know, then they can solve their own risk-reward ratios. Suppose somebody proved it does some kind of permanent damage. Okay. So the user has to figure out if there is any point in his remaining in optimum condition for a minimum kind of existence. For me, it was relaxing in a way, the couple of times I've had enough to feel it. But it gave me the giggles, warped my time sense, and made things too bright and hard-edged. Also it bent dimensions somehow. Buildings leaned just a little bit the wrong way. Rooms were not perfectly oblong any more. It's a kind of sensual relaxation, but it gave me the uneasy feeling somebody could come up behind me and kill me and I would die distantly amused instead of scared witless."

"I am trying to imagine you giggling."

"I can still hear it."

"What about it being sunken treasure, Travis?"

"I am thinking back to the money. How it was packaged. Hundreds on the bottom, then fifties, twenties, tens. Some had fives on top. Tied with white cotton string, in both directions. With an adding-machine tape tucked under the string. Bricks of ten thousand. Somebody very neat. It smacks of retail business, my friend. Think of it this way. Suppose you are taking in a lot of cash from various sources, and you use that cash to buy from several other sources, after removing your own share. Assume you do not want to change little ones into big ones at your friendly bank. Okay, if you put all the hundreds together, you have some thin little bricks to buy with. But at the other end you've got some great big stacks of little bills to add up to the same kind of round number. So you mix them up, and you have fairly manageable sizes."

"Sounds less and less like doubloons," Meyer said.

"Yes, it does."

"When I get this pain right between my eyes it means I've done enough thinking for now—on a conscious level. Now the subconscious can go to work. Do you have the gut feeling Jack Omaha is dead?"

"Yes."

"Then that makes the *Christina III* a very unlucky vessel."

"Jack, Omaha, Carrie Milligan, and Cal Birdsong."

"And," he said, "the invisible planetary body which warped the other orbits. Good night."

After I had puttered around aimlessly and had at last gone to bed, I found myself reliving the memory of Boo Brodey when he tried to recruit me. He's big and red and abraded by life—by hard work and hard living, by small mercenary wars and thin predatory women. Yet there is something childlike about him.

He paced up and down in front of me, his face knotted with anxiety and appeal, chunking his fist into his palm, saying, "Jesus, Trav, you know how I am. Somebody tells me what to do and when, it gets done. I work something out myself and it's a disaster. Trav, we're talking about the money tree. Honest to Christ, you wouldn't believe it, the kind of money. Kids, weird little kids, are bringing in bags of grass right and left. Anything that'll fly, that's the way to do it. You can lease an airplane to fly up to Atlanta and back. Okay, you put it down on the deck and go to Jamaica and buy ten thousand worth and come back, and you got thirty thousand before the day is over. It's coming in on boats and ships and everything, Trav. Come *on!* The narcs aren't all that hard-nose about grass. They know they can't keep it out, and a lot of them, they don't know for sure it hurts anybody anyway, right? Come on in with me and help set it up. You know, the contacts and all. Help me out, dammit!''

When I told him I didn't want in, he wanted me to set it all up for him. I could stay outside and get a piece of it in exchange for management skills. I said no, I didn't want to go down that particular road. If you make it with grass, you find out that hash and coke are more portable and profitable. You kid yourself into the next step, and by the time they pick you up, your picture in the paper looks like some kind of degenerate, fangs and all. And all you can say is, Gee, the other guys were doing it too.

If I were really going to do it, I would refit the *Muñequita* for long-range work. Tune her for lowest gas consumption and put in bigger tanks. She's already braced to bang through seas most runabouts can't handle. Then I would . . .

Whoa, McGee. There is larceny in every heart, and you have more than your share. So forget how far it is across the Yucatan Straits, leaving from Key West.

7

IT WAS an overcast morning with almost no wind at all. The wide bay was glassy calm, the outlying headlands misted, looking farther away than they were.

There was a narrow, scrabbly, oyster-shell beach beside the cottage at 28 Mangrove Lane where Carrie Milligan had once lived. A narrow wooden dock extended twenty feet into the bay. It was still solid, just beginning to lean. It was good, I guessed, for another couple of years. Two old skiffs were high on the beach, overturned, nosing into the sea grapes.

Jason sat on the end of one of the skiffs. He wore a white shirt and white trousers. He had a big plantation straw hat shadowing his face. He was playing chords quite softly on a big guitar with a lot of ornate fretwork against the dark wood. The chords were related but did not become any recognizable song. They were in slow cadence, major and minor.

Meyer and I joined the group, standing a bit north of most of them, in the shade of a small gnarled water oak. I saw Harry Hascomb and the young man who had been counting stock in the warehouse. I saw Mrs. Jack Omaha, Gil from Gil's Kitchen, Susan Dobrovsky, Frederick Van Harn, Oliver from the marina, Joanna from Superior Building Supplies, and a man it took me a few moments to place. He was Arthur, the younger of the two cops who had subdued Cal Birdsong.

There were seven young ladies in long pastel dresses. The dresses were not in any sense a matched set. They were all of different cut and style, but all long and all pastel. Susan wore a long white dress which was just enough too big so that I suspected it was borrowed. Susan and the other girls all had armfuls of the lush Florida flowers of late springtime.

A young man stepped out of the group and turned and faced us. He had red hair to his shoulders and a curly red beard. He wore a sports jacket and plaid slacks.

In a resonant and penetrating voice he said, "We are here today to say good-bye to our sister, Carrie." The guitar music softened but continued. "She lived among us for a time. She touched our lives. She was an open person. She was not afraid of life or of herself. She was at home being Carrie, our sister. And we were at home with her, in love and trust and understanding. In her memory, each one of us here now most solemnly vows to be more sensitive to the needs of those who share our lives, to be more compassionate, to give that kind of understanding which does not concern itself with blame and guilt and retribution. In token of this pledge, and in symbol of our loss, we consign these flowers to the sea."

He moved to the side. The guitar became louder. One by one the pastel girls walked out to the end of the dock and flung the armloads of blooms onto the gray and glassy bay. There were tear marks on their cheeks. The flowers spread and began, very slowly, to move outward and in a southerly direction with the current. It was a very simple and moving thing. I had the feeling of a greater loss for having so undervalued Carrie. I excused myself by saying I had really not known her very well. But that was what Red-beard had said, that we should be more sensitive to the needs of others—and more sensitive, I added, to their identities as well. If she had meant this much to these people, then I had slighted her value as a person.

The music trailed off and stopped. Jason stood up and bobbed his head to indicate that was all. The murmur of voices began. Susan went a little way down the beach and stood, watching the floating flowers.

I looked at the twenty or so people I did not know, and I realized anew that there is a new subculture in the world. These were mostly young working people. Their work was their concession to the necessities. Their off-work identities were contra-establishment. Perhaps this was the only effective answer to all the malaise and the restlessness and the disbelief in institutionalized life, to conform for the sake of earning the bread and then to step from the job into almost as much personal freedom as the commune person.

I realized Meyer was no longer at my elbow. I looked around and did not see him. Jason nodded to me and said, "Was it okay?"

"It was beautiful."

"I figured if I just noodled around it would be better. If you play something, people start making the lyrics in their heads and they miss the other words. Robby did fine, I thought. He's an architect. Cindy wanted to make it to the service here, but she's still too shook."

"She shouldn't have even thought about it."

"Well, she thought a lot of Carrie. When Cindy was sick last year, Carrie came over and straightened out the books. It took her a whole weekend to do it, the way Cal had screwed things up. Look, I think I ought to talk to Susan. You think it would be okay?"

"I think it would be fine."

He moved off down the beach. Meyer came up to me and said, "There's a hex nut on the bottom of the gas tank. The undercoat is off it on one of the surfaces, and the metal is shiny where the undercoat flaked off."

I stared at him in disbelief. "With all these people around, you were damn fool enough to—"

"I was flipping my lucky silver dollar and catching it, like this. I dropped it and it hit the toe of my shoe and rolled under the Datsun. I didn't get a good look or a long look."

"Don't try to be cute about these things."

"Don't try to be McGee, you mean?"

"Don't get huffy. If you want to travel with the team, learn the ground rules. I've told you before. Don't *ever* take a risk you don't have to take, just to save time or inflate your ego."

"Now wait a minute—"

"There are a lot of things you can tell me that I would never know or guess unless you told me. You have a lot of special information in your head. So have I in mine. My information can make you live longer. And better."

"Better than what?" a girl asked. I turned. Joanna. Miss Freeler, recently of Superior Building Supplies. Dear friend of Harry Hascomb. Ex-friend. Slender girl with a delicate and lovely face, long fall of ginger-colored hair. Green eyes, slightly protruding and very challenging. The girl challenge, old as time.

"Live better than Harry is going to live for a while."

"That wouldn't be hard," she said. "Bet your ass. Harry is going to have to give up a lot of goodies. I know you from the office yesterday, when I quit. I remember you because you've got weird eyes. And for other reasons too, I might add. I bet you hear that from all the girls. You know, you got eyes the color of gin. What's your name?"

"McGee. And this is Meyer. Joanna Freeler."

"Hello, Meyer," she said. "Hello, McGee. What are you two dudes doing here at the memorial?"

"Friends of the deceased," I said. "From Lauderdale."

"Sure. That's where she married that muscle bum. Why didn't she marry you? Weren't you available, McGee?"

"Weren't. Aren't. Won't be."

"Now you're singing my song," she said.

She was wearing a long orange dress. The color was not good with her coloring. She had thrown her flowers farther and spread them wider than any of the others.

"You seem to be in good spirits," I said.

She clenched her jaw and glared up at me. "That's a shitty thing to say, friend. I miss her like hell. And in one way or another, I'll always miss her. Okay?"

"I didn't mean anything by what I said."

"Then apologize for letting your mouth run with your head turned off, McGee."

"I do so hereby apologize."

She hugged my arm and smiled and said to Meyer, "You run along, dearie. I have to ask this man something."

Meyer said, "I'll walk back to the boat."

"You've got a boat here? At Westway? Hmm. A fast boat?"

"If you really really press her, she'll do seven or eight knots."

"You a pilot? Like in an airplane?"

"No."

"Come along. I just don't like to say some kinds of things in front of two people. All right?"

She led me well away from the others, over to the far edge of the lot. One water oak had sent out a huge limb, parallel to the ground, the top of it almost as high as my shirt pocket. Joanna gave a little bounce and put her palms on the limb and floated up, turning in air to sit lightly. She patted the limb beside her. "Come into my tree, friend."

I sat beside her. She took my hand and inspected it carefully, back and front.

"Hmm. You've had an active past."

"You could have said that in front of Meyer."

"It's hard to say what I want to say in front of just one person. I mean it's so easy for you to get the wrong idea. I'll miss Carrie. But she *is* dead, right? And the world goes on. One thing I know from all this, maybe the same thing Carrie figured out, there's got to be more to living than sitting on your butt forty hours a week in an office and getting laid once in a while by the joker who signs your paycheck. I could retire, maybe. If I play it right. But what I want is more interesting work. Like what Carrie was doing."

"What was she doing?"

"Don't try to get cute, McGee. Listen, I *knew* that girl. There's four of us in the cottage now. Me and Betty Joller and Nat Weiss and Flossie Speck. So before she moved out and since, Carrie was supplying the cottage with free grass for her friends, like a paper bag this big half full. We must have two pounds left. Do I have to spell it out? What I wasn't told, I can guess. So it all fell apart for you people. She went to Lauderdale. Now you are here to put it back together again, right? So this is a job application. I'm very smart and I know how to keep my mouth shut."

"I wouldn't say you know how to keep your mouth shut."

"This one time I have to take the chance, or where am I? Outside, as usual."

"Who do you think I represent?"

"You are sitting in my tree playing stupid. You look smart and rough. You're in distribution after the crazy people bring it in. I want to be a crazy people because I need something weird to do, and the money is nice. I told Carrie she shouldn't be involved, and here am I asking to get involved. What did happen to Jack?"

"Didn't Carrie tell you that?"

"She said he got scared and probably grabbed his share and ran. But that doesn't . . ."

"Doesn't what?"

"Never mind. Skip it."

"Did Harry know what was going on?"

"Cowboy Harry? He's a jerk. How could he know what was going on? It takes him both hands to find his ass. Why did you come to see him anyway?"

"To talk to him about Carrie."

"Why would you want to talk to him about Carrie?"

"You can keep your mouth shut?"

"You know it!"

"Just trying to get a line on who pushed Carrie in front of that truck."

The color drained out of her face. She wiped her mouth and shuddered. "Come on, now!"

"She was killed. I guess you could call it an occupational hazard, right? If you want to accept that kind of risk, maybe we can find something for you."

"But who . . . who . . . ."

"The competition, probably."

She looked down and plucked the orange dress away from her body. "I'm getting all hot and sticky. I better change. Don't go away, huh? I want to think this over, okay?"

Joanna dropped lightly from the limb and went to the cottage, striding long, and disappeared inside. A lot of the people had left. Some had gone into the cottage. Others were talking, by twos and threes. I saw Susan walking toward the Datsun, so I dropped down and got to the car just as she did. Her eyes were red, but she managed a smile.

"I think Carrie would have liked it," she said.

"I'm sure she would. Yesterday I walked off with her rings. I forgot to give them to you. And I left them on the boat. We could go get them now."

She frowned and shook her head. "There's no hurry. I have to be here a few days anyway, Fred . . . Mr. Van Harn says."

"Do you want me to go and pick up that package from Mr. Rucker?"

"Oh, no, thanks. I already talked to Betty about it, and she's coming with me now and we'll go over there before two o'clock. It's perfectly all right, really. But thank you."

A sturdy girl in a yellow dress came hurrying to the car, saying, "Sorry, Sue. I got to talking to somebody."

'Betty, this is Travis McGee. Betty Joller.'

She had one of those plump pretty faces which go with wooden shoes and beer festivals. Her eyes were Dutch blue, and her smile was totally friendly and not the least bit provocative. "When I saw you standing with Meyer, I figured it had to be you," she said. "Carrie told me once that the only really happy time she could remember was when you loaned her and Ben your houseboat for their honeymoon. We're all going to miss her so much around here."

They got in, and Susan hitched her white dress up above her knees and then backed smartly around and they left. At my elbow Joanna said, "Now that Susan is some kind of great package."

"And Jason has his eyes on it."

"I noticed that. She's too young for you, chief."

"So are you."

She laughed so hard it bent her over. The laugh was silver bright under the shade trees, unfitting for the occasion. "Me? Me?" she gasped. "I'm the oldest person around anywhere." She wore little salmon shorts and a soft gray top. She had wound her ginger hair into a pile atop her head and pinned it in place casually. Ends were escaping. It made her throat look very slender and vulnerable.

She looked around. "Where did you leave your wheels?"

"We walked over from the marina."

"So I'll walk back with you, okay?"

"Okay, Joanna."

"We haven't made our deal yet."

"Deal?"

She carried a small white canvas beach bag. She twirled it by its draw cord. "Keep playing dumb and I'll brain you, honey."

So we went out to the sidewalk and walked through sun and shade, past little frame houses and new little stores, to the marina. Jason was back at work. He was in his khaki shorts standing on the bow deck of a big Chris, hosing it down, washing off the salt, and the new arrivals, a pair of small round white-haired people in bright boat clothes, stood sourly watching his every move. "Get that cleat too," the man yelled. "The cleat!"

"Yessir," said Jason the musician. "Yessir, sir."

Joanna was loudly enthusiastic about the below-decks space of *The Busted Flush*. While she was trotting around, oh-ing and ah-ing. Meyer told me he had some errands. I gave him the car keys. I did not know if he had errands or a sudden attack of discretion.

I caught up with her in the head, standing in front of the big mirror, touching her hair, turning and looking back at herself over her shoulder. She saw me in the mirror and said, "This is really some kind of floating playpen. It's funny. I keep feeling left out. I keep thinking that it isn't right that all this has been going on without *me*. After all, I'm the best in the world. You didn't know?"

"You hadn't mentioned it before."

"Don't tell me you designed all this?"

"No. It was as is when I won this barge in a poker game."

"Ah, Hence the name."

"There was a Brazilian lady that went with it, but I wouldn't let him bet her."

"Are Brazilians so great?"

"I wouldn't know. Anyway, I kept the decor."

She was smiling. Then suddenly she slumped her shoulders, shook her head, her face somber. "It's so great to kid around, isn't it? I guess the real reason I'm quitting the job is because it wouldn't be the same there without Carrie. Can I have a beer?"

"Of course."

We sat in the galley booth, facing each other across the Formica top. She was pensive, silent, unreadable.

Finally she said, "So it isn't any game. So I don't want in, thanks just the same. Sorry I bothered you."

So I told her the truth about my relationship to Carrie. And why I was here with Meyer. She turned beet red and had to get up and pace around to control her restless embarrassment. It took me about five minutes to get the record straight. I left out the part about the money.

"You must have thought I'd lost my mind!"

"I decided you weren't too tightly wrapped, kid."

"You encouraged me, damn you!"

Finally she calmed down and sat down, sipped her beer, and said, "Okay, I can see why you think she was killed. The purse and the gas and so on. But why? She wasn't into anything *that* rough. Everybody and his brother is hustling grass into Florida. There's absolute tons of it coming in all the time. It's about as risky as running a stop sign.''

"Did she tell you how it worked?"

"Not in so many words. It was no secret they used Jack's cruiser. There is no way this coast can be policed. Too many small boats and little airplanes and all."

"Didn't anybody at the cottage ask Carrie where she got it?"

"Betty always did, and Carrie would say something different every time. Like she'd say they had a special on it at Quik-Chek. It was top quality, cured right. Jason says it's the best he's ever run into. It was fun, the four of us. Betty and me, Carrie and Floss. Betty got a little machine and made cigarettes. And we had the cookbook, too, and made those hash puppies. Like on an evening, there'd be eight or ten of us sitting around, and maybe Jason making music, and we'd get onto a real nice level. And there'd be good relaxed talk that made sense, not like when everybody is drinking and people get ugly or silly. They say now it can mess up having babies, and it can lower your resistance to colds and flu and infection and so on. So? Automobiles can kill you, and people don't stop driving."

"The imperatives aren't the same."

"The what aren't what?"

"Excuse me. Let's not get into a hard sell."

"Are you opposed?"

"Joanna, I don't know. A fellow who was pretty handy with a boat once said that anything you feel good after is moral. But that implies that the deed is unchanging and the doer is unchanging. What you feel good after one time, you feel rotten after the next. And it is difficult to know in advance. And morality shouldn't be experimental, I don't think. I find that the world is full of things which are unavoidable and which cloud my mind. When my mind is clouded, I am experiencing less. I may *think* it is more, if the mind is warped, but it is less, really. The mind looks inward, not outward. So I just . . . try to make sure there's always somebody in the control room, somebody standing watch."

"Somehow it sounds dull."

"It isn't."

She wrapped her fingers around my wrist. "Okay, smart-ass. Do you think you'd feel good after me?"

"If the reasons are right, sure."

"Is there more than one reason, friend?"

"The biggest and most important reason in the world is to be together with someone in a way that makes life a little less bleak and solitary and lonesome. To exchange the I for the We. In the biggest sense of the word, it's cold outside. And kindness and affection and gentleness build a nice warm fire inside. That's okay. But if you want to set some new international screwing record, or if you want to show off the busiest fastest hips in town, forget it."

The fingers slackened their hold on my wrist and she pulled her hand back. Tears stood in her eyes. She smiled and shook her head and said, "No way, McGee. Whatever it is you're selling, I can't afford it. I went that route once, and it stung. It stung a lot. If that's the kind of dressing you want on the salad, eat elsewhere. I am a very good lay for the Harry Hascombs of the world, and I always feel good afterward, thanks.''

"Always?"

"Go to hell!'' she said and got up. "All I am is your garden-variety man-eater. I like it. Go to hell!''

"To each his dagnab blue-eyed own.''

She smiled. "And I'll always miss Walt Kelly too.'' She held her hand out to me. "Friends? I didn't exactly come here to set up a friendship. But it'll have to do. God! I am starving. What have you got here?'' She had opened the refrigerator. "Is this corned beef? Cheese. Where's the bread? I have this terrible food engine inside me. I eat enough for three truck drivers and I'm always hungry and I never gain one little ounce. I could give you bone bruises, dear.''

I sat and watched her make sandwiches. She was very deft, and she made a lot of them. She ate about twice as much as I ate. She ate with such enthusiasm it made her sweaty, even in the air conditioning. She ate with such a lusty, bright-eyed joy that I had the wistful wish to have played her game and bundled her into the sack five minutes after Meyer stepped off the boat. She was intensely alive, as vital and immediate as anyone I had met in a long time.

"How often did she bring the samples?"

"What? Oh, when we were about to run out. Her moving to that Fifteen Hundred place had something to do with the deal. She told me she was getting a free ride on the apartment. But she missed us.''

The phone rang. It startled both of us. I went into the lounge and answered it. It was Meyer. "About the autopsy on Birdsong, it was heart. Some kind of aneurysm. Thought you'd like to know. I hope I . . . haven't disturbed you by phoning.''

"You can come back aboard any time.''

"Oh.''

"What's this with the Oh?''

"Just Oh. Nothing complicated. Oh.''

She sauntered into the lounge and stretched out on the yellow couch, placing her second mug of milk on the coffee table. "This is truly some great boat.''

"What is Chris Omaha like?''

"Nobody can ever figure out how come Jack stayed with her so long. She's dumb, loud, and greedy. Rotten to him and rotten to the kids. Ever since the kids got old enough to be sent off to school, they've been away. She likes to be alone in the house in case something wearing pants comes by to make a delivery or fix something. Jack caught her a couple of times. But leave her? No. Carrie thought for quite a while maybe he would leave Chris and marry her. I don't know what the hold is. It was a kid marriage for them. Seventeen and eighteen they were. It finally got to be an arrangement, I guess. He could have Carrie, and she could have anybody who happened to come along.''

"Like Ready Freddy Van Harn?''

"Ready Freddy? Wow, you read him right. I'll have to tell Floss what you called him. No, Fred is the lawyer for the business, and he's Jack and Harry's personal lawyer, and he'll be handling the estate, what's left, but he wouldn't boff around with old Chris, not when he can tag the best there is."

I recounted my reasons for contradicting her. She looked astonished. "What *about* that! What do you know? I guess old Chris snuck up on his blind side or something."

"He was Carrie's lawyer?"

"From being the lawyer for the business. When she wanted to make out a will so that Ben couldn't get her savings or her car or anything like that, she asked Fred one day when he was in to see Harry about something, and he made some notes and drew up a will and had her come into the office and sign it. I guess he made himself the executor. That would be okay by Carrie. And Betty told me she'd warned Susan about Fred. Susan seems like such a nice kid. Fred even got to Betty one time. I guess it was sort of a challenge to him. Betty is sort of sexless, you know? She has all the equipment and she's pretty, but something's left out. Fred got her a little bit bombed on wine and then he took her. It wasn't exactly rape, but it was as close as it could get and still not be. She hates him. He really hurt her, because she's built small, and that Fred has . . . well, all I can say is that you'd never know, looking at him, so kind of slender and girlish almost. And pretty. But he's a bull. He's huge. He's so huge he's sort of scary. And . . . he likes to hurt. I don't like kinky things. I like it, you know, for fun. It doesn't seem to be fun for him. Oh, he knows a lot of tricks and so forth. But it's more like he read up on it in engineering school. Once was enough for me. He's with you but he isn't. He's . . . I don't know to say it."

"Remote?"

"Ri-i-ght! I think Fred is trying to score every girl in Bayside and surrounding area. He's real hell on wives. Maybe that's why he put Chris on his list. Men have tried to beat up on him for messing around, but he is just as quick and just as mean as a snake. He's a good lawyer, but he's not a very nice person. I don't know how marriage is going to work out for him. He's going to get married. It was in the paper. Jane Schermer. Very social and very very rich. It's grove money from way back. He has some ranchland out near all her groves, lots of it, but nowhere near as big. The Van Harn family used to have money, but about the time Fred was in Stetson Law, his daddy shot himself and it turned out he was almost totally busted. It was something to do with letter stock. I don't even know what that is. But that's what they say. Something about pledging letter stock for bank loans, and him being the lawyer for the bank. Fred works hard. I think he's maybe made back a lot of money. Everybody says he does a good job. But I think that way down deep he's a creepy person."

"Bayside seems like a busy place."

"It's okay, I guess. I really don't know whether I'll stay around. I left once before and came back. Maybe I'll come to Lauderdale and live on this boat with you for a while. Okay?"

"We'll keep your name on file, Miss Freeler."

"You are *so* nice to me."

My alarm bell bonged as Meyer stepped aboard, onto the mat on the stern deck. He knocked and came in and smiled at pretty Joanna on the yellow couch. "I like to see healthy young girls drinking milk," he said. She had set aside a couple of sandwiches for him, neatly packaged in Saran. She stirred herself and got up, yawning, and said she was going back to the cottage for a nap. I took her by the shoulders and turned her around and gave her a little push toward the staterooms. She trudged off, scuffing her heels, and when I looked in on her she was snoring, a large snare-drum sound for such a small lady.

I sat with Meyer while he ate at the booth in the galley.

"I tracked it down," he said. "The place Carrie had her car serviced. It's a big Shell station right across from the entrance to Junction Park. It was handy for her because she could leave her car there while she was working. It was in last Tuesday. They looked up the ticket. They changed the oil and the filter and put on new wiper blades—and filled the tank."

"And if it was filled Tuesday, and she didn't go on any trips . . ."

"She worked all Tuesday and Wednesday."

"Very nice work, Meyer."

"Thank you."

"About that planet theory of yours, how they find the invisible one by seeing what it does to the orbits of the others. I have a candidate for planet. One attorney by the name of Frederick Van Harn. He impinges on the lives of too many of the people we're interested in."

"Including Mrs. Birdsong."

"Huh?"

"He was coming out of her motel unit when I drove in."

"Oh, that's just great. Anyway, he's top priority. All we can find out. Right?"

"Yessir, sir."

And despite my protestations that it wasn't all that urgent, he headed on out again after reborrowing the car keys.

8

JOANNA WOKE up at four and said a sleepy farewell and went tottering off. I wrote a note to Meyer and left it where he would see it. I locked the *Flush* and walked all the way to 1500 Seaway Boulevard, estimating it at a little less than two miles south of the marina. At first it was very hot, but then a quick thunderstorm came slamming in. I stepped over a hedge and took refuge under a tremendous old banyan. A small white dog yapped at me from a screened porch, some of his yapping drowned by thunder. A pale woman came out onto the porch to see why he was making such a fuss. Over the rain sound I yelled, "I'm trespassing!"

"You can trespass on the porch here if you want."

"I'm terrified of the savage dog. Thanks anyway."

She smiled and went back into the house. When the rain stopped, mist rose from the pavement. The air was washed clean and was much cooler. I stepped along faster than before.

Fifteen Hundred was a jumble of villas and town houses, of joined and separate structures interconnected by arcades and roofed walkways. The layout established small courtyards of various sizes. It did allow for a maximum privacy of approach and departure, but at the expense of security. In a world where violence is ever less comprehensible and avoidable, people—especially the middle-aged and the old—settle more comfortably behind barred gates, locked lobbies, roving guard dogs. They seek to die in bed, of something gentle and merciful.

I roamed, looking for Walter J. Demos. His was number 60, the ground floor of a town house near the back of the property, looking out at the pool area. A pretty lady in jeans and work shirt and tousled hairdo opened the door and said, liltingly. "No vacancies, none at all; so sorry." She started to close the door.

"I want to talk to Mr. Demos."

"He isn't even adding any names to the list, it's so long now." She had sweat beads of exertion on her forehead and upper lip. Behind her I could see a mop pail with a wringer fastened to it.

"I don't want to live here."

"Then you must be out of your tree. If it's about something else, well, let me think. Mary Ferris was after him to do something about her disposer. I think he'll be there by now. That's Twenty-one. Go past the pool and through that arch at the right and it will be . . . the second? No, the third doorway to your right. Go up in the stairs and come back toward the front of the building."

*   *   *

Walter J. Demos wore gray coveralls and an engineer cap. The coveralls were wet-dark around his middle in a wide irregular band. He did indeed look something like a shorter broader Kojak, his face and jaw massive, almost acromegalic.

He showed me what he had in his hand. It looked like a tangled ball of dirty string.

"Do you know what this is? Can you guess?" he asked.

The woman giggled. She was plump and coy and underdressed.

"I wouldn't know."

"Miss Mary here had a lovely artichoke yesterday, and she put all the inedible parts of it into her disposer. Artichoke leaves, my friend, are made of string. And in a little while the string wound itself into a tangled mess and stopped the machinery."

Mary giggled again and switched back and forth, chewing a knuckle, scuffing her sandaled foot.

She thanked him and he gave her the string to dispose of in a less damaging manner. He picked up his tin toolbox, and we left to walk slowly back toward his apartment.

"I could tell them all to call the repair people. I could spend all my time in the pool. But it would drive me quite mad, I think. I have to keep busy. That's the way I am, Mr. McGee. And it saves my people money, which is increasingly important these days. Everyone chips in and helps whenever and wherever they can. We're a family here, helping and protecting each other.''

"Meyer told me he got that impression.''

"Oh, then *you* must be the friend he mentioned. I chatted with him for just a few minutes, but he struck me as charming and highly intelligent. I like intelligent people. That's the way I am.''

"Have you found out who trashed Carrie's apartment?''

"What? Oh, no, we haven't. And I doubt we ever will. No one resident here would ever do a thing like that.''

"Even though she was resented by the other . . . members of the family?''

He stopped and peered at me. "What would give you that idea?''

I was tempted to remind him of Meyer's intelligence, but I thought I could make a little more mileage by using the dead lady, so I said, "Mrs. Milligan was quite aware of it.''

He grunted and we walked on, right to his door. The lady had stopped sweating. He took her hand in both of his. "Thank you so *very* much, Lillian. You know how much I appreciate it.''

She went smiling off, purse in hand. He closed the door and looked around. "Nice job," he said to himself. "Very nice." He turned to me and made a wry grimace. "I have to be so very careful. If one of them cleans up for me too often, the others get jealous. Please sit down. You were telling me that Carrie had some fantasy about resentment.''

"Purely a paranoid fantasy. She thought that because you put her at the head of the list and gave her the first empty apartment, the others resented her. She thought that because she was getting a rent-free ride, they resented her. She thought that because she didn't care to mingle, they resented her. She would rather have stayed with her friends in the cottage at Mangrove Lane. Maybe you should have told the whole family that Carrie wasn't a very special and dear friend, but just part of the pot distribution system. Jack Omaha, Cal Birdsong, Carrie Milligan, and you.''

He was good. He stared at me. At first he chuckled and then he laughed and then he roared. He slapped his thighs and rocked back and forth and lost his breath. Finally he held his wrists out and, still choking, said, "Okay, officer. I'll go quietly. You've got me.''

"Why the special treatment she got from you? Tell me so we can all laugh.''

He lost all traces of mirth. "You're beginning to annoy me. It's no business of yours, but I'll tell you anyway. A friend of mine asked me to make the apartment available to Mrs. Milligan. Jack Omaha asked me. My books show the rent paid every month. She may have had a free ride, but it wasn't from me. Probably Jack felt that it would be more pleasant to have . . . more privacy and more access to the lady.''

I lifted eyebrows and looked at him politely. "I'm beginning to annoy you, Mr. Demos?''

"Frankly, yes.''

There are a lot of choices in every instance. And it is easy to make a bad choice. A man will react badly to the promise of some unthinkable punishment. The musician will buckle at the thought of smashed hands. The choice cannot be made with the thought of taking any pleasure in the choice. It has to be businesslike, or it will not be convincing. This man was the benign daddy, the solid meaty big-skulled patriarch, full of such amiable wisdom and helpfulness that he would appeal to the little girl in any woman who might be still searching for poppa. A gregarious man. A sensualist. A skilled, success-ful, and unlikely womanizer who had built himself a profitable world teeming with prey. He was pleased with himself, and evidently still greedy.

"I'm thinking of alternate ways of annoying you, Mr. Demos."

"What do you mean?"

"We have a specialist we could import. His nickname is Sixteen Weeks. He's very bright about guessing just how much punishment a given person can endure and still recover. He can guarantee you sixteen weeks in the hospital. At your age you might not ever get about as well as you do now."

His attempt at a smile was abortive. "That's grotesque."

"Or, if we decide to head in another direction, I'd turn the problem of disposition over to Meyer. He works things out so there isn't any fuss. As you noted, he's highly intelligent. We gave him the problems of Mr. Omaha, Mr. Birdsong, and Mrs. Milligan. He'd find something plausible for you. They could find you on the bottom of the pool some morning."

I think he tried to smile again. It gave his mouth an odd look. "Are you quite mad? Why are you saying such terrible things? What do you *want* from me?"

Rhetoric, all by itself, is too abstract. It needs punctuation. Show and tell. I stood up, smiling. I moved slowly. He watched me with some agitation. I walked slowly around to the back of his chair. He leaned forward and craned his neck around to watch me. I knew he was wondering whether or not to get up out of the chair.

It takes a reasonable amount of precision. In the clavicle area, where the muscle webs of the trapezius and deltoid are thinned out, the descending brachial plexus, which includes the big ulnar and radial nerves to the arm, is close to the bone. I chopped down, a short swift smashing blow, and hit him just as he started to move, hit him on target, mashing the nerves against bone with the bone ridge of my knuckles.

Walter J. Demos screamed in a very aspirated hissy way and came floun-dering up out of the chair. His right arm hung dead. He clasped his right shoulder in his big left hand. He stared at me with bulging eyes and roared with pain. Tears ran down his face.

There was a flurried rapping at the door. "Walter?" a woman cried. "Are you all right? Walter?"

"Tell her to call the cops," I suggested. "We can all sit around and talk about how much pot you moved out of this place."

"Walter?" she yelled.

"Everything is fine, Edith." he called. "Go away!" He sat down again and said, "You broke my shoulder!"

"It isn't broken. It will be okay again in a week."

"But I can't move my arm. It's numb."

"The feeling will come back, Wally."

"Nobody ever calls me Wally."

"Except me. I can call you Wally, can't I"

"What do you *want* of me? Were they really killed? Really?"

"What we want is an established outlet in Bayside. Your previous source has dried up, Wally. Now tell me how you got into it and how you've been operating.

He found a hanky with his left hand and patted his eyes and blew his nose. He rubbed his numb arm. He talked and talked and talked.

He had always purchased supplies for apartment repairs and redecorating from Superior. He became friendly with Jack Omaha and they would have coffee together at a diner near the industrial park, within walking distance. One day he told Omaha that a lot of his tenants had become ill from smoking grass adulterated with some unknown compound. Jack said that his personal supplier, his milkman, had recently been busted, and he was buying it at a gas station and paying too much. Omaha had taken a lot of his vacation time in Jamaica. Half joking, he had told Demos he was tempted to go get his own, but it wasn't worth the risk unless he arranged to have a lot of it brought in and he couldn't see peddling it. Demos told Omaha that quite a bit could be absorbed at 1500 Seaway Boulevard, and some of his tenants could probably get rid of a lot more at the offices where they worked.

It wasn't long before they had talked themselves into it. Omaha came back from Jamaica with guarantees, having talked to local hustlers named Little Bamboo, Popeye, Hitler, John Wayne, and so on.

At that point it was decided that Walter would be better off if he did not know any of the details of the smuggling operation, and if Omaha did not know a thing about his wholesale operation. The first shipments were small. As they got bigger, Demos brought in his most trusted tenants and it became a cottage industry, taking the bulk and weighing, measuring, and bagging it for the smaller wholesalers and the retail trade.

"We thought we'd be able to avoid getting mixed up with any—excuse the expression—hoodlums. We didn't see that there was anything terribly sinister about it. We were filling a demand at a fair price. We tried to cut our risks. Bringing Carrie here to live was part of the risk-cutting. She'd tip me in advance as to when a shipment would be coming in. I'd get my people ready. On those nights she'd be driving one of the little panel trucks from Superior instead of her own car. When it was unloaded, checked, and weighed, I'd give her the money. We'd work all night. I wanted it all out of here by the following morning. Except personal supplies, of course."

"When was the last shipment?"

He looked dispirited. He nursed his shoulder. He sighed. I could feel a certain satisfaction in having diagnosed him so precisely. But with satisfaction there was also regret. Demos had been full of himself, full of a big-bellied confidence, sure of his place in his world. But in had come the pale-eyed stranger who had said terrifying things and who had sickened him with pain. His world had become fragile all of a sudden. He heart was heavy. He was not a bad man, everything considered. He had been a jolly sly man, a manipulator, a greedy chap, over-confident. He had changed.

"Do you want me to annoy you some more, Wally?"

"Nol! No, I was trying to remember exactly. A Tuesday night. That would make it May fourteenth. Yes. I can't remember the exact time, but it was before midnight."

"How much was there?"

"An average shipment. Ten sacks, I think. Forty kilos each. Over eight hundred and fifty pounds. I think I gave her about ninety thousand dollars."

He described, by request, the way the money was wrapped. It fitted the way it had been packaged when Carrie gave it to me. The adding-machine tape was from his office machine. He handled the money, figuring the commissions to his peddlers.

I pressed him to find out how well he had done. He was evasive. In the beginning he had plowed everything back into increasing shipments. He guessed Jack Omaha was doing the same. They were on a cash-and-carry basis with each other. When they got to maximum weight coming in, he had started to skim, and he guessed that Omaha had started too. He said he was having a problem legitimizing the cash, trying to work it out in such a way that he could apply it to the outstanding mortgages on Fifteen Hundred. He guessed that probably Jack Omaha was having the same problem, but he hadn't discussed it with him. He started to ask me about Jack Omaha and changed his mind. He didn't want to know anything about Omaha. Or Carrie.

I asked to see Carrie's apartment. He said that a Miss Joller and a Miss Dobrovsky, Carrie's sister, had gone through everything and packed up some things for shipment to New Jersey, and had called Goodwill to come pick up the rest. It had been cleaned and the new tenant was moving in tomorrow morning. So there was nothing to see.

He said he had a headache and would like to lie down. I told him we had some more ground to cover first. I asked him what Carrie did with the money.

He said he had the impression she took it down to Superior and put it in the safe. It seemed logical that she would have some safe place to put it.

"What do you want from me?" he asked again.

"You have a nice operation, Wally. It's cleaner than some loft or old warehouse or a trailer parked in the woods. And you have those nice clean little clerks and bank people doing the pushing and being very careful because they don't want to mess up this great life-style you created for them. I don't have to put you out of business because you're already retired. You've got no supply, right? Do you know what I'm going to recommend? I'm going to say you should be our exclusive distributor in Bayside. How *about* that?"

I couldn't detect any genuine enthusiasm in his response.

"What does . . . it entail?"

"We'll guarantee top quality. We'll guarantee no hassling by the law. We'll expect you to absorb, say a ton a month, cash on the line, half again what you were paying Omaha. In time we'll have you broaden the line. Coke and hash."

"Oh, I just couldn't handle that, Mr. McGee. I really couldn't. That quantity and price . . . This has been just a small operation. An amateur thing. You know. I just couldn't . . ."

I stood up, smiling at him. "It's all settled."

"Don't I have any choice?"

"Choice? Of course! You stay right here and hang onto the cash, because when we make a delivery, you have to be able to pay. You have to accept what we send you. Don't try to look for another supply source. You just wait. If you want to fuss and bob and weave and make trouble, that's your choice. If so we'll kill you and make our deal with whoever takes over this place. It might be a couple of months before we set you up as a distributor, Wally. Hang in there.''

He didn't move. I let myself out. I was a little depressed by my own childishness. It was a fair assumption it could work exactly as I had outlined it to Demos. The contact would probably be a lot less melodramatic than I had made it. Actually the setup would probably not appeal. It was too unusual. Hoodlums are the true conservatives. When you are winning, never change the dice. Distribution would be limited to the candy-store, horse-room, bartender, cocktail-waitress, coin-machine, call-girl circuits. Demos's arrangement was too fancy and made too much sense.

I took a small detour to go around by the pool. The after-work residents crowded the pool area. They made a youngish, attractive throng in their brown hides and resort colors. The scene looked like a commercial for swimming pools.

They made gay little cries of glee and fun. A game of water tag was in progress.

Wally's Paradise. There was one thing wrong with it, and that was what probably created the slightly frantic gaiety. They all loved it here. They were all going to stay. They were going to obey all the rules, and pay the rent, and stay and stay and stay.

It was a life-style designed for the young. Twenty years from now it was going to look a lot less graceful and productive. Unless all leases were canceled at age thirty-five, and your family throws you out. It was a pretty problem for Wally, and a dreadful one for his tenants.

I skirted the jolly crowd and walked back to the marina. I needed the long walk in order to sort out everything I had learned from Walter Demos and fit it into the facts and inferences I had acquired before chatting with him.

9

THE DAY was darkening prematurely by the time I got back to the marina. As I passed the office there was a bright blue click of lightning, a white dazzle, and an enormous crash of thunder. I ran through the first heavy drops and boarded the *Flush*.

It was still locked, the security system still operative. Meyer was not back yet. My note to him was still where I had left it. He arrived, soaking wet, ten minutes later.

After he had changed, we sat in the lounge and exchanged information.

"Frederick Van Harn is a very impressive young man," Meyer told me. "In a very short time he has built up a very wide-ranging and profitable practice of law. He has been pulling together the shattered remnants of the Democratic Party in this county. He will very probably run for the state legislature and very probably will make it, after he marries Jane Schermer. Her Uncle Jake is the power and money behind the party. Van Harn can speak very persuasively in public. A lot of people don't care for him person-

ally, but they have a grudging respect for the way he came back and started
building a career right on the top of the ruin his father made of *his* life. About
two years ago Van Harn bought the Carpenter ranch twelve miles west of
town. The Schermers live out that way. Jane has extensive grove land out
there."

"From what Joanna said, I'd think this reputation as a womanizer would
get in the way of his electioneering."

"The general feeling around the area seems to be that he has a way with
the ladies, but he'll settle down after he marries Jane. It isn't doing him any
harm that I could see. And I spent my time drinking beer in a place across
from the courthouse. Bail bondsmen. An investigator for the state's attorney.
Bartender. A lady from the tax office. There was just one questionable area
that turned up."

"Such as?"

"Gossip. About money. It just seems to the spectators that Freddy has
bought too much too fast. They wonder if maybe Freddy's father killed himself because he couldn't avoid being caught, but left a stash of cash around
somewhere. They say the ranch he bought is twelve hundred acres, high and
dry. It had to be at least a million one, even without the ranch house and the
man-made lake and the airstrip and hangar. So even if he made out well in
the law, how could he pay his taxes and still have enough left over for his
life-style? He's about thirty years old, and he's been at it here just six years,
but he started slow and small."

"Did you get any information on how well his father lived?"

"Oh, very well, apparently. Cars, boats, hunting lodges, women."

"You've come back with a lot."

Meyer smiled. "It's a cozy bar. The conversation was general. Everybody
joined in. Freddy has charisma. He's one of the people that other people like
to talk about. So it was easy. Besides, due to constant pressure from you,
I'm getting better at being a sneak."

"That isn't a word I would have chosen."

"Once you face up to reality, everything is easier."

From time to time the rain came down with such a roar we couldn't hear
each other. Wind buffeted the *Flush,* thudding her against the fenders I had
put out and made fast to the pilings. Then the rain steadied down into a hard,
continuing downpour. I opened two cans of chili, and Meyer doctored the
brew with some chopped hot pickled peppers and some pepper seeds. He
does not approve of chili unless the tears are running down his cheeks while
he eats. His specialty, Meyer's Superior Cocktail Dip, is made with dry
Chinese mustard moistened to the proper consistency with Tabasco sauce.
The unsuspecting have been known to leap four feet straight up into the air
after scooping up a tiny portion on a potato chip. Strong men have come
down running and gone right through the wall when they missed the open
doorway.

It was a good night to stay aboard. It was a good night to conjecture, to try
various possible patterns of human behavior and see how well they fit, much
like kids in the attic trying on old uniforms, wearing old medals.

I got out charts of the Caribbean and worked out alternate routes from
Bayside to Kingston and to Montego Bay. It was easier to route back in pre-

Castro days. (Maybe everything was easier.) I made it 650, if you were a straight crow. But avoiding Fidel's air space with enough of a margin of comfort made it 1,000 miles. No great problem for the huskier variety of private aircraft, provided fuel was available at the Jamaica end.

So add in the Bertram. From predawn to after dark would give you, say, sixteen hours. Allowing for variations in wind and weather and the size of the seas, call it an outside distance of 120 or 130 out and the same back. That would also allow some time at the far end, for rendezvous.

As I had to start somewhere, I picked 220 mph for the aircraft cruising speed. Give it an hour at the far end for gassing and loading. Ten hours would do it. Leave in daylight, return by daylight. Okay, so why push the boat so hard? Probably two reasons. First, because the seas close to Florida are so full of small craft, you have to go a long way to get out of the traffic. Second, once you are in open empty water, you are too hard to find from the air. So you have to head for some distinctive land mass that the aircraft can find without too much trouble.

I drew a 130-mile half circle on the chart, with the point of the compass at Bayside. Of the areas included, I was willing to vote for the north side of Grand Bahama, over away from the folks and the casinos, where the water is tricky. Big stuff goes way north to come around into the Tongue of the Ocean. Little stuff stays inside, south of Grand Bahama. If they picked a tiny island off the north shore, a pilot could orient himself by the configuration of Grand Bahama, head for the tiny island, and the rendezvous point could be, for example, a mile north of that crumb of land.

If they had a source in the Bahamas for the Jamaican weed, then I was wrong. But that was not likely. Too much risk and too low a margin.

And our Freddy Van Harn has an airstrip and a hangar. And he was Jack Omaha's lawyer. Chris Omaha's lawyer. Lawyer for Superior. Lawyer for Carrie, and Susan, and the marina.

"The invisible mass," Meyer said, "distorting the orbits."

"Distorting the orbits, or removing the planets?"

"But why?" Meyer asked.

"You know, that's really a rotten question."

"It has to be answered. Otherwise there's nothing."

"Let's find out first if he has an airplane."

"How?"

"The direct approach. Let's go look. Very very early tomorrow."

Somebody came hurrying out of the rain and boarded the *Flush*. We both heard the warning bell. I snapped on the aft floods, and through the rain curtain we saw Joanna scuttle close to the door for shelter. She was holding a package.

I let her in. She was one very damp lady.

"Hey!" she said. "This is such a rotten Saturday night, all things considered, I decided we ought to have some kind of celebration. Okay?" She turned and put her package on the table, her back to me. "And it just so happens—"

There was a huge white ringing crash, blinding light, deafening sound, and I was spun and dropped into darkness, hands out to break the fall that never ended . . .

*   *   *

I opened my eyes and looked up at a white ceiling. There was an annoying whining ringing sound going on which made it difficult to think clearly. I looked back up over my head and saw the familiar white tubular headboard of your average hospital bed and thought, Oh, Christ, not again! A quarter millimeter at a time I rolled my head to the left and saw a narrow solitary window with the venetian blinds almost but not quite closed. A white floor lamp beside the window was turned on. The chair in front of the window was empty. My head made a funny sound against the pillow as I rolled it back into place. I brought up from beneath the covers a slow brown enormous hand and willed it to feel of my head. It felt bandage and then moved dumbly back to lie inert against my chest. So. The other arm worked. Both legs worked. I wished somebody would turn off the ringing. I rolled my head to the right and saw a closed door. A long sigh ended in sleep.

I woke up. The ringing was not quite as loud. There was night instead of sunshine between the slats of the blind. I thought nothing had changed until I found I couldn't move my right arm. I turned my head and studied the arm. It was strapped to a board. There was a needle in the vein inside my elbow. The needle was taped in place. I saw a rubber tube that went up to a bottle hanging over me. It seemed to be about half empty. The stuff in it was gray-white and semitransparent. I reached around in my head for the nurse word: I.V. Meaning . . . intravenous. Meaning I was having dinner.

After considerable fumbling around I found a push button safety-pinned where I was least likely to be able to reach it with my left hand. But I managed, and I thumbed it down.

After a few minutes the door was slung open and a dainty little white-haired nurse about fifty years old came trotting in, "Oh, hey!" she said. "Oh, good!" Then she said something I couldn't hear because of the ringing.

"What? Somebody turn off the damn bell."

She leaned close. She laughed. "Bell? It's in your ears, sweetie. From the bomb."

"Bomb?"

She checked the I.V. and said, "You're doing okay here. They're not going to have to go into your skull, sweetie. Now be patient. I'm supposed to get Dr. Owings to check you."

"Where am I?"

"Ask your doctor, sweetie." And she was gone, the door hissing slowly shut behind her.

Dr. Owings really took his time. I found out later that he was out of the hospital. And I found out that one Harry Max Scorf wanted to be present when I came out of it, if I came out of it.

After an hour, Dr. Hubert Owings came in, wearing that familiar look of the distracted, overworked professional. If you ordered a doctor type from central casting, they wouldn't have sent Hubert. He looked like a cowhand in a cigarette ad, even to the lock of hair falling forward across the hero forehead. The man who followed him in was small and spare and old. He wore a thick ugly gray suit, a frayed and soiled shirt in a faded candy stripe. It was buttoned at the throat, but he wore no tie. He wore a gleaming white ranch hat, the Harry Truman model, and, as I found out later, gleaming black boots. His face was small, withered, and colorless.

"Mr. McGee," said my doctor irritably. "Captain Scorf may want to read you your rights."

"Now, Hube," Scorf said in a plaintive voice, "it's nothing like that. Son, I'm Harry Max Scorf, and I just want to know if you'll freely and willingly answer any questions I might have about the death of Miss Freeler."

I stared at him. "Miss Freeler?"

"Captain, if you would just sit over there and let me handle the usual questions?"

"Sure, Hube. Sure thing."

Hube shone a sharp little light into my eyes, first one and then the other. "Your name?"

I gave it at once. He straightened up and stared down at me in perplexity. I didn't know what was wrong, and then like an echo, I heard my voice giving my name, rank, and serial number.

"I don't know why I did that," I said.

"What do you remember doing last?"

"While waiting for you, doctor, I've been trying to remember. The last thing I know is that I was standing in a heavy rain under a banyan tree, and a little white dog on a screened porch was barking at me. I was on my way to see . . . someone at Fifteen Hundred Seaway Boulevard, but I don't know if I ever got there. I don't know how I got here, or why. This *is* Bayside?"

"It is. You were brought in unconscious with a severe concussion and a deep laceration on the back of your head, triangular, with a flap of scalp dangling."

"What about Meyer?"

"At the time you were brought in—"

"What about Meyer!"

"He's jes' fine." Harry Max Scorf said.

"Thanks, Captain."

Looking annoyed, Hube said, "If you'd remained unconscious any longer we were going to have to—"

"What day is this?"

"Thursday evening. Nine thirty on Thursday evening, Mr. McGee. The sixth day of June."

"For the love of—"

"Hold still, please. I'm trying to check you."

I became aware for the first time of the catheter. He sent Scorf out of the room for no good reason while he uncoupled me from the input and output tubes. He asked me if I thought I could stand up, as if I felt like trying to stand up. I did, in the ridiculous hospital long bib, and walked carefully and shakily around the bed and got back in, sweating with the effort it had taken.

He left me with Scorf, saying, "If you feel you are getting too tired, just say so, and the captain will leave."

After the door closed, Scorf said, "Now just why did you and your friend come up here from Lauderdale, McGee?"

"No answers at all, Captain. Not until the blanks are filled in. What happened? I remember now that Joanna's last name was Freeling."

"Freeler. Now what I know about the bomb comes from the two experts we had come in and check it all over. You and Meyer were on your houseboat Saturday night. It was raining hard. That girl came aboard with a package.

She put it on the table and bent over it to unwrap it. It went off. You and your friend were lucky because you were both standing behind her and not too far apart, so her body took the major force of the explosion. It blew the girl practically into two halves. She never knew what happened. It knocked both of you down, you and Meyer. You hit your head and he didn't. He's lost the hearing in one ear, but they think it's coming back."

"What did it do to the boat?"

"Blew out all the glass. Blew a small hole in the deck, and blew a great big hole in the overhead, like ten feet by ten feet. Then it rained into the hole all night long. It's a mess. They're working on it now."

"They?"

"At that Westway Harbor Marina. Jason and Oliver and a friend of theirs. With Meyer helping."

"Where's Meyer?"

"Waiting for me to get out of here. He got called the first thing. Anyway, it was what they call a primitive-type bomb."

"Primitive?"

"No timing device or anything like that. They explained it to me after they found enough to know how it probably worked. The package was about so big, tied with string. There were four sticks of dynamite in there, taped together and taped into place. There was a battery and a cap and a little switch, a contact switch. What the fella who made it did, he stuck a thick piece of cardboard between the switch terminals. Then he tied string to the cardboard and led the string out a hole in the side of the box and fastened it to the string he tied around the box. So anybody unties it and pulls the string off, they pull that cardboard out and contact is made and it all goes *bam*. It went off about eight inches from the middle of that girl. Bombs are so damned ugly and messy. I can't get inside the head of a fella who'd use a bomb."

"Who are you, anyway?"

"Harry Max Scorf."

"I mean your official capacity."

"Oh, I should have said. I'm with the City and County of Bayside. Used to be just with the County. What I am, I'm kind of a special investigator. Odds and ends of this and that. I work when I please and how I please."

"Must be nice."

"It's worse than having hours. A man works longer. Then again, there isn't anything I'd rather be doing. No family. No hobbies. Tuesday I drove on down to Fort Lauderdale and I walked around that Bahia Mar Marina and asked questions about you and Meyer. You don't seem to have much visible means of support, McGee."

"Salvage work. Here and there. It's spotty."

"I combed every dang inch of what's left of your houseboat."

"What's left of it!"

"Steady there. It floats. I came to a conclusion."

"Which is?"

"I don't really think you came up here to straighten out the distribution of pot in Bayside County.

"Thanks, Scorf."

"Somebody will come along soon. No place along the coast can stay amateur. They'll take in the ones who'll play along and kill those that won't, and turn it from nickels and dimes into big money, like it is other places. I thought they were already here. Maybe they are. But it's not you and Meyer.''

"Why not?"

"Because the job calls for running the hard stuff, and running women, and selling to everybody, grannies and little kids. It calls for buying the law and buying the courts, and you and Meyer are quick enough in your own way and hard enough in your own way, but you got stopping places that are way short of what it takes. If you got a stubborn bartender and you bust both his arms and change his face, the replacement bartender is willing to do business with you. Bars are a nice distribution point for off-premises use.''

"Are you working on a book?"

"Don't get snotty with an old man. I could write one.''

"Why *are* we here?"

"Well, Harry Hascomb has one story, and that Miss Dobrovsky, she's got another, and Jack Omaha's wife has another. They add up to Carolyn Milligan having been a friend of yours. But if you though that girl was killed, and you came here to find out who did it and why, and you didn't check in with us and show credentials—which you haven't got—then you're in trouble, aren't you?"

"I know she was killed and so do you. I just wonder if it was entirely an accidental death. That's all.''

"And you wanted to attend the service?"

"Right!"

"Now you lunged at that like a bass, boy.''

"Remember, I hit my head when somebody killed Joanna.''

"We can set here and josh each other from now till the end of time. And you can duck and bob and weave all you want. The thing I've got the most of is time. If somebody did kill Carolyn on purpose, who is your guess?''

"Shouldn't this be some kind of a trade?"

"It is. You've been busy. You've been lying to people. Maybe you've been obstructing justice, or concealing the evidence of a crime, or impersonating an officer. Things like that, I won't act on any of that, at least right now. That's the trade.''

"Take me in, officer. Read me my rights.''

He sighed and shoved his white hat farther back on his head. "Well, let's see now. What have I got to trade? How about this? So far we've kept a lid on that autopsy on Cal Birdsong. It was heart, all right. But Doc Stanyard didn't like the way it looked, that big soft clot in the pleural cavity and no real sign of any aneurysm. He checked it slow and small and found that something went into there on Cal's left side, between the ribs, smaller than a knitting needle or an ice pick. It could have been a piece of stiff piano wire, sharpened to a needle point. A person could roll it between thumb and forefinder like one of those Chinese needles, to make it go in easy. The heart really hops around in there when it beats. Run that needle in there back and forth a couple of times, and you'd probably pick an artery open or puncture the sac around the heart or mess up a valve somehow. Doc found the entrance track and laid it open and took slides. I saw them this morning, all developed. The track shows up nice.''

"And what was Birdsong doing?"

"Seems he was dog tired. They tried to keep him awake on account of his being hit on the head. They don't like people sleeping with head injuries. But he was pooped and he slept hard. And forever. It wouldn't probably wake him, just that little prickle when it went through the skin."

"Does his wife know this?"

"She was one of the ones with him. We're keeping the lid on while we watch how people act."

"One of the ones with him?"

"That's all the trading material you get for now. Your turn."

"You probably know everything I could tell you."

"Try me."

"Well . . . Adding two and two, the *Christina* came in on May fourteenth, on Tuesday night, with over eight hundred pounds of marijuana aboard. Just two people went out before dawn Tuesday: Jack Omaha and Cal Birdsong. Sometimes Carrie Milligan went, but she didn't go that day because she was sick and said she would be in when she felt well enough. I would guess that Carrie went to Westway Harbor that night in a panel delivery truck owned by Superior Building Supplies. The board is docked in a good area for privacy. It's beyond the range of the dock lights, but you can drive up close to it. The grass was loaded onto the truck, and Carrie took it to Fifteen Hundred Seaway Boulevard. After it was off-loaded, Mr. Walter Demos took over, and he paid Carrie in cash for the delivery at the rate of a hundred dollars a pound. My guess is that she drove down to Superior and parked the truck where she had picked it up. She had left her own car there. Standard procedure was for her to put the money from Demos into the office safe. She and Jack Omaha had the combination. End of trade. Anything new?"

"Here and there." he said comfortably. "Here and there. Of course you spoiled any chance of us finding anything at all by scragging Demos in his big love nest. There won't be a scrap anywhere."

"He's anxious to . . . wait a second. It fades in and out, like a bad projection bulb. Sorry. My memory quits when it comes to Demos. Your turn," I added.

"Let me see. Oh, here's something you wouldn't know. In that rain Saturday night somebody had left off a package on the porch of the cottage, well back under the overhand, for Joanna Freeler. Betty Joller told me that when Joanna came home she knew what was in the package. She said it was some wine and cheese and like that, for a snack, a present from somebody who couldn't keep a date that night. Now there was just going to be the three of them in the cottage that night. Joanna and Betty Joller and Natalie Weiss. I think it was inteded for the package to be opened with the three of them there. Instead, on an impulse, that girl came running through the rain with it. She was a girl who'd rather be with men than girls any time. Your turn, McGee."

I thought it over and then I decided. What the hell, why not? I went through the whole Carrie Milligan death item by item, stressing the illogic of her supposed behavior. The gassing of her car the previous day, and the signs of fresh tampering with the gas tank drain cock.

He glared down at a freckled fist and said, "Even after years, you miss the damnedest things. You know, I decided that what she was going to do was cross the road and walk to a lighted house and ask to use the phone. With her purse setting there on the front seat in an unlocked car? Nonsense! It was right there and I missed it cold." He thought it over, and finally said, "That should do for now."

"You owe me one."

"I don't have any more to trade." He was distracted by the conjectures swarming in his head. He wanted to be up and off and away. I had put him onto the possibility of a new pattern.

He stood up. I said, "When do you lock me up?"

He focused on me completely and silently. Harry Max Scorf was no figure of fun. He was one hard and determined little man.

"I'll do whatever needs to be done," he said, and turned and left, tugging his hat to the correct angle as he went through the doorway. Before the door had wheezed entirely shut. Meyer came bursting in, grinning.

10

"WELCOME BACK!" said Meyer.

"Thanks. What about the *Flush?*"

"It floats."

"Really, how is it?"

"There's nothing that about ten thousand dollars can't fix. Don't worry about it."

"Good God, what's left of it?"

"Don't *worry* about it. You do a lot of talking about the way possessions hold us all in thrall. Pretty things are chains and shakles."

It made me gloomy. I could see a listing hulk with huge holes, with wisps of smoke rising from the interior debris. And it worried me that I should care that much. The important loss was the death of that lively girl. Blown in half. Into two girl parts. Such a great and bitter waste.

I realized that if the *Flush* were entirely gone, if it had burned to the waterline and sunk, I would be able to adjust more easily than to the uncertainty. Baubles and toys should disappear, not become broken litter.

Meyer sat beside the bed. He looked like an apprehensive owl as he said, "I kept wondering what the hell to do if you didn't wake up. People stay in a coma for years. They seem to have families to look after them."

"And you could see yourself stuck?"

"I could see myself tottering down to the drugstore saying, Yep, he's still asleep. Been nineteen years now. Gimme some more of that goo for bedsores."

"Look, I blank out during my walk that Saturday afternoon. Tell me about Joanna."

He told me. I could not make it seem real. It was easier to make the service seem real. They did the same thing for her as they did for Carrie. One less girl in a long dress to throw flowers. Good-bye, my sister Joanna. Her widower father attended, full of indignation and stiffness at such an informal heathen ceremony. But, Meyer said, it melted him quickly and he wept with the rest. It loosened the adhesions in his heart, freeing him from other rituals.

"We're losing too many girls," I told Meyer.

"You've added a new one."

"Hmm. The spry nurse lady."

"No. Cindy Birdsong. She's spent a lot of time here, so someone would be with you when you woke up. She was sure you would. Then she missed by a few minutes. She left a little while before you came out of it, apparently. She's out there now, waiting her turn."

"Why the devotion?"

"I don't know. It's some kind of penance, maybe. Or maybe she is the kind of person who has to have somebody to fret about. Cal is gone. You were at her marina when we got blown up."

"What did it do to you."

"Gave my back a little wrench and gave me a sore shoulder and one deaf ear."

"So this is Thursday, everybody keeps telling me, June sixth, they keep saying, and it is five days gone out of my life, and what useful thing have you done with those days? I don't like it any more around here, Meyer. I want to go home. Every time I get blown up by a bomb I get that same feeling. Let's go home."

"That wrapped head makes you look strange. It's like a turban. Lawrence of Arabia, or some damned mercenary. You're dark enough for any Arab, but the pale eyes make you look very savage somehow."

"Meyer, what did you find out?"

"Oh. While you were unconscious? Let me think. Oh, yes. That's quite a nice hangar out there at the ranch. Quonset-type construction. That's where ranch equipment gets repaired and maintained too. There's a slow charger for batteries, and a battery cart to boost the aircraft batteries when starting the aircraft up cold. There's a fifteen-hundred-gallon gas tank and a pump to service the aircraft and the ranch vehicles. There's about six employees out there, which means a pretty good payroll, wouldn't you say?"

"Meyer!"

"Are you supposed to sit up like that? There, that's better. Okay. Travis, he has . . ." Meyer paused and took out his little pocket notebook and flipped through the pages, grunting from time to time.

"Meyer!"

"He has a Beechcraft Baron, designation B fifty-five. It has two two-hundred-and-sixty-horsepower Continental engines, designation Ten four-seventy L. The fuselage is twenty-nine feet long, and the wingspan is thirty-seven feet ten inches. At ten thousand five hundred feet, at a long-range cruising speed of two hundred and twenty miles per hour, with optional fuel capacity of a hundred and thirty-six gallons, he can carry two people and over eight hundred pounds of cargo for sixteen hundred miles, less ten percent safety factor, which gives us fourteen hundred and forty miles. It has an automatic pilot and a lot of other things which I didn't write down here. He bought it used a year ago for sixty-five thousand. He financed it. It can carry four people. It is white with a blue stripe."

I stared at him. "And you went out there and went in the hangar!"

He stared back. "I wish I could say yes."

"What did you do?"

"You reminded me to be cautious when I looked under that Datsun."

"What did you do?"

"I did what all economists do. I went to the library. And after a two-hour search I found an article about him and his place in a magazine called *Florida Ranchorama*. It had a picture of the hangar, with airplane inside. Then I went to the airport, over to the private airplane area, and talked with some mechanics there about airplanes. I asked some questions and then I did a lot of listening. I found out more about airplanes than I care to know."

"You did very very well, old friend."

"Shall I blush and simper?"

"If you don't keep it up too long. I hate blushing and simpering in a grown man when it goes on and on."

"You seem to be doing a lot of yawning."

"I am dead tired for some unknown reason, and I am starving. I've never been so empty."

We got hold of the sprightly little old nurse, who said the kitchen was closed and who then went off and checked with Dr. Owings to see if it was all right for Meyer to bring food in. He said fine, and he would approve it because I had a private room.

When Meyer left on his errand it was after eleven, and I did not expect Mrs. Birdsong to be waiting that late. But she was. She came in, and her face went from somber to beautiful in the glow of her smile. She came around and sat on the chair and then stood up again. Awkward moment.

"Please sit down" I said.

"I am so used to sitting right here without . . ."

"You don't need any invitation, really. Meyer told me how faithful you've been."

She had seated herself again, on the edge of the chair. She wore khaki slacks, fitted and faded almost white. She wore a tan shirt with silver buttons. She clutched a brown leather purse with both hands. She wore a trace of lipstick, nothing more. When she looked down the dark glossy hair would have swung forward, would have softened her face, had she not worn it cropped so desperately short. In manner and looks it was almost as if she were trying to deny her femininity, or perhaps she was so shrewdly aware of herself, she knew that any attempt to deny it merely emphasized it.

"Faithful," she said, giving the word a bitter emphasis. "Sure, I guess so. I . . . didn't want you to wake up and not have anyone close by to tell you what happened. But I missed out on that . . . too."

"I appreciate it. Maybe it was good to have someone nearby. I think that people are never totally completely one hundred percent unconscious. I think that they are always aware to some degree of what is going on around them. I think I knew you were here."

"How could you know it was me?"

"Maybe just that someone was here who cared."

"Cared. Yes, that word is okay, Mister McGee. Cared if you lived or died. I'll buy that word."

"I'll give it to you free."

She smiled and again that transformation, but the smile did not last long enough. She flushed visibly and said, "I didn't think about it being hard to talk to you when you woke up."

"Is it hard?"

"Well, I don't know what to say. We buried my husband Monday. I've hired another person. With Jason, Oliver, and the new man, Ritchie, everything can go on . . . as before. After the insurance people told Meyer that you're not covered, he said it was okay if I told the boys to work on your houseboat whenever they have the time."

I sat up. "I'm covered!"

"For lots of things, yes. If your tanks had blown up, yes. Or sinkings or collisions or fire or running aground. But not for people bringing a bomb on board, you're not covered. Should you be sitting up like that?"

I settled down again. She reached and gave a quick shy pat on my arm.

"It's sort of in their spare time, so I'm only billing you for supplies."

"It wasn't your fault."

"I don't know. Sometimes things happen that maybe a person could have stopped."

"And people can take too much onto themselves. If I had done this . . . or that . . . or the other, then maybe this or that or the other would never have happened. The world-mother syndrome."

She thought it over. "I guess I am sort of that way."

She looked down and away, lost to me, wandering in the backwoods of her mind. It was a strong clear face, clean and dark and timeless, like the face a young monk seen in an old drawing. It was somber and passionate, withdrawn yet intensely involved. The curve of the lips, shape of the throat, set of the eyes, all spoke of fire and of need carefully suppressed, held down in merciless discipline.

Meyer came back. She stirred to leave, but he had brought food for her too. He said it had not been easy at that time of night. Quarter-pounders with cheese, in square cartons, still hot. He had brought six of them, and a container of milk and two containers of coffee. Meyer sat on the foot of my bed. I was certain I could eat three of them. I was famished. Yet it was all I could do to finish the first one. I drank the milk. I sagged back. I thought I would close my eyes for just a moment. I heard them talking, and their voices sounded strange to me, as if I were a child again, half asleep in the back seat while the parents talked together in the front seat. When the little white-haired nurse woke me up to find out if I wanted a sleeping pill, Meyer and Cindy were gone and the room was darkened. I heard a siren far away. I turned back into my sleep, wormed my way back to dreaming.

*   *   *

On Friday at eleven thirty Dr. Hubert Owings changed the dressing on my head, making it much smaller, getting away from the turban effect. He checked me over and approved me for release. I phoned the marina and got hold of Jason, who got hold of Meyer. Meyer said he would be along to pick me up in a half hour. I told him to bring money. And clothes. The clothes I had been wearing when I arrived were too badly dappled with the blood of Joanna to ever consider wearing again.

I borrowed a shower cap and took a shower. Meyer arrived and said he had stopped at the cashier's office and bought me out, and given the release ticket to the nurse at the floor station. I got up too quickly and felt dizzy. I had to sit down for a minute before I could get dressed. Meyer was worried about me.

"Hube said I'm fine. A heave concussion. No fracture. I came out of it okay, he says. If I start to have fainting spells, come back in for observation. They are short of beds or they'd keep me longer."

The world looked strange. There were little halos around the edges of every tree and building. I did very deep breathing. It is strange to sleep for five days and five nights and have the world go rolling along without you. Just like it will keep on after you're dead. The wide busy world of tire balancing, diaper changing, window washing, barn dancing, bike racing, nose picking, and bug swatting will go merrily merrily along. If they were never aware of your presence, they won't be overwhelmed by your absence.

On the way back Meyer told me that Cindy Birdsong had made arrangements for me to have a unit at the model, next to hers. I could not get any rest aboard the *Flush* because of all the sawing and hammering. I was supposed to get a lot of rest. The prescription would make me drowsy. I said it was a lot of nonsense.

But when I got out of the car I gave up all hope of walking out to look at my boat. I saved everything I had left for the immense feat of tottering over to the motel and collapsing onto the bed which Cindy and Meyer guided me to.

I slept through lunch and woke up at five o'clock. I put my shoes on and latched my belt and went on the long walk out to the *Flush*. The sun was still high and hot. I heard the power saw long before I recognized who was running it. Jason was brown and sweaty, and he was cutting some heavy-duty marine plywood to size. He let go of the trigger on the saw and put it on the uncut sheet and stuck his hand out. "You don't look so bad, Mr. McGee."

"Neither does my vessel."

"Not so bad on the outside until you notice it blew all the ports out of the lounge. It isn't so great in there."

"Do you know how to do . . . what you're doing?"

"Does it make you nervous? I can cut plywood to fit, for God's sake. The thing is to get it sealed before it rains again. We're into the rainy season now. I fixed the two broken cross members, those beam things. They were splintered. I cut out the bad parts and bolted in new pieces. It's okay now. Stronger than before."

"In case I get another gift bomb?"

"Nobody around here makes any jokes about that."

"I'm sorry.

"Joanna was an okay person. Not like Carrie, but okay. I mean there was no need for anybody to blow her to pieces."

I climbed aboard and up the side ladderway. There was one hole left, a neat rectangle about two feet by five feet. There was new plywood over an area at least sixteen by thirty feet, the major portion of the sun deck. Jason came up with the last piece and laid it in place. It fit so snugly he had to stomp it into place with his bare heels. He knelt on it and took the nails from his canvas apron and smartly whacked the nails home. He threw one to me. It had a twist like a screw, and it was heavy-duty galvanized.

"These won't let go." he said.

"You're doing a good job."

"Ollie and I both think we are. He did part of this. What I plan on doing is caulk all these seams with a resin compound before I lay the new vinyl decking. It doesn't exactly match this stuff but it's close. Here's a sample. Close enough?"

"Nobody will ever notice. What about the ports?"

"That's another story. I got a guy coming to make an estimate tomorrow morning. At ten, if you want to be in on it."

I left him to his hammering and went below and went down into the forward bilge area. It took thirty seconds to make certain nobody had located my hiding place between the fake double hull, not even the impressive Harry Max Scorf himself. I checked out three weapons. If he found them, he had had the sense to leave them where they were, entirely legal.

The lounge was a sorry mess. It was damp as a swamp and already sour with mildew, a gray-green scum spreading across the carpeting. The yellow couch lay with its feet in the air, a dead mammoth from earlier times. Shards and splinters of coffee table and chairs lay here and there in profusion. A large splinter protruded from the precise center of a stereo speaker. Another had pierced a painting I was fond of, right between the Syd and the Solomon of the painter's lower-right corner signature. There were thick brown stains of dried blood. There was a chemical smell, like cap pistols and ammonia.

Meyer came hurrying in, "Hello! Should you be roaming around like this?"

"I'm roaming around crying."

"I know. I know."

"Is the wiring messed up? Would the air conditioning work?"

"It kept blowing circuits at first, and I found out that it was the lamp that used to be on this bracket over here. It smashed the inside of it. But now things work."

"Then instead of letting the place rot, let's get some sheet Pliofilm and staple it over the ports and get the air conditioning going to start to dry it out in here. And let's pull up this carpeting and get it trucked away."

"All right. But spare me the 'us' part of it. Go back and rest."

"Is there any ice?"

There was. I assembled a flagon of Plymouth and carried it topside and sat at the controls and sipped and watched the sun sliding down the sky on the other side of Florida. That drink really slugged me. I had to pay special attention to every shift of weight and balance as I walked back to the motel. Every footfall was an engineering problem. My ears had started ringing again.

Cindy heard me and opened the interconnecting door and stood staring at me. I realized that I was visibly smashed, and I realized she'd had all too much of that in her marriage.

She shook her head. "Travis, good God. Sit down before you fall down."

"Thank you very much indeed."

"Are you going to be sick?"

"I don't think so. Thank you very much indeed."

"Here. Let's swing your legs up. Let me get your shoes."

"Thank you very much indeed."

11

I OPENED my eyes. It was night. There was a small lamp with an opaque shade on a table in a corner. Cindy Birdsong slept in the wing chair beside the table, long legs extended, ankles crossed, head tilted way over to rest on her shoulder, mouth slightly agape. I spied upon the privacy of her sleep. She rifled the closets and drawers of memory while her body lay a-sprawl, clad in gray cardigan, pink blouse, dark blue slacks.

I looked at my watch. I pressed the button. No display. The batteries had died. I had such an evil taste in my mouth I knew I had been asleep a long time. I felt as if I could eat a bison. Raw. With a dull fork.

I tiptoed to the small bathroom and eased the door shut before I turned the light on. I looked at a gaunt, weathered, and mostly unfamiliar face. I brushed my teeth with foaming energy and drank four glasses of water. My tan looked yellowed, as if I had jaundice. The white scar tissue in the left eyebrow seemed more visible than usual, the nose more askew. The eyes looked shifty and uncertain. Some kind of hero. Some kind of chronic girl-loser. Some kind of person on the edge of life, unwilling and/or unable to wedge himself into the heartlands.

When I turned the light off and opened the door, Cindy was sitting bolt upright on the edge of the chair, knees together. She hugged herself, rubbing her left shoulder, and said, "I must have dozed off. I'm sorry."

"Why be sorry? What time is it?"

She gave a little start as she looked at her watch. "Good grief, it's quarter to four! I . . . I really haven't been sleeping well lately. Until now. I guess you were so deep in sleep it was contagious. How do you feel?"

"I'm starving. You asked. I have to tell you I'm going to faint from hunger. I'll fall heavily."

At her invitation I followed her into the larger unit she had shared with Cal. There was a kitchenette arrangement behind folding doors, scrubbed to a high shine. We inventoried the possibilities, and I opted for Polish sausage and lots of eggs. She went into the bathroom and came out with minty breath and brushed hair.

She made an ample quantity and served herself a substantial helping. It was not a meal where conversation was encouraged. It was a meal which required more eggs, and she hopped up and scrambled more. She served good coffee in big mugs.

At last I felt comfortable. I felt cozy. I leaned back. She caught my eye and flushed slightly and said, "I haven't been eating hardly anything. Until now. I've lost about six pounds in the past week or so. I want to keep it off."

"You seemed about the right size and shape when I checked into your marina, lady."

"I get hippy. That's where it all goes."

The silence between us was comfortable—and then uncomfortable. The awareness grew, tangible as that ringing in the ears. She looked down, flushing again. When she got up I reached for her and caught her wrist, then tugged her gently around the corner of the table toward me. She came with an unwillingness, looking away, murmuring "Please." I pulled her to stand by me, against my thigh, and slid my hand to her waist, slid it under the edge of the pink blouse to clasp the smooth warm flesh where the waist was slimmest.

"No." she said in a soft dragging voice, far away.

"I have been losing girls," I said. "It has to stop."

"I'm not a girl. Not any more, I'm not."

I stood up and put my hands on her shoulders, felt a gentle shuddering that was awareness, not revulsion.

"Cindy, I could say an awful lot of dumb things. What it would boil down to is, I'm alive, glad to be alive, and I want you."

"I . . . I just can't quite . . ."

And I steered her slowly and gently to the relative darkness of my connecting unit, through the door ahead of me, arm around her waist, blundering together to the bed.

At the bed, after she sat and I began to undo the buttons of her blouse, she pushed me away and said, "I have to say something first. Before anything happens. Listen to me. Wait. Please. When I heard he was dead there was . . . some kind of dirty joy in me. I cried and carried on because people expected me to."

"It's like that sometimes."

"I don't want it to be like that for me." Her voice was uneven. "I know what they think: It was all just dandy great until he got on the booze. Well, it wasn't all that great. It wasn't even half good between us. He wanted it to be great. I couldn't really love him. I tried to imitate loving him, but he knew it had all gone away for me. He knew I felt empty. That's why he started drinking like that. People got it all backward. And I feel so . . . so rotten. So sick. So really terrible about . . . what I did to him."

It was all the confession she could handle. Guilt broke the dam inside her. I held her and she rocked herself back and forth in her inner agony. Guilt is the most merciless disease of man. It stains all the other areas of living. It darkens all skies.

I held her and eased her and soothed her. When she was nearly quiet, except for the occasional hiccup sob, I wondered if she was too spent for love. I peeled her gently and quietly out of her clothes. When we were naked and enclasped, facing each other on the motel bed, there seemed to be a great deal of her, long and firm and rich, with a body heat degrees above mine.

We were the wounded, she from all the trauma of her tears, me from the concussion and the five lost days. So it was not a physical, sexual greed that motored us.

It was an affirmation, a way to be less alone. In fact for quite a long time it seemed as if it would be lovemaking without climax, with only slowness, tenderness, and affection.

With the first of morning light she found a slow and lasting release and faded from that crest into the downslope of sleep. I eased out of the bed to close the slats of the blinds and shut out the increasing brightness. As I went back to bed I carried an uneasy afterimage of something, some shadow or substance, flickering swiftly away from the space under the window, out of sight.

*   *   *

On Saturday afternoon I left Meyer and Oliver to finish stapling the Pliofilm over the ports and over the smashed doorway, and went back to the motel, feeling pleasantly tired, and curious as to how she would accommodate herself to this new fact of her life.

She wore a brief yellow sun dress. She came toward me and looked cautiously beyond me to see if we were observed. Then she kissed me quickly on the lips and pulled me inside her quarters for a more emphatic kiss after the door was shut.

She was smiling. She said, "I don't know what I ought to say. But what I want to say is, Thanks for a lovely evening, for a lovely late date."

"You are most very certainly absolutely welcome, ma'am."

"Can you eat beef stew?"

"Indefinitely."

"I want you to keep your strength up."

"That the best invitation I've had today. You're blushing."

"The stew is canned, dammit. I had to spell Ritchie at the office and didn't have time to fix anything special. But I added a couple of things to make it taste better."

It was excellent stew. We sat across the table from each other, by the window. We could see most of the marina from the window.

I said, "Cindy, my darling, I want to ask you some things. You might wonder why I have to ask them. But it would be a very long story, and I will tell you that long story some day but not right now. Okay?"

"Questions about what?"

"About a lot of things. First question: When Cal went off before dawn on those boat trips with Jack Omaha, where were they going?"

She tilted her head, frowning. "Off Grand Bahama Island after billfish, dear. Sometimes little Carrie Milligan went too. Jack's secretary and . . . well, playmate. I think it was a chance for them to play while Cal ran the boat. The other times they were after tuna and marlin and so on."

"Was Cal getting any extra money from anywhere, in large amounts?"

"Cal? God, no! He was good at spending it, not making it."

"Did you think those trips were strange in any way?"

"Listen, darling. I didn't much care if they were strange or not. I didn't think very much about what Cal did or didn't do. There was very limited communication between us. Before I met him I had been going with someone and I was in love with him, very deeply in love. We had the most horrible fight ever, and he went off and got married. So I went off and got married. He showed me and I showed him. I married Cal, and it is a lousy reason to get married. It was sort of okay in a limited way. The physical part was okay at first, and then it didn't hold up very well, especially not when he was drinking. About his trips, if I thought about them at all, it was to wish they'd happen oftener and last longer. And there was no extra money from anywhere. I guess I ought to tell you that these are almost the same questions our lawyer asked me."

"Fred Van Harn?"

"Yes. He was very solemn and insistent. He said that he wanted to make certain I wasn't mixed up in anything that Cal might have been doing that was against the law. I told him exactly what I've been telling you. He said that he couldn't protect me unless I was frank and open with him. He said that anything I told him was privileged information. I had to say I just didn't know anything, and that it had been a long time since Cal and I had talked much about anything. It wasn't exactly the friendliest conversation in the world."

"What do you mean by that?"

"Oh, it's just that Fred is . . . well, constantly horny. About a year ago he made a pretty startling pass at me. It was in his office. He came up behind me and hugged himself up against me and had both hands roaming all over me. I'm a very strong person."

"I noticed."

"Hush. I picked his hand up and set my teeth in his thumb. He screamed. He had to have a tetanus shot. He got over his problem very quickly. So we haven't been very chummy with each other."

"I wouldn't think so."

"Men like that have an instinct about wives, when they might be vulnerable. Something must show, somehow. For one little instant when he was doing what he was doing, I thought, Well, why not, what the hell? But then I realized that if I was going to say what the hell with somebody, it wouldn't be with Freddy. He's too conscious of those long black eyelashes of his. So I bit him to the bone."

"That pleases me."

"What *was* Cal doing on those trips?"

"Smuggling narcotics."

She stared at me. "You've got to be kidding! You really have got to be kidding!"

"Jamaican marijuana."

"Oh. Just grass. Well . . . ."

"What's the matter?"

"*That's* where he got that stuff. He insisted I try it. A sloppy cigarette, twisted at the ends. A toke, he called it. A joint. He showed me how you're supposed to do it. Then we made love after he knew I was feeling it a lot. Love was strange and dreamy. I could hear the sound his hand made on my skin, a little brushing sound. Things went on forever, and I knew every part of it while it was going on. And I started crying and couldn't stop. It was so sweet and sad I couldn't stop crying. That made him angry and he went storming out. That was the last time we ever made love together, and that was . . . months ago. I guess that was part of what he was smuggling, he and Jack?"

"Probably."

"I liked it and I didn't like it. I would like to try it with somebody I really love sometime, but not until I'd tried everything else first with that person."

She got up and took the dishes to the sink.

I watched her, appreciating the way the brief yellow dress made her legs look uncommonly tan and uncommonly long.

Yet I had the curious feeling that I had not really made love to her. We could make small bawdy jokes together. We could kiss in excellent imitation of newfound lovers. I could look upon her in happy memory of the last time and steamy anticipation of the next time, but at the same time feel as if we were theater people, trained to give a convincing imitation of desire. We were close. We knew all the motions. Yet in a way I could not define we were insulated from each other, not quite touching in some deep and important way.

As a test I went up behind her and put my arms around her and pulled her close. She tilted her head back and said, "You risk a tetanus shot, sir."

"Worth it, ma'am."

"Listen. Where did the money go? If he was taking risks like that, where is the money?"

"I don't know. Maybe he hid it in some safe place, or somebody was holding it for him."

As I turned her around she said, "He used to worry so much about the money we owe on the marina. He used to fret and fume. Hey! What are we doing now?"

"It's siesta time. This is called getting you ready for your three o'clock nap."

"Don't you think you better move back onto your houseboat?"

"Right now?"

"Well . . . not exactly right now, okay?"

*   *   *

By Sunday afternoon the air conditioning was making good headway against the dampness aboard the *Flush*. A milky light and blurred outlines of nearby boats shone thorugh the Pliofilm. The carpeting had been jettisoned, and Meyer had samples to study, before rendering advice.

The ninth day of June. I hadn't adjusted to the five-day gap in my memory. I was being hustled along too fast into the time stream. Ears ringing. A sweet and greedy lady to be with.

"Make some sense of things," I asked Meyer.

He stopped playing solitaire with his carpet samples. "I cannot come up with an overview," he said. "I can sense no paradigm that later events will prove out. I can construct no model from what we have."

"Thanks."

"Believe me, it's nothing."

"I know. I know."

"How about this blue? Indoor-outdoor. Won't fade."

"It's truly lovely, Meyer."

"Come on. Don't you care how it's going to look?"

"Intensely."

"All things considered, you should be jollier, Travis."

"Than whom?"

"Than whom has not such a handsome lady tending his convalescence."

"I feel disoriented. I have a dull ache in the back of my head, and I live in a motel."

Further discussion of my melancholy was terminated by the arrival of Jason-Jesus with Susan Dobrovsky. She looked sallow and subdued, with smudges under her eyes and a listless manner. Jason was being very firm and forthright. The protector. No social strokes. No discussion of the weather. He planted his feet and got right into it.

"Susan and I have been developing a useful dialogue about her situation here. We've decided that it is more important for her to get away, to get back to Nutley, than it is to hang around while Van Harn takes care of the last little legal details regarding Carrie's death."

She sat on the edge of the yellow couch which was going to have to be recovered. "I want to leave," she said, in a very small voice. "Everything here has been so rotten."

"Mr. McGee, Susan told me that you told her that you owed Carrie some money. You paid off the funeral home in cash. Is there more money Susan should have?"

"Yes."

"How much?"

"What's your special interest in this, Jason?"

"Somebody has to care about situations like this. People have to take care of people."

"Granted. Let me talk to Susan alone. Meyer, why don't you go topside with Jason?"

When they had left and the Pliofilm curtain had fallen back into place, I went over and sat beside her on the couch. She became very still, quite rigid. It seemed a curious reaction. I touched her arm and she made a huge flinching motion, ending up two feet farther away from me.

"Hey," I said. "Whoa. Settle down."

"I'm sorry. I'm sorry. It's just that I'm not reacting to things . . . normally. To being touched by anybody. I can't help it."

"What happened to you?"

She gave me a wide, bright, terrible smile. "Happened? Oh, I was a guest at the V-H Ranch yesterday and the day before. That's all. Mr. Van Harn raises Black Angus and breeds horses. He has twelve hundred acres out there, and the old Carpenter ranch house was built out of hard pine in nineteen twenty-one and it's still as solid as a rock I . . . nothing . . . can't . . ."

She bent abruptly forward, face in her hands, hands resting on her knees. I reached to touch her and pulled my hand back in time.

"Were you forced?"

Her voice was muffled. "Yes. No. I don't know. I don't know what to say. He kept after me and after me and after me. It went on and on. I got so tired. So I thought . . . I don't know what I thought. Just that if I let him that would be the end of it."

"Susan, I have to know something. Did he ask you anything about Carrie?"

"There wasn't much talking."

"Did he ask you anything at all about Carrie?"

"Well, he wanted to know the last time I'd talked to her, and so I told him about the long phone call, the one I told you about too. He made me remember everything she said. One part that I told him was about you. You know. Carrie said to me that if a person named Travis McGee got in touch with me I was to trust him all the way."

"Did he seem interested in that?"

"Not any more than in any of the rest of it. He just kept me going over it and over it until he saw there wasn't any part of it I hadn't told him. That was the only talking there was, mostly."

"When did this conversation take place?"

"Yesterday, I think. Yes, yesterday. Early in the morning, I think. I remember the sounds the birds were making. Early sounds."

"How did you get back?"

"He drove me in and let me off at the Inn. He had a meeting. Maybe it was three o'clock yesterday afternoon. Jason came over this morning. I . . . told him about it. I wanted to tell somebody about how damned dumb I was."

"How did Jason react?"

"He wants to go kill him. What good would that do anybody? I shouldn't have gone out there with him. Joanna told me enough about him so I should have been careful, more careful. Mr. McGee, is there any more money? And you still have Carrie's rings. I remember Mr. Rucker giving them to you. He tried to give them to me and I couldn't take them then. I can now. Is there any money?"

"A lot of money."

"A lot?"

"Ninety-four thousand dollars in cash."

Her face went quite blank as she stared at me. She rubbed the palms of her hands on her forearms, one and then the other. "What?"

"Ninety-four thousand two hundred, less six hundred and eighty-six fifty that I paid Rucker. Ninety-three thousand something."

She rubbed the palms of her hands together. She narrowed those tilted gray-green eyes. She swung her hair back with a toss of her head. "Where would . . . Carrie get that?"

"From something she was involved in."

"From smuggling marijuana?"

"Did someone suggest that to you?"

"Betty Joller. It had something to do with why she left the cottage and went to live at that Fifteen Hundred place, Betty said. Would she make that much all for herself?"

"It's possible."

"She always wanted to have a lot of money."

"On the other hand, maybe the money is Van Harn's."

Her sallow round face looked stricken. "Would she be mixed up with him in anything? I wonder if he ever . . . made love to my sister. Jesus! That word doesn't fit. Love!"

"I wouldn't know."

She looked thoughtful. "She was always a stronger type person than me. I mean she could probably handle that kind of a man better than I could. Being older and married and so on. I never knew about men like that. He just kept confusing me. I guess I want that money now. Where is it?"

"In a very safe place."

"Can you get it for me?"

"Do you want to travel with that much in cash?"

"Oh. No. I guess not."

"I can get it to you later. What are you going to do with it when you get it?"

"I don't know. Put it in a deposit box, I guess. I don't know about taxes and so on. And her estate. On the phone something she said made me think she gave you some money too."

"She did. I hope it's going to be enough to get my houseboat fixed up. It was a fee for services. I am trying to find out who killed her."

"Who killed her! You're confusing me."

"Fly out of here. Fly home. I'll bring the money."

"When?"

"When I find out what went on here."

"And you'll tell me? Did somebody actually kill Carrie?"

"It's a possibility."

"Because of what she was doing? Because of the smuggling?"

"I would think so. In the meanwhile, Susan, not one word to anybody. Not even Jason."

"But I am very—"

"Not even Jason. Damn it, she told you to trust me. So trust me. Don't stand around dragging your feet."

"Well, then. Not even Jason."

As I went out onto the side deck with her, I saw Oliver trotting toward the *Flush*. He looked solemn. "Judge Schermer wants to talk to you, Mr. McGee."

"Send him along then."

"Oh, no. He wants you at his car. He's up there by the office."

12

IT WAS a spanking new Cadillac limousine, black as a crow's wing. It had tinted glass. I saw the black chauffeur walking offstage toward a shady bench.

A young woman stood beside the car. She put her hand out. "I'm Jane Schermer, Mr. McGee. Sorry to disturb you like this, but my uncle is anxious to talk to you."

She was a young woman with a sunburned flavor of ranchlands, cattle, and horses. She had a prematurely middle-aged face, doughy and slightly heavy in the jowls. She was oddly built, tall and broad, with vestigial breasts and very little indentation at the waist. The accent was expensive finishing school, possibly in Pennsylvania.

Jane opened the rear door and said, "Mr. McGee, Uncle Jake."

"How do you do, Judge Schermer," I said politely.

"Jane, you go take a little walk for yourself. This is man talk. Give us fifteen minutes. McGee, come on in here, but don't sit beside me. You can't talk to a man sitting beside you, damn it. Open up that jump seat and sit facing me. That's fine. Please don't smoke."

"I had no intention of so doing."

He chuckled. "No intention of so doing. You ever read for the law? Can't get the stink out of the upholstery."

He looked ludicrously like Harry Max Scorf. He looked as if somebody had taken Harry Max and inflated him until his skin was shiny-tight and then had spray-painted him pink. His round stomach rested on his round thighs. He wore khakis and a straw ranch hat. The motor purred almost soundlessly. The compressor for the air conditioning clicked on and off.

"You're one sizable son of a bitch, aren't you?" he said. "That's some goddamn pair of wrists on you. You go about two twenty-five?"

"Few people guess it that close."

"I guess a lot of things close. It's been a help over the years."

"Do you want to get to some kind of point?"

"Saving us both time, eh? I have a protégé."

"Named Freddy Van Harn, who is engaged to be married to your niece, Jane Schermer. People think he has a political future. Then there could be those who don't think he has any future at all."

"You are a quick one, all right. You surely are. Frederick and I discuss his future and his current problems from time to time. You came up as one of his current problems."

"Me?"

"Pure bug-eyed astonishment, eh? Frederick is a lively young man. It's entirely possible for a fellow like him to become involved in something foolish out of a sense of risk and adventure. At his age—he's only twenty-nine—a single man can do some foolish things, never quite realizing that he might be destroying his whole future and destroying the dreams of the people depending on him. A man can have his sense of values warped by expediency sometimes, McGee. In Frederick's case, he's wanted to make money fast and make it big to wipe out the local memories of his father, a man who made a terrible mistake and took his life. Frederick became overextended, and he took a foolish risk in an effort to make some quick money. I've been very severe with him about that."

"What kind of risk?"

"We don't have to go into that here."

"Then let's say he was flying in grass, dropping it to a friend in a power boat. That would be profitable and foolish enough, don't you think?"

"Out of the goodness of my heart, I would advise you not to get too smart-mouth and high-ass around me. It makes me irritable, and when I get irritable, I'm harder to deal with."

"I'm not after a deal."

"You might be sooner than you know."

"Whatever that might mean."

"Frederick Van Harn is a very talented attorney, and he has that special kind of charisma which means he can go far in public service. It's past time that me and my little group had somebody in Tallahassee speaking up for this county and our special problems here. We've all he'ped him along ever' way we could, ever since he got out of Stetson and set up practice here. Once he's married to Janie he won't have any more money problems to fret about and do foolish things trying to solve them. You get what I mean. Janie inherited ten thousand acres of the most profitable grove lands in this whole state."

"How nice for her."

"McGee, we're talking about image here. We're building an image people are going to trust. You ought to hear that boy give a speech. Make you tingle all over. What I wouldn't want to happen, I wouldn't want anybody to come here, some stranger, and try to make a big fuss based entirely on the word of some dead thieving slut."

"You wouldn't?"

"Especially when it would be bad timing for Frederick in his career. A man shouldn't lose his whole future on acount of one foolish act. It wouldn't be fair, would it?"

"To whom?"

"To those of us working hard to see dreams come true."

I shook my head. "Judge, you picked the wrong protégé. You picked a bad one."

"What are you talking about?"

"This Ready Freddy is kinky, Judge. He's all twisted in the sex areas."

"By God, there's nothing twisted about a man liking his pussy and going after it any danged place he can find it. When I was that boy's age I was ranging three counties on the moonlight nights."

"He likes it to hurt them, Judge. He liked to force them. He likes to scare them. He likes to humiliate them. He leaves them with bad memories and a bad case of the shakes."

"I'd say you've been listening to some foolish woman with too many inhibitions to be any damn good in bed. I'd stake my life that boy is normal. And when he's got a wife and career he'll be too busy to go tomcatting."

"That sexy wife ought to keep him at home, all right."

"Watch yourself! You got a lot more mouth than you need."

"Judge, we have arrived at the end of our discussion. Weird as it may seem to you, I think your protégé is a murderous, spooky fellow. I think he has been going around killing people. I think he killed two friends of mine. Tell him that."

I reached behind me for the door handle. "Wait!" he said sharply. "What are you trying to pull? You can't believe that shit!"

"But I do!"

We locked stares for ten long seconds. And then he looked down and away, lips pursed. "We couldn't be that far wrong," he said softly wonderingly. He shook himself and glowered at me. "You want to raise the ante. All right. Here is your deal. Twenty-five thousand dollars cash to get out of this county and stay out."

"Not for ten times the offer, Judge."

"You are dead wrong about Frederick. Believe me."

"I'll have to prove that to myself in my own way."

"Stop reaching back of you for that door handle. Set a minute. Everybody wants something bad. What is it you want?"

"It isn't nice to go around killing people."

"Frederick wouldn't kill anybody. Have you got some romantical notion about getting even for Carrie Milligan? My God, McGee, these people that get into drugs, they've got the life expectancy of a mayfly. That girl probably didn't know where she was or what she was doing. She walked into traffic."

"Like Joanna."

"A bomb? Frederick Van Harn fooling around with bombs? That's ridiculous. What do you want? What are you after?"

"Nothing you'd understand, Judge."

"I understand a lot of things. I understand the world is too full of people and half a billion of 'em are starving this year. I understand there's a few million tons of phosphate under the ranchlands down in the southeast corner of this county, and the ecology freaks have kept National Minerals Industries from strip-mining it, and there's a group of us thinks if we put Fred in the State Senate, that might get changed around and a lot of people might make out pretty good. I understand that we're not going to stand for anybody coming in here and messing up our plans. People are starving because of the shortage of fertilizer. Phosphate is high priority, McGee. Now who's going to do the most good in the world, Van Harn or you?''

"It's nice to know why you're so interested in me."

"You know what I'm going to do for you? I'm going to set up a little session between you and Frederick, and I'll let him tell you just what his involvement was."

"Are you sure you want to do that?"

"What's the matter? Afraid he'll shoot your theories full of holes?"

"I met him once. He didn't impress me, Judge."

"You caught him at a bad time. He told me about it."

"Why should he tell you?"

"I asked him if he'd ever met you."

"I'll talk to him, sure. Send this car back with him in it, and I'll talk to him right here. Like this. Alone. If he's willing."

"He's willing to do what we want him to do."

"Let's make it tomorrow. There isn't enough of today left. I seem to get tired easily."

"Tomorrow morning."

I got out. Jane Schermer was strolling slowly toward the limousine. When she saw me holding the door for her, she quickened her step. The Judge kicked the jump seat back into its niche. I handed her in and closed the door. The driver climbed in and chunked his door shut, and the car moved off through the late heat of the day, with barely audible hum of gears and engine.

Cindy was in the office. A man from Virginia was settling up, preparatory to leaving in the early morning on Monday. He was signing travelers' checks. He wore red-white-and-blue shorts and a yellow shirt, funny shoes, and a funny hat. He had narrow little shoulders and a yard of rump. He was telling Cindy how great it had been, except when the bomb went off. She said she was sorry about that bomb. He said he didn't know what people were thinking of these days. Like in Ireland.

He went out with his receipt and with Cindy's wishes for a good cruise back to Virginia. The door swung shut and she said, "You look practically gray. What is it, dear?"

"The Judge wore me down. I'm going to lie down."

"Before you fall down."

"I'm going to swim in that motel pool first."

"Should you?"

"If I don't get the dressing wet."

"Somebody ought to be with you."

The new fellow came in. Ritchie. A little older than Ollie and Jason, a lot less hairy. He said Jason was out on the docks and sure, he'd take the desk.

I went to the *Flush* and got swim trunks. Meyer wasn't aboard. I changed in the motel, and by the time I got to the pool Cindy was there, taking long sweeping strokes, a fast crawl from end to end, using kick turns. The dusk light was turning orange, making the world look odd, as though awaiting thunder. I sat on the side of the pool and admired the smooth flexing of the muscles of her back and hips and thighs as she made those turns. Then I lowered myself into the pool and paddled lethargically around, keeping my head high. She wore a white suit, white swim cap.

When I clambered out, refreshed and relaxed, she was still swimming hard, but she was beginning to labor, beginning that side to side roll of exhaustion. At last she came to the edge and clung, panting audibly. I went and took her wrists and hoisted her out. She stumbled against me and recoiled, turning away from me.

"What was that all about?"

"What was what all about?" She walked over to her towel and mopped her face, tugged the cap off, shook her dark hair out, and sat on an aluminum chaise and closed her eyes.

I sat on the concrete beside the chaise and took hold of her hand. It was brown and boneless, without response. "What was the compulsive swimming all about?"

"Exercise. That's all."

"All?"

"Well. I guess I was fighting us. Working off anger."

"Why?"

"It just seems too pat. Just too damned easy, that's all. Nothing comes for free. Everything costs. I walk around all day wanting to be in bed with you. Knowing I will be. But maybe I won't be."

"Why not?"

"Weren't you listening? I said it was too easy for us."

"And that makes it bad? That makes it ugly?"

"I didn't *say* that."

"Meyer is the one with the erudition. Meyer is the one with all the smarts. I can give you something secondhand from Meyer which might help. It comes from a smart tough old Greek by the name of Homer. I'll tell you what he said . . . if you'll use it."

"I'll try."

"He said, 'Dear to us ever is the banquet and the harp and the dance and changes of raiment and the warm bath and love and sleep.' "

She kept her eyes closed and her face told me nothing. Finally she said, "Dear to us ever. Yes." She turned her head toward me and opened her eyes and linked her fingers in mine. "Maybe that old Greek meant that a thing in and of itself is okay, without deadlines or promissory notes or anything. Just in and of itself alone."

"In and of itself together."

"Well, sure."

And so we went into the motel where there was a last pink tinge of sunlight dimly reflected on a far wall. Out of the wet suits our bodies were enclasped clammy cool, but swiftly heating. There was no constraint in her, only a fp merging and changing energy, quite swift and certain of itself, strong and searching.

When I awoke she was gone. There was a rusty old projector in the back of my mind, showing underexposed film on a mildewed screen. The projection bulb kept burning out and the film kept jamming in the gate, but by watching closely I could make most of it out. Memory was healing itself, taking me from banyan shelter in the rain to Fifteen Hundred to my talk with the bald man. It was all of a piece, but with murky places which I hoped would become more clear to me as time went on.

It was four in the morning. I was on the edge of sleep, beginning to hallucinate back into my dreams, when the creak of the interconnecting door brought me awake. I smelled her perfume. Her groping hand touched my shoulder. She whispered my name.

I turned the sheet back for her and she came shivering in beside me, chattering her teeth. She wore something gauzy and hip-length.

"What's the matter?"

"I dreamed you were d-d-dead too, darling."

"I'm not."

"I just had to come in and hold you. That's all I want."

"Everything is all right. It's all right."

"I'll be okay in a little wh-while."

I held her, close and safe. She felt restless for quite a long time, and then gradually her breathing slowed and deepened. I tried to visualize her face but could not, and at the edge of sleep I had the nightmare vision of face without features, of a rounded, tanned expanse of flesh, anonymous as the back of her shoulder.

When I awoke at dawn she was still with me. I thought I was aboard the *Flush,* and for a time I did not know who she was. Her leg jumped twice and she made a whining sound before turning back into heavy sleep.

As once again she became restless, I tried to find the answer to my feeling that I could not seem to get truly close to her. I did not know enough about her. Had she fallen out of apple trees, ridden a red bike, built castles in a sandbox, scabbed her knees, worshiped her daddy, sung in a choir, written poetry, walked in the rain? She did not tell me enough. I wanted to know all of the complex of experience which had finally brought her to this place and time, to this moment with her dark hair fragrant and pressed against the edge of my chin. A widow, now indulging herself in the delights of the flesh, so long denied by the hulking drunken husband, and feeling guilt for such indulgence. I was being used, and wanted a deeper and truer contact. I wondered if I wanted her to be in love with me, as a sop to my ego, perhaps.

There was a change in the feel of her, in the textures of her, that told me she was now awake. Gently, gently, she disengaged herself as I feigned sleep. She sat on the edge of the bed and groped for the short nightgown, then stood and put it on. Through slitted eyes I saw her put a fist in front of a wide yawn, a yawn so huge it made her shudder. She moved silently across the room and slipped through the interconnecting door. I heard the soft click of the latch and the second metallic sound that meant she had locked the door behind her. A gesture for the motel maid? A disavowal? Or the end of the episode?

13

FREDERICK VAN HARN sat in the same rear corner of the limousine as had the Judge. The black chauffeur sat upon a different bench because the shade patterns were different at ten o'clock on that Monday morning. The engine ran as quietly as before, the compressor clicking on and off.

I sat on the same jump seat, turned to face him. I wore boat pants, sandals, a faded old shirt from Guatemala. He wore a beige business suit, white shirt, tie of dark green silk, dark brown loafers polished to satin gloss. As he looked directly at me I saw that his sideburns were precisely even. The sideburn hair was long, brushed back to cover the ears. Neat little ears, I imagined. Maybe a bit pointed on the top. Olive skin, delicate features, long dark eyelashes, brown liquid eyes.

I had been an annoyance to him when we had met at Jack Omaha's house. He studied me quietly, very much as ease, not the least bit uncomfortable. His hands were long and sinewy, and he clasped his fingers around a slightly upraised knee.

"Mr. McGee, you got under my skin pretty good when we met at Chris's place."

"You went into a massive tizzy."

He smiled. "Are you trying to do it again?"

"I don't know. What are *you* trying to do?"

It was an engaging smile. Very direct. "I'm trying to get you off my back. Uncle Jake thinks you could hurt me."

"Don't you?"

The smile faded. He looked earnest. "I really don't see how. Oh, if you were politically inclined you could give me some static by bringing up the dumb-ass bit about flying marijuana in, but you'd have no proof of that, and I think I could deny it convincingly. Besides, I don't think people are as dead set against it as they used to be. The use of it is too prevalent. I hear that a long time ago the rumrunners were folk heroes along this coast. It's getting to be much the same with grass. I'm not sure you could hurt me."

"What if somebody got notarized statements from Betty Joller and Susan Dobrovsky? Do you think your kinky love life could hurt you any if it came out?"

He colored but recovered quickly. "People must find it remarkably easy to talk to you, McGee. I don't think there's anything kinky about enjoying the hard sell. Reluctance stimulates me. Maybe in retrospect they see it differently than it was. But in both those cases there were plenty of squeals of girlish joy."

"Joanna thought you were tiresome."

"Please stop trying to bait me. Let's try to get along at least a little bit. Try to understand each other."

"What do you want me to understand?"

He shrugged. "How I was such a damned fool. I'd flown to most of the islands. I'm a good pilot. I've got a good airplane and I keep it in first-class condition. As lawyer for Superior Building Supplies, I knew Jack and Harry were in bad shape and things were getting worse. I think it was Jack who brought it up, like a joke. I had said something about falling behind on the ranch payments and trying to get an extension on the loan. He said we ought to work out a way to bring grass in. He said he could find a nice outlet for us. We met again and planned how we could do it, still treating it as a joke. Finally I went down and lined up a source in Jamaica and then we . . . went ahead. We couldn't afford much the first time. But it all worked out okay.''

"Tell me about it."

He shrugged again. "We'd rendezvous off the north shore of Grand Bahama. The coast was always clear because it's difficult water. I'd circle and drop the stuff. We would have put the big bags inside plastic bags from Omaha's stock and tied the neck so they'd float and the seawater couldn't get to the grass. They'd gather them in with a boat hook. Very simple.''

"How about the last trip?"

"What about it?"

"Who was involved?"

"Just the four of us. Carrie went with me. Jack and Cal were aboard the boat. I had headwinds and I was a little late coming to the rendezvous point. At about five fifteen Carrie started horsing those sacks out the door. She was a strong person. They picked them up. Nine, I believe there were. So I put my ship right down on the deck and crossed the coast north of here and came down to the ranch and landed. She got in the little truck and went to the marina late that night, and they loaded the stuff into the truck. She drove it to the outlet and got paid off and took the money down and put it in the safe at Superior.''

"What happened to Jack Omaha?"

"I have a theory."

"Such as?"

"I think some professionals were moving in on us. It was too easy to score. I think they got to Jack and scared him badly. I think that he stayed with Carrie and they went down and emptied the safe and went their separate ways. A lot of that money was supposed to be mine. It would have helped me a lot to have it. As it was I had to arrange to . . . borrow it.''

"From Uncle Jake Schermer?"

His smile was ironic. "And a lot of advice went along with the money. He was upset about the whole thing. I couldn't make him understand that it wasn't as important as he was making out. It was . . . a caper. It was fun, damn it. Everybody in the group got along all right. Low risk and good money. We were planning on making one or two more trips and then splitting the money and calling it a day. I wanted to come out of it with two hundred thousand clear. And that's what Jack Omaha felt he needed to save the business.''

"Harry Hascomb wasn't in on it?"

"Harry talks to make himself important. He talks in bars. And bedrooms. Harry is a jerk. I'm talking to you now, McGee, but there is no part of this you can prove. There is no basis for indictment by anybody.''

"And the Judge and his group are going to make certain you have a nice clean record because you are going to make them all rich and happy."

After a flash of anger he spoke slowly and judiciously. "I don't know how much good I'm going to do them. I really don't. The timing is right. I can get elected. The campaign will be well financed. The incumbent is senile. I've built a good base here. I plan to announce right after the wedding. I love this part of Florida. I'm not at all certain I'd be in favor of a new deepwater port and a lot of phosphate mining and processing. It's a dirty industry. The port will bring in other industries. Maybe a refinery. But those are low-employment prospects. They won't keep young people from leaving the Bayside area. And they will pollute the water and the air. On a risk-reward basis I can't make it add up. I have the feeling I want to work in the best interests of the people who will vote me into office, not the few men who have been grooming me for office."

He was impressively convincing. He emanated a total sincerity. Right at that moment he had my vote. I could see what it was about him that made the Judge label him charismatic. He talked to me as if I were the most interesting person he would meet this year.

"What do you think I ought to do?" he asked me.

"Do what you think is right."

"That sounds so easy. Right and wrong. Black and white. Up and down. It divides the substances of life unrealistically. The world is often gray and sideways. According to the game plan, if I go to Tallahassee I ought to be able to move the situation along in five to six years. If there is world famine by then, it will be the thing I should do."

He sighed and shrugged.

"Well, it's my problem and I will have to make the decision. I know I'm going to run for the office. I'll just have to take one step at a time, McGee. I want to thank you for listening to me. I haven't killed anybody. I don't know where the money went. I got into a foolish situation because I didn't weigh all the consequences. And I'm glad now that it's over. I know that the chemistry between us is not good. I can't help that. I don't expect everybody to like me. I'll depend on your sense of fair play."

I found myself shaking hands with him. I got out of the car hastily, and after it drove away I wiped my hand on the side of my trousers. I felt dazed. He had focused a compelling personality upon me the way somebody might focus a big spotlight. He had that indefinable thing called presence, and he had it in large measure. I tried to superimpose the new image upon the fellow I had met in Jack Omaha's house, listlessly tying his tie after a session in Jack Omaha's bed. That fellow's anger had been pettish, slightly shrill. I could not overlap my two images of the man. I wondered if my previous image had somehow been warped by the great blow on the back of the head when the explosion had hurled me off my feet.

This man had been engaging, plausible, completely at ease. He made me feel as if it were very nice indeed to be taken into his confidence. There were dozens of things I wanted to ask him, but the chance was gone. The chance had driven away in a gleaming limousine, cool in the heat of the morning.

Yes, if he could project all that to a group, he could be elected. No sweat.

Yet where were you, Van Harn, when Big Cal Birdsong was dying in the hospital, with a thin wire sticking him in the heart? Were you beside the bed, charismatic and relaxed? When your men clear new ranchland, do they blow the pine stumps with dynamite? Did those lean sinewy hands hoist Carrie into the front corner of the Dodge truck? Exactly how did you make Susan look so sick at heart, so defeated and sad?

I had been trying to make it all a single interrelated series of acts of violence. But his convincing presence was making it all come unstuck, turning it all into unrelated episodes.

Harry Max Scorf said, "Have a nice chat?"

Usually I can sense people who move up close behind me. Something gives me warning. Not this time. I leapt into the air.

"Jesus!"

"Nope. Only me. Harry Max Scorf."

"Of the City and County of Bayside. I know. I know."

"Your nerves aren't real good, son."

"Yes, I had a nice chat. What else is new?"

"Let's sit," he said, leading the way to a shady bench.

I sat beside him, leaning back, squinting from the shady place out at the white dazzle of boats at the marina. I could see a brown lady in lavender bikini prone on the foredeck of a Chris, her head near the gray bulk of a big Danforth. Nearby was the silen gleaming bulk of Jack Omaha's muscular Bertram. Was it beginning to look slightly dingy? The unused boat so quickly acquires that abandoned, unloved, uncherished look. Chrome gets foggy. Bronze turns green. Aluminium pits and flakes. The lines get whiskery and the fenders get dirty. By looking to my right I could see into the office to where Cindy Birdsong stood working on a ledger, elbow on the counter, fingers clenched in her hair, tongue sticking out the corner of her mouth. Looking beyond the Bertram, beyond the bikini, I could see Meyer and Jason working, sweat-shiny, on the sun deck of the *Flush,* setting and cementing the vinyl sheets. Behind me was the traffic roar of the busy Monday streets and highways. Florida no longer slows down for June. A pity.

Harry Max Scorf produced a blue bandanna and flicked a shadow of dust off the toes of his gleaming boots. He took off his white Truman hat with care, wiped the sweatband, and placed it between us on the weathered wood of the bench. He seemed to doff force and authority along with the hat. His head was oddly pointy.

"What is new." he said, "is that the special task force hit Fifteen Hundred Seaway Boulevard at first light this morning. And some sight it was. Nine cars. Twenty-five men. Feds and state people. I was local liaison, sort of observing. They tested me out long ago and know I can keep my mouth shut. I went along with the four who hit Walter J. Demos's apartment. He'd been entertaining a little schoolteacher person in his bed. They found about thirty pounds of cannabis in a plastic bag hanging on a hook about three feet up inside his fireplace. I can tell you it was sorry shit, my friend. Weak and dusty, a lot of big lower leaves cured bad, powdery as senna leaves. Well, those two had got some clothes on and they stood in the living room, both of them crying. The little schoolteacher was crying because she was ashamed and scared for her job, which she will lose. And that ball-headed Demos was crying because he was so goddamn mad at himself he couldn't hardly stand it. All the other men were going through the other apartments. There was one crazy scramble of folks trying to get back to their own beds. I think I've got the figure right. They made fifteen arrests for possession, not counting

Demos and the teacher. Of course with Demos with that quantity, it will be for dealing, and that is heavier. You want to put it together for me?"

"You already have."

"I know. I know. But you tickle me. You've got cop sense."

"I can't remember a word of my little talk with him."

"What do you think you might have said?"

"Oh, something to open him up. Come on very very heavy, like somebody from the Office taking over the operation. An amateur like Demos would buy an act that wasn't exactly plausible. Then I suppose I would have told him to hold onto his money and wait for a delivery and not get impatient."

"You just suppose you might have said all that?"

"And left him in a posture he couldn't maintain. He is big jolly old Uncle Walter, head of the family. He is supposed to take care of everything and provide everything to make life juicy for his tenants. So when somebody showed up with some product, Uncle Wally bought it, and then they turned him in. I'd say that he was put out of business by the real professionals, easily, quietly, no fuss. He was buying enough for Fifteen Hundred, to maintain the life-style there. The squire of swingleville. The professionals wouldn't bother to work him over. The professionals use the law to weed out the amateurs."

"Did they weed out that girl, that Carolyn Milligan?"

I didn't have to think long. "You don't like that any better than I do, Captain. Makes no sense. I could never believe that."

He sighed and said, "Neither can I. I tried to figure they'd wipe out the supply group: Omaha, Birdsong, Milligan. Then go after distribution. The trouble is, they wouldn't get into that much trouble for the sake of one channel of supply in Bayside County. There's three or four other groups. It isn't all that big. It's all businesslike. Nobody kills anybody unless there is absolutely no other way at all. This whole thing won't hang together because I don't know some things I ought to know. That's always the way it is. When you know enough, all of a sudden you know it all."

"What about Carrie? Did you look into that?"

"I got with Doc Stanyard on that. We went over his autopsy notes. Her left arm was badly abraded on the outside of the forearm and upper arm, with some paint fragments driven into the skin. See what that means?"

"No."

"Use your thick head, McGee."

It took about twenty seconds before light dawned. "Okay, if she was sober enough to pull her car off the road, then she was alert enough to have the normal instinct of lifting her arm to ward off the truck bearing down on her. She would step out and try to ward it off and dodge back. Her arm was hanging at her side when she was hit, so the assumption is that she was unconscious."

"Or suiciding. Waiting for the right vehicle. Left her purse in the car. Shut her eyes and stepped out. *Bam.*"

"Which do you think?"

"I think that unless I learn more, I won't ever know what it was. Why did you have a conference with the Judge yesterday and a talk with Freddy this morning?"

"We were talking about his appeal to the electorate."

"His daddy was pleasant. Weak and pleasant and crooked. Funny thing. They say Freddy won't ever have his hand in the till because of what happened to his daddy. It did him good instead of bad. They like the way he's come up so fast."

"Too fast, Captain?"

"They changed the retirement rules when it got to be City and County of Bayside. I've got thirteen months to go. If somewhere down the road, before thirteen months are up, I get thrown off, I ride an old bicycle and eat dog food. If I last it out, I'm better off than I would have been under the old rule. If Judge Jacob Schermer and his buddies are playing poker some night and somebody at the table says they've got tired of my face, I'm through the next day."

"Scare you?"

He turned and looked at me. Those old eyes had seen everything, twice. They had looked into a lot of people. An echo of a smile touched the corner of his mouth. "Scared shitless," he murmured.

"Then I better not tell you Freddy was flying the grass from Jamaica and air-dropping it to Omaha's boat off Grand Bahama."

No, you shouldn't tell me because it would fit too close with the arithmetic I've worked up about Freddy. He dresses fancy, drinks fancy, drives fancy. He's got the ranch and the airplane and forty pair of boots. But then you got to remember that Miss Janie has ten thousand acres of grove, and under management it must turn her sixty dollar an acre a year net, on which she can afford Fred Van Harn as a play toy, but if I were Jake I wouldn't be hoping my niece would marry up with a fellow with some kind of wrong twist in his head. Two years ago something got hushed up. They got delay after delay so by the time it was ready to go to court that girl had grown some inches taller. It's said he claims he never had any idea she was only fourteen. Anyway, she got taller and older and smarter, and settled for the money. They've been grooming him for politics, first the State Senate, then maybe Governor. They really don't give a damn what kind of a man he is. What they care about is that, he goes on local television on a public issue, you never seen such mail as comes in. Begging him to run for office. That's all they care about. In fact the other stuff kind of helps them out because it makes it easier to control him. Oh, they'll have him married to Miss Janie, and she'll be a good hostess, and she'll bear him some healthy kids, and there you are. He can turn that charm on. He can charm a five-thousand-dollar fee out of a five-hundred-dollar case and make the sucker come back for more advice. What did he tell you?"

"He told me he didn't kill anybody."

"My hunch is he probably didn't. But he sure got into the pants of just about ever' woman involved in it. You got a list?"

"Carrie Milligan. Joanna Freeler. Betty Joller. Chris Omaha. He made a try at Miz Birdsong, but she bit him."

"Good for her."

"And Susan Dobrovsky."

He stared at me, registering shock. "That girl too? Son of a *bitch!*"

"He took her out to the ranch. She was suppoed to leave for home this morning. Jason was going to see her off."

"Ever since that boy was fourteen damn years old, he's been lifting every skirt he sees. There's stories about him. He goes after ever' one as if there was never going to be any more. And there's something about him, they say. The ones you'd never expect, their eyes cross and they lay back and put their heels in the air for him. There's no law against it, at least no law anybody enforces. And he doesn't seem to ever get tired of looking for it. And he finds it places you wouldn't even think of."

I admit to myself there were, indeed, a lot of places I would never think of. And a fair portion of every day when I did not think of it at all, at all.

"Vote for Van Harn," I said.

"They'll do that. Senator Van Harn. They need a man up there riding point on what they want around here. Deepwater port for the phosphate down in the south county. Refinery. And all the goodies that go along with it that only a few fellows get a piece of."

"The Judge offered me twenty-five big ones to go away and forget all about Freddy."

Harry Max Scorf looked mildly startled. "What do they think you know?"

"No more than I've told you. That he's a kink. He rapes people and kills people and spends too much money and flies grass in."

He stood up and carefully fitted his white hat back over the pointy skull, tugging it to the right angle. He gave me a sharklike smile. "What the hell do they want for a front-runner? Some kind of nance fellow? See you around, son."

                                *   *   *

When I went into the office, Cindy looked up with her customer face, cool and polite. Then the great warm smile came. "Hello," she said. It was just one word, but it was about fifteen words long.

"And hello to you. Books balance?"

"They do now. What I did, I wrote a hundred and sixteen dollars when it was supposed to be a hundred and sixty-one. I saw you out there. Captain Scorf has been around forever, and they say he's always looked exactly the same. Was he being rough with you?"

"No. He says I've got cop sense."

"Is that a good thing to have?"

"They have finished the noisy parts of repairing the *Flush*. I think I better pay my motel bill and move my toothbrush back to the boat."

She showed quick sharp dismay and disappointment before she caught herself. "Anything you wish, dear."

"If you want to bring a small portable fire extinguisher, I'll talk Meyer into cooking some of his renowned chili tonight."

"That would be nice," she said, forcing it.

"Anything wrong?"

"Nothing at all, thank you."

"Are you sure?"

"Certainly I'm sure!"

There is no going past that point. All the roads are barricaded and all the bridges are blown. The fields are mined and the artillery has every sector zeroed in.

So I went and moved my toothbrush and accessories out of the unit, went to the front, and paid a fat lady my accumulated charges. She asked me if I was feeling better, and I said I was feeling just great. She said, "It's so nice that Mrs. Birdsong has a friend nearby in her time of need. Have you known her long."

"A very long time."

"He drank, you know."

"Yes. Cal drank."

"In a way, it's a blessing."

"There are a lot of ways of looking at everything, I guess."

"Oh, yes, that's so true."

A small fire fight, with no decision. Both sides retreated.

*   *   *

When I got to the boat, the glass people had arrived. There were four of them, in white coveralls, with the pieces all cut to size, tempered glass for marine use. The foreman said they would be through by four at the latest. Jason and Meyer were celebrating the completion of the vinyl job on the sun deck by having a cold beer in the shade of the canopy over the topside control panel. I inspected the job and gave my approval.

I am skeptical of all of the so-termed marvelous advances of science. And I am suspicious of anything which tries to look like something it isn't. Thus it would seem that a coal-tar derivative patterned to look like bleached teak would turn me totally off. But it is so damned practical. If you should ever have an artery which can't be repaired, it can be replaced with woven Dacron. And, wearing that in your gut, it would be unseemly to go about muttering about the plastic world full of plastic people.

So I stand on my plastic deck and mutter whatever I please. When did I make any claim about being consistent? Or even reasonable?

I went below and checked out my stereo set. I put on the new record, Ruby Braff and George Barnes. It is nece to have one that is just out and know that it is destined to become one of the great jazz classics. I knew I had lost one speaker. I suspected I had lost more. Delicate microcircuitry cannot take that kind of explosive compression. When the noise came out, sounding like someone gargling a throatful of crickets, I snapped it off in haste.

Back to the shop. No new components. Get the Marantz stuff fixed. I did not think I could placidly endure another gleaming salesman tell me that I had to have quadraphony sound, coming at me from all directions. I have never felt any urge to stand in the middle of a group of musicians. They belong over *there*, damn it, and I belong over *here*, listening to what they are doing over *there*. Music that enfolds you, coming from some undetectable set of sources, is gimmicky, unreal, and eminently forgettable.

Jason went back to work his turn in the office. Meyer and I made some sardine sandwiches. He was glad to learn I was back aboard for good. We sat at the booth in the galley and ate. And compared notes and reports.

"We are absolutely nowhere." Meyer said.

"A perfect summary."

"Are you sure you feel okay?"

"Don't I look okay?"

"Glassy. You stare at me in a . . . goggly way."

"Come to think of it, I feel goggly and glassy."

"Just this minute. Or . . ."

"Most of the time. The light seems too bright."

"When the windows are done—"

"The ports."

"When the windows are down, we could go."

"Home?"

"And forget this whole mess, Travis."

"Tempting. Who are we supposed to be, going around finding out who did what and why?"

"That's why they have police."

"Right!"

We beamed at each other, but we both knew we were talking nonsense. The habit of involvement is not easily broken. It is even more pervasive than the habit of non-involvement, the habit of walking away when the action starts.

I told him we couldn't leave because we had a guest coming for dinner. I told him he was cooking chili.

14

We three had sat with tears running down our cheeks and told each other in choked voices that the chili was truly delicious. She and Meyer had cleaned up, telling me that I was still on semi-invalid status.

By the time they were through, there was a large dark night outside, wide as a country, high as the stars, and hot with the night winds of June.

We killed the lights and went topside to a shadowed part of the sun deck, out of the reach of dock lights. The sky was pink-orange over Bayside, all its outdoor advertising glowing against a mist made of hydrocarbon fartings of trucks and other vehicles. We aligned deck chairs on the newly repaired decking so as to look out at the stars over the Atlantic. We were into the rainy season now. The night of June tenth. Bulbous black lay low to the southeast, sullenly flickering an unseen artillery of lightning.

She on my left, Meyer on my right, the night air stirring across us and then fluttering back to stillness. Her hand crept over to my thigh, stealthily, nudged a welcome, and was enclosed by my hand, unseen by Meyer, as if we were children in church. With my thumb I rubbed the thick warm pads at the base of her fingers. I wondered if she had been told or had guessed that her husband had not died of natural causes. They would have to tell her, sooner or later, no matter how pessimistic the law felt about catching whoever had done it. Harry Max Scorf had indicated quite plainly that she was on his list of suspects. Though I knew her very well in certain limited ways, I knew her not at all in many aspects. But I could not imagine her killing in that stealthy way, jabbing a wire into the great chest while the king slept.

Harry Max Scorf, in a dogged and plodding pattern, would have long since established the identity of every person who could have gotten close to Cal Birdsong long enough to do him in.

"It always seems such a waste when it rains way out there," she said. "Sort of badly managed, to rain into the sea."

"It's moving this way," Meyer said. "But your average thunderstorm has a total life span of fifty-five minutes."

She sat up and looked across me at Meyer. "You've got to be kidding."

"Believe him," I said.

"When the conditions are right a pod will be forming in the area as the older pod is dissipating its energies. Thus we get the impression of one single storm lasting for hours. Not so."

She settled back and made a small sound of mirth and wryness. "The rest of my life," she said, "I'll see a thunderstorm and say to myself they only last fifty-five minutes."

Her hand still rested in mine, her hand warm and dry. I thought of lies and polygraphs and biofeedback. One type of biofeedback machine requires strapping a pair of electrodes to the palm of your hand. When you are tense and nervous, your palm is moist and cool and the conductivity of your skin is increased. The machine has a dial and a little electronic tone, thin and insectile. As you make yourself more calm your hand becomes more dry, the dial needle swings slowly downward, and the electronic note moves down the scale. By giving you the visible and audible results of different mental and emotional postures, in time you learn, without the machine, how to impose a great calm upon yourself, an alpha state, if you will.

Soon she would be told her husband had been murdered. The required Grand Jury hearing could not be delayed indefinitely. I rubbed my thumb back and forth across the pads on the palm of her hand, and tried to think of how to word my trick remark, and felt disgusted with myself. A rotten game to play with this woman.

Suddenly, without a word being said, I felt her palm go cold and wet. She tugged her hand away and got up and moved over to the rail and turned to lean against it, her arms folded, her shoulders hunched forward.

"What's wrong, Cindy?"

"I guess somebody walked over my grave."

She was silhouetted against the intermittent glow of distant lightning. "Did you think of something that upset you?"

"I think I'll go home now," she said.

"I'll walk you."

"I'm okay."

"No trouble."

I tried to make conversation as we walked to the motel, but she gave one-word responses. She unlocked the door and pushed it open and turned to me. I took her in my arms. Her lips were cool and firm. There was no response in lips or body, and then there was a lot. A hungry lot.

We went in and the door clicked shut. "No lights," she said. "Don't let me think about anything. Don't give me time to think about anything. Please."

The bed was by big windows. The draperies were open. The storm moved closer. The lightning flashes were vivid. Each one made a still picture of her in black and white. Black eyes and lips and hair and nipples and groin. White, white, white all the rest of her. The lightning arrested movement. It caught her in a fluid turning, mouth agape with harsh breath and effort. It froze a leg, lifting. It stopped her, astride, arms braced, halting the elliptical swing of hips, turning her into a pen and ink drawing of greatest clarity. I kept her for a long time within the prison of her own tensions, though she escaped to partial release from time to time. Each lightning stroke seemed to be brighter, each stroke bringing the thunder closer and sharper. At last the lightning made a ticking sound, filled the room with a strange hard blue light, and the great following bang of thunder made her gasp and leap. The ensuing crashing downpour of the rain was like a signal to us.

We lay damp and slack in a close and sweaty embrace, content, heavy-breathing, detumescent. The storm air moved across us, cooling our bodies. The intensity of the downpour began to slacken, but it was still a heavy tropic rain.

"Ruthie took those pills," she said.

"What?"

"You didn't know her. It was a long time ago. Bud—he was her husband —ran off a curve and hit a big tree. They gave her pills to make it easier. God, she took so many pills you couldn't talk to her, hardly. Huh? she'd say. Huh? Wha'? And sleep? She'd sleep twenty hours a day. Toby—you didn't know him either—his wife went back to see her sick mother and the airplane fell out of the sky. For Toby it was booze. After a year they had to put him away and dry him out. People use things, don't they? I'm using sex. I want it to be more and more, every time with you. It was more this time than ever. When it's so much, I can't think about anything else. The thing about me is, I'm not like this. Not really. I told you Cal hadn't touched me in ever so long. But it didn't make me feel . . . deprived. I mean it was okay. I guess I'm the way I am now, with you, because I try so hard to get my mind turned off. I try so hard, I get way way into the sex thing, like I couldn't before. I always felt a little odd about it. Ashamed, almost. I mean being so big and strong and healthy and looking . . . as if I would like it."

"You need never feel odd again."

"I won't. I won't."

"And you've got a talking jag."

"I know. And you have to listen, don't you? We don't really know each other. It's strange. I guess the way men think about these things, without me sounding like an egomaniac, what you did was luck out. You came along at the time when any presentable and sympathetic guy would be right where you are right now, doing what you are doing."

"Flattery will get you everywhere."

"Trav, please don't make flip little remarks. What our relationship is, it's backassward. It started at the end, and I want to find our beginnings. I want to know you as a person, not just want you terribly for the way you can turn my head off. It's a genuine compulsion, really."

"Okay. No flip remarks. No bedroom comedy. I saw the vulnerability and

I took advantage. So that makes it seem unreal to me too. But it's more than pure physical hunger.''

"What else is it?''

"Liking you. Wanting things to be right for you. Wanting the world to be a special place for you. Also, there's guilt.''

"About what?''

"About knowing that Cal was murdered. Harry Max Scorf told me. I don't know if he knew I'd tell you.''

She sat up, with sharp hissing exhalation. "How?'' she whispered.

I told her. She made a sick sound and closed her fingers around my arm with impressive force.

"Jason,'' she whispered.

"Are you sure?''

"I can't prove anything. Once . . . after things had been very bad—Cal was drunk and he beat me—Jason came to me and said that there were ways Cal could be killed that nobody would ever know. I made him be still. I knew he was going to say he'd do it for me. And he would have. He's a strange boy. He can't stand any kind of cruelty. He was a battered child. He nearly died of it. And he has been . . . a little bit in love with me, I think.''

"It showed, after Cal knocked you out.''

She settled slowly back down again, cheek against my chest, arm heavy across me. "I thought I saw him at the hospital the evening Cal died. I was going out to eat. I thought I saw Jason riding his bike toward the hospital at the far end of the parking lot. I didn't think any more about it until now. When I came back from eating, all those people were working on Cal so frantically. What it probably was was a piece of stiff leader wire. Cal was in one of those security rooms, single rooms, but he wasn't guarded. But I don't really *know*. So I don't have to go and tell anyone, do I?''

"Are you angry at Jason?''

"I don't *know*. Cal was killing himself in any case. They'd told him his liver was going bad and he shouldn't drink at all. I can understand why Jason did it. If he did it. Trav, help me.''

"Captain Scorf will ask questions of you, sooner or later. It would look better if you went to him. Ask him if your husband died of natural causes. If he levels with you, register shock and then tell your suspicions. It will have to be your choice as to whether you tell Jason you're going to go see Scorf and, if Jason runs, how much lead time you give him.''

"Okay. I'll do it that way. But I wish you hadn't told me anything, dear.''

"Why did you get upset tonight when we were looking at the stars and the storm?''

"Upset? Oh, I just remembered a nightmare Cal had, about a week before he died. He woke up roaring. I couldn't seem to make him wake up. I looked up at the dark sky and remembered. He had a nightmare about something falling toward him out of the sky that was going to kill him, that was going to land on him and kill him, and he couldn't get out from underneath it. He was so really terrified that I guess it left a mark on me. Half nightmre and half delirium, I guess it was. His mind had gone all warped and nasty from the drinking. Then he didn't want me to tell anybody about his nightmare! As if anybody in the world would give a damn! Tonight I remembered, and it made me feel weird and crawly.''

The rain stopped. Another pod formed and came grumbling toward us through the night. She talked in a slumbrous, murmurous voice, and then the voice ended and her breathing changed, slow, deep, and warm against my throat. I watched the flashes against the window and against the ceiling. The new storm moved closer, and at last the thunder became loud enough to awaken her. She started, then settled back. "I was dreaming," she said.

"Pleasant dreams?"

"Not really. I was in front of a judge's bench. It was very high, so high I couldn't see him at all. They wouldn't let me move back to where I could see him, and it made me angry. I knew he would never believe me unless I could see him and he could see me. I was accused of something about Jason, doing something wrong.''

"Such as?"

"I don't *know*. I guess I was guilty of something, all right. I mean when somebody is attracted to you, you know about it. And it feels good to be admired that way. So you . . . respond to it. Do you know what I mean? It changes the way you look at the other person, and the way you walk when you walk away from them, and it changes the pitch of your voice when you laugh. So I guess . . . those little things would add up, and maybe that's why he did what he did. *If* he did it.''

"Don't go around looking for guilt.''

"I miss Cal. I miss him every single day of my life. It had gotten to be a rotten marriage, and I miss him terribly.''

"Involvement doesn't have to be good or bad. It just is. It exists. And when it stops, it leaves emptiness.''

"Something happens, and I think how I'll have to tell Cal about that. Then I know I can't. Oh, hell.''

She began to weep, without particular emphasis. Gentle tears for a rainy night. When they subsided she began an imitation of need, a faking of desire. But the textures of her mouth were unconvincing. The storm time had worn us both out. I was glad she did not persist, as male pride would have made the responsive effort obligatory. The second storm was upon us, the wet wind blowing across weary bodies. I covered us with the sheet. The lightning once again took still pictures of the room, of her head on the pillow beside me. After the crashing downpour turned to a diminishing rain, she slept. When the rain stopped I slipped out of the bed, closed the draperies, groped my way into my clothes, and left without awakening her, testing the door to be sure it had locked behind me.

The storm had knocked the power out. There were stars in half the sky. My eyes were accustomed to darkness. I found the path without difficulty and walked between the black shapes of shrubbery, down the slope past the office, and out onto the dock.

Meyer had locked the *Flush* and gone to bed. I found the right key by touch. In the darkness of the lounge I gave my left shin a nasty rap against the new coffee table. I limped to the head and, by darkness, took a long hot sudsy shower. The great bed swallowed me up like a toad flicking a fly into the black belly.

15

By the time I came out to fix my breakfast, Meyer was having his second cup of coffee.

"You are running for office?" he asked.

"I thought you knew I owned a white shirt and a tie."

"I guess I'd forgotten."

"I want to look safe and plausible."

"To whom?"

I poured my orange juice and selected a handful of eggs.

"Five eggs?" he asked.

"These are the super supreme extra large eggs, which means they are just a little bit bigger than robin eggs. Stop all this idle criticism and take a look at the back of my head, please. I took the dressing off."

I sat on my heels. He came from the booth and stood behind me and turned my head toward the light. "Mmm. Looks sort of like the stitching on a baseball. Nice and clean, though. No redness that I can see."

He went back to his coffee. I broke the eggs into the small skillet, sliced some sharp cheddar and dropped it in, chopped some mild onion and dropped it in, folded that stuff in with a fork, took a couple of stirs, and in a couple of minutes it was done.

When I sat down to my breakfast Meyer said, "You were saying?"

"I'm saying something new now. We've been playing with a short deck. With a card missing, the tricks won't work. Maybe it is a variation of your invisible planet theory. I'll describe the missing card to you. The Van Harn airplane comes winging through the blue, and in the late afternoon it spots the Bertram off the north shore of Grand Bahama, as before. There are eight or nine bags of gage, plastic-wrapped to keep the water out. They are about a hundred pounds each. Van Harn makes a big circle at an altitude of a couple of hundred feet. The circle is big so that each time he comes around, Carrie has time to pull and tug and wrestle one of the bags to the passenger door and shove it out on his signal. That would be the way to do it, right? Nine passes. They hope to drop them close enough so they can be picked up quickly with a little maneuvering and a boat hook. Cal Birdsong and Jack Omaha are busily and happily hooking the bags aboard. Probably Birdsong is running the boat and Omaha is doing the stevedore job. Van Harn and Carrie are having a dandy time too. A little bit of adventure, a nice piece of money, and all the bugs have been worked out of the system. The payoff is big. Have you got the picture?"

"It seems plausible. What are you getting at?"

"Cindy told me that a week before he died Cal had a nightmare about something falling out of the sky and killing him."

"I saw Meyer's face change. I saw the comprehension, the nod, the pursing of lips.

"One drop was too good." he said.

"And Jack Omaha was careless. He wasn't watching. He was maybe leaning to get the boat hook into a floating bag. There would be a hell of a lot of impact. A good guess would be that it hit him in the back of the head and

261

snapped his neck. And all of a sudden it wasn't a party any more. It wasn't fun any more."

Nodding. Meyer spoke in an introspective monotone. "So Birdsong wired weights to the body and dropped it into the deeps, after dark. Van Harn flew back to the ranch with Carrie. When Birdsong was due in, she was waiting here at the marina with one of the little panel trucks. Birdsong loaded the sacks into the truck. They got their stories straight. She drove to Fifteen Hundred where the truck was unloaded and Walter J. Demos paid her off. She drove the truck down to Superior Building Supplies. She had probably left her car there. She put the money into the safe and took her share, because she knew the game was over. And she brought her share to you to hold. Travis, how do you read Van Harn's reaction?"

"Sudden total terror. I don't think the money mattered one damn to him any more. Marrying Jane Schermer would take care of the money problem forevermore. He knew he had been taking a stupid chance, perhaps rebelling against a career of fronting for Uncle Jake and his good old boys. He would know that if it all came out, it would finish him. It wasn't a prank. He was involved in the death of a prominent local man while committing a felony. Good old Jack Omaha of Rotary, Kiwanis, and the Junior Chamber. He wouldn't even keep his ticket to practice law. So I think that all of a sudden he was very anxious to please Uncle Jake."

"The eyewitnesses were Carrie Milligan and Cal Birdsong."

"Exactly, Meyer. A hustling lady and a drunk. I just thought of something else: Freddy's matinee with Chris Omaha. There probably isn't a better way of finding out how much the lady knows about anything. He wanted to know how much Jack had told her about the smuggling, or if he had told her anything at all. He evidently hadn't."

"And the burgled apartment?" Meyer said.

"Same reason. Find and remove any written evidence."

"What about Joanna and the bomb?"

"That won't make any sense until we know more."

"If you can ever make sense out of a bomb. The Irish tried it. Except for the people getting killed, it's turned into a farce to amuse the world. The Irish have forgotten why they set off bombs, if indeed they ever knew. It's probably because there's so damned little else to do in that dreary land."

"You won't be popular in Ireland."

"I've never had any urge to go back, thank you."

"Joanna came aboard bearing goodies. A little feast left off at the cottage for her. Meyer, we were both moving toward as she started to open the box. If she had been a string-saver, a careful untier of knots, we'd both be dead. But she was the rip and tear type. God, I can still smell the stink of explosion in here."

"I know. It's a little less every day."

After I finished off the eggs, I answered his first question. "I am going to visit the brilliant young attorney at his place of business. And I may have to see Judge Schermer. And I may have to see the Judge's niece."

"With what objective?"

"Application of pressure."

"What do you want me to do?"

"Be right here where I can get you if and when I need you."

*   *   *

Cindy Birdsong was alone in the office when I walked up there from the docks. She got up from the desk and came around the end of the counter quickly, then glanced guiltily out of each of the windows before tiptoeing to be kissed. A brief kiss, but very personal and emphatic. "You sneaked away." she said.

"Like a thief in the night."

"I slept like dead. I woke up and didn't know where I was or who I was, darling."

'I'll try to keep track."

She became more brisk and businesslike as she backed away from me. "Something strange, Travis. Jason was supposed to tend the office this morning. Ollie says he isn't around. And Ritchie has got some kind of a bug."

"Where does Jason stay?"

"He and Ollie have been living board the *Wanderer*. Over there at the end. It's ours : . . mine, I mean. But she needs new engines and an awful lot of other things."

I could see that the *Wanderer* was an old Egg Harbor fly bridge sedan, white hull and a rather unhappy shade of green topsides, something under forty feet in length.

Ollie came into the office, round, brown, and sweat-shiny, and gave me a good morning and gave Cindy a dock slip and said, "I put that Jacksonville Hatteras in Thirty-three instead of Twenty-six. It's new and he can't handle it worth a damn. It's easier to get in and out of Thirty-three. Okay?"

"Of course."

"They'll sign in personally when they get it hosed down. They're very fat people, both of them. Not real old. Just fat."

"Oliver," I said, "do you think Jason took off for good?"

He stared at me. "Why would he do that?"

"I don't know. He's missing. That's one possibility, isn't it?"

"I didn't think of him exactly as being missing, Mr. McGee."

"Did you notice if his personal gear was gone?"

"I didn't even think to look."

"Could we take a look right now?"

He looked at Cindy and when she nodded he said, "Why not?"

We both stepped aboard the *Wanderer* at the same moment, making it rub and creak against the fenders. As we went below Oliver said, "We slept here in the main cabin. Jason in the port bunk and me over here. If anybody was entertaining anybody, the other person slept up in the bow. There's two bunks up there. You can see that he slept in his bunk at least for a while and . . . you know something? I don't see his guitar anyplace."

We checked the locker and stowage area. His personal gear was gone.

"What kind of car does he have?"

"No car. A bicycle. Ten speed. Schwinn Sports Tourer. Blue. He keeps it chained to a post behind the office under the overhang. His duffel bags are the kind that hang off the back rack on a bike. Panniers, they call them. The guitar has a long strap so that he can sling it around his shoulder so it hangs down his back. He loves that bike. He does the whole bit. Toe straps. Racing saddle. Hundred miles a day. That's how come those fantastic leg muscles.''

I sat on Jason's bunk and said, "I don't even know his last name."

"Breen. Jason Breen." he said, sitting facing me.

"Okay to work with?"

"Sure. Why?" He looked defiant.

"How much do you really know about him?"

"What business is it of yours?"

"The boss lady has had enough trouble, don't you think?"

He looked uncertain. "I know. But what has that—?"

"Jason could have done something very bad and very stupid, because he thought he was helping Mrs. Birdsong. I want to get a reading from you about his capacities. You strike me as being very bright and observant, Ollie."

He blushed. "Well, not as bright as Jason. He reads very heavy things and he has very heavy thoughts."

"About what?"

"Free will, destiny, reincarnation. Stuff like that."

"What kind of person is he?"

Oliver pondered, his forehead wrinkling. "Well, he's a mixture. He likes to be with people. People with him. When there's a group, people end up doing what he wants to do without him having to push. When he's having a good time, everybody is having a good time, and when he isn't, nobody is. At the same time he's a loner. You never really know what he's thinking. He does nice things for people without making a big fuss about it. The ladies really like him a lot. You saw how he sort of stepped in and took care of Carrie's sister, Susan. Got her on the plane and everything. About doing anything wrong, I don't think he'd do anything *he* thought was wrong. But there would be no way in God's world of stopping him from doing something if he thought it was right."

"Did he have a thing about Mrs. Birdsong?"

Oliver blushed more deeply. "No more than . . . anybody. I mean she's a very decent person. And she looks . . . so great. And Cal was such a son of a bitch to her. Really dirty mean. He's no loss to anybody."

"Except to her. She misses him."

"That's her, all right. She's the kind of person who could even forgive that rotten bastard. Look, I know what's going on with you two. If you give her a hard time, I'm going to take my best shot."

"I think you really would."

"Believe it."

"What do you think is going on, anyway?"

"Jason told me. He's never wrong about things like that. He sleeps a couple of hours at a time. He prowls around a lot. He always knows what's going on over at the cottage and on the boats and in the motel and the whole neighborhood."

"How did he act about it when he told you? Just how did he tell you? Can you remember the words?"

"Close enough. I came in the other night and he was in the bunk reading and he looked over and said, 'McGee is screwing Cindy.' It was just a statement of fact. It stung me, you know. I said you were a bastard to be laying her so soon after Cal died, and he told me that was a sentimental and stupid attitude. I couldn't tell what he thought about it.''

"Current girl friend?"

"He hasn't got any particular person at the moment that I know of. He goes over and sees Betty Joller. You know, she's alone in the cottage now. Unless she can get somebody to come in with her, a couple of girls, she can't swing the rent and upkeep.''

"Wasn't there another girl there?"

"Two. Nat Weiss and Flossie Speck. After the bombing, Nat went back to Miami and Floss decided to try it out in California. She was bored with her job here anyway. She was working for the phone company.''

"Didn't Jason have something going with Carrie and with Joanna?"

"Probably. Sure. It wouldn't be any great big deal in either direction. It would just have to be the right time and place is all, and it would just happen.''

"Would Carrie have confided in him?"

"What about?"

"Anything that might have bugged her.''

"I don't see why not. People talk to Jason about the goddamnedest things. He doesn't pass it along. You know you can tell him things. Funny, come to think of it, how he never tells things about himself to other people. I guess he's had a hard life. He was in foster homes. They took him away from his own folks because they nearly killed him beating him. He wasn't even two years old. That's the only thing he did ever tell me. He had about six broken bones. Maybe more. I forget.''

"Did the storms wake you up last night?"

"Hell, yes!''

"Was Jason in his bunk?"

"Let me think. No, he wasn't. I could see in the flashes of lightning. I mean it wasn't anything unusual. He's always roaming around by himself. Or visiting people. He's a very restless person.''

"But he's been here two years, ever since they opened.''

"I don't mean restless like that. We've talked about moving on, but we never do. You get kind of hooked. Boats and water and working outside mostly.''

"But now he's packed his gear and moved on.''

"I can't believe he'd just go without a word. But maybe he would. Maybe he would. He'd have pay coming. I don't know why he'd leave without picking up his pay. Maybe he figures on sending for it. Or maybe he didn't leave. Maybe he moved into the cottage.''

"Want to check that out for me?"

"For myself too. Sure.''

As I walked slowly back to the office, alone, I could guess at what would convince Jason Breen it was time to pack and leave. If he had been under the open awning windows, crouched a couple of feet from the bed, he would have heard a conversation about Cal's murder. A little bonus for the restless voyeur of the marina. A little lead time on the blue bike, I wondered if he had sheathed his guitar in rainproof plastic.

I briefed Cindy and we waited for Oliver. He came back panting for breath, overheated. "Not there," he said. "Betty hasn't . . . gone to work yet. She said . . . she hasn't . . . seen Jason."

After Oliver left Cindy said, "You don't suppose Jason . . . could have listened?"

"Could be. He'd know you were going to talk to Scorf."

"But does a person . . . flee on a bicycle?"

"A person flees on what they have at hand, if they are anxious to flee."

"It makes me feel . . . sort of rotten to think anybody could have been listening."

"Ollie says Jason did a lot of prowling."

"But he seemed so nice!"

"We like the people who like us."

"I suppose. Rats. Phone call! Sure. Here's the book."

I phoned the offices of Frederick Van Harn, Attorney-at-Law, in the Kaufman Building. A soft-voiced girl answered by speaking the number I had just dialed.

"May I speak to Mr. Van Harn, please?"

"Who is calling?"

"A certain Mr. McGee, my dear."

"Is it a business call or a personal call?"

"Let's say business."

"He won't be in the office today."

"Out of town?"

"No, sir. He won't be in today."

"Where can I get in touch with him?"

"You could phone here tomorrow, Mr. McGee."

"What if I said personal instead of business?"

"You already picked one, sir."

"Is he out at the ranch? What's the number there, please?"

"Sorry, sir. That is an unlisted number. You can reach him here tomorrow morning."

I thanked her and hung up. I wondered vaguely if Freddy was stupid enough to be making another run to Jamaica and decided he wasn't. I asked Cindy if she could aim me toward the Van Harn ranch. She was blank on that, but she knew the road to take to get to Jane Schermer country, out amongst the grapefruits, and Meyer had told me they were adjacent.

I threw jacket and tie into the back seat of the bright little oven, opened all windows, and headed a little bit south and then turned west on Central Avenue. At first it was a six-lane avenue fringed with motels, the Colonel's chicken, steak houses, gift shops, dress shops, savings and loans, and small office buildings. After a few blocks of this, I was in used-car country speckled with tired old shopping centers and convenience stores. After a mile or so of that, the road became divided and I went through a long expanse of decaying residential. The pseudo-Moorish and old frame houses had once been impressive—and expensive. They were cut up into apartments and rooming houses. The yards were rank and littered, and the palms in the medial strip looked sickly. The road became two-lane, and I went through an area of huge new shopping centers and small dreary-looking developments where, on the flatlands, the developers had peeled off every tree and had big bonfires before putting in the boxy little houses. As these dwindled I saw For Sale signs on raw acreage, and at about nine miles from where I had made my turn, I came to the first ranchlands, with some Brahman, some Black Angus, some Charolais. Windmills flapped near the water holes. Salt blocks were set out in little open sheds. Where there were trees, the cattle had eaten the bottoms of the boughs off in a straight line, so that at a distance it had something of the look of African landscape.

There was more contour to the land on the right of the road, and more of that was used for geometric groves, laid out with a painful precision. I saw some spray trucks working the groves, tall booms hissing white into the trees, agitating the leaves and the young fruit.

Big trucks used the narrow road and used it fast. Their windy wake snaped at my little rental. The landscape was beginning to turn a rich and glorious green with the heavy rains. Kingfishers sat on high wires, looking optimistically down into the drainage ditches. Grease-fat bugs burst on my windshield.

The entrance was so inconspicuous I nearly missed it. The narrow driveway was marked with two gray posts. A varnished sign not much larger than a license tag was nailed to one post, saying V-H Ranch. The entrance drive was lumpy and muddy. Wire fencing was snugged close on each side of it. Ahead was a distant grove of pines. On either side was a hell of a lot of empty space, flat as a drafting table with some faraway clots of cattle wavering in the heat shimmer. The fencing on both sides turned away from the road just before the grove. The grove was a huge stand of ancient loblolly, home for hawk and crow and mockingbird and some huge fox squirrels which menaced me with fang and gesture and profane chatter. Once through the grove I could see the house a couple of hundred yards away, spotted in the middle of giant live oaks hung with moss.

It was squarish, two stories, with two broad verandas which encircled it completely, one at each level. Steep tin roof, big overhang. Porch furniture. The house looked rough and comfortable. A pair of dogs came around the corner of the house at a full run, arfing toward me. They were part German shepherd, but broader across chest and brow. One put his feet up on the side of the yellow Gremlin and grinned at me, tongue lolling. He lifted his lips to show me more tooth and made a sound like a big generator running in a deep basement. My window was up before he could draw breath.

An old man came out onto the porch, shaded his eyes, and then put fingers in his mouth and blew a piercing blast which silenced birds and dogs and could possibly have stopped traffic on the distant highway. The dogs backed away and dwindled. They walked sideways, knees bent, tails tucked under. They swallowed, lapped their jowls, and looked apologetic.

"Git on out back!" he yelled, and they did git, in scuttling fashion. Then he stood on the porch, feet planted, arms crossed, and waited for me to approach, and waited for me to say the first word. He was a tall scrawny bald man with tufts of white over his ears. He was all strings, except for his watermelon belly, and he wore crisp khakis and new blue sneakers.

"It's nice to see animals pay attention," I said.

"They know I kicks their ass nine feet in the air ef'n they don't. State your business."

"I would like to see Mr. Van Harn."

"Sorry."

"He isn't here?"

"I didn't say that, did I?"

"Then he is here?"

"He could be."

"My name is Travis McGee. To whom am I speaking?"

"I'm Mr. Smith."

"Mr. Smith, your loyalty is commendable. I would like you to take a short message to Mr. Van Harn. I think he will want to talk to me."

"I don't know as I want to do that. He's in a real bad temper this morning. He had to shoot Sultan. Busted his fool leg. Fifteen-thousand-dollar horse. He don't want no help with it. He's got a backhoe down there, and a jeep with a blade, and he's burying that fool horse by himself. He sent Rowdy and the boys off to string fence. Wants to be alone with the fool dead horse. I don't want to mess into that, Mister McGee."

"The message is very important to him."

Smith studied me for long long seconds. This was a character reading. "You say you snuck by here after I told you to git?"

"I put my car back in the pines and snuck by. Where did I go to when I snuck by, Mr. Smith?"

"You followed the ruts there to the side of the house. Two hundred yards, you come to a plank bridge. Cross it and turn left past a stand of live oaks and you can see the stables and some storage sheds, and past that the hangar and the landing strip. He'll be on high ground right across from the stables. You'll see the backhoe and jeep before you can make him out."

"Mr. Smith?"

"Yes."

"What about those dogs?"

He took me around the house. The dogs crawled forward and I extended my hand. They both snuffed my hand. "Leave him alone, hear?" Smith roared. The dogs nodded. "They won't bother you none," he said.

Smith was right. I saw the vehicles first. The yellow jeep with a front-end blade was crawling slowly across the infield of a rough track, dragging the glossy red-brown body toward the slight ride and the cabbage palms at the far side, where the backhoe stood near a large mound of dirt.

Van Harn saw me walking toward him and stopped the jeep.

"What are you doing here, McGee? How'd you get past the house?"

"Smith told me to get lost. I parked in the pines and snuck around. Sorry about your horse."

He had wrapped chain around the hind legs and fastened it to the tow hook on the back of the jeep. The great head of the horse was at rest. I had seen it bobbling across the stubble. The visible eye bulged nastily from the socket. The shot had been perfectly centered, above and between the eyes, making a caked mess of the brown gloss. A swarm of bluebottle flies settled onto the horse when the jeep stopped. He was a grotesque parody of a horse at a full run, front legs reaching, back legs extended, head high.

"What do you want?"

"I tried the office first."

"What do you want?"

"Why don't you go ahead and bury the horse and then . . ."

"What do you want?"

He wanted the leverage right away, right in the blazing sun of midmorning, in the infield of his little track. He wore big oval sunglasses, aviator type, and a white canvas cap. He was stripped to the waist. He wore dirty khaki pants and old white boat shoes. I was surprised at how tanned his body was, and how slender and fit he looked. Thin tough musculature made ridges and knots under the tan hide at each slight move. He had a medallion of black hair in the middle of his chest, big as a saucer, turning into a thin line of black hair that disappeared behind his brass belt buckle.

Plausibility is the key. I said, "When we had our little talk in the limousine, there was an area we didn't get to."

"Such as?"

"Uncle Jake offered me twenty-five thousand to pack and leave. I wanted to talk to you about whether it is all the traffic will bear."

"It sounds like too much as it is. What can you do?"

"I can put things together. Carrie gave me enough to go on. It's a case of filling in the blanks."

"Blanks?"

"Such as who decided to fasten ballast to Jack Omaha and drop him in the sea after he got hit by the bag of grass when you and Carrie were air-dropping the stuff to Cal and Jack aboard the *Christina III*."

He opened his mouth and closed it, opened it again, and said, "You lost me on the first curve, McGee."

"I think you waited too long."

"Maybe I did. I've got to bury Sultan." He started the jeep up and once more the big head bounced along the ground, tongue protruding between the big square teeth. I followed along at walking speed. He went to the left of the big hole, as close as he could get to it, and cut to the right as soon as he was past it. When he stopped, the horse lay with his back at the edge of the hole. He backed the slack off on the chain, got out and unfastened it from the jeep and the horse's legs, and dropped it into the jeep. Next he bent and picked up the hind legs and pushed at them, rolling the horse onto its back. It slipped over the edge of the hole and fell four feet, turning the rest of the way over, gases bursting out of its body as it thudded against the bottom.

I backed out of the way when he got back into the jeep, after setting the blade to its low position, and began shoving dirt into the hole. It was pale dirt, a mix of sand, topsoil, and surface limestone which contained billions of small fossil shells.

A buzzard began a big lazy circle overhead. I squinted up at it against blue sky, wondering how it knew. The abrupt roaring of the jeep shocked me out of my stupid trance. The onrushing blade was a yard from my legs by the time I took a frantic sideways leap, like a man going into second base in a headlong slide. I sprawled and rolled and came up onto my feet with the jeep right behind me. I feinted one way and dived the other way, came to my feet, and ran around to the other side of the horse grave.

He idled down and stopped. Oval lenses looked at me from under the stubby bill of the white cap.

"You move good for the size of you," he said.

"Thanks. And what's one more dead person?"

"At this point in time, not very much."

"But you can't make it, not the way you've tried to make it, Freddy. You dropped the rock in the water, and you can't move around fast enough to flatten out all the ripples."

"I can give it a goddamn good try. I didn't know if you had a gun. I guess you don't."

"I should have. It was an oversight."

"Final mistake."

"What was Carrie's final mistake?"

He seemed puzzled. "Mistake? Walking in front of a truck?"

"Didn't you close her mouth for good?"

"Didn't have to. Carrie was bright. She was involved in Jack's death too, you know. And she had less leverage than I have."

It was convincing. I felt confused. I couldn't see him as the murderer of Cal Birdsong or the builder of the bomb which killed Joanna. So why was he so obviously intent on doing away with me?

"I think we ought to talk," I said.

"Make your move."

"What move? Run for it? How far would I get?"

He gunned the jeep toward the right. I lunged to the left, dipping to scoop up a handful of ancient oyster shells from the pile of dirt. They were thick, calcified and heavy, dating back to the time when the V-H Ranch had been on the bottom of a shallow sea. I wound up quickly, stuck my leg in the air, threw a shell with a followthrough that brought my knuckles to within an inch of the ground. I really whistled it, but it curved low and outside, missing his right shoulder narrowly. He backed away quickly and, out of range, stood up and pulled the windshield up and fastened the wing nuts before rolling back to position.

"That was very cute," he said.

"Freddy, I've talked to a lot of people about you."

"I'm sorry about that. But it doesn't change anything."

"Your odds are impossible already."

"You don't know how bad they really are, McGee. But they are the only odds I've got, and it's the only game there is."

I tossed the other shells away. They weren't going to help me. I could guess what he would do. He would start circling that big grave as fast as he could go. I could stay out in front but not for long, not in such heat. And as soon as I slowed, or headed for the trees or the stables, he'd have me. I didn't have much time to do any thinking.

In such a situation it is difficult to believe it is completely serious. A yellow jeep is a jolly vehicle. Pastureland is not menacing. The hour before noon is not a likely time for dying. It was some odd game of tag, and when it ended the eventual loser would congratulate the winner. Let's try it again someday, pal.

But it was real. A jeep with or without a blade is a lethal weapon. I could tell from the way it tracked that he had it in four-wheel drive. He was skilled, and the jeep was agile.

I thought of alternatives and discarded them as fast as they came up. I could head across the field and try to trap him into a circle out in the open. I could turn a smaller circle than he and maybe get near enough to the side of the jeep to jump him. No chance. He would read it, accelerate out of the circle, and swing around and come back at me. Or I could slow him enough, maybe, to go up over the blade and hood and drop in on him. But how do I slow him down that much?

Suddenly I thought of one slim chance. If I couldn't make it work, I was going to be no worse off. I was going to be dead. And if I didn't try it, I was going to be dead. A mockingbird flew over, singing on the wing, a melody so painfully sweet it pinched the heart. I do not want to leave the world of mockingbirds, boats, beaches, ladies, love, and peanut butter from Deaf Smith County. Especially do I not want to leave it at the hands of a fool, at the hands of this Van Harn who thought he could wipe out an event by killing anybody who knew anything about it. It has been tried. It never works. Any lawyer should know that.

I had to get him going counterclockwise around the horse grave. So I moved to my left and he gunned the motor and took the bait. He came on so fast he gave me a very bad moment. The big hole was a sloppy rectangle about ten feet by eight feet. Before I could get my feet untangled and get around the first corner, he nearly clipped me. He had shoved about three blade loads in on top of the dead horse, and so that side was filled to within about two feet of the original ground level, the whole front half of the horse still uncovered.

He pressed me. I had to lope around pretty good, with a constant fear I might slip and fall on the corners. He held it in an almost continuous controlled skid, the back wheels staying farther away from the hole than the front wheels. His reasoning was obvious. In such heat I could only make so many circuits. I had to make enough circuits to lull him. The sweat was running into my eyes. Each time I passed the decision point, I mentally rehearsed exactly how to do it. And I had to do it soon, before I was exhausted.

At last I felt ready. I rounded the corner, dropped down two feet onto the loose dirt, spun and leapt up beside the jeep, and dived for the top of the wheel. He tried to accelerate but I was able to stretch the necessary few inches. I snapped my right hand onto the top of the wheel and pulled it hard over, toward me. The jeep swerved into the horse grave, dropped, and piled into the straight side of the hole, over where it was deeper.

The left rear fender had popped me in the side of the thigh, throwing me into a deep corner of the hole, in considerable torment. I scrabbled and pulled myself up and saw Van Harn fold slowly sideways out of the jeep. The four wheels were still turning, settling it deeper, and then it stalled out.

His legs were still hung up in the jeep. One eye was half open, the other closed. He had a high white knot in the middle of his forehead, growing visibly. I hobbled to him and bent over him. He hit me in the mouth and knocked me back into the same corner of the hole. Before I could get up, he sprang out of the hole and went racing toward the backhoe. I came lumping along behind him, with no hope of closing the distance.

He went to the back of it and wrenched a spade out of some spring clips, a spade I wished I had seen earlier.

He darted to meet me and swung the spade, blade edgeways, at my middle.

During my screeching halt I managed to suck my stomach back out of the way. He swung back the other way, from left to right, aiming at my head. I couldn't back away in time. I dropped under it, dropped to my hands and knees, felt it whip the hair at the crown of my head. That made everything real and deadly. A tenth of a second faster and he would have cleaved my skull.

From knuckles and knees I launched myself forward, getting one foot under me, coming up under him like a submarining guard, getting a shoulder tucked cozily into his gut, clapping an arm around his heels as he tried to bicycle backward. He smacked down hard and lost his spade. I crawled up him, straddled him. He was yipping, bucking, writhing. I didn't want to break my hands on the bones of his skull or face. I came down with a forearm across his throat, my other hand locked on my wrist for leverage. I tucked my face into the curve of my arm as protection from his flailings. After a frantic spasm he fluttered a little and went still. I kept the pressure on to be sure of him. Then I rolled off and got onto my knees and sat back on my heels, blowing hard. His white cap lay nearby. I picked it up and wiped the sweat off my face and out of my eyes.

His face was puffy and suffused with blood. His chest was moving. It seemed very quiet out there in that pastureland. I listened to the songs of the midday bugs and the liquid call of a distant meadowlark. Time to wrap him up and make delivery.

16

WHEN AT last I felt partially restored and was not gagging with each breath, I got up onto my feet. My right thigh was cramping with the muscle bruise the jeep had given me. I managed a deep knee bend without screaming, and the second one did not hurt quite as much.

The jeep offered the best chance of something with which I could tie him up. I trudged toward the horse grave. If he could have come the whole distance across grass, he would have had me. He had to cross some of that dirt from the hole. The brittle limestone crackled under his running feet. I jumped sideways, ducked, and spun all in a single terrified bound. I heard the spade hiss past my head. His momentum carried him toward the hole. He tried to turn, tripped, stumbled, fell and rolled down the slope, and ended up beside the jeep.

I was after him quickly and got there as he lifted the spade over his head. I reached up and got hold of the handle. As soon as I had the handle he let go of it and hit me three very fast and very good shots. He had screwed his feet into the dirt. He had very good leverage, and he was too able to attempt the roundhouse blows of the beginner. He slammed them home, very close straight shots. They darkened the sky. The spade slid out of my hand. I stepped into him and hugged him like a big sick bear. I bore him down and suddenly he was in back of me instead of in front of me. I was on my hands and knees in the soft dirt and he had a wiry arm locked around my throat.

My air was shut off. Dazed as I was. I could not get the leverage to get out of that position or to throw him off. I tried to crawl to the jeep. He somehow held me back. I scraped with both hands like a dog digging a hole as I tried to plunge forward. The world swam. My lungs heaved against the obstruction. I began to feel a lazy floating pleasure. Oxygen starvation. Rapture of the deeps. I folded down and with darkening sight stared into the hole I had dug with my hands. I saw a piece of blue pipe, very pretty blue pipe. And just under it, as in some grotesque still life, I saw an unmistakable segment of suntanned wrist, dirt caught in the sun-bleached curling hair.

The dimming brain works slowly and with difficulty. Clean blue tubing. An azure blue. The size used for a bicycle frame. And why was that fellow under it, under the dry dirt that had come from a hole too deep for all the recent rain to reach? There was a stupid rhyme in the fading brain: Jason Breen and his Azure Machine.

The realization pierced the darkness that was closing in on me. What happened in my mind was not fright, not anger. It was an overwhelming dismay. A veritable crescendo of dismay, enough to galvanize my slackening body into a few moments of a terrible, terminal strength. I will never know how I was able to come to my feet with Van Harn plastered to my back. I took a single wobbly step and then fell toward the jeep, turning as I fell, so that I smashed him against the metal. I rebounded onto hands and knees, the stricture gone from my throat. I stretched out and breathed until the shadows lightened and the sun came out again. In sudden fright I pushed myself up and spun around. Freddy lay on his side.

I had the feeling he was going to bound to his feet and we were going to have to do it all over again, as if he were some mythological creature which could not be slain.

First I got the chain from the jeep. I rolled him onto his face and chained his wrists together, tying a clumsy knot, and used the surplus to chain his ankles.

Then I knelt by the hole and carefully pulled the dirt away until I could see a hand, and most of a forearm, and more of the tubing of the blue bicycle.

From the angle, the rest of him was under the jeep, and under a foot of dirt. Somewhere under there could be found the stillness of the Jesus face, the wire glasses, the crushed guitar, the brown legs sturdy with the bicycle muscles. And somewhere in his head, lost forever in the death of the synapses, were the jellied memories of why he had come out here and what Van Harn had done to him. The idea had been splendid. Dig a big hole and bury the body under a horse. Who would ever look farther than the horse?

I dragged Van Harn up the slope toward the back of the jeep and left him in the shade of the rear overhang. I felt his throat. The pulse was strong and regular. Except for the knot on his forehead, there wasn't a mark on his face. The left side of my underlip felt like half a hot plum. When I opened my mouth to yawn width, experimentally, the hinges creaked. I had a dull headache behind my eyes. He could blow them in pretty good. His dark glasses were missing. I looked around and found them, stomped flat.

Just as I climbed out of the hole I heard the oncoming drumbeat of a galloping horse. It was one great big dark brown horse, and she looked good in her cowgirl hat, yellow shirt, and twill britches. But when she pulled it up short and slid off, she turned back into Jane Schermer, with pudding face, minimal neck, and neuter body.

"Smith said Frederick had to shoot . . . ." She saw Freddy in the shade of the jeep. "What are you *doing* to him?"

"Nothing, at the moment. But he's kept me pretty busy."

"Get that chain off him at once!"

"First come take a look at this."

She hesitated, then dropped down into the hole. She had let the reins hang free. The big horse made munching and ripping sounds in the stubbly grass. I pointed to the hole, big around as a bushel basket and half as deep, with the arm and hand and the portion of blue bike in the bottom of it.

She stared and sprang back and turned quickly, making a shallow, gagging little coughing sound. "Who? What—?"

"I'm pretty sure it's Jason Breen. He worked at Westway Harbor Marina."

"But did you . . . ."

"Did I? For God's sake! Sure. I came out here and sort of borrowed that backhoe, which I don't know how to operate. Then I dug this big son of a bitch of a hole. Then I put Jason and all his gear in the bottom of said hole and covered him over good. Then I shot this horse and . . . look. Forget it."

"But Frederick couldn't have done it."

"Lady Jane, I don't think there's anything in this world that you or I could think of that Freddy wouldn't do, if he happened to feel like it."

She hustled over and knelt by Freddy. She felt his forehead with the back of her hand. She put her ear against his bare chest to hear his heart. She stood up and looked at the visible half of the horse. "Poor darling," she said softly. "Poor Sultan. Poor beast. My Graciela foaled him. He grew up on my place. I gave him to Frederick."

"That's nice."

She went to the front legs of the horse, lifted, and tested with strong hands. "Must be a hind leg," she said. "Take that stupid chain off of Frederick right away!"

"I don't think it's a hind leg either."

She stared at me. "What do you mean?"

"I think Freddy needed a dead horse."

"He has other horses here. Sultan was valuable."

"He needed a dead horse that was so valuable and he liked so much that it made sense for him to send his ranch hands off on other work while he took care of it himself."

"What makes you think a hind leg isn't broken?"

"I watched him slide it up to the edge of the hole and roll it in. By then he didn't care what I saw because he had already decided to put me in the hole next to Jason. Under the horse."

"You make him sound like a . . . Could you uncover those back legs? Please?"

I walked over and got the spade and went to work. Once I got into the rhythm of it, it didn't take long. Before I finished, her fool horse finally caught on to the fact there was a dead horse in the area. He came over and stared into the hole, then screamed and backed away, shaking his head, rolling his eyes, and clacking his teeth. Jane hustled and caught him and led him all the way to the trees and tied him to a branch and left him there, squealing and pawing at the ground.

She hunkered down and checked each back leg in turn, then stood up and dusted her hands and climbed up out of the hole. I followed her. She looked thoughtfully down at Freddy, and she didn't say anything about the chain.

"I raised Sultan," she said.

"I better go to the house and use the phone."

"Phone?"

"To report a body."

"Oh, of course. There's one in the tack room, an extension. Are you going to leave Frederick . . . like this?"

"I know. That chain looks as if I'm overreacting. But I feel a lot better with it wrapped right where it is."

She looked at me and through me. Her eyes were small and of no particular color. Dull hazel, perhaps. "The things people said about him. I knew they were all lies. They were jealous." She focused on me. "Is this all some kind of terrible trick? Did you shoot Sultan?"

"I am not terribly fond of horses, but I've never shot one."

"I have to believe somebody."

"It might as well be me. Freddy tried to kill me. He made some good tries. He tried with the jeep. He tried with the spade. He tried manual strangulation. He is a very tough animal. He is about twice as strong as he looks."

"Jane?" Freddy said weakly. "Jane, dear?"

"Yes?"

"Help me, please."

"You shot Sultan because he broke his leg?"

"No other choice, dear. Please help me. Unfasten the chain, please."

She moved closer, looking down at him. "I don't think I can help you, darling. I don't think anybody can help you. Just be patient. We're going to make a phone call. You won't have to stay there very long."

I was halfway to the stables and the tack room before I could no longer hear his voice calling her name. She cantered past me when I was almost there. I found the phone while she was shooing her horse into an empty box stall.

Captain Scorf was not available, so I asked for someone to whom I could report a dead body, a murdered body. Then I gave a very simple report and explicit directions.

Jane Schermer sat with her back against the box stall door, her knees hiked up. There was a broad overhang shading the walk which led by the stalls. I sat beside her.

After a long time she said, "They were telling the truth and he was telling the lies."

"What?"

"Nothing. I've been going over things that troubled me, that I asked him about. I've been such a fool."

"That is a very convincing fellow when he wants to sell you."

"I was too easy to sell. I wanted to get married."

"So you'll get married. But not to Freddy."

She turned and looked at me. "Men have never paid much attention to me. I know when it's the money. A person can tell. I wondered about him. I was never sure."

"Maybe it wasn't."

"You're trying so hard to be kind, aren't you? Why would he . . . spoil everything for himself?"

"In big ways, and little ways too, people do that all the time to themselves. We can't stand prosperity. We have to tinker with the machinery."

She looked out across the track at the distant scene, at the canted top half of the yellow jeep. She touched my arm suddenly. "Look!"

I looked out there and saw that Freddy had performed a feat I would have called impossible. With wrists chained behind him and ankles chained together, he had managed to worm his way out from under the back end of the jeep and get himself up out of the hole and onto his feet. He was on the far side of the hole, hopping up and down with terrible demonic energy, managing somehow to retain his balance, though without seeming to make any progress. He was springing high into the air. I thought I heard a distant shouting. Then we saw him fall, roll, and disappear back into the hole.

We both got up. Jane said, "Something's the matter with him."

"I could make you a list."

But she had started off at a flat-out run, too concerned to remember she could ride that big horse out to him. I loped along, feeling the lumpy pain in my thigh with each stride. When we got there she jumped down into the hole where he was flapping and churning around and yelled, "Fire ants! Fire ants! Help me with him."

I think he had five thousand ants on his face, arms, and torso, swarming and biting with that dedicated aggression peculiar to that innocent-looking little red-brown ant.

I jumped down and grabbed him and wrestled him up out of the hole and half carried, half dragged him about forty feet and put him down on the grass. All this while he was moaning, cawing, and whimpering, and Jane was slapping and brushing at the ants. About a hundred turned their eager attentions to me, so after I dropped him I hopped and slapped and brushed until the frequency dropped to a random nip from time to time. They are called fire ants because the bite feels like a very tiny red-hot coal on the surface of your skin.

She kept on getting rid of the ants while I quickly took the chain off ankles and wrists. He had stopped being a dangerous person. Though his gestures seemed weak and uncertain, he was of some help in removing the ants. The ones that were being brushed off were climbing back onto him, so I got him onto his feet and trundled him another fifty feet before he stumbled and fell.

When he was down I pulled his shoes and socks off, undid the brass buckle, and pulled his khaki trousers off. The ants were thick on his legs, way up to the upper thigh and the groin. I pulled his underwear shorts off and wadded them up and used them to brush away the ants. I noted that, dimensionally, he more than lived up to the billing Joanna had given him. I rolled him over and over, away from the area where the brushed-off ants could get back on him.

They are aggressive, these red ants, but they are certainly not the menace the farming fraternity and the petrochemical industry would have us believe. If you stand too near a nest, they will come out and climb up your shoes and sting your ankles. You know immediately, and you move away and knock them off. The bites make little white blisters which, if untended, are likely to fester. The easiest remedy is rubbing alcohol applied as soon as possible after being bitten. Vodka or gin will do.

Ninety-nine out of a hundred fire-ant horror stories are false. Freddy was the one in a hundred. I had never heard of anybody being so completely bitten. We had him free of the ants at last. He made sad weak sounds as he rolled his head from side to side. He was gray and sweaty. I wedged him back into his pants and clinched the big brass buckle.

I now knew why he had been so anxious to do me in. But it seemed idiotic to have killed Jason Breen.

I leaned close to him and said, "Hey! Why did Jason come out here?"

"Money," he said in a dull voice. "Called me at four in the morning on the private line. I chained the dogs. Waited in the grove. Twenty thousand."

"Why?"

"He'd snooped. Figured it all out. Saw the *Christina* come in without Jack. Told me he had killed Cal with a wire and he had to run, and unless I gave him money he'd claim I paid him to kill Cal. I said okay. He was very jumpy. Then he said he was going to beat up on me anyway, on account of what happened with the Dobrovsky girl. He hit me and I hit him. I caught him in the throat. It broke something. He grabbed his throat. Tried to breathe. Fell onto his knees. Made choking noises. Fell over dead in less than two minutes. By dawn light his face was black and his eyes bulged out. I dragged him down to the stables. Wheeled his bike down. Oh, Christ, everything is getting so . . . so far away."

He was looking worse by the moment, face bloating, tongue thickening. His lips were fat. He was close to blacking out.

"He told me once a bee sting can make him real sick," Jane said. "What's *keeping* them!"

A moment later we both heard the distant hooting as a cruiser blew its way through the highway traffic. When in another minute it hove into sight around the stand of trees, I stood up and waved my arms at it. It came bounding across the track and the infield, stopped near us, and two deputies piled out, very smart in pale blue shirts, dark blue pants, and trooper hats. They were big, young and ruddy, creaking with equipment.

"Hey, Miz Jane!" one of them said.

"Why, hello, Harvey!"

"Now just who is this here, Miz Jane?"

"You know him! This is Frederick Van Harn."

Harvey stared. "You've got to be kidding," he said in an awed voice. "What in hell *happened* to him?"

"He got into fire ants," I said, "and he's allergic. He's going into shock. Can you get a radio patch through to hospital emergency?"

"Yes, but—"

"You better get on it and tell them you're heading in there wide open. Tell them it's shock from insect bites. They'll know what to have ready. I think it's called anaphylactic shock."

"But—"

Jane stepped closer to him and said, "Maybe you *want* to explain to my Uncle Jake why you let Frederick die?"

That is one of the interesting things about power. Everybody who really has it seems to know exactly how to use it. The ones who pretend to have it make the wrong moves.

While he was on the radio, the other deputy and I lifted Freddy and put him in the back of the cruiser, on his back on the seat. The deputy said, "There's supposed to be a body here?"

"There is."

"Harv, I'll stay here and look into what the call was about. You come back or have them send somebody, okay?"

Jane had gotten in the back and she was kneeling on the floor, holding Freddy's hand. Harvey made a tight circle and went bucketing out of there. We heard him hooting his way down the highway toward the city.

The one left behind said, "Those far ants are mean."

I inspected the bites on the backs of my hands and between the fingers. "They're very convincing."

He took out his notebook. "Who was it phoned in?"

"Me. Travis McGee."

"My name is Simmons. Frank Simmons." He almost started to shake hands and apparently decided it wasn't professional.

"Have you been a deputy long?"

"Just over three weeks. Address, Mr. McGee?"

He wrote the ID information down, slowly and carefully. "Now where'd this dead body be?"

"Over there in that hole."

"Is it a real old dead body? I mean dead long?"

"Only since last night."

We walked to the hole. In a higher voice he said, "That there is a dead *horse!* You funnin' me? What's that jeep doing in there?"

"Frank, there's a small hole I want you to look in, there by the front of the jeep."

He went over and looked down into the smaller hole. There were some flies on the brown arm. He swayed slightly, then whirled and took two big steps and threw up. When he was finished he straightened up slowly and said, "That didn't give me a damn bit of warning. It just come on me all at once."

"It can happen that way."

"This is my first one on duty. Jesus! Look, don't tell Harv about me barfin', okay?"

"I'd have no reason to."

"He rides me. He thinks I won't make it. I'll make it. Now, who discovered the body? You or Miz Schermer or Mr. Van Harn?"

"I discovered it."

"Who put it there?"

"Mr. Van Harn."

"The *hell* you say?" He bent and slapped at his ankles. "Far ants all over the place. Let's get out of this here hole. You think there's a water tap around here anyplace?"

"Over there at the stables."

"Let's us walk over there. Now, you got any idea who the deceased is?"

'I think it is a fellow named Jason Breen."

"From Westway Harbor? With the beard?"

"Right."

"I'll be a son of a bitch," he said softly and stopped long enough to write the name in his notebook.

17

CAPTAIN HARRY MAX SCORF questioned me at the scene. By the time he was through they had Jason and his bike and his smashed guitar and his duffel bags out of the ground. I followed Scorf over and took a look at the body. The eyes glared up at the sky. The beard was chalked with limestone dust, giving me a hint of what he would have looked like as an old man, had the world given him a chance to live that long.

It had taken Mr. Smith a long time to notice that something was wrong. He came trotting across the field as they were loading Jason. "What are all these damn cars coming in and out? Is that fellow dead? He looks dead. Where is Mister Fred? Who's in charge here anyways?"

Scorf settled Smith down with an admirable economy of word and gesture. Then he suggested that I drive him to the hospital in my rental car, which would give him a chance to go over my story with me once more.

We turned the vent windows so the hot air blew in. I drove slowly. I went through the play-by-play description of our battle again. He chuckled and I told him that it did not seem funny at the time, and it did not get any funnier with the passage of time. I told him that he could maybe think of a nice funny way to tell Uncle Jake that he was going to have to arrest Frederick Van Harn.

"While we're both being funny, McGee, you can tell me how you happened to know that Breen was buried under that dead horse."

"As I said, Captain, I was scrabbling in the dirt, trying to get a purchase, trying to crawl to the jeep so I could grab onto it and stand up. Which I finally did. But I uncovered part of Breen and the bike first."

"It's nothing you can prove, and I want to see just how Van Harn's story matches yours. I'll buy the story about how he killed Jason, because Jane Schermer heard that part of it too. And maybe the autopsy will verify. We know the autopsy verifies the way Birdsong died. But I would be a happier man if I could get a better way to tie Breen to that killing. He was on my list and looking better every day. But it isn't solid."

"I can make you happier. I think Cindy Birdsong will be willing to tell you without much urging that once upon a time after Cal beat her up, Breen went to her and said he could arrange to kill Birdsong very quietly for her. No one would suspect. She was horrified and told him to forget it. The same day I arrived, when Birdsong got ugly with me, he backhanded his wife in the office and knocked her cold. Jason Breen was the one who got to her and picked her off the floor.''

He turned in the seat and I could feel him looking at me. "That means that I can't let you go back there alone. You could coach her. I want to come up on her cold with this.''

"Captain, what difference does it make anyway? You don't have to build a case against Jason Breen. It doesn't have to stand up in court. It gets Birdsong off your books.''

"I am a careful man, McGee. I like people, alive or dead, to get charged with what they did, not what somebody else did.''

When we got to the hospital, we were told that Frederick Van Harn was in Intensive Care. I followed Scorf up to the fourth floor. A young doctor was sitting in the small waiting room outside the closed double doors, talking quietly to Jane Schermer. Tears were running down her prematurely middle-aged face. The doctor came and talked to us in the corridor. He said they had tried, but they just couldn't reverse the severe shock, not even with every radical treatment they could think of. He had responded slightly to massive injections of digitalis but had faded again until his heart had stopped and they had been unable to restart it. An intense allergic reaction, he said. Massive fluid imbalance. A pity, he said. Such a young man.

Harry Max Scorf looked indignant. One cannot ask questions of the dead. People were eluding him. He acted as if he thought it was unfair, a kind of trickery.

*   *   *

The murder and the poetic justice of the macabre death made the event a twenty-four-hour sensation. The wire services picked it up. It had the right words. Prominent attorney. Political hopeful. Possible blackmail. Involvement in drug smuggling suspected. Murdered man believed intimate of ex-model recently slain by bomb aboard houseboat.

But a news story is a fragile thing. It is like a hot air balloon. It needs a constand additive of more hot air in the form of new revelations, new actions, new suspicions. Without this the air cools, the big bag wrinkles, sighs, settles to the ground, and disappears.

Judge Jacob Schermer put the clamp on any flow of additives. He and his minions spread the word. They apparently had leverage to use on the local radio stations and the Bayside television station and the monopoly newspaper. They also had the City and County Police Department, the banks, the Chamber of Commerce, the service clubs, and every phase of local government.

No one knew a thing about anything. A blank stare was better than no comment. The reporters who had come in from Jacksonville, Miami, and Orlando went hurrying right back out of town toward the next story. People could barely remember what Van Harn looked like or what he did. The usual eruption of sick, sad, violent events continued throughout the nation and the world, like an unending, eternal string of those little Chinese firecrackers called ladyfingers.

By Saturday morning, when Harry Max Scorf came to see us aboard the *Flush,* the news story was so dead it might as well have happened in some other year.

He sat in the cool lounge, took his spotless white hat off and wiped the sweatband with a bandanna, and placed it back on his head carefully, at exactly the right angle.

"My feeling," he said to us, "is that I ought to waltz you people to and fro and bounce you up and down gentle like until you let loose of something that makes sense out of where you fit in this picture. But it's one of those feelings I don't get to enjoy."

"Orders?" I asked.

"The official position is that there're no loose ends at all. Everything is solved and filed away. The Milligan woman was an accident. Jack Omaha lit out for places unknown. Jason kilt the Freeler girl with the bomb and kilt Birdsong with a wire. Then Freddy kilt Jason and the ants kilt him. And that's all she wrote, boys. You two fellas know, just like I know, that it adds up to a crock of shit."

"We really can't help you at all," Meyer said.

He sighed. "Anyway, one thing looks better. There's pretty fair grass coming in at a reasonable price. Somebody has knocked all them amateur wholesalers into a tight line. Some professional outfit has moved in like overnight and took over the whole county. Speaking purely as a cop, it's a relief. It's the amateurs who screw everything up. With these pros, I know which way they'll jump, and what will make them jump and what won't. If they keep it tidy, we'll lay back and let it roll. When customs picks up forty-two tons at a time on the Mexican border, it's a signal that it is too big a business to hope to stop entire. If these pros start to get into any heavier action around here, then what we'll do is make their operation so expensive it'll take the cream off, and they'll back off to what they've got right now. It's the amateurs who drive you crazy. That Walter J. Demos would drive anybody crazy, the damned fool. Every time I try to talk to the son of a bitch, he starts crying. He sits down, wraps his arms around his bald head, and start bellering. What I come by for is to say you can make everybody very happy by going back where you come from, as soon as you can untie your ropes and start your engine."

"This is a roust, Captain?" I asked.

"Not right at this minute, it isn't. It starts to be a roust when I tell somebody you won't move. Then that somebody goes to all the city and county departments that have got anything to do with boats and navigation. Then they come around here and they check you and your boat for every little paragraph in city, county, state, and federal law going back to when Lincoln got shot. Like any boat operating in county waters has got to carry two brass kerosene lanterns at least fourteen inches high as spare equipment, one with green glass and one with red glass, and if you can't show them to the inspector, it's a hundred dollars a day and costs for every day of violation, whether you're tied up or running. That's when it gets to be a roust. Want any more?"

"When you want us to move out, Captain," I said, "you just give the word and we'll move. You've convinced us."

He looked puzzled. "I thought I'd just given you the word."

Meyer cleared his throat and said, "I suppose you could change that official position you described if you could come up with something new?"

Scorf frowned. "It would have to be hard evidence. Very hard. I told you, people want this all forgot. Right now. If anything gets stirred up and it comes to nothing, I am retired with no pension."

"Sometimes you can't help thinking," I said.

"About what?"

Meyer said, "We did a lot of thinking and talking last night, Captain. We decided to check just a little bit further and then bring it to you. But you've rushed us. It's still all theory."

"Theory," he said, and seemed to be looking around for a place to spit.

I said, "Carrie Milligan's share of the ill-gotten gains was a little better than a hundred thousand dollars."

He snapped his head around and stared at me. "That sounds more like a fact than a theory, McGee."

"She gave it to me to hold for her, and to give to her sister if anything happened to her."

"We can come back to that," Scorf said. "Where does it lead you?"

"We had four people in business together. Carrie Milligan, Freddy Van Harn, Jack Omaha, and Cal Birdsong. Carrie had her own kind of twisted integrity. She'd take no more than what was hers. But she was afraid somebody might take her share away from her. With Freddy supplying the plane and Jack supplying the boat, and probably the two of them supplying financing, would Carrie have been in for a full quarter of the pie? I'd say no. I would say a top of twenty percent. Jack was the banker. He was keeping it in the safe at the business. Carrie was the bookkeeper and courier. New buys were financed out of that money in the safe. When they eventually decided to call it quits, they would have divided it up according to the formula and gone their separate ways. If a hundred thousand equals twenty percent, then there was four hundred thousand left in the safe after she took hers."

"Four hundred thousand!" Scorf said slowly.

"Maybe more," Meyer said. "It is hard to read the motives of a dead man you never met, but it struck us last night that Jack Omaha was setting himself up for total departure, deserting hearth and home, cashing in everything, even cleaning out the partnership. Maybe he left that money in the safe with the group funds, or maybe he hit it somewhere where he could get to it quickly."

"So maybe he did take off," Scorf said, "and took Van Harn's money and Cal Birdsong's money with him."

"Or, like I told you before, a bag of grass fell on his head and killed him, and that's why Freddy told me that Jason saw the *Christina* come in without Jack Omaha."

Scorf frowned. "So . . . Van Harn would want his money and he'd know where it was and who could give it to him."

I said, "There's a chance he would want to leave it right there for the time being. Jack and Carrie had the combination. Jack was dead and he could trust Carrie. It would be there when he needed it."

"You mean it could still be there?" Scorf asked, frowning in puzzlement.

"Suppose," Meyer said, "that Harry Hascomb walked in on Carrie when she was taking her share out of the pot that night of the day Jack Omaha died. He would know there was big money there, but no way to get to it. Harry was the outside man. Because Omaha and Carrie handled all the accounts and financial records, they would be the only ones who needed to know the combination to the safe. Insurance people like to ask that the number of people with access be kept to a minimum. Two is ideal. Because Harry saw her take the money, it would account for her being uneasy and leaving the money with Travis McGee in Lauderdale. Just in case.''

Scorf displayed the quickness of the cop mind by saying, ''And after he found out that Omaha was planning to clean him out, and maybe guessed from the Milligan woman's reactions that Omaha was already dead, the simplest way into the safe would be to have the Milligan woman die by accident so he could call the safe company and have them drill it open. It would be the reasonable thing for him to do.''

I said, ''We can assume Van Harn went there as soon as he heard of Carrie's accident. All Harry would have to do is act totally blank about there being any money in the safe. Van Harn wouldn't dare press it. Besides, Uncle Jake had already taken him out of his financial bind.''

Scorf sighed. ''All theory. Pretty theory.''

''How about some fact?'' Meyer asked him. ''In the building supply and construction supply business, Hascomb either handled dynamite and caps and wire and batteries and knew how to get what he needed. He was the outside man, not the desk man, and apparently had some mechanical training or ability.''

''And,'' I said, ''Joanna Freeler told me she could retire, if she played it right.''

''Are you trying to say she could have known that Hascomb killed Carrie, and she would blackm—''

''No! It really shook her when I told her I thought Carrie had been pushed in front of that truck. I think Carrie told Joanna there was a bundle of money in the office safe. They were the only two girls working in that office. And that would give her some leverage to use on Harry Hascomb. That could have been her retirement. If she played it right.''

''She didn't play it right,'' Scorf said.

Meyer said, ''We decided last night that if Harry had asked Joanna for a date she would have accepted. They'd had an intimate relationship for several years. Then, if he couldn't keep the date, he could have left off a consolation prize, a box of wine and cheese.''

''Loud wine and cheese,'' Scorf said. He got up and roamed the lounge. He stopped and looked around. ''This place was one damn mess when I checked it out. Sickened me. Dead girls get to me. A bomb is a cruel and ugly thing. Any kind of death is cruel and ugly, I guess. Except as a merciful end to pain. The worst are bombs and fire and knives. Look, I know about girls in offices. Jack Omaha and the Milligan woman were the two supposed to have the combination. Bet you a white hat Joanna Freeler knew it too, or knew where Miz Milligan wrote it down. Know where every damn person in America writes down the combination to a safe? They write it on tape and stick it to the backside or underside of the top middle desk drawer. Half the safe jobs in the country are easy because everybody knows where to look for the combination.''

''We don't want to start the voyage home just yet,'' I said.

''Whatever you've given me, I can handle,'' he said. ''It's all theory. If Joanna let it be known to Hascomb that she accepted the date so they could have a little chat about how the Milligan woman died, she set herself up with wine and cheese.''

"If we worked it out right," Meyer said, "it would be . . . gratifying if we could be present when you interview Mr. Hascomb.''

Scorf looked bleakly at him. "Gratifying, eh?''

"So few things in life work out neatly, Captain Scorf, it would be reassuring to be in on one that does.''

"And you think that this whole mess is neat?''

Meyer looked troubled. "Not in the usual sense of the word.''

Scorf thought it over. "It's hardly one damn thing to go on. I don't want a committee, for God's sake. McGee, you can come along with me and watch me mess it up. Meyer, you better stay right here and get this thing ready to move on out into the channel. My orders are clear. I have to get you started on your way. And we'll be back soon.''

*   *   *

I had expected Scorf to sit bolt upright behind the wheel of the dark blue unmarked Cougar and fumble it along at a stilted thirty-five. Instead, after he had belted himself in, he tipped his white hat forward to his eyebrows, lounged back into the corner of the driver's seat, put his fingertips on the wheel, and slid through heavy traffic like an oiled eel. He moved to where the holes were, moving the oncoming traffic over, and was able to avoid accelerations, decelerations, and the use of the brakes. He had looked too underprivileged to be an expert, but he was, indubitably. And I said so.

With mirthless smile he said, "I wasted a lot of time and money ramming stocks around the dirt circuits. I felt easy riding with you the other day. Except you're not good on picking lanes at the lights.''

"Is there a secret I don't know?''

"Always haul in behind the local plates on older cars with kids driving and crowd them a little so they'll pile on out of your way. Haul in behind local delivery trucks. On three lanes run the middle one, and swing to the curb lane when you're going to miss the light. A man turning is out of your way fast.''

"Where are we going?''

"Pineview Lakes Estates. Twenty-one Loblolly Lane.''

*   *   *

It was low land, five miles out. The developers had used the fill from the dug lakes to lift the ranch-type homes out of the swamp. It was eleven in the morning when we pulled into the river-pebble driveway of number 21, a long low cypress house with a shake roof out of some kind of fireproof imitation of cedar. It was stained pale silver and had faded blue blinds by the windows, the kind that are fixed in place and never cover the windows.

Two tanned skinny boys were working on a stripped VW with wide oversized tires. They gave us a sidelong glance and no further acknowledgment of our existence, even when we stood beside the VW.

"Either of you a Hascomb?" Scorf asked.

"Me," the skinnier one said.

"Your daddy around?''

"No."

"Miz Hascomb?''

"No."

"If it wouldn't strain your brain, sonny, maybe you could break down and tell me where I could find your dad."

The boy straightened up and stared at him in bleak silence. "What's this shit about brain strain, gramps?"

"I am Captain Harry Max Scorf, and I am tired of the hard-guy act from young trash. I get cooperation from you, and I get manners from you, and I get respect from you, sonny, or you go downtown for obstructing a police officer in his line of duty."

The bleak stare did not change. "Oh, goodness me," the boy said in a flat voice. "I did not for one moment realize. Tsk tsk. From what I overheard I believe you will find my dear father down at his place of business, Superior Building Supplies, at Junction Park. Actually it is no longer his place of business because the silly shit has lost it because he didn't know how to run it, and his partner screwed him and ran with the cash. But Cowboy Harry is just as bigmouth as ever. He is down there because some pigeon from Port Fierce wants to buy the junk that didn't get cleared out in the clearance sale. And now if you will give me your gracious permission to get back to work here."

Scorf smiled sadly and shook his head. "Thank you kindly, sonny. I am sure we will meet professionally one day."

"You can count on it," the boy said.

As we drove out Scorf said, "What makes so many of them so damned angry at everything lately?"

"It's a new preservative they put in the fried meat sold at drive-ins."

"As good an answer as any."

* * *

There was one car behind Superior Building Supplies, a recent-model Ford station wagon with local plates, dinged and dusty, with a cracked window and a soft tire. One of the big sliding doors that opened onto the loading dock was ajar about three feet. We climbed onto the dock and went into the shadowy echoing areas of the empty warehouse. The air conditioning was off.

"Hascomb?" Scorf shouted.

"Yo! Who is it?"

Harry came out of the shadows, a pair of pliers in his hand. He peered and said, "Oh, hey, Harry Max! You were against the light." He looked at me. "What was your name, friend?"

"McGee."

Hascomb was stripped to the waist, the sweat rolling of his soft torso. His cowhand pants, cinched with a wide belt, were sweat-dark around the waistline. His abundant red-brown hair was carefully coiffed and sprayed into mod position, covering his ears. His boot heels clicked on the cement floor.

"You caught me, Harry Max," Hascomb said. "What I'm doing, I'm taking off the big junction box over there. I don't rightly know if it's mine or the owner's, so in case of doubt I'm taking it. The fellow from Fort Pierce offered twenty bucks, and that is twenty bucks I wouldn't otherwise have. He took a lot of the small stuff and he's sending a bigger truck back for the desks, safe, chairs, and those two generators over there. And that cleans me out."

"Sorry to hear it." Scorf said.

Hascomb sighed and shrugged. "Hard times and a thief for a partner."

"What are you going to do?"

"I think we'll head out to Wyoming. Out to the mines. I can fix any damn thing that's got moving parts. New start. The equity in the house will give us a stake. Were you boys looking for me?"

I wondered how Scorf would approach it. Suspicion without proof is a dangerous thing and a clumsy thing.

Scorf said, "Harry, I hope you won't take this wrong, I surely do. In my line of work I have to do a lot of fool things I don't believe in, but I guess every line of work is the same. Anyways, I guess your prints are on file from army duty, but it would take a time to get them out of Washington or wherever the hell they keep them, and so they said to me, Captain, you go bring Harry Hascomb in voluntary and take his prints. You won't put up a fuss, will you?"

"Me? No. Hell, no. I won't put up a fuss, but what in the world is the point of it, Harry Max?"

"Maybe I shouldn't even tell you this, but we've known each other a long time. Maybe you know or don't know, a fragment of a print isn't worth a damn. This piece they got looks like it is one half of the pad of the third finger right hand."

"A print of what?"

Scorf scuffed at the cement floor. He shook his head. "Now you've got to understand how they think, Harry. It certainly wasn't exactly a big secret around the town that you and Joanna Freeler had a lot more than a business relationship. And lovers can have quarrels. Anyway—and don't get sore— the bomb experts, they recovered a piece of battery casing about so big, and they used some kind of chemical treatment to bring out the fragment of the print enough to photograph it. Once they compare yours, then you're off the list for keeps, Harry. It's something I plain have to do, and I'm sorry. I'm really sorry."

Harry Hascomb whacked the smaller man on the shoulder. "Chrissake, Harry Max. Don't feel sorry. I know when a man has a job to do, he has to do it. Right? You want me to go in right now? Let me get my shirt."

I noticed that Harry Max Scorf drifted along behind Hascomb as the man got his shirt, and I noticed that Scorf's heavy, drab suit coat was unbuttoned, and I could guess at the presence of the belly gun clipped to the waistband of his trousers.

Hascomb shouldered into his ranch shirt and tucked it in and buttoned it as we walked out. He slid the big door shut and snapped the heavy padlock on the hasp and smiled and said, "Have to finish stealing that box later." We were parked beside the Ford wagon, just to the right of it. Hascomb started to get into the Cougar and then he said, slapping his pocket, "Just a second, Harry Max. Let me get my other pack of cigarettes."

He leaned into the wagon and thumbed the button that dropped the door of the glove compartment. He was very good. Scorf was standing outside the open door of the two-door Cougar, holding the driver's seat tilted forward so that Hascomb could climb into the back. I was opposite the hood, walking toward the door on the passenger side.

Hascomb snatched an ancient weapon out of his glove compartment. Officers have smuggled them home from the last five wars. The Colt .45 automatic. I caught a glimpse of it as he turned and fired at Scorf at point-blank range.

Scorf got his left hand up to ward off the big slow slug. He was reaching for the belly gun with his right hand. The big slug went through the palm of his left hand and hit the shelf of brow over the left eye. The resistance of the thick ridge of bone snapped his head back and broke his neck. The white hat went sailing over the hood of the car. The relentless chunk of lead plowed through the brain tissues and took off a hunk of the back of the skull as big as an apple. It was all very immediate and messy. It spattered blood and tissue over the front half of the Cougar. I saw it all in slow motion. It was in the hard and vivid light of the hour before noon. It was a day of almost stagnant air. The wind had been moving steadily from north to south, bringing to Florida's east coast all the stained and corrosive crud of Birmingham and the rest of the industrial South. The horizons were whiskey-stained, and the sky above was a pallid saffron instead of blue. The bleared sun made harsh studio lighting on the parking-lot scene. And Harry Hascomb saw Captain Scorf's horrid death under the dreadful lemon sky.

Scorf lay poised halfway across the dark blue hood. Meyer had been so right about the vivid reality of death. Harry Hascomb's face was absolutely slack, his eyes blank and dulled. He had expected to see the picture of the dead grackle. Here was the genuine article, smashed, leaking, stinking, and so sickeningly vivid that it immobilized him, froze him in an incredulous horror. I was caught on tiptoe for an instant, knowing that we were in a deserted parking lot in a deserted area, knowing that I could not expect any Saturday noon curiosity-seekers.

Scorf's coat was spread, showing the gun butt. With a swift and insane delicacy, with a mind-bulging awareness of my own madness, I leaned into the field of fire of the big automatic, snatched Scorf's weapon free, and fell to the cement on the far side of the Cougar from the immobilized Hascomb. He fired as I disappeared from his view, and like an afterecho of the hefty *bam,* I heard the slug chunk into the loading dock. An instant later Scorf slid off the hood onto his side, landing with a heavy clopping and thudding.

Doubtless Harry Hascomb had some sort of a script in mind. Maybe the automatic was due to end up in my dead hand, and Harry was due to end up in Peru.

I am not one for the shootout at the O.K. or any other corral. I have no wish to stand in full view with steely nerves and draw a bead on the chap trying to blow my head in twain.

I hitched quickly into the prone position and steadied the short-barreled weapon by grasping my right wrist in my left hand and pushing outward. I aimed under the low road clearance of the Cougar, and I aimed at the front ankle creases in his Western boot and did not miss at that range. He yelled and started gimping around. I missed the other boot the first try and then got it on the second try. All of Harry Hascomb came tumbling down, making shrill sounds of total dismay. He thought to return the fire in the same manner, aiming under the car. I was after his hand or wrist, but I hit the automatic by accident. The slug spanged and went screeing off in ricochet, and the Colt killed the muffler on the Cougar before it went spinning away from him.

Without any conscious thought and without the awareness of any lapse of time, I found myself standing over Hascomb, picking a place right between his eyes.

Then I realized it would mean I would spend the best years of my life in Bayside, filling out forms and answering questions. He was not going anywhere, but to be safe I took both sets of car keys. I walked all the way to the phone booth beside the gas station, the one Carrie had patronized.

18

A WIND had come up and blown all the smutch into somebody else's sky. Cindy and I sat on the deck chairs on the sun deck, side by side, and looked up at all the diamonds in the sky.

"You said they found it, Trav, but where was it?"

"In a box labeled Camp Stove. He was getting ready to go camping. And get lost in the woods. Forever."

"He said he killed Carrie?"

"Knocked her cold. Waited for the right kind of traffic and then took her by the crotch and the nape of the neck and slung her into the farm truck."

I sensed the way she shuttered.

She said, "I suppose, in a way, some of the money is mine."

"In a way. But your chances of getting it . . ."

"I know. I'll just have to make it anyway."

"Couldn't you sell out?"

"Sure. But then what?"

"What do you mean?"

"Trav, darling, I like to work. I like to run things. And I like to have security. I've got a hundred thousand mortgage to pay off, and the place is worth ten times that. I am really going to have to pitch in."

"And I was going to ask you to pack a bag and come cruising."

"Well . . . someday, maybe."

"I gather that you are underwhelmed."

"Male pride talking. Can't you accept the fact that I'm tied to this place?"

"And you want to be tied to it."

"Please. I don't want to fight with you. Please, dear."

I stretched until my shoulders creaked. "Okay, Cindy. You are very realistic and diligent and all that. Maybe I have a grasshopper philosophy, but it strikes me there are a lot of dead people around here. Given advance warning, they could have done more living."

"We don't know each other."

"What does that mean?"

"I found out from you I'm a more physical person than I thought I was. Okay, so it makes me skeptical of myself and impatient about things. So, being a careful person, I need time. I just can't go mooning and dreaming around here and letting important things slide."

"Mooning and dreaming are very good stuff."

"Sure, sure, sure. We really don't know each other at all. I'm not a drone. I'm a worker. A builder. Maybe I can learn to play someday. But I have to have something solid, all built, before I'll dare. Please understand."

I gave up. I lifted her hand up and opened it and kissed the palm. She shivered. I said, "Give me a call when you get all your ducks in a row. When you feel like getting acquainted."

"Could you call me?"

"I suppose so. Why?"

"It's very strange to feel so shy about somebody you've been to bed with. But I do."

"Cindy, I will call you. But when?"

She inhaled and exhaled deeply, a sign of relaxation and contentment and eventual anticipation.

"Just try me every once in a while, okay?"

And it was okay because it had to be. There wasn't any other choice. Sometimes it is a relief not to have a choice. I will have to get Meyer to explain this concept to me.

The Empty Copper Sea

❖

*Dedicated to all the shining memories
of those last two passenger ships
which flew the United States Flag,
the* Monterey *and the* Mariposa,
*and to the mariners
who sailed aboard them.*

*A man needs only to be turned around once
with his eyes shut in this world to be lost.*

THOREAU

1

VAN HARDER came aboard *The Busted Flush* on a hot bright May morning. My houseboat was at her home mooring, Slip F-18 at Bahia Mar, Fort Lauderdale. I was in the midst of one of my periodic spasms of energy born of guilt. You go along thinking you are properly maintaining your houseboat and your runabout, going by the book, keeping a watchful eye on the lines, the bilge, the brightwork, and all. But the book was written for more merciful climates than Florida, once described to the King of Spain by DeSoto as "an uninhabitable sandspit," even though at the time it was inhabited by quite a lot of Indians.

Suddenly everything starts to snap, rip, and fall out, to leak and squeal and give final gasps. Then you bend to it, or you go live ashore like a sane person.

Crabbing along, inch by inch, I was replacing the rail posts around the whole three sides of the sun deck, port, starboard, and stern, using a power drill and a power screwdriver to set the four big screws down through the stainless flange at the foot of each post. I had sore knees, a lame wrist, and a constant drip of sweat from nose and chin. I wore an old pair of tennis shorts, and the sun was eating into my tired brown back.

It had been six, maybe seven years since I'd seen Van Harder. He had owned the *Queen Bee III* in charter-boat row. He had been steady and he could find fish, and so had less trouble finding customers than a lot of the others. I knew he wasn't going to overwhelm me with a lot of conversation. I knew he'd had some bad luck, but that was a long time ago. A frugal man, he had saved his money and finally sold the *Queen Bee III* to Rance Fazzo, had acquired a shrimp boat and a large debt, and had moved around to the other coast.

I finished the post, walked over, and mopped my face on the towel. We sat on the two pilot chairs, swiveled away from the instrument panel to face astern, toward all the shops and towers of Bahia Mar, both of us shaded by the folding navy top.

Van Harder was a lean, sallow man. Tall, silent, and expressionless. I had never seen him without a greasy khaki cap with a bill. Florida born for generations back, from that tough, tireless, malnourished, merciless stock which had scared the living hell out of the troops they had faced during the War Between the States. His eyes were a pale watery blue. He was about fifty, I guessed.

297

"They tell me Fazzo is fishing out of Marathon now," he said.

"Doing okay, from what I hear."

Silence.

"Meyer still around?"

"Still around. He had some errands over in town today."

Silence.

"Guess you heard I lost the *Queen Bee Number Four*. Shrimp boat. Sixty-five foot."

"Yes, I remember now. Wasn't that four years or so ago?"

"Two month shy of five year. Run down by a phosphate ship headed for Tampa. Forty mile west of Naples. Three in the morning. Lost two men. One of them had the helm. No way to tell what happened."

"Insurance?"

He spat over the rail, downwind, with excellent accuracy and velocity. "Enough to pay off what I owed on her. Got a job hired captain on another shrimper. Bigger. New. Hula Marine Enterprises."

"Hula?"

"That's the *h* and *u* off the front of Hubbard and the *l* and *a* off the front of Lawless. Hubbard Lawless. Hula run six shrimp boats at the time, and seven by the time they sold out a couple of years ago. What happened was Hub seen the handwriting on the wall, and he sold out to Weldron, which is a part of Associated Foods, own markets and all. I could have stayed on with Weldron, like most of the others did, except the ones so old they would have been in retirement too quick, and Weldron wouldn't take them. But Hub Lawless, he offered me a job skipper of the *Julie*. Real nice cruiser."

"I've seen her over at Pier Sixty-six, way out at the end. Nice."

"Dutch built. Big twin diesels. Fast. Good range. White with blue trim. How'd you know it was the same *Julie?*"

"I remember that name. Lawless. I asked who the owner was."

"If it was a year ago, I was captaining her. Year ago April. Had some time to come over here and see who was around, how things were going. Didn't happen to run into you then, McGee."

"But this time you looked me up." Not quite a question, but at least a leading remark. It sailed right by him. No response. I slumped in the chair, chin on my chest, ankles crossed, staring patiently at my big brown bare feet, at some paler cleat marks on the outside of the left ankle, and at the deep curving ugly scar down the outside of my right thigh.

"Funny thing about it all," he said, "was that Hub took me on because he knowed I was steady. The captain he had before, I won't mention no names, he got into the whiskey and he took a cut for himself when he ordered supplies, and he had brought women aboard when Hub was off on business trips."

"Why do you say that's funny?"

"Funny meaning strange how it came out, is all. I become a born-again Christian when I was twenty-eight years old. Clawed my suffering way up out of the black depths of sin to walk in love and brotherhood with our good Lord Jesus. Now Hub knew that. And he respected that. Until that night he never had no women aboard except his wife and his daughter."

"What night?"

He turned and gave me a long, watery blue stare. "The night Hub Lawless got drownded! What night you think I was talking about? There wasn't a newspaper in Florida didn't have the whole thing in it."

"When did it happen?"

"March twenty-two. Fell off the *Julie* somehow."

"I've been gone since early March, Van. I got back a week ago. Duke Davis had a party down in the Grenadines on that big ketch of his, the *Antsie,* and he had a bad fall and tore up his back, and he cabled me to come down and help him bring the *Antsie* all the way home. I didn't have any time to read the papers or listen to the news."

"Thought you look darker than I remembered."

"What's this all about, Van?"

He gave it about thirty seconds of thought before answering. "I know maybe more than I should about the time you he'ped out Arthur Wilkinson when he was way down, and it was right after you he'ped him, he married Chookie McCall. What I heard that time was that if somebody lost something important to them, you'd try to get it back, and if you did, you'd keep half what it's worth."

"That's close enough. So?"

He leaned toward me, just a little. I sensed that this was something he had thought about very carefully, turning it this way and that, not certain whether he was being a fool. His wisdom was the sea. So he took onto himself more dignity.

"They is stolen from me my good name, McGee."

"I don't see how or what—"

"Now you wait a minute. I got marked down as a drunken man, a fool who lost the owner overboard and nearly lost his vessel. They had an inquiry and held I was negligent. I haven't got my papers and I can't work at my trade. I have talked it over with Eleanor Ann, who has got a nursing job there in Timber Bay, and she says if it is what I want to do, she'll help out. I would say that by and large, my good name is worth twenty thousand dollars anyway, so what I'll do, I'll give you a piece of paper. You can word it any way you want, and I'll sign it. It will say that if you can find some way to show it wasn't my fault at all, I will pay you ten thousand dollars, not all at once, but over whatever time it takes me to make it and pay it."

Everything he had was wrapped up in that request: his pride, his dignity, his seafaring career, his worth as a man. And I sensed that this was the very last thing he had been able to think of. Travis McGee, the last chance he had.

"You better tell me exactly what happened."

"You'll make the deal?"

"After you tell me what happened, I will sit around and think about it, and I will probably talk to Meyer about it. And then I will tell you if I think I can help at all. If I can't, I'm wasting your time and mine."

He thought that over slowly, pursed his lips, and gave a little nod of acceptance. And told his story.

At about four in the afternoon of March twenty-second, Hubbard Lawless had phoned the *Julie* from his country office out at the grove and asked if the cruiser was okay to take a night run on down to Clearwater. It was a pointless question because Van Harder always kept the *Julie* ready to go. Van reminded Mr. Lawless that the mate, DeeGee Walloway, had been given time off to go up to Waycross, Georgia, where his father was close to death with cancer of the throat. Lawless said there was no need for the mate. There would be four in the party, and one of them would be available to handle the lines, if necessary, and they could certainly serve their own booze and peanuts.

Harder thought it would be four businessmen; he had often made short trips up and down the Florida coast when Lawless wanted to meet with people without attracting too much attention. The boat made a good place to hold a conference. It couldn't easily be bugged, a fact that politicians seemed to appreciate.

They came aboard at nine. They came down to the marina dock in John Tuckerman's big blue Chrysler Imperial. John Tuckerman was a sort of unofficial assistant to Hub Lawless. He didn't seem to hold any particular office in any of Hub's many corporations and partnerships, but he always seemed to be around, laughing, making jokes, making sure of air reservations, hotel reservations, dockage space, hangar space, and so on. They brought two young women aboard. Half the ages of Hub and John Tuckerman. Tight pants and airline carry-ons. Perfume and giggles.

Van Harder didn't like it one bit. The *Julie* was a family boat, named after Mr. Hub's wife. Women like those two didn't belong aboard. Harder knew from what people said that Hub Lawless was very probably a womanizer, but until that moment, when the two came aboard the *Julie,* it had been just talk as far as Harder was concerned. When he had been doing charter fishing, he had been known to turn back and come roaring to the dock and refund the unused part of the charter if people started messing around aboard the *Queen Bee III.* He couldn't exactly refuse to make the run to Clearwater, but he did not want to stay on as captain of a floating whorehouse.

Still puzzling over what to do, Harder took the *Julie* on out of South Cedar Pass. It was an unseasonably chilly night, with a northwest wind and the sea foaming white across the bars that bracketed the tricky channel inshore of the sea buoy. Once he was in good water, he set the course for a point offshore of Clearwater, put the steering on automatic pilot, and watched the compass carefully to see if, in the following sea shoving against the stern starboard quarter, she would hold at that speed without too much yawing and swinging and searching.

As was their custom, when Hubbard Lawless felt the *Julie* settle into cruising speed, he built Harder's single drink, a tall bourbon and water, and brought it up to him. Harder decided it was a poor time to speak to Mr. Lawless about the women. He did not feel that the single drink was in conflict with his religious convictions. It never led to another.

"Not long after I drank it down, I remember I had a buzzy feeling in my head, and then it was like the *Julie* climbed a big black wave that curled over at the top. I woke up sick and confused. I didn't know where I was, even, but we were tied up back at the regular dock. Hack Ames, he's the Sheriff, he was kicking me awake and yelling at me. He didn't want to try to pick me up, I stank so from having throwed up on my clothes. I reached up and got hold of the rail and pulled myself up, but I was so dizzy I couldn't dare let go. I couldn't make out what all the yelling was about."

"What had happened?"

"John Tuckerman testified at the inquest. He said one of the girls felt a little sick and went topside to get some air and went hurrying below again to tell them I was unconscious on the deck. Hub and Tuckerman came up and they checked me and thought I looked pretty bad. They thought maybe I had a stroke or some damn thing, so the best thing to do would be get me to shore. They had both run the boat, but neither one of them had come back in South Cedar Pass at night with a sea running. The way they worked it out, Hub Lawless went way up on the bow while Tuckerman eased it in. They steered at first by the city lights, and then by the sea buoy, and slowed way down to hunt the next marker. The girls stayed below, out of the cold wind. The boat was rocking and pitching in the chop. Hub was hanging on and trying to spot the sandbars. Tuckerman said that all of a sudden Hub pointed to the right. Tuckerman thought he meant turn hard right, and that's what he did. The instant he hit the hard sandbar, he knew Hub Lawless had been pointing out the problem, not pointing out where to steer. The jolt tore Hub's grip loose and he went overboard off the bow. The waves were picking the bow up and dropping it back onto the bar so hard Tuckerman knew he had to back off or start to break up. He put it in hard reverse and yanked it back off, and he couldn't find the switch to turn on the overhead searchlight so he could hunt for Hub. He threw a life ring over, slinging it toward the bar, hoping Hub could find it. He didn't know how to work the ship-to-shore, and even if he did, he didn't dare leave go of the wheel and the throttles. He yelled for the women and they finally heard him and came up to help look for Hub. It was a wild dark night and the only thing he could think of to do was try to find the markers and find his way in and get help. I stayed passed out through all of it and didn't come out of it even partway until, like I said, Hack Ames was aboard trying to kick me awake."

"Funny thing for him to do if he thought you were sick."

"He testified he thought I was drunk. He said I looked drunk, talked drunk, walked drunk, and smelled drunk. There was other testimony at the hearing, about how small boats had gone out hunting for Hub Lawless, and one of them found the life ring and nothing else. I testified I had that one drink that Mr. Lawless brought me like always. They asked me why I'd refused to go to a doctor, and I explained that once I started to come out of it, I felt groggy but I didn't feel sick, not in any particular place or particular way. They decided that Hub Lawless was missing and believed to be dead by . . . I can't recall the word."

"Misadventure?"

"That's the one. His body never has showed up."

"What is it you think I could do anyway?"

"There's a lot of talk around Timber Bay. People say Hubbard Lawless is alive. They say he's in Yucatan, living like a king."

"There's always talk like that when the body isn't recovered, and when the person had some money."

"But what if he *is* alive? You see what I mean?"

"Then he and Tuckerman had to plan the whole thing, and they had to knock you out."

"What I didn't tell you, I was drunk a lot when I was a sinner. I was jailed for drunk, time and again. I gave it up all the way for twenty year. Took it up again, just the one drink when Lawless would fix me one, showing myself there was no holt on me any more. They asked about that at the hearing and I told them. I told them I'd been passed-out drunk and remembered it clear, and this wasn't like it.''

"Why would the man fake his own death?''

"Money trouble. Woman trouble. Insurance. That's what they're saying. I got to have some help. I don't know what to do with myself. I don't know which way to turn any more. That was in March, and here it is May, and I haven't had one real good night's sleep since.''

"Van, I don't want to say yes or no this minute.''

"I can understand that.''

"I want to walk it around a little.''

"Want I should come back about evening?''

"Where can I reach you?''

"I got one day of work, crewing for Billy Maxwell tomorrow, for walk-around money. I'll bunk aboard his boat tonight. It's that thirty-eight-foot Merrit with the—''

"Down at the far end. I know the boat.''

"Remember, I'll sign a paper for the money, and I'm good for it.''

"I know you are. I'll be in touch tomorrow. Or why don't you come here after you get through with the charter?''

After he left I sat there and watched him walk along the pier, a big sad sallow man, with a little bit more than his share of pride and rigidity. The world had tried to hammer him into the ground a few times, but he had endured and survived. Maybe this time he could not. Maybe it was too much.

2

AS I DROVE into town with Meyer that bright evening, we got onto a familiar complaint. Back not long ago when all the action in town was located in the rectangle bounded by the Beach, Sunrise Boulevard, Andrews Avenue, and New River, you could not go into the city without seeing a few dozen people you knew. Meyer had spent a whole day doing errands without running into a single person he knew. And it depressed him. He is the sort of man who manages to know people. He knows at least six people for every person I know. His little bright blue eyes sparkle with pleasure when he meets anyone he has ever met before, and the splendid computer between his ears immediately furnishes a printout of everything they had ever confessed to him. Meyer can suffer bores without pain. He finds them interesting. He says the knack of being able to bore almost anybody is a great art. He says he studies it. So if my hairy amiable friend had been unable to find a familiar face in downtown Lauderdale, the world was in deep trouble. He is seldom depressed.

At least the tourist influx had died down to about 15 percent of peak, and we did not have to hunt for one of those places where locals go to avoid the crush. We settled for Dorsey Brannigan's pub atmosphere and Irish stew, and a couple of bottles of stout.

I knew that Van Harder's story would get Meyer over his identity crisis, and so it did.

He had followed the news story of Hubbard Lawless's untidy end in local papers and could fill me in a little on the man.

"About forty, as I remember. An achiever, Travis. One of those twenty-hours-a-day fellows. Wife and teenage daughters. A florid life-style, I believe. Lots of small corporations and partnerships. Housing, fishing, citrus, ranch-land, and construction. The follow-up stories hinted that he was in very serious financial difficulties at the time of his death. And there was an enormous life insurance policy. Two million or more. I can't remember the exact amount."

"Anything about how maybe he took off, faked it all?"

"Nothing direct. Mystery surrounds the disappearance of Timber Bay tycoon. The body has not been recovered. I think it safe to assume that if the papers were hinting, then the public was talking more directly about that possibility. Then it died down, I'd guess about mid-April."

"What do you think about Van Harder's story?"

"He's a reliable man. So let's say it was a heart attack, a stroke, a savage bout of food poisoning, or somebody put something in the drink. In any event I think we can say that Lawless left the boat before it returned. He left on purpose or by accident. And in either case, he died or left town."

"I don't know what I'd do without your help."

"It's simple mathematics, Travis. Permutations and combinations. You have three sequences—of four choices, two choices, and two choices. So there are sixteen possibilities."

I stared blankly at him. "Such as?"

"It was a heart attack. Lawless fell overboard by accident. He made shore and realized what a good chance it was for him to try to disappear forever. Or—Lawless put something in the drink, went overboard on purpose, miscalculated the risk, and drowned. Do you see why I say there are—"

"I see, I see. You don't know what a help that is."

"Break it down and you can't find one of the sixteen where Harder is at fault."

"Should I try to help him, dammit?"

"Would you like to know why I am saying yes, you should?"

"Yes, I would."

"Because as you told me this heart-stirring tale, you kept loading all the dice in Van Harder's favor, so that when you came to the point of asking me, I'd say yes. Okay. Yes."

"I'll be *damned* if I will. I am not in the business of salvaging the reputations of broken-down fishermen. I visited the city of Timber Bay once upon a time. It was closed. I am sick of red-hots, of overachievers, of jolly-boy Chamber of Commerce types. I've stashed enough money to last until Christmas week, and I've got work to do on the *Flush,* and when the work is done I want to ask about eight good friends and you to go on a nice little lazy cruise down to—"

"Will we need some sort of a cover story for Timber Bay?"

"We?"

"You don't think I'd let Harder down, do you?"

I stared at my friend with fond exasperation. I said, "You have a small piece of boiled onion on your underlip."

"Sorry," he said, and removed it.

"How about a bottle of Harp?"

"Splendid!"

"No, we won't need a cover story. People will want to talk about Hubbard Lawless. All we have to do is get them talking and then sort it all out."

"I'm glad you talked me into going," Meyer said. "Life has been too restful lately. And here comes somebody I *do* know. Life is improving." I looked where he was looking and saw Cindy Thorner and her husband, Bob, just leaving. They saw us at the same time and came over and sat with us for a while in one of Brannigan's big oak booths. They are South Miami people, and we had met them during a couple of skin-diving fiestas down in the Keys. Cindy is a perky soul, looking far too young to have grown kids, a blue-eyed blonde with enough energy for three ladies.

They had been in Lauderdale for some sort of bridge thing, some determined pursuit of master points about which I know less than nothing, and were about to head back. Meyer got off into his diatribe about not meeting anyone he knew all day, and how depressing it was, and how everything is changing so fast.

Then he told us all his new insight into the problem. Florida can never really come to grips with saving the environment because a very large percentage of the population at any given time just got here. So why should they fight to turn the clock back? It looks great to them the way it is. Two years later, as they are beginning to feel uneasy, a few thousand more people are just discovering it all for the first time and wouldn't change a thing. And meanwhile the people who knew what it was like twenty years ago are an ever-dwindling minority, a voice too faint to be heard.

They had to go. As Cindy got up she said, "Meyer, a Florida conservationist is a fellow who bought his waterfront property last week."

"And wants us to make room for two or three of his friends, and then shut the door forever," Meyer said.

Then she told me that the best reef for snorkeling she had ever seen was at Akumal in Yucatan, fifty miles down the coast from Cozumel. She said they were there at Easter and I should promise myself not to miss it.

After the Thorners left, Meyer said, "A person can go for months without hearing anybody say Yucatan, and now I have heard it twice in the same evening. A more primitive soul would take it as a sign."

"A sign that Hub Lawless is down there snorkeling away, drinking booze out of green coconuts, and finessing the señoritas?"

"We could go look there first, maybe?" said Meyer.

*   *   *

I drove back through the thinning traffic a little past ten. My ancient electric-blue Rolls pickup whispered along, silent and smooth as one of the great cats a-hunting. We decided there was no need to keep Van Harder in suspense once the decision was made, so, once I had stowed Miss Agnes in her parking slot, we walked down charter-boat row, past *Windsong* and *Dream Girl, Amigo* and *Eagle, Playtime* and *Uzelle, Pronto* and *Caliban,* all the way down to where Billy Maxwell's *Honcho* was moored and dark, the dockside lights slanting down into the dark cockpit.

I put one foot on the stern quarter of the *Honcho* and leaned my weight on it and let it rock back. Within seconds Van came up from below, silent and quick, a short gaff in his hand. Even though the *Honcho* was rocking a little in a fresh sea breeze that pushed against the tuna tower, that subtle change of motion was enough to bring Harder up out of sleep, instantly alert to repel boarders.

"Oh, it's you fellows," he said in a sleep-rusty voice. "Come aboard and set?"

"No thanks, Van. I stopped by to tell you we'll go over to Timber Bay and see what we can turn up."

After a long five seconds he said, "I do surely appreciate it. You fix up that paper to sign?"

"No hurry on that."

"They aren't going to care for people nosing around there."

"Who isn't?"

"Reporters came around, and all. Government people and law people and bank people. They asking questions, handing out legal papers, and so on. So the family and the people that worked for him and the people tied into it all, one way or another, they're sick of it now, even though it slacked off a lot by the middle of last month. How you, Meyer?"

"I've been fine, Van. Sorry to hear about your bad luck."

"It do seem to come at me in bunches lately."

"Forgive me for asking, Van, but did you see a doctor and get checked over?"

"Hoped he could find some reason I passed out. Doc Stuart. He said he couldn't find any evidence I'd had some kind of heart spasm or something go wrong in my head, but then again he said he couldn't find any reason to say something like that hadn't happened. But if it had, it might probably happen again, and that would help pin it down. Aside from kid stuff, I never had a sick day in my life. Not ever. How soon are you going on over there?"

"We can talk about that tomorrow," I told him. We ambled back and sat for a time on the transom of Meyer's chunky little old cruiser, the *John Maynard Keynes,* looking at the overhead stars, faint through the particulate matter which jams the air of the gold coast night and day, never dropping below twenty thousand particles per cubic centimeter, except when a hurricane sweeps it away briefly, blowing it all into somebody else's sky.

"A cover story will help. I was wrong," I said.

"I'm working on it," Meyer said. From his tone of voice I decided not to ask any more questions.

I went back alone to the *Flush.* My security system advised me I'd had no uninvited guests. I was still worn down by the weeks aboard the *Antsie,* working that ketch north into the teeth of a hard wind that never quite became a gale and never died out. Cold food and safety lines, chafing and salt rash, constant motion and noise, and the deep fatigue, like a bone bruise all over. I wanted to drift *The Busted Flush* down through glassy bays, past mangroves

⌐and pelicans and the leaping of mullet. I wanted to take her down through Biscayne Bay and Florida Bay, and up by Flamingo through Whitewater, and out the mouth of the Shark River, and up past Naples, Fort Myers, Boca Grande, Venice, Sarasota, Bradenton, Tampa Bay, Clearwater, all the way on up to Timber Bay.

Once I was in the big bed in the master stateroom, I traced the route in the Waterway Guide all the way up to Cedar Key, which would be the last overnight before Timber Bay. I hadn't run any part of the lonesome leg from Egmont Channel a hundred and fifty or so nautical miles up to Lighthouse Point beyond St. Marks in quite a few years, and so was pleased to learn they'd put in a new chain of sea buoys nine to sixteen miles off the shoreline —nineteen-foot-high dolphins with slow flashers I'd be able to see six miles away in clear weather. Timber Bay lies twenty-seven nautical miles north of Cedar Key, and that pinpointed the city halfway between the marker number 16 for Pepperfish Key and marker 18 for Deadman Bay.

I reached for scratch paper and made a rough estimate of four hundred and seventy-five statute miles from Bahia Mar to Timber Bay. Running a ten-hour day at my cruising speed of a dazzling seven knots, I could just do it in six days, if absolutely nothing went wrong. As something always does go wrong, I always add a fudge factor of 50 percent. Nine days.

The *Flush* and I used to make nine knots. Then it was eight. Now we are down to seven, even when the bottom is clean and fresh. The problem seems to be in the efficiency of the two smallish Hercules diesels. They have many, many miles thereon. They are nosier than when I won the boat long ago. Some day they will have to be replaced. I have replaced almost everything else, a bit at a time.

I checked the accommodations at Timber Bay in the Guide and found a map of the waterfront and a description of the facilities. Cedar Pass Marina looked just fine. Ten feet on the approach and ten feet alongside. They could accommodate up to seventy-foot craft, so my fifty-two feet was no problem. Everything I needed was available at the marina, from electric to diesel fuel to repairs, showers, laundromat, groceries, restaurant, and even a motel.

I had a distant memory of its being a small and sleepy place. Like Cedar Key, it had been one of the towns supplying the timber which was barged south down the coast to build hunting and fishing lodges for gentlemen from the Midwest before the southwest Florida area was available by road and railroad. Again like Cedar Key, it had supplied the wood for a few billion lead pencils, until the wood finally ran out. Both of them were well off the main north-south tourist routes, with Timber Bay being about fifteen miles west of Route 19, down State Road 359, a long straight two-lane road through a tangle of dankness, smelling of snake.

Now, apparently, as they had found Cedar Key, the tourist and the retired had finally found Timber Bay—just as, inevitably, every square foot of the state except the state parks is going to be found and asphalted and painted with yellow parking lines.

I woke up at two in the morning with the light still on and the Guide open and face down on my chest. I stayed awake just long enough to be sure I didn't sink back into the same dream that awoke me. I had been underwater, swimming behind Van Harder, following the steady stroke of his swim fins and wondering why I had to be burdened with tanks, weights, and mask while he swam free. Then he turned and I saw small silver fish swimming in and out of his empty eye sockets.

As I faded down toward sleep I realized the dream had told me something. I should give up my rationalized cruise. When the cavalry went riding to rescue the wagon train, they never took the scenic route.

3

THE NEXT morning, Wednesday, the eighteenth day of May, after I finally gave up trying to find Meyer, he found me. He was beaming with pride and satisfaction. We went into the lounge of the *Flush* and he showed me the three identical envelopes, all addressed to him, hand-delivered, not mailed.

The stationery was uncommonly crisp, and it was a ribbed creamy forty-pound bond, bearing at the top the corporate logo of one of America's most successful conglomerates.

Up at the top left was printed in very small letters, "Office of the Chairman of the Board of Directors."

My dear Meyer,

This letters confirms our conversations regarding our potential interest in various enterprises and holdings large and small, which are now available or may become available in the Timber Bay area.

Knowing our long-range plans for the area, you will be able to determine if there are properties or enterprises there which should require our further attention with a view to negotiation.

In the event we do acquire anything there, with such acquisition based upon your recommendation, we both understand that you will be due remuneration on a percentage basis, just as we have operated in the past.

You are, of course, authorized to use your best judgment in showing this letter on a confidential basis to those who might have a need to know, and you are authorized to instruct them to get in touch with me personally if they should have any doubts as to your credibility.

Cordially yours,

Emmett

Emmett Allbritton
Chairman of the Board

"All three are alike," Meyer said.

"How the *hell* did you manage this?"

"I had breakfast with good old Emmett aboard his little hundred-and-twenty-foot play toy at Pier Sixty-six. Back when he was CEO of his corporation, I saved him from stepping in something nasty. They were acquiring a company which had a patent infringement suit filed against it. Emmett's legal people didn't think the suit had much chance. I was doing a Eurodollar survey for them at that time, and I came across something that indicated the suit would be large and nasty and successful. I went directly to him. He delayed the closing until the suit went to trial. And was very glad. So he owed me one. He had stationery aboard, and I took it to a public stenographer I know and composed the letter and took the three originals back to him for signature."

"You *do* know what you've got here?" I said.

"Travis, what I have here is a con man's dream. Emmett knows I won't misuse it, and he knows I'll destroy all three letters the instant there's no more need to use them."

"What about Van Harder? He can't lie worth a damn."

"Who says anything about lying? I am going to ask him if it meets with his approval if I kill two birds with one stone by checking into some property over there some friends might want to buy. Actually, if I do find something that looks very good, I think Emmett *would* be interested."

"Have you figured out my role in all this, pal?"

"If you are my friend, you are going to be accepted. Avarice is the longest lever in the world. Everybody is going to be very anxious to help me. Nobody will want to risk offending me. If they offend me, I won't make them independently wealthy. Of course, it would be easier if Van Harder wasn't there, giving them cause to wonder if we are what we say we are."

"Ha!" I said.

"Whyfor the Ha?"

"He could bring the *Flush* all the way around. As a favor. So we could come back home the slow way."

"Some likely people around here could fly over and help us come back the slow way," Meyer said, nodding and nodding, smiling and smiling. "How long will it take him?"

"Six to nine days."

"Do you trust his luck?"

"He's used up all the bad part."

"I stopped at Zzest Travel and had Peggy look up the best place to stay in Timber Bay. It's the North Bay Yacht and Tennis Resort. Suitable, apparently, for a man of my influence and know-how. They should have some humble accommodations for you as well."

*   *   *

When he came back from the charter, Van Harder said he'd be glad to take my houseboat on around to Timber Bay, but couldn't he be more help to us in Timber Bay, telling us who everybody was?

While I fumbled the question Meyer said that maybe it was best if we went in cold; then we could tell Van our impressions by the time he arrived at the Cedar Pass Marina.

It took until noon the next day to teach Van the little eccentricities of the engines, bilge pumps, generators, two banks of batteries, automatic pilot, air conditioning, water tanks, fuel tanks, engine gauges, RDF, SSB-VHF, tape deck, marine head, freezer, bottled gas, and so on—and to lay aboard provisions enough for the trip, get the needed new charts, estimate the cash he would need, and recommend the places to hole up. He marveled most at the giant bed, the enormous shower stall, and the huge bathtub, shaking his head and saying, "My, my, my."

I showed him the security system—the concealed switches for the Radar Sentry and the Audio Alarm and the fail-safe bulbs he would find lighted if the devices had been activated when he was ashore.

Meyer kept Harder busy while I removed my working capital from the double-hull hidey-hole on the port side in the forward bilge area. After Harder left at noon—warping the *Flush* out with an offhand competence that would have erased any doubts if I'd harbored any—I put the better part of my funds into a safety-deposit box.

It was an odd feeling to be at Bahia Mar without the *Flush*—different from when I had to put her up for bottom work. This was more of a betrayal. She was burbling happily along, down toward Dania and Hollywood, and all I had left in the slip was the overpowered runabout, my T-Craft *Muñequita*, tarped and tied off, bobbing whenever the power squadron boys went by.

*   *   *

By six thirty that same Thursday we were settling into a two-bedroom suite on the second floor of the North Bay Yacht and Tennis Resort. We'd flown from Lauderdale to Gainesville and then caught a little feeder-line Bonanza from Gainesville to Timber Bay, with one stop at Cross City. At the trim new little Timber Bay airport I rented a light gray Dodge Dart. The girl at the rental desk gave us a map of Timber Bay. The basic layout was simple. Imagine a capital H with a backward capital C jammed up close to it: ƆH The interior of the C is all water. Some small islands and unusual outcroppings of limestone block the open mouth of the C, leaving South Cedar Pass at one end and North Pass at the other. The crossbar of the H is the urban continuation of State Road 359, which comes from the east and dead-ends right at the bay shore. There it intersects the western vertical line of the H— inevitably called Bay Street—where Bay follows the C curve of the bay shore for a time before straightening out. The south end of the bay is where the marinas, commercial docks, and fish houses are located. The north end of the bay is more elegant, and beyond the top of the C a lot of sand has been dredged up and imported and a lot of fill put down to make a beach development area north of North Pass. The other up-and-down line of the H is Dixie Boulevard, named after the county. When it gets out into the country, it changes to Road 351A, going north to Steinhatchee and south to Horseshoe Beach. The northern open end of the H is residential, getting more pleasant the farther you get north of the crossbar until you get too far north into an area of shacks and junk trailers, abandoned wrecks, bedsprings, and refrigerators. South of the crossbar is mostly commercial. The crossbar itself is called Main Street. Between Dixie Boulevard and Bay Street, on Main, are the banks, office buildings, and better stores. Urban sprawl reaches out to the east, north, and south, with franchise food service, small shopping plazas, automobile dealerships, drive-ins, and housing developments.

The North Bay Yacht and Tennis Resort was just north of the top of the C, with boat basin and dredged channel, with a private slice of the handmade beach, with tennis courts, pool, children's playground, cocktail lounge (entertainment nightly—Billy Jean Bailey at the piano), Prime Western Beef, closed-circuit television movies, and a wealth of other irresistible advantages.

When I had stowed the few items of gear I had brought along, I went into our sitting room and found Meyer standing out on the shallow balcony, with the sliding doors open. I joined him and stood beside him, leaning on the concrete rail. Directly below us was a putting green, where a fat man labored mightily to improve his stroke. Off to the left was the big pool, with a few swimmers. Off to the right was a slice of the boat basin, where the brightwork winked in the last of the sunlight of the May evening. Directly ahead, beyond the putting surface, were the tennis courts. In the nearest one, two girls in pastel tennis dresses engaged in deadly combat. They looked to be about fifteen. The one on the right, a blonde in pale salmon, had a lovely style, drifting with dance steps to the right place, setting, stroking, following through. The one on the left, in pale aqua, was shorter and stockier, with cropped dark curly hair. She was a scrambler. She was often out of position. She made improbable saves. She went to the net when she shouldn't have but managed to guess right a lot of times about where the passing shot would be. When she hit it on the wood, it tended to drop in. She tried for shots that were beyond her abilities—long-range drop shots, topspin lobs—and made them pay off just often enough. She was sweaty and grim. She fell and bounded up. They had a gallery of about a dozen people. One point went on and on and on. Had it been a faster surface, the little dark-haired one couldn't have beaten the blonde. Finally she went racing to the net after an angled return of second serve. The blonde whipped it right at her, apparently trying to drive it right through her. But in desperate reflex she got the racket in the way. The ball turned the racket and rebounded, touched the tape, and fell in for the point, and the people clapped and whistled. The winner held her hand out, and the blonde looked at it and turned and strolled away. The winner went and got her big towel and mopped her face, wobbled over to the grass, and spread the towel and fell on it, gulping for air but smiling all the while. The winners smile. The losers holler "Deal!"

*   *   *

We went out and explored the city in the fading light of evening, drifting the gray Dodge back and forth through the social and commercial strata, snuffling the flavors of change, the plastic aromas of the new Florida superimposed on the Spanish moss, the rain-sounds of the night peepers in the marsh, the sea smell of low tides, creak of bamboo in light winds, fright cry of the cruising night birds, tiny sirens of the mosquitoes, faraway flicker of lightning silhouetting the circus parade of thunderheads on the Gulf horizon —superimposed on all these old enduring things, known when only Caloosas made their shell mounds and slipped through the sawgrass in their dugouts. Here now was the faint petrochemical stinkings, a perpetual farting of the great god Progress. And a *wang-dang* thudding of bubblegum rock from the speakers on the poles in the shopping-plaza parking lot. And screech-wheeling vans painted with western desert sunsets. And the lighted banks and the savings-and-loan buildings, looking like Bauhaus wedding cakes.

We found a place called the Captain's Galley, with a parking lot full of local cars. There was no table for two, sir, not for fifteen or twenty minutes. The smell of fried grease was so heavy we hesitated, but I looked into the dark bar and saw captain's chairs for the customers facing the pit where the barkeeps worked. And when I asked for the brand of gin we wanted the iced martinis made from, there was no confusion or hesitation. The young man in the sailor suit whipped the blue-labeled square bottle of Boodles out of the rack, poured generously, made us the driest of the dry, glacial and delicious.

I overtipped at the bar, a device useful in all such circumstances because it caused some secret signal to pass between the bartender and the fellow with the sheaf of menus. With more warmth than he had shown when we arrived, he led us to a corner booth set up for four, whipped away the extra setups, and said it would be his pleasure to go personally and come back with our second drinks if we were now ready, and we were. It is all a kind of bullshit, of course, to pry special treatment out of busy service people, but it improves taste and appetite. If you feel valued, it makes a better evening. And to busy service people everyone falls into a known category. It is enough merely to imitate the habits and mannerisms of that category which expects and gets the very best service. Hub Lawless would have expected it, gotten it, and probably tipped well, in the familiar style of the sun-belt businessman.

A pretty waitress with frosted hair told us the flounder was exceptional tonight, and yes, she would see that they picked two very nice ones to broil for us. And they were indeed splendid, as was the salad with herb dressing, hot fresh rolls with sweet butter, the carafe of house Chablis, and the es- presso.

The throng had thinned out by the time we left. Meyer went out of his way to tell the manager how pleasant the evening had been. He asked if we were passing through, and Meyer said we were in town on business, looking at property, and staying at the North Bay Resort. I went on out to the car. Meyer came out in five minutes, humming happily to himself.

As I drove off he said, "That manager's name is Bellamy. Moved down here from Atlanta three years ago. He owns a piece of that place, so he works lunch and dinner seven nights a week. If we want a quiet table any time, we can phone him. Just ask for Dave Bellamy."

"And he is one of your dearest friends."

"Is that supposed to be some form of humor? Dave is a nice man. He said the best real-estate broker for commercial properties is George Glenn. Glenn- more Realty. First United Plaza. I wrote it down."

He had been writing lots of things down. While I had been provisioning my houseboat and explaining her eccentricities to Van Harder, Meyer had been going through microfilm copies of the two-months-old newspapers at the li- brary, writing down the facts he had related to me on our flight across the state.

We found a more detailed map of Timber Bay and all the rest of Dixie County in the newsstand area of a big drugstore in the Baygate Plaza Mall. We found a phone book and wrote down addresses in Meyer's pocket note- book.

We went poking around, looking. We found HULA MARINE ENTERPRISES A DIVISION OF WELDRON/ASSOCIATED FOODS (the sign read), down at the south end of the bay, with hurricane fencing closing off access to the big dock, warehouses, and processing plant. Bright lights shone down on the whole area from high poles, discouraging intrusion. We cruised slowly by the Hubbard Lawless residence at 215 South Oak Lane, a winding mile of asphalt in the northeast sector, off Dixie Boulevard, bordering the Timber Bay Country Club. It was a very long low white structure set well back behind a low concrete wall. There were dim lights on in the house. In the glow of a streetlight some distance away, the wide yard looked unkempt. The three overhead garage doors were all closed.

We found some of the other identities left behind by Mr. Lawless, like so many cocoons shed in some startling metamorphosis. Lawless Groves. Double L Ranches. Hula Construction. Hub-Law Development Corporation. At Hula Construction the hurricane-wire gate was chained shut. A single guard light shone down on the empty area where equipment had once been parked. Grass was beginning to poke up through the thin skin of asphalt.

"How old was he in March?" I asked Meyer.

"Not quite forty-one."

I aimed us back toward the North Bay Yacht and Tennis Resort. Those birthday years that end in a zero are loaded. A time of reevaluation. Where the hell have I been and what have I been doing and how much is left for me, and what will I do with the rest of my short turn around the track? I had one of those zero years coming up, not too many birthdays from now. Maybe Hub Lawless had felt trapped in his own treadmill, hemmed in by his juggling act, tied fast to success. The most probable catalyst was the random female who had come along at the wrong time in his life.

"Can you remember the names of those two girls?" I asked Meyer.

"Felicia Ambar and Michele Burns."

"They still around this town?"

"They were both employed here in Timber Bay. Maybe they moved on. Probably you could find out about that better than me, Travis."

*   *   *

So I began to find out about it as soon as we got back. Meyer went on up to bed at my suggestion, and not at all reluctantly. Billy Jean Bailey was having a slow night in the lounge. It was called the Western Sky Lounge because, I suppose, of the hunk of glass the size of a basketball court standing on end, facing west. She looked no bigger than a half a minute sitting at her little pink sequined piano at the foot of that giant window. One spot shone down on her from the ceiling fifty feet overhead. She had a platinum natural, a pink sleeveless blouse which matched the piano, and silver slacks which matched the sequins. I sat at the bar, turning to watch her and listen to her. There were a few couples whispering together and groping each other in the shadowed privacy of banquettes. There were some noisy salesmen at the bar, at the far end. Billy Jean had a deep expensive-looking tan, a round and pretty face, a button mouth, an amplified piano, and a baritone voice.

She played a medley of old standards. She did a lot of flowery, tinkly improvisations, moving far away from the melody and then sneaking up on it again. I like a firmer structure, a more emphatic rhythm. Then the improvisation is supported, as with Joe Pass on that incredible guitar of his. But she did well enough. And looked good while doing it. And seemed to sigh at one point, looking around, seeming to grimace.

I got up and walked over to her. It was a long walk. She watched me arriving, her smile polite. She kept the music going with a little bit of right hand and hardly any left at all.

"Maybe 'Lush Life'?" I asked.

"My God, a thousand years ago I used to do that. I'll have to fool around with it and work into it. Sure. And?"

"And a drink with me on your break?"

"If you can hum it, I can fake it."

I went back to the bar. She found her way into "Lush Life" and, with but one stumble, got the words out of the music box of memory, did it very straight, and then moved into it with enough class to silence the salesmen for all of thirty seconds. She closed it off with her theme and came over, standing small at my elbow.

"As always, Mitch," she said to the barman. "Over there," she said to me and headed for a narrow booth for two. I paid the tab and carried her drink and mine to the booth.

"Thanks, friend," she said, "for bringing that old one up. I don't know how it fell out of the repertoire. It goes back in. I am Billy Jean Bailey and you are . . ."

"McGee. Travis McGee. Been working this lounge long?"

"Practically forever. Hell, it's all right. Good people own and operate this place. I used to do the resort-tour thing when I was first down here. I started in Youngstown. I used to do the Maine coast thing, and the Catskills and Poconos in the summer, and down the other coast here in the winter. Lauderdale, Hollywood, Miami, and so forth. But that can kill you off before your time. Then Danny died. He was my agent and kind of boyfriend. And they wanted me back here. That was three years ago. And here I am. Still. McGee, you drive one of those shrimpers for Hula? No? I thought you looked sort of the type. Like around boats and so forth. Jesus, this is one dead night here. Been in town long?"

"Checked in here this evening. I don't know anything about the town."

"There's no action, if that's what you mean. Oh, there's a couple of discos like everywhere, mostly all kids."

"No games?"

"You've got to be kidding. Oh, they probably play for lots of money over at the Elks or maybe the Legion. But you don't mean that."

"No, I don't mean that."

"So you can look at it this way, McGee. We're right at the heart of all the Thursday-night action there is in Dixie County."

"You're all the action I need, Billy Jean Bailey."

Her mouth hardened. "If you mean what that sounds like, you are in for one hell of a sudden disappointment."

"Whoa. I meant it is nice to sit and talk and have a few drinks and listen to the piano lady."

She studied me, head cocked. "Okay. Maybe I keep my guard up too high. But you know how things are. I don't even sit with guys much. I don't know why I did this time. You dint come on strong, and I liked what you requested, I guess."

"Friends?" I asked.

"Sure."

"I'll be around for a while. I'm over here from Lauderdale with a man named Meyer. He's my best friend. He's gone to bed in the suite, but I didn't feel like folding yet. What he's here for, he's looking into property that some bank might be liquidating that belonged to a man named Lawless."

"Oh, Jesus, *another* one."

"What do you mean?"

"McGee, dear, you have no idea the people who have come to town because of that Hub Lawless thing. My God, there is the IRS and people from the Department of Agriculture, the bank examiners, and investigators from the Justice Department, and FBI people, and insurance people. It is a real mess. You have no idea what a shock it was to this town. And still is. It has really sort of put this place into a depression."

"Did you know him?"

"And the *newspaper* people and the *television* people. The town was full up already, it being March, the end of the tourist season, and some of them were even sleeping in their cars. Did I know him, did you say? Just casual, like he came in sometimes, always with a bunch of people. Hey, Mitch is making motions. I got to go earn my bread. Don't go away." She finished her drink, patted my hand, slid out, and ambled to her pink piano, swinging along in her silver pants, patting her silver hair, tapping her mike with a fingernail as she swung it close to her lips, saying in her oddly deep voice. "Well, here we are again, back into it, dears, don't all of you go away, because . . . recognize this? Of course you do. Made famous by a lot of people including me, your own Billy Jean Bailey. . . ."

Above her and beyond her I could see the night stars. Though the room was nearly empty, she didn't dog it. She worked her stint, making music, including one very showy arrangement of "Flight of the Bumblebee" based on the old Red Norvo arrangement, but without as much drive as the way Norvo did it because she did not have the power in her left hand to roll the heavy bass. She moved from that into her theme, at which point I went over and got another pair of drinks and got back to the table with them just as she arrived, delicately winded from the session, saying, "And that is all for this here Thursday night because it is ten past Cinderella. Saturday we go until two. Friday until one. Monday not at all, thank God."

"I enjoyed it."

"Good. It was kind of for you. I'm glad you happened along tonight. I don't know why, but I've been down. You know. All blah. What do you really do for a living anyway, McGee?"

"Free-lance salvage work."

"Like sunken treasure?"

"Sort of like that."

"But you're not working on this trip? You're just here with your friend whatzis."

"Meyer. I can help him out on . . ."

She beckoned to someone beyond and behind me. He came over. He dragged a chair over from a table and plonked it down beside the shallow booth and sat down, saying, "Hi, B.J."

"How you, Nicky? I want you should meet my friend Harris McGee. McGee, this is Nicky Noyes. Nicky used to work for Mr. Lawless."

Noyes looked like an American Indian fullback who broke training five years ago. He had a lot of long black hair, a drooping pistolero mustache, rubbery brown jowls, flinty little eyes deep-set under thick black brows, buffalo shoulders, a lacy white guayabera stretched taut across chest and stomach, a lot of dangling gold trinkets on a thick gold chain nested in the black chest hair, and a sharp tang of some kind of insistent male perfume.

He looked me over with skeptical thoroughness. "So I used to work for Hub. Isn't that damn fascinating?"

"It makes me tingle all over," I said.

Chemistry was against us. We shared a simultaneous loathing for each other. No special reason. It was just there.

He turned toward the piano player, hunching his left shoulder forward to close me out. "You want to go over to Stel's?" he asked her.

"I don't know. I guess not tonight."

"You rather sit around and let somebody pick your brains about what you know about Lawless?"

"Come *on,* Nicky! McGee isn't in town about Lawless, honest."

He stared at me. "And you don't know the first thing about it, I bet."

I shrugged. "I heard some hick businessman and one of his business buddies took a couple of hookers out on a cabin cruiser and everybody got slopped and the hired captain passed out and the local big shot fell overboard and drowned, and everybody got all worked up about it. But I guess there isn't much to get worked up about around here anyway."

It made his big neck bulge. It made his face darker. It turned big hands into fists and made his voice uneven. "Sure, you know a lot. All you know is that newspaper shit. I never see Hub Lawless liquored up in my life. Not once. And I happen to know the fellow ran the *Julie* for Hub, and old Van wouldn't take more than just one drink ever. As for what you call hookers, Hub didn't fool around. I wouldn't say not ever, but anyways not around here, where he was a director in the bank and a deacon in the church, with a good marriage and those two daughters. Who are you calling hookers anyway? 'Licia Ambar, she works in Top Forty Music over in the Baygate Plaza Mall, and she's a good kid. Michele Burns, she works waitress over to the Cove. She's no hooker."

"Nicky, she's about as close as you can get and not be. Jack had to tell Mishy not to come cruising this bar, remember? Come on, you guys. What's to get so edged up about?"

He gestured toward me. "People like McGoo here who know everything about everything, they gripe my ass, B.J."

"McGee," I said. "I think I know how *you* spell *your* last name."

"Hey, guys!" she said sharply. "You'll get me in trouble, dammit."

"Lawless didn't drown," he said to me, almost inaudibly.

"Nicky!" she said nervously.

"Shut up, B.J." He held up a big hand and ticked the items off on his fingers. "One. He sold off the trucks for cash, cheap. Two. He stopped paying all the accounts coming due, and at the very end he cleaned out the bank accounts. Three. That girl left town the next day."

"Girl?" I asked.

He hesitated and then sighed. "What am I doing? It isn't any business of yours anyway."

"Tell me one more thing, Noyes."

"What?"

"Do you believe in the tooth fairy too?"

That did it. He got up very nimbly for a man that size, leaned his perfume close to me, gold trinkets a-dangle, and said, "Outside, McGoo. Now!" And he left.

"I shouldn't have even noticed he was here," she said dolefully.

"It's okay," I said.

"You're not going out there!"

"Why not?"

"Because it's childish, and because he's really mad enough to really kill you. I've never seen Nicky so worked up."

"Do you know if he was ever a fighter?"

"I don't think so. He's never said anything. He was Mr. Lawless's super-intendent, building those houses on that ranchland south of Baygate Plaza Mall. Please don't go out there, McGee."

"It's been too long since I've been childish, I guess. Want to come watch?"

She responded with a certain unwholesome anticipatory delight that she tried to conceal. Stripped down to essentials, it was a primitive situation. The two bull males and the nervous skittery female. He was in the parking area near the entrance to the lounge, standing near a blue Chevy pickup. It was a balmy night. He had shed his expensive guayabera, exposing an impressive mat of black hair. I told Billy Jean Bailey to stay where she was, under the palm trees, and I went on out to him, and he tried to finish it with one big looping right-hand lead. I got my left arm and shoulder up in time and moved a little bit inside it, but the inside of his wrist and forearm thumped the side of my head over the ear, enough so I knew he could hit. A lot of big men can't hit. A punch has to have snap in it, terminal whipping velocity; otherwise it is a big slow push.

I wanted him to be in a big hurry to finish it. I got my shoulders high and my arms high, and tucked my chin into my chest, bobbing under some of the roundhouse rights and lefts, taking others on my shoulders, elbows, forearms, moving in the direction of the punches to soften them as much as I could. But they still hurt, laming my arms a little. He gave whistling grunts of effort with each swing. Canvas shoes squeaked and flapped on the asphalt. I wondered how the thumping and the thudding of the blows sounded to B. J. Bailey. When he began to tire, I encouraged him by backing away toward a pale car nearby. I encouraged him further by turning to my left and bending over so my back was toward him, my fists covering my ears, risking the chance he might know enough to take a really punishing shot at my right kidney.

"Had enough?" he gasped. "Had enough, you son of a bitch?"

It was not much of a risk—I had guessed from his style what he would probably do. He would put his left hand on my right shoulder, spin me around to face him, and pop me with that big right hand.

I felt the grasp of the left hand, resisted it for a moment, then spun with it, feet and heels braced just right, using all the momentum of the turn to drive my very best left hand deep into the sweaty meat just below the V of the floating ribs. I covered my jaw with my right arm as I swung, chin tucked into my elbow. To make a blow truly effective, you have to hit through the target. I tried to hit so far through it I would feel the knuckles of his spine against the knuckles of my left hand.

It burst the air out of him, drove him back, and dropped him. His right hand had hit me just over the left eye, lightly, as my punch landed. I felt the warmth run into my eye and down my cheek. Nicky rolled, groaning, onto his hands and knees and fell onto his side, hugging his middle. B.J. came running to me, gasped, and cried, "You're all bleeding!" Nicky rolled to his pickup and managed to climb up the side of it, hand over hand, until he was on his feet and could lean against it. I took the wad of tissue B.J. handed me, wiped my eye with one, and pressed the rest against my eyebrow. I walked over to the pickup.

Nicky had his right forearm pressed across his middle. "I think you bust something inside," he said huskily.

"What's my name?" I asked him. The ritual of the schoolyard, the necessary childishness.

"McGee," he said, with no hesitation and no resistance. "I can't hardly breathe at all."

I opened the truck door, turned him, helped him hoist himself up to sit behind the wheel. He dug into his pocket slowly and found the keys, sighed, sorted the right one out and sighed again, and put it into the switch.

"I'm hurt real bad," he said.

"Go home and get some rest," I told him. He started the truck, turned on the lights, and drove away.

"Do you have to call a doctor or anything?" she asked.

"I don't know."

"Jack isn't going to like it at all."

"Who's Jack?"

"The manager here. He doesn't like for there to be any kind of trouble."

"I don't think it's much. I think we could pull it together with some adhesive."

She had some in her cabaña beyond the pool. We kept to the shadows. She babbled nervously in a semiwhisper. I gathered that Jack wouldn't care for this sort of thing, either. She said these cabañas had been designed to look out toward the beach, but then they had to put up the tennis courts and the locker rooms, and so her windows looked at the back of the locker rooms and you couldn't see much of anything at all, but then again it went with the territory, and beggars couldn't be choosers, and there you are.

She unlocked the door and let us in, and pulled the heavy draperies across the windows before turning on the lights. She was, as she had explained, clean but not neat. Her three-quarter bed had not been made back into a couch. There was a bright spill of lady-clothes on the available furniture, sliding stacks of *Billboard* and *Variety* and sheet music. She had a little Sony music center and a tumbled cupboard of records and tapes. She had show-biz glossies of a lot of people I'd never seen before scotch-taped to the walls.

She broke out some ice, and I wrapped some in a hand towel and got the bleeding slowed to where I could get a good look at the gash. It was an inch and a half long, quite shallow, close to the eyebrow, and slanting toward my left ear. The impact had evidently broken a little bleeder close to the surface. I had her cut a dozen very narrow strips of adhesive tape with her nail scissors. I sat on the closed lid of the toilet and held a hand mirror so I could instruct her in just how to pull the wound shut, lacing it with the narrow strips of tape in a series of X's. Then we placed a small gauze compress against it and taped that in place.

She said she knew how to get the dark dapplings of blood off the chest and shoulder of my pale blue shirt, and she took it into the tiny kitchen alcove and set it to soaking in something.

She told me she had thought he was giving me a terrible beating and it had made her start to cry. She told me it had been a funny time for her lately, kind of bored and listless and lonesome, like waiting for something to happen. She said if I was to happen to her, it would be okay, no matter what she said earlier. She said she knew what she was doing. She wasn't any kid. In the right light she could pass for twenty-five because she'd had a real good Mexican lift, "but don't ask how old I really am because I always lie." She hung on me, and I took her to bed, but after a while she got up and put a yellow towel on a small lamp on the other side of the room and turned the other lights out and said she always slept with a night light on. She said she had some really good grass, and did I want to share a joint? I said I didn't, thanks, and she said she had some coke too, not very good because it was cut too far down, and maybe I'd like some. I said no thanks, and she said it really didn't mean anything to her one way or the other, except she didn't believe in the hard stuff, ever, but would I mind if she had just a little grass?—because then she could be sure of getting it off. I said I didn't mind, so she got a saved butt out of a little box in the nightstand drawer, good for five deep drags, well spaced, then pressed it out and came back down to me with that sad, sweet, oriental tang on her breath.

4

I AWOKE a little after four in the morning. I could look across her to her improvised night light. It made yellow highlights on the sprawl of her small lean naked back and small mound of buttocks. She had her face pressed against my ribs, and I felt the long, slow heat of each exhalation from the depths of her sleep. She had one leg linked over mine, her right arm across my middle. A frizzle of that kinked platinum hair tickled me just under the armpit with each breath I took. The night bugs made small whirring sounds, and a wind made a sudden rain-sound in the palm fronds.

I sighed in a kind of habitual dismay at my own involvements. This one had a locker-room drabness about it. Hey, guys, the first night I stayed there, I screwed the piano player.

How was it, fella?

Well, to tell the truth, not bad. A lot of little extra frills and trills and improvisations, just like her piano playing, but not much real intensity, you know.

The why and when of the inadvertent affair is never simply explained. I remembered a few years ago, Meyer pressing a book upon me by one L. Rust Hills, entitled *How to Be Good*. Mr. Hills was explaining to his peer group how one might retain a modicum of goodness in a sadly corrupt world. One chapter in particular seemed appropriate to the situation in which I now found myself. He described the awkward union which he terms "the charity fuck." This is when a person finds himself in a situation where he suddenly realizes that the other party is ready, willing, and eager to make love, and because the place is available and private, and the time is available, and both parties are reasonably healthy, the only possible reason for saying no thanks is because you find the other party physically unappealing. Any excuse at that time—not in the mood, have this little headache, and so on and so on—will be so feeble as to lead the spurned party to the inevitable conclusion that she is indeed sexually unappetizing. This is such an unthinkable blow to give to another person's ego and self-esteem, it is far more charitable to gird the old loins and hop to it.

So here she was in the sweet depths of her postcoital slumber, reassured once more of her sexuality and desirability. As I was wedged back against the wall, there was no hope of stealthy departure. I took hold of her shoulder and gave her a little shake.

"Whassawharra?" she said into my ribs.

"Got to leave, B.J."

She groaned and hoisted herself up onto her elbows and lifted a bleared face to stare at me. "Whachawannago?"

"Daylight soon. Don't want old Jack watching me creep out of here, do you?"

"Shidno, swee."

I clambered over her and got into my clothes.

"Shirdsonahanganashar."

"What? What?"

"When I got up before, I hung your shirt on a hanger in the shower, but it probally isn't dry."

"Oh."

It wasn't. Not quite. I pulled a sheet up to cover her. I kissed her lazy mouth and patted her rump, and she told me to make sure the door locked behind me. It did. I felt a dampness in the cool touch of the predawn air. My brow felt fine, but my arms were leaden and dulled by the deep ache of the bruises from Nicky Noyes's big fists. Hell of a night, all told. Too much travel, too much to drink, a stupid brawl, and finally some romping with a small wiry tanned lady who was lonely enough to be potential trouble. By diligent effort I seemed to be prolonging my adolescence to total absurdity.

On impulse I turned away from the walk and found my way by starlight down to the beach, and out of my east-coast habit looked for that touch of light along the horizon which would warn me of the new day. Then I realized it would come up behind me, over the land. I walked to a chaise and stretched out on the damp canvas.

Between love and sleep, she had given drowsy answers to my elaborately casual questions.

—What did Nicky mean about a girl leaving town the next day?

—Huh? Oh, her. She left town the next day.

—Who?

—Who what?

—Who left town the next day?

—Well, they said she and Hub Lawless had something going. Then there were other people said there was always talk about a woman like that, like Kristin Petersen, whoever she was working for, and they said Hub and Julia Lawless had too good a marriage. Then her leaving town the very next day while the Coast Guard and everybody was hunting Hub's body . . .

Her voice had faded down into a muttering and then into slow, heavy breathing. A little bit more for Meyer's notebook. One Kristin Petersen, who had worked for Hubbard Lawless in some capacity as yet unknown and who was a natural target for gossip. A veritable battalion of women were thronging the Timber Bay scene: B. J. Bailey, Felicia Ambar, Michele Burns, Julia Lawless, and now Kristin, who had departed.

There was beginning to be such a subtle additive of light that I could make out the ghostly shape of a marker off to my left, where North Pass entered Timber Bay, and beyond it some shadowy tree shapes on the outcroppings that sheltered the bay. The Gulf was quiet, with a gentle lap and slap of small waves on the packed wet sand. I heard a deep-throated diesel chugging through the wet noises of the sea and soon saw the outline of a shrimper heading out. There was a pale yellow rectangle in the amidships area, with a man standing against the glow, and I saw him lift his arm and realized that he was lifting a cup of coffee to his lips. It was so vivid I could smell the coffee.

And I had a sudden wrenching urge to shed my own identity and be somebody else. Somehow I had managed to lock myself into this unlikely and unsatisfying self, this Travis McGee, shabby knight errant, fighting for small, lost, unimportant causes, deluding himself with the belief that he is in some sense freer than your average fellow, and that it is a very good thing to have escaped the customary trap of regular hours, regular pay, home and kiddies, Christmas bonus, back yard bar-B-cue, hospitalization, and family burial plot.

All we have, I thought, is a trap of a slightly different size and shape. Just as the idea of an ancient hippie is gross and ludicrous, so is the idea of an elderly beach bum. I dreaded the shape of the gray years ahead and wished to hop out of myself, maybe into the skin of the coffee drinker now far out of sight in the just-brightening morning. And he, the poor deluded bastard, would probably have changed places willingly.

I stood up and stretched my sore arms again and decided, What the hell, when in doubt turn to the obligations of the moment. Van Harder was a tough, humorless, competent seaman, and I had given him my word, and he deserved my best effort. If I questioned my own value, then he was likely to get less than his money's worth. He was the innocent bystander who'd been run down by somebody else's fun machine, and all I had to do was repair his reputation somehow. And stop moaning about myself.

I went up to our second-floor suite, showered, changed, and looked out at the early slant of sunshine, and at two young men in warm-up suits volleying on the farthest tennis court, one strung so much tighter than the other that the sounds were in different keys—*pink—punk—pink—punk*. A shirt-sleeved, necktied man, thick around the middle, came hurrying out. The boys looked up at the windows of the hotel and shrugged and moved slowly and disconsolately off the court, picking up the yellow balls and putting them back in the cans. I guessed that the necktie was Manager Jack, doing his managing. Beyond the courts I could see the roof of the row of cabañas and estimated the exact place where B.J. lay deep in sleep in the yellow glow, surrounded by all the silent music, still and dead in the grooves of the records, frozen into the emulsion on the tapes, locked into the calligraphy of her sheet music and the stilled cleverness of her piano hands.

"You up?" Meyer said, astonished. He had come out of his bedroom into our shared sitting room. He plodded to the corridor door, looked out to see if there was a morning paper there, and gave a grunt of annoyance on finding that service not provided. He wore a robe in awning stripes of pink, yellow, and black, and he looked and acted like a cross performing bear which had escaped a small circus.

"You want some morning news?" I asked. When he stopped and glowered at me I said, "Mystery woman Kristin Petersen, employed by Hubbard Lawless, disappears the day after alleged drowning. Nicholas Noyes, onetime superintendent of Hula Construction, states that Lawless sold equipment for cash before disappearing. And cleaned out bank accounts. One of the two young ladies aboard the *Julie* the night of the accident was one Michele Burns, known as Mishy, who is a waitress at the Cove and is reputed to be a part-time hooker. The other, Felicia Ambar, known as 'Licia, works at Top Forty Music in the Baygate Plaza Mall."

The glower was unchanged. "So?" he said.

"Don't you want to write it down?"

"What happened to your face?"

"Nicky Noyes took an instant dislike to it."

Meyer nodded. "I can see his point." He went into the bath, and soon I heard the shower. Meyer is not a morning person. Neither am I. But he is one of the non-morning persons who set the standards for all the rest of us.

After his breakfast and after the morning paper, Meyer was ready for communication.

"Officially," I said, "I ran into that jungle-gym thing in the dark."

"Why?"

"Both combatants were last seen with one Billy Jean Bailey, who is the piano player here and has been for three years, and Jack the Manager does not like to have piano ladies causing fusses between bar patrons. Or guests of the house."

"Who fixed it?"

"Miss Bailey."

His nod was approving. "Neatly done."

"I've been wondering about the best way to use that great letter of yours."

He found the right page in his notebook. "The top man at the Coast National Bank and Trust is Devlin J. Boggs. And it is not a chain bank, a situation that gets more rare every day."

"Should I go along with you?"

He studied me, head tilted, and finally nodded. "I think so. We're going to be linked anyway. You'd better be working for me."

"As what?"

"Maybe . . . as knowledgeable in the area of groves and construction and marine holdings. And ranchland."

"I can handle that. I'll carry a pack of Marlboros and grunt a lot and look open-air sincere."

*   *   *

The Coast National Bank and Trust Company occupied most of the ground floor of a ten-story office building at the corner of Bay and Main. All the window glass had an orange-yellow tint, making a golden glow inside. The executive offices were glass cubicles along the left wall as you went in the main entrance on Bay. There were lines at the tellers, and people crisscrossing the broad expanse of carpeted floor. Friday is a busy banking day.

Boggs was talking to two men seated across his desk from him. Meyer gave the secretary his plainest and most impressive card after writing on the back of it, "Representing Emmett Allbritton." She started to put the card down, read what he had written, looked at us again, got up and tapped on the door and took the card in and placed it by Boggs's elbow, and came back out.

Within moments he was ushering the two men out. He came out with them and took us in and got us properly seated before he went around and sat in his judge's chair. Devlin Boggs was about fifty, a tall and very erect fellow with a long and lugubrious face, an iron-gray military haircut, a lantern jaw, and a dark and elegant suit.

After introductions, Meyer handed him the letter. Boggs read it and said, "I had the pleasure of meeting Mr. Allbritton about, I think, fifteen years ago. He spoke to the Association in Houston about future problems in energy supply. Prophetic indeed. It is quite . . . heartening to know that they have long-range plans for this area." He looked inquiringly at Meyer.

Meyer said, "I wouldn't, of course, be at liberty to discuss the little I know of those plans at this time."

"Of course. What sort of"—he looked at the letter again—"holdings large and small would he be interested in?"

"Anything available."

"Raw land, developed land, actual business operations?"

"He would expect me to make recommendations."

"But I assume you are coming to me because of the possible availability of some of Hubbard Lawless's holdings. We have all been terribly shocked by what has happened. We had great confidence in Hub's energy and judgment. He was one of our directors, you know. Things were slow this year. Everybody complained, Hub included. He had borrowed up to the statutory maximum percentage from the bank. Three million dollars. These loans were to four corporations he controlled, and also to himself as an individual. The loans were secured by the assets of the corporations. After . . . it happened, we were able to inventory, or try to inventory, the assets. The books were in . . . very untidy condition. It would seem that for many weeks he had been systematically selling off the assets of his companies for cash, out of town." He took out a snowy handkerchief and wiped his lips. "He had been ignoring his accounts payable, making a special effort on collections. During the week before he disappeared, he drained every single one of his corporate accounts down to minimum balance. He even took out the compensating balance against his personal loans, which he had agreed to leave untouched. Understand that the company accounts included tax reserves, FICA monies, retirement debits, money due for his upcoming payroll. He was down to about forty people from the hundred and twenty he employed at this same time last year.''

"How much did he get away with?" I asked.

"There are too many ways to compute it, Mr. McGee, for me to make a valid estimate. My horseback guess would be between six and seven hundred thousand dollars. I would say that those assets remaining behind which can be converted into cash would result in a recovery of maybe one and a quarter million dollars, and most of that value would be in the appraised value of the ranch and grove lands.''

"So the bank stands to take a bath of one and three quarters million dollars," Meyer said.

Boggs wiped his mouth again and said dolefully, "If it were only that simple. There are a lot of other claims and liens against those assets. We may have the senior debt instruments, but we might have to prove it in court. It is such a terrible tangle that it might drag on for years. Legal fees and court costs will eat up a great deal of the remaining equity. In the meanwhile, such a huge write-off against our loan-loss reserves might mean that we would have to . . . give favorable consideration to an acquisition offer we have been rejecting. I have always felt that a locally owned, locally managed bank is far more responsive to the needs of any community, and . . . excuse me. Our banking problems are of no interest to you.''

Meyer gave a sympathetic sigh and said, "And I suppose that the state banking authorities and the examiners from the FDIC are stating that you didn't exercise prudence and good judgment in so setting up the loans to Mr. Lawless that he was able to market the assets without your knowledge and able to withdraw his compensating balance.''

"I see you know banking, sir."

"Everybody is always full of wisdom after the event."

"Hub was in and out of the bank a couple times every day. He was a director. He was on the Loan Committee of the board. He was a very hardworking man. And very . . . personable. Anyway, I wish we were in a position to be able to offer to sell some of the remaining real-estate assets to Mr. Allbritton's corporation. But, with no legal decision as to whether Mr. Lawless is dead or alive, you can see the terrible legal tangle we are in here.''

"Do you believe he is dead?"

Boggs hesitated a long time, choosing the right words. He said, "I did at first. Now I am not so sure. Neither, of course, is the insurance company. Julia Lawless is the owner of that two-million-dollar policy. It was taken out seven or eight years ago, for half a million, and as his affairs kept getting more involved, he kept adding to it. She owns the house free and clear. The land it's on was a gift from her father when they got married. I think she has some sort of very small income from her father's estate. Not enough, I wouldn't think, to run the house. I suppose . . . she is another of the victims of this disaster.''

Meyer said, "I don't imagine you would have any objections if I set up a hypothetical situation. Suppose, just for instance, that Mr. Allbritton made a decision, based on our examination of the properties, to make an offer of one million dollars for Tract So-and-So. Could the various claimants be brought together to reach an understanding? Could title be passed somehow?"

For an instant a faint gleam of hope illuminated Devlin Bogg's long sad face, but it faded away. "I wouldn't think so. I don't know. It's a bureaucratic tangle as well as a legal tangle. Some kind of accommodation would have to be reached with the IRS . . . I suppose Harold Payne might be able to give you better answers than I can. He is the bank's attorney, and he handled Hub's affairs as well. Elfording, Payne and Morehouse. They're in this building. Seventh floor."

I awaited Meyer's next move. He was doing very, very well. One door had been wedged open. Duplicity was hard on Meyer. It frayed his nerves and upset his digestion.

"Mr. Boggs," he said, "it is quite evident from what we have heard so far that . . . people asking questions are not exactly welcome in Timber Bay lately. I can always show my letter of authority, but I would rather not do that except when dealing with a man of your position. Perhaps you might be able to give us . . . some sort of notes, possibly on the back of your business cards?"

Once he started, Meyer kept him going. Fifteen minutes later we were out on the broad sidewalk. Meyer leaned against the bank. I leafed through the little packet of cards. Devlin J. Boggs wrote in a very neat small black legible hand.

They were directed to Harold Payne, to Walter Olivera of the *Timber Bay Journal,* to Lou Latzov of Glennmore Realty, to Julia Lawless, and to Hack Ames, the Sheriff of Dixie County; and one read, "To Whom It May Concern."

In his tight little script he said that we had his confidence, and any help they could give us would be deeply and personally appreciated by Devlin J. Boggs.

Meyer was breathing deeply, eyes closed. "How was I?"

"You'll never be better. We start now from the top. A new sensation for Meyer and McGee. Tools of the power structure. Servants of the establishment."

He smiled modestly. "No, I was never better."

So we walked to where I'd parked, got into the car, and split up the cards. He took the lawyer and the real-estate broker. I took the Sheriff and the newspaperman. His were downtown, so I took the car.

5

HAGGERMANN "HACK" Ames maintained his headquarters in the East Wing of the County Court House. Once it had been determined I was not an emergency, I was told to sit and wait in a cramped and dingy little room. The tattered magazines on the table were all hunting, fishing, and firearms oriented, looking as if some very sweaty-handed people had tried to escape into them.

Florida elects its sheriffs on a party basis, a shockingly bad system. Elections come around too often. Unqualified men can slip in. People with political clout are seldom harassed by the Sheriff. Good politicians do lots of favors. Every time when, by a change in state law or by local option, they try to set the office up on an appointive basis with specific qualifications, thousands of loud right-wing nuts rise up out of the shrubbery and start screaming about being deprived of their democratic rights and their voting franchise. Law enforcement has become so complex, technical, and demanding, so dependent on the expert use of expert equipment, one might as well say it would make as much sense to elect brain surgeons from the public at large as sheriffs.

A surprising number of them are very good in spite of having to be political animals in order to survive. An unsurprising number of them are ninety-nine-point-nine percent worthless. Having heard from Van Harder of the attempt to kick him awake, I expected the second kind.

But as time passed, I began to revise my judgment. The people who hurried by the waiting-room door were slender and young and in smart uniforms, male and female. No fat-guts, pearl-handled, hat-tilted-over-the-eyes, good-old-boy deputies. I could almost make out the words of the woman handling communications, calling the codes for various types of alarms.

Finally I was sent in to the Sheriff's small office.

"Just a minute," he said. "Sit."

It was a tiny office with a steel desk, steel chairs, dark gray carpeting, off-white walls, and no window at all. A big steel floor lamp hurled so many watts against the white ceiling, it was bright enough in there to make a television series. Me and Hack. He was signing what appeared to be requisition forms. He was a medium man with dusty brown hair and an unhealthy pallor. He was carefully reviewing the list of items on each requisition.

When he had finished he pushed a button on the base of his fancy telephone, and a uniformed woman came briskly in and took the requisitions away.

"Between the damned state auditors and the goddamn nitpicking Washington desk jockeys, a man can spend his life doing the paperwork," he said. He stared at me carefully for the first time. His eyes were brown, and they looked as dry and dusty as his hair. "Didn't you get picked up here in Dixie County five-six years back?"

"No, Sheriff."

"I could have swore. Do me a favor. Stand up."

What can you do? I stood up. He came around his desk and stood in front of me and looked up at my face. He backed off and bent and took a good look at my shoes.

He sat down again, and said, "No lifts. The one I mean, the one that looked like you, he was about six foot even. Once a man gets his height, he don't grow any more than that. Sure looks like you in the face. What's your name again? McGee. From Lauderdale? What's that you got there?"

I reached across the desk and handed him Boggs's card. He read it, looked at me, read it again, and put it down in neat alignment with the corner of his desk. He reached his hand across to me and we shook hands.

"Nice to know you, Mr. McGee. Now just what is it that I can help you on? You just tell me and we'll give it a try." It was as if I had suddenly turned into a Dixie County voter.

"What's the current status of the investigation of the Hubbard Lawless disappearance?"

"My investigation isn't the only one in town."

"I didn't think it would be."

He shifted around in his chair. If he'd had a window, he'd have gotten up and stared out of it. "Our investigation so far tends to show that Hub Lawless is still alive."

"Where is he?"

He picked up Devlin Boggs's card again and asked me if I would mind stepping out of the office and closing the door. He said it wouldn't be more than a couple of minutes, and it wasn't. He called me back in and I sat down.

"You've got to keep this quiet, Mr. McGee."

"I intend to."

"I gave one of my deputies, a man name of Wright Fletcher, that speaks pretty good Mexican, leave of absence to go on down to Mexico with an investigator from the insurance company has the big policy on Hub's life. Both those men thinks there's a pretty good chance of getting a line on him, and if they can locate him, there's enough federal heat involved, we should be able to get him extradited."

"So how did he get from the Gulf of Mexico to Mexico?"

"You know how he turned everything he could into cash, picked everything clean; that gave us the lead on premeditation."

"But wasn't there a hearing and a verdict that he was missing and presumed dead?"

"That was when the whole thing had just happened. Everybody liked Hub. What it looked like, he was just getting a bunch of cash together to put it into something good where he could turn it over fast and come out ahead. He'd done that kind of thing before. And nearly everybody knew he couldn't swim a stroke. It's like that with a lot of Florida native born. Me, I've lived all my life close enough to the Gulf to near spit in it, and I can't swim no more than Hub could. And the Gulf water is right cold in March. Once we get a line on Hub, we can open the whole thing up again. That insurance company sure-God doesn't want to presume him dead. And Julie Lawless wants to take them to court to get the money."

"What do you have to go on?"

"First there is kind of negative reasoning. We can show how he was turning stuff into cash. Hundred-dollar bills is all you can get hold of nowadays without attracting attention. You know how much space and weight is involved in six hundred thousand dollars? That is six thousand pieces of paper. It will weigh right around twenty pounds. If it was all mint, which it wasn't, it would make a package six inches by seven and a half inches, and ten inches high. We've not found it or any part of it. And we have looked. We've looked good.

"The next part is negative reasoning too. When they got around to inventorying the stuff on the books of those four corporations of his, there was a jeep missing he used a lot. An old yellow jeep with dune-buggy tires that he could run cross-country at the ranch and the grove. It has never turned up. His other two cars were here, but the jeep is gone."

"Do you have any positive reasoning, Sheriff?"

He looked at me, and in those dusty brown eyes I could read a very serious message. Though he looked like a mild man, I would not want to irritate him and not have a little card from Boggs to keep him in check. He exhaled and let his white knuckles relax.

"We got a lot of calls. After the whole thing went on the wire services, we got calls he was seen in Tacoma and on Maui and in Scranton, P-A. People called up and said that if there was a reward they'd tell us where to come pick him up. Key West, Detroit, Montreal. Everybody knew right where Hub Lawless was hiding. When a man has money and you can't find the body, these calls always come in."

"But that is—"

"Wait until I finish. We don't have the budget to check out all that nonsense. But we check out what looks possible. Just ten days ago in the Tuesday mail we got a letter from Orlando. There was a slide in it, in a cardboard mount. There was a typed note in with the slide. I've got a copy here of what the note said, and a print made from the slide."

He read me the note. " 'The man in this picture I took looks like the man in the newspaper pictures. I took this picture on Friday April eighth in Guadalajara. I can't give you my name or address because my boyfriend thinks I was in San Diego visiting my sister.' "

The print was a four-by-five, sharp and clear. It showed a sidewalk café, a sunny street, traffic, buses, buildings in the distance, nearby shops with signs in Spanish. There were several tables occupied. A man sat alone at one of them, off to the left. He was almost facing the camera. He was carefully pouring what was evidently beer into his glass.

Hack Ames came around the desk, leaned over my shoulder, and tapped that beer-pouring fellow with his finger. "Hub. No doubt of it. We projected that slide as big as we could with the best projector we could locate. Hell, it even shows the detail of his ring, the little scar at the corner of his mouth. The experts say it was taken on Ektachrome X with a good-quality lens that was a medium-wide angle, like maybe thirty-five millimeters. It was developed at one of the Kodak regional labs, and the date stamp in the cardboard of the mount says April. You can see that she wasn't trying to take a picture of Hub. I think she didn't even know what she had until she got the slides and used a viewer or a projector."

Hubbard Lawless was wearing an open khaki jacket with short sleeves over a yellow T-shirt. He had a blunt cheerful face, snub nose, bland brow, thinning blond hair combed and sprayed to hide the paucity of it. His hands were big, his forearms thick and muscular. He wore a small frown of concentration as he poured his beer.

"So it places him in Guadalajara a month and a half ago. That's where your deputy and the insurance investigator went?"

"With copies of this picture. Wright Fletcher is a very hard worker. He'll show that picture to ten thousand people if he has to. But they're going to concentrate on the clinics.

"Clinics?"

"That's the world center for cosmetic surgery. Lifts, nose jobs, hair plants. There are dozens of very qualified surgeons working down there."

"Makes sense."

"If he's been and gone, there'll be before-and-after pictures in the files. That and this picture and the date of the operation would prove he didn't drown when he allegedly fell off the *Julie*."

"What about Kristin Petersen?"

"You mean is she with Hub? It looks that way. Funny thing. A man gets to be forty and he gets itchy, and it's usually a woman sets him off, trying for a different kind of life. It happens every day. But most men, when they go off the deep end, they don't influence the lives of so many other people. They don't raise such hell with a community. This has upset a lot of applecarts."

"We're staying at the North Bay Resort. Maybe you could let me know if your deputy finds out anything."

"I don't exactly see where you fit into this."

"We fit where Mr. Boggs said we fit."

"Sure," said the Sheriff. "Great."

"Can I keep the picture?"

"If you want it. We had a lot made."

"Are the city police in on this in any way?"

"There aren't any. There was a referendum and the county took over law enforcement for everything inside the county. They get more service for less money this way. We absorbed their staff and equipment and gave up their office space two years ago."

"Where is the *Julie*, Sheriff?"

"Over to Cedar Pass Marina. The fellow that was mate, DeeGee Wallo-way, he's living aboard and keeping an eye on it."

"Can I tell him it's okay with you if I take a look at it?"

"Now why would you want to do that?"

"It can't hurt anything, can it?"

"I guess not. But there's been enough people trying to be some kind of Shylock Holmes around here."

"Was Harder really drunk?"

"He looked drunk, smelled drunk, talked drunk, walked drunk, and all-around acted drunk. So, like it said in the paper, I didn't get him tested for drunk. So I can't swear he was passed-out drunk. Besides, he'd done a lot of jail time for D and D."

"Before he was born again."

"Those born-again ones fall off too, McGee. And hate to admit it. One drink, Van said. Like the ones we pick up wavering all over the road. Two little beers, they say. John Tuckerman and those girls swore Hub took Van up just that one drink. But he could have had a pint bottle in his coat, sucked it dry, and heaved it over the side. He comes from here, you know. And a lot of people remember the hell he raised when he was young. He finally left here and moved on down to Everglades City, did some guiding and gator poaching, got in trouble down there, found Jesus, moved to Lauderdale, and finally wound up back here again. The ones that swear off, most of them they go back onto it sooner or later, get pig drunk and locked up.''

"Something special you've got against drunks, Sheriff?"

"Married to one for a long time. Too long. She finally drove into a tree one night."

"Nice of you to give me so much time, Sheriff."

"What happened there, over your eye?"

"I cut across the grounds last night, heading toward the beach, and ran into some of that playground stuff in the dark. Nothing important. Appreciate your help.''

When I stood up, he tilted his chair back and looked up at me. "There have been some people coming into Timber Bay, nosing around here and there, thinking to come up with the kind of leverage that might would get them a piece of the money Hub is supposed to taken."

"I can well imagine."

"It would hurt me to find out that you people had conned Devlin Boggs and you're after the same thing as those other sharpshooters."

"You mean they think the money is here?" I asked, trying to look as though I were stupid enough to ask such a question.

With patient exasperation he said, "They hope to get a line *here* on where he went *from* here. And then they hope to go to wherever they think he is and take the money away from him."

"Oh."

"Hub Lawless could be a real surprise to anybody who found him and had ideas."

"What do you mean?"

"One time some red-hots up from Tampa tried to take the payroll money at Hula Marine—that was before he sold out to Associated Foods. There were three of them and Hub shot one in the stomach, threw one of them into a wall, and broke the wrist on the third. He moves fast. I've hunted with him. He's got real good reflexes, and he stays in shape. Jogging and so on. Weights.''

I thanked him again and left. This was one complicated man, this Sheriff Ames. He had a mild look. But those dusty brown eyes kept asking more questions than were spoken. He made me wonder if I had actually come to Timber Bay to get a line on all that money. He made me feel guilty for things I'd never done. He made me conscious of that capacity for blackhearted evil which every one of us shares with everyone else—and never speaks about.

6

I WAS the first to arrive at the Captain's Galley for lunch, having set up the date by phone with Walter Olivera, phoned Dave Bellamy for the reservation, and left word at the desk at the North Bay Resort for Meyer to join us. I had a one-drink wait at the bar, and then Bellamy brought Walter Olivera over.

At first glance I thought he was a high-school kid. Tall, skinny, with long dank blond hair, a goatee, embroidered jeans, two strands of heishi, and little Ben Franklin glasses. But each time I got a better look at him, I added five years, and finally guessed him at thirty.

Meyer arrived right after him, and Bellamy gave us the same booth as on our first visit. Olivera sat on the inside, and I sat across from them. The place was full of locals from the marts of trade—secretaries, brokers, salesmen, and city-hall types, along with lawyers, dentists, and contractors. It made a cheerful midday din of voices, ice, silverware, and laughter.

Olivera said, "Sure, my by-line was on almost all the Hub Lawless stories, and on almost everything else too. What it is, we don't have the horses to put out the *Bay Journal* seven mornings a week, and we don't have the budget. It is an ABC figure of fifteen thousand, and we were picked up two years ago by Southern Communications, Incorporated, which has maybe twenty smallish papers and a dozen FM rock radio stations. They sit up there in Atlanta with their computer printouts, looking at the gross and the net, and they write ugly letters to Harry Dister—he runs the paper and has ulcers on his ulcers—asking how come he paid fourteen cents more a ream for copy paper this year than last year. They don't give a shit what our editorial position is or our politics. They make us buy the cheapest syndicated crud on the market, and they make poor Harry hustle his ass off for advertising linage." He picked up his glass of white wine. "No point in telling you *all* my problems, gentlemen. Yes, I covered the Lawless mess, and I didn't do any digging because I can't spend or spare the time."

Meyer said, "I hope you understand our position, Mr. Olivera. If Lawless is alive and well, we have to go after the available property in one way, and if he is indeed drowned, then we go after it another way."

"I can see that, sure."

"So I guess what we are looking for—with Devlin Boggs's help—is an educated guess on what to expect," I said.

Walter Olivera took his time. "I see it this way," he said finally. "Mr. Lawless was a proud man. He was born right here in Timber Bay. When he was in his second year at the University of Florida at Gainesville, his mother, father, and older brother were killed in a light-plane accident. His brother had rented the plane. Hit power lines trying to set it down in a field when the motor quit. After everything was settled, there was just enough left to see Hub through school. He took business courses. He came back here and married Julia Herron. Her father was D. Jake Herron, who was a state legislator for this area for thirty years, right up to when he died.

"Hub borrowed some money from his father-in-law to get started in the construction and land-development business, and paid it all back with interest. He worked hard. He worked all hours. Every time he got a little bit ahead, he'd branch out. He started Hula Marine Enterprises, Double L Ranches, and Lawless Groves and nursed them through the early years and turned them into profitable businesses. It was a process of constant expansion. I think he was a millionaire, on paper at least, by the time he was thirty-five. He *liked* making things work out. But luck always enters in. He had no way of knowing everything would start to go sour at about the same time."

"Everything?" Meyer asked.

"Just about. He took the money he got from selling Hula Marine to Associated Foods, and he put it into two big tracts of land, one about two miles east of the city line on State Road Three fifty-nine, and the other way out beyond the south end of Bay, down on a little road that winds on down toward Pepperfish Key. Good waterfront land, and a lot of it. The land on Three fifty-nine was to be a shopping center, a big one. You can drive out and take a look at it. He got the land prepared, roads paved, foundations set. The waterfront land was going to be a big condominium development. Six high-rise buildings, fifteen hundred units. He'd borrowed right up to the hilt, and he was counting on the cash flow he could generate from his other interests to keep the new ventures going."

Meyer nodded and said, "Hard freeze?"

"You bet it was. A little freeze is okay. It even helps make the crop juicier. They say Hub was up all night long, roaring around in that yellow jeep. They burned smudge pots and tires and ran big fans off generators. They tried everything. But when there is absolutely no wind and the temperature stays below eighteen degrees for almost five hours, there isn't anything anybody can do. It froze and split some of his older trees. He didn't even end up with cattle feed. And you know what has happened to the price of beef and beef cattle in Florida. They say he could have squeaked through, by getting the shopping center up as fast as he could. The center was going to be anchored by a big store, one of the big chains. He had a good lease, all signed. And a lot of little people were beginning to flock around on account of the traffic that would be generated by the chain store. And all of a sudden they went the way of Grant's. Bankrupt. Finished. And his lease was worthless. He wanted to make the condominium project first priority, but all of a sudden the state came into the act and said that the project was going to damage valuable wetlands. They wanted a setback from the beach that would have made it impossible for him to put the buildings up in the area left, and they asked for an environmental-impact study, which would have delayed it at least eighteen months even if the answer had been favorable to him.

"He was a very up-front guy. He admitted everything wasn't going too great. But he smiled a lot and he was confident, and everybody figured Hub Lawless would work his way out of it the same as other times when he had been caught in a narrow place. I heard rumors he was sleeping on a cot out at his ranch office, and that his marriage had gone bad and he had something going with a woman named Petersen. She was an architect, and she was supposed to be helping with the designs of the shopping center and condominium project. If he had something going, then maybe he wasn't thinking too clearly. As I said, he was proud. If he hung around, he was certainly going to go steadily and inevitably down the tube. He was going to have to see those corporations go into bankruptcy, and he was going to have to go into personal bankruptcy, resign from the board of the bank, resign from a lot of civic activities and church things. It was certainly going to spoil his image with his daughters, Tracy and Lynn. Sixteen and fourteen are tough years to suddenly go broke. So he decided to milk every dime he could out of every account, every source of funds, fake his own death, and go on the run, realizing that nobody could step in and grab the proceeds of the big insurance coverage on his life away from Julia Lawless. I want the lentil soup, please, a big bowl, and an order of the whole wheat toast, no butter.''

After we had all ordered, Olivera made his little summary. "He had no really good choices. He had no way of knowing that it would look so suspicious that the insurance company would refuse to pay the claim. He did so many things so well, it's funny he didn't manage his own disappearance better.''

"Would you guess he's in Mexico?'' I asked.

"That seems to be the current rumor. I wouldn't fault it. He went down there quite a few times. He liked the country. He and John Tuckerman used to go down and hunt a lot. Hub spoke enough bad Spanish to get by. Apparently he started squirreling away cash about the first of the year. It would give him a lot of time, almost three months, to establish a new identity.''

"With the lady architect?''

"And lots and lots of pesos," Olivera said cheerfully.

"Apparently Tuckerman was in on the deception,'' Meyer said.

"Had to be. And I think it was very, very rough on John Tuckerman. He thought Hub Lawless was the finest man who ever walked. Hub had a way of generating a lot of loyalty. If Hub had asked John to set himself on fire, he'd have run after the gasoline and the matches. Unquestioning. Okay, John helped him, and did exactly as he was told. And after it happened, John crawled into the bottle and he's been there ever since.''

"What was his position anyway?''

"He was supposed to be a vice-president of each of the four corporations. What he did was make sure the cars were gassed and maintained, and he made reservations and carried luggage and told jokes. He has no family except a sister. Hub Lawless was his family, and the Lawless enterprises were his home.''

"What's he doing now?''

"Drinking. He has a beach shack down there on the land Hub bought for the condominium project. The ownership of that land is in limbo. He's a squatter, technically, but I don't think he'll be rousted out of there right soon. If I had to make a guess, I would say that Hub probably gave John enough cash to keep him going.''

"*If* you had to make a guess," Meyer said.

Olivera turned and stared at Meyer and then over at me. "Look, you guys. This is a favor, okay? Boggs, the big man, asked me to cooperate.''

Meyer looked wounded. "Please don't misunderstand, Walter. Did I sound disapproving? I wasn't. We're here to make guesses. Good newspaper people make guesses based on hunch and experience and then check them out to find the facts, right?''

Olivera relaxed again. "What I'm working on is not exactly the *Washington Post*.''

"Does the paper do any crusading?'' I asked.

"If it doesn't cost anything.''

"Here's one that might not cost much. If we assume Hub Lawless had the whole thing planned ahead, and if we assume John Tuckerman was in on it and helped out, then it follows that Van Harder, running the boat, was given a funny drink. So he lost his license to skipper a boat carrying passengers for hire. So he got labeled a drunk who passed out while the owner fell overboard.''

Olivera thought it over, frowning, turning it this way and that. "I suppose we could have an editorial. But to get his case reconsidered, there would have to be some hard facts.''

I decided to run a little test. "Hard facts. For example, a reliable eyewitness who'd swear to having seen Lawless in Mexico in April?''

"That might do it,'' he said. "That would be great, sure.''

So either he was a great actor or he didn't know about the photograph. I resisted the temptation to be a nine-cent hero and take the picture out and explain it to him.

"What's all this about Harder anyway?'' he asked.

"He's just a sample of all the people who get hurt when somebody pulls something off, when somebody sets up a conspiracy to defraud,'' I said.

While we ate, quite a few people who passed our booth on their way out spoke to Walter Olivera. He kept grinning and nodding and flapping his hand at them. And it seemed obvious that every one of them was wondering who we were. Small cities have a very compact power structure, and it is always more evident when the tourist season is over.

"It was really a hell of a blow to this town,'' Olivera said, when his lentil soup was gone. "High hopes. You know. Two big projects. More jobs. The best thing that could happen would be if some organization could come in and pick up right where Hub left off, iron out the bugs, and get those projects moving again. I would think most of the creditors would listen to reason.''

"If we knew who to buy the rights from,'' Meyer said.

"I know. The official result was: Missing, presumed dead by misadventure. Now the general feeling is: Missing, presumed alive. If seven years pass with no trace of him, I think they can declare him dead. And that is too damned long to wait.''

He had to get back to the paper. He shook hands around, thanked us for the lunch, told us he would be glad to help in any way he could. And he said that everybody he could think of would be glad to help us too.

After he was gone we ordered more coffee. I told Meyer the Haggermann Ames story and gave him a stealthy look at the picture of Hub Lawless in Guadalajara. He was enchanted, but agreed with me that it was the kind of evidence that would not stand up in any court of law. It would have to be backed up by direct examination of the person who had taken the photograph.

He had spent all his time with Harold Payne and said, "One very cool and cautious fellow. Very reluctant to violate any client-attorney relationship, even after I hinted that, if Mr. Allbritton's firm came in here, I would recommend they use his services for local legal matters. That didn't thaw him. He said he had been Mr. Lawless's personal attorney for many years and that he had set up the corporations Mr. Lawless had controlled and had advised him on tax and estate matters. He said he had blocked an attempt by the IRS to proceed with a computation of estate tax and had contested a writ to have his client's personal safety-deposit box opened. He had not filed a copy of the will and would not do so until there was positive proof that Hubbard Lawless was deceased.''

"Did he have any opinions about what happened?''

"He didn't express any direct opinion. He said it was entirely possible that, had his client not met with an accident on the night of March twenty-second last, he would have been able to explain his very good reasons for having enhanced his cash position."

" 'Enhanced his cash position'?" I said.

"A direct quote," Meyer said. "Payne is okay. The firm represents the bank, too. It puts him in a curious position, a sort of ex post facto conflict of interest. So he is doing the smart thing, following the letter of the law, keeping his head down, keeping everything in stasis until more information comes to light."

"Are we getting anywhere?" I asked. "Are we doing Van Harder any good? That's what this is all about. Remember?"

"To replace the fledgling in the nest, one must first climb to the top of the tall tree."

"Oh, boy."

"About five or six o'clock back at the Resort—forgive the expression?"

"Have a nice afternoon."

7

THE VAST expanses of the parking areas at Baygate Plaza were less than half filled, and I wondered at the wisdom of Hub Lawless's decision to build another big shopping center in Timber Bay.

Once I found my way into the Mall, I located an orientation map, one of those YOU ARE HERE! things, and found where I was in relation to Top 40 Music. I plodded along the tile-finished concrete under the perpetual fluorescence, past all the jewelry stores, shoe stores, cut-rate blue-jeans stores, gift marts, caramel-corn outlets, and health-food hustles. I plodded along in the din of canned music, in the perpetual carnival atmosphere of everyday, past the custom T-shirts, the pregnant ladies eating ice cream cones, and the lines of children on school holiday waiting to get into another revival of *Star Wars*, shrieking and jabbing at one another and pretending to die of serious wounds.

When I came to Top 40 Music, I turned out of the slow parade and went in, feeling as if I were leaning into the blare of somebody electronically amplified, yelling "Babybabybabybaby . . ."

There was an extraordinarily beautiful young woman in there, in white slacks and pink top, with flawless figure and flawless complexion. She had one disconcerting flaw, though—she had such a mouthful of big white projecting teeth that she couldn't quite close her lips. She had a smoky drift of dark hair, dark eyes, and a fine way of holding herself, of walking. I could almost read her lips and knew she was asking me if she could do anything for me.

I leaned toward her and yelled into her ear, "Miss Ambar?"

"Yes?"

"Can we go somewhere and talk?"

"What about?"

"Hub Lawless."

"No way!"

I handed her the To Whom It May concern card signed by Devlin Boggs. She looked at it and shrugged, then handed it back.

"Please?" I shouted.

She looked me over more carefully. I tried to look responsible and respectable. I could almost hear her sigh. She hurried into the back and came out with a small white-haired lady with a smudge of dust on her cheek. Then Miss Ambar walked by me and out into the pedestrian traffic. She turned back and looked at me. "So come on!" her lips said, inaudible in all that *babybabybaby* din.

*   *   *

We sat at a counter fifty yards from the music store. I had coffee and she ordered a tall Red Zinger tea with honey. She had the ghost of an accent. We kept our voices down.

"What she did, what Mishy did, she call me up like I guess it was two o'clock that day, and she said, Hey, 'Licia, you wan we go on a boat tonight down to Clearwater? I said I din wan to do nothing like that at all, I had a date and so on, but she begged and begged and said how it was such a nice boat and all, real fast, real lovely, and where she works, the Cove, she had heard Mister Tuckerman, he was saying they were going down in the boat, and she asked maybe a fren of hers and her could come along, and he said, Hell, why not? So she wouldn't go without me and she said she had a girlfren there in Clearwater, we could stay in her place, and then her girlfren's boyfren, he could drive us back up here next day. Chee, I tole this seven tousand times, I think. Over and over and over."

"Are you originally from Mexico?"

"From Honduras. When I was a little kid. I got no accent now at all. How you can tell?"

"I just guessed."

"Okay, so I got to the Cove about eight thirty all set to go, and pretty soon Mr. Tuckerman, he picks us up, and then he picks up Mr. Lawless from downtown, and we go down to the marine place and get on, and it was beautiful, it really was. I didn't know they were so nice inside. Just like in some kind of high-price trailer, television and hi-fi and everything, and ice and booze. I thought that what it was, it was some kind of pass. You know, like we were going to put out on account of we were so grategul to be on that boat. What Mishy does is her business, but I wasn't going to, no matter what. But it was no problem on account of they acted like maybe we weren't there at all. They were in the other end of that living-room-type place, having a drink, talking in low voices, talking business. After we had been gone from the dock about twenty minutes, maybe less, Mr. Lawless made a drink and took it up and gave it to that Captain Harder. I din know his name then. I found out his name later on. Okay, so they were talking again, Lawless and Tuckerman, and the boat was going up and down, kind of, and I began to feel kind of sick. I said I was feeling sick, and Mr. Tuckerman said I should go up topside and the cold air would make me feel better. I went on up there and it really was cold and the wind was blowing something scary. Then I saw that

Captain Harder on the floor up there, like he was dead. I ran back down there screaming and the men went running up, and then Mr. Tuckerman came back down and said they had decided to go back to Timber Bay, which was just fine with me, because by then I was sorry I'd ever said I'd come along for the ride, and Mishy was sorry too because she wasn't feeling real great either. It was more bouncy on the way back, and it seemed to take longer, which I found out later it did, on account of Mr. Lawless was driving it by hand. What Mishy and I were doing, we were running in and out of that funny little bathroom, throwing up, taking turns. Then finally the wind wasn't so strong, but we were bouncing up and down terrible, and there was one awful jolt that threw me right on the floor—I mean deck. Then Mishy thought she heard somebody yelling for us and then I heard it too, and neither of us would go up alone, so we both went. We were inside the pass by then, I think. Mr. Tuckerman yelled to us that Mr. Lawless had fallen overboard and we were to help look. The Captain was still on the deck passed out. It was a real nightmare. You couldn't see nothing. Nobody could run the radio they have on boats like that. So we had to go in. Mr. Tuckerman banged the boat something terrible against the dock and there was some man there who came running to help with the lines, and pretty soon the police and everybody were there, and by then, I can tell you, I didn't give a damn what anybody did with me, I was so glad to have my feet back on the ground again. I was so glad I could hardly stand it. I thought it had to be about three in the morning, but you know what? It was only about an hour and a half, just a little more than an hour and a half from the time we'd left. It was a terrible experience, I can tell you. We had to make statements and wait and sign them after they were typed up for us, and later we had to testify at the hearing. I'd never done that before. It isn't as bad as I thought it would be. It was the worst night of my life. I din wan to go in the first place. That damn Mishy. She gets me into bad things. I doan wan to do anything with her again. But you know how it is when somebody keeps calling up. What the hell. She's some crazy person, that Mishy. She likes a lot of stuff happening, and it sure happens aroun her. I tole all this nine tousand times. It's been in the papers, every word of it.''

"Weren't you going to get into Clearwater pretty late?''

"Like four in the morning. Something like that. It was a crazy thing to do, but that's how Mishy is.''

"Why were Mr. Tuckerman and Mr. Lawless going there by water? Did you get any clue to that?''

"Some kind of business thing. Nobody really said.''

"And the Captain was really out?''

"Man, I thought he was dead!''

"Were they drinking?''

"Little bit. Not much.''

I smiled at her. "Somebody said last night over at the North Bay Resort lounge that you're a nice person.''

She lighted up. "Hey! Who says that?''

"Nicky Noyes.''

She lost the sparkle. "Oh, *that* one. I see him around. I doan go out with him. He used to work for Mr. Lawless, you know? Some kind of good job, he says. I couldn't say. Lunchtime some guy I know was in buying tapes and

he said Nicky was in the hospital from being in some kind of fight someplace.''

"Does he get in fights a lot?"

"Not often on account of he's so big. But he comes on evil—bigmout',
you know. He was over to North Bay last night. Huh! What happen over
your eye anyhow?"

"I ran into something in the dark."

"Something like Nicky?"

Her very dark eyes were merry. So take a chance, McGee. "What if it
was?"

"Good for *you!* That sumbitch likes hurting. He busted Mishy's finger
once. He walk into a room, she walks out, you bet." She looked at me more
carefully. "No more marks? Just one? Maybe you had a stick?"

"Footwork."

"That bank card says help you out. From the president yet. And you go
around hitting. That doesn't sound like a bank."

"Did the fellow say how Nicky is?"

"Oh, he is okay. He said they were letting him out. He was just in, you
know, for overnight. He goes to Emergency a lot. Nicky is always worried
about his bod. If he feels hot, right away he wants to find out his temperature,
and he thinks maybe he's dying. He was some kind of big person around here
in high school, and then he went to play football in Tallahassee, but he got
sent home for some kind of gambling. He had a good job with Mr. Lawless.
I doan know what now. For a little bit, he drove beer. Now he seems to be
okay for money, but they say he's a dealer, nothing real real heavy, just grass
and coke and hash. Mishy is into that sometimes when she feels real down,
but not me. Never. It's too scary. I got to know where I am and where I'm
coming from."

"Is Mishy a special friend of John Tuckerman?"

"Huh? Oh, you wanna know if it's all that special? Maybe. It wouldn't
mean all that much to Michele. I mean he's kinda nice and funny. But she
never mentioned it especially."

"Is it okay to tell her I talked to you?"

"Sure. But why bother anyway, with me or her?"

"I'm working for people who want to buy Mr. Lawless's land. So we need
to find out if he's dead."

"Chee, we can't help. I'm telling you, there was a hell of a lot of black
water out there, all bouncing up and down, and me knocked on the fl—deck.
They say he couldn't swim at all. They say he's in Mexico. What that means
is he didn't have to swim. Mishy and I talked about that. So if he comes
ashore, he's in Timber Bay, where all around the bay it's built up. A wet man
walking around? They say the tide was going out strong. What was there? A
boat? I doan know, mister. You said your name is what? McGee? I just doan
know. I theenk that sumbitch is dead. Hey, I got to get back or Carol'll kill
me dead. Sure. Talk to Mishy. But for what?"

*   *   *

The Cove was about two hundred yards south of the North Bay Resort, a
rambling frame sun-bleached structure which extended out over the bay,
supported by thick pilings. The dining area was the farthest from the shore,

beyond a large bar area hung with nets, glass floats, mounted fish, and funny sayings. They were having their midafternoon lull. A salesman was playing pinball, hammering the corners of the machine with the heels of his hands. A chubby white-haired couple wearing identical horn-rimmed glasses sat at a corner table drinking draft beer and playing gin. A tall hollow-chested bartender with a gay-nineties mustache and hairstyle was polishing stemware and inserting it upside down into the overhead racks.

I slid onto a padded bar stool and said, "Mishy Burns around?"

"She comes on at four," he said.

"Draft beer, please."

He served it with a nice head. He said, "When she does come on, she's working. She has to set up the tables. When she comes on, she's not on her own time."

"Are you trying to be unpleasant?"

"I'm just telling you the way it is, friend. What she does on her own time is her business."

"You own this place?"

"I'm one of the owners."

I was getting very tired of contentious attitudes. I smiled at him. I said, "I've always wondered about places like this."

"Wondered what?"

"Suppose, just for the hell of it, you took a list of all the regulatory agencies that have any kind of authority over the way you do business here. County, city, state, federal. You know, the food-handling ordinances, and the tax people and the liquor people. Then suppose you went through this place and made a list of every single violation of every law, ordinance, and regulation."

"We run a good clean place here. We don't violate anything!"

"Nonsense, good buddy. There is no way to avoid being in violation of something. The rules are contradictory. You know it and I know it. Right now you are subject to fines, suspension of licenses, civil suits. That's the way the establishment keeps you in line. If you get feisty, they come and look you over and tell you you have to build a whole new kitchen, or replace all your wiring, or put in ten more parking spaces."

"Who the hell *are* you?"

"I am the fellow who came in here a little while ago, very quietly, and sat right here and asked you if Mishy Burns was around, and got a big discussion of her working hours and who pays her. We can start over again. Okay? Mishy Burns around?"

"She comes on at four," he said.

"Draft beer, please," I said, and he took the empty and refilled it and moved down the bar and left me alone, which was exactly what I wanted.

Michele came in ten minutes later. I had been building a mental picture of her, and so I was totally unprepared for a twenty-two-year-old Doris Day. She came a-dancing and bubbling in, full of warmth and life and high spirits. She brightened the place up. The salesman knew her and the gin players knew her. The bartender motioned to me and she came over and put her hand out and said, beaming, "Hello! I'm Mishy Burns."

"Travis McGee. The man says you're on his time and you can't talk to me."

"About what, love?"

"I've been talking to 'Licia about your cruise."

She made a face. "Oh, God. That again!"

She was in constant motion, constant changes of expression, posture, tossing her hair back, rocking from heel to toe, so much so that one wanted to clamp firm hands on her shoulders and settle her down, position her, quiet her. I realized that all the animation gave the impression of prettiness, and that perhaps in repose her face would look quite plain.

"Harley gets itchy, don't you, Harley? Look, love, let me go put on the house garments and brush up the dining room a little and then we can talk, because things will be dead as a snake until five past five and all the car doors start chunking shut out there in the lot."

I saw her in a little while, trotting back and forth in the dining room, wearing a crotch-length tennis dress with a sailor collar and a little white yachtsman's cap. Another waitress had joined her. A couple of construction workers—off at four—came in for beers. Somebody started the juke. I watched Michele. She had absolutely great legs. I felt guilty at the way I was going to try to booby-trap my question. Not very guilty. Anticipatory guilt, the kind that Meyer calls chessboard guilt, when you realize that the weaker player is making a frail response to a standard opening, and you are about to ram your bishops down his throat.

When she beckoned to me, I went into the dining room and followed her over to a service bar where she had coffee waiting. She said, "Coffee? Black? Okay. Look, I have talked myself out on that boat ride. Believe me, it was a long, long time ago. To me, two months is long. Lots and lots of things happen in two months. I have told about it so much that what I remember now is not the boat ride but all the times I talked about it."

"It can happen. Felicia is just as tired of it, I guess."

"You would never believe how sick we got. Maybe I would have been okay, but as soon as she lost it, I was gone too."

"There was just one thing I wanted to get straight, Michele."

"Such as?"

"Exactly how did John Tuckerman word it when he asked you to come along for the ride and bring a friend?"

"You got it wrong. I asked him if we could go along."

"'Licia says that's what Tuckerman told you to say."

"Why, God *damn* her! She agreed never to tell anybody—"

And suddenly she stopped all motion. She was a subdued, plain-faced blonde with deeply bitten fingernails, staring at me from way inside herself, like an animal looking out of the brush.

"You rotten bastard," she said in a low voice. "You faked me out, didn't you?"

"Look at it this way. If Lawless is still alive somewhere, the whole thing was a conspiracy to defraud. He needed bodies to dress up the conspiracy."

"That shows how much you know, you bastard."

"I know this. You lied under oath. Right? So far, that's between the two of us. And Felicia. But you keep on with the garbage mouth, I see no reason to keep your little secret."

We stood facing each other, each with an elbow on the service bar. For a few moments the wary creature stared through her eyes at me, out of the thickets at the back of her mind, and then dropped out of sight, and she was Miss Cheerleader again, all bounce and joy, all twinkle and grin.

With breathy laugh and salacious wink, she said, "What it was, and I'll trust you, I really will, John Tuckerman has this thing about Felicia. You wouldn't believe how horny he is for her, right from the first look he got at her. He said he would give me a nice present if I could get 'Licia to come along. What it was, it was a way of getting maybe a good chance to set her up. She didn't know what was coming down. She's a funny kid. She's not much for sex. She lived with some cat for a while but she'll never talk about it, and I think it was some kind of bad start for her, so now it's all yeck to her. What happened was we got seasick, and then Harder passed out and we had to come back and you know what happened. Right in the beginning John Tuckerman had told me to say it was me asked him if we could come along. Later on he said it was even more important I should say that, because if it got out he asked us, it would look bad. Mr. Lawless wasn't real turned on by having us come along. He hardly spoke to us at all. The way Felicia found out was, after the testimony and all, I got a little high and started kidding Felicia about Tuckerman giving me a hundred dollars to talk her into that terrible boat ride. She was really pissed off at me. She wouldn't talk to me for a week, but then she began to see how funny it was and she forgave me. She said even if it had been the best boat ride the world ever saw, Tuckerman wasted a hundred dollars. I don't see why she's like that. He's sort of old for her. He's thirty-eight, he says, but probably forty. I told her he's not kinky or anything like that, and very sweet and generous, and he lives on that great beach, but she doesn't want anything to do with him. It isn't as if she thinks she's the world's best. She has this idea she's ugly. Somebody told her once that with those teeth she could eat a Big Mac through a venetian blind. She doesn't see why anybody would want her."

"Which finger did Nicky Noyes break?"

Her face got red. "She's got all those big white teeth and she's got a great big mouth too."

"Here come customers."

"Oh, God, with four kids yet. We close the kitchen at ten and I'm off by ten thirty."

"If I'm not at the bar there by ten thirty, give up on me."

"But you'll be around?"

"Sure. For a while."

8

I WENT right from the Cove to 215 South Oak Lane, to the long white house with the three-car garage. I arrived at about quarter to five. There were two cars in the drive, a weatherbeaten old Cadillac convertible, rusting out under the white paint, and a new little gray Honda Accord. The front door was open. Through the screen I heard women laughing—not social laughter, but contagious yelps of delight.

I had to ring the bell a couple of times. A woman came hurrying to the door and looked out at me, brows raised in query. She was small and lean and sunbrown in yellow shorts and a T-shirt. The black-gray bangs of her Prince Valiant hairstyle came almost to her black brows. Her face was sun-weathered, hollow-cheeked, with deep squint lines, deep brackets around her mouth. Her eyes were dark blue.

"Mrs. Lawless?" I said.

"Yes, but I don't want a thing, thanks."

"I represent a group trying to purchase Double L Ranches and Lawless Groves, and I would appreciate a little of your time."

I sorted out the calling card which said on the back "Dear Julia" and was signed "Dev." She opened the door a whole quarter inch to receive the card and then latched it again.

After she read it slowly and carefully, she frowned at me and said, "I can't sell that land. You certainly know that much."

"If your husband is alive, the problem is more complicated."

"Hub is dead."

"Perhaps you could help us ascertain that fact."

"I'm through talking to people about my husband."

"Because they wouldn't listen?"

"Something like that."

"I listen pretty good. Not as good as D. Jake Herron used to. But pretty good."

Her face softened slightly. "You knew my father?"

"Just slightly. A friend of mine and I helped D. Jake nail a game warden some years back who was in the alligator-hide business as a sideline. The warden took a couple of shots at us."

"I *remember* hearing about that!"

"I remember him saying that night that nobody ever wasted their time listening."

"Well . . . come on in. Maybe you'll buy something."

"I don't understand."

"We're tagging stuff for the biggest garage sale ever presented on South Oak Lane. Maybe the only garage sale."

I went through the house with her and out to the area in the rear. There was a big screened cage, a swimming pool, a flagstone terrace beyond the cage, and a barbecue area beyond the terrace. Two women were working with Julia Lawless. There was a beefy cheerful redhead named Doris Jennings and a sallow and mocking blonde named Freddy Ellis. One Lawless daughter was there, introduced as Lynn. She looked familiar, and I suddenly remembered where I had seen her.

"Nice going, tiger," I said to her.

"For what?" she said, looking at me with that apathy they reserve for ancient male strangers.

"For whipping Miss Languid in the salmon dress over at the North Bay Resort courts. She wouldn't shake hands on it, I noticed."

She gave me a quick, warning wink. "Thanks. That was Sandra Ellis. I never beat her before."

Freddy Ellis said, "Hey. You mean my snitty little daughter lost ungraciously?"

"I didn't mind, honest," Lynn said.

"*I* mind," Freddy said ominously.

Doris Jennings asked me if I would be willing to look at the prices they had put on Hub's possessions and see if they were out of line. She said she had gotten advice from the sporting-goods stores which had sold him a lot of the things. They were arranged on display in the nearest stall of the garage.

I moved slowly and carefully past Hubbard Lawless's golf clubs, golf cart, tennis equipment, bowling ball and bowling shoes, shotguns, rifles, target pistol, fly rods, spinning rods, surf rods, tuna rods, reels and reel cases, boxes of lures, boxes of flies, weights, punching bag, Nikon cameras, lenses, lens cases, strobe lights, tripods, slide boxes, slide projectors, movie cameras, movie projectors, light stands, ten-speed tour bike, binoculars, sheath knives . . .

The man liked nice things, and he kept them in good shape. He didn't buy things and put them away. They showed signs of wear and signs of care.

A splendid custom shotgun caught my eye. It was in a fitted pigskin case, with an extra set of side-by-side barrels. Spanish walnut stock. Initials inlaid in gold. H.R.L. Beavertail forearm. Single nonselective trigger. Ventilated rib. English scroll engraving on white steel. It was Orvis Custom, built to Hub Lawless's physical dimensions, and I knew it had to represent a minimum three-thousand-dollar investment. A dandy toy for a grown-up boy. It was priced to move at five hundred. I assembled it and tried it. The drop at the comb and the heel were wrong, trigger distance wrong. And the initials were wrong. A man the same size as Hub Lawless could find a great bargain here.

I moved along and then went back to the billfish tackle, and fended off a lust to buy some of it. The man had good taste in equipment.

"Well?" Julia asked.

"You got good advice. The prices of the things I know about are in line. Fair for the buyer and the seller."

"He never stinted himself," she said flatly. "Good old Hub. The best was just barely good enough."

"Mother!" Lynn said, defending the beloved daddy.

"Sorry, chick," Julia said, reaching to ruffle the girl's hair. "Thanks for easing my mind about the prices. They seemed kind of low. I know what he paid for some of those things."

"I know nothing about golf equipment or bicycles."

"Oh, those prices are okay. I didn't know about the outdoor jock stuff."

The next stall of the garage was filled with standard garage-sale household items, Julia's and also items brought over by Doris Jennings and Freddy Ellis, for a joint effort. It was a predictable array: Cribs and high chairs. Ornate beer steins and souvenir plates. Bonus books from book clubs. Floor lamps and suitcases. Rotisseries and bulletin boards. Tricycles and feather headdresses. End tables and tablecloths. On being pressed, I said it looked as if they had a lot of good stuff there.

Finally, as a reward for my patience and help, and for having known her father, she took me back into the living room for the obligatory conversation.

She sat curled in a corner of a large couch. I sat across from her, with a glass coffee table between us.

"It's so damned depressing," she said. "I've still not tackled his dressing room. I've got to get rid of all that stuff. Goodwill, I guess. Or the Salvation Army or somebody."

"A lot of people seem to think he's in Mexico."

"Say the rest of it too, Mr. McGee."

"Such as?"

"He stole the money and ran. He took off with his Norwegian piece of ass to live happily ever after."

"He was having an affair with her. An architect, wasn't she?"

"Okay. So he was having an affair. His very first. Believe me, it was his first. It started last year. In the summer. She was recommended to him. She was supposed to be some kind of an expert in the design of shopping centers. She did a big one in Atlanta and one in Jacksonville. When everything went to hell with the one he was supposed to build here, she should have taken off, right? But she stayed on, drawing pay from the big shot who was going broke. Oh, I am so goddamn sick of these little Scandinavian broads with their little breathy accents and no makeup, maybe a trace of lipstick, and their pale green eyes and their big boobs and no more morals than rabbits. I don't mind telling you I was really really hurt. I couldn't believe it at first. Then when we had a nose-to-nose battle, he wouldn't deny it. Finally he confessed and promised he would break up with her, but he didn't. He claimed he tried, but he didn't try hard enough. I asked him if he gave a damn about Tracy and Lynn. It marks a child terribly when there is family trouble when they're in their mid-teens, just sixteen and fourteen. We had more rotten fights and then he started sleeping out at the ranch, in a room back of the ranch office out there. That was in late January. I've had a chance to think lately. And I can . . . almost begin to understand this Kristin business. Hub had a dream. He admired my daddy so much. What he wanted to do was build a base. Money and power. And then one day he was going to run for governor and become somebody in Florida. But last year, when times were hard and things began to go bad, he could see his dream fading. He had been too confident. He'd made a bad judgment of the situation. It was going to spoil his track record to be brought down after forty. And there wouldn't be enough time to build it all up again. He was really seriously upset. He always had such great drive and spirit, and he couldn't find a way out of the spot he was in. Some men would go a little crazy. Some would take to the bottle or go onto Valium. Hub took up with that architect person, proving his manhood, I guess. Maybe she kept telling him he was a great man. Maybe I should have done that so she wouldn't have to. Maybe I nagged him some. And maybe it was Hub's way of going a little bit crazy. Am I making any sense?"

"I think you are."

"You *really* listen, don't you?"

"I'm interested."

"You have been sitting there, looking right at me, and nodding and making little sounds in your throat. You are so damned earnest about listening to me, you made me rattle on and on and on."

"You wanted to talk about it. That's all."

"So I open up to you and I don't even know you."

"That's the easiest way of all, when you don't know the other person."

"Maybe."

"What makes you so sure he's dead?"

"We were always very close. Very close, until the last eight months of his life. We were in touch with each other on some kind of level most people don't have. Once I had a feeling of blackness, of terrible fear. He'd gone hunting with John Tuckerman. I wrote down the exact time it happened. I couldn't get in touch with him. I was beside myself with worry. Finally he phoned me from Waycross, Georgia, and said he'd been bitten on the wrist by a big cottonmouth, but he'd been treated and it was going to be okay and he would be home in two days. When we compared my note with the time he had been bitten, it was correct to the very minute. He knew the time because it had bitten him on the left wrist, near where his wristwatch was. Once when the girls were both in school, in the first and third grades, he came charging home in the middle of the afternoon, convinced something was wrong. I'd fallen from the shed roof and wrenched my back so badly I couldn't stand up. I couldn't even crawl to the phone or to the neighbors, it hurt so badly. I'd ruptured a disc. I knew that if I waited he'd come. I knew that he knew I was in trouble, and he came. There were lots of little things like that that happened between us. Those are just two of the biggest ones. When they told me that night that Hub was lost off the *Julie* and believed drowned, I didn't believe it. I kind of reached into that private world where he and I were always in contact, and I knew he was still there, so he couldn't be dead."

"I don't understand."

"It was a distasteful situation—with those two young girls going with two middle-aged men out on that lovely boat named for me—but not some kind of disaster, really. I didn't know what was going on. I got to sleep quite late. The girls were terribly upset, Tracy and Lynn, and I had to get them settled down. They loved their father so much. They couldn't understand what was happening to their world. I am very concerned about them, about Tracy particularly, she's getting so strange and secretive. Anyway, I took a sleeping pill and I didn't wake up until after ten the next morning, March twenty-third. Everything came rushing back into my mind and I reached out, or over, or down, in some direction I can't describe, to find the same reassurance I'd felt the night before, and there was nothing. Absolutely nothing. It was a cold, dead abandoned place in my mind. I knew he was gone. There is no doubt at all in my mind. My husband is dead."

"Forgive me, but that is not exactly the sort of evidence that will mean much to the insurance company."

"I found that out. They want any excuse not to pay, because it is a very big policy. I wouldn't be at all surprised if they hadn't started all these rumors about Hub being in Mexico. He loved Mexico, granted. *If* he were alive, it would be a reasonable place for him to run to, if he wanted to hide."

"Cleaning out those bank accounts makes it look as if he had running and hiding on his mind."

"Maybe he did. I don't know. We weren't communicating. I suppose it would have eased his conscience about me and the girls if he could fake his own death and leave that insurance for me."

"What if he tried to fake it, and something went wrong and he died?"

"That would fit the way he acted before he disappeared, and it would fit the way I feel about his being so definitely dead."

"Hypothetical question. Suppose somebody showed you a picture of Hubbard Lawless taken at a sidewalk café in Guadalajara on the eighth day of April, sitting and pouring dark beer into a glass?"

"I would have to say the picture is a fake."

"Who would bother to fake it?"

"The insurance company, of course. To muddy the waters and hang onto their two million dollars. The insurance is mine. I am the owner of that policy. It's all in the records of the trust department at Coast National Bank and Trust. You can ask Rob Gaylor all about it. He's the Senior Trust Officer. He handles what my daddy left in trust for me. It isn't enough to maintain this house and raise two girls. Thus the garage sale, and also, I am going to list the house and look for something smaller and less expensive to maintain."

"It's a beautiful house, Mrs. Lawless."

"Julie, please. I know. But houses can go sour on you, all of a sudden. You remember too many birthdays and Christmases. What do people call you?"

"Travis. Trav. I wonder if you could tell me who could give me the most information on Kristin Petersen, Julie."

"She wasn't the sort of person who goes around making dozens of new friends. She subleased a condo apartment at North Pass Vista. That's just north of the North Bay Resort, where you saw Lynn beat Sandra Ellis—"

"And where I'm staying with my associate, Meyer."

"North Pass Vista is a kind of town-house arrangement. They have a rental office there where you could ask."

"If I think of more questions I want to ask you, may I come back again?"

"Of course. But you are not really interested in buying land, are you?"

"My associate is."

She looked at me steadily, with care. "I think he probably is, but not to the extent you'd have me believe. You're here for something entirely different. To find out something. To help someone."

"You know, you could make me pretty uncomfortable with all that."

"I don't want to. I'm not a witch. I just can read some people sometimes. Whatever you do, Travis, you are very damn good at it."

"Thank you. I'm not sure you're correct."

"I've got to get back out there to the old-table-lamp department and start pricing. Will you tell me some day why you're here?"

"If you're interested."

"I wouldn't ask if I weren't."

*   *   *

I got back to the North Bay Yacht and Tennis Resort at quarter past six, feeling grainy, listless, and depressed. There was no Meyer and no note from Meyer. I peeled off the little compress and then, with great care, pulled off the thin strips of adhesive. The skin held together nicely, so I dabbed some disinfectant on it, purchased from a drugstore near the bank, and covered it with a flesh-colored waterproof Band-Aid from the same source. I stared into my own pale and skeptical eyes. An unenamored lady had once termed them "spit-colored." Deepwater tan, a few little white scars here and there, a nose but slightly bent, a scuffle of sun-baked hair, responding to no known discipline and seldom subjected to any.

Out on that ketch, the *Antsie,* beating our interminable way up from the Grenadines to the Virgins to Keasler's Peninsula, I had wanted the night lights and the gentle ladies and the best of booze, with enough music to make them mix properly. And here I was, up to my hocks in all such ingredients and wishing I was back aboard the *Antsie,* being yanked and hammered and pounded by the ever-insisting sea. Life is a perverse art indeed.

I left a note for Meyer that he could find me in the lounge. Feeling somewhat better after the shower and the change of clothes, I went on down and walked in on a very busy bar, plus Billy Jean Bailey tinkling away on background music as opposed to the performance numbers she did later at night. When she saw me, her smile lighted her up from inside, like candles in a pumpkin, and my heart sank. She had on a silver-blue cowboy shirt and tight white jeans. She switched the music to tell me that I had come along from out of nowhere, and then she had me walking out of a dream, and then the music said that she was in love, in love, in love, with a wonderful guy.

"No, no, no," I yelled, in the back of my brain, and beat on the cell bars. "No way. Please."

When she took a break, she came around to the far end of the bar and wormed her way in to stand close beside me, with maximum contact. She put her hand on my neck and pulled my ear down to where she could talk into it. "I've had the most goddamn delicious day of my whole life, thinking about you, bun."

"Uh."

"I've never turned on like that before. Couldn't you tell?"

"Uh."

"We're so fantastic, I can almost get it off just thinking about how it was. I can get right to the edge, bun."

"Bun?"

"Bun rabbit. My dear darling bun rabbit baby. Oh, God, time is going so slow, it will *never* be midnight."

"Don't you go Friday until one?"

"Oh, Christ! It *is* Friday."

"Yes. It sure is."

She kissed me on the ear and went switching back to her piano. I was conscious of considerable amusement among the bystanders. She had not exactly concealed the relationship. My ears felt hot. Visitor makes immediate dear friend of the piano player.

I wrote her a very short note, paid for my drink, took the note over to the piano, and put it where she could read it. She did so and made a kiss shape with her small mouth and then a big happy smile, and I went lumbering out and met Meyer just as I got outside the door.

"Where are *you* going?" he asked.

"It's very close in there."

"With that ceiling?"

"Take my word. Close. Very close. Let's . . . uh . . . have a drink at the Cove. Very close by. Walking distance."

"I know, I saw it. Are you all right? You act strange."

"Tell me about your afternoon, Meyer."

"Mr. Glenn and Mr. Latzov drove me all over this county and showed me fantastic bargains in ranchland, grove land, raw land, development opportunities, waterfront land, and swamplands. They told me this area is right on the threshold of fantastic, unbelievable growth, and every dollar put into land values here would be like investing in St. Petersburg Beach in nineteen fifty. Every time I tried to bring up the Lawless holdings, they would whip me out into the scrub country and show me something much better, available right now."

Once we were wedged into a corner of the long bar at the Cove, I asked him what Mr. Glenn and Mr. Latzov thought about the Lawless affair.

"A terrible tragedy. A legal tangle. A sorry affair. You never know what a man will do when he's pushed too far. They said that considering how smart Hub Lawless is, the odds are very small that anybody will ever find him. And they estimated his getaway money at closer to a million."

It was payday in Timber Bay. The noise level at the Cove was overwhelming. Waitresses worked at a dead run. Harley had two helpers behind the bar. Suddenly I noticed Nicky Noyes over in a corner of the bar area, at a bare table beyond the row of pinball machines. He sat behind a round table, and the two couples with him looked as if they had just climbed down off their big road cycles. They looked quaint. They are fading into history, like Pancho Villa's irregulars. All the macho whiskers and the leather clothes and the dead eyes and their feral, abused little women. Hundreds of them roar up and down the highway in formation, making formal protest about the law forcing them to wear a helmet. It is a violation of their freedom and liberty, they say. Very macho. But when they don't wear helmets, they abuse the taxpayers, taking a couple of weeks to die in intensive care, their primitive brains jellied by hard impact with the concrete highway. Somebody has to pick them up when they go down and deliver them to Emergency, regrettably.

I saw Noyes gesture toward the bar, and moments later all five of them were looking directly at me, a stare of speculation and obscure challenge.

I said to Meyer, "Beyond the pinball machines at the round table, the fellow with his back to the wall, facing us directly, is Nicky Noyes."

"With the headband and all the gold trinkets?"

"Himself."

"Wholesome company he keeps."

"Isn't it, though? I keep getting the feeling that Nicky isn't very tightly wrapped. He could be working himself up to jump me."

"Right here?"

"Or wait outside for me."

"For us."

"Thank you, Meyer. Very nice instinct. Here he comes, incidentally."

Nicky came plodding toward me. He walked oddly, putting his feet down with care. His strong cologne arrived three steps before he did. I shifted carefully, coiling all my springs without appearing to do so. Nicky came inside my normal space and stopped, broad belly almost touching me. His gaze moved rapidly side to side, up and down, back and forth.

"You are part of the trial," he said, chanting it in such a way he sounded like a Sunday television preacher.

"Trial?"

"Certain things are going to happen, and you are part of them, and when it is all over, we'll all be back at the beginning, every one of us but you."

"Have you been sampling your own merchandise, Noyes?"

"Soon you'll see the shape of everything yet to come and the part you're going to play, but it will be too late by then. It is up to me to turn it on and turn it off. It mustn't go too fast. You understand? Everything is part of it now."

And he turned away from me and walked to the door and on out, still walking with that strange care, as if he might step too heavily, break through the floor of the world, and fall forever. One worn-out-looking woman at the table where Noyes had been sitting caught my eye, smiled wearily, and circled a forefinger near her temple.

A big young man was standing near us at the bar. He turned his red whiskers toward me and said, "Don't you mind ol' Nicky, hear? He's okay. I drove a truck for Hula Construction for nearly three years, and Nicky was the foreman part of the time, and superintendent the last year I was there."

"I hope he used to make more sense."

"He did. He didn't used to be at all like the way he is now. He's weird now. You know about Hub Lawless taking off with all the money?"

"Yes. I've heard about it."

"Well, Nick thought Lawless was the finest man ever walked the earth. He worked all kind of hours for Hub. He sprained a gut for Hub. And the hell of it was, Hub took off owing Nicky two months' pay. I tell you, it soured Nicky. It turned him kind of mean. He used to laugh a lot, and he used to fight for fun, and not very often. Now it's like he's against the world. I don't even speak to him any more because I don't want to get into some kind of argument with him. He always treated me fine."

"Could you hear what he was saying to me?"

"Sure could. Didn't make any sense. I guess from what you said to him, you know he's a dealer now. It's a small-potatoes thing with him from what I hear. He lives okay on it, maybe even pretty good. A couple of times he give me and my wife Betty free samples, but we flushed them down. I don't make enough driving for the county to want to pick up any habit where I got to buy it from Nicky. They say he is using his own stuff, and they say he's messing up his head."

"Sometimes he's better than other times?"

"That's right, but I'd say that each time he gets weird he seems to get a little weirder than the time before, and I never heard him so far out over the edge as he was tonight." He put a big hand out. "My name is Ron Shermerhorn."

"McGee. And this is Meyer. Ron Shermerhorn."

"Pleased to meet you. I don't want to talk about Nicky too much, you know. He was always okay to me. I just didn't want you to think he was just another one of your ordinary crazies, is all."

"He jumped me last night," I said. "In the parking lot outside the North Bay Resort lounge. I don't really know why. I walked out with the piano player, Billy Jean Bailey, and there he was, ready and waiting, shirt off, spitting on his hands."

Ron was looking me over for signs of damage. "Talk him out of it?"

"No, we went around a little, and then I helped him climb into his truck."

"You've got to be pretty good."

"I faked him out."

He was still staring dubiously at me when a man on the other side of Meyer spun around so violently he knocked Meyer back against me. The man then went charging toward the men's room, back of his hand pressed to his mouth, and disappeared.

"What's all that?" Meyer demanded indignantly.

"Oh," Ron said, "that's just Fritz Plous. Works for the paper. He's in here a lot. Throws up a lot. It takes him sudden. It's what they call auto—auto—"

"Autointoxication?" Meyer suggested.

"That's it! The doctor has told him not to think about throwing up. But he sorts of gets it on his mind and he can't get his mind off it and all of a sudden he has to make a run for it."

"You have your share of unusual people here in Timber Bay," I said.

"No more than anywhere," Ron said with a trace of indignation. He drained his glass and put it down. "See you guys," he said, and went on out into the evening.

Meyer and I stood silently side by side. The man named Plous came back to the bar, gray and sweaty. We stood in a blur of ambient noise, of Muzak and laughter, tinkle and clatter, rumble and chatter, and *tink* of ice.

Ever since Noyes had delivered his cryptic speech I had felt even more depressed than had been my usual quota lately. I was aware that Meyer was studying me thoughtfully, carefully.

"What's with you?" I said in irritation.

"Where has gone all that lazy mocking charm of yesteryear?" he asked. "Where is the beach wanderer, the amiable oaf I used to know?"

"Knock it off. Okay?"

"What the hell is making you so edgy!"

I had to use a surprising amount of control to quell the impulse to yap at him again, like a cross dog. I forced the deep breath and said, "I don't know. Maybe I'm coming down with something. I'd like a bowl of hot chicken soup and a feather bed. An empty feather bed. I can't relate to this paragon, this splendid fellow who left with the money. I can't get used to all the leverage we have, Meyer. Everybody wants to be nice to us because we might represent new money in town. The Sheriff makes me very nervous. I met a lovely girl who hates her own teeth. All the way up from the Grenadines to the Virgins I had no one to talk to but Duke Davis, and you know how he is. Two words a day does it. Then one hell of a three-day party at St. Croix, and more weeks of silence. I think I got used to it, Meyer. I am getting edgy talking to these people. I hate the sound of my own voice. And not too far from here, not far enough, there is a hundred-pound piano player fixing to fasten onto me the way a King's Crown attaches itself to a clam, and I have to shake her off somehow."

"I think you *are* coming down with something."

"Julia Lawless is bitter and angry at the world. She's selling Hub's toyland. At a garage sale, for God's sake. You should see the Orvis rods and shotguns. Is there a name for what I'm coming down with?"

"Some kind of culture shock. It manifests itself in an inability to see a reality untainted by temporary hang-ups."

"And yesterday when I was waiting to cross the street near the bank, I could look into all the cars roaring by, and the people in them had a kind of a dead look. As if they were hurrying so as not to be late for their own funerals. Is there any cure for my disease?"

"When Harder comes waddling into the marina with the *Flush,* you'll perk up. Hermit crabs get very nervous when they have to scrounge around without their shell."

"I can't wait that long. I feel as if some absolutely unimaginable catastrophe was getting itself ready to happen. And I feel as if, for no reason in the world, I was going to suddenly—for God's sake—start *crying!*"

He looked at me then with a startled compassion, intently, somberly. "Hey," he said softly. "Hey, Travis."

"Sorry."

"I thought it was just a little everyday weltschmerz. We're not here on some great big thing, you know."

"It's as big a thing as Harder can possibly think of."

"Did you and Duke Davis stand watches all the way up?"

"Yes, why? We decided it was best because the automatic pilot wasn't reliable in any kind of chop, and we were in shipping lanes most of the way. Besides, we didn't get any really long reaches on the way up. We fought wind all the way."

"What did you think about all that time?"

"Come *on!* I played all the games of What if. I counted the ladies I have known. I replayed the hard shots—given and taken. Remembered grief, remembered pleasure. I thought of all the choices made, the doors I've slammed shut, the seasons which have closed down on me, games called on account of pain. All that shit, Meyer. You know. A man's head goes round and about. Filth and glory. The whole schmear."

"But mostly . . . Who am I? Where am I going?"

"I guess."

"And the answer?"

I shrugged. "Answer shmanser. In the immortal words of Popeye, I yam what I yam. I know my patterns and limitations, needs and hang-ups. So I go on. Right? I endure. I enjoy what I can. There aren't any more forks in the road to take. Keep walking."

"You have felt that horrid rotten exhalation, Travis, that breath from the grave, that terminal sigh. You've been singing laments for yourself. Laments, regrets, remorses."

"Light the pyre. Float me out on my boat. Come on, Meyer. I've always been perfectly willing to accept the risks as they come along. If I make it, I make it. And if I don't, I had one hell of a time trying."

"And what you *do,* the services you render, are important."

"Are they?"

"Aren't they?" he asked.

"If you get somebody out of one bad screw-up, haul them out, brush them off, and send them on their way, they will head right back into some other kind of screw-up."

"Ah-hah!"

"What's with this Ah-hah?"

"You question the validity of the mission. Thus you question the validity of the missionary. A loss of faith. That is corrosive. At that point you question existence itself, the meaning of it. A common human condition. Those with no imagination never really feel despair. Congratulations!"

"Good God, Meyer!"

"I'll phone my new friend, and we shall have Boodles and beef at the Captain's Galley."

"Everybody has to be somewhere, I guess."

Meyer learned that there would be a table. We walked back to the lot and got the rental and drove on out to the Galley.

Meyer was turning something around and around in his mind. He had that look. One does not make conversation when Meyer has that look. At the table he finally sighed and smiled and gave it a try.

"Travis, I've mentioned to you the second law of thermodynamics."

"Which is?"

"That all organized systems tend to slide slowly into chaos and disorder. Energy tends to run down. The universe itself heads inevitably toward darkness and stasis."

"Cheering thought."

"Prigogine altered this concept with his idea of dissipative structures."

"Who?"

"Ilya Prigogine, the Belgian mathematician."

"Oh."

"He used the analogy of a walled city and an open city. The walled city, isolated from its surroundings, will run down, decay, and die. The open city will have an exchange of material and energy with its surroundings and will become larger and more complex, capable of dissipating energy even as it grows. I have been thinking that it would not warp the analogy too badly to extend it to a single individual."

"The walled person versus the open person?"

"The walled person would decline, fade, decay."

"Meyer, dammit, I have a lot more interchange of material and energy with my environment than most."

"In a physical sense, but you are not decaying in any physical sense. Great Scott. look at you. You look as if you could get up and run right through that wall."

"The decay is emotional?"

"And you are walled, in an emotional sense. There is no genuine give-and-take. There is no real involvement, lately. You are going through the motions. As with the piano player. As with Nick Noyes. You are vaguely predatory lately. And irritable. And listless. You are getting no emotional feedback."

"Where do I go looking for some?"

"That's the catch. You can't. It isn't that mechanical. You merely have to be receptive and hope it comes along."

"Meanwhile, I am being ground down by the second law of thermodynamics?"

"In a sense, yes."

"Thank you so much. I never would have known."

"Like I said. Irritable."

9

AT TEN o'clock on Saturday morning, I took a chance on some strong black coffee. My throat clenched and my stomach worked and leaped, but settled down slowly. I felt of my face carefully.

"What's the matter?" Meyer asked.

"My face feels as if it had been sliced off, Cuisinarted, chilled, and slapped back on. If I turn my head too fast, it will slide off. Is there a pile driver working nearby?"

"That's tennis you hear."

"How was I?"

"I would say you weren't listless. And you were audible. Lord, yes! You were audible."

"I thought I had long since outgrown that kind of thing."

"You had enough screwdrivers to empty your average orange tree. I lost count."

"What happened to me?"

"You had a large wish to stop thinking, to turn your head off. You were not happy with yourself, so you decided to dim your lights. And you did. You became someone else. Completely."

"Anybody we know?"

"McGee, you were loud, amiable, patriotic, and on key. You let me drive. We seemed to accumulate quite a group of new friends. We stopped at the Cove and picked up one blond Mishy Burns and we brought the whole pack here to the Cove. B. J. Bailey did not approve of you at all. Jack the Manager did not approve of the group. We were deprived of the chance of a midnight swim in the pool, but there was no way he could close the beach. You passed out on one of those canvas chaises. The piano player came after you at about quarter past one. There was some serious contention between the piano player and Miss Burns over your recumbent body, though I must say you seemed of very little value to anyone. There were some brisk face-slappings, some pungent dialogue, and then some yanking of hair, at which point they fell to the sand and went rolling over and over down the slope of the beach, yelping and biting. I chose that opportunity to yank you to your feet and walk you away. You began singing again, but not loudly. It was another rendition of 'Ragged but Right.' You had favored us with an estimated twenty renditions."

"What did I do to deserve all this? No, don't tell me. The question was rhetorical. God, Meyer, my hair aches and my skin doesn't fit and all my teeth feel loose."

"Last night we agreed the next thing we should do is go see John Tuckerman. I know how to find his place. It's about nine miles down the coast. Feel well enough to leave?"

"I am going to feel absolutely rotten wherever I happen to be, so I might as well be in the car as out of it. You drive."

I sat lumpily beside him, feeling squalid and faintly nauseated as he headed south, making the big half circle around the bay front, past the marinas and commercial docks and fish houses. Two blocks before we came to the end of Bay Street, Meyer turned right. We went through a couple of blocks of waterfront enterprise, ship's chandlers, old rooming houses, saloons, and sundries stores, and soon the street had turned into two-lane rough country asphalt, past trailer parks and junkyards, running between shallow ditches where coarse weeds and grasses grew high. By the time we were in empty country, the road was much worse. The potholes were deep. In places the wind had drifted sand across the road. The occasional hawk sat atop a phone pole, watching the clumps of marsh grass.

An armadillo trundled across the road, delicate little head upraised, full of false security, trusting too much in its body armor.

To keep my attention off wondering how soon I was going to be sick, I said, briskly conversational, "In Texas they scoop those out and make baskets out of them and sell them in roadside stands."

After a few moments of silence, Meyer said, "It is to be hoped that on some planet far beyond our galaxy a race of sentient armadillos is busy scooping out Texans and selling them at roadside stands, possibly as Lister bags."

That did it. "Whoa," I said in a small chastened voice. He whoaed and I sprang out and made it to the ditch, there paying one of the more ordinary penalties of abuse. I went back to the car and looked in at him. "How much farther?"

"I'd say three miles."

"Please drive straight ahead two miles, park, and wait for me."

The road curved. Two miles took him out of sight. The May sun was hot on my shoulders. I swung along, taking big strides but feeling clammy. And unwell. With a monstrous effort I kicked myself into a trot. For a little while I thought I would pass out, but suddenly I began to sweat properly. I stopped gasping and began to breathe properly. I stopped landing on my heels, jarring myself, and got up onto the balls of my feet. At the end of an estimated mile I began to get that good feeling of having all the parts of the machine working, thighs lifting properly, lungs filling deeply, arms swinging in cadence, lots of muscles flexing and relaxing.

"You'll live," Meyer said when I got to the car.

"I'm beginning to feel as if I might want to."

"We have to look for a sand road that turns off to the right at a shallow angle. With a yellow mailbox at the corner."

The yellow mailbox had an aluminum sign on top if it, the kind of sign where you buy the letters and slide them into a groove. The letters said TUCKERM.

The sand road wound between big bushes, angling toward the beach. We came upon a large faded sign which announced to nobody in particular, "Future Site of Pepperfish Village. A Planned Condominium Community. 1500

Units. Complete Recreation Facilities. Private Beach. Yacht Club. Golf Course. Shopping Plaza. A Hub-Law Development. Planning and Design by Kristin Petersen, AIA. Construction by Hula Construction, Inc. Occupation of first phase by   " Somebody had obliterated the rest of it with a big broad slap of red paint.

"So ends the dream," Meyer said.

"They could have built a better mousetrap."

"The world is beating a path down to this improbable peninsula, mousetraps or no. But it does seem to be a strange location."

Soon we came upon Tuckerman's place, off to the right of the road. It was atop spindly pilings ten feet high. The house was about thirty feet square. A veranda deck extended ten feet beyond it all the way around. The peaked roof was of galvanized sheet metal, weathered to a powdery white. The house and deck were of native pine, slapped up green and now weathered to gray, warped and twisted, with long-ago paint scoured off by the wind-driven sand. There was an old Fiat parked under the deck, square and green, sagging in the off right haunch with some kind of sprained underpinning.

Out behind the house, between the house and the long row of sand dunes, a woman stopped poking into a 55-gallon drum with a long stick and turned to look at us through the thicket of pilings supporting the house. She'd spent a lot of weeks in hot sun. She wore the bottom half of a string bikini, in red-orange Day Glo. Without haste or emphasis, she turned and located the bikini top, slipped it on, hammocked herself into it, and tied it in back. She then peered into the drum and began prodding again with the stick.

We walked around to where she was. There were two clotheslines hung with damp clothing. The drum was up on concrete blocks. There was a driftwood fire under it, flames almost too pale to see in the bright sunlight. Steam came off the soapy water in the drum. Bright clothing came into view and sank again as she prodded away.

"If you are the guys from Maytag," she said, "it is about time. This thing don't cycle worth a hoot."

"How is it on spin dry?" Meyer asked.

"Beyond belief." As she spoke, water began to spill over the top of a second drum a dozen feet away. She sprinted to a small plywood shack and turned something off. A pump gasped and died. She came back and took the hose out of the newly filled drum. She was sweaty from working so near the fire. She was a big woman, middle twenties, tall, with solid bone structure, slender waist, great shoulders. Muscle rolled in her back as she dug into the drum with her thick piece of driftwood. She levered a sopping wad of clothing up and looked at it.

"I can say," she said, "without fear or favor, that all this stuff is cleaner than it was. Beyond that I will not go."

With a grunt of effort she levered the mass out of the drum and carried it to the other drum and dropped it in, and the displaced water sloshed out.

"Have you come to take him away?" she asked

"No," I said.

"Which leaves me with mixed emotions."

The next wad of wet clothing was too heavy for her. I stepped in and carried it over to the rinse-water drum. She had brown hair, coarse with sun and salt, looking as if she had cropped it herself. She had a solid jaw, a broad mouth, dark brown eyes, and a jutting, high-bridged, no-nonsense nose.

"But you're looking for him?"

"For a talk," Meyer said.

She fished the final garment out of the hot water and put it in the other drum, turned and stared at us, seemed to see something that reassured her, smiled, and put her hand out. "I'm Gretel Howard."

After introductions, Meyer explained that we were trying to get the title cleared up somehow on some of Hubbard Lawless's holdings so that an offer could be made.

She looked at him and then at me. "Real-estate people? Not really."

"Not really," I said. "He's doing a favor for a friend. I'm with him."

"You look like the sort of man who can fix an antique Kohler five-thousand-watt generator, McGee."

"I can look at it and make reassuring noises."

"Follow me."

We went to the plywood shed. It was a big brute. The gas was in a drum on a scaffolding arrangement behind the shed. Plenty of gas. I couldn't check the condition of the batteries. It was rigged to start up at power demand. Turn on a hundred watts anywhere in the circuit and it would or should begin. A thin little metal leaf, like a spring, was supposed to be activated by the demand and bend over and touch a terminal. I pushed it over against the terminal, and with a great popping stuttering roar, the generator came to life.

Gretel sprang backward and hit the back of her head against the frame of the low doorway into the shed. Meyer backed into the little gasoline water pump and burned the back of his ankle on the still-hot housing. They each made appropriately fevered statements in the silence after I had released the little contact leaf. I examined it carefully. The vibration of the generator had caused the setscrew to work loose. I tightened it with the edge of a dime until the leaf was a sixteenth of an inch from the contact. There was a light in the shed, a hanging bulb. I turned it on, and the generator roared into life. I turned it off, smiling, smug and happy.

"My undying gratitude," she said. "We'll go find John. But first I have to churn my rinse a little."

As she churned, Meyer said, "You *have* heard of Laundromats?"

"I know. You're being ironic. Yes, love, and I could have bundled all this scrungy stuff into Brenda—that is little green Brenda over there, my dear lopsided auto—and gone Laundromating with a lot of gratitude for the benefits of civilization and so on. But I have this pioneer hang-up. I love doing things the hard way."

Making it evident we weren't going to be given the reason.

"I didn't mean to pry," Meyer said.

"Of *course* you didn't. I can wring this stuff out and hang it later, gentlemen. Let's go up on the deck and see if we can spot John pursuing lunch."

We climbed the warped and weathered stairway to the deck, climbed from one world into another. From the deck one could see across the top of the dunes, out to the blue Gulf dotted with infrequent whitecaps in the morning breeze. To the south was a curve of beach and the continuing line of dunes. To the north, far away, were a few white towers of Timber Bay rising up out of the city smudge. To the east was the north-south wavery line of the old asphalt road, heat shimmering from it.

She went into the house and came out with binoculars, and located him far up the beach. They were big old Navy ten-power, hard to hand-hold. She gave them to me, stood beside me. I was very conscious of her there, of a radiation of her body heat as we stood in the shade of the overhang, of the way the top of her brown head came higher than my eyes. Few women stand that tall in bare brown feet. I guessed her at a fraction of an inch over six feet.

I focused on John Tuckerman. He was a mile away, standing to mid-thigh in the waves, casting out beyond where they were beginning to lift and break.

"You can walk up there and talk to him," she said. "But don't . . . expect too much. He's quite confused."

"How so?"

"I thought when I got every last trace of alcohol out of his system, he would be like he used to be. Poor John. It's a wonder I haven't killed him, running him up and down that beach. I asked Dr. Sam Stuart about it and he said it was due to alcoholic spasm destroying brain tissue. He changed during the month after Hub disappeared. He was drinking so very heavily, I understand. He was . . . the way he is by the time I got here, by the time I *could* get here."

"Should we both go?" I asked her.

"It might make him anxious to see two of you coming. Just you alone would be better, I think."

*   *   *

He noticed me when I was a hundred yards from him. He saw me when he had drawn back his arm to cast. He stayed frozen in that position for a few moments and then lowered the rod and stood waiting. He looked like a Clark Gable gone seriously to seed. His dark hair was tangled and long. His black mustache had grown down over his lip. He had a four-day stubble of beard. But the cheekbones were high and hard, the brow jutting, the eyes dark, deepset, and merry. He was bigger than I had expected, almost as tall as I am, and wider, but soft. Tan helped hide the softness, the sagging belly, the varicosities on the husky legs. He wore ragged shorts. There was a tackle box on the sand and a stringer staked close by, with the line leading into the wave wash.

"Any luck?" I asked.

"Not good today. Just some of those little suckers that taste like iodine. And a little shark I let go."

"What are you using, John?"

"I got these tired pieces of cut bait. They're beginning to smell. Say, how'd you know my name?"

"Gretel pointed you out up the beach here and told me you're fishing for lunch. She seems like a nice person."

"Oh, she's a wonderful girl. Just wonderful. She's taking real good care of me. I can't remember the last time I had a drink. What's your name?"

"McGee. Travis McGee. I came out here with a friend of mine. His name is Meyer. He's back at the house with Gretel. We came to Timber Bay a few days ago to find out about buying Hub's ranch and grove land. We wondered if you could help us."

"No, I couldn't help you with anything like that. I was just a friend. That's all. We grew up together and went to school together and stayed friends. Hub was the smart one."

"I thought you were a vice-president of those companies he had."

"Oh, I was, sure. I guess I still am, come to think of it. But it didn't mean anything, not anything at all. He said it was so I could be expensed. I don't know why what I got paid couldn't have come out of just one of the businesses. I wasn't getting a free ride, though. I did a lot of things for Hub. And for Julie and the kids too. Pretty important things, sometimes. Like making sure something would get delivered on time to the right person."

Finally I was able to put a name to what was so strange about him: it was his childlike quality. The amiable open manner, the pleasant eagerness were those of a manly child, eager for approval.

"Deliveries can be *very* important," I said.

"You just bet they can!"

I saw some action out beyond the waves and wondered if I could find him some better bait. I took off shoes and socks, rolled my pant legs up, went down to the edge of the water, and began digging in the soft wet sand. After a little while I dug up a sand flea, oyster-white, multilegged, and snatched him before he could burrow back into the wet sand. He was as big around as my thumb and half as long. I took him and impaled him on John Tuckerman's hook.

"That's an *ugly* thing!" he said. "Where did you find it?"

"There should be a lot of them along this beach. Cast out over in that direction and reel in fast."

"Fast? Okay."

In the first ten feet of retrieve he got a hard strike. He yelled with excitement and pleasure. He worked the fish expertly, but when we got a look at it, his shoulders sagged. "Oh, nuts. Another kind of trash fish. A darn jackfish."

He had a fish knife in his tackle box. I pulled the four-pound jack farther up the beach, slit its throat, and pulled it back into the water, holding it captive by the leader. It pumped strings and strands of dark blood into the water until it weakened and died. The sea had washed away all the pink blush of blood.

"What did you do that for?" he demanded. He looked upset and disapproving.

"Because it is second cousin to a pompano, and now the meat won't be dark and heavy, and it makes a good panfish."

As the knife was sharp enough, I filleted the fish on the spot, washed the two slabs of meat in the sea, and threw the rest out beyond the surf, where the crabs would clean it up quickly.

"You sure did that fast," John Tuckerman said.

"Lots of practice."

"Say, were you ever a guide? Did you do guiding out of Marathon, ever? You look like a fellow me and Hub hired down there a long time ago. No, you couldn't be. That was maybe fifteen years ago. He'd be a lot older by now than you are."

"I've found fish for a lot of people, but not for hire."

"What did you say your name is?"

"Travis McGee."

"Trav?"

"Sure."

"I used to remember names real good. It is sort of a trick. You know. You find some way to match up the name to the way the people look. Like if there is a woman named Fowler with a big mouth and a real loud voice, you say to yourself, She is Fowler the Howler, and then you never forget. But I have stopped remembering somehow. I used to be able to tell ten thousand jokes. I was known for telling jokes. The other day I was fishing and I tried to remember one. Just one. And I couldn't."

"If this fish is lunch, we ought to get it back to the house."

"Hey, you're right!"

We picked up our stuff and walked back along the beach toward the cottage. The roof gleamed white in the sunlight on the far side of the dune. I could see the dark shade on the veranda and a sudden glint, and knew she was taking a look at us through the binoculars.

Trite and repetitive thoughts march endlessly through every mind. I cannot use or even think of binoculars without my memory banks making a printout of the overly familiar fact that in World War II the Israeli hero Dayan, serving with the British, lost his eye when a sniper slug hit the binoculars he was using. I do not need to know this all my life. I do not need my memory dredging it up. We have no way of turning these things off. Every brain, including those of Kissinger breadth and force, is cluttered with these bits and snippets, these everlasting echoes.

"House been there long?" I asked him.

"A long time. I don't know how long. It was there when Hub bought the whole tract. That damn Kristin talked him into buying it. It was unique, she said. It sure is unique. It is too far from anything. Hub said I could use it as a beach house. I fixed it up a little. Got a new well dug. Put the generator in and did some wiring. But the generator won't work now."

"I fixed it."

"You did? So quick!"

"A setscrew had worked loose. It wasn't much."

"Gee, Gretel and I are sure glad it's fixed."

"And now you live out here?"

"With no money coming in at all, I couldn't keep the nice apartment I had at North Pass Vista. It was more like a whole house than an apartment."

"Kristin lived there too?"

"She lived in Melody unit. I was over in Symphony, nearer the beach. They're named after music things. Concerto, Harmony, Opera, and so on. The wife of that guy that put them up was a harp player. There are four town houses in each unit. Like Symphony One, Symphony Two, and so on. Mine was Symphony Four. I put my stuff in storage. I didn't want to bring it down here to the beach to this place. I don't think I can keep up the payments on the storage. I'll probably lose that too."

"Too?"

"Like I lost the car. They say I ran it into a tree, but I don't remember. I shouldn't have been driving anyway because my license was suspended. The car was totaled and the insurance company wouldn't pay a dime because I wasn't a licensed driver any more. How do you like that? I was with them sixteen years! It was right about then that Gretel got here, thank God. Now that she's here, everything will be okay.''

"When we got here she was doing the laundry in those big drums. Are you two so hard up you can't spare quarters for a coin laundry? We passed one back at the edge of town.''

"Oh, we could afford that, but Gretel is stubborn. And she gets these ideas about things. She wants to see just how independent of everything we can be. No telephones or power companies. She's trying to grow stuff in a garden she planted way the other side of the hard road, on the edge of the marsh, but the birds and rabbits are giving her a hard time. And the mosquitoes eat her when she goes over to work on it. But she won't give up. Not on anything. Ever.''

We came to the path that wound up to the crest of the dune and down the other side. Gretel and Meyer were on the deck. John Tuckerman held up the fillets of jack, and Gretel applauded him.

She came down and got the fish. Once she had hefted it, she asked us to stay to lunch. Meyer sidestepped the question and left it up to me. I said we'd be delighted, and thanks very much for asking us.

We tipped the soapy-water drum downslope, and she grilled the fish over the embers from the driftwood fire. While I had been with John Tuckerman, Gretel and Meyer had wrung out and hung up the clothes. We had lunch off chipped blue willowware plates at a table by the windows in the small bare living room of the beach cottage. We had the grilled fish, canned peas, and black coffee. The biggest object in the room was the fireplace. There were seashells on the windowsills and the mantel. Gretel put on a blue work shirt over her bikini before coming to the table. She glowed with strength and health and vitality. I envied John Tuckerman. There were golden flecks in the deep brown pigment of her eyes, near the pupils. The whites of her eyes were the blue-white of peak physical condition. Through the meal we talked fishing, and over coffee I said, "Where were you before you came here, Gretel?''

"I came out of the nowhere into the here.''

"We don't answer questions,'' John said earnestly. "That's one of the rules. She says I could get into real—''

"Hey!'' she said. "We don't have to explain why we don't answer questions.''

"Okay,'' he said grumpily. "But you sure are bossy.''

"There are reasons,'' she said. She smiled at Meyer. "We've had other visitors.''

"Like Fletcher. Like that damned Fletcher.''

"Hush, dear,'' she said.

"A deputy sheriff?'' I asked. "Now in Mexico with the insurance investigator?''

"He said they were going there,'' John said.

She glared at me, her face darkening in anger. She said, "I think it is pretty damned low to keep digging and digging away at somebody who . . . who . . .'' She didn't know how to say it in front of him.

"You're cute,'' I said. "Both of you. You make a cute couple. Speaking about low. Sure, John Tuckerman. Keep your mouth shut. And deprive a very decent hard-luck man named Van Harder from making a living at his trade. There is a smell of money in the wind, lady, and you seem to turn toward it like some kind of weathervane. You came out of the nowhere into the here to brush up an old affair and get closer to the money.''

She stared at me, aghast. "You think I'm his old lady?"

"She's his sister," Meyer said. And as soon as it was said, I could see it. Bone structures, coloring.

She thumped the table with her fist, making coffee dance in the cups. "I came here to help John any way I can, because there isn't anybody else left in the world who will help him."

"In spite of all your marvelous motives and family spirit and so on, Gretel, it still leaves Van Harder on the beach."

"He ran the *Julie*," John said. "Hub put half of one of those horse capsules in—"

"John! Shut up, shut up, shut up! Jesus God! They can nail you for conspiracy to defraud, or whatever the right words for it are. Now tell me, John, what really happened to Van Harder?"

"I guess he must have had that big drink Hub gave him on an empty stomach. Or else he brought some liquor aboard with him and drank it too. He passed out when we were on automatic pilot, and one of the girls got sick and went up there and saw him and came down and told us. We decided we'd better go back to Timber Bay. When we found the pass and started in, Hub went up on the bow and—"

I interrupted him. He had been reciting it. He had learned it by rote. "Okay, okay," I said. "Van got half a horse tranquilizer. I know the other story by heart too."

John looked at Gretel for guidance. She said to me, "I guess you can understand why we can't help your friend. Why John can't help your friend. The establishment took such a beating, they would be glad to stuff anybody in jail."

John Tuckerman made a muffled sound. We all looked at him. His eyes had filled and one tear broke and ran down his cheek. "He could have taken me with him," he said. "Everything would have been all right. If he had to go, he could have taken me. Instead of that bitch architect. That dirty rotten bitch architect." His voice broke.

Meyer said in his jolliest tone, "John and I are going to clean up here, while you and Travis take a walk on the beach, Gretel."

She looked at him and then she looked at me, a steady, suspicious, interrogatory look, trying to see through my eyes and into my skull. There was a sudden impact, almost tangible. I wanted to be more than I was, for her. I wanted to stop being tiresome and listless and predictable. I wanted to be thrice life-size, witty and urbane, bright and reliable, sincere and impressive —all for her. She merited better than the pedestrian person she stared at.

The hostility and suspicion faded into a look of doubt, a lip-biting tension. "So come on," she said, and I had to hurry to catch her halfway up the dune.

We stopped at the crest, the early afternoon sun speckling the sea with silver mirrors, aiming arrows of light at us. To the south, birds worked a moiled area of bait.

"We have to trust somebody," she said. She looked sidelong at me. "I've had terrible luck in the trusting department."

Before I could respond she was off down the slope, leggy and swift, heading south down the beach.

10

"You can't really appreciate the change in John unless you'd known him before. So quick and funny and exasperating. If he'd just had the motivation, he could have been a successful person. Well, maybe he was a successful person. At least he had sense enough not to try marriage. He would have made a terrible husband. As bad, I guess, as the one I married too young, Billy Howard. I think John has always been more than half in love with Julie Lawless anyway."

We were two miles down the beach from the cottage. A driftwood weatherworn section of wooden dock projected from the shallow slope of the dune —a shelf for sitting. She poked at the sand with a stick as she talked, making small avalanches.

"He tied his life to Hub Lawless's life. And when everything went sour for Hub and he decided to run, he shucked John off. John has been an intensely loyal person. He drank for oblivion, and I think he found some . . . permanent kind. He is . . . a simplified personality now. At the time of the hearing and the investigation, he was himself. I couldn't be here then, but I could tell from the newspaper stories. He could handle it. He couldn't get through that sort of thing now. He can be tricked, like a child."

"The way I was tricking him."

"Yes. It made me angry."

"You didn't hide it."

"Short fuse, friend."

"Short fuse and long talk. You talk around and around it, and you keep on wondering if you should tell me anything, or if you should keep on waffling."

"I just met you a few hours ago."

"I came here at Van Harder's request, to clear his name."

"You're a private detective, then?"

"Me? No. Those people have to have licenses and be bonded and carry insurance and report to the law people wherever they go. They charge fees and have office phones and all that. I just do favors for friends. Sort of salvage work."

"But Van Harder is paying you?"

"No. He offered me ten thousand dollars in time payments if I could do it. He thinks his good name is worth twenty thousand. When I find things for people, I keep half. But I won't take that kind of money from him. I'll have to find some way of saving his pride, *if* I can get his situation reconsidered. He's spent his life on the water. It isn't fair that he should be victimized by some sharp operator rigging his own disappearance with other people's money."

"And leaving his best friend, as he always called John, flat broke in the bargain."

"Self-preservation. A strong instinct."

She poked away at the sand, bent so far forward I could not see her face. I looked at the smooth brown legs, the flow of the complex curves, one into the next, lovely as music. She had shed the work shirt. It lay on the weathered wood between us. The bikini string bit into the skin of her warm brown back, and I followed the way her back narrowed down to her waist, then flared to the hips. I read the calligraphy of the round knuckles of the bent spine, and of the twinned dimples farther down.

She turned sharply and caught me staring at her. She said, "I suppose your hairy pal is worming it all out of John anyway."

"I could say yes in hopes it would open you up. Actually, I don't know. He may be leaving it up to you to decide."

She laughed. "When we were alone he gave me a little lecture on how people have washed their garments, down through the ages. He's really a nice person."

"Maybe we both are."

"I have a track record that tells me not to trust my instincts. I have been undone by scoundrels, sir."

"And probably scoundrels have been undone by you."

"Sometimes. Thanks for the confidence. Anyway . . ." She told me what she had learned from her brother, little by little.

When things had begun to go bad, Hub had begun joking about escape. He and John had made up wild plans, as a sort of running fantasy. But as things got worse, the jokes became strained, and the planning became more serious. John had not learned until very far along in the planning process that it had been Hub's wish, all along, to take Kristin Petersen with him, or to meet her there. John had thought this ironic, as the architect was really the person who had encouraged Hub to make the land purchases which had finally foundered him. Apparently, according to John's observations, the affair between Hub and Kristin was intensely physical, the kind of obsessive infatuation which seemed to blind him to all consequences.

The most delicate and intricate chore had been the conversion, over three months, of assets into cash, with frequent trips to Tampa, Clearwater, and Orlando. They had taken a four-day trip to Mexico in late February, ostensibly to hunt cat in the mountains, actually to arrange for surgery in Guadalajara at a later date, and to set up a hideaway for Hub and Kristin after the operations.

When I asked where, she said that John didn't know, that he had remained in Guadalajara while Hub flew off somewhere, but John had the impression Hub went to Yucatan.

They had done a lot of the planning right there in the cottage, arguing, picking flaws, finding solutions.

The cash had been hidden at the ranch. On March twenty-second, Hub Lawless had put the cash in the yellow jeep and driven out to the cottage. John Tuckerman had driven out there and picked him up and taken him back into Timber Bay. John had arranged for the two girls to come along on the *Julie* so that there would be innocent witnesses to the accident. Hub had made certain neither girl saw the powerful tranquilizer in powder form being dumped into Harder's token drink.

Just when it was about time for one of them, John or Hub, to go topside and "discover" Harder, one of the girls became seasick and went up and saved them the trouble. After she came down, they went up to see, then turned the cruiser around to go back. Hub went below and told the girls what they were doing, and also told them that now they were going into the wind, and it was very cold and ugly up above.

Hub went back up. John had taken the *Julie* as close inshore as he dared. When they came opposite the harsh gleam of the Coleman lantern John had left lighted on the deck railing of the beach cottage, Hub clapped John on the back, thanked him, shook his hand, and went overboard. When he was in the sea, he quickly yanked the cord that inflated the life belt he was wearing. They had tested it several times in rough water off John Tuckerman's beach. Hub was confident using it and could make good time through the water.

John piloted the *Julie* to Timber Bay, went in the pass, thumbed the bow onto the sandbar, began yelling for the girls, and threw the life ring over. He stayed and answered all questions, over and over and over. It was very late when he got back to his apartment. In the early morning he drove out to the cottage and, to his consternation, saw that the yellow jeep was still there. He found Hub Lawless on the cot in the corner of the living room, gray, sweaty, and short of breath. Hub had the feeling, he said, that some round heavy weight was pushing down on his chest. It was more of a feeling of pressure than of pain. He had been much farther from shore than he had realized when he went overboard. He had struggled for a long time and had finally come to shore, exhausted, a long way south of the lantern light. The cold wind chilled him as he walked up the beach, and he had a nagging pain in his left arm and shoulder. It was not until he had climbed the dune that he had fainted. He did not know how long he was out, but he did not think it was very long. He got himself up the stairs and into the cottage, stripped off his sodden clothes, and dressed in the fresh dry clothing. The nausea had started then, and the weakness. He did not feel equal to driving the jeep to Tampa, as planned, and anyway he had already missed his early flight from Tampa to Houston and thus also his Houston-Guadalajara connection. The tickets and the tourist card were in the false name he had selected, Steven Pickering, the name he had used with the clinic in Guadalajara.

He told John Tuckerman to drive back to Timber Bay, contact Kristin Petersen, and tell her what had happened and to come to the cottage. In the original plan she had been supposed to hang around for a week, mourning Hub, and then go back to Atlanta, where she had lived when they met. Later —originally—she was to fly to Mexico and join him at some unknown place in Yucatan. But now, Hub gave John a sealed note to give her. He told John to conceal the jeep nearby in the brush before he left and to stay away from the cottage for a few days.

When John went back to the cottage, there was no one there. Hub was gone. The jeep was gone. There was no note and no money. John had understood that Hub was going to leave him some of the money, which he was to tuck away in a very safe place and not dip into for as long as possible.

"So they went off together in the jeep? With the woman driving, if he couldn't."

"That's what it looks like."

"What was going to happen to the jeep if they'd followed the original plan?"

"Hub was going to leave the claim check for the jeep and the jeep keys in an envelope at the National Airlines desk, and John was going to get down there somehow and claim the jeep and bring it back and take the back roads to get onto the ranch property, and then just park it somewhere on the ranch, as though Hub had left it there."

"Why a jeep, not a car?"

"This road and the hard road become almost impassable five miles south of here. A storm tore it all up. A car couldn't make it, but the jeep could. He was going to come ashore and change, drive the jeep south, and be in Tampa before dawn."

"Carrying money, lots of money? Oh, sure. No baggage check leaving this country, and no baggage check disembarking in Mexico."

"Especially for the first-class passengers. And he had been in and out enough times to know the routines."

"Having the woman leave Timber Bay on the twenty-third, with its being pretty much common knowledge there was something between them—that made it look more like an arranged disappearance."

"Yes, it did. My brother worried about that. He says that Hub worked so hard and carefully to make sure Julia would get the insurance money, it's a shame that all these rumors started. I suppose it was unavoidable. If he couldn't manage the running all by himself, the woman had to help him."

"It seems Hub made it to Guadalajara. Deputy Fletcher and the insurance investigator are down there now."

"Who told them about Guadalajara?"

"When a case like this breaks in the papers, the police get a flood of crank mail and phone calls. They sort them out. Some young woman in Orlando sent an anonymous letter with a color slide to the Sheriff. She had taken the pictures on a Friday, April eighth, at a sidewalk café, of a street scene. She recognized the man in the left of the picture later as being the man whose picture was in all the area newspapers. She said she couldn't come forward because her boyfriend thought she was visiting a friend in California. Sheriff Hack Ames made the connection with the big face-lift and cosmetic-surgery business there."

She stabbed the stick viciously into the sand. "I could spit," she said. "He sits down there fat and happy, and he left all this ruin behind him. Will they find him?"

"I don't know. Bringing him back would be something else. We have an extradition agreement. But he didn't hold anything up with a gun. Right now there isn't any warrant out for him that I know of. And if he has any political friends down there, it could take a long, long time."

"Was that woman in the picture too?"

"No."

"She must be a real charmer. A dandy person."

"Hub Lawless must have been vulnerable."

"Like my dear little husband, Billy Howard, was vulnerable. Vulnerable and full of big schemes. God! I was eighteen when I married him. We got a job managing a ski resort forty miles from the end of the earth, and I learned to ski well enough to teach beginners. I cooked and kept the books and waited table and cleaned the rooms and drove the bus and sold the gear too. We crapped out. Too much snow. They couldn't keep the roads clear. The customers couldn't get in. We operated a tennis camp for an old pro who gave the lessons and kept trying to hustle me into the bushes. I cooked and kept the books and waited table and cleaned the rooms and drove the bus and sold the gear, and got to play pretty good tennis. Until the old pro dropped dead on the court and his sister fired us. Shall I go on? Why am I telling you all this?''

"Because I want to know all this."

"Sure. We ran a summer camp for little rich kids. I taught archery, riding, swimming, diving, woodcraft, judo, finger painting, and track. I cooked and kept the books and waited table and drove the bus and pitched softball. Billy made a pass at one of the young mothers who came up to visit, and she told the owners, and we got hurled out in the middle of August. More?''

"Can there be more?"

"You can believe it. So we got a job running a fat farm for California ladies. A dietician cooked. Local high-school girls waited table and cleaned the rooms. All I had to do was run all the exercise classes, keep the books, keep the weight charts, organize their day to keep them all busy, drive the bus, and so on and so on. So I was taking them on a little jog, and I looked back, still jogging, to see how the stragglers were coming along, and one of them ahead of me fell down, and I tripped over her and broke my wrist. See, it wasn't set exactly right. It's a little bit lumpy.''

I examined her right wrist. The bone seemed to jut out a little. Her forearm was baked to a warm golden brown, with the fine hairs, scorched white by the sun, lying against the brown with a tender, infinite neatness. I said it didn't look lumpy.

"We're coming to the best part," she said. "I couldn't keep the books and records. The owners had to hire a bookkeeper. They cut my pay. The bookkeeper was cute. Dear darling Billy ran off with her. She couldn't even keep the books right. She was one of those helpless ones with the big melting eyes. She sighed a lot. I don't think she bathed as much as her mother might have wished. And the reason I couldn't come here sooner, after I had seen the whole mess in the papers and called John, was because I was not supposed to leave the state until I got the final papers of divorce. The lawyer said it might gum things up. He said I could go if I wanted, and it would probably be all right. But I wanted to be very damned sure that my seven years of marriage were over. Aren't we supposed to change completely every seven years, all the cells or something? I was ready. Wow, was I ever ready! I put in seven years of sixteen-hour days. Seven years of hard, hard labor.''

"What are you going to do afterward? After all this?"

"When the time comes, I'll think about it."

Our eyes caught and held for a few moments. When she looked away, I had a very strange feeling. I felt as if I had shucked some kind of drab outer skin. It was old and brittle, and as I stretched and moved, it shattered and fell off. I could breathe more deeply. The Gulf was a sharper blue. There was wine in the air. I saw every grain of sand, every fragment of seashell, every movement of beach grasses in the May breeze. It was an awakening. I was full of juices and thirsts, energies and hungers, and I wanted to laugh for no reason at all.

I reached and caught the lumpy wrist, and she looked at me with surprise and faint irritation, gave one tug to get away, and then did not resist. I did not have to worry about her reaction. I could make her understand anything.

"Gretel, thanks for telling me all you know. Thanks for trusting me. I'm going to help you with this. Meyer and I will help you, and we'll get it all sorted out."

"For half of what?"

"For half of the way you look right now."

"Come on! You've been in the sun too long."

She snatched her work shirt and we headed back. She seemed to have been infected by some of my exuberance. At one point she sprinted away from me, running on the packed sand where the tide had receded. She ran well, and it took a determined effort to overtake her. She stopped when I clapped my right hand on her left shoulder. She was breathing hard, and she inspected me and discovered I wasn't.

"Good shape, huh?" she gasped.

"Better than my usual. I helped a friend bring a big ketch up from the Grenadines to Lauderdale. Lots of wind, all from the wrong direction. A person could get in the same kind of good shape by spending a month working with weights while rolling downhill."

"Are you a freak about condition?" She was recovering her wind quickly.

"I guess to a certain extent. I get into situations where it is nice to be quick, and healthy to be persuasive. I get into them oftener than most. If I get bloated and slow, somebody is going to put me out of business. So when I get the slow bloats, I get the guilts, and when I'm in shape I feel righteous and smug—but what I do is keep going from one extreme to the other, and getting it back gets rougher every year. How about you? Freaky?"

"Not really. But I'm sort of a jock. You know, born with good coordination and good muscle memory. I learn physical things quickly. I like competition. I don't have to tell you I am one big girl. Six foot one-half inch. One hundred and forty-eight pounds of meat. Solid meat. You are one man who doesn't make me feel all that huge, though. I guess I like to stay in shape because you can do things better, and you feel so much better. It's kind of a . . . a hummy feeling. You know your motor is running."

We went back to the cottage. Meyer was on the veranda deck reading a copy of the *Reader's Digest* for July 1936. He said it had a lot of uplift in it. He said he had learned that the ideal article for the *Reader's Digest* would have a rather long title: "I Dropped My Crutches, Abandoned My Electronic Submarine, Climbed the Undersea Mountain and Found God." He said John Tuckerman was napping. He had felt very tired.

John came yawning out as we talked. He sat in an old rocker and nodded from time to time as Gretel told him that she had told me all about the plan he had cooked up with Hub for the disappearance. He did not seem especially concerned.

He smiled at me and said, "I tried to talk Hub out of it. I really did. I told him he was letting all his friends down. He was letting down the people who were still working for him, who were still loyal. He wouldn't listen. He said everything had gone to hell and there was no way to salvage any of it, except to leave and take what he could with him. All he could really think about was getting into the Petersen woman's pants. Excuse me, Gretel.''

"Was she all that great?" Gretel asked.

"Depends on what you like," John said. "She's kind of pale and round-faced, but with hollows in her cheeks, pale green eyes, soft quiet little voice, silver-blond hair that she braids a lot, and a slender body, but with real big tits. She's quiet but she's used to giving orders, and when she tells somebody to do something she has a way of making them jump and do it. She walks into a room and you know she is . . . somebody. Somebody important."

"How did she act when you gave her the message?" I asked him.

"Oh, she was upset. She paced around her place, nibbling her thumb knuckle, telling me to shut up whenever I tried to say I was leaving."

"She had opened the note?"

"Yes, but she didn't tell me what it said."

"But the verbal message," Meyer asked, "as I think you told me before your nap, was to tell her to come out to the cottage, was it not?"

"Yes. To tell her he'd had some kind of mild heart attack, and to come out. He told me to stay away from the cottage for a few days and to hide the jeep in the brush before I left."

"Then," said Meyer, "the written message had to be some kind of instruction to her, to do something *before* coming out, because if he was going to see her out there, he would be able to tell her any other instruction. And it had to be something he didn't want to tell you."

"I don't know what that would be. He knew he could trust me."

"We have one problem to solve first," Meyer said. We looked at him. He looked very pleased with himself. "It's so obvious," he said. "Certainly she didn't *walk* out here from the town!"

In the silence, Gretel said, "It's like that game of logic where you have to get everybody across the river in one boat in so many trips. What kind of car did she have, Johnny?"

"A small rental car. A red Mazda five-door hatchback. Hub rented it for her from Garner Wedley, owns the Texaco station out on Dixie Boulevard and has the franchise for Bonus Rental. I know because I had to take it to be gassed and serviced a few times. It drove nice."

"Oh, John, did you have to do things like that for him? Putting gas in his girl friend's car?"

He shook his head as if in irritation at her denseness. "Honey, you just don't understand. Anything that Hub asked me to do, I was *glad* to do. It didn't matter what. I worked for him, and I was his friend too. And I still am, no matter what."

"Did the Texaco station man get his car back?" I asked. I saw Meyer nod his approval out of the corner of my eye.

John Tuckerman frowned. "My memory has gone so rotten. It seems I remember Garn chewing at me about something or other, about that car. But a lot of people were chewing at me about a lot of things back then, that last little bitty part of March. My feeling is he got it back but there was something wrong with it, wrong with the deal somehow."

We asked more questions. What sort of container was the money in? It was in a fake gas can chained and padlocked to the rack on the back of the jeep. How much money? Hub never said. But it was a lot. A real lot. Hub said he was sorry he'd never see his daughters again, and never see John again. But a man had to do what he had to do.

Where had the money been hidden out at the ranch? As they had collected more and more of it, turning pieces of paper and equipment and supplies into cash, Hub had kept it in various places, moving it every time he got nervous about it. And the more it got to be, the more often he got nervous.

What did you mean by a fake gas can? It was one of those heavy-duty GI gas cans, tall and narrow and painted yellow like the jeep. There were two of them, and they fitted in brackets in the back, on either side of the spare-tire bracket. Hub had hacksawed a can in half and soldered a flange on the inside of the lower half, so the top half could be fitted back on. He packed all the money in there, put the can in the bracket, ran the heavy-duty rubberized chain through the heavy handle that was part of the top of the can, pulled the chain tight, and padlocked it. From then on he felt easy about the money. He could park it right down near the bank. Whenever he left the jeep, he took the distributor rotor along with him. He made jokes with John Tuckerman about the kind of gas in the gas can. He told John some of it was his and would be left behind.

I said to John, "I suppose you've hunted for the money, for what he was supposed to leave here for you."

John looked at me. He wore the somewhat defiant expression of a sly child. "I won't say."

"We looked for it," Gretel said wearily.

"We never did!" John yelled. "Never!"

And from the subtle gesture she made, I knew it was time for us to go.

*   *   *

It was almost four fifteen on Saturday afternoon when we headed back toward Timber Bay.

Meyer said, "I haven't heard that infuriatingly tuneless whistling of yours for a long, long time. Congratulations."

"On what?"

"On coming back to the land of the living."

"It shows? I was that bad?"

"You were that bad, and for a long time. You were, in fact, committing the eighth deadly sin."

"I was? What is that?"

"You were boring, Travis. Very boring."

"Oh?"

"Self-involved people are always boring. Nobody can ever be as interested in them as they are in themselves."

"Sorry about that."

"You probably couldn't help it. It's been coming on since before we went up to Bayside that time."

"If I've been so depressing, why didn't you just bug off?"

"There was always the chance you'd come out of it."

"I feel as if I had."

"She seems to be an exceptional person."

"Gretel? Yes. Yes, she is. I like these dunes. They give it a nice wild unspoiled look. We'll have to cruise this coast sometime. Maybe head north from here."

"What are you smiling at?"

"Me? Was I smiling?"

11

THE LIGHT breeze was out of the southwest. The sky was cloudless. The late afternoon sun was hot. Shopping centers were jammed. So were the beaches and tennis courts. Meyer took the Dodge to go find out about the rental Mazda. I walked north along the uplands above the beach until I came to North Pass Vista.

I walked around the place for a few minutes and located Symphony, where John Tuckerman had lived, and Melody. Each was a cluster of four small two-story town houses. Melody Three was where Kristin Petersen had lived. Someone else was in there. A slight baldheaded man was in the narrow carport, painting a small chest of drawers, biting his lip as he made each careful stroke.

The office was in a unit farthest from the water. There was a sign stuck into the lawn and another over the doorbell. A man opened the door and looked out at me. He had half glasses and a boot-camp haircut. He looked to be about forty.

"Yes?" he said, managing to inject hostility and disbelief into that single syllable.

"I want to ask some questions about Kristin Petersen, please."

"I have no interest in answering them."

As he started to close the door I put my palm against it and gave a hearty shove. It drove him back and banged the door open.

"Hey!" he said. "You can't force your way in here!"

The foyer was a shallow office, with a secretarial desk, two chairs, and a gray file cabinet. He picked up the phone and dialed the operator. I took my time finding the To Whom It May Concern card from Devlin Boggs. He asked the operator for the police. I held the card up in front of him. He told the police it was a mistake and he was sorry. He took the card, turned it over and read the message, and handed it back.

"What's your interest in Miss Petersen?"

"My interest is enough to drop subpoenas on you if I think you are holding back."

"Oh. You're an attorney?"

"What is your name?"

"Stanley Moran."

"Mr. Stanley Moran, I don't want you to keep asking me questions. I am not here to answer questions. I am here to ask them. Maybe you would like to phone Mr. Boggs and get his opinion on whether or not you should ask me a lot of questions.''

"But how do I know you—"

"Or I can come back with Hack Ames, or Deputy Fletcher, or anybody you might think of who can reassure you.''

"Why are you smiling like that?''

"Because the angrier I get, the more I smile. It's a form of nervous anxiety. When I break out laughing, I usually hit people.''

He sat down behind the desk, picked a pencil up and put it down, and moved a stapler a few inches to the left to line it up with the edge of the small desk.

"There's nothing I've said or done to get angry at.''

"When did she leave here?''

"Do you know how many times I've had to answer—"

"Stanley, I'm smiling again.''

"Oh. She left here on the twenty-third. The precise time cannot be established. She had a visitor at ten thirty that morning. The police were very interested in that, and they finally were able to identify the visitor as Mr. Tuckerman, who was then living in Symphony Four. After he left, she drove out and was gone the rest of the day. People were interested in her movements because of her—cough—relationship with Mr. Lawless, who at that time was believed drowned out in the bay. They were searching for the body. Her car was seen back in her carport at about eleven on the night of the twenty-third; however, it was gone when I walked around the area at six the following morning. I rise early. So the assumption is that she departed during the night of the twenty-third, or very very early on the morning of the twenty-fourth.''

"She took everything with her?''

"Well . . . *practically* everything. All her personal things, of course. But she left a few things she had bought for the unit. Let me see now. Two very primitive-looking pottery bowls. Ugly things, actually. One small table, of blond wood with the top inset with blue and green tiles. One framed print that I can't make head or tail of—you can hardly tell which way up to hang it. Our storage space here is very limited. There's a limit to how long I can hold these items. I might say that Miss Petersen was not exactly my favorite tenant here at Vista. She made *very* disparaging remarks about the decor and the architecture. My wife and I have worked very hard to make these units attractive and livable. She had no reason to call them vulgar. We do not set ourselves up as moral arbitrators or—"

"Arbiters.''

"What?''

"I have been listening to a man named Meyer too long. Go ahead. You were saying?''

"People's morals are their own affair. But she did, time and again, 'entertain' Mr. Lawless here overnight. His car would be parked in her drive and I would sometimes see him leave in the early morning.''

"Shameless!'' I said.

"What else do you want to know?''

"Did mail keep coming for her?''

"Yes, until I filled out a permanent change-of-address card and signed her name to it. I had it sent to the Atlanta address she gave me when she rented Melody Three. Of course, I have told all of this so many times that—"

"Did she have any particular friends among the other renters?"

"Not one that I know of."

"And you would know."

"I like to think so. After the projects for which Mr. Lawless had hired her were indefinitely delayed, we thought she would probably go right back to Atlanta, but she stayed on. She would go over onto our beach for a little while every day, and she would swim in the pool. I know that quite a few men tried to strike up a conversation with her. She was quite . . . noticeable in her swimming attire. But she never responded at all."

"What do you think happened to her, Mr. Moran?"

"Why do you want to know what I *think?*"

"Why do you always answer a question with a question?"

"Do I? Excuse me. My wife and I think she ran away with Mr. Lawless. We think they are living in Mexico under new names."

"Why would she leave her profession?"

"Because of being in love with Mr. Lawless, I would guess. Anyway, I don't know that she was really good at being an architect. They say that the other things she has designed were really not great successes. They say she wasn't in great demand, actually."

"Did she leave owing you money?"

"Heavens, no! We ask for the first and the last two months in advance. Technically you could say she was paid up through this month, through May."

"Did she pay by check on an Atlanta bank?"

"Yes. I can tell you which bank. Just a moment. I noted it on my copy of the lease."

He got it out of the file. "The first check was for fifteen hundred and sixty dollars, including tax, on Atlanta Southern Bank and Trust, check number eight-twenty, account number four-four-eight, four-four-one."

I wrote it down and said, "You keep good records."

"Thank you, mister—"

"McGee," I said, moving toward the door. "And thank you for everything."

"No trouble at all," he said. "Any time."

The world is full of contention and contentious people. They will not tell you the time of day or day of the month without their little display of hostility. I have argued with Meyer about it. It is more than a reflex, I think. It is an affirmation of importance. Each one is saying, "I can afford to be nasty to you because I don't need any favors from you, buster." It is also, perhaps, a warped application of today's necessity to be cool. Stan Moran in his half glasses and brush cut and improvised office, managing the Vista in order to save rent, was all too conscious of being nobody, and it had curdled him. I guessed he would have some sort of disability pension from somewhere. Or maybe he was a retired enlisted man who had been company clerk for too many abusive officers. If I were King of the World I would roam my kingdom in rags, incognito, dropping fortunes onto the people who are nice with no special reason to be nice, and having my troops lop off the heads of the mean, small, embittered little bastards who try to inflate their self-esteem by stomping on yours. I would start the lopping among post-office employees, bank tellers, bus drivers, and pharmacists. I would go on to checkout clerks, bellboys, prowl-car cops, telephone operators, and U.S. Embassy clerks. By God, there would be so many heads rolling here and there, the world would look like a berserk bowling alley. Meyer says this shows a tad of hostility.

*   *   *

As Meyer was not yet back, I decided to walk all the way around to the Cedar Pass Marina and take a look at the *Julie* and have a couple of words with DeeGee Walloway, resident aboard. It was a fine time of day for walking, and there was lots to look at around that great curve of Bay Street. I whistled one of my tuneless tunes, strode my loose-jointed, ambling, ground-covering way, squinted when the sun shone between the buildings on the bay shore. I smiled at a brown cocky city dog and nodded at a fish-house cat nested into a windowsill. Gulls tipped and dipped, yelling derision and dirty gull-words. Steel tools made music when dropped on concrete floors. Cars and trucks belched blue, gunning at the lights. A paste-white lady with sulfur curls, wearing bullfighter pants and a leopard top, slouched in a doorway and gave me a kissy-looking smile. Spillane had shot her in the stomach a generation ago, and she was still working the streets. I told her it was a lovely evening and kept going. Even the wind-sped half-sheet of newsprint that wrapped itself around my ankle had some magic meaning, just beyond the edge of comprehension. I picked it off and read that firebombs had crisped four more West German children, that 30 percent of Florida high-school graduates couldn't make change, and 50 percent couldn't comprehend a traffic citation. I read that unemployment was stabilized, UFOs had been seen over Elmira, the latest oil spill was as yet unidentified, and, to make a room look larger, use cool colors on the walls, such as blues and greens and grays.

I wadded it to walnut size and threw it some fifteen feet at a trash container. The swing lid of the trash container was open about an inch and a half. If it went in, I would live forever. It didn't even touch the edges as it disappeared inside. I wished it was all a sound stage, that the orchestra was out of sight. I wished I was Gene Kelly. I wished I could dance.

*   *   *

I went into the marina office. It was shipshape, clean, efficient-looking. The man in white behind the desk looked like a Lufthansa pilot. "Sir?" he said with measured smile.

"My name is McGee. I phoned from Lauderdale earlier in the week, about dock space for a houseboat."

He flipped through his cards. "Yes. The arrival date was indefinite. I have it here you will arrive between the twenty-fifth, next Wednesday, and the twenty-ninth. Let me see. Marjory took the call. I assume she told you it is no problem this time of year. Fifty-three feet. *The Busted Flush?*"

"As in poker, not as in plumbing."

"Length of stay indefinite?"

"That's correct. I'll let you people know as soon as I know." I hesitated, and decided to try it out. "Captain Van Harder is bringing her around for me."

It did startle him. The eyes of eagles clouded for a moment. The muscles of the square jaw worked. "I probably should not say anything to you. Van is as good as there is around here. I don't think he should have lost his license. Did you know he had?"

"Yes."

"This is something a lot of people do not know—if you hire a man to operate your boat and he doesn't have a license, if there is any trouble, you might have difficulty with your insurance company."

"I knew him years ago when he fished charter out of Bahia Mar at Lauderdale, before he went into shrimp and had his bad luck. He's bringing it around as a favor to me. No hiring involved and no passengers aboard. So I think it's okay."

He nodded. "I would think it's okay too."

"What is the status of the *Julie?*"

"The legal status? Clouded. The bank has put a lien on her. So she just sits, God knows how long. I know that nobody is going to move her until we get our dock rental. The mate is living aboard."

"Is he there now?"

He started to say he didn't know, but a smallish, dark, and pretty woman came in from the room behind the office. He introduced us. She remembered my call. He asked Marjory if she'd seen Walloway leave the marina and she said she thought he was still aboard.

I remembered the *Julie* from having seen her at Pier 66. She looked even better in the dying day. She sparkled from one end to the other. The brightwork was like mirrors. Varnish gleamed. Lines were smartly coiled, all the fenders perfectly placed. The boat basin had two main docks at right angles to the shoreline, with finger piers extending out on either side of the main docks. Small stuff was moored at the finger piers between the two docks, where there was less maneuvering room. The *Julie* was on the outside of the left-hand dock, moored to one of the middle finger piers, stern toward the dock, starboard against the finger pier.

A hinged section of rail was turned back amidships to make space for the little boarding ramp. Its wheels moved very slightly as the breeze moved the hull of the vessel.

DeeGee Walloway came toward the ramp, stuffing his keys into the pocket of his tight whipcord cowboy pants. He wore boots, a silver-gray shirt with lots of piping and pearl buttons, a blue neckerchief, and a Saturday-night cowboy hat. He looked like Billy Carter, except he was half again as tall and twice as broad.

I knew at once why that name had rung a small bell in the back of my head. He stopped and stared at me. He snapped his fingers, rubbed his mouth, shoved his hat back, and said, "McGee!"

"How you, Deej?"

"Son of a bitch! Hey, is Van bringing your houseboat around from the other side?"

"Word sure gets around."

"What happened, he phoned Eleanor Ann the other day, and she said he sounded a little more up than he has lately, and he told her everything would be working out for him, but I don't see how the hell it can. He told her he was bringing a houseboat around—and it would take maybe seven or eight days—for a fellow name of McGee he used to know in Lauderdale. So I figured it might just be the same one. I only knew you that one time, but I never forgot it."

Somebody had brought him to Meyer's annual birthday chili bash one year. After enough drinks he had decided to whip people. He told me later that it usually came out that way. Not ugly, not loud, not mean. Just an urge to whip people for the fun of it. If I had gotten him fresh, I don't think I could have handled it. But he had whipped Jack Case and Howie Villetti before Chookie looked me up and told me some jerk named Walloway was spoiling the party. Jack and Howie had put quite a strain on Deej. He had a little sprain in his neck that made him hold his head funny, and he wasn't going to be able to see out of his left eye much longer. We had the party that year on a sandspit called Instant Island. He was grinning and chuckling. He was a happy man, doing what he liked best. I spent a disheartening fifteen minutes before he finally stayed down. He came at me the next day and, because I had learned his tricks, it took about ten minutes. He came at me the third day, and that was the day I saw one coming at me so late that all I could do was duck my head into it. It broke his hand and left me with double vision for two weeks.

"I just *know*," he said, "that I should have been able to whip you."

"No, DeeGee. No. Get your mind off it."

"It still bothers me. But what the hell. I'm not in no kind of shape like I was then. Look at the gut on me. And I hardly got any wind at all. You, you look like you're in training for something. You get yourself lean and mean to come over see old DeeGee Walloway?"

"Get your mind off it."

"The only way I could take you now is sucker-punch you first. And that isn't my style. There's no fun in that."

"Can you whip everybody in Timber Bay?"

"Pretty much most of them."

"Nicky Noyes?"

"Oh, *hell*, yes! He hits like he was throwing rocks, but he don't aim. What you doing right now? Want to walk around to a couple of places and check the action? We can find us some ass and bring it back here to the boat. It isn't widespread like you got it in Lauderdale, but it's around if you look. That's what I was planning on, it being Saturday night."

"Can I take a look at the *Julie?* Don't mean to trouble you."

"Hell, no trouble."

He gave me the tour. I looked it all over. In spite of my protests, I had to look at the engines. He lifted the hatch and shone a light on the big GM diesels. The daylight was almost gone.

"A man could *eat* off that block there," he said proudly. "That's one thing ol' Van always yapped about. And I ain't slacked off an inch since he got busted."

"What's going to happen to her?"

"God only knows. The bank is giving me walk-around money for staying aboard her and keeping her up. I expect they'll get the title cleared and sell her."

"I understand you were out of town when the trouble happened."

"That's right. I was up to Waycross, where I come from. My daddy was bad off. It had been coming on a long time, but he was a stubborn old coot. He got hoarse and it hurt him to swaller. And his neck started getting bigger. My mom noticed that and she nagged him and nagged him until he went to the doctor. Soon as the doctor told him he wasn't a-going to make it, my daddy started going fast. He was nearly gone when I got there, but he could smile and nod at me, and write words on a pad. You know, I never made that man happy with me. Not one time. I damn almost did when I got into the University of Georgia on a football scholarship, but then I got throwed out of the first two games I got into. I was a right tackle, and then I got throwed out of the school itself, signed on in the Navy, and got throwed out of that for discipline problems. He wanted so bad for me to be somebody. But, shit, I'm all I want to be. I think my daddy lasted two days and a half or so after I heard Mr. Lawless got lost overboard. I was holding his hand there at the end. His hand gave this little quiver and then lay slack. Felt weird."

I went forward to the spot where Lawless was supposed to have fallen overboard. There was a bow rail, braided cable threaded through stanchions, ending abruptly about eight feet from the bow, where the cable was angled down from the final stanchion and made fast to a fitting in the deck. So, if he was on the starboard side, say about seven feet back from the bow and pointed out to the right, bracing himself for the vessel to turn sharp left, and it had instead turned sharp right, then the angled cable would have hit him in the shins and he would have tripped over into the chop and into the night's blackness. They had worked the story out nicely.

"Seen enough?" he asked. "Let's go get a drink, McGee."

As we walked by the lighted office, the little dark-haired lady waved. "Don't futz with that one there," DeeGee said. "Marjory is Coop's old lady. He's the one right there, in the white, runs the place. She acts like she'd fool around, but she doesn't."

"What do you think about the Hub Lawless situation?"

"I wouldn't tell you this if you weren't my friend. Anybody whips me like you did, they're my friend. I think they decided there was no way they could buy Van off. He's straight. So they give him a mickey. Hell, I know the routine. Whenever we got rolling, whenever we settled into cruising speed, Mr. Lawless would bring a couple of drinks topside, one for me and one for Van. He'd check the dials and the course and look around at the weather and either stay with us and have his drink up topside with us, or go on back below with whoever he had aboard."

"Women passengers?"

"No way. Not even that Norway ass he got mixed up with. Jumpin' B. Jesus, but I would have liked me a chop at that one. She was steamy, I'm telling you. She had a fire burned all the time. A tilty little swivel-ass like to break your heart, and she knew it and she waved it. And really great wheels. Mr. Lawless got into that and stopped giving a damn for much of anything else, and no man would blame him too much. But he never brought her aboard. I couldn't hardly believe that he and John Tuckerman had Mishy and that Mexican friend of hers aboard. Mishy is okay. I'd guess offhand that Tuckerman chopped her once in a while. She isn't exactly a pro, but she likes to work you, you know? She needs room rent, or some damn thing, or something to send her poor old mother for her birthday. The way I see it, it was easy to give Van a mickey because of the way Mr. Lawless always gave him a drink. The two girls were below, and I think they were just to dress up the act a little. I think there was somebody in a boat waiting for him to jump, and they took him to an airplane somewhere, maybe a seaplane. They say he took off with a million dollars. You can buy a lot of help for a small piece of that kind of money.''

"And he's in Mexico?"

"Sure. He went there a lot. Him and John Tuckerman, hunting, fishing, horsing around. They were best friends of each other. John has been way into the sauce ever since. Bombed out of his mind. What did he ever have besides being Hub's best friend?"

"You liked Lawless?"

"Hell, yes. *Everybody* that worked for him liked him. It really hurt him bad when he had to start laying people off from the businesses he ran. And I know for a fact he was trying to sell the *Julie*. Some people came aboard and looked her over. But it's hard to move a boat like that. She won't suit people with really big money, and she's too much for the average boat fella. I guess if he'd sold her, he'd have had to disappear some other way that would look like he died, so the insurance would go to Mrs. Lawless and the girls.''

"Did they come out on the boat much?"

"His family? Oh, sure. But a lot oftener before than after things started to get tight for him. I mean you can run a lot of dollars through those diesels just to move that thing out for an afternoon picnic. She's way overdue for bottom work right now, too. Like the man said, if you have to ask, you can't afford it.''

He stopped and motioned me ahead of him, and we went into a place called Lucille's. It was long and dark, with a mahogany bar, a brass rail, sawdust, spittoons, Victorian nudes in gilt frames, bowls of salted peanuts, and a game show on the television perched over the far end of the bar. Lucille squeezed past one of her bartenders to come down toward the entrance and take care of us herself. She was roughly the same size as Walloway, and of only slightly different dimensions. She wore what looked at first glance like a blue bath-robe. She had curly shiny black hair, like a poodle. Her face was white and stiff as wallboard, and she wore lots of eye makeup and lots of burgundy lipstick. I guessed her at about sixty.

"No thumping anybody tonight, Deej!" she ordered in a whiskey contralto.

"Meet my friend name of McGee. He whipped me three times."

She looked me over. "Looks as if he could do it again if he had a mind to. Welcome to my place. Deej, you start anything, you can bet your bucket I'm calling the law early.''

"I was only funnin', honey."

"What would you done to him was you serious?"

"I've never been serious in my whole life. Double Bellows and a Millers chaser.'' I settled for the chaser. He was almost offended, but I explained I had other places to go and I didn't want to start more than I could arrange to finish. I said the previous night was still too fresh in my memory, what I remembered of it.

He told Lucille we had been talking about Lawless and Tuckerman. "If I had a shiny dime for every time I've heard those names in the last two months, I could quit and live ladylike," she said.

"Seen John Tuckerman lately?" he asked her.

"No. He's down to that shack on that land nine miles south Hub bought for his girl friend to design apartments on, and they say his sister is there and she has got him dried out and she's keeping him dry, but his brains are still mush. I don't never want to see him back in here. He was flat-out pitiful. I don't want to see people that make me sorry I sell the stuff. I don't need that kind of guilts. I got more than enough other kinds to go around."

"Did you know Hubbard Lawless?"

"*Everybody* knew Hub. The business people in this town, of which I am one, aren't never going to find it easy to forgive him for what he done to the town. He left us in a depression here. Everything is tied into everything else, and when something quits, other things get hard up on account of it. They say we got fourteen percent unemployment here, and I can feel it in my gross, believe me. But at the same time, everybody knows Hub worked hard to make things work, and he did things for the good of the place too. He contributed to everything when he was doing well. Community Chest, Boys' Club, Cedar Pass Park, bandstand, the Pirate Pageant. He didn't keep regular hours. He was out at that ranch by dawn. He'd work at getting stuff shipped in the middle of the night. Nobody ever knew when that man slept. He always had a smile and a little joke. The way it looks to me, when he got the money for Hula Marine, he should have used it to shore up the other businesses instead of buying the wrong land at the wrong time for the shopping center and that condominium thing."

"What you forget, Lucille," DeeGee said, "he wasn't thinking straight. He had a bad case of nooky disease."

"I don't allow dirty talk in here, and you know it."

"I would have said it nice if I knowed how, Lucille, dammit. You know as well as I do that architect woman had him going in circles."

"Well," she said, "nobody is perfect, and I hope that wherever he is, Mexico or wherever, he's found some kind of peace, because he sure got awful jumpy before he took off. The town will make out. People will keep coming down from the north. Things will keep going. They always have."

"You have a kind heart, Lucille," DeeGee said.

"Not kind enough to set you up a freebie."

"Okay. Hit me again anyway. Same thing. You, McGee?"

I excused myself and left. He seemed disappointed to have me go. I imagine he got over it in about forty seconds. It would take him about that long to get a good look at the two young women who were going in as I was leaving.

12

I FOUND Meyer in a booth in the lounge. Business was better than usual. Billy Jean Bailey was tinkling away at her compulsory background-music stint, with no one listening. She looked at me and through me, with no change of expression, and looked away, smiling and nodding at someone else.

After I brought a drink back to the booth, Meyer reported on the rental Mazda.

"I had to wait quite a while for Mr. Wedley. He was out with the tow truck on a pickup. Shorthanded. The boy pumping gas did not know anything about anything. When Wedley came back he was busy on the phone for ten minutes. Finally he was able to tell me about the Mazda. Five days after Lawless disappeared, he got a collect call from airport administration at Orlando. The car had been left in rental car return with the keys behind the sun visor. No one knew when it had been left. Airport administration got into it when Hertz complained that it was their space and they needed it. Garner Wedley's Texaco station address and phone was on the key tag, so they had phoned him and he had arranged to get it picked up. He said that Bonus Rental was a small operation and he had an area franchise, and it said on the rental contract that the car had to be returned to him, but it wasn't. It made him angry to talk about. He said that Hub had rented it for that Scandihoovian female of his, and it worked out to ninety-five seventy-five Hub owed him that he would never see. He told the Sheriff about it, and after an investigation the Sheriff said that it was reasonable to assume that Miss Petersen had driven the car to Orlando, arriving during the morning of the twenty-fourth. He had obtained a picture of her, from the files of the *Bay Journal*, taken when Lawless had given a press party to announce the plans for the new shopping plaza, and had carried the picture over to Orlando and questioned the airline personnel, but found no one who remembered her. He questioned the rental-car people as well, because it has apparently become a popular device to abandon an automobile in an airport parking area and immediately rent another and drive away. Did you know that?"

"Not until this minute."

"If there is any point in it, I suppose we could get one of those pictures from Walter Olivera. But we seem to be getting far afield from Van Harder's problem."

"We are and we aren't. I don't think anybody in authority would take anything Tuckerman might say seriously enough to get Harder some kind of reconsideration. One thing we might do is ask that doctor if Harder's symptoms were consistent with the brand of horse tranquilizer Lawless used at the ranch."

Meyer looked into his notebook, thumbing the pages over. "Here it is. Dr. Sam Stuart. Tuckerman's doctor too, apparently. Shall I make a note of that for Monday? And do it myself?"

"Who else have you got written down there, that we should see?"

"There's Van Harder's wife. Eleanor Ann Harder. She's a nurse at Bay General. And the insurance investigator. I found out his name, by the way. Frederic Tannoy. The company is Planters Mutual General. Tannoy is a troubleshooter for a consortium of middle-sized insurance companies, working on a fee-and-percentage basis. The local agent who sold the policies is a general agent named Ralph Stennenmacher, in the Coast National building."

"Tannoy is with that deputy in Mexico," I said. "Meanwhile, I'll see Stennenmacher on Monday."

B. J. Bailey walked past our booth, giving me one brilliantly venomous glance as she went by. It depressed me. I often wonder what basic insecurity I must have to make me so anxious for approval. I touched the tape over my eye. It had not been entrapment, or even pursuit. No promises made. It had been a happening, not important, happening only because of the time and the place and the shared, nagging sense of depression. There in the yellow-glowing darkness, she had been small, limber, greedy, slightly sweaty, her hair stiff from sprayings, humming with her pleasures and making them last. I knew the reason for the hate. No matter how she thought of herself, she was a severely conventional little person and could not accept pleasure for the sake of pleasure, but had to cloak it in romantic rationalization. Like one of her lyrics—it must be love because it feels so good.

I found it ironic that I shared her disease, that puritanical necessity to put acceptable labels on things. The quick jump had always made me feel uneasy. Life cannot become a candy box without some kind of retribution from the watchful gods. I had shared her bed with such a familiar anticipation of the uneasiness that would follow that I had been unable to enjoy her completely. This is the penalty paid by the demipagans, always to have the pleasures diluted by the apprehensions, unless all the labels are in order.

She had found the only label which permitted her all the customary fictions. She was woman betrayed by a scoundrel, a low fellow who had won her with promises, promises, and then turned his back on all her bounty. I leaned out of the booth and looked for her, saw her in the center of a small group of men, laughing with them, drinking with them, eyes a-sparkle. I decided that, when the chance occurred, I would give her a further fiction to apply like a fresh dressing to her pride. Maybe I was in danger and sought to avoid endangering her. Or I was an alcoholic, or dying of something, or had a wife and six kiddies—anything, in fact, which would fit into your average morning soap opera as something worth dramatic dialogue. Meanwhile I would have to accept being an object of hatred, one of your good old boys, one of your male-chauvinist-pig types that went around thinking of women as being something you used when you felt the need, receptacles rather than persons.

"As I was saying," Meyer said.

"Sorry about that."

"Now that I have your attention, let's go over the actual movements of the vehicles and people, as we understand it at the moment. Let this matchbook be the beach cottage. And this one be the Vista. And this one way over here is Orlando. This match is the jeep. This match is the car Tuckerman no longer has. This match is the Petersen Mazda. Here is Tuckerman driving down to the cottage on the morning of the twenty-third to find that Lawless is still there, and sick. Here he goes back to the Vista. He stays there. Kristin goes down to the cottage in the Mazda, let us say in the late morning of the twenty-third. Tuckerman stays away, as Lawless asked, and goes back on the twenty-fifth or -sixth, and finds nothing. The Mazda had been driven to Orlando, where it was discovered on the twenty-seventh. Now let's see how many assumptions we can make about the vanished jeep."

"How many? Lawless recovered enough to drive it on south, over that bad portion of the road, down to Horseshoe Beach, and then he cut over to the main road, and went on down to an airport somewhere, and flew to Mexico."

"And if he didn't recover enough to drive?"

"Let me see. Kristin drove to the cottage on the afternoon of the twenty-third. She finds he is too sick to drive. If he wasn't, they could have stayed with the original plan, for her to hang around mourning her drowned boy-friend for a week or so before following him to Mexico. But with him too sick, she goes back to the Vista after dark, packs, loads the stuff into the Mazda, and comes down and gets him. She could have had him in the back with the luggage, covered with a blanket or something, when they went back through town. They abandoned the Mazda in Orlando, took a flight to Miami, let's say, traveling separately, and flew Mexicana from there over to Cancun, Yucatan."

"You've developed an interesting point, Travis. About their adhering to the original plan if he was well enough to drive the jeep. But what happened to the jeep, if we follow your scenario?"

I shrugged. "Ran it into the swamps or into a deep pond."

"If he wasn't well enough to drive, he wasn't well enough to hide a jeep."

"I see her as an intelligent woman, and physically competent. It wouldn't be anything she couldn't handle."

"Let me change your scenario in one respect. Rather than make two trips out to the cottage in a conspicuous red car, she could have brought Lawless back in with her when she packed up her belongings and left her apartment."

"I'll buy that. It was dark when she drove back. It's a better guess than two trips."

We sat at the booth, staring at the matchbook covers and the matches. "Whichever," I said, "he got to Mexico."

"Whichever," Meyer said, nodding.

There was a deep-throated din of male voices in the big room. Piano tinkle had begun again. I did not want the half drink left in my glass. My stomach felt close to rebellion. This room was not real. It seemed misted and murky, like the contrived visuals in French movies of the second class. Nine miles south reality began, in the long flowing line, that most gentle curve, of the top of a caramel thigh. It began in flecks of gold set close to the black pupil. It began with that elegant balance of the upper body on the pelvic structure, moving in grace to a long long stride.

"Who *was* Gretel?" I asked Meyer.

"She was pretty shrewd. She held an old chicken bone out of the cage for the witch to feel, to hide the fact she was getting plump enough to cook and eat."

"How about a nice beach picnic tomorrow?"

"Nine miles from here?"

He looked at his notebook again. "Eleanor Ann, Stennenmacher, Dr. Stuart."

"Monday we see them. Okay? Monday."

When we walked out of the place, Noyes lurched into me. It seemed half intentional, half inadvertent. He was sweating heavily. His pistolero mustache looked dank and defeated. He had a pale blue guayabera on, so wet the matted chest hair showed through it. The flinty little Neanderthal eyes stared at me, hostile and slightly unfocused.

"B.J. told me the whole thing, you son of a bitch."

"Hey. Take it easy."

"Don't tell me how to take anything, nark."

"Nark?"

"And it's supposed to look like I resisted arrest, right? You don't like people out on bail, right?"

"You must be drunk."

"Check with Mitch. I haven't had drink one."

"Get out of the way, please."

"You think I'm going to let you kill me?"

"You are boring us, Nicky. You are boring me and you are boring my friend Meyer. And you were boring the people at your table at the Cove last night. You are making a new career out of boring people."

"You want to come outside?"

"Walloway says you can hit, but you can't aim. Save yourself a short walk."

He stepped sideways to catch his balance, putting a hand out to grab at the edge of the bar. He muttered something I could not quite hear.

*   *   *

We left. Meyer said we were in a rut, but we might as well try the Captain's Galley again. We were in no special hurry. I looked back and was surprised to see Nicky Noyes, burly in the shadows, following us toward the lot. I stopped and he stopped. Meyer missed me and turned and saw him.

"What's he going to do?" Meyer asked.

"Nothing at all. Trying to bug me a little, I guess."

We went on and he followed. When I looked back again, he was angling over toward his pickup truck. As we neared the gray rental Dodge, I heard the pickup door chunk shut. We reached the Dodge. Meyer reached for the door handle on the passenger side as I took a stride to walk around the front. I heard a very small squeak of tennis shoe rubber on asphalt. I heard a dual *snick-snick*, oily and metallic and horridly efficient. There is some good elemental machinery in my skull, left over from the million years of hunting, of eating and being eaten. I am delighted to have that machinery. If I didn't have it, I would long since have been forcibly retired from my line of work. Primitive computers worked out the direction of the sound, the distance, the probable angle of fire. I spun and dived in a flat trajectory at right angles to the line of fire. My shoulder hit the partially open door and slammed it shut again, a microsecond before I hit Meyer at mid-thigh and tumbled him and myself all the way back to a point six feet behind the right rear wheel. There was a bright-throated *blam-blam,* two great sounds not quite simultaneous, deafeningly close to us, and as I rolled up to one knee I saw Nicky Noyes stagger back and fall heavily.

He broke the gun open, fumbled something out of his pocket, snapped the old shotgun shut again just as I ran through the powder stink, caught the warm double barrels, and ripped it out of his hands.

"Kill you!" he yelled in a raw high voice as he was struggling up. "Kill you!" He turned and ran. For a fellow so unsteady on his feet, he was running pretty good. He was barreling right along. He ran right toward the long curve of Bay Street. Traffic was heavy and fairly fast.

"Oh, no," Meyer said softly, beside me.

Nicky tripped slightly just before he reached the curbing. He went out into traffic in that head-down, forward-tilting manner of the fullback when it's third and one. He ran his head, shoulders, and chest across the hood of a big pale Cadillac, and the front right post of the windshield hit him at waist level. It was slanted enough to hurl him into the air, and more slanted after it had done so. It was almost horizontal, with the white roof buckled into big lumps. His momentum and the impact threw him farther out into traffic, with one sodden bounce and then a floppy roll. Tires of a half-dozen vehicles screamed torment. There were two heavy metallic chunking noises of rear-end collisions, also some thinner sounds as grilles gnashed at fenders. The pale Cadillac had swerved violently to the right to miss running over what remained of Noyes. It came across the curbing and wedged itself between a pair of young banyan trees. People began the yelling and the screaming. People ran out of the North Bay Resort. A car horn began a seemingly endless braying.

I put the shotgun on the front seat of the pickup. I trotted after Meyer. A trucker was lighting some highway flares and setting them out. Meyer hurried toward Noyes, then swerved and galloped to the pale Cadillac. It hadn't wedged itself between the trees as far as the doors. In the reflected brightness of headlights and the red glow of the flares, I saw a white-haired man slumped against the horn ring and, beyond him, crouched low under the bent post and car roof, a plump blond lady. When Meyer eased the man back off the ring, the huge horn-noise ceased.

"He ran right in front of us!" the woman shrilled. "Right in front of the car!"

Meyer stuck his fingers into the side of the driver's throat. He looked at me and shook his head. And so, ignoring the woman, we tugged that old gentleman out of his Cadillac and stretched him out supine on the nearest flat ground. Meyer knelt on the left side near the shoulders and put his left hand under the nape of the man's neck, his right palm on the man's forehead. He pulled up on the neck and pushed down on the forehead to give the head a pronounced backward tilt and clear the airway. He put his ear close to the man's mouth and looked along the chest as he did so, to detect any movement. I knelt at the man's right side and found the place to brace the heel of my right hand, two finger widths above the sternum, left hand atop right hand, elbows straight and locked. Meyer checked the pulse again and gave three quick exhalations into the man's mouth, holding the nose clamped shut with the thumb and finger of his right hand.

After the third exhalation, I began my chore, pushing down hard and releasing, saying my cadence out loud. "One—and—two—and—three—and—four—and—five—and—one—and—two—" I pushed down on the number, released on the "and." The cadence was ninety pushes a minute. When the heart stops, irreversible brain damage starts after four minutes. I guess he'd been about forty seconds to a minute from the time of cardiac arrest until we went to work on him. The air we breathe in is about 21 percent oxygen. The air we exhale is about 15 percent oxygen. Meyer was oxygenating the lungs. I was pumping the heart by compressing it between the sternum and the spine. Done properly, this can establish a blood pressure and an oxygenation of the brain adequate to sustain the brain undamaged.

The woman was not making things any easier. She had crawled out of the car and was dancing around us, yelling, "Get a doctor! Get an ambulance! Stop that! Stop that this minute!"

She tugged at me and then at Meyer, and between breaths he yelled at her, "I am a doctor, madam!"

"Is he dead?" she yelled. "Is he? Is he?"

We had attracted a part of the crowd. The crowd was fragmented, watching different parts of the show, as at a carnival midway. A couple of women in our crowd grabbed the wife and hauled her away.

I kept counting, and at one point I felt a gentle crackling sound under my hands and knew it was some ribs going. When it is properly done, you will almost always break some ribs. The choice is clear—a dead person with nice whole ribs, or a potentially alive person with some rib fractures. I checked the position of my hands and kept going. I wondered where the hell the official medics were. Suddenly the unconscious man vomited. Meyer, leaning toward him, caught quite a bit of it. Meyer did what everyone does in such circumstances. He turned aside and threw up too. A husky kid about sixteen dropped to his knees beside Meyer and swabbed the man's mouth with tissue, rolled his head to the side and then back. Meyer tried to give the next breath and couldn't manage it. The kid muscled him aside and took over, doing the job with perfect timing. It is essential not to break the rhythm, because it can set the person way back. Meyer got up slowly, gagging and coughing. I heard the sirens coming. We kept going. Though it seemed longer, I imagine we gave that man cardiopulmonary resuscitation for about twelve to fourteen minutes before the medics moved in with their specialized equipment and their direct electronic links to hospital Emergency.

Ambulances were soon leaving. Tow trucks were untangling the torn metal. The flares were extinguished, traffic resumed, and the spectators began drifting away.

The kid said, "That's the first time I used it for real. You done it often, mister?"

"Second time for me. The first was a drowning. Didn't make it."

"You take the CPR course?" he asked.

"Nobody should ever try cardiopulmonary resuscitation without taking the course. You could do more harm than good."

"That's what they told us too. You think that old guy will make it?"

"I hope so," I said. I saw B. J. Bailey heading back toward the main building of the Resort, and I hurried and stopped her by clamping a hand on her shoulder.

She turned and said, "And what the hell do you want?"

"I want to know how you got Nicky so charged up about me. What the hell did you tell him?"

"I didn't tell him anything."

"Listen to me, Billy Jean. Whatever you told him, it made him come after us with a shotgun. He shot to kill. Believe me. He missed. He tried to reload. I took the gun away from him. He ran out into traffic and got hit and killed."

"Killed!" she said, aghast. "You're joking. You got to be joking."

"You killed him, Billy Jean."

We stood near a driveway lamp, and it shone pale yellow across her small face. Her mouth broke and she hunched her shoulders high. "No, I didn't! I didn't! I told him you came here after him. He gets kind of weird about maybe there are people after him. He's on crystal. It makes people like that. I thought he would fight again, is all. I thought maybe he'd beat you up this time. I didn't think he would . . . oh, no. Oh, no."

She stood hunched and sobbing.

I gave her some clumsy pats on the back and said, "Look, I didn't mean to hurt your feelings last night."

"You came back here with . . ."

"I know, I know. That was dumb. I do some very dumb things like that. Frequently. Forget you ever knew me."

"I can't stop thinking about Nicky. I just can't. I can't work tonight. Oh, Jesus. Look. One thing. You get the hell away from me. Okay? Get away and stay away. Okay?" She glared up at me out of her grief-swollen face. I stood and watched her walk away.

Meyer came up behind me and said, "More diplomacy?"

"Are you all right?"

"I'm going up to the room for a few minutes. Where will you be?"

"Right here, waiting for the Sheriff."

"You called?" Sheriff Ames said, at my elbow. He said we could both come with him—sit in his car and chat a while. I explained Meyer's problem, and he pointed to where he was parked and let Meyer go to freshen up.

13

I TOLD him the story while we sat in his car waiting for Meyer to return. When Meyer returned, he had Meyer tell it again. He got the shotgun out of the pickup and found the right barrel loaded with a fresh shell of number 12. We went over and studied the rental Dodge. The first barrel had blown a hunk the size of a cantaloupe out of the right front tire at seven o'clock. For a time we couldn't find where the second one had gone, and it was Meyer who spotted the tiny streaks of ricochet atop the mound of the trunk cover. So he had been swinging it when he fired, and the first one had slain the tire and kicked the muzzle up, so that only the bottom few pellets of the pattern touched the trunk when the rest of them sailed off toward the tennis courts. I could estimate that the second pattern had been directly over us as we tumbled past the rear of the car. I had one skinned elbow and the knee was gone out of my slacks. Meyer had taken a crack on the back of the head and slid through grease on his behind.

Ames drove us to the hospital, and we went in through Emergency. Meyer and I sat in wicker chairs in a small waiting room while Ames went wandering off after information. The clock ticked. Nurses rustled by. A child was crying. The available magazines were devoted to health, diet, maintaining the right attitude toward life, and how to manage a hospital. Two young, thin black girls came in and sat on the couch, hugging each other and sniffling. A nurse came and got them, and a little while later I heard a terrible grieving desolate scream, and wondered if it had come from one of them.

Ames sauntered back in, pale, worn, and dusty-looking, a drab man of no particular emphasis or importance. He sat and said, "They're still working on Noyes, still operating on him, but I get the feeling they're giving up. Now they're doing what's called the practice of medicine, with Dr. Ted Scudder running the show. He'll come on down here shortly, I'd say."

"What about that old man?"

"That was a Mr. and Mrs. Whittaker Davis, from Watertown, New York, looking for a place to retire. Safe to say it won't be here."

"Was?" Meyer asked. "Or is?"

"Oh. Sorry. Is. At least for now. They're breathing for him, but they've got heart action. He's in cardiac intensive care, all wired up to the machinery." He turned so as to look directly at Meyer, frowning. "His wife says a man who looks like you, who worked on him, and who would be you, wouldn't it?—she said he said he was a doctor. There's a law I'd have to look up about impersonating a licensed profession."

"I'm a doctor," Meyer said. "I didn't tell her my specialty."

"What would that be?"

"Economics. I misled Mrs. Davis. Guilty. She was trying to interrupt the CPR."

"They say you knew what you were doing."

"We are DC Number Two Basic Rescuers, both of us," Meyer said proudly. He gave me a smug nod. I sighed. He had insisted. He had nagged at me until I agreed. What was the result? Two dreadful hours of hard labor on a drowned and dark blue girl before finally the professionals had shown up and told us we were wasting our time. She was gone. And now a dying old man whose ribs I had broken. Great.

A round, weary, red-faced man dressed in operating-theater green came scuffing in and collapsed into a wicker chair. There was a brown spatter of blood across his chest. His plastic mask dangled. He shoved his little green hat back, took his glasses off, and began cleaning them on a tissue. "Official time of death, Hack, make it nine twenty-five. Ten minutes ago. But he was dead as chopped liver the minute the car hit him. Busted all to hell inside. Ripped and ruptured. Liver, spleen, kidney, bowel. He was nearly torn in half. The certificate will say internal injuries."

The Sheriff introduced us, explaining that we were in town on business, seeking to arrange the purchase of some of the Lawless holdings.

The Sheriff said, "I told them up there I want a blood sample and urine sample to go to the lab. Damn fool ran right into traffic. Check for booze and foreign substances, I told them, and they'll tell my deputy when he gets over here."

Scudder got up and sighed. "My turn in the barrel. Four to midnight. I draw that one on Saturday night once every five weeks. Try to keep everything quiet for the rest of my tour, Hack."

"Try to."

We checked on Mr. Whittaker Davis again before leaving. No change. Because there was a fatality, possibly two, Ames wanted our statements on tape. He said they'd be typed up for signature in the next few days. Probably by Tuesday afternoon.

He made it sound like routine, but once he got me into his office and over at a small conference table at the side, with the tape all hooked up and tested, with me on record as saying I was giving the information of my own free will, he did more digging than I had anticipated. He covered my first encounter with Noyes, the absurd fight in the parking lot, the second encounter at the Cove, and what had been said back and forth on all occasions. And the third and final encounter. Very final for Nicky Noyes.

Hack Ames was good at his job. He had all the tricks. For a time I found myself going along in his rhythm, but then the alarm bells began to sound and I hauled back on my own reins. A good questioner will ask a question, get what sounds like a complete answer and sit there in silence, mildly quizzical, until you qualify or add to the answer. A good questioner will ask very simple questions requiring short and simple answers and slowly increase the pace until when he throws a curve, the silence seems to last too long, and you feel a compulsion to give an answer quickly. Any answer. A good questioner will ask a dozen questions about situation X, and then a dozen questions about situation Y, and finally he will start a series about situation Z, but the fifth question may be about Y and the seventh may be about X, questions you have already answered, but phrased just a bit differently. A good questioner will give you back your answers, twisted very slightly, and wait for the corrections. And he will ask you a question that is absurd, or grotesque, stop you before you can answer, and throw in a much better question while you are still off balance from the earlier one. There is always this problem. If you can know and anticipate and deal with the skilled questioner, you slowly begin to realize that you are doing so much bobbing and weaving that, in itself, it becomes significant. You cannot start refusing to answer. You cannot fake anger. You become aware of little inconsistencies here and there, and he gives you no chance to patch them up.

He turned off the recorder. He scratched at his dusty head, yawned, and said, "You're almost good enough, McGee."

"For what?"

"For playing games with tired old county sheriffs on a Saturday night."

"No games."

"Unless a fellow is trying to borrow money, Dev Boggs will just about believe anything you want to tell him."

"Meyer has a letter from—"

"I saw the letter he left with Boggs. I phoned that big man Friday afternoon, that Allbritton. Never could get him. Imagine if I got him, he'd back it up, but that letter, you know, doesn't really say much of anything. I checked back through your registration there at the North Bay Resort, and I called a friend over in Fort Lauderdale. He looked around and called me back. You two keep a low profile over there. This Meyer seems to make out doing talks at conferences and being a consultant once in a while."

"He's sort of an investor."

"Sure. And you are sort of a salvage consultant or some goddamn thing. And Billy Carter is a field hand."

"What are you trying to say to me, Sheriff?"

He cracked his knuckles and blinked his tired brown eyes. "What I am saying is that I get sick of being insulted. I've got a job here and I do it and I do it damn well, if statistics mean anything. For two months now I've had federal employees and state people coming into Dixie County and padding around, fumbling into this and that, screwing up the detail, living on travel and per diem, without the courtesy of checking in with me. A lot of them are supposed to be officers of the law, though what law and what office is often hard to tell. The general attitude is maybe I am involved in whatever it is they are overpaid to try to look into. Or I am some dummy barely competent to set up speed traps and arrest drunks. Hub Lawless is responsible for a whole batch of them coming in. I am getting tired of it, McGee. I am going to start throwing asses into the little slam here, and I can't see any special reason why I shouldn't start with yours. The way I read you, you are either U.S. or state level, and you are over here on the Lawless matter, or you are here on the new drug thing, and the one phone call I'm going to let you have, it better work out because you're not going to get two.''

"Wrong on all guesses," I said.

"Bullshit, McGee! You think I don't know when a man is being evasive? You think I can't recognize fancy footwork?"

"Okay, okay. Van Harder asked me to come over and see if I could find out enough to get a rehearing on his license. He's bringing my houseboat around. I got a reservation for it at the Cedar Pass Marina."

He looked startled and incredulous. "You some kind of lawyer?"

"No."

"Licensed investigator?"

"No. It's just a favor for a friend."

"A friend? How come Harder is a friend of *yours*?"

"Because he fished charter out of Bahia Mar. He had the *Queen Bee Number Three*. He sold her to a man named Fazzo when he went into shrimping. Harder was already there when I began living there. All the permanent people around a marina know each other."

"Why did he ask *you*? What qualifications have *you* got?"

I waited a while on that one and finally said, "Indignation."

"All right! Okay! It's justified. It wasn't at the time. At the time, McGee, it looked exactly like what it was supposed to look like, a reformed drunk who fell off."

"And his friendly Sheriff tried to kick him back up onto his drunken feet."

"I've been sorry about that ever since. I did it because I was angry, dammit. I like Van. It scalded me he should be such a jackass. Since then things have shaped up different. I'll go along with what he kept saying, that there had to be something in that drink Hub took up to him. All the rest of it was staged too perfect. Van could have come to me. I mean it. He can come to me and I can get that license give back to him, and I kindly think I'll go ahead and get it done anyway without his asking."

"Sheriff, if you really know Van, you know why he won't come to you."

For just an instant he looked puzzled, and then he nodded. "I know. I kicked him. Not hard or anything. But I kicked him. You don't kick a man like Van Harder. Those people that gave Hub a dollar and a half of work for every dollar of pay, they've certainly got cause to despise that man. Harder, Noyes, all of them."

We sat in silence. I wondered what on earth Meyer would be thinking, sitting out there waiting.

"I ought to chase your ass right out of my county," he said. "I really should."

"Mr. Boggs still has Meyer's letter."

"Don't try to keep conning me with that. Okay?"

"Okay."

"Maybe you decided to help Van Harder out because you knew about this case and thought you might run across some money."

"The thought crossed my mind, Sheriff."

He grinned for the first time. "Crossed a lot of minds. But it has all pretty much died down. It's pretty certain Hub is in Mexico and he took it with him, and got that lady architect with him too. Walking hand in hand into the Mexican sunset. Smiling a lot. Hard to believe Hub Lawless did that to his own town, to all of us. Wife, kids too. With them, of course, he told himself the insurance would take care of them. Except, on a big policy, they look for any loophole to keep from paying off."

"But you don't know all the answers yet, Sheriff. Things don't quite fit."

He tilted his chair back and stuck his thumbs inside his belt. He squinted at the desk top and said, "Now if I wasn't tied hand and foot by the restrictions of this office, I could churn around here and there, telling lies, making jokes, pushing buttons, hustling and scrambling. Maybe some pieces would fall out of the box and I'd get to know more. No! Don't tell me you understand a damned thing, because I don't want to hear anything about your understanding. There isn't any understanding. You might come back in here some day and have a chat, if you have some interesting conversation. I get bored a lot in here. I spent fourteen years in a car out on the roads. It gets tiresome in here."

"Before I go, it was kind of a shock to have Noyes trying very hard to kill me, or both of us."

"It knocked Nicky way off balance when Hub took off. He went away for a little while and came back with merchandise. We knew he was dealing, and we got a pretty good customer list. It's easier to keep your finger on a network you know than to try to unravel the next one that starts up. He got to hitting his own goods. Dr. Sam Stuart knows more about it than I do. He's worried all to hell lately. Something the kids are taking. We had a thirteen-year-old girl sit on a gravel pile last month and swallow gravel, a chunk at a time, until she had four pounds of rock in her belly. Weird. God only knows who'll take over where Nicky leaves off. Maybe the others we got will just start handling more."

"Meyer is waiting out there."

"Oh, sure. Send him in. It will only be a few minutes for him. I'll expect to see you around?"

I nodded. Meaning clear. See me around or he would come and get me. I went out and sent Meyer in. I sat and waited. A sturdy woman typed slowly. I could just hear the dispatcher. A gigantic deputy came in slowly and said to the woman, "What's it about?"

"You know what it's about."

"Not the damn charts again. Don't tell me it's the charts."

"You're sixteen over again, Rudy."

"But, damn it all, I'm not fat!"

"He says you got to be no more than two twenty-five. Weren't you in high school with Nick Noyes?"

"Junior and senior. Four years of him."

"He's dead."

"No shit, Marie! OD'd?"

"Hit by a tourist Cadillac while crossing the street."

"You've got to be kidding."

Meyer came out, and the deputy went in to take his chewing for being overweight. We went out and suddenly realized we had no transportation. After we phoned a taxi and stood waiting, Meyer said, "What took you so long in there?"

"He thought I was being cute about something, so he went around and around, coming in at me from new angles. He finally decided I was some kind of out-of-town law, so I told him why we're here."

"So he said go back to Lauderdale?"

"Almost. Not quite. Without saying so, he sort of appointed me official cat's-paw."

"How nice for you!"

"I didn't tell him what we've got so far."

"Which is next door to nothing at all. What we know changes nothing."

"It locates Lawless as of the next morning, ashore and alive."

"Which he is conceding anyway, Travis," Meyer said, opening the cab door.

We stopped at the Galley to make certain that it was really too late to get anything to eat, but it wasn't. Dave Bellamy said he was delighted to take care of old customers.

Good ol' Dave. He supervised the preparation of a pair of extra-dry Boodles gin martinis. Meyer looked beat. He beamed at the drink when it was placed in front of him. And, as on other occasions when the martini is badly needed, he quoted Bernard De Voto on that subject: "The rat stops gnawing in the wood, the dungeon walls withdraw, the weight is lifted. Your pulse steadies and the sun has found your heart. The day was not bad, the season has not been bad, and there is sense and even promise in going on. Prosit."

"Saved a life. Maybe," I said.

"And almost lost one or two. But didn't," he said.

"About that picnic tomorrow."

"Maybe that lithesome person hates picnics."

"She's living a picnic out there. I saw a deli next to the supermarket at Baygate Plaza Mall. I can get one of those big wicker hamper things, and a big cooler. I'll set up a picnic like she never saw before, from shrimp to champagne."

"What you're talking about is a Care package."

"What do you mean?"

"When you start hauling great quantities of food to a female person, it means you really care. It always has. I think it is some primal instinct. The hunter bringing spoils to the cave."

"Hmmm. Meyer, would it offend your sense of fitness if I called Gretel a girl?"

"Instead of a person or a woman or some such? You want to be patronizing and chauvinistic, eh? Look down upon her?"

"Cut it out, Meyer. I can go with all that approach right up to a point.

When it doesn't mean much one way or another. You know. But here we have one of the truly great, all-time, record-breaking, incomparable girls. And I want to call her a girl."

"And take her a ton of food. Ah, me. Ah, so. And so it goes. Let's order before I faint from hunger. You are a child of your times, McGee. And so am I. Call *her* what you will, but call *me* a waiter."

14

THERE ARE days you can't ever forget. It doesn't mean that anything really startling has to happen. It was a great glowing golden day in May. A Sunday numbered twenty-two. There you are in the midst of life, and one of those days comes rolling at you, and it is just like one of the magical days of childhood, like the first Monday after school is out.

We couldn't warn John Tuckerman and Gretel Howard we were coming. We had to hope they'd be glad to see us when we showed up an hour before noon. And they were. Demonstrably glad. She knew how to accept gifts. None of this "Aw, you shouldn't have." She went through the hamper and the cooler, giving little yelps of delight. "Hey! How about this! Wow! Look here, Johnny! Hey, you crazy guys. A jar of red caviar! Have you gone nuts, bonkers, utterly strange?"

I was glad that Meyer had realized it would be best not to bring any booze, or any beer. Tuckerman seemed slightly dazed. He wore a gentle smile. He rocked back and forth, heel to toe. You had to speak to him twice to get an answer.

"I said is the fishing any good?"

"Oh. Sure. I mean, I guess so. Haven't done much good. But they're out there, all right. They're out there."

He looked much better. It took me a few moments to realize that not only had he shaved; his mustache and hair had been trimmed back a little. He seemed to want to be part of the festivities, but he could not quite keep track of the chatter. We were not trying to dazzle him with repartee or profundities. It was just your normal picnic conversation, but it was as if he were a foreigner among us, looking back and forth with a slightly baffled expression, able to speak the language, only not all that well.

One odd little incident happened. Gretel stopped in the middle of a sentence and stared at John. He sat with his eyes squeezed shut and his jaw knotted. She put her hand on his rigid arm.

"Are you going to be all right?" she asked.

He nodded. And in a little while the tensions went out of him. I asked her about that later, after we had swum down the beach and were walking back, and she said that it was hallucinations. They happened now and again. Some sort of a cousin of delirium tremens, the result of the booze with which he had almost killed himself. She told me that was the reason she did not want to leave him alone. She didn't want to take him into town yet, or go in without him. Hence her magic washing machine. She thought that I had guessed the problem, and that was why I had brought enough food for fifteen people. By great exercise of character I made myself admit I hadn't guessed it.

We sat on the side of a dune. We could have been the only two people in the world. I wanted to kiss her. My heart was in my throat. I felt fifteen again. I looked into her eyes and saw her amused acceptance of us, and knew I could. It was immediately intense, astonishing both of us, as was admitted later. We lay back against the slope of the dune, as closely enclasped as we could get, and it was all very delicious for a long time, and then it began to get a little bit too yeasty for the time and place. "Hey!" she said in a muffled voice. "Hey you! McGee!" And then, with a muscular squirm, she kicked us over far enough so that we began rolling, and we rolled over and over down to the bottom of the dune and had to go into the Gulf again to rinse off the sand that had caked on our sweaty bodies.

It was a great day. Eating and swimming and napping, walking and talking. A simple day. I can remember the precise pattern of the white grains of sand on the round tan meat of her shoulder, and the patterns of the droplets of seawater on her long thigh. Gretel filled my eyes. I learned her by heart, wrists and ankles, mouth corners and hairline, the high arches and slender feet, downy hollow of her back, tidy ears, flat to the good skull.

There would never be enough time in all the world for us to say to each other all the things that needed saying, time to tell all that had happened to each of us before the other had appeared—a sudden shining in the midst of life. In so many ways she was like a lady lost long ago, so astonishingly like her—not in appearance as much as in the climate of the heart—that it was like being given another chance after the gaming table had already been closed for good. She had a great laugh. It was a husky, full-throated bray, an explosion of laughter, uncontrolled. And she laughed at the right places.

The second strange incident happened in late afternoon when the four of us were up on the roofed deck of the cottage, sitting in the ragged old deck chairs and the unraveling wicker ones, squinting into the sun glare off the broad Gulf.

Meyer had talked a little bit about the odds and ends we had unearthed, Mr. Wedley recovering his red Mazda, the items Kristin had left behind, DeeGee Walloway's guess as to what had happened. Things like that. I realized that Meyer was sidestepping the big dramatic incident. When he ran down I said, "Leaving it to me?"

"Why not?" he said.

"Leaving what?" Gretel asked.

"Nothing at all. Really." I became Lawrence of Arabia. "Chap tried to blow some large ugly shotgun holes in us last night. Number twelve. Range of fifteen feet. Missed. Wounded our vehicle."

"He missed," Meyer said, "because that slothful-looking beach bum sitting there with the rotten imitation accent has one of the most fantastic reaction times you would ever care to see. I heard a strange little clicking behind us and suddenly McGee slammed into me, and as I was tumbling along the asphalt I heard a deafening pair of explosions."

She had worn a half smile, anticipating some sort of joke. But when she realized Meyer was quite serious, her jaw dropped and her eyes went wide in consternation. "How terrible!" she said.

"He jumped up and ran over to the fellow and yanked the gun away from him before he could reload and aim again, and the fellow ran right out into the Bay Street traffic and got hit by a car. We saw him get hit. We knew no one could survive that kind of impact, especially a man that heavy. He died on the operating table.''

"Who was it?'' Tuckerman asked.

"Nick Noyes.''

Tuckerman boggled at me. "Nick,'' he said. "Nick. Nick.'' It was not a sound of anguish or dismay. It was a puzzled expression he wore, as if he were trying to remember something about Noyes.

"He worked for Hub too, didn't he?'' Gretel said. "In construction or something? Johnny, didn't the two of you hang around together after Hub left? Isn't that what you told me?''

I sat between Tuckerman and his sister. Tuckerman reached over and put his right hand on my forearm and clamped down. I would not have believed him that powerful. "Nicky is dead? Really?''

"Very dead, John.''

The grip slowly softened and he took his hand away. His smile came slowly, and grew and grew. It was one of the contagious smiles of childhood, a big candy-apple, cotton-candy, roller-coaster smile.

"I won't have to kill him?'' John Tuckerman said joyously.

Gretel inhaled sharply. "Johnny!''

"Well, I won't. You heard him, Gretel. Nicky is dead, and I won't have to even think about killing him any more. That's the best thing I've heard in a long time.''

"Why would you think you had to kill him?''

"Oh, I've known I'd have to.''

"But *why?*''

"Because he was after me.''

"After you? How?''

"Just after me, dammit.''

"But if he was after you, dear, wouldn't he have come out here?''

"Oh, he's been here. A lot. Sneaking around. You wouldn't know about it. I didn't tell you. I didn't want to worry you, that's all. Now he won't be around here any more. Unless . . . .'' He stopped and stared at me and began to glower.

"What's the matter, John?''

"You two could be helping him. You could be lying, to make it all easier for him.''

We couldn't ease his suspicions until Meyer remembered he had the Sunday edition of the *Bay Journal* down in the car. He got it, and Tuckerman was at last willing to admit Noyes was dead. He went down to ground level and climbed the dune and sat just over the crest of it with his back to us, silhouetted against the sea glare.

"Let me apologize,'' Gretel said. "We've been through this before. I thought he was over it. So I asked about Nick Noyes, trying to lead John into it in . . . a less squirrelly fashion. From what I gather, Nick looked John up to commiserate with him, to get drunk together and cuss Hub Lawless and talk about their bad luck. That was while John was still living at the Vista, and before he had smashed up his car. I think Nick suspected that Hub's disappearance was planned and that my brother was in on it somehow. I think he was trying to pry information out of John. John is quite sure he did not reveal anything. He's not really sure, of course, but he thinks Nick Noyes was so angry at the whole thing, and so sure Hub had left with Miss Petersen, that if he thought John had any part in it, he would have blown the whistle. It *would* be actionable, wouldn't it?''

"Accessory to fraud, or conspiracy to defraud," Meyer said. "Something ominous at any rate."

"Also, that Wright Fletcher, the Sheriff's deputy, was out here prodding away at Johnny. He came several times after I was here, and I finally told him to make an arrest or stay away. He didn't seem to have anything to go on except the idea that, inasmuch as John was Hub's best friend, John had to know about anything Hub planned and did."

"He believes Noyes was out here prowling around?''

"Practically every night. He was very sure one night. He said he could hear him. We'd had a hard rain earlier in the evening. It dappled the sand and took out footprints and tire tracks. There was just that one hard rain. The next morning I made him walk the perimeter with me. There wasn't a footprint or a tire track for a hundred yards in any direction. I almost convinced him Nick hadn't been here. At noontime he told me that it was pretty obvious Nick had a special pair of shoes with soles which imitated the marks rain makes. He was serious. It breaks my heart. He was always so damned sane and practical and fun. At times—I don't know—I get the feeling he's putting me on, that it is all some kind of a weird game, and then I will realize he means it, he really means it all."

"Any idea why he thinks Noyes was after him?''

"No. None. It's an obsession. Nick was after him, just after him. No reason. Look at him out there! God only knows what sick thoughts are crawling through his head. He's better than he was. He let me trim his hair. You noticed? He finally got over the idea that if it was trimmed the hair ends would bleed. Yeck. Every day a little bit better, I keep telling myself."

Aside from those two incidents, it was one of your great days. We stayed into the night and built a fire of driftwood on the beach. A sea breeze kept the bugs away from us. We had stars by the billion. Meyer was in his best form. He came up with a tale I had never heard before, about a time years ago when he had attended a monetary conference in Tokyo. He was slated to deliver a paper he had written on the effect of interest rates on gross national product in the emerging nations. It was over an hour long. The taxi driver took him that morning to the hotel where he was to deliver his paper. Eager underlings led him to a big hall. He was pleased and surprised at the size of the audience. He gave his talk, shook hands with what seemed to be dozens of Japanese men, and left, still savoring the applause.

That afternoon he was called before the executive committee. They wanted to know why he had failed to appear and deliver his paper. He said he had. They proved he hadn't. He began to realize that he should have been made suspicious by the fact that the audience was entirely Japanese, quite a few of them were women, and, of the men who shook his hand afterward, not one of them thanked him in English. And he remembered a small elderly Japanese man who stood in the wings while he talked and kept looking at his watch in a troubled way.

Meyer then told us of the lengths he went to to find the hotel again. He never found it. So he would never know whom he had talked to, or what they had expected. He had always remembered how their applause had warmed his heart. A polite people indeed.

He did it well. He had Gretel chuckling and groaning a long time after he finished. When it was late, she made some chicken sandwiches for us to take along, so we could collapse into bed at the Resort.

On the way back along the nine miles of lumps and potholes, I realized how ready I was for sleep.

"You and Gretel make an extraordinary couple," Meyer said, apropos of nothing at all.

"How?"

"Hard to describe, exactly. You give the impression of having been close for years. You are tuned to her in some fashion. The two of you look larger than life somehow. Of course, you *are* larger than couples one runs across every day. There is some sort of aura about you two. You had it in place when you came back down the beach that first day. I don't know why it should, but it makes me feel drab."

"For a drab man, you tell a funny Japanese story."

"I felt compelled to do my best. She makes you want to dig deeply into your bag of tricks. With no insistence at all, she seems to demand some kind of excellence."

"I don't happen to have any of that around."

"I think she thinks you do, or she wouldn't bother."

"How is she bothering?"

"Don't you know how she looks at you?"

"Okay, okay. Sure."

He sighed. "That fellow—what was his name?—Billy Howard. Billy must have been the prize damn fool of all the world."

"Maybe he couldn't stand the pressure of her expectations—the need to be as much better than the next guy as she was better than the next woman."

"Interesting idea. The retreat from excellence. But she isn't demanding excellence in that sense, Travis. All she demands is honesty, really."

"At this point in the life of McGee, how do I go about telling the truths from the lies? When I say something this time, how can I tell that I really mean it?"

"If you can't tell, we're all in trouble."

"How so?"

"In spite of your poses, old friend, you have a strange, tough, anachronistic sense of honor."

"Oh, sure."

"You bleed over your despicable acts. But like our friend Rust Hills, you tiptoe past the edge of corruption in a naughty world, and you genuinely suffer if you do not live up to your own images of your various selves."

"Are you telling me I need not fear meeting the lady's requirements?"

"Whatever they might be, Travis. Whatever they might be."

"Look at that hole. You could hide a coffee table in that hole."

"Be careful. We have no spare, remember."

I wandered the road, finding the smooth parts, feeling underneath the deep-water tan the heat of the long May day in the sun. I had a stack of those old-fashioned photographic plates in the back of my mind. The big camera had been made of brass and oak. I had spent a lot of the day ducking under the black cloth, raising high the T stick with the magnesium powder in the groove along the top of the bar, focusing the big lens, waiting until she held still, then triggering the powder. *Poom.* And a cloud of white smoke, and another image of Gretel tucked away forever.

Long ago a picture must have been an event. Capturing a living image has become too ordinary a miracle, perhaps. They go about with their automatic-drive Nikons and OM-2's and their Leicaflexes, and put their finger on the button, and the hand-held machinery makes a noise like a big toy cricket. *Reep, reep, reep, reep.* A billion billion slides, projected once, labeled, and filed forever. Windrows of empty yellow boxes blow across the Gobi, the Peruvian highlands, the temple steps at Chichicastenango. The clicking and whirring and clacking is the background sound at the Acropolis, at the beach at Cannes, on the slopes at Villefranche. All the bright people, stopped in the midst of life, looking with forced smile into the lenses, then to be filed away, their colors fading as the years pass, caught there in slide trays, stack loads, view cubes, until one day the camera person dies and the grandchild says, "Mom, I don't know any of these people. Or where these were taken even. There are jillions of them here in this big box and more in the closet. What will I do with them anyway?"

"Throw them out, dear."

15

I SLEPT like a winter-bound bear and awoke refreshed to a morning of misty rain. Meyer was up and gone. He does not leave long chatty notes. This one said, *8:10. Bkfs dwnstrs. Then Dr. S.*

He was gone by the time I got downstairs. The waitress showed me to a table for two in a window corner of the small dining room. It looked out across the wet and empty courts. Between the far trees I could see segments of gray sea, almost flat calm.

I ordered, and as I was drinking coffee, waiting for the food to arrive, I saw Jack the Manager appear in the arched doorway to the lobby. He wore a black sport shirt and white slacks. The shirt was strained across the round front of him. He stared at me. He looked like an emperor penguin disapproving of a dead fish.

He came directly over to my table and said, "Mr. McGee!"

"Good morning. Join me?"

"I would like to point out—"

"Sit down and point out. Please."

He eased into the chair facing me. He looked nervous and uncomfortable. "There have been complaints," he said.

"About what?"

"Your group was very noisy Friday night. And there have been two altercations in the parking area."

I nodded. "Of course. Shots were fired. Then all those tires screaming, and then the sirens. Very upsetting."

He looked slightly relieved. "I'm glad you're taking this attitude. It makes it easier for me. Our guests are used to a—"

"Just one moment," I said, stopping him. I took out the pocket notebook which Meyer had convinced me was useful. I leafed through the pages, nodding to myself, frowning. When he started to speak, I stopped him with upraised hand.

I put the notebook away and smiled reassuringly at him. "I know what is basically bothering you. Right? And I am really not authorized to tell you anything at all. But you've been so pleasant, such a good host, that I am going to level with you, and I hope you appreciate what a rare thing that is."

"I don't know what—"

"From what I can guess, and from what I know of procedure, there is really very little chance of your being subpoenaed."

"Of being . . . for what . . . I don't . . ."

"And there is even *less* chance of the Resort here being either fined heavily or closed under the provisions of Chapter Twenty-one, Paragraph C-Six, Subparagraph *a*."

"But I don't—"

"So you don't have to *worry*. Right? You can relax! It isn't hanging over you any longer. At least, I am *reasonably* sure they won't come at you in that manner. But nobody knows, of course, until they have an executive session."

His face had turned red. He grasped the edge of the table and leaned toward me. "Mr. McGee, I haven't the faintest idea what the hell you are talking about!"

My food came. It looked very good indeed. I smiled at Jack the Manager, and I winked at him and said, "None of that now."

"NONE OF WHAT?"

"Shshsh. Please. You know I can't go any further with this. I shouldn't have mentioned it at all. I was only trying to do you a favor."

"But I want to know what this is all about!"

"Please forget I said anything to you. I violated a confidence. And for God's sake, don't say anything to anyone else, because if it was leaked out and got back to the Supervisor, there's no way in the *world* you could avoid a subpoena."

"I must insist—"

"Do you want to ruin everything for yourself? Have you got some kind of economic death wish?"

I chomped the good Canadian bacon. I beamed and winked and nodded at him. His choice was clear. Either I was certifiable as a maniac, or he and the Resort were in violation of the rules, somehow. In serious violation. I could guess his thoughts from his expression. It has all become regulation by blackmail, of course. Every small businessman lives with the knowledge that he is always in violation of some of the rules. Safety regulations, consumer protection laws, wage and hour laws, pure food and drug statutes, IRS regulations —and on top of all these are the interwoven, supplementary, conflicting regulations of the state, county, and city.

He fills out the forms and sends them in because he knows that, if the forms do not come back in, the computer flags him. He fills in the blanks with lies because it would take more hours than there are in the week to fill in the forms arriving each week. He knows all these lies go on record somewhere, and that at any time a field inspector can happen along and check out the old lies and apply pressure. So all he can do is contribute to both political parties, support local, state, and national candidates, and hope for the best.

It was easier for him to believe he was in some kind of trouble than that I had lost my wits.

He got up and said, "Uh . . . thank you, Mr. McGee."

"Believe me, I was glad to do it."

"Uh . . . enjoy your breakfast," he said, and walked away. He turned in the archway, stopped, and stared back at me, his expression troubled, eyes clouded. He shrugged and walked on, out of sight.

It was a small and childish pleasure. I ate with appetite. Great eggs. Days of misty rain are fine. Jack the Manager would leave us alone. He would do a lot of wondering, but he would keep his mouth shut and stay out of the way. And we would refrain from chousing anyone out into traffic. And we would duck away from all shotgun blasts to avoid messing up the parking area.

Gretel was alive in this rain-mist day, in the same dimension, time sector, and hemisphere. She fitted in with any recitation of one of my lists of good words: pound sweet apples, song by Eydie, pine forests, spring water, old wool shirts, night silence, fresh Golden Bantam, first run of a hooked permit, Canadian geese, coral reefs, good leather, thunderstorms, wooden beams, beach walking, Gretel. We all have the lists. Different lists for different times of day and of life. Our little barometers of excellence, recording inner climate.

*   *   *

The first chore after breakfast was another call to the hospital to get the word on the old party we had restored to momentary life. They said that Whittaker Davis was in serious condition, but no longer in critical condition. I asked if his condition could be considered grave. She said they didn't use that word any more because people got it confused with being buried. She said if they did use it, Mr. Davis would be a little bit better than grave, that it sort of would come between critical and serious, but don't count on it.

Meyer points out that fewer and fewer people in this country speak English any more, and that the trend is toward the guttural grunt. As a case in point, he quotes the earnest newscaster he heard one time over WTVT Channel 2 in Utica, New York, speaking of an emergency operation performed upon the wife of one of the nation's most important citizens. With expression of concern he read from his script that she was being operated on because they had "found a noodle on her breast." The song lyrics, Meyer says, presage the future shape of the language.

I was glad the old party was hanging in there. At least we had provided time for the Davis clan to gather at the bedside, if there was a clan, and if the hospital permitted clans to gather.

While at the phone I found the number for Ralph Stennenmacher, General Agent, in the Coast National building. The girl said he was in, and tried to get my name and make an appointment, but I said I would wander on up and take my chances.

A neat little sign on the corner of her secretarial desk said, "Dora Danniker, Serf-Person." She was as tiny as B. J. Bailey, but had a lean pale little face, big glasses, and mouse-blond hair pulled back into a knot. You half expected a toothy actor to pull her to her feet, take away her glasses, fluff her hair out, and say, "But you are beautiful, Dora darling!" Then they would dance.

She looked me over with considerable speculative care, from my tan Eagle shirt to my green brushed-denim slacks and buff-colored After Hours shoes, and back up again.

She said, "It would be nice if you could at least say you'd seen me someplace before, McGee."

I thumped my forehead with the heel of my hand. "Friday night?"

She nodded and smiled an evil smile. "You called me your little pal for a while. You said I should fly away with you, and we would sail the seven seas, climb the highest mountains. And all that stuff."

"Have mercy."

"Even smashed as you were, friend, plotzed out of your wits, you were using your head. You were trying to sign me on to solve the big problem you were having with B.J. and Mishy. You weren't exactly what I would call some kind of a prize. I think it was because those two hate each other and needed an excuse. Do you get like that often?"

"Every night in the week, love."

She studied me, nodded to herself. "You couldn't look the way you look and do that. You were pretty funny for a long time. Life of the party. And finally, of course, you passed out."

"You were still there?"

"Because the guy I was with was still there and I was exhausted from trying to drag him away. You want to see my boss?"

"When convenient."

"He's got somebody in there with him now. Have a seat. Have a paper. I've got to get something done here or I'd spend a little more time working you over. How was your hangover?"

"Didn't your boyfriend object to this 'sail the seas and climb the mountains' routine?"

"Sure. But you finally got tired of him yapping at you. We were walking, the whole bunch of us. You threw Timmy up into a tree."

"I what?"

"You picked him up and threw him up into a tree. You threw him pretty high. He's sort of a small guy. He grabbed a branch and you kept right on walking and talking. He really hates you."

"Please tell him I'm sorry."

"Don't worry. He hates everybody your size. It's just a general attitude—"

The office door opened and a man came out, speaking back over his shoulder, saying, "If they get any line on him, Ralph, like I said, I'll go on back down. But this ought to be enough for our purposes."

He smiled and nodded at Dora Danniker, gave me one quick flat glance, and went on out, a lean man in a wrinkled pale blue suit, carrying a gray tweed dispatch case. After he was gone I tried to fasten his face firmly in my memory, but it faded before I could begin to identify any distinctive feature. Ralph Stennenmacher stood in his office doorway and looked at me with a genuine smile of welcome.

Dora said, "This is Mr. Travis McGee. He hasn't had a chance to tell me what he wants to see you about."

He shook my hand and tugged me toward his office. He liked me. That is the secret. That's what had made Ralph a success. He was interested in me and he wanted to know more about me. He wanted to sit me down across his big blond desk and listen to my life story. When that genuine and unmistakable warmth is combined with good sense and good products, then you have a great salesman—and a happy man. One wall was hung with certificates, awards, commendations, and group photographs, hung frame to frame. He had white hair, big black-framed glasses, and a comfortable belly. He had little broken veins in his nose and cheeks, big knuckles, a resonant voice, and laugh lines around his eyes. He aimed a big finger at me and said, "Hey, I saw you and another man at the Cove having lunch with Walter Olivera. Excuse me, dammit, at the Galley. Mmmm. Friday?"

I said that was right. This Timber Bay had begun to give the impression of being a risky place for intrigue. Everybody seemed to keep an eye on everybody. I gave him the Devlin Boggs explanation of our presence in town, and he was glad to tell all.

"I wrote the coverage on all Hub's activities and on his personal life too. In the beginning we were thinking of having business insurance, of having insurance at his death go right into the company or corporation so that it could be used to buy out the widow's interest in the partnership or her stock interest, whatever. But I wasn't satisfied that it answered his problem, on account of the way he ran things. Understand, Hub was a good businessman, but he was a loner and a high roller. He wanted to run whatever show he was in, and he had an instinct about pushing his luck—right up until the end, of course. So it began to appear to me like there wouldn't be much of anything left of Hub-Law, Double L, Lawless Grovers, or Hula Construction if Hub died. For one thing, nobody would know what was going on. He kept terrible records and he kept a lot of information in his head. And second, because of the way he liked to keep moving money and debt around, it might be that the businesses, each one of them, might have to be liquidated to pay off what was owed. So we started quite a while back with three hundred thousand ordinary life, with Julia the beneficiary, and built it to a half million, million, million and a half, two million, two million two hundred thousand as of the alleged date of death. The girls were contingent beneficiaries. We set the policies up with Julia as the owner, and we put them in her trust downstairs at the bank, the one her daddy Jake Herron set up for her when she turned eighteen. Her daddy helped me get started, by the way. A finer man never lived. . . ."

"Where was I? Oh, the trust paid the premiums on the policies, and it left Julia in a pretty good condition. You could just about figure that after expenses and all, and knocking off the mortgage, she'd have anyway one point seven million, plus the little she gets from Jake's estate, which goes to the daughters, share alike, when Julie dies. That money could bring her in about ninety thousand a year tax free, more than enough right now to be mighty comfortable on in Timber Bay, but who can say if it will be enough tomorrow? Tomorrow it might cost ninety thousand a year to hire a truck driver. But it's all, like they say, academic. Hub Lawless is alive down there in Mexico somewhere, according to the report that free-lance investigator that just left here gave me."

"I heard that a Mr. Frederic Tannoy was going down there with Deputy Fletcher to see if they could—"

"Gone and got back late last night. Tannoy was the one in the blue suit leaving as you came in. He gave me a copy of this thing he wrote up, which he now turns in to Planters Mutual General Insurance in Topeka. A good solid old-line company. Conservative investments, and they treat their policyholders right. I've worked with them a number of years, and this is the first sour one we've ever had. I'd give an arm if this hadn't have happened. Things like this hurt everybody. This says confidential, so I better not let you have it to look at, but I can read you off here what it says."

He frowned at the document, lips moving, and said, "What happened was that Tannoy and Wright Fletcher went down to Guadalajara with pictures of Hub, and they've got here a little list of five people swearing they saw Hub Lawless in Guadalajara after the twenty-second of March, the date Hub was supposed to have fallen off the boat. It also says here that they picked up Xerox copies of the office records from the Naderman-Santos Medical Clinic, where they had a set of presurgery pictures taken for the record and placed on file under the name Pickering. He made a firm date for Wednesday, March thirtieth, to sign himself in. He paid five hundred dollars down when he made the date in late February. He signed up for—these are hard words—rhinoplasty, rhytidectomy, and, uh, blepharoplasty. Nose job, face lift, and work on the eyes. He had used the name Steven Pickering, and he had a tourist card in that name and had signed as Pickering on the formal release for surgery. He didn't show up for his appointment. It doesn't matter, as far as the investigation is concerned. There's enough in this report so they can back off from paying the face amount of the policies. They can assume he went somewhere else to get the work done. It would be foolish to sue them. No chance of a recovery, or even any compromise. He's down there somewhere with that Petersen woman. I just wonder how he feels about what he's done to everybody around here."

"Maybe he doesn't care."

"Oh, no. Hub cares. That's how come people can't understand it, really. He's a good man. Everything just got to be too much for him. I've been thinking about it a lot. I think that if everything had worked out just fine for him in a business way—the new shopping plaza and that huge development nine miles south of the city—he would still have done something nobody would be able to understand. Maybe blown his own head off."

It surprised me. "Why?"

"Things aren't all that great. You play craps?"

"Once in a while. I'm no big fan."

"Imagine a man like Hub Lawless at a great big crap table. He's keeping a dozen bets going all the time. He's on the come line and the field. He's betting with fours and tens, against sixes and eights. He's bending over that table, sweating, changing bets, doubling up, drawing down, watching the dice and the stick man and the other players. He keeps winning because he is working harder than anybody else, and he's figuring the odds closer, and he's keeping track every minute. For a long time it's fun. And one day he finds out that they've chained him to the table. That's it, his whole life, piling up counters. He can still keep going as hard as before, but it's different. Choice is gone."

It was a striking analogy. "He used to get away a lot."

"No. Not a lot, and not for long. Everybody thought he was such a happy guy, such good spirits, so friendly. I knew him real well, Mr. McGee, and in the last few years he seemed to me to be kind of . . . wistful. He was getting heavy and out of condition, and he smoked too much. He didn't have time to stay in shape. He didn't have time for much social life or home life, either. Nice home. Lovely wife and daughters. But he had chained himself to the table without realizing it. He knew, or had started to realize that the rest of his life was going to be pretty much the same."

"One of those evaluations that come along at forty?"

"I suppose so. But he felt the weight of the people who depended on him for jobs. I guess he even felt my weight. I wrote all his coverage, and I don't mind saying I'll miss the business. I guess a man gets to feel the need to experience more lives than the one they give him a chance to lead, no matter how well he does at it."

"And along comes the lady architect."

"Sure thing. Ever shoot a sandhill crane?"

"No."

"I got talked into going over to Texas one time with some old buddies of mine and shooting crane. They put me in the tall grass downwind from this little sort of marshy pond. And after a time this big gawky old bird starts to soar in for a landing. They yelled to me to shoot it. So I stood up and I shot it. It was about as tough a shot as standing on the end of a runway and shooting a seven-forty-seven. Blew most of his feathers off, and he landed thump dead about eight feet from me. Made me sick to my stomach. People will do some funny things in the name of sport. That's the way Kristin Petersen shot old Hub down. She blew all the feathers off him and he landed thump. He was ready for her. He was ready for anything that was going to change things around for him. Nothing tasted good to him any more. He stopped giving a damn what anybody thought of him. When the dice came to him, he wanted to show off for Kristin, so he bet the whole pile and lost it, and there was nothing left for him to do, if he wanted to keep her, but steal and run. And that is just what he did."

"He didn't do it very well."

"If he'd done it well, he'd have left Julia with her pride and with plenty of money. That was how he justified it, I guess."

"I certainly appreciate your being so open with me. Mr. Stennenmacher."

"Nobody in Timber Bay calls me that. It is too damned long a name. I'm

Ralph to everybody. You come back any time you want to talk about Hub Lawless. I knew him about as well as anybody except John Tuckerman. Poor John.''

"He's off the sauce. His sister has it under control."

"I heard she was taking care of him down there. I remember her when she was in high school here. Gretel was a beautiful girl."

"Still is."

"I get to know all the high-school kids. I do my magic shows."

"Magic?"

He smiled and pulled a long yellow pencil out of his ear, snapped it in half, threw the pieces up in the air, and caught the pencil as it came down whole. "When you think of magic, think of Ralph the magician. And think of insurance because it will be magic if you can get by without it."

"Oh."

"I get them in junior high, before they get too sophisticated. Levitation. Magic rings. Mystery fire. The multiplying rabbits. I practice one hour every morning of my life. I get up that extra hour to get the practice in." He stopped smiling as he thought of Tuckerman again. "John went downhill very very fast after Hub left. He drank himself into the hospital that first month, and that's where what little money he had left went to. I hope he works himself out of it. But I certainly don't know what will happen to him. He lived off Hub's energy and luck all his life. I can't think of anyone around here who'd hire him. There was something besides booze involved. Dr. Sam Stuart knows more about that than I would."

"Drugs?"

"Something like that. Something that bent his head out of shape."

I thanked him again, and I waved good-bye to Dora, the Serf-Person, as I left. I hesitated when I got off the elevator, then decided it was as good a time as any to see Devlin Boggs about Kristin Petersen's banking affairs.

I waited near his office. He was somewhere in the back of the bank. Soon I saw him striding across the carpeting, erect as a doorman, neat as an undertaker, lugubrious as a liberal in Scottsdale. I told him what I wanted to find out, expecting that he would turn the chore over to an underling, some pathetic little vice-president, but he wanted to handle it himself.

I sat and listened to him call the Atlanta Southern Bank and Trust and say those mystic words which enabled him to pierce the secretarial barricades and get through to a certain Mr. Chance McKay. I thought that a dashing name for a banker—maybe not for an Atlanta banker. Finally Boggs made it through to him, and it is to be noted that the southern businessman and banker tends to relate to the telephone the way a four-wheeler relates to CB nineteen. Regardless of regional origin, he becomes just a big mushmouth.

"Hey, Chance? Thishere's Dev Boggs down at Timber Bay, Florida. . . . Sure. . . . Just fine, mostly. . . . No, I couldn't make it this year. Surely missed it, too. . . . Old buddy, I need a small favor from you, won't cost you a dime. We're looking at a big loss down here on business and personal loans to a skip. Maybe it wouldn't look big to you, but it is king-size for Timber Bay, and it might could eat a hole in our loan-loss reserve that'll take a time to fill back. This skip took off, we think, with a girl friend who's one of your customers up there, and if we could get a clue on where checks are maybe coming in from on her account, or where the closeout balance was sent, it might help us find the skip. The name is Petersen, first name Kristin with a K. Account number four-four-eight, four-four-one. . . . Sure, take your time. . . . What? . . . Oh, okay.''

Boggs kept the phone at his ear and covered the mouthpiece and said, ''He thinks he had an earlier request on that. An official one.''

''It would be likely.''

''Right here, Chance. . . . Yes, go ahead.'' Boggs listened and wrote down numbers. ''Yes. . . . I see. . . . Sure. Listen, I want to thank you. 'Preciate it. . . . What? . . . I do hope to make it this year for sure. Our best to Molly, hear? 'Bye.''

He read to me from the scratch paper. ''Her checking account balance is twenty-one hundred and twenty dollars and five cents. The last check was dated March twentieth, a check made out to cash for five hundred, and there has been no activity in the account since. She has passbook savings of about eleven hundred dollars. She has a one-year Certificate of Deposit at six and a quarter percent in the amount of seven thousand dollars, due in July, and two four-year CDs for fifteen thousand each, due year after next. She also has a safe-deposit box.''

''A prudent lady. A tad over . . . what? Forty thousand? One assumes she's planning to return.''

With mournful look he said, ''If she's prudent, she wouldn't want to lump her money in with what Lawless absconded with. If anything went wrong, she could lose hers too. I imagine she's woman of the world enough to know that the affair can cool off at any time. She left herself a place to go back to.''

16

WHEN I couldn't find Meyer, I decided it was a good time to locate Eleanor Ann Harder. I had the address and phone number Van had given me. She answered the phone and said she had just gotten off duty, but if I came right over, we could talk.

It was a small frame cottage on a small lot, with so many trees and bushes it was almost hidden from the street. She was a big woman, thick and solid rather than fat. She had a pale, rectangular face, small features, erect carriage. She could have been thirty or fifty. She wore her white uniform. We sat on the little screened porch at the side of the house and talked.

''We're so grateful to you, Mr. McGee, for anything you can do. Take Van's occupation away from him and he's lost. He's a very proud man. He's a very decent man.''

''We should be able to work it all out. The Sheriff is cooperative. The whole situation looks different today, not like it looked two months ago.''

''He phoned me yesterday afternoon from Sarasota and said things were going well, and wanted to know if I'd seen you. I said not yet but that you would probably stop by. I told him about Nick Noyes and how the paper said

he had fired shots at you and your friend before he was killed accidentally.
Van was very upset about that. He couldn't understand why Nick would do
such a thing. He hadn't thought there would be any danger involved in your
coming over, or he would have warned you."

"He's making pretty fair time."

"He'll be here Thursday, he thinks. Should I tell the marina?"

"They're all set. No need. I would imagine you are certain Van didn't get
drunk that night."

Her chin came up and her eyes got smaller. "Mr. McGee, I met my husband almost five years ago. I worked at Tampa General at that time. His
shrimp boat was run down by an ore ship, and he spent four days out in the
Gulf before they were rescued. He came down with pneumonia, and he was
on my station. He is a fine man. We were married two weeks after he got out
of the hospital. As an RN I know the symptoms of the abuse of alcohol. I
knew of the ceremony of taking one drink aboard the *Julie* at the beginning
of each cruise. It was his . . . I don't know how to say it."

"I know what you mean. Proving to himself each time he had whipped it."

"And he had. I know he was given something very strong to knock him
out like that. He was fuzzy-minded for days. His memory was quite disorga-
nized."

"But he didn't go to a doctor."

"I begged him to. A doctor might have detected something in specimens.
Van is one of the world's most stubborn men. By the time he went to Dr.
Stuart, it was too late for anything like that. He had three strikes on him
around Timber Bay anyway. You see, he came from here."

"I didn't know that."

"It's hard to find out very much about Van from Van. As a young man he
was a notorious drunk. He broke places up and was thrown in jail dozens of
times. You knew him in Lauderdale after he'd sobered up and become a
respectable citizen. A reputation hangs on. For example, when he lost his
shrimp boat, there was talk around Timber Bay that he'd been at the helm,
drunk, when it happened. When Hub hired him at Hula Marine, people said
Hub would live to regret it. Hub Lawless enjoyed hiring . . . misfits. I think
he enjoyed gratitude."

"Then it was pretty damned cruel to feed Van a mickey."

"It was wicked in the way that word is used in the Bible."

"It was part of the plot he dreamed up."

"So he could escape punishment as a thief and adulterer. His soul will
scream in hell forever."

She meant it. She was not the mild lady I had thought. Her knuckles were
white and a muscle under her eye twitched and leaped.

"Mrs. Harder, I wanted to make something clear to you. Van thinks that I
am undertaking this venture for money. I'm not. I'll take expenses, if he
insists. But no ten thousand. I pretended to go along with that because if I
said I would do it as a favor, he wouldn't have wanted me to come over here
at all."

"I know. He's planning to pay it. It might take three years, but he'll pay
it. You can't stop him. If you do what you promised to try to do, then nothing
on earth can stop him from paying you the money, as long as he is alive and
working."

"Is there some way I could sneak it back to you?"

"I would never betray him like that. He'd walk right out of my life if he ever found out. I wouldn't blame him. I couldn't stand losing him."

*   *   *

When I told Meyer about her, when we met at the bar at the Galley, he said that when he had been little an elderly aunt had given him an image of the devil which had lasted all his life. "The traditional figure, of course. Lean, very white face, all in black, black goatee, cloven feet, bat wings, a tail with a strange pointy end like an arrowhead. And a pitchfork with little barbs on the tines. Whenever a wicked person dies, there is a final exhalation. The soul emerges on that final breath, looking a bit like a small graveyard spook, a little evanescent thing in a white sheet with black eyeholes. The soul tries to rise up to heaven, but the devil is right there, making his rounds of the dying wicked ones, and he spears it with his fork and stuffs it into a specimen bag he wears on his belt. When the bag is jammed full he turns it over to a messenger-type demon. That demon gives him an empty bag and takes the full one on down to hell. He goes down the nearest well, or mine shaft, or newly dug grave, and keeps right on going. He dumps the bag out and picks up an empty one. The resident in-house demons set upon the bagged souls and start all that frying, basting, slicing, and so on we hear about."

The bartender forced a laugh. Meyer stared at him. "You don't believe in hell?"

"Well, not *that* one, thank God." He wandered away, touching his throat.

"So what about Dr. Sam Stuart?"

"I'll tell you at the table, Travis."

As we finished our drink, awaiting the table call, I told him about Kristin's idle forty thousand. And I told him about how Tannoy and Deputy Fletcher had nailed down Hub's presence in Guadalajara subsequent to the supposed drowning.

At the table he told me about Dr. Stuart. "He's younger than I expected him to be. Sort of a jumpy, impatient, high-strung type. He has a crusade going. But he thinks it's lost before he can even get it off the ground. But he is going to try. He seems to be that sort of a person. What do you know about PCP?"

"Is that the name of his crusade?"

"It's an animal tranquilizer. Phencyclidine. It was developed for use in hypodermic guns to knock down grizzly bears in national parks and keep them down while they were transported to less accessible areas."

"If it's also called angel dust, I've heard of it. It makes a very rough trip, I've heard."

Meyer looked in his notebook. "It is known by different names in different areas. Hog, crystal, peace pill, blasting powder, and sugarino. Range of symptoms: it can produce a staggering walk, slurred speech, and slowed reaction times, imitating the effects of alcohol. It can produce bizarre sensations and hallucinations. People act out violent fantasies. It upsets the neural linkages in the brain. With repeated use it can cause permanent brain damage, with the lingering effects of paranoia, suspicion, anxiety, tendencies toward inexplicable violence, distorted memory, sporadic amnesia. It can duplicate acute schizophrenia."

"Nicky Noyes?"

"He's pretty sure of it. He thinks that it is the root cause of a lot more death and violence than people realize. One-car accidents, suicides, mass murders, sniping, stranglings. The effects are almost completely unpredictable, varying with each individual. He says the whole situation terrifies him."

"Isn't that just a little bit strong?"

"You should hear him, Travis. He made a believer out of me. He's had a couple of fifteen-year-old kids blind themselves with their fingernails."

I stared at him. "That made my stomach turn right over. They better stop that stuff at the source."

"That's the problem. Any college chemistry student with four or five hundred dollars can set up production in a shed and be turning out phencyclidine in a few days out of easily available materials. They turn the liquid into a crystalline substance. A marijuana cigarette doctored with a pinch of angel dust goes on the street for ten dollars, and five or six little teenagers can turn on on one cigarette, and the chemists who set up the lab can make five figures a week wholesaling the stuff. He says there is an underground lab somewhere in the Timber Bay area. He says he thinks Noyes was one of the several local dealers."

"Oh, great."

"Dr. Stuart says Noyes wasn't too stable to begin with. He'd been in various kinds of trouble before Lawless ever hired him. Lawless straightened him out."

"I wonder if Nicky gave Tuckerman some of his free samples."

"I wondered about that too, and I asked Dr. Stuart if that could be possible. He thought it over and said that it would be impossible to separate the effects of angel dust and the effects of acute alcoholism. He said Tuckerman had been a heavy drinker for years, thinking of himself as a social drinker but getting ever nearer the edge, and in the process doing quite a bit of physical damage to himself. He said that after Lawless left, Tuckerman drank himself into a series of alcoholic spasms in April that destroyed a lot of brain tissue —maybe as much as a dozen series of electroshock treatments. Tuckerman has fatty degeneration of the heart, twenty percent liver function, coronary artery disease, and borderline diabetes."

"Does Gretel know all that?"

"He did mention that he had talked to her about John's condition, so I guess she was given all the bad news. He said he told her that John was erratic but probably not dangerous."

"She'll have to stay with him, then."

"There isn't anyone else," Meyer agreed.

And I knew that Gretel was not the sort of person to sidestep any obligation of the blood or the heart. Tuckerman would probably hang on for years. Nice timing, McGee. Your usual luck.

After lunch we went back to the suite at the Resort. I felt restless. I talked it all over again with Meyer. We had been up one side of it and down the other. We had done a lot more prying than our limited function warranted. We knew more about Timber Bay than we had wanted to know. Good ol' Hub Lawless was down there in Yucatan trying to turn his personal clock back to the steamy days of his young manhood.

I wandered around the sitting room, wishing I was on Gretel's beach with

Gretel. I stopped at the windows and looked out, and saw a small familiar figure coming around the edge of the tennis courts, beyond the backstops, heading for the pool. By leaning close to the window, I saw her take up position on a chaise on the apron of the pool.

So I went down there and came up on her quietly, and sat cross-legged on the tile beside her chaise without invitation. Billy Jean wore giant sunglasses with rose-purple lenses, a yellow turban, yellow bikini, and a quart of coconut oil.

"I'm still supposed to stay the hell away?"

She shrugged. "Stay. Go. It doesn't matter, does it?"

"I was wondering if Nicky was on angel dust."

"You mean often, or just the other night?"

"Both."

"Okay, yes to both. He hit it pretty good, but like he said, it's okay for some people and it isn't okay for other people. I guess it wasn't so great for him either, shooting off a gun like that in the parking lot."

"B.J., he was trying to kill me."

"You say."

"Please believe me. He really tried, and if he hadn't been so unsteady, he would have done it."

She got up and pulled the back of the chaise out of the stops so she could lay it flat. She got back onto her towel face down.

"Okay," she said wearily. "So he really tried. And if he hadn't missed, I could have gone to your funeral. Just think."

"But it was an extreme reaction. It was crazy."

"Nicky was a crazy kind of person. Nobody ever really knew what he'd do next. He did whatever he felt like. You always knew things would be lively around Nicky. So the crystal rotted his head out. Okay, he's dead, isn't he? Why are you worrying about him? I thought the only person you ever worried about was Travis McGee."

"Did you try crystal?"

"Ha! Once, baby. Just once. That is a hit like you can't believe. Christ! There I am crawling around on my floor, and it keeps bending under me, and I'm scared shitless I'll fall through. I sit in a corner where I think it's safe and I look at my hands and my fingers had all grown together so my hands were like—you know—flippers. Like pink mittens. I saw a kid like that on television. His mother had taken the wrong kind of medicine when she was pregnant. I had these pink flippers instead of fingers and I started screaming and screaming and screaming. But they said afterward all I did was make a little mewly sound and I kept staring at my hands with the tears running down my face. No way I would ever try that crystal again. Nicky said I might get a real good ride out of it the next time, but it wasn't worth trying. I still dream about my hands looking like that. I'm at the piano and somebody asks for something that's tough to play, and I look down and there are those goddamn flippers again. No way. I stay with a little grass now and then, and not much of that either. And some hash when I'm on vacation."

She turned her head and looked at her hand and spread the fingers, worked them, closed the hand into a fist and put it under her cheek.

"B.J., I'm sorry I screwed up our friendship."

"I could certainly have done without you showing up with that pig Mishy, especially after the nice note you gave me when you left the lounge earlier."

"I apologize."

She rolled onto her side and plucked the purple glasses off and squinted intently at me.

"If you want to pick it up where we left off, forget it. You hurt me. You really hurt me, and the kind of person I am, I can't ever . . . you know . . . recapture a mood, not after I've been hurt. I thought you were a truly great person. It just goes to show."

I nodded. "You're right. It goes to show. I will cherish the memory of the little time we had."

"You will? Honest?"

"Yes, I will."

She grinned and put her glasses back on. "Okay. So will I. And that's the best way. A wonderful memory. Right?"

"One of the best."

"Maybe you're okay, McGee. Maybe you've got some heart after all. Listen, I'm sorry I got Nicky all worked up about you. I had no way of knowing he would do anything like he did. I mean, who could ever guess?"

I went back up to the suite. Meyer read me perfectly, and was amused I should take the trouble to placate Miss Bailey. I don't know why it should amuse him to have me try to get back in the good graces of people I have offended. It is just the sort of thing he does. But I offend more than he does. Oftener and more thoroughly.

I went into my bedroom and got the four-by-five color print of Lawless out of the nightstand drawer where I had put it. I straightened it out. It had cracked a little bit where I had folded it before. I took it to the bright light at the window and studied it.

Okay, so it was taken April eighth in Guadalajara, according to the accompanying message. And that would date it just seventeen days after a heart attack. He looked substantial, hearty, and cheerful, sitting there pouring his beer. So maybe it wasn't a heart attack. Maybe some kind of violent attack of flu. Or maybe he mended very quickly.

And Sheriff Hack Ames had received the slide in the mail just about one month later.

Probably, if it was a heart attack, he would not be anxious to undergo a lot of complicated surgery, and that was why he had never showed up at the Naderman-Santos Medical Clinic. So why hadn't he gotten his five hundred back, or at least rescheduled his appointment? Lawless could not have felt he had left a trail leading directly to Guadalajara. John Tuckerman knew where he was going, but John was loyal. But how loyal does a man remain when you take off and leave him penniless?

Some woman in Orlando had been projecting her Mexican slides and had recognized Lawless as being the man pictured in most of the newspapers in Florida, and featured on TV newscasts. And now Tannoy and Fletcher had nailed it down. Lawless had been seen in Guadalajara subsequent to the twenty-second of March.

The photograph wasn't telling me a thing. I looked at his clothing. The short-sleeved khaki jacket was bleached by sun and age to an off-white. I wondered what other clothing he had taken with him. Whatever he had decided to take, he had probably left packed in a suitcase in the jeep, down there under the cottage on stilts. It might be of some vague help to know what was missing from his wardrobe. It might be a clue to where he intended to hole up with the architect. Beach stuff would give one answer, and a lot of sweaters missing would give another.

I interrupted Meyer's somber inspection of the Monday *Barron's*. "I think maybe I'll go check something with Julia Lawless."

"Do you owe her an apology too?"

"No. I thought it might make a difference to know what clothes he took with him."

"If you're that restless, Travis, why don't you drive down and see Gretel? I'm sure she'd be happy to see you."

"Am I being busy for the sake of being busy? Is that what you think?"

"All I know is you're making me nervous. Go somewhere. Please."

"Where will you be?"

"Right here. Asleep, if everything works out."

17

WHEN I arrived at 215 South Oak Lane, I saw that the garage-sale sign was still planted in the lawn. The sallow housewife with the dark blond hair and bitter smile sat in a folding chair in the shade just inside the overhead doors of the big garage. A very pretty young girl was standing at a table nearby, polishing a brass candlestick.

"Hey, McGee," the woman said. "We met the other day. I'm Freddy Ellis. Did you meet Tracy Lawless?"

The girl gave me a quick glance. "Hi," she said and turned her attention back to her chore.

"Looks as if you did well," I said.

"Damn well, considering. The gang of locusts came and went over the weekend. Several times. We're down to the dregs."

"Is Mrs. Lawless around?"

"She'll be back after a while," Tracy said. "What is it you want?"

"She told me I could stop back if I wanted to ask her anything else."

"About what?"

"Tracy!" Freddy Ellis said warningly.

"I'm sorry, but there've been enough people bothering her. This has been very hard for her. This sale and all. She's exhausted."

"When she gets back, if she doesn't want to talk to me, I won't push it."

She studied me and then nodded. She polished the last of the white residue from the candlestick and placed the pair on display. I looked around and noticed that all the guns and fishing tackle were gone. Most of the photographic equipment seemed to be gone. His ten-speed bike, rowing machine, and bowling ball were still there.

Tracy said, at my elbow, "I found out that they drill holes in a bowling ball to fit whoever buys it. I don't think my mother knew that either. I guess it won't sell. I don't know why the bicycle won't sell. It cost nearly six hundred dollars, and we've got it priced at two hundred, and it is practically new. He was going to get in really good shape. He was going to ride with me and Lynn every morning, and then he was going to ride it to work. I think we did that three times. Maybe even four." She did not sound especially bitter. Just factual.

A tall surfboard was propped against the wall. When I looked more closely at it, she said, "I'm holding that for a girl that has to ask her father if she can buy it. It used to be mine."

"It's a good one."

"I know. But it is dumb to have a surfboard here. When is there any surf to ride? Just in storms, sometimes. I didn't even ask for one. He just bought it as a surprise year before last. He threw away a lot of money that way."

"It's fun to buy things for people you love."

"That's one of the reasons, I guess," she said, and turned away. The bitterness had been visible for a moment.

Julia drove in and got out of her car, carrying a bag of groceries. The daughter went to her and took it and apparently asked her if she wanted to talk to me. She nodded and smiled at me, and the girl went into the house with the bag.

We talked once again in the living room, with the coffee table between us. Yes, she had heard that the investigators had established that Hub was in Mexico subsequent to the twenty-second of March. She said that was nonsense. He was dead, and she knew it.

"Did Hack Ames show you a picture of Hub taken in Guadalajara on April eighth?"

"He tried to show it to me. I said it was impossible. It just couldn't be. I wouldn't even look at it. I said it was some kind of a trick. He got very annoyed with me. He really did."

"I've got a print of that picture here."

"Don't try to show it to me!"

"Julia, please. I was wondering what sort of clothing he planned to take with him. It could indicate *where* he was intending to go, whether he got there or not."

She hesitated, and then with a sigh of resignation she took the picture and turned it toward the light. She closed her eyes for a few moments, then studied it again, and handed it back.

"You can't learn much from that bush jacket," she said. "That's the last one of four he bought at Abercombie and Fitch at least fifteen years ago. They were made out of their special Safari Cloth. They wore like iron. That was the last one. Shoulder straps. Four pleated pockets with buttons. I remember mending the left sleeve in front. You can see the mend. He ripped it on a branch."

"Do you know what other clothes he took?"

"I have no idea. He'd moved a lot of his stuff out to the ranch, you know. He was supposed to be sleeping out there."

"Could you tell by looking to see what's missing?"

She heaved a great sigh. "Well, I've got to go through that stuff sooner or later."

"Maybe it would be better to put it off for a while."

"No. I'll go look. Not that it will do any good."

She came back in five minutes, taking long strides for such a small person. She was bent forward, eyes glaring, jaw set.

"Here, damn you!" she yelled and hurled something at me. I got a hand up in time and caught the wadded cotton. Julie stood over me. "I told him and I told you that goddamn picture was nonsense. Look at it! Look at the sleeve! What did he do, smart man? Wear that to Mexico and sneak back after April eighth and slip it into his closet with the rest of his stuff? I *told* you. I told everyone. Hub is . . . is . . ." She collapsed onto the couch and began to weep.

"Julia? Julia!" I had to say her name very sharply to bring her back for a moment from the self-involvement of her tears. She stared at me, her face small, lined, and anguished.

"I agreed to tell you why I came here," I said.

"If it was to prove he's really dead . . ."

"To clear Van Harder. To get his license back. A favor for a friend. That's all."

Her stare showed she found it hard to believe. "Just for that? My God, you go plunging around, kicking and thumping, just for that? What kind of an idiot project is that?" Tears were drying.

"Your husband and his dear friend left Harder way up the creek. Harder was loyal to your husband. They gave him a very cheap shot."

"What do you think he gave me? And his daughters?"

"And his bank and his friends and his other employees too. I guess I stepped in just now because I didn't want to see some grown person crying for him."

"He was my husband!"

"When I was small there was a neighborhood kid who had a lot of toys. Whenever we played with him we all knew that whatever the game was, we had to let him win. If we didn't, he would pick up his toys and leave. He was kind of a fat kid."

"You've got some sort of adolescent infatuation with the idea of gallantry and fair play," she said. "He was doing what he thought was right. Damn you, why have you got me defending him? Would you leave? Please?"

*   *   *

Sheriff Haggermann Ames saw me in his little sterile windowless office at quarter to four that Monday afternoon.

He looked at the paper bag I brought in. "What have you got?"

"You won't like it."

"Would you like a list of the things that happen every day that I don't like and never expect to like?"

I sat opposite him and took the bush jacket out of the bag. I shoved the print he had given me in front of him, unfolded the bush jacket, and pointed to the mended rip in the front of the short left sleeve. His face did not reveal a thing. He told me to stay put. He came back with a slide projector, the kind which comes in a small tin suitcase which opens up into a tent-shaped ground-glass screen. The slide is projected onto the back of the ground-glass. He plugged it in, turned it on, inserted the slide, turned it to sharp focus. Then he compared the shirt I'd handed him to the shirt in the photograph. He compared the shoulder straps, collar, mend, the buttons on the flap pockets. He turned the projection lamp off, tilted his head back, and stared at the ceiling.

"Get it from Julia?" he asked.

"Yes. She did the mending. He bought four of them a long time ago. This was the last one left."

"What the hell made you go ask?"

"I don't know. I began to wonder if too many trails led to Mexico. I wanted her to look and see what sort of things he took. I had the idea that if he took snowshoes and thermal underwear, it might mean people were looking in the wrong place. I sort of fell into this."

He looked at the shirt as if he wanted to set fire to it. "I fall into things too. They are like accidents, but not quite. Something in the back of a cop's head keeps nibbling away."

"I'm not a cop."

"Maybe you should consider it."

"I don't think so, Sheriff."

"Well . . . where the hell are we? As near as we can tell Hub was down in Mexico sometime in February. Maybe the woman took the picture then and got confused about the date. I don't like that. She was too positive."

"She was selling that date. She was selling the idea Hub is alive."

"And she was steering us toward Guadalajara," he said. "What if that architect lady wanted the whole pie? What if she was just using Hub? The way I read it, her career wasn't exactly climbing. Okay, so they meet the morning after he was supposed to drown. Maybe they meet at the place where he stashed the money. I don't think he jumped overboard with it. She knows the plan is to go to Mexico, get plastic surgery, hole up somewhere, and have a long happy life. But she doesn't like that kind of risk, being tied to him, maybe caught with him. So she pops him, buries him, and leaves with all the cash. To lay the false trail, she sends the slide to me."

"If she did that, Sheriff, the best and safest thing she could do would be go back to Atlanta, keep the money hidden away, and pick up the strings of the life she led up there. But there's been no transactions in checking or savings for two months, and she's got forty thousand dollars up there in the Atlanta Southern."

He gave me one of his mild, tired, dusty looks. He scratched the back of his head. "Dig, dig, dig."

"I was curious about her."

"Sure. So am I. The couple who subleased her apartment up there are curious too. And she took a leave of absence from the firm she was working with. They are wondering."

"Mr. Boggs was glad to make the inquiry."

"Sure. What else do you know you haven't got around to mentioning?"

"I brought that bush jacket right to you."

"Yes, you did. And sidestepped the question too."

"Can I ask a question?"

"Such as?"

"Who paid for Deputy Fletcher's trip to Guadalajara?"

He focused a bleak stare on the wall behind me and then turned and pushed a button on his intercom. "Pull Fletcher in from wherever, on the double, in my office."

He looked at me and said, "One thing about Wright Fletcher, he ain't too god-awful bright on the best of days. The script I'm going to try is that the body just now come ashore, positive ID from the dental work."

"He was going down to that shack where Tuckerman is staying and putting pressure on Tuckerman until the sister ran him off."

He smiled. I wouldn't want him smiling at me like that. "Now that's nice to know."

Ten minutes later I had my first look at Wright Fletcher. He was as big as the side of a house. He was as big as Walloway. He came creaking and jingling in, all leather and whipcord and the metallic necessities of office. At Ames's suggestion, I had moved back into a chair against the wall, almost behind the chair where Fletcher had to sit.

He looked uncomfortable. There were two rolls of sun-baked fat on the back of his neck.

"That was a real nice break for you, flying down to Mexico like that with Mr. Tannoy. You know we could never have pried loose the money to send you down there. And we couldn't have sent you down official without probably an act of Congress, Wright."

"Well, Mr. Tannoy really needed me. He doesn't speak any Spanish at all. I'm not what you'd call fluent, but I was able to help him a lot."

"That's nice. I'm glad you were able to help him. And you are one thousand percent sure Hub Lawless is down there?"

"Well . . . I'm a thousand percent certain he *was* there. We found that sidewalk café place where that picture was taken, about three blocks from the main square, and I took another picture of it and gave it to you."

"That was a big help. Now let's say a body came drifting in and we just got a positive on the dental work, and it is Hub Lawless, not looking too good after two months in the water."

"Honest to God? Did the body come in?"

"Wait a minute, Deputy! You seem pretty ready to believe that it did. I thought you had him all nailed down in Mexico. Is there something the matter with your investigation work down there?"

"N-no, Sheriff. No, there wasn't nothing wrong."

"It works out nice for Tannoy if the company doesn't have to pay off, doesn't it?"

"I think he gets some kind of a percentage commission."

"On two point two million! Must be a nice commission."

"I guess so."

"Now you have five people on the report you gave me, each ready to swear they saw Lawless down there after March twenty-second. Five good sound reliable witnesses. People we could put on the stand?"

"Well . . . we didn't tell them they'd have to do that."

"Did Mr. Tannoy give them something for their trouble?"

"A couple of hundred pesos, Sheriff. Like about ten dollars. As, you know, a courtesy."

"I know. He put you up in a good hotel?"

"Very nice."

"Good food, good booze, a little night life?"

"Aw, Sheriff, like Mr. Tannoy said, it was kind of like a vacation anyway. Nobody should mind if we enjoyed ourselves, as long as we got the job done."

"Maybe there was a little bonus for you too?"

"Not really a bonus."

"Well, what?"

"Just a silver belt buckle, for a souvenir."

"And?"

"Well . . . a necklace for Madge."

"Silver?"

"Yes, sir."

"How many people did you talk to who remembered Hub Lawless, but remembered him as being there back in February?"

"Quite a few."

"Ten?"

"Well, more."

"I don't see their names on the report."

"Mr. Tannoy said they wouldn't do anybody any good. He said it was all perfectly clear that Hub took off with the money and it wasn't right he should get to rip off an insurance company at the same time. He said that whenever people rip off an insurance company, the rates go up for all the rest of us."

"Get out of here!"

"Sir?"

"Get your fat sly ass out of here, Fletcher. It makes me feel sick to look at you. I'm going to think up an assignment for you you'll never forget. Git!"

After the door closed, he said, "So much for the Mexican connection. Can't blame Tannoy too much. A professional company man. Any company that'll pay him. Where are we now? It would be a pretty safe guess that Hub hasn't been to Mexico since February. Maybe he sent along the slide. False trail."

"After going to all the trouble to make it look like accidental drowning?"

"Okay, so then he realized it wasn't going to work. Remember I didn't get the note from Orlando with the slide until the tenth of this month, McGee."

"Nobody was talking about Guadalajara until you got it. So even if he knew what was going on around here, even if somebody was keeping him up to date, the escape route was still safe. And the complete change of appearance was still a good idea."

Ames thought in silence for a few moments. "We have to remember that he had already missed his appointment at the clinic by the time I got the picture of him." He pinched the bridge of his nose, squeezing his eyes shut. "Let's back up. Who would know about Guadalajara? Lawless, Kristin Petersen, and John Tuckerman. I put in a lot of hours back there toward the end of March, working on John Tuckerman. I couldn't move him an inch. He wasn't giving me the story word for word every time. That would have tipped me off. But it was damned close to word for word. All right, so he had to be in on the scheme. Those two were always close. I had to back off. I had nothing to go on. Harder was no help. Those two girls backed up Tuckerman's story. So if he was in on it, he certainly didn't get paid off. He had to give up his place. He wrecked his car. He was in the hospital screaming at the big polka-dot lobsters that were crawling all over him and up the walls. What would he get out of sending that slide to me? How would he manage it?''

He took the slide out of the projector. "Number eleven," he said. "Out of twenty or thirty-six. Developed by Kodak in April. Along with the thirty-nine billion other slides they processed in April." He looked at his watch. "We can make it to Ben's Camera House before it closes."

18

BEN HAD a florid face and a curly red beard. He said, "Hack, there is absolutely no way to tell a thing about this slide. It is just about perfect exposure, but these days of automatic, through-the-lens, CD cells and all, the exception is when we get things through here that are over or under.

"Now because it has Hub Lawless in the picture, it could be like thousands of other slides and prints that have come through here with the Lawless family on them. They talk about other people having a hard time on account of Hub taking off the way he did—I am the one really hurting. I can't even guess the thousands and thousands of feet of Super Eight movie film he took of those girls and his wife. And every time Hub went off hunting or fishing or cruising, he'd be back in with a dozen rolls of color to be developed. And he was gadget-happy. I must have sold him forty different cameras over the years. And lenses and tripods and monopods. Flash attachments, viewers, projectors, screens. Name it and he'd buy it. I took back a lot in trade, of course, but I can tell you Julia had a lot left out there for that garage sale. I went out and helped her price it out to move it, and I hear they did well getting rid of it at the prices I suggested."

"Did John Tuckerman ever bring the film in and pick it up?" the Sheriff asked.

"John? Sure. He was Hub's errand boy. It would be more often John than Hub when it came to picking up film."

"Did John take any of his own?"

"You know, I don't think he owned a camera. I know he used to take some pictures sometimes, for Hub, when Hub wanted himself in the picture, like with a big fish, something like that. Snapshots. Aim and fire. Maybe he owned a camera. Maybe Hub gave him one. But John never seemed much interested."

"Did John pick up any film after Hub disappeared?"

"No. There wasn't any here. Hub stuck me for a hundred and something dollars on the books, on open account, when he took off."

"Did Hub get his pictures developed soon after he took them?"

Ben laughed. "Nearly always. But the man had too many cameras. And he had a habit of leaving exposed film in the cameras and forgetting what it was taken of. You can't do that with professional film and expect to get much. But you can leave amateur color film in a long time and not lose much. They know people tend to leave film in their cameras. They build it to last."

"So this slide here, developed in April, that could be a picture taken in February?"

"Or even last year sometime. I can tell you this wouldn't have come through my store here, seeing as how it is April, and assuming it was Hub's. It wouldn't have to go through any retail store, you know. A person can buy a slide mailer and send it to Kodak and get the slides back in the mail."

"Did Hub use those mailers?"

"Sometimes he bought some, when he was going to be away awhile. He'd mail in the film and then the slides would be waiting at home for him when he got home."

The Sheriff drove me back to the courthouse, where I had parked. I sat in his car with him for a few minutes. "What we've got so far, based on too damn many assumptions," he said, "we've got Hub in Guadalajara in early February, with John Tuckerman. We know they went down there hunting cat, but we didn't know they went to Guadalajara. We got Hub asking John to take a picture of the street there, with Hub over to the left. He isn't even looking into the camera, like a man does when his picture is being taken. What would make John want to sneak a picture way back then?"

"Maybe in the next slide, number twelve, Hub Lawless is smiling into the camera. Maybe John took it too soon."

"Why would there be any picture taking anyway?"

"You mean if they—if Hub—was planning the escape route, setting up the clinic appointment, and all? I suppose he was trying to stick with his normal routines. He always took pictures. He always came home from trips with pictures."

"Maybe. We assume the film was left in the camera, and Tuckerman got it developed and managed to mail one print from Orlando. Too much, McGee. Too damned thin. Too damned improbable. And why the hell would John Tuckerman want to screw up Hub's plans after helping him carry them out?"

"Because he didn't like getting the short end."

"You're getting along with him all right?"

"Pretty good."

"Maybe you could see if he wants to talk any photography or if he acts funny. Just to satisfy your own curiosity."

"Not yours?"

"No. If I want to learn anything about anything, all I have to do is have Deputy Fletcher saddle up and ride. Besides, I'm not permitted to deputize anybody unless we have a declared state of emergency."

"Sheriff, if I happen to find out anything I think you might want to know, I might want to tell you about it." I had my hand on the car door, ready to get out.

"Set quiet one minute longer, McGee."

"Yes, *sir!*"

"You could aggravate me pretty good if you put your mind to it, McGee. Be that as it may, I dropped by to see a man this morning, and he swore up and down you told him you were a lawyer."

"No way!"

"Stanley Moran."

"Oh. I told him I'd lay a subpoena on him if he didn't behave. I didn't pretend to be a lawyer. He asked me if I was a lawyer. I didn't answer the question."

"It bothers me, too, the way that architect lady up and left so sudden. Looked like she packed up and left and drove over to Orlando and flew out, never to come back. Meant to look like that, you think?"

"I don't know exactly what you mean."

"This morning I looked at the stuff she left behind. I wondered if it was anything worth taking with her. I borrowed the painting she left. Only so big. Hardly bigger than a legal-size piece of paper. Frame is light. It had the name of a gallery down in Clearwater on it, on the back. Can't pronounce the name of the artist. The title was *Tide Watch*. I phoned the gallery about it and they said it was purchased by a Miss Petersen in January of this year for seven hundred and fifty dollars, plus tax. It would fit in a suitcase easy, between clothes. A fifty-dollar painting, a hundred-dollar painting, a person could be so absentminded on account of wanting to leave in a hurry, they could overlook it. But seven hundred and fifty dollars?"

"And a person could pack her stuff, put it in her car, drive to Orlando, buy a cheap ticket, check the stuff aboard, leave the car at the airport, miss the flight, take a bus to practically anyplace, and the luggage would end up in an airline warehouse somewhere."

"Which fits nice with the information she hasn't touched her checking account since before the twenty-second of March, over two months."

"Or, if you are in a rush and traveling light, why bother with a seven-hundred-and-fifty-dollar painting when you are on the run with eight hundred thousand or so?"

"If somebody knew the entire scam, McGee, if they intercepted Hub and his new lady, took the money, buried them deep, then pulled that picture trick to steer everybody toward Mexico . . ."

"Somebody like?"

"I know. I know. Not like Tuckerman. Certainly not Julia Lawless."

For a moment, for one moment, I was tempted to tell him what I had learned from Gretel and John about the whole scheme as devised by Hub, and about the heart attack, the yellow jeep, the message John took to Kristin Petersen. But Gretel had trusted me, and she had induced John to trust me. If my luck ran really bad, one day this dusty dangerous little man would find out what I had held back and find out I had held it back. In a perfectly ordinary manner, with his ordinary face and gestures and tone of voice, he had a knack of creating a respect that bordered on dread.

* * *

In late afternoon I aimed the gray Dodge Dart southward, pretending I was intent on my mission of involving John Tuckerman in some small talk about photography. But Gretel filled my head, and I leafed through the hundred pictures of her, taken by a personal invisible camera which had produced instant three-dimensional colored shots, vivid, never fading. I whistled. I decided that the unraveling of the Hubbard Lawless mystery was just a nervous reflex on my part. None of my business. Van Harder would be absolved and relicensed. The Sheriff was willing to arrange that without much further urging.

For all of me, the whole area could strangle in angel dust. All I wanted to do was find some way to pick up my woman and run, preferably in *The Busted Flush,* once Van Harder had turned her back over to me.

I steered around the deeper potholes. The sun was sliding down the sky, off to my right. A rabbit sat up and stopped munching as I drove slowly by. There was a small hawk perched on the mailbox, and it went arrowing off as I turned in. Soon the stilt house was in view, with the square green Fiat still parked under it. I popped the horn ring a couple of times as I drove into the yard. I got out and looked up, expecting to see her come out onto the veranda. Empty. There was not the slightest breath of a breeze. There was not the slightest stir of leaves or grass. Nor any bird sound.

The creak of the weathered stairs seemed loud as I went quickly up to the veranda deck.

"Hallo? Hey! Gretel? John?"

Nothing.

I walked around to the Gulf side of the deck, looking in the windows as I passed them. I tried the screen door and it opened. The table was set for two. There was driftwood and paper in the fireplace, ready to light against the possible evening chill.

"Hallo?"

I noticed the old ten-power binoculars. They were on the deck, looking as if they had fallen from the rough railing. I picked them up, thinking that probably Gretel and her brother were somewhere along the beach and I would be able to spot them. When I tried to look through them, it felt as if my left eye was being pulled out of the socket. Apparently they had fallen, and the prisms inside the left half had been knocked a little out of line.

There were clouds on the horizon, the sun moving down toward them. Squinting against the sun, I looked through the right half, adjusting it to my vision. I swept the beach off to the right and saw no one. I swept around to the left, looking south, and saw no one. I saw something against the concave seaward slope of a dune where the beach swung slightly westward. The sun made a bright glare against that angle of sand. I braced the binoculars against one of the uprights that supported the overhanging roof, made an additional adjustment to the focus, lost the object, found it again, and suddenly saw that it was a figure flattened against the sand, face down. It was a female, I thought. It was Gretel. It was too far away for anybody to be sure it was even female. I would have needed a forty-power spotting scope on a tripod to make it out properly. It could not be Gretel. But I was over the dune and on the beach and running hard on the packed sand, groaning as I ran, still telling myself it was not Gretel, running with no clear memory of ever having left the veranda.

It is curious how many things can go on in your mind simultaneously. If it was Gretel, she was sunbathing. She was upslope to present a better angle to the late sun. Of course. She would laugh when I came running at her like a maniac. (But she had looked too flat and too still.) A person can fall asleep in the sun. (Face down in the sand?)

When I was fifty yards from her, I heard that flat, sharp, lathe-snapping noise which a small-caliber high-velocity rifle shot makes in the open air. I had the general impression it was fired from somewhere in front of me, somewhere beyond where Gretel lay. I made two more long running strides before, simultaneously with the second crisp, abrupt sound, something tugged at the short sleeve of my sport shirt and burned my upper right arm. I plunged through soft sand, away from the wet packed beach sand, running as I had been taught long ago, moving without pattern from side to side, keeping low, and feeling once again that area of belly-coldness which seems to mark the spot where the whistling slug will impact. I dived and scrambled the last twenty feet, rolling fast to end up close to Gretel. There had been nobody on the beach, nobody visible on the dunes. The rifleman had to be up on the crest, just over the crest, peering over to aim and fire. Here the slope was so steep that when I looked up I could not see the crest, only a smooth round of sand partway up the slope.

Her dark hair was matted to a chocolate thickness at the crown of her head. Two green-bellied flies walked on her hair. Her face was turned slightly away from me. Her fingers were stubbed into the sand as though she had been trying to pull herself up the slope. She wore rust-colored shorts and a white T-shirt, dappled on the back with the brownish spots of dried blood. She wore one white boat shoe. On the left foot.

A great desolation chilled my heart. It was an emptiness stretching from here to infinity, from now to eternity.

Slowly, slowly the whole world was suffused with that strange orange glow which happens rarely toward sunset. The clouds turned to gold as the sun moved behind them, and the reflection of the clouds colored the earth. I have never seen the Gulf so quiet. There were no ripples, no birds, no sign of feeding fish, no offshore vessels moving across the horizon. I had seen this strange coppery light in Tahiti, in Ceylon (before it became Sri Lanka), and in Granada and the Grenadines. The world must have looked like that before the first creatures came crawling out of the salt water to spawn on the empty land. I turned my head and saw, beyond the shoulder of my beloved, the empty copper sea, hushed and waiting, as if the world had paused between breaths. Perhaps it was like this in the beginning, and will be like this again, after man has slain every living thing. Sand, heat, and water. And death.

A lone gull came winging in across the water, angling in, at a height just sufficient for him to clear the ridge of the dune.

The gull would have crossed the crest about two hundred feet ahead of me and to my right. When he neared the crest he suddenly squawked alarm and veered to the left of his line of flight and sharply upward before flying on.

So there he was. X. For unknown. The rifleman. I raised up very quickly and dropped flat again. If you lift slowly, you give them time to put a third eye in the center of your forehead. I retained the afterimage of the empty crest. Nothing. No glint of metal. No round shape of head or bulk of shoulders. Just the wind-smoothed tan sand. I took another look. And another. Nothing at all.

The terrain promised no advantage. I could not hope to run up the slope. I could get up there to the crest by churning and floundering and clawing my way up through the coarse sliding sand, as easy to shoot as a deer in deep snow. I could make good time down the slope, right down to the open beach, where I would make a pretty good target there as well. I could move laterally, but not very far. The slight concavity which hid me from the crest grew shallower to my left and was gone within twenty feet. Ten feet to my left I saw an object protruding from the sand, the end of something thrown up by a storm of long ago. It looked as if it might be wood, but it was diffiuclt to tell in that golden-red glow. I wanted a stick, a stone, a switch—anything. It is an ancient instinct. Man is the tool user. Even as the saber-toothed tiger was disemboweling him, man was reaching for a branch to club the beast. It did not matter that nothing I could find on a beach would help me ward off the tiger or the bullet, I wanted something in hand. A tool. Comfort of a kind.

I edged over to it. Wood. A good shape and size for grasping. Was it too short or too long? Too short to use, too long to extricate from the sand? I worked it back and forth and pulled it free. It was the handle end of a canoe paddle. The piece was two feet long. I had grasped it near the break. On the other end, the end normally grasped, there were dead barnacles, tough, sharp, and firmly seated.

It had an incongruity like the red light that filled the beach. Canoes were summer lakes, frocks, big hats, and music coming across the water.

The initial panic had settled into a reliable flow of adrenaline. It is my fate and my flaw to have learned too long ago that this is what I am about. This is when I am alive and know it most completely. Every sense is honed by the knowledge of the imminence of death. The juices flow. In the back of my mind I tried to tell myself that I had been turned into a murderous machine by the sight of Gretel. But it was rationalization. There was a hard joy in this acceptance of a total risk. I knew that if he got me—whoever he might be— he was going to have to be very damned good at it, and even then I was going to create some astonishment in him. I would live totally on this thin edge until it was over, and then I would either be dead for good or partially dead until the next time.

The copper sea made no sound at all. I eeled slowly upslope, angling to my right, knowing that I would be exposed to him, would be in his line of fire before I could reach the crest. I worked it slowly, peering toward the area where the bird had veered. I kept muscles poised and bunched so that in an instant I could hurl myself back and to the left, hoping to fall back into the sanctuary of the concavity near Gretel. As I came closer to the crest, I diminished the chance of regaining the concavity undamaged. On the other hand, it was easier to watch for him. Or her. Or them. Or it. The dune was about fifty feet high, much higher than in front of the shack. Perhaps if someone suddenly appeared to fire at me again, at shorter range, it might be better to plunge over the crest, race and roll down the shaded side, taking a chance of finding some kind of cover.

At last I was close to the crest. The wind had given it a sharp, wandering edge. I was on about a fifty-degree slope. I dug my fingers into the sand just short of the ridge. My chin touched the sand. I was absolutely certain that somebody was waiting, alert, ready for the target to appear above the ridge, silhouetted against the slow-motion bonfire of the sky.

So I worked my legs up under me, adjusted my grip on the piece of paddle, and began to take slow, deep breaths. In the total silence of the world, my best way to get over was to bound over, letting out a yell which would shock the rifleman into a momentary rigidity, or into panicky unaimed shots. There was the hesitation much like that remembered from childhood, standing on the edge of the roof, a reluctance to make the first commitment.

In that great stillness a monstrous breathing sound began. A great snuffling intake, and then a long breathing sigh. *Snuff-sigh. Snuff-sigh. Snuff-sigh.* As though a winded dragon lay beyond the ridge, slightly to my right and far down the landward side of the dune. It was very steady and regular. I tried to identify that sound. It seemed, somehow, very homely and familiar. Suddenly there was a metallic clank at the end of the snuffing sound, a hesitation before the sigh.

I knew then what the sound was. It had been unfamiliar only because it was so incongruous when compared with my state of tension. There could be two of them, of course. It was still a time for caution, but a time to discard the large bad idea of bounding over the rim and down the slope, yelling and waving my paddle.

I dropped back a little and then moved laterally until I was directly above that breathing sound. And then, instinctively holding my breath, I looked over the edge.

It was darker on the landward side of the dune. The red light that bathed the world was all shadows and wine.

There, below me, John Tuckerman shoveled the dry, loose sand. *Chuff* of the shovel blade into the sand, then the soft sound, like an exhalation, as he swung the sand out in an arc behind him. As he dug, the sand slid down the slope, rivulets filling some of the space he had shoveled. The muscles of his back and shoulders and upper arms slid and bulged under the sun-scorched flab. He worked with the metronomic energy of the demented. He was naked. It was a labor assigned in hell. From the blazing sunburn on his body, and from the look of the piles of sand he had shoveled, he had been at it all day.

He was excavating the yellow jeep. It was aimed south, parallel to the ridge. The wheels and fenders on the right side of the vehicle, in fact the whole right side of it, was still covered by the slide of brown coarse sand. There was a figure behind the steering wheel. It sat, arms in its lap, chin on its chest, looking like a crude sand sculpture made of a slightly darker shade of sand. An imperceptible movement of the air brought the faint, sweet, gassy stink of decay, and I nearly gagged as I realized that the sand was darker because it was clotted by the fluids released by the tissues. In the passenger seat a slight knob had begun to appear, in just the right place and the right size to be the back of a head.

I looked for the rifle, finally saw it about thirty feet beyond the front of the jeep, leaning against a leafless stunted bush.

He stopped shoveling. He spoke at conversational pitch, but in a strange tone of voice, a sweet wheedling tone pitched so much higher than his normal tone that he sounded almost like a woman.

"Now you shouldn't talk to me like that, Hub! I'll get you out of here and you can be on your way. Don't I always do what you want me to? Don't I?"

He waited, leaning forward, seeming to listen.

"No, it wasn't like that," he said. "What she was going to do was take all the money and leave all by herself. But I made her wait, Hub. I made Krissy-bitch wait, and she's right there beside you, isn't she? And that's proof. You and she can go on off together soon as I get you dug out and get the engine started.''

Again he listened.

Again he answered. ''Well, goddarn it, Hub, I forgot. That's all. I knew I had something to remember and I forgot. When I covered you up so you'd be safe, I just jammed it against the dune, put you in the driver's seat, climbed on up with the shovel, and spilled enough down to do it in ten minutes, no more. That's how I didn't know it would take me this long to get you out. You two will be fine in Mexico. They've about stopped hunting you. Now you stop complaining and let me work, will you?''

That high sweet tone of voice made the skin crawl on the back of my neck and the backs of my hands. And it was no longer a person-against-person conflict. He was a mechanical toy, and I had to get to him and turn him off. A mechanical man will walk into a wall and try to keep walking. He will fall down and his legs will still make walking motions, little gears and springs ticking as he winds down.

19

HE WAS working at the rear of the jeep, and as I tried to decide on my best and safest move, more sand spilled toward him, revealing the head and shoulders of the figure sitting next to the body of Hubbard Lawless. It was as dark and silent as he.

I moved to my right behind the crest, so no movement would catch his eye, and stopped when I was directly opposite the small-caliber rifle.

I timed my lunge so that it came just as he was lifting a full shovel of sand and beginning to pivot to throw it behind him. I came down the slope in giant plunging strides. The whirling shovel caught me just below the knees, whacking a leg out from under me in such a way that I landed face down on the hardpan at the bottom of the dune, losing my good canoe-paddle club in my effort to break my fall. I got up on what felt like two broken legs as he whirled with the rifle in hand. I dived for my club, grasping it, rolling over and over toward him, heard the brokenstick sound of the shot, and felt both fire and numbness in the left cheek of my behind just before I rolled against his legs and knocked him down. He sprang up again with a rubbery monstrous agility, with a frightening strength. I'd grasped the gun barrel in my left hand, and I took a swing at him with the club as he was bounding at me, wresting the gun away from me. There was such a slight feeling of impact that I knew I had only grazed him with the club.

He backed away from me and aimed at the middle of my forehead. I could practically see the little round hole it would make where it went in, and the shattered suety ruin it would make where it came out.

''Johnny!'' she cried, a long desperate wailing sound, full of an absolutely final despair. I was kneeling, as though in homage to my executioner. I looked back over my shoulder and saw her standing tall, teetering, on the crest of the dune, outlined against the burgundy light. He moved the sight from me to her, aiming up at her, as I threw the club at his face as hard as I could. He fired, and I turned again and saw her tumble toward us. She slid down the slope, creating a small avalanche of sand which almost covered her head when the sliding stopped.

With no thought of the gun, I went stumbling, crawling, floundering to her, and grasped her shoulders and pulled her head out of the brown sand. She made a dry spitting noise, trying to expel the sand caked in her mouth.

John Tuckerman was acting strangely. He seemed to be trying to aim the gun at us, holding it in one hand. With his other hand he was clutching at his own throat. As I leaped toward him to try to take away the rifle, he dropped it and put both hands to his throat. He was making a wet hissing sound. In what light was left I could see the sheen of the bright arterial blood which came out between his fingers and ran in a broad band down through the chest hair, down the belly, into the groin, and down both thighs.

He looked puzzled. Then he seemed to smile at me, one of those small shy smiles people use when they have committed some vulgar social blunder. A girl who had just lost her contact lens in her chicken chow mein once gave me a smile very like that.

He took two slow steps toward the jeep, then lowered himself gently to his hands and knees. He crawled a little farther, blood pumping out of the throat wound. He seemed to dwindle in size as I watched. He collapsed onto his face a yard from the jeep, with a final exhalation that made him smaller yet. There was a strange overlay of sentimentality about it. Faithful hound returns to master. I turned and hobbled back to Gretel. I had rolled her onto her back when I had pulled her face out of the sand. As I looked at her, the last of the red light went, leaving us in a darkening, gray-blue edge of night. Her face was so slack I could see what she had looked like asleep in her crib long ago. She was breathing, her respiration slow and shallow. Her pulse was heavy, steady, reassuring.

I checked my personal damage. The slug had gone at an angle through the right gluteus maximus, and it had been so undamaged in transit the exit wound was as small as the entrance wound. I could not get a very good look, of course. It was bleeding, but not inordinately. More of a seepage. And it had begun to hurt. A lot. That is the big walking muscle back there. Grab yourself a handful of right buttock—your own—and walk a few steps and feel what happens. A lot of clenching and unclenching goes on. I pulled my pants back up and fastened my belt. I looked around for a moment. Stillness. Stench. Hubbard Lawless and Kristin Petersen sat motionless in the jeep, heads bowed.

For a moment the world veered and tipped, and I had the ghastly conviction Hub would lift his head, give me a sandy and horrible smile, start the jeep, and go roaring down the rough track with the remaining sand spilling out.

The reserve gas can was chained and locked to the rear bracket on the jeep. I had the momentary image of myself using the shovel to break the lock, then checking the money and burying it in the sand where only I could find it.

But the lady was breathing, and the rental Dodge was one hundred million miles away. With an enormous effort, I scooped her up. I held her cradled in my arms. I began the long walk back to the car through the increasing blackness of the night, feeling the tickle of blood on the back of my right thigh, feeling the leaden ache of the wound plus the shrill yank of pain with each step. At last I made it and stretched her out on the back seat. I drove slowly to Timber Bay, sitting in a puddle of my own blood. I went directly to the hospital and into the archway reserved for ambulances.

As I clambered slowly out, an old man in uniform was dancing around me in utter fury, slapping the pistol holstered on his belt, telling me I could not park there. I smiled and nodded and started to try to pull Gretel out of the back seat. Then more people came. Helping hands. I did a lot of smiling and nodding, and they paid no attention to me until someone noticed that I was leaving bloody footprints on their shiny gray vinyl floor. . . .

*   *   *

They did not have to do much to me. Some suturing, antibiotics, observation. Keep me a few days. Find a tall enough crutch so I could take pressure off the ham muscles. It should have been routine. I had been in so many hospitals. I had been hurt so many times. But they disorient you. Their white lights burn all the time. They come by in the night. They change your habits, your hours, your diet, and the climate inside your head. You are an object, subject to their manipulations.

I wanted to see Gretel. I wanted to be with Gretel. I wanted to hold her hand. Their whole establishment seemed designed to keep me away from her. The red-faced, endlessly weary Dr. Ted Scudder had sutured my butt and had assisted in the emergency surgery on Gretel's skull. He was perfectly willing to tell me how Gretel was and what they had done.

The injury was consistent with someone's chasing her along the beach and clubbing her in the back of the skull, perhaps with the flat of the blade of a shovel. It had given her a depressed fracture of the occipital bone on the right side of the back of the skull. It seemed almost inconceivable to them that she could have been able to climb the dune.

"Extraordinary vitality," Scudder said. "We've got a very good man here. Townsend. I assisted. Two and a half hours of very careful work. Freeze those little bleeders. Tiny stitches in the tear in the dura. Fit the pieces where they belonged. Just three. Bit of wire. Considerable traumatic amnesia. Thinks she's in California. Thinks she's missing work. No visitors. Not until she gets herself sorted out better. Avoid emotional shocks. Also, it keeps Hack Ames from bugging her. My orders. Includes you, McGee."

When bluster doesn't work, when begging is useless, try guile. I lied my way right to her door and put my hand against it to push it open. Didn't. There was already one perilously deep black hole in the middle of my head. I had seen the flies and thought her dead. Never thought of checking. Made the worst possible assumption merely because that seemed to be the way my luck was running, and would run forever. Just one touch on the neck to find the pulse—that was all it would have taken. So, having made an almost fatal blunder of omission, I paused just before the blunder of commission, took my hand away, crutched myself back to the service stairway, and grunted my way down the stairs. I had thought of her . . . instead of my own dramas and concerns. Could I possibly be growing up? After so long?

On Friday at noon, with me sitting on my inflated rubber ring, Meyer drove slowly and carefully down to the Cedar Pass Marina. He had checked us out of the North Bay Yacht and Tennis Resort and moved our gear aboard *The Busted Flush*. Home is a good place to be when you hurt. I was so damned glad to see my old-crock houseboat squatting there that my eyes stung and misted. Van Harder was there, giving me that limp, dry, callused handshake so curiously typical of many men who spend their lives out of doors. We went to the lounge, and I got comfortable on the long yellow couch, rubber ring under my aching tail.

"I took my stuff off this morning," Harder said. "Had a talk with the Sheriff. Should have my license back middle of next month. Once I'm working again, I'll start payments on what I owe. Hack apologized for kicking me. He said he never should have done that, never. And I told him he was right, he never should have."

"You don't owe me anything," I said.

"A bargain is a bargain."

One long look at him was enough to convince me there was no point in argument. "Okay. Okay. But open a savings account here in your name. And when it gets up to the full amount, let me know."

He thought that over, nodded, and put some bills and change on the coffee table, along with a piece of yellow paper with figures written on it. "This here is what's left from the expense money bringing her over here. Forty-two seventy-five. It's all writ down. Eleanor Ann made sure the figures add up right."

"Thanks. She looks great. She really does."

"I had plenty of time to do this and that. Drains and screens and packing. Some splicing. Stuff like that. I'd rather be busy than setting around." He coughed. "She needs bottom work, and you got a soft spot on the transom, outboard, port. I chalk-marked it. Could be dry rot. Should be looked at."

I thanked him again and he said I'd be hearing from him, and off he went. Meyer brought me a cold beer and sat on the other side of the coffee table. "I saved the papers," he said. "Over there in the corner. Big sensation in the press."

"They tried to get to me. Hack Ames had the lid on. Walter Olivera was the only one who slipped by. I told him no comment. Hack's orders."

He went over and leafed through the stack and brought back a copy of the *Timber Bay Journal*. "Did you see this front page?"

I hadn't. It was a night shot, a floodlit picture of the jeep, the two occupants still in it, Tuckerman still on the ground beside the jeep. It had been taken by somebody who had squatted down in front of and to the left of the jeep, with wide-angle lens. Grisly and effective.

I had, of course, read and heard the news and the story of the official reconstruction. Hub Lawless's autopsy had shown plugged coronary arteries. Miss Petersen had died of suffocation under the sand after having been struck a terrible blow in the face which had fractured her jaw and cheek and most probably rendered her unconscious. In the original conspiracy, Lawless had gone overboard from the *Julie* at night opposite the shack. The jeep, with the $892,000 jammed into the big auxiliary gas can, was already there. Tuckerman went out the next morning and found Lawless dead of a heart attack brought on by struggling to get to shore. Either Miss Petersen was with Tuckerman or he went and got her. There was a quarrel about the money.

Tuckerman killed the woman and put both bodies into the jeep after driving it to where the dune slope was high and steep. Covered it deep by avalanching enough sand down the slope. Two months later his sister came upon him when he was trying to dig the money out. He had struck her on the head, injuring her seriously. A Mr. McGee, a friend of Tuckerman and his sister, had arrived and had struggled with Tuckerman. In the struggle McGee had suffered a bullet wound, and Tuckerman had died of an injury sustained in a fall. McGee, wounded, had brought Mrs. Howard in to the hospital and had informed the Sheriff before undergoing treatment for his wound.

"I'm never around when things are going on," Meyer said.

"Be glad. This time, be glad."

"How lucky it was that John Tuckerman died of a fall."

"You remind me of the Sheriff."

"He keeps saying that?"

"We had four conferences in the hospital. He is a very diligent man. He is a very stubborn man."

Meyer peered out through the windows of the lounge. "And here he comes again."

Meyer went and invited him aboard and led him in. He was carrying the solid hunk of canoe paddle with the barnacles firmly fixed to that curved part which was supposed to fit into the palm of the hand of the paddler.

He sat down and sighed and smiled and accepted a beer. He bumped the paddle gently against his knee. "We got the lab report back, McGee. The tissue and blood they got off this thing, off the edges of these barnacles, match Tuckerman's type."

"So he must have fallen on it!" I said.

"You claim you missed him clean both times, when you swung at him and when you threw it at him."

"Startled him both times and missed him both times."

"From the shape and location of the wound, the lab people think that it struck the throat, moving from left to right at high velocity, and tore a hole in the artery and a hole in the windpipe. Are you sure there wasn't some slight little impact when you swung at him?"

"Positive."

"McGee, you were defending your life against a madman with a gun. The booze and the PCP had turned his brain to hog slop. You thought the sister was dead and he was going to kill you. And you could see the dead bodies in the jeep. What the hell do you think I am trying to do? Railroad you into Raiford, for Christ's sweet sake? I want to wrap this all up, all the way. I want a grand jury verdict of justifiable homicide. I don't want a file that says Tuckerman fell down onto some barnacles, dammit."

"He fell down."

"What's wrong with my saying that you hit him a lucky shot anyway, no matter what you say?"

"Sheriff," Meyer said mildly, "Travis McGee might find the attendant publicity somewhat constraining in his chosen profession of, shall we say, salvage expert. And he would have to be charged, of course, to be exonerated. And in this computerized world, the charge would be a part of his record. Secondly, of course, he is quite interested in Mrs. Howard. If she should recover as fully as they anticipate, she might find it awkward to feel any unmixed emotion toward her brother's executioner. Lastly, sir, McGee and I are accustomed to exchanging confidences, and if there was any doubt at all in his mind about whether or not he missed the deceased when he swung or when he threw that object, I am certain he would have told me. And you have my word of honor that such has not been the case. Oh, and one other possible solution. Were the object wedged into the ground at about this angle, and were the deceased to fall, left side first, he being a tall and heavy man, the wound might look as though—"

"All right, all *right!*" Hack Ames said. "You do go on. He fell. The most timely fall in the history of grand larceny and felony murder. You know what I am going to do with this half of a paddle? I am going to hang it on my office wall, and the moral is going to be for me not to get too cute." He finished the beer and stood up.

We both stared at him. I said, "Cute about what?"

"Remember the way we went around and around about that slide, once you found out the bush jacket was still in his closet at home? Hub's jacket?"

"It still bothers me," I said. "I can't see Tuckerman being sly enough to work something out like that, aiming the whole search toward Mexico, knowing Lawless was buried in the sand out there, in the yellow jeep."

"Stop worrying about it. The little lady that sent us the slide turned up. She came over to see us because she was absolutely certain the body we found couldn't have been Hub Lawless if the body had been under the sand ever since March twenty-third. She came over because she had broken up with her boyfriend and didn't have to be careful about talking about Mexico any more. And she wondered if she could cut in on any part of the reward for information in the case. Little bit of a thing. Very excitable and fast-talking. Hops around from this to that. Hard to follow her. Well, it took almost two hours to unravel it. She had gone down to Guadalajara twice. She went down in February with three other girls from the insurance office where she works. A winter vacation. One week. And she met a young Mexican there. An assistant manager of the hotel where they stayed. She went back to see him in April. She took pictures on only one day. Friday, April eighth, when her Roberto was busy and she walked around alone. She had the camera with her. A little Konica range-finder camera with automatic exposure. Had she taken the camera with her the first time she went? Yes. Taken pictures? Yes. Did they get mixed up together? No. Because they were dated. The date of development was stamped right into the cardboard. One batch said F-E-B, and one batch said A-P-R. Did you use the camera between trips to Mexico? No. So then came the key question. Did you take part of a roll and leave it in the camera between trips? She got real still and stared at me, and those pretty eyes got bigger and bigger, and finally she hit the desk with her little fist and said, 'Boy, am I some kind of dumb!' We walked all around it, McGee. She felt terrible. She apologized and apologized. I told her she had been a big help, really. She had helped us unravel Hub's plan, the one he would have followed if he hadn't had a heart attack. The warning is clear. Don't get too cute. Always think of the simplest solution. Tricky stuff will snarl up your head."

"You do the tricky stuff pretty well, Sheriff," I said. "Like that expensive painting the Petersen woman left behind."

He shrugged again. "I'd counted her dead before that. John Tuckerman took her keys after he'd killed her, drove in after dark, packed her stuff, loaded it in the red car, and drove it to Orlando. That was before he was so far gone. His head was still working. Remember your guess? I think he bought a plane ticket to somewhere. Maybe Miami. Checked her baggage through and tore up the ticket. So it's in an airline warehouse somewhere. Left the car in a rental car space. Probably took a bus right back to Timber Bay."

After he left, Meyer said, "I don't think John Tuckerman was sane from the moment he came back with Kristin and found Hub Lawless dead or dying. He'd given his life to Hub. Clown, errand boy, hunting companion. And probably the woman turned her back on Hub lying there and demanded the jeep and the money. Or just the money. So he hit her and buried them both, and that was the end of him. Maybe on a half-conscious level his relationship to Hub was something he couldn't admit to himself, something a good ol' boy is not *ever* supposed to feel."

"Thanks for helping with the Sheriff."

"Just don't tell me whether you did or didn't."

"I don't plan to."

epilogue

ON A July afternoon, late, we came trundling down the Gulf in *The Busted Flush,* just the two of us. We came down the length of Longboat Key, where the condominiums stand tall off Sarasota, and when we passed St. Armands Key, I told her about the famous shopping circle there and promised her I would take her to it and buy her something ridiculously expensive. It would be something useless and important and would have to do with some of the slice of the recovery awarded me by the committee headed by J. Devlin Boggs.

Some days we made good miles, some days zero. She had fallen deeply in love with the old houseboat, had learned how to cope with the trickeries of the galley and the cranky plumbing in the head. She wasted fresh water in long showers when we had it and did without when we didn't. She learned how to read the charts and operate the radio and the RDF, synchronize the diesels, and cook up Chili Meyer.

On this uncounted day in July, we came into Big Pass at dusk, on a tide so low I had to creep through the shoaling waters, bumping lightly twice. The charter boats were coming in off the Gulf. The sun was a forest fire in the west, and the distant downtown windows winked red in response. I chugged slowly by Sand Dollar Island and over to an anchorage area I had used before, happy to see no other craft there swinging on their hooks. We were well out of the channel, in about seven feet of water and about a hundred and fifty feet off a sandy beach, when I put down the two bigger Danforths, cut the power, swung on the lines, tested them, and found them firm.

While I made drinks, Gretel checked the larder and said she'd better make out a list in the morning. We had both spent all day in a sun so hot, so burning bright, that we radiated heat. Her brown hair had grown out to about an inch and a half. She had been shaved bald as an ostrich egg, and had given me no glimpse of her skull during the bristly time. Now it was revealed. Crowning glory, she called it. The constant sun was baking it lighter. I might end up with a blond person, she told me. She thought it made her look like a boy, hair that short. I told her that from the eyebrows up, in a certain light, at a certain angle, she might look somewhat like a boy. But include any other parts of her, and the illusion was lost. Smashed-all-to-hell-and-gone lost. That kind of lost. She asked if I was trying to call her hippy. I said she was hippy, busty, waisty, lippy, throaty, that she was all thighed, bellied, eyelashed, ankled, all ladied up just fine.

Today she had been quieter than usual, and I knew she had been thinking about the life I wanted for us.

After we ate and had tidied up, I went on deck to check the weather and the bugs. It was a splendid night, mild and sweet, frosted with stars. The western sky was black, where thunder bumped and muttered, and the breezes came from there. I got the inflatable mattresses out of the locker, put them side by side on the sun deck, pumped them firm with the pedal pump, spread a blanket over them.

There was a strawberry glow over the city. The lights winked out in the houses along the Siesta Key side of Big Pass. We lay on our backs and identified the constellations, and we both saw the same shooting star.

"Hey, do you wish on those?" she asked. "I forget."

"There's no rule against it. I wish you'd make up your mind. That is, if I'm entitled to a wish."

"I think maybe I have. To review the proposition you made me, you want me to share your life on any basis I choose, just so long as I understand it's permanent."

"Properly stated."

"I think it is very probably exactly the right time in your life for this to happen, maybe even the last chance you'll have."

"Something has been happening to me these last few years," I said. My voice sounded rough and uneven. "A bleakness. I don't know what to call it."

"No, darling. Don't go grasping at me. I'm not saying yes. Let go. There. Now listen to me. I really do love you. And much as I love you and want you, I can't be . . . somebody's remedy. Some kind of medicine for the soul."

"But that isn't—"

"Listen to me, please. I have to be my own person. I have to take complete charge of my life. I did the hard-scrabble years for somebody else, for some idea that was never going to work anyway. I'm not talking about lib or chauvinism. I've got kind of an alarming capacity for blind loyalty. Like my brother had. Fierce loyalty. I know that in some very final way, dear, we are all absolutely alone. The relationships people have are an attempt to deny that aloneness, but it doesn't go away. I want my loyalty to be to me for a while, and maybe for all the years I might have left. I have to be complete within myself and stand by myself in order to really become a person."

"You *are* a person, a damned wonderful—"

"Hush! I'm not going to run away. I love you. I want to stay near you, but if you won't accept my terms, I'll *have* to run away. I'll come to your town to live and work. We'll find me a place. I want demanding work that I can be good at and get better at. We will be friends, and from time to time, for as long as we both want, we'll be lovers. But nobody is going to try to manipulate or change or control or smother anybody else."

"But I don't—"

"Think about it, darling. Tell me tomorrow. I'm trying to be wise about myself. I can't be rushed. I have to reinvent myself. By myself. I don't want to sign on."

"But you'll be nearby."

She got up and went over to the rail. I followed and stood beside her, resting a hand on the warmth of her waist through the T-shirt. She moved to lean against me, head against my shoulder. She was a strong and accessible magic.

"I don't think he would have hit me," she said. "I've thought about him all day."

"You've been quiet."

"I know. I think there was somebody else there."

"There could have been," I lied. "We'll never know."

"No matter what that stuff did to his brain. I can remember up to the point where he sprang up out of bed in his room and went yelling outdoors as if he was answering somebody. I just can't remember past that."

"Don't keep trying."

She looked at the lights of Sarasota. "We don't know anyone here. We're not in their minds," she said. "So in some kind of funny way, we're dead. Nothing stopped in Timber Bay. They're stirring around up there tonight, laughing and hurting and hating and making love. Some are trying to live and some are trying to die. We're fading out of their minds. I'm fading out of the memories of the people I've known back in my other life. And as they are fading out of my memory, it is as if they were dying. Dying is all forgetting, maybe. Nothing more. You are not dead until there isn't a crumb of memory left anywhere in the world."

"You come up with some pretty strange stuff, lady."

"So why do you want me around for keeps anyway?"

"Two or three minor reasons. Nothing important."

"Settle for my being sort of a neighbor?"

"Like you said, I'll let you know tomorrow."

She turned into my arms. The thunder boomed closer. It was using up more of the sky.

It was clear that the rain would come. We went back to the mattresses. When the first big drops did come, they fell splatting unheeded and almost unnoticed upon my bare back and on her upturned face, vivid in the first stroke of lightning.

The Green Ripper

❖

To Maxwell P. Wilkinson
Representative and Friend

Fanaticism is described as redoubling your effort when you have forgotten your aim.

GEORGE SANTAYANA

1

MEYER CAME aboard *The Busted Flush* on a dark, wet, windy Friday afternoon in early December. I had not seen him in nearly two months. He looked worn and tired, and he had faded to an indoor pallor. He shucked his rain jacket and sat heavily in the biggest chair and said he wouldn't mind at all if I offered him maybe a little bourbon, one rock, a dollop of water.

"Where's Gretel?" he asked as I handed him his drink.

"Moved out," I said. He looked so dismayed I quickly added that she had found herself a job, finally, way the hell and gone over in the suburb of Tamarac, west of North Lauderdale and west of the Turnpike, out in the area of the shiny new developments and shopping plazas, near University Community Hospital and Timber Run Golf Club. "Couldn't get any farther away and still be in the same metropolitan area. It takes at least forty minutes to drive over there."

"Doing what?"

"The outfit is called, excuse the expression, Bonnie Brae. It is a combination fat farm, tennis club, and real estate development. She works in the office, lives in one of the model houses, gives tennis lessons to the littlies, exercise classes for the fatties, and is becoming indispensable. She can tell you all about it. She'll be here about six or six thirty."

"I was afraid you two had split."

"No chance. I'm not going to let that one get away."

"Splendid judgment."

"It's a phase, Meyer. She did hard time in a bad marriage and says it stunted her. She has to make it on her own, she says, to become a complete person, and when she is, then we can think about what kind of arrangement we're going to have."

"Makes a certain amount of sense."

"Not to me."

"But you're not . . . being derisive or patronizing?"

"Hell, no. I am being full of understanding, and all that."

I didn't want to try to tell him what a vacuum she left when she packed and moved out. The houseboat was dismally empty. When I woke up, if I wanted to hear clinking sounds from the galley, I had to go make them myself. The winter boats were beginning to come down, filling up the empty berths, spewing out their slender and elegant ladies to walk the area, shopping and smiling, providing what in times past had been like one of those commercial hatcheries where you pay a fee and catch your own trout and take it home to cook. But Grets had made all the pretty ladies look brittle, bloodless, and tasteless, and made the time without her seem leaden and endless.

In another season there were the girls of summer, robust and playful in their sandy ways, and now here were the winter ones, with cool surmise in the tended eye, fragrant and speculative, strolling and shopping, sailing and tanning, then making their night music and night scent, searching for something they could not quite name, but would know once they found it.

"How did the conference go?" I asked.

He shook a weary head. "These are bad days for an economist, my friend. We have gone past the frontiers of theory. There is nothing left but one huge ugly fact."

"Which is?"

"There is a debt of perhaps two trillion dollars out there, owed by governments to governments, by governments to banks, and there is not one chance in hell it can ever be paid back. There is not enough productive capacity in the world, plus enough raw materials, to provide maintenance of plant plus enough overage even to keep up with the mounting interest."

"What happens? It gets written off?"

He looked at me with a pitying expression. "All the major world currencies will collapse. Trade will cease. Without trade, without the mechanical-scientific apparatus running, the planet won't support its four billion people, or perhaps even half that. Agribusiness feeds the world. Hydrocarbon utilization heats and houses and clothes the people. There will be fear, hate, anger, death. The new barbarism. There will be plague and poison. And then the new Dark Ages."

"Should I pack?"

"Go ahead. Scoff. What the sane people and sane governments are trying to do is scuffle a little more breathing space, a little more time, before the collapse."

"How much time have we got?"

"If nobody pushes the wrong button or puts a bomb under the wrong castle, I would give us five more years at worst, twelve at best. What is triggering it is the crisis of reduced expectations. All over the world people are suddenly coming to realize that their children and grandchildren are going to have it worse than they did, that the trend line is down. So they want to blame somebody. They want to hoot and holler in the streets and burn something down."

"Whose side are you on?"

"I'm one of the scufflers. Cut and paste. Fix the world with paper clips and rubber bands."

"Are you *trying* to depress me, old buddy?"

"On Pearl Harbor Day?"

"So it is."

"And with each passing year it is going to seem ever more quaint, the little tin airplanes bombing the sleepy iron giants."

"There you go again."

He yawned and I noticed again how worn he looked. The international conference had been held in Zurich. There had been high hopes—the newspapers said—for a solution to the currency problems, but as it went on and on and on, interest could not be sustained, nor could hope.

"How was the trip back, Meyer?"

"I was too sound asleep to notice."

"Did you all just sit around and read papers to each other?"

"There was some of that. Yes. But most of it was workshop, computer analysis. Feed all the known, unchangeable factors into the program, and then add the ones that can be changed, predicating interdependence, making the variations according to a pattern, and analyzing the shape of the world that emerges, each one a computer model. Very bright young specialists assisted. We came out all too close to the doom anticipated by the Club of Rome, no matter how we switched the data around. It comes down to this, Travis—there are too many mouths to feed. One million three hundred thousand more every week! And of all the people who have ever been alive on Earth, more than half are living right now. We are gnawing the planet bare, and technology can't keep pace with need."

I had never seen him more serious, or more depressed. I fixed him a fresh drink when Gretel arrived. I met her, and after the welcome kiss, she looked over my shoulder and gave a whoop of surprise and pleasure at seeing Meyer. She thrust me aside and ran into his delighted bear hug. Then she held him off at arm's length and tilted her head to give him her brown-eyed measuring stare.

"You look *awful!*" she said. "You look like you just got out of jail."

"Fairly good guess. And you look fantastic, Gretel."

"It goes with the job. I got sort of sloppy living on this barge, eating too much and drinking too much. Today I jogged with four sets of fatties. I must have done seven miles. I've got the greatest new job."

"Travis was telling me about it."

"You'll have to come out and let me show you around." Quite suddenly the enthusiasm had faded out of her voice. I couldn't imagine why. She gave me a quick look and looked away, and went to the galley to fix herself one of her vegetable juice cocktails.

I followed her and said, "Is something wrong out there?"

"No. Of course not."

"Hey, Grets. This here is me. Asking."

"I hear you asking. I think I might fall right off the wagon right now. I'm down to where I can spare a few pounds. Straight Boodles and rocks, okay?"

"When you come down off it, you come down a way."

She leaned against a storage locker as I fixed her drink. I looked at her, a great lithe woman who, on tiptoe, could almost look me in the eye. Thick brown sun-streaked hair, dark brown eyes, firm jaw, broad mouth, high-bridged imperious nose. A woman of passion, intensity, good humor, mocking grace, and a very irritating and compelling need for total—or almost total —independence. During all the lazy weeks aboard *The Busted Flush* when, after the death of her brother in Timber Bay, I had brought her all the way around the peninsula to Fort Lauderdale, we had arrived at last at a relationship she had decided did not threaten her freedom. She was a hearty and sensuous woman, and for a long time she was suspicious and reluctant in lovemaking, apparently feeling that my increasing knowledge of her body's resources, its needs and rhythms and special stimuli, was somehow an exercise in ownership. But after she decided to accept completely, she became herself—forthright, evocative, and deliciously bawdy when the mood was upon her.

After she took a sip of her drink I put fingertips under her chin, tilted it up, kissed her gently on the lips, and then said, "Whatever it is, I would like to know. Okay? Like management trying to slip up on your blind side?"

She grinned. "*That* I can handle, McGee. What makes you think there's a blind side?"

"If there isn't, what are you doing *here?*"

She frowned into her drink. "I think I'll tell both of you. I think I could use more than one opinion."

We went back in and she sat next to Meyer on the yellow davenport. "What it is," she said, "I think something other than what is supposed to be going on out there, is going on out there."

"Bonnie Brae is a front for something else?" I asked.

"Not really that," she said. "I mean, it's pretty big and elaborate. Mr. Ladwigg and Mr. Broffski borrowed a fantastic amount of money to buy the land. It's twelve hundred and eighty acres. There was a big stone-and-cypress house on it, and outbuildings. It was called the Cattrell place and was empty for years while the estate was being settled. They put a half-million dollars into renovating the house and some of the other buildings. And they put in roads and a sewage-treatment plant, water supply, and all that. And they fixed the old airstrip near the barns. They are digging lakes, and building and selling houses, and selling building sites. We can accommodate twenty-four fatties in the main house at one time, feed them from the diet kitchen, and keep them busy. They pay twelve hundred a week, and there's a waiting list. And there's a waiting list for membership in the tennis club too. I mean, without knowing all the financial details, I'd say it's going very well. Mr. Ladwigg and Mr. Broffski have both built houses for themselves in the best part of the development, where the lots have to be two acres each, and Mr. Morse Slater, the manager, has a new house near theirs. There are twenty-five or thirty new houses occupied, and room for an awful lot more, of course. There are some staff quarters in the back of the main house, because it is sort of like a small hotel, or hospital. There is a nice flavor. I mean it's a good place to work. We have some laughs. People get along." Her voice trailed off and she sipped and frowned.

"And now something doesn't seem right?" Meyer asked, prompting her.

She smiled and leaned back. "Maybe I was lied to for too many years. Husband Billy was a world-champion-class liar. Brother John wasn't exactly clumsy at it."

"What's my rating?" I asked.

"All the returns aren't in. What I'm saying, maybe I get suspicious when there's no real need."

"We've got the whole evening, my dear," Meyer said. "If we're all patient, you'll probably get to the point sooner or later."

"I guess I'm dragging my feet because it sounds so weird I hate to mention it. Last week I had a batch of fatties down by the barns in the middle of the morning, making them do exercises, when a pretty little blue airplane landed on our strip. When I went back to the office, I asked Mr. Slater who had come in and he said that it was somebody to see Mr. Ladwigg, he didn't know what about. I asked because sometimes a buyer flies in, and when they buy something, it means more paperwork for me. Now we come to the coincidence part. I woke up real early the next morning. It was brisk and clear. The model house I'm living in is about a half mile from the office. A couple of days before, I lost a pin I like very much while leading a group jogging. So I put on a heavy sweater and went out to retrace our route, thinking maybe I could find it in the grass. I was over by the airstrip, searching near a patch of palmetto, when I heard a motor. For a moment I thought it was a plane, and then I stepped out almost into the path of Herman Ladwigg's Toyota, going cross-country. It's like a Land Rover, tall and open, with winches and things, and huge tires. It's white with red trim. Mr. Ladwigg was driving, and it startled him as much as it did me, I guess. I dodged back, and I was on the passenger side of it as it went by. So the face of the man riding with Mr. Ladwigg was not more than a yard away from me. I saw him very very clearly. And I knew in that split second I had seen him before. He looked right at me, and I saw the flicker of his recognition. He knew me too. But I couldn't remember where or when. All I could remember was that it had been an unpleasant experience."

"You can describe him?"

"Oh, sure. Big, but not fat. Big-boned. About forty, maybe a little less. Kind of a round face, with all his features sort of small and centered in the middle of all that face. Wispy blond hair cut quite short. No visible eyebrows or eyelashes. Lots and lots of pits and craters in his cheeks, from terrible acne when he was young. Little mouth, little pale eyes, girlish little nose. He was wearing a khaki jacket over a white turtleneck. He was holding onto the side of the passenger door because of the rough ride. His hands are very big and . . . well, brutal-looking."

Meyer said, "It doesn't sound as if there could be two like that. But it's possible, of course. Maybe his change of expression was not recognition, but surprise at seeing somebody pop up like that."

"No. He knew me. Because I remembered two nights ago, in the middle of the night, where I'd seen him. As soon as I remembered, I knew it was the same man. Five years ago Billy's sister, my kid sister-in-law, Mitsy, disappeared. The family was frantic. She'd been in school up near San Francisco. She had just taken her things and gone away. Billy got time off from work and went up to San Francisco and nosed around and found out she had been hanging around with some kids who were connected with a religion called . . . damn! It will come to me."

"The Unification Church, the Moonies?" Meyer asked. She shook her head. "Hare Krishna? Scientology? Children of God? The Jesus People? The Church of Armageddon?"

She stopped him and said, "That's close, that last one. It's like Apocalypse. Wait a minute. Apocrypha! The Church of the Apocrypha."

"Very *interesting!*" Meyer said.

"What's an apocrypha?" I asked.

"It's plural," he said. "Fourteen books or chapters which are sort of an appendix to the Old Testament and are not acceptable to the establishment. Seldom printed. They are bloody, merciless, and, some say, divinely inspired. Authorship unsubstantiated. I suspect that a religion based upon them would be . . . severe indeed."

"A postcard finally came from Mitsy," Gretel said. "It was mailed from Ukiah, California. It was to her mother, father, her two brothers, and me. All it said was, 'Remember that I will always love you, but I will never see you again in this life.' You can imagine how that hit us all. Mitsy was such a . . . such a *merry* little gal. Pretty and bouncy and popular. Your standard cheerleader type. No steady boyfriend. She wanted to be a social worker and work with handicapped children.

"Anyway, her father hired an investigator, and he located an encampment of the Church of the Apocrypha about twenty miles southwest of Ukiah, off in the woods. He had tried to get in to find out if Mitsy was there, but he couldn't learn a thing. Just about that time, her father—my father-in-law—had a stroke, a severe one. His right side was totally paralyzed, and he couldn't speak or understand what anyone said. He died of pneumonia about four months later. Billy's younger brother was working in Iran. So when we could, Billy and I drove up to the encampment, using the map the investigator had marked.

"There were little winding roads, and finally we came to the private, no-trespassing signs he had told us about, and the wire gate across the road. A young boy came out of a lean-to. He wore a dirty white smock and he was trying to grow a beard. We said we wanted to visit Miriam Howard, Mitsy Howard. He nodded and walked away up the curving road beyond the wire gate, and out of sight. We waited and waited and waited. Billy got very angry. I had to keep talking him out of going over the gate. It was over an hour before that man came down the road. That *same man.* He was five years younger, of course. He wore a white tunic with a Chinese collar, and white trousers tucked into shiny black boots. He came right to the high fence and looked us over very carefully. He completely ignored the angry questions Billy was shouting at him.

"Finally he spoke to us. There was so little movement of his lips it was as if he were a ventriloquist. He had a soft little voice. 'I am Brother Titus. I am an elder of the Church of the Apocrypha. You are inquiring about someone we now know as Sister Aquila. She has asked me to tell you that she is quite happy here and she does not wish to see you or anyone from her previous life.'

"Billy demanded to see her. He swore at Titus. It had no effect. He said it wasn't possible, not now, not ever. She was happy in her new life, he said. Billy said he was going to see his sister Mitsy, and if it took a court order for a conservatorship, he would get it. He'd gotten that information from the investigator.

"Brother Titus thought for a little while and told us to wait. In twenty minutes a little crowd of them, about nine or ten, came down to the gate. We didn't see Brother Titus again. The people ranged in age from, I would guess, sixteen to twenty-five. Three or four girls, and the rest boys. At first we thought they had come without Mitsy, and then we recognized her. It was a shock. She had become such a worn, skinny, subdued little thing. She wore a dirty white smock and she had some kind of serious rash on her face and throat and arms. They looked badly chapped. The smock was too big for her. All of them had exactly the same look. It's hard to describe. Sort of bland and smug and glassy.

"They stood very close to her as she stood at the gate. She said, 'Hello, Billy. Hello, Gretel. I don't know how you found me, but I'm sorry you did.' Billy said, 'What have they *done* to you, Mitsy?' She said, 'My name is Sister Aquila now. They have made me very happy. I am full of peace and happiness and the love of God. Please don't ever try to find me again. Tell Mama and Papa I'm happy here, happier than I've ever been before.' Billy said, 'You better come home. Pop has had a very bad stroke. Things are in terrible shape. We all need you.' She didn't turn a hair. She looked at him with that contented half smile and said, 'All of that is in my previous life. It has nothing to do with me now. My life is here. Go away, please. God bless you.' They all turned and went up the hill together, so close together they made each other stumble from time to time. They all had exactly that same *look*. It took the heart right out of Billy."

"Did you make another try?" Meyer asked.

"Billy did. He went up there several weeks later, but they told him she was gone. They said she had been 'called' to another place in the service of the Lord. If it wasn't for the stroke, maybe the family would have taken some kind of action through the courts, but money was scarce, and God knows Billy and I couldn't finance a court order and deprogramming her and all that. The brother came back from Iran about six months before Billy ran out on me. Carl, his name is. He couldn't understand why we couldn't get her away from those people. He wasn't here. He couldn't know how it was. He lives in Houston now, at least he did the last I heard, and their mother lives with him and his wife."

"So you saw Brother Titus here, last week?" I said.

"Definitely. He was so . . . so out of context, it took a while to remember where I'd seen him before. But I am positive. Trav, there's another thing that seems odd. After they went by me, they headed for the airstrip, and a little later the blue plane took off. I *saw* it take off and head west. When Mr. Ladwigg drove back home, he drove on the road. Why did he take Brother Titus on such a roundabout way? Was it because Titus didn't want to be seen by anybody?"

"Maybe he was showing him some land. Maybe the Church wants to set up an encampment here," I said.

"Where there isn't any available? That piece was sold months ago."

"To whom?" Meyer asked.

"To some kind of foreign syndicate, headquartered in Brussels. I was told they plan to put up a hotel-club where members can come for holidays in the States. They took twenty undeveloped acres over on our western boundary near the airstrip."

"For foreign members of the Church of the Apocrypha?" Meyer asked with a sweet smile.

"Oh, no!" Gretel looked horrified. "Mr. Ladwigg and Mr. Broffski and Mr. Slater would have fits. It can't be that, really. Could it, Travis? Could that creep . . ."

"Not at the price they're probably getting out there."

"Two hundred and twenty-five thousand. It was a special price because of no roads or water supply or sewer."

"Maybe Brother Titus left the Church," I suggested. "Maybe he's into real estate. That has the status of a religion in south Florida."

She didn't laugh. She was scowling. "I keep thinking of Mitsy. Her hands were grubby and her hair was caked with dirt. She had sores on her ankles. She looked exhausted. I am damn well going to find out exactly what that man is doing around there. And it can't be anything good."

"You two are well-matched," Meyer said. "You both have the same kind of compulsive curiosity. I will tell you what I tell Travis, my dear. Proceed with caution. The world is full of damp rocks, with some very strange creatures hiding under them."

"Herm Ladwigg is an old honey bear," she said. "He would not be involved in anything tricky or dirty. And if I can think of the right way to ask him, he'll tell me what's going on."

The next time we looked at Meyer, we found he had fallen asleep in the chair. He would bitterly resent our leaving him like that, so we stirred him awake. He said he was too tired to eat, and over Gretel's protests that she could stir up something in a hurry, he went clumping on back to his stubby old cabin cruiser moored just down the pier from my slip, the *John Maynard Keynes,* sighing in consternation at the state of all the money in the world.

We buttoned up *The Busted Flush.* Gretel kicked off her shoes and hung herself around my neck and grinned into my face and said, "Well . . . will it be before or after the crab-meat feast I am going to fix us?"

I gave it judicious thought. "How about a little of both?"

"How did I know you were going to say that?"

"Because I usually do."

"Shut up and deal," she whispered.

So the gusty winds of a Friday night in December came circling through the marina, grinding and tilting all the play boats and work boats around us, creaking the hulls against the fenders, clanking fittings against masts. While in the big bed in the master stateroom her narrowed eyes glinted in faint reflected light, my hands found the well-known slopes and lifts and hollows of her warmth and agility. We played the games of delay and anticipation, of teasing and waiting, until we went past the boundaries of willed restraint and came in a mounting rush that seemed to seek an even greater closeness than the paired loins could provide. And then subsided, with the outdoor wind making breathing sounds against the superstructure of the old barge-type houseboat, and the faint swing and dip of the hull seeming to echo, in a slower pace, the lovemaking just ended. With neither of us knowing or guessing that it was the very last night. With neither of us able to endure that knowledge had we been told.

2

BECAUSE GRETEL had too many jobs at Bonnie Brae, she went back out Saturday morning to catch up on her desk work, driving off in the little Honda Civic I had helped her find and buy. It had belonged to a hairdresser at Pier 66 who had decided to marry her friend and go live in Saudi Arabia. It was pink, with a special muffler.

She planned to come in again early Saturday evening and stay until Monday morning. It was a bright breezy day. My two best Finor reels were overdue for cleaning and oiling, and I had the first one apart when Grets phoned me from work.

Her voice was hushed. "Darling, there is one hell of a mess out here. Herm is dead."

"Herm?"

"Ladwigg. Mr. Ladwigg. One of the owners."

"Heart attack?"

"They don't know yet. He's been bicycling early in the morning lately, for exercise, riding around the new roads they put in. And they found him in the middle of the road, face down, next to the bicycle. He either blacked out and the fall killed him . . . they just don't know yet. He was forty-six. What I wanted to say, don't expect me tonight, huh? Catherine—Mrs. Ladwigg—is in shock. They gave her a sedative. I'm here at the Ladwigg house trying to get in touch with her son and daughter. The son is a lawyer in Anchorage and the daughter works for the U.S. Embassy in Helsinki, and I haven't got through to either of them yet. When I do, I'm going to stay here until one or both of them get here. There's nobody else to do it. Stan Broffski's wife is a total loss in a situation like this."

"Want me to come out and help you wait around?"

"That's nice of you, but no, thanks."

"Let me know when you think you'll be free, when you have an idea of the time."

"Sure. Bye, dear."

So I went back to my fish reels. It was just ten o'clock, Saturday morning, December 8. They were having their weekend in Helsinki and in Anchorage. No telling how long it would take to find either of them. In the meanwhile, poor Herm had succumbed to the age of the jock. The mystique of pushing yourself past your limits. The age of shin splints, sprung knees, and new hernias. An office-softened body in its middle years needs a long, long time to come around. Until a man can walk seven miles in two hours without blowing like a porpoise, without sweating gallons, without pumping his heart past 120, it is asinine to start jogging. Except for a few dreadful lapses which have not really gone on too long, I have stayed in shape all my life. Being in shape means knowing your body, how it feels, how it responds to this and to that, and when to stop. You develop a sixth sense about when to stop. It is not mysticism. It is brute labor, boring and demanding. Violent exercise is for children and knowledgeable jocks. Not for insurance adjustors and sales managers. They do not need to be in the shape they want to be, and could not sustain it if they could get there. Walking briskly no less than six hours a week will do it for them. The McGee System for earnest office people. I can push myself considerably further because I sense when I'm getting too close to the place where something is going to pop, rip, or split.

Meyer stopped by a little while after I'd finished the reels. He said he had slept fourteen hours and still felt tired. I told him about the trouble out at Bonnie Brae, and he agreed with me that Ladwigg had probably pushed himself beyond his ability. A fall onto asphalt paving from a ten-speed bike going twenty miles an hour can easily be fatal, especially without a helmet. I doubted Ladwigg would wear a crash helmet while cruising his own development in the early hours.

Gretel phoned again at half-past noon to say she had located the son in Alaska and told him the news, and he expected to be able to get to Lauderdale late this same night.

"You sound a little beat," I said.

"Do I? The phone has been driving me crazy. But I do feel sort of blah. As if I'm coming down with a bug."

"Can you get somebody to take over?"

"I'm trying."

"I think I'll come on out."

"I . . . I'll be glad to see you."

Meyer left. I locked up the *Flush,* went over to the parking area, and cranked up my ancient Rolls pickup, the electric-blue Miss Agnes. The replaced power plant yanked her along too fast for her tall antique dignity, like a dowager blown into an unwilling trot by a gale-force wind. I made a stop on Spangler and picked up a pair of quarter-pounders with cheese, on the assumption that Gretel wouldn't have had time for lunch either.

I went all the way over to the University Drive intersection and turned north past the new plazas and shopping centers, the caramel-colored condominiums, the undeveloped flatlands where the palmetto still grew, the clusters of wooden town houses with roofs cut into steep new architectural clichés to shed some unimaginable snow load. Bonnie Brae had marked their entrance with squat fat brick pillars on either side of their divided-lane driveway. It curved off to the right to the big parking area near the renovated Cattrell place now used as clubhouse, fat farm, and administration building. When the gusty wind slowed, there was heat in the sun. I could see people bobbing and trotting about over on the tennis courts.

I went into the foyer of the building, hoping to find somebody who would direct me to Ladwigg's new house. A man came out of a room at my right and walked up to me, hand out.

"Mr. McGee?" He was a boyish thirty-something, with apple cheeks, a bushy blond mustache, thinning blond hair carefully adjusted to hide the thinning, bow tie, gray tweed jacket with leather elbows. When I nodded he shook my hand heartily and said, "I'm Morse Slater. Maybe Gretel has mentioned me."

"The manager, yes." He had a bumbling kind of effusiveness about him, a shoe-clerk willingness to please, which was given the lie by the ice-blue eyes, intent, aware, measuring. I said, "What I want to know is how I find the—"

"Gretel told me to look out for you. I just took her up the Drive to the hospital. Got back minutes ago."

"What happened?"

"Some sort of bug, I think. She seemed to be in a half faint, and she felt so hot to the touch it frightened me. So I took her right to Emergency and signed her in. They took her temperature and checked her into the hospital and began tests. A Dr. Tower seemed to be the one giving the orders. We accepted financial responsibility, of course. All our people have insurance which . . . but you're not interested in that. Room one thirty-three."

I think he tried to say something else, but I was already on my way. The hospital was on the same side of University Drive, and a little more than a half mile away.

I managed to talk my way to the nurses' station and then down the corridor to the room where Gretel was. It was a two-bed room with an old woman asleep and snoring by the windows, with a curtain drawn between the two beds. I pulled a straight chair close beside Gretel and took her hand. It felt dry and hot.

"What's going on?" I asked her.

Her lips were swollen and cracked, and her brown hair was damp and matted. She moistened her lips and gave me a small wry smile. "It's one of those days," she said. "Oh, boy. I got up and busted my favorite coffee mug that you gave me. Herm Ladwigg died in the street. A bug gave me a hell of a sting in the back of the neck. Later on, when I began to feel dizzy, I fainted and fell and broke one of the big lamps in the Ladwigg house. And here I am. It's one of those days."

"What do they say is wrong?"

"They don't say. Fever of unknown origin. My ears are ringing so loud you should be able to hear them. I really feel weird."

"They're running tests, aren't they? They'll find out what you've got."

A little bit of a sallow blond nurse came hurrying in. She had a fifty-year-old face and a twenty-five-year-old body. She gave me a disapproving glance, took a temperature reading with an electronic gadget, then took blood pressure on the left arm, pursed her lips, came around and displaced me, and took the pressure on the other arm. She trotted out. I moved close. Gretel found my wrist with her hot dry hand and held tight. "Trav, I feel so hot. I'm burning up. I feel terrible, Trav. Terrible."

When I spoke to her again, she didn't answer. She seemed to be asleep, her eyes about one third open, breathing so rapidly and shallowly through her mouth, it scared me.

I went plunging out to find somebody and ran into a couple of orderlies pushing a stretcher. I asked them what was going on, and they said they were taking a patient named Gretel Howard to Intensive Care. Other than that, they knew nothing.

I followed along, after they had raised the bed and pulled her across onto the stretcher. They tried to keep me from getting into the elevator with her, but it didn't work. But they did stop me at the door of the Intensive Care area. I told a very large white-haired nurse that if somebody didn't come and tell me within ten minutes what was going on, I was coming through that door.

The doctor who came out said his name was Tower. Vance Tower. He led me over to some rattan chairs near a window and we sat down and he said, "I need some background here."

"What's the matter with her?"

He had taken a little Pearlcorder out of his pocket and put it into dictation mode. "Name, address, and occupation, please," he said, and held it up between us. They make you play their game their way, and if you want a lot of delays, just refuse to go along. Travis McGee. Slip F-18, Bahia Mar Marina. Salvage Consultant.

"Relationship to patient?"

I hesitated, then said, "Common-law husband." After all, she had lived aboard the houseboat with me for a lot of weeks.

He was a dumpy-looking man, soft and pale and too heavy, going bald, short of breath, looking out of tired little brown eyes at me, showing no reaction at all to my answers.

"How can we contact her close relatives?"

"There aren't any. Parents and only brother are dead. She is divorced from her first husband. No children. I think there may be some distant kin, second cousins and so on, but I would have no idea how to reach them."

"Where has she been lately? Geographically, that is."

"Lately? Up until May she was living in Timber Bay over on the west coast. Then we came around to Lauderdale aboard my houseboat. We took our time. Got here in early August. She lived aboard and then moved to one of the model houses at Bonnie Brae to be closer to her work. A temporary arrangement."

"Did she go out of the country at any time since last May?"

"No."

"Has she been in swamp country?"

"No. Why?"

"Do you know if any of the people she has been associated with have been taken seriously ill, quite suddenly?"

"I don't know if this is what you mean, but one of the owners of Bonnie Brae fell off his bicycle this morning and—"

"I know about that. I mean an illness like hers, characterized by extremely high temperatures, sporadic delirium, cardiac arrhythmia, and fading blood pressure."

"I can't think of anyone we know who's been sick lately. What's wrong with her?"

"I've ordered every lab test I can think of. I don't approve of the shotgun approach to antibiotics, but I'm giving her a wide range of those. If we can't knock that fever down any other way, I'm going to try packing her in ice." He sighed heavily. "The big problem with treating something when you don't know what it is, you can make diagnosis all that more difficult."

"Can I see her?"

He thought it over, then nodded. "They'll be busy in there. You can see her five minutes out of every hour. I'll approve that. It won't be pleasant for you, and I doubt if she'll know you're there."

A nurse came out and motioned to him, and he got up and plodded in, through the double doors. Man at work. A very tired man. But he was an empathetic man because, about ten minutes later, he beckoned to me and took me to her bedside. The rapid shallow breathing had eased. There was an I.V. rigged, dripping into the vein in her arm. Her cheeks seemed hollower than they had looked an hour before, in her room, her eyes more sunken.

He said in a low voice, "We knocked the fever down almost one degree. First sign of progress."

We walked out together and he said, "I'm making a full report of all our findings to Disease Control in Atlanta. Do you know anything about the red welt on the back of her neck?"

"She told me she was bitten by a bug this morning. She said it stung her."

"Symptoms bear no relation to anaphylactic shock. We've taken some tissue from the area. It's being packed in dry ice and flown to Atlanta, along with blood samples and so forth. Got more sophisticated analysis systems available up there. Paper chromatography. Thin-layer chromatology techniques."

The hours blurred. I went in as often as I could. Night and day inside hospitals are too much alike. Saturday night. Sunday. Sunday night. She kept changing, little by little, going further away from me. They did a tracheotomy, and from then on a machine was doing her breathing for her, pumping her chest up and down. When I bent close to her to touch my lips to her dank forehead, I could detect the faint sour smell of mortal illness. At one point, early in the vigil, I went out to the car and made the mistake of trying to eat one of the clammy hamburgers and was sick on the asphalt.

Meyer came out, bringing a change of clothes and my toilet kit. A nurse found me a towel and took me to a place where I could shower and scrape the pale stubble off my tired brown jaws.

Somebody forgot to stop me and tell me. I went in a little after eleven on Monday night, and she was gone. The bed was empty. The equipment had been moved away.

"Where is she?" I roared, and they came running toward me, hushing me, ushering me toward the door.

A big black nurse, big as a tight end, had been answering questions for me during other visits during that shift. She took hold of my shoulders and gave me a shake. "Easy now! Easy now!" she said in a husky whisper. "It's better we lost her."

"Better than what?"

"Hush now. You hush down. A temperature like that, for so long, it cooked her brain. She would have been a vegetable. Terrible thing, a strong young woman like that." She had led me out into the corridor. "Who you got to come get you?"

"I'll manage." I tried to smile. The tears were running down my face. No sobs. No shudders. Just eyes running. "Where is she now?"

"They're doing an autopsy."

"Who said they could!"

"It's a law, Mr. McGee. When the cause of death is unknown, they have to. There's no way anybody can stop them, and that's a good law. Whatever is killing people, we have to find it out."

"What finally happened? There was that machine . . ."

She shrugged. "Total kidney failure, and then the heart gave out right about the same time." She shook her head. Her eyes were shining with unshed tears. "I don't know. We get so many old ones here. Not young strong women like her. Whatever it was, it came and wore her right down to nothing. It took the life right out of her. It ate her up, like it was some hungry thing.'' She caught herself. ''Sorry. I talk too much. Listen, if you're the only one she had, what you've got to do now, you've got to make the arrangements. She's got to have a burial.''

I walked on out of their hospital, snuffling from time to time, marveling that I could walk with so little thought and effort. Long strides, heels thudding against the tile floor, hand lifting without conscious command to flatten against the push plate on the big glass door, push and let me out into the chill night, spangled with stars that were faint above the security lights of the parking area. I walked to the tall dark shape of Miss Agnes, my ancient Rolls, and leaned against one of her high front fenders, my arms folded, ankles crossed, eyes running again.

Cessation. Ending. A stopping of her. I heard the night sounds of country and city. Yawk of a night bird nearby. Faraway eerie pulsing of siren. Whispering drone of light traffic on University Drive, lights in moving patterns. Grinding whine of trucks moving fast, a mile or so away. Random night wind clattering palm fronds. This was the world, bustling its way on through its allotted four billion more years of time, carrying its four billion souls gracelessly onward. A lot of them had stopped tonight, some in blood and terror. I tried to comprehend the enormity—the obscenity—of the fact that Gretel Howard had been one of them, just as dead as the teenagers who impacted a tree at a hundred and ten miles an hour near Tulsa, the flying dentist who didn't see the power lines, the Muslim children dead by fire in Bangladesh, the three hundred elderly in Florida who would not make it through the night in their nursing-home beds.

I could not fit my mind around the realization of finality. There seemed to be more that would happen for the two of us, more of life to be consumed and completed. My body knew with a dreadful precision all the contours of her, the shapes and fittings, the sighs and turnings, gasps and pressures.

I sought refuge in a child's dreaming. They had spirited her away, mended her, and would soon spring the great surprise upon me. She would come running, laughing, half crying, saying, ''Darling, we were just fooling you a little. That's all. Did we scare you too much? I'm sorry, Trav, dear. So sorry. Take me home.''

And on the way home she would explain to me how she had outwitted the green ripper. I had read once about a little kid who had overheard some adult conversation and afterward, in the night, had terrible nightmares. He kept telling his people he dreamed about the green ripper coming to get him. They finally figured out that he had heard talk about the grim reaper. I had told Grets about it, and it had found its way into our personal language. It was not possible that the green ripper had gotten her.

Not possible.

3

MEYER TOOK care of practically everything. I couldn't have managed. I was too listless and too depressed. We both remembered that after her

brother's death at Timber Bay, Gretel said she preferred cremation, just
as he had. Cremation and maybe a small nondenominational memorial
service for close friends. Not many people had attended John Tuckerman's
memorial service in Timber Bay. He had been too closely associated
with Hubbard Lawless, the man who had taken all the money and tried to
run.

I did not think there would be many people who would want to come to
Gretel's memorial service. Meyer arranged it at a small chapel up beyond
South Beach Park, at eleven in the morning on Saturday, ten days before
Christmas.

Ten or so people came in from Bonnie Brae. And a lot of people from the
Bahia Mar area. Meyer calls it a subculture, the permanents. The great waves
of tourists and boat people flood the area and recede, leaving the same old
faces, most of them, year after year. I did not see all of them come in. When
it was over and we walked out into December sunshine, they were there,
moving toward me to touch, to shake hands, to kiss, to say some fumbly
words: We're sorry. That's what it was about. Together we form a village.
And share the trouble as much as we can. Take as much of it upon ourselves
as is possible, and we know it is not very much. Okay?

There was Skeeter, and there were Gabe and Doris Marchman—Gabe's
metal crutches glinting in the sun. From charter-boat row there were Billy
Maxwell, Lew and Sandy, Barney and Babs, Roxy and his nephews. There
was the Alabama Tiger, and Junebug was with him, looking strangely subdued. Raul and Nita Tenero were there, up from Miami, with Merrimay
Lane. There were Irv Deibert and Johnny Dow, and Chookie and Arthur
Wilkinson, back together again. And there were others, from the hotel and
the shops, the boatyards and the tethered fleet.

My village and my people. They seemed to know what I needed most, a
sense of place, the feeling of belonging to some kind of resilient society. A
man can play the game of being the loner, moving unscathed through an
indifferent world, toughened by the diminished expectations of his place and
time. I spoke to them, thanked them, managing to keep myself together. As
I did so, I thought of the ones who weren't there any more. Lois, of course.
Puss Killian. Mike Gibson, of the world before I came to the marina. Nora
Gardino. Barni Baker, who went down with her 727 into the swamp short of
the airfield. Too damn many of them. I could just barely stand losing them,
but I couldn't handle having Gretel gone too. She was destined to be a part
of the life that would come after the marina. But she was gone and I was fixed
there, embedded in time, embedded in a life I had in some curious way
outgrown. I was an artifact, genus boat bum, a pale-eyed, shambling, gan-
gling, knuckly man, without enough unscarred hide left to make a decent
lampshade. Watchful appraiser of the sandy-rumped beach ladies. Creaking
knight errant, yawning at the thought of the next dragon. They don't make
grails the way they used to. She had deserted me here, left me in this now
unbreakable mold, this half-farcical image, trapped me in my solitary, fussy,
bachelor hang-ups from now until they turned me off too. I shook hands, I
hugged and was hugged, and I tried to smile into reddened eyes, and they
left, slowly, car doors chunking, driving away from the sunlit ceremony of
farewell to my girl.

I had parked Miss Agnes two blocks away. An electric-blue Rolls hand-hewn into a pickup truck seemed too conspicuous and frivolous for a memorial service for my dead.

After we got in and I waited for the chance to move out from the curb, Meyer said, "Did it go all right? Did he pick the right things to read?"

"It was fine."

"I tried to ask you ahead of time, but I couldn't seem to get through."

"It was fine."

I thought of the fine running we had done, Gretel and I, on the beach near the shack where her brother was living. I thought of making love with her on the sun deck at dusk, in a hard warm summer rain. I had never really told her how much it all meant. There was going to be plenty of time for that. All the rest of her life. I could make a list of the things we were going to talk about someday. When we had the time.

"Good turnout," Meyer said.

"For God's sake!"

"So I'll keep my mouth shut."

"Fine."

I wanted to apologize, but couldn't find the right way to begin, and so the rest of the ride was silent. He sat beside me like a gloomy bear. I knew his feelings weren't hurt. He was sad because I had lost Gretel, and because we had lost Gretel.

"I picked out an urn," he said, as we pulled into the parking place. "Nothing ornate. Bronze, though. Seventy-two something, including tax. He wrapped it up in a box and brown paper, ready for mailing."

"I might take it out there."

"I told him you might do that," he said. "I've got the box at my place. I'll bring it over. Unless you'd like to have me go on out there with you."

"I'll let you know, Meyer. Keep it for now. And thanks."

He headed over to the newsstand to see if his copy of *Barron's* had come in, and I walked back to *The Busted Flush,* anxious to get out of the suit and get the necktie off. And anxious to see how much Boodles gin I could fit into a king-size old-fashioned glass.

Two men had boarded my houseboat. They were on my little back porch aft the lounge, one sitting on a folding stool, the other leaning against the rail. They were of a size and age, middle height, middle forties, a tailored three-piece gray suit, with white shirt, black shoes, blue necktie with a white figure; a tailored three-piece chocolate-brown suit, with white shirt, brown shoes, tan necktie with a small figure. Gray Suit wore a gray tweed snap-brim hat, and Brown Suit wore a dark brown hound's-tooth tweed hat. Soft jowls, pale faces, horn-rim glasses on one, metal-rim glasses on the other. One stood up and the other pushed off from the rail as I came aboard.

"Mr. McGee?" said Gray Suit.

The brain is a swift and subtle computer. I have perhaps become more sensitive to the clues which exist in mannerisms, stance, expression, hand gestures, and dress than most people. If you are in a line of work where a bad guess can give you a pair of broken elbows, you tend to become a quick study.

They were not going to try to sell me anything. They did not have the twinkle, the up-front affability. They were not here to enforce one of the idiot rules of a bureaucracy that grows like high-speed cancer. They did not have that look of fatuous satisfaction and autocratic, patronizing indifference of fellows who come to tell you that you forgot to file Form Z-2324, as amended. Or to tell you that you can't cut down your pine tree without enlisting the services of an approved, accredited, licensed tree surgeon.

They looked important. As if they had come to buy the marina and put up a research institute. Lawyers? Executives? They were not very fit. They moved heavily. They looked out of place aboard my houseboat, as if it was a little closer to the outdoor life than they cared to be.

"I am not exactly cheered up by people coming aboard without being asked," I said.

"Forgive the intrusion, please," Gray Suit said. He had been the one sitting. "I am not familiar with marine protocol, Mr. McGee. We were told this is your houseboat, and we have been waiting for you. My name is Toomey. This is Mr. Kline."

"I am not in the mood for visitors or transactions or conversation about anything."

"We are anxious to talk to you," Kline said. He had picked up a dispatch case I had not noticed before. It matched his suit color. "I think it would all go more smoothly if you did not put us in the position where we would have to insist."

I studied him. "You are telling me that if you have to insist, you have the leverage to make it stick?"

"We do indeed," said Toomey. "And we would rather not."

So I unlocked and we went into the lounge. I have played respectable poker over the years. I won my houseboat on a broken flush, four pink ones up and a stranger down. I can sense when a bluff is a bluff is a bluff. They had the leverage, and the clothes and manner to go with it.

Before I invited them to sit down while I changed, I asked to see credentials. They looked vaguely like passports, small with the dark blue cover and great seal of the U. S. of A. Inside were the color ID pictures, the thumbprint, the name of an agency I had never heard of before.

"We do not usually go out into the field," Toomey said. "We have access to another agency for investigative matters. But after a conference with our superior, it was suggested that we take a firsthand look."

"At what?"

"Excuse me. I thought you'd guessed."

"Guessed what?"

"We want to ask you what you know about Gretel Tuckerman Howard."

"I just came back from her memorial service."

"We know that," Kline said.

"Sit down. I'll be back in a minute."

I took my time changing into old flannel slacks, Mexican sandals, and an old wool shirt. There was a small chill spot at the nape of my neck. A warning of some kind.

They had moved a couple of chairs close to the coffee table. Kline had a little Sony TC-150 opened up, and he was breaking the seal on a new cassette. "I hope you won't mind that I tape this."

"Go right ahead."

He put the tape in, put it on Record and counted to ten, rewound, played it back, rewound again, and said, "December fifteenth, one ten P.M., initial interview by Toomey and Kline with Travis McGee aboard his houseboat moored at Slip F-Eighteen, Bahia Mar Marina, Fort Lauderdale, Florida.''

Toomey took over. ''Please describe your relationship to the decedent. Wait. Excuse me. Where and when did you meet her?''

''Earlier this year. May. At a beach shack where her brother was living. John Tuckerman. South of Timber Bay, over on the west coast of Florida. The northwest coast. Her brother died a little while later. I went with Gretel when she flew out to California to have his ashes buried in a little cemetery in Petaluma. We flew back to Timber Bay and, sometime in June, we left Timber Bay in this houseboat and came down around the peninsula and back up here to Lauderdale. We made it a leisurely trip. We got here in August. She lived aboard until she located the job at Bonnie Brae in early November and moved out there, to one of the model houses.''

With great delicacy Toomey asked, ''Would you say that you and she had a . . . significant relationship?''

''I didn't care what rules we went by, as long as we both agreed that it would be a permanent thing. Why do you have to know stuff like this?''

''We want to know whether the relationship was such that she would confide in you.''

''Confide what?''

''Let us just say details of her workday, her life out there. That sort of thing.''

''Are you looking into something fishy at Bonnie Brae?''

''Did Mrs. Howard say something fishy is going on at Bonnie Brae?''

''No. No, she didn't. I mean, she called up last Saturday morning before she got sick, to tell me about one of the owners, Mr. Ladwigg, dying in an accidental fall on his bicycle, if that's what you mean.''

Kline took over. ''Let me set up a hypothesis, Mr. McGee, and see if that helps. Suppose Mrs. Howard, in the course of her employment out there, learned that something curious was going on. Say that part of the operation was a cover for something else, like gambling or smuggling or something of that nature. Would she have confided in you?''

''Of course.''

''Would she have confided something like that to anyone other than you? Or as well as you?''

''I can't see that happening.''

''And she talked to you about her work?''

''Certainly. About her exercise classes of fatties, and the tennis lessons she was giving to children, and the forms she had to complete on each sale of land, houses, and so forth. She liked her work.''

The two men looked at each other, and Kline reached over and punched the key to turn off the recorder. Toomey said, ''We do appreciate your cooperation, Mr. McGee.''

''Wouldn't you say you owe me some kind of explanation . . . why you are interested in Gretel Howard?''

Toomey smiled sadly. ''I wish we could. I really wish we could. There was a possibility she could have acquired some information which would have been useful to us. Unfortunately she became ill before we had a chance to speak with her.''

"If I happen to remember something later on, how do I get in touch with you?" I asked. "I'm pretty upset right now and I'm not thinking too clearly."

Kline tore a sheet out of a small spiral notebook and wrote a number on it: (202) 661-7007. I thanked him. They put the recorder away in the dispatch case, smiled politely, put on their hats, and marched off, down my little gangplank and off toward the parking area, in step, arms swinging in unison.

Three minutes later Sue Sampson arrived, bearing a casserole of hot beef stew. She apologized for having to miss the service and took off just as Meyer arrived.

I made the delayed drinks. Meyer put the stew over low heat while we sat and he listened to the saga of Toomey and Kline.

"All right," he said, "so you sidestepped. You left out Brother Titus and the blue airplane and the twenty-acre sale to a syndicate in Brussels. But you make them sound very authentic."

"While they were boring in, I was deciding several things. First, that I am not in very good emotional shape to spar with anybody about anything. Second, that I could get in touch with them later. Third, that they were almost too perfect. Too cold and clean. They had no regional accent that I could detect. They said they did not usually go out into the field. That implied some importance to talking to me. But it never came off as important. They wanted some hearsay about what might be going on at Bonnie Brae. Colloquial American pronunciation, but a stilted kind of sentence structure. Almost like you when you are at your most professorial."

"Didactic is a better word. The tendency to lecture others."

"Kline made those little continental crossbars on the sevens in the phone number. See?"

"But that came after you had decided to hold off."

"Before that, their pants were too long. Long enough almost to step on the back of the cuffs. Like Kissinger. The necktie knots were wrong. Frenchmen tie them that way. When Kline cleaned his glasses and held them up to the light, I looked through them too, and I saw no distortion."

"So the glasses were a very minor correction. So both of them have lived and worked abroad. So they spoke another language before they learned English."

"I know. I know. But, dammit, it seemed like such an invasion of my personal privacy to have strangers here asking me to talk about Gretel. I am not ready to talk about Gretel to anybody. I am not impressed by official credentials. Not by Mr. Robert A. Toomey or Mr. Richard E. Kline, on the staff of the Select Committee on Special Resources in the Senate Office Building."

"Are you sure you remember that accurately?"

"I'm sure."

Meyer wrote it down on Kline's piece of paper. "No great problem to check it out on Monday, if you'd like."

"I'd like."

"Ready for stew?"

"Right after the next drink. If it all checks out, I'll forget my paranoia and phone them and tell all."

"And what if it doesn't check out? What if your instincts were accurate?"

"Then I'm going to have to try to figure out what they were really after. The cover story was very elaborate. I wouldn't think they'd have gone to all that trouble just for me. I would be incidental to something more important to them, or to someone."

I had one drink more than I needed. Meyer dished out the stew. I managed almost half of what he served me. He wanted to clean up, but I shooed him out, sent him home.

After I washed the dishes, I locked up and went over the pedestrian bridge to the beach. A high gray overcast had moved in, pushed by a cool fitful breeze off the sea. I had put on good shoes for walking, and I headed north on packed damp sand, lunging along, carrying with me my sorrow, my mild headache, my sour stomach, and the dull pain in my right thigh which cold and damp will cause. I plodded along the beach all the way up to Galt Ocean Mile, and from there on I alternated between the beach and A-1-A, depending on obstacles. The cold and the oncoming dusk had emptied the beaches. The glassy facades of the condominiums glittered down at me.

I pushed hard, but even so it had been dark a long time when I crossed back over to the mainland on the Atlantic Boulevard bridge at Pompano Beach. I walked the seven short blocks to North Federal Highway. They were promoting Christmas carols at the big shopping center, pumping them out into the night wind. Jangle bells. And the silent stars go by.

When I found a saloon, I had a small draft beer and phoned a cab. One Oscar Lopez arrived in a rattle-bang rig that smelled strongly of cigar and faintly of vomit. He was dubious about the length of the trip compared with the appearance of the passenger, and I had to show him that I had money. Though he played loud rock and drove badly, he did not have to be told to turn east at Sunrise. He let me off at the marina. I walked to my houseboat, let myself in. It was empty. I had gotten used to a certain amount of emptiness after she had moved way out there to Bonnie Brae. But it had been a conditional emptiness. She could and would return. But now it was a hollowness beyond belief. Even the promise of life and warmth had been drained out of that clumsy old hull. She was hollow, brittle, tacky, and old, sighing in a night wind, smelling faintly of onion, unwilling to admit that Gretel had ever lived here with me. My legs were leaden with fatigue. The small beer was caught in the back of my throat. Gretel was turned to ash and confined in bronze. The green ripper sailed by on the night wind, looking for more customers. I suggested, politely, that I would give him no big argument this time. But there were others with a higher priority tonight.

4

I GOT through Sunday—with a little help from my friends. It was a day of cold December rain. I uncrated and hooked up my new speakers. They had been delivered ten days ago. Once they were positioned and adjusted, I tied them down. I had been going to give the old ones to Gretel to give to a friend, but I couldn't remember the friend's name.

The new ones had a great big full rich sound for such small enclosures. They worked all day long. Big music and Bloody Marys. People came by and brought bottles and food and stayed for a time and left again. When it would begin to get too noisy, somebody would remember that too much merriment was probably in bad taste, and things would quiet down, but not for long. It was a party related to a wake.

At the bitter end of the day there was but one guest left aboard. I had heard about her but had never met her. She was the third or fourth wife of some old party from Long Island whose hundred-and-twenty-foot ocean-going yacht was moored at one of the big berths, with a permanent crew of five. The *Madrina,* meaning "godmother," a nice enough name for a ship. The *Madrina* had been at the marina for a month because her owner had a very bad stroke the day before they were to sail for Bermuda. I did not know who brought the wife aboard my vessel, or left her there with me. Smallish, dark-haired, and very nice to look upon, she was a creature of many subtle perfections. Named Anna. An accent I could not place. Some Portuguese, she said, and Chinese, and a lot of White Russian, born in Hong Kong, and with a degree in engineering from the University of Alabama.

Anna wore a woolly white jump suit with a turtleneck, a heavy-duty gold zipper all the way down the front of it, and some little marine flag signals embroidered over the pocket. At five of midnight, after the others had left, there we were. She was curled into a corner of my yellow sofa, brandy glass in hand, looking over at me out of dark eyes under dark brows under the wing of smooth jet hair across her forehead. She stared with a total focus of her attention, watchful as a cat. The white outfit fitted so closely no one with figure flaws could have managed it. I couldn't remember who had brought her into the group.

"We have very much the same kind of trouble, Travis," she said.

"We do?"

"They told me the day before yesterday, at the hospital, that Harvey won't live."

"I'm sorry to hear it."

"Just two short years. That's all we had."

"Yes. That's too bad."

"Any day now."

"Those things happen."

"I need advice about the *Madrina.*"

"What kind of advice?"

"They told me you know all about boats."

"I don't know anything about ships. Over a hundred feet is a ship, unless it is a submarine, and then it's still a boat."

"Advice about selling it. If I should sell it here or have them take it back home. I don't trust Michael."

"Who is Michael?"

"He is the captain. Maybe if it is best to take it home to sell it, you could help me."

"A boat is a hole in the water into which you throw money. A ship is a bigger hole into which you throw more money. If you don't want it, move off it right now. Get rid of the crew and all perishables, cancel the telephone hookup, and turn it over to one of the brokers. There are good ones here."

"I really can't do that until after all that will and executor thing is taken care of."

"And he isn't even dead yet."

"The way you say that, you make me sound . . . terrible."

"Not intended."

"I didn't think it would be unreasonable, Travis, to suggest that we might help each other. And comfort each other." She added a slight arching of the back, for emphasis. A very subtle movement of her left hand indicated that I should come over and sit by her.

I stood up and said, "I'm dead, Anna. I'll walk you back around to the *Madrina*."

She tossed off the rest of the brandy, frowned, shrugged, and let me walk her home. She hung onto my forearm with both hands and contrived to bump a hip into me every now and again.

"What if I want to fire Michael and he won't let himself be fired by me?"

I was supposed to volunteer assistance. "Then you'll have to let the executor fire him, I guess."

"He's worked for Harvey for twenty-three years."

We stopped at the gangplank. She said, "Would you like to come aboard and look around?"

"Not really."

"You're not very gracious, are you?"

"Not very."

"Well . . . if you feel terribly lonely and want someone to talk to who . . . faces the same kind of sorrow, I'll be nearby. Okay?"

"Okay, Anna. Sure. 'Night."

I walked slowly home to *The Busted Flush*. There was a sour smell in the night air, like a broken drain. Anna was a very tidy little biscuit, with her old dark eyes set in that child's face. She exuded a tantalizing flavor of corruption, of secret, unspeakable experience. There had been times in my life when I would have been happy to help her pass the time until old Harv died and then talked her into letting me help her take the *Madrina* home, by way of a lot of nice islands.

But I had seen the crocodile tears bulging in her dark eyes when she had said, "Any day now." And I had seen the greed behind the tears, the impulse to break into laughter. Everything old Harv had is now mine, fella. All, all mine. During those past two years she had probably been dreadfully afraid that he would live forever.

When you see the ugliness behind the tears of another person, it makes you take a closer look at your own.

We are all at the mercy of the scriptwriters, directors, and actors in cinema and television. Man is a herd creature, social and imitative. We learn the outward manifestations of inner stress, patterning reaction to what we have learned. And because the visible ways we react are so often borrowed, we wonder about the truth of what is happening underneath. Do I *really* feel pain, grief, shock, loss?

It is as if we look inside and take a tentative rap at some bell that hangs in there. I had the horrid feeling that *maybe* my pain was tempered by some sick measure of relief, that I had escaped the trap of a permanent twoness.

Take a rap at that bell, dreading a possible flat, cracked, dissonant sound of self-pity, of a grubby selfishness.

But it rang true. It rang for her, for my lost girl. The loving and the losing were still larger than life. Than my life. The sound of the bell was almost unbearable. I was like a rat in a cage, subjected to supersonic experimentation. They run back and forth and roll at last onto their backs, chewing their paws bloody. I wanted to swim straight out into the sea. Or go visit Anna and help her into bed. Each was a form of drowning.

5

On Monday morning I awoke glum, got up glum, dressed glum. The sky was a bright pewter, a radiance that cast no shadow but made people squint and walk hunched over, as if searching for something. It would be windless and silent one moment, then a hard blast would come slamming past, picking up dust devils and scraps of paper before subsiding into stillness. At sea on a day like this I would have been laying a course to the nearest shelter and checking the fuel level to see how fast I dared go to get there. It was the kind of weather that makes people cross.

Meyer was cross when he arrived at eleven for reheated coffee.

"How are you?" he asked, peering at me.

"Peachy."

"I'm sorry. It is the standard question one asks. How did you get rid of little Anna?"

"Walked her back to her personal ship. What made you jump to the conclusion I got rid of her?"

"Not such a big jump. Why shouldn't you get rid of her? There'd be no reason to keep her around."

"Who brought her and dumped her on me?"

"Lili MacNair. And it wasn't her fault. She just couldn't get the Farmer woman to leave."

"Farmer?"

"Anna Farmer."

"Don't look so exasperated, Meyer. I never caught her last name. Is she worth talking about, even? And does it matter a damn one way or another what I do or don't do with my days or with my nights?"

"Aha!" he said. "Tragic figger of a man."

"Meyer, I know what you are trying to do, and I forgive you. But don't keep it up. Understand?"

He stared and finally nodded. "All right. I was out of line. A transparent, clumsy attempt to cheer the troops. What I came over for, aside from dispensing hollow cheer, was to complain about the bureaucracy. And to give you a conundrum to occupy your mind."

"A riddle?"

"Somewhat. I was on the phone at a reasonable morning hour, calling old friends in Washington. There are a lot of offices up there. And strange titles. Deputy Director to the Assistant Director in charge of the Policy Committee on Administration. The phone directory is gigantic. I gave them the information and set them to scurrying about. I gave the same mission to three quite different people in three quite different departments, and then waited for the results. The last call came in fifteen minutes ago. That phone number they gave you is not an operating number. There is not now and never has been, at least in living memory, any Select Committee on Special Resources. The central register of all civil servants has no Robert A. Toomey, but it does have two Richard E. Klines. One is twenty-five and works for the Department of the Interior in Alaska. The other is sixty-one and based in Guam. Interesting?"

My head was too full of fragments, like a kaleidoscope, making its bright patterns of nonsense. I had decided that when they had visited me, my reaction had been paranoid.

"I don't know what to think, Meyer. Don't they have departments sort of hidden away, without public records and so forth?"

"So why give you a bad phone number?"

"Maybe you would like to try to make sense out of it."

"Too many parts missing," he said. He got up and roamed around the lounge, sighing audibly, pausing to look out the port, then resuming his circuit. "High-level inquiry," he said.

"What?"

"Excuse me. I'm talking to myself."

He roamed and muttered and finally sat down. He gave me a bright false smile. "It's all too melodramatic. There is but one way I can make the parts fit together, and it offends me."

"See if it offends me."

"It will more than offend, Travis. All right. Postulate X. X is an unknown force, group, movement, with unknown objectives. X is powerful and has high-priority objectives. Secrecy is imperative. Brother Titus represents the syndicate in Brussels, and he came down here from another part of the country to take a look at the land and make contact with Mr. Ladwigg. The odds against anyone seeing him and recognizing him are astronomical. But that is one way in which life is consistently quirky. It keeps serving up unlikely coincidences. Gretel told us her story about Brother Titus on December seventh. And she said she had seen him 'last week,' if I remember correctly. Not 'this week,' 'last week.' The last week in November. Brother Titus went back to X and reported being recognized. For some reason, this created a great danger to the high-priority objective. They had a week in which to plan and move. Their representatives were in the area by midweek, perhaps, or earlier. On Saturday morning Ladwigg fell off his bike and died. Gretel was taken ill on Saturday. They are the only two, we can assume, who saw Titus face to face. Toomey and Kline came here Saturday to find out if Gretel told you about him. From what you told me of the questioning, they would have gotten the information from anyone less wary than you."

"What the hell are you trying to say?"

"I *told* you the reconstruction is so melodramatic it offends me. If you had told them all about Brother Titus, as related by Gretel, right now you might be in the hospital, fading fast."

I thought it over. I could not make it seem real. "Okay, why the charade? If what is going on is so important, why not just wait until dark, thump my skull, and let me go out on the tide?"

"They do not want to create curiosity. A man falls off his bike and dies. One of the young women who work for him falls ill and dies. The authorities can accept that as routine. But what if the woman's best friend should then die accidentally, or be taken ill in the same way?"

"The authorities would assume the friend caught it from her, whatever it was."

"But that would create a big flap. Gretel's illness and death were reported, you said, to the Center for Disease Control in Atlanta."

"By Dr. Tower."

"Having it turn out to be contagious would make headlines."

"Mental games are your specialty, Meyer. But it does not amuse me one goddamn bit to have you making a lot of assumptions based on Gretel being murdered, poisoned somehow. For God's sake, you saw her that one time there! She was sick. She was terribly, terribly ill. Know what her last words were? 'I'm burning up. I feel terrible, Trav. Terrible.' Great last words to remember. Comforting. Dammit, she could have mentioned Titus to those people out there at Bonnie Brae. She could have asked about him. She could have asked the other partner, or Slater. And she could have told them about the fellow just the way she told us."

"The way she told us, remember, was to start by saying she thought there was something funny going on out there. And she would not be likely to bring that up with the people she was working for. Or with. And one good way to prove I am totally wrong is to find out if Broffski and Slater have been questioned, just as you were. I don't think that pair came here from out of town to talk to you alone."

I looked at him. "If I thought for one moment that somebody had . . . poisoned her . . ."

"I am not sitting here, Travis, trying to dream up a cheap plot line for a grade Z movie. You asked me to try to make sense out of it. I can make melodramatic sense out of it, *if* I make the assumption that both Gretel and Ladwigg were killed. If they weren't, the sense of it all eludes me."

"You're *serious!*"

"Enough to want to try to prove it out one way or the other."

"Where would you start?"

"By finding out if Broffski and Slater were questioned too."

*   *   *

So once again I drove out to Bonnie Brae. I could not have guessed how difficult it would be. Memories of her were of a painful clarity, a vividness in the back of the mind.

Slater, the manager, was out for lunch. Stanley Broffski was in his office. What did we wish to speak to him about? the woman asked. I said it involved some negotiations with Herman Ladwigg. She trotted off and soon reappeared, beckoning us in.

Broffski sat behind a big white desk covered with piles of correspondence and blueprints. He was plump to the point of bursting out of his sport shirt. He had black hair combed across his forehead and a Groucho mustache. He had an air of jolly impatience, amused exasperation.

He waved us into chairs, saying, "Honest to Christ, I wish to hell Herm had the habit of writing things down. Nothing against him, you understand. Nobody ever had a better partner. But he carried around too much in his head alla time! It's driving me up the wall trying to find out who did what to who."

"I suppose," Meyer said, "you divided up all the responsibilities you have here."

"I've got the fat farm and the tennis club, and we'll have a riding stable going pretty soon. They're working on the stalls down there now." He swiveled his chair half around and pointed through the wide window to an old barn a hundred yards away. Two pickup trucks and a van were parked there, near a pile of fresh lumber. Off to the left a clutch of fatties trotted heavily down a long gentle slope. They were mostly women in their middle years, with a few men and a few adolescents, boys and girls. Despite the age differences, the fat at that distance looked the same, bouncing and flapping under the sweaty shorts and shirts. A lean woman was galloping along beside them, clapping her hands, running back and forth.

"We work the tract-house part together," he said. "I mean, we did. Herm handled the land sales. He was a wizard at that. We're all going to miss him. Of course, we both worked with the manager, Morse Slater. Morse keeps everything running smooth. If he wasn't around at this time, I'd be whipped. We lost a hell of a good girl right after we lost Herm. Some kind of legionnaire flu, they say. She wasn't here long, but Morse says she was the greatest. Everything from doing the billing to teaching tennis. Hell, it's a sound operation here. Everything will turn out roses. We've got a nice community coming along. We're keeping a lot of open space, and nothing tacky gets built. What was it you had going with Herm, gentlemen? Was it something to do with the commercial area?"

"Actually," Meyer said, "we're trying to find out who it was who flew in almost three weeks ago, maybe November twenty-eighth or -ninth, to talk to Mr. Ladwigg, and flew out the next morning."

"In a little blue airplane," Broffski said. His voice was no longer amiable, his face no longer jolly. "I am getting damn sick and tired of that fucking blue airplane. I am going to close that strip. Who needs it?"

He bounded up and went around us to his office door. "Morse! Get in here a minute."

Morse Slater came in, recognized me at once, and came over to me. I stood up, and he shook my hand and said, "I'm terribly sorry I had to miss the service, Mr. McGee. I thought until the last minute I would make it, but something came up."

I said, "Sure. Understood. Meyer, this is Morse Slater. I told you about him."

As they shook hands Broffski said, "What's going on? What service?"

"Gretel Howard," I told him.

There was a sudden look of comprehension. "McGee! Right. I heard about you from her. What has all this got to do with the fucking blue airplane?"

Meyer said politely, "Has someone else been interested in it?"

"We had the FAA out here. You tell them what it was about, Morse."

We all sat down and Morse said, "Apparently it was some sort of serious violation of the air safety rules, flying too close to a commercial liner, something like that. It was a Mr. Ryan from Washington, a field investigator, and they had traced the plane here. He was a very stubborn man. He couldn't seem to accept the idea that no one except Mr. Ladwigg knew where the airplane came from or who was flying it. He insisted on talking to some of the other employees, and he even had me take him over to the Ladwigg home and let him interrogate Mrs. Ladwigg."

"Catherine didn't know from nothing," Broffski said. "She never saw the guy. She said Herm put him up in the guest wing and talked business in there from the time he arrived until late at night. Herm told her not to bother about dinner, and when she checked the guest wing after the man had left, she found paper bags and cups from one of the fried chicken places down the Drive, so she thinks Herm went out and brought food back. The next morning early she heard Herm drive out in the Toyota. All Herm ever told her was that it was a big deal for a good-sized tract, and they were talking construction and deadlines. Damned imposition for him to go bothering Catherine."

Morse Slater said, "Ryan said to me that he wanted to find out if the aircraft had flown in from the islands with a load of coke or grass. He said he wanted to get that pilot out of the air. He just couldn't understand why we didn't have some record of the identification number on the plane. I showed him the strip, of course. A grassy strip, an old shed, a wind sock, and a padlocked gas pump. There's nobody there to check anything in or out."

"We let Ryan look through Herm's desk notes and appointment calendar," Stanley Broffski said. "He said he'd come back with a subpoena if we didn't. There wasn't a clue."

"When was Ryan here?" Meyer asked.

Slater stared at the ceiling for a moment. "Last Thursday, the thirteenth. He disrupted the day, most of it."

"Remember his whole name?" Meyer asked.

"Ryan, Howard C. In his forties. Pale, broad, soft. Very autocratic. An irritating fellow."

"I still don't understand why you two men are here," Broffski said. "Why should you give a shit who flew in and out in that airplane? What should it have to do with you?"

I reached into the deepest pocket in one of the old bags of tricks and came up with a useful inspiration. I leaned forward, adjusting my face to maximum leaden sincerity, and I secretly apologized to Gretel. "Mr. Broffski, I was able to be with Gretel for a little time every hour, while she was dying. Toward the end there, she came sort of half-awake, and she said, 'Blue airplane. Blue airplane.' I thought she was out of her head from the fever. If she wasn't, then she was trying to tell me something, I don't know what it was, and then when I heard from somebody at the funeral that a blue airplane had landed here the week before she died, I thought . . . well, it wouldn't be any harm in asking, because you were her friends."

"No harm! No harm at all!" Broffski said. "She was one terrific personality. She had star quality around here. Now I know why you're asking, but I still don't see what it has to do with anything. Herm knew who came in, and it seems as if whoever it was wanted to keep a real low profile."

"I wonder why," Morse Slater said, frowning.

"Who knows?" Broffski said. "Maybe some kind of deal he wasn't ready to tell us about. So if somebody is still interested, they'll contact us. If they do, I hope it's better than that Brussels deal of his."

"Brussels?" Meyer asked politely.

"Twenty acres, undeveloped, on the west side of the property," Slater said. "We're holding a ten percent deposit in an escrow account. The purchaser is something called the Morgen Group. Morgen with an 'e.' "

"Fascinating name," Meyer said.

"What's so fascinating about it?" Broffski asked.

"It's an obsolete land-measurement term which used to be used in Holland and in South Africa. A *morgen* is approximately two acres, and the translation, of course, is 'morning.' It derived from approximately how much land one man could plow with horses in a single morning."

Broffski stared at him. "You got a lot of stuff like that in your head? What line of work are you in?"

"I'm an economist. Semiretired."

"The address is a bank in Brussels. I tried to pick it up where Herm left off, and I made four phone calls to that bank. They deny any knowledge of the Morgen Group. All they would say is I should write to that name care of the bank, and if there was a Morgen Group, it would probably be delivered to them. I sent a cable, and the call-back on it said it was undeliverable. I wrote, and we're waiting."

Meyer nodded and said, "The Morgen Group is probably equivalent in law to what we call a blind trust here. And Brussels is quietly taking the place of Switzerland. Their secrecy is guaranteed by Belgian law. They have number accounts and investment services and they have no reverse interest, as the Swiss do. Thus, with a blind trust, there is a double layer of legal confidentiality. Impenetrable."

"Why so secret?" Broffski said. "Herm told me that a bunch of Belgians wanted to build their own hotel-club on the twenty acres, so the members could come here on vacation."

"Maybe it was going to be a front for something," Slater said.

Broffski looked across the desk at Slater, a look of annoyance and derision. "Sure. Right here in our back yard they are going to build a warehouse for the drug business. Or a studio to make porn movies."

"Sorry," Slater said. But he didn't look sorry.

Broffski sighed. "Well, there isn't anything I can do about it. The land sits there. Eleven months from now we can take the money out of escrow and put the land on the market again. Or develop it. Whatever." He stood up and reached across the desk. "Sorry we can't give you any more help." He shook hands, and we went out with Morse Slater.

"Can we look around the property?" Meyer asked.

"Certainly," he said, and gave us a brochure with a map of Bonnie Brae, showing the existing roads and the ones to come later. He pointed to the area on the map where the Belgians had planned to buy—and maybe still would. We thanked him and went out into the silver daylight, squinting against the high hard dazzle of the sky.

6

WE WALKED across a field to the airstrip. We walked through a healthy growth of sand spurs and stopped and picked them off socks and pants cuffs when we got to a cleared space. Meyer thumped the surface of the landing strip with his heel.

"Probably some kind of soil cement," I said. "You plow it up, mix the cement with the dirt, grade it, water it, roll it down. Quick and easy."

We could hear the unrhythmic whacking of a lot of hammers as workmen were framing a house a hundred yards away.

Meyer said, "If Ladwigg was coming over here to the strip from those houses there, cross-country, he would have to pass that patch of bushes and palmetto over there."

We went over to look for tire tracks. They would be about three weeks old. There was a faint pattern in the heavy grass, a mark of rugged tread in dried mud, and some grease stains on the tallest grass.

"So she stood here, I'd guess," Meyer said.

"Out in the early morning, looking for her pin," I said. "Yes. And so what?"

Meyer shrugged. "I don't *know* what. Every action we take, every thought we have, they are all based upon some form of information. We know more now than we did before. It is difficult, I think, and erroneous, to try to decide in advance whether additional facts will be useful."

"So if she stood here, and heard the motor and stepped out in this direction, okay, the car would pass close, and the passenger would be three feet away, as she said. And we could backtrack the vehicle to old Herm's house. Incidentally, coming around to the airstrip overland instead of on the road doesn't mean much. The people who own those four-wheel-drive brutes like to take them bouncing through the fields and woods. It does something for their glands. It could be preference instead of secretiveness. On the other hand, he did avoid meeting Mrs. Ladwigg, and the two men ate in the guest wing. Anyway, Meyer, where the hell are we *going* with all this?"

Roaring at Meyer seldom does any good. He gave me the mild smile, the bland nod. "Let's see where we've been. On the thirteenth of December, two days before Toomey and Kline paid a visit to you, a Mr. Ryan visited Bonnie Brae. I do not think the Federal Aviation Administration gets into the business of tracking down small planes which endanger scheduled airline flights. I think that is the Civil Aeronautics Board's chore. And, whoever was looking into it, surely if there was danger of a collision, somebody would have picked up the identification numbers of the small airplane. They are required to carry the numbers in very large contrasting colors. Additionally, the customs people are monitoring all small planes in flight along this coast. And, finally, there seems to be a telltale monotony about the names of the three alleged officials—Howard C., Robert A., and Richard E. If any more turn up, we can expect William B. and Thomas D.''

Meyer will never cease to astonish me. That heavy skull is loaded with microprocessors. Information is subject to constant analysis, synthesis, storage and retrieval. But when this makes him seem too intellectual, too somber, I have but to recall him at Bailey's, our neighborhood disco, cavorting like a dancing bear with three blond chiclets who adore him, and who listen to him when he sits like a hairy Buddha, declaiming instant legends and inventing instant folk-song lyrics. The dancing Meyer, pelt gleaming under the disco lights, little blue eyes shining, is the antidote to the data-processing machine under the skull bones.

We moved over into the semishade of a young live oak. The shadows had no edges under that white fluorescent sky.

He leaned against the tree. I sat on my heels and poked at the hard dirt with a piece of branch.

"It's too much!" he said irritably.

"How do you mean?"

"Pretend for one moment that Gretel never told us about Brother Titus. She might not have said anything, you know. Then where would we be? You would have accepted their story that they were looking into something that might be going on at Bonnie Brae. Let's hope they accepted your statement that Gretel had told you nothing. The Ryan person convinced them out at Bonnie Brae that he was what he said he was. Toomey, Kline, and Ryan were mopping up. There is no other answer. Ladwigg and Gretel were both killed.''

"No!"

"Yes, Travis. Both deaths were made to look routine. An accident and an illness. They would not make waves. It was somehow terribly important that no one be left alive who could talk about Brother Titus. The secrecy of the whole business indicates that there might be people who might possibly recognize him. It was a remote chance, but one that X could not accept. Remember, I am using X to indicate an individual or an organization. Because of the emphasis on secrecy, I am assuming some link between Brother Titus and the twenty acres on which the Morgen Group made a down payment.''

"But there wouldn't be any point in killing Gretel! What if she did recognize him? No matter *what* is going on, isn't that one hell of an overreaction to being recognized?''

"That's where I draw a blank, Travis. I have been trying to think of something big enough and bad enough and important enough for an organized group—and believe me, they *are* organized—to wipe out every possible trace of a visit from an official of an obscure religious sect. Eradication per se would not be difficult if one had the stomach for extreme measures. Float you out on the tide, and me also, to be totally safe. Eliminate Catherine Ladwigg, Stanley Broffski, Morse Slater, and anybody else Gretel worked with. Eradication of every trace without arousing suspicion is a lot trickier. It requires thought and organization and great care. If Gretel had not talked to you, it would have been successful. If you had been entirely truthful with

Toomey and Kline, it would have been successful, because they would have dealt with you.''

"Melodrama.''

"I know. I know. But fit the facts together in any other way and you get more nonsense instead of less.''

"So the Morgen Group was going to build some kind of top-secret installation at Bonnie Brae. Or a heroin refinery. Or maybe Brother Titus was the fellow behind the grassy knoll in Dallas. Come on, Meyer. How many coincidences can we string together?''

I stood up and headed back across the field to the new asphalt road. I saw something glint in the grass, and bent down and pushed the grass aside and picked it up. I had seen her wear that pin several times when we had gone ashore from *The Busted Flush* during our long slow trip back around the peninsula. It was of Mexican silver, framing a three-dimensional Aztec face carved out of a mottled hard green stone. It was crudely made, and the clasp was not very secure.

How many coincidences can we string together? Sure. If, retracing her jogging route, she had found the pin before Ladwigg drove Titus back to his airplane—if she and her ex-husband had not traced her sister-in-law to that California encampment—if she had found a different job in Lauderdale . . .

Looking down at the primitive green face in the palm of my hand, I felt dizzy. The world was all tied together in some mysterious tangle of invisible web, single strands that reached impossible distances, glimpsed but rarely when the light caught them just right.

The biggest if of all. If she had never met me. Because I had brought her here.

If her mother had never met her father.

If her aunt had wheels.

If.

An empty path to walk. It leads toward superstition and paranoia, two whistle stops on the road to incurable depression. Once upon a time I took a random walk across a field. I went hither and yon, ambling along, looking at the sky and the trees, nibbling grass, kicking rocks. The first jeep to start across that field blew up. So did the people who went to get the people who'd been in the jeep. And I stood right there, sweaty and safe, trembling inside, while the experts dug over ninety mines out of that field, defused them, stacked them, and took them away. That's the way it goes sometimes. Philosophy 401, with Professor McGee. Life is a minefield. Think that over and write a paper on it, class.

I put the pin in my pocket. Talisman of some kind. Rub the tiny green face with the ball of the thumb. Like a worry stone, to relieve executive tensions. The times I remembered seeing it, she had worn it on the left side, where the slope of the breast began. She had bought it, she said, at a craft shop in San Francisco at Ghirardelli Square. I hadn't been there with her. All the places I hadn't been with her, I would never be with her. And at those unknown places, at unknown times, there would be less of me present. There can be few things worse than unconsciously saving things up to tell someone you will never see again.

"Coincidence,'' I told Meyer. "Maybe there was somebody thinking about hustling her on her way, but they didn't have to. She got sick. And antibiotics wouldn't touch it. And she died.''

"Maybe," he said. "Maybe it was that way.''

*   *   *

My phone aboard the *Flush* rang at eight fifteen the next morning, and when I answered it I heard the click of someone hanging up. Fifteen minutes later it rang again, and when I answered it, a voice said, "Remember this number, McGee. Seven-nine-two, oh-seven-oh-one. Go to a pay phone as soon as you can and call this number. Seven-nine-two, oh-seven-oh-one.''

He hung up. The voice was soft. There was no regional accent. I wrote the number down and finished my coffee while I thought about it. Then I locked up and walked to a pay phone.

The same voice answered. "This is McGee," I said.

"What was your mother's maiden name?''

"Devlin. Mary Catherine Devlin.''

"Drive to Pier Sixty-six and park in the marina lot. Walk to the hotel and go in one of the lower-level entrances that face toward the marina, the one nearest the water. Turn right and walk slowly down the corridor toward the main part of the hotel.''

"Why?''

After a pause he said, "Because you want to know why somebody died.''

"Who the hell are you?''

"Can you remember what I told you to do?''

"Of course.''

He hung up. I went to Meyer's stubby little cabin cruiser, the *John Maynard Keynes,* and roused him. He came out, blinking into the sunlight, carrying his coffee onto the fantail, looking grainy and whiskery. I repeated the two conversations as accurately as I could.

"Mother's maiden name. Standard security procedure. Not generally available.''

"I know that. Somebody wants to tell me why Gretel died.''

"You're going, of course.''

"That's why I came over to tell you. So you'll be able to give somebody a lead if I don't show up back here. If somebody wants to take me out, forget the hotel. It will be the marina parking lot. Drop me there at long range, and untie the lines and take off.''

"I'll come along.''

"If you wouldn't mind. He didn't say to come alone. You could wait in the truck. Armed.''

"But not very dangerous.''

"What we will have are those stupid walkie-talkies, the little ones you bought as a gag. With fresh batteries. The mysterious strangers are probably in one of those rooms. I am assuming more than one. I can keep my unit in my pocket. Without my aerial up you should be able to read a signal from me based on Off-On. We can test them here.''

With fresh batteries we found out that he would receive a definite alteration in the buzzing sound when my unit was turned on, even at a hundred yards. I could give him numbers. Short bursts for numbers from 1 to 9. A steady blast for a zero. Room 302 would be *dit-dit-dit daaaaah dit-dit.*

"In a building with a steel frame?" he asked.

"Listen harder. They'll take it away from me pretty quick, I imagine. I'll give you the room number soon as I can."

* * *

There are a lot of trees in that parking lot, and it has a considerable depth. I circled around the back of it, walking swiftly through the open areas. Then I circled back to an arched entrance, went in, turned right, walked slowly. The rooms were on my right. So they could have watched me through a window.

I kept my hand in my pocket, finger on the switch. A door opened behind me and I spun around. Room 121. Very easy. A sallow young man, tall, with a lot of nose and a lot of neck, motioned to me to come in. He wore pale-blue trunks, and he had a bath towel around his neck. His hair was still wet from his morning swim.

The familiar voice was right behind me, and I had neither heard him nor sensed him. "Hand out of the pocket. That's nice. Move right on in. Fine. You're doing fine."

With the voice still behind me and the room door closed, the swimmer patted me down and took the little gadget out of my pocket. He read the label on it aloud. "Junior Space Cadet." He grinned and tossed it onto one of the double beds. "Clean," he said.

"Sit right down over there, in the straight chair by that countertop, Mr. McGee," the voice said. Large room. Two double beds. Pile carpeting. Small refrigerator. Recently redecorated. Between the half-open draperies I could see beach chairs and a table on the tiny ground-level terrace outside sliding doors, and I could look out toward the marina parking lot.

When I sat down I got my first look at the voice. Like Swimmer, he seemed to be in his late twenties. Mid-height, with the shoulder meat of one who works out with weights. Glossy dark hair, square jaw, neck as broad as the jaw. Metal-rimmed glasses with a slight amber tint. A pleasant smile.

"My name is McGee," I said.

"I think we'll try to get along without names."

He took the toy off the bed, inspected it, pulled the sectional aerial to full length, and went over and opened the sliding door. "Dr. Meyer? Everything is in order here. Why don't you come on in?"

When there was no answer, he tossed the unit to me. I pushed the little piano key and said, "No reason why you shouldn't, Meyer."

"Okay." The voice was tinny and remote. "Shall I bring your hat?"

"No. Leave it in the car and lock up. Room One-two-one."

When Meyer arrived, Swimmer frisked him, declared him clean, and then winked at me and said, "I was looking for your hat."

"Was it all that obvious?" I asked.

"Don't worry about it," Weightlifter said. "It's good procedure. Simple and useful. Keep it. Because it doesn't work with us doesn't mean it isn't any good. But, Dr. Meyer, I'm curious."

"Just Meyer, please."

"Fine. What if he'd asked you to bring his hat?"

"There are several ways he could have asked me to bring it. Each one is an option. If he felt the two of us could handle things, I would have been ready when I came through the door, and so would he."

"Nice. Very nice," Swimmer said.

"You seem to know a hell of a lot," I said.

Weightlifter shrugged and sat on the edge of a bed, and motioned Meyer over to a wing chair by the sliding doors. "Not as much as we tried to find out. I'll give you credit. You have some very solid friends around that marina, McGee. We didn't have much time to work on it. We put a lot of people on it. We pulled your military record. We put some tourists into that Bahia Mar Marina. We had somebody at Timber Bay. We sent somebody to Petaluma. We know—or at least we feel able to assume—that you are not wanted anywhere, that your identity is correct, that you are not into the coke or grass trade, and that you are not political."

"Who is we?" Meyer asked.

"We won't go into that. Just as I told Mr. McGee, we won't go into names either. And we won't show identification. And if you check the register later, it won't do you a bit of good. And, I'll be frank with you, the names and the connections wouldn't mean much to you. We are going to ask questions. Lots of them. This might take a long time. But we start with evidence of good faith."

Swimmer went to the closet and came back with a nine-by-twelve manila envelope and handed it to Weightlifter.

"Before I show you these," Weightlifter said, "I must explain how we happened to luck out. Dr. Tower reported the symptoms to the Center for Disease Control in Atlanta. They have had standing orders for over a year to report any case which has those same symptoms to a certain branch of the Federal Government. An expert in forensic medicine flew down to Atlanta from New York, starting about an hour after word came to Washington. When it became obvious to Dr. Tower that Mrs. Howard was going to die, he phoned Atlanta. The expert came down here in time to participate in the autopsy. He found what we had instructed him to look for. Take a look at these prints."

I had been watching him covertly. He was left-handed. He wore a sport shirt that hung outside his trousers, and once when he moved I had identified the bulge on his right side, halfway between the belly button and the point of the hip bone.

He handed me the print, and when he turned to take the other one over to Meyer, I let mine slip to the floor, moved quickly behind him, locked his left arm, and reached around and under with the right hand and yanked the belly holster out, gun, belt clip, and all, and then slammed him into Swimmer, who was heading for the closet. They went into a lamp table and snapped a couple of slender legs as they brought it down.

By then I had the short-barreled revolver properly in hand, and Meyer was standing beside me.

"Slow and easy," I said, and they did indeed move slowly as they separated themselves from each other and from the pieces of lamp and table. There was nothing pleasant about their faces, but nothing ugly either. No sign of strain or worry. A watchful competence, like a very good boxer waiting for the opening.

I have to go on instinct. Sometimes it has betrayed me. Never fatally, fortunately. Most of the time it works for me.

I said, "We'll play it your way, gentlemen. I didn't want you to go away with the impression we're a pair of clowns. It is a matter of pride with me. Let's say our relationship has reached a new level. First names would help."

I tossed the gun onto the nearest bed and extended my hand to Weightlifter. As he took it and I pulled him to his feet, he said, "Max. He's Jake."

Jake got up and cocked his head as he stared at me. "Maybe if I hadn't read off the name of that walkie-talkie?"

"Maybe. I don't know."

Max slid the revolver into the holster after checking it over, and clipped the holster to his pants and smoothed the sport shirt down over the bulge. He looked thoughtful. "McGee, you may be half again as big as I expected, and you are certainly twice as quick as anybody your size I've ever seen, but it was still a hell of a risk. It was a stupid risk. You miss the gun and maybe I kill you as I am falling. From instinct. From training. From too long doing what I do."

"He wanted to make an impression on you," Meyer said.

Jake said, "There are some folks we work with and work for who would never let us forget how we got taken."

"And never understand it," Max said.

"But they weren't here to watch," I said.

I saw the tension go out of him, little by little. Jake had a bad bruise on his shin. It was swelling and turning blue. I had torn a fingernail snatching the revolver.

Finally Max grinned at me and said, "Now I understand a little bit more about some of the things I found out about you. Now they make more sense. But it was still stupid."

Meyer made an odd sound. He looked up from the print he was holding. He looked questioningly at Max and said, "Markov?"

"Yes. And you better tell me how you know about that!"

7

MEYER LOOKED at Max, his expression puzzled. "But why wouldn't I know about it? It had a lot of publicity."

"But how would you make the connection from these photographs?"

Still puzzled, Meyer said, "The details made an impression on me." He looked toward the ceiling, frowned, closed his eyes, and said, "A sphere of platinum and iridium—I forget the percentages of each in the alloy. One fifteenth of an inch in diameter, with two tiny holes drilled into it at right angles to each other, with traces of an unknown substance in the holes."

"But you glanced at these photos and made the connection."

Meyer straightened and glared at him. "If you are pretending to be professional, *act* like a professional. If I had any trace of guilty knowledge, would I have revealed it? The people who *do* have guilty knowledge are certainly too professional to reveal it."

I interrupted, saying, "Let me explain something. Meyer has a fantastic memory. I don't know what the hell either of you are talking about. What I've got here is a picture of what looks like a lumpy silver bowling ball with the holes drilled badly."

"The scale, Travis," Meyer said. "Look at the scale."

Yes, it was very small. Maybe not quite as small as the head of a pin, but almost.

"That item," said Max, "is a twin to the one removed from the right thigh of a Bulgarian defector in London named Georgi Markov after he died—with the symptoms of high fever, sharp drop in blood pressure, and renal failure. That was quite some time ago."

"Somebody jabbed him with an umbrella," Meyer said.

"Yes. That one. This is a photograph of an identical object removed from the right side of the back of the neck of Mrs. Howard. The traces of the poison found inside those holes are being analyzed. They did not get a complete analysis of the poison in the Markov case, or in the Kostov attempt which happened a month before Markov was killed. The pellet hit Kostov in the back in a Paris subway. We can assume a better delivery system was devised to take care of Markov. Kostov recovered."

I sat heavily and stared at the picture of the dull silver ball. Somebody had stuck that thing into the back of the neck of my woman and killed her. I had been trying not to accept the fact that such a thing could happen, and had happened.

"I'm burning up. I feel terrible, Trav. Terrible."

Her face had become gaunt so quickly. Fever had eaten her up, eaten the quickness and happiness, eaten the brightness.

The reason for doing that to her seemed beyond any comprehension. But somebody did it. And from this moment on, the only satisfying purpose in life would be to find out exactly, precisely, specifically who.

I came back from a long way off and heard the last part of Meyer's question. "—many more since the Markov case?"

"Classified information."

"Who *does* such a thing?" I demanded.

Jake took the answer to that one. "We could say that we have reason to believe the poison itself, a complex chemical structure, was developed by Kamera, a section of Department V of the KGB. We have reason to believe they have been working for many years on poisons which, after injection, break down into substances normally found in the human body. They killed Vladimir Tkachenko back in 1967 in London when, we think, he tried to defect. Method of delivery unknown. Poison unknown."

"It's like you're speaking a foreign language. This is Fort Lauderdamndale. This is the palm-tree Christmas coming, with Sanny Claus in shorts, and the tourists swarming. What has all this Russian stuff got to do with Gretel and me?"

Max said, "It has something to do with everyone who lives on the planet, in one way or another."

"Philosophy I don't need," I said.

"Okay. Markov, most probably, was killed by an agent from the Soviet bloc. He was making the big man in Bulgaria, Todor Zhivkov, very unhappy by his broadcasts over Radio Free Europe. We can guess that Zhivkov asked for help to get him silenced. But when it comes to the assassination of a young woman in Florida, we can't make the same kind of reasonable assumption. Put it this way. Russia and the United States are each supportive of various groups and movements all over the world. Arms and ammunition move toward areas of tension. There is no way to exert final control over the use of a weapon. The two major powers try to supply those whose goals are closest to their own, and then they hope for the best. This is a very advanced and exotic assassination device. We can assume the KGB would be cautious about supplying it to anyone over here. We could have missed it easily. When they took a scrap of tissue for biopsy while Mrs. Howard was still alive, they could have gotten that platinum bead along with it, missed it when they sliced a section for the microscope, and thrown it out without ever knowing. So the intent was to simulate a natural death. That leads us to the point. Why could she not be permitted to live? Why did it have to look like a natural death?"

I looked at each of them in turn. "And that's it? You don't know who did it?"

Max shook his head. "We have no idea. We can't find a starting point, except with you two."

Meyer asked, "What kind of people would it be rational for them to supply over here with a thing like that?"

Max shrugged. "A mole, maybe. Somebody who was put in place a long time ago. An agitator of any consequence. Weathermen, Symbionese, anybody trying to alter the political equilibrium by violent means. But that doesn't make it sound rational. It doesn't seem like a useful target. One would expect it should be a visiting shah, a premier, or a red-hot research physicist. Let's get to it. Mr. McGee, do you have any reason to believe that Gretel Howard was connected in any way with any political action group?"

I looked down at my fists as I sought the right way to say it. "We had a lot of intense time alone with each other. A couple of months aboard my houseboat. We talked a lot. We opened up to each other all the way. We tracked each other from childhood right on up to the moment. She was as apolitical as I am. We both lived in the world, and didn't get too red-hot about who was running it. Maybe that's wrong in your eyes. But it is the way she was and the way I am."

"And she could not have been conning you?"

"Absolutely no way."

"When and how did she get the alleged insect sting?"

"No idea. She was telling me over the phone everything that had gone wrong with her day. No, sorry. She didn't tell me about the insect bite until I saw her in the hospital. She broke a mug I had given her when she was having breakfast, and then she learned her boss had fallen off his bike and died, and then a bug bit her, and then she had fainted and fallen and broken a lamp in the Ladwigg house. From the sequence I'd say she got bitten, or shot, between eight and ten o'clock that morning. How was it done?"

Jake shook his long sandy head. "The thing is so damn small, delivery systems are difficult. It has so little mass it makes a poor projectile. Like a man trying to hurl a single grain of rice. One of the groups . . . I mean to say, we've experimented with silver beads which closely approximate the size and weight of one of the deadly ones. The propulsion force can be compressed air, a spring mechanism, or a small charge of propellant. Compressed air seems to provide the most convenient, quiet, and compact unit. But for it to penetrate the skin, the maximum effective range is about ten inches. Beyond that, the lack of mass reduces velocity and penetrating power drastically. So someone had to put the weapon within a few inches of her neck. It could have looked like a book, a camera, a walking stick, a tobacco pipe, a purse —almost any small unremarkable portable object. The best time and place would be out of doors, in a crowd.''

"Like a crowd around Ladwigg after he fell?" I said.

"Yes, like that," Max said. "Here's the scenario. Ladwigg's early morning bike ride had been cased. Somebody picked the right spot, out of sight of any of the houses, where they could step out and chunk a rock into the front of his face as he came along at twenty miles an hour on his ten-speed. When the body was discovered, the sirens arriving brought people out of the houses widely scattered around there. And the people from the offices. It's a new community. For the most part, the people are strangers to each other. An unfamiliar person would be assumed to be a new homeowner. When they got Markov, they poked him in the back of the leg with an umbrella tip. Mrs. Howard got it in the back of the neck, so, as I said, the weapon could have looked like any innocuous familiar object. And the crowd watching them load Ladwigg's body provided enough diversion. After we learned what had killed the woman and went back in time and took a closer look at the way Ladwigg died, it became obvious they were part of the same assignment for somebody.''

"If you know that," I said, "then you've probably done a lot more homework. Why don't you tell us what you know, so we won't be repeating stuff?''

"It's better this way. It's a check on our own information.''

"And on us.''

"Why not? Memories aren't flawless. Don't have such a low boiling point. Your honor isn't at stake any more," Max said.

"So ask me something.''

Meyer interrupted. "Gentlemen!" he said. "Let's all be friends. I think that what I will do at this point is relate the details of a visit by two men to Mr. McGee last Saturday, a visit by one man to Bonnie Brae on Thursday, the thirteenth, some phone calls I made yesterday morning, and a visit to Bonnie Brae which we made yesterday afternoon. But before I get into that narrative, I will first tell you what Gretel Howard told the two of us on the evening of Friday, December seventh. Knowing your area of interest and suspecting the extent of your training, I shall tell this in what may seem like infinite detail, adding my suspicions, inferences, and conjectures as I proceed. Will that be useful?''

"Very.''

"Before I begin, let me say that I am taking you two on faith. I am assuming your hats are white. Left to my own devices, I would not be so revelatory. But when my friend Travis threw the revolver onto the bed, he was exercising his right to have a hunch, and because I have seen how his hunches usually work, I am following it.''

I moved over to a more comfortable chair. Jake taped the extraordinary performance. Meyer remembered so much more than I did, I wondered if my brain was slowly turning to mush. He spoke in sentences, in paragraphs, in chapters. Max scribbled a note to himself from time to time. Whenever I thought Meyer was going to leave something out, he came around to it in the next few minutes. When he was through he was slightly hoarse, and we took a break and ordered up a late room-service lunch. Jake intercepted the cart at the door, signed, and wheeled it in.

During lunch there were some obligatory comments about the weather, the price of hotel rooms, the Miami Dolphins' season, and how much vitamin C you take to ward off the common cold.

After the cart was wheeled out again by Jake and the door closed, Max got up and paced, frowning, chunking his fist into his palm from time to time.

He went back to the desk and looked at his notes. "Give me her description of this Brother Titus again, please. As close to her words as you can make it."

"I can make it exact," Meyer said.

"How the hell can you do that?"

"Give me a couple of minutes," Meyer said. He closed his eyes and began to breathe slowly and deeply. His eyelids fluttered. His mouth sagged partly open. I had seen him do it before. It was a form of autohypnosis, and he was projecting himself back to the evening of the seventh.

He lifted his head and opened his eyes. Jake inserted a fresh cassette and punched the tape on again. Meyer spoke in his own voice and diction. "Big, but not fat. Big-boned. About forty, maybe a little less. Kind of a round face, with all of his features sort of small and centered in the middle of all that face." It made the backs of my hands tingle and the back of my neck crawl. It was Gretel's word choice, phrasing, cadence, pauses. It was Gretel, speaking again through Meyer, telling us whom to look for.

"Wispy blond hair cut quite short. No visible eyebrows or eyelashes. Lots and lots of pits and craters in his cheeks, from terrible acne when he was young. Little mouth, little pale eyes, girlish little nose. He was wearing a khaki jacket over a white turtleneck. He was holding onto the side of the passenger door because of the rough ride. His hands are very big and . . . well, brutal-looking."

He stopped and gave himself a little shake, and all three of them looked questioningly at me.

"Absolutely exact," I said. "Just as I remember it. I mean, better than I remember it." I was too boisterous, too jovial, too loud, the way you get when you want to disavow being moved by something. I caught Meyer's look of concern. I envied him his ability to regress himself to the actual scene, to be with her in that way. I had no way to be with her. Memory has a will of its own. When I forced it, she would blur out. It had to come to me in sudden takes, little snippets from the cutting-room floor of the mind. They came smoking in, stunning me.

The tape was stopped. Jake had put the cassettes in a row, in order. He began numbering them, dating them.

Max looked at his notes. "When there is a near collision in the air, NASA is the investigating agency. They recommend to the FAA the action to be taken. So do the controllers and airport managers. We'll recheck the three of them—Toomey, Kline, and Ryan, but will come up probably with just what you have, Meyer."

Meyer nodded and said, "I keep thinking, Max, wondering what those three *do* represent. Travis caught that faint continental flavor. But he says the speech was colloquial American."

"Buffalo, St. Louis, or Santa Barbara," I said, "or anyplace in between. Middle height, middle age, no distinguishing features. Office fellows. Flabby and pale. Both with glasses. Invisible men. Clothes off the rack, not cheap and not expensive. Hell, if you walked through any downtown past the banks on a Tuesday noon, you'd see them walking together to lunch. If you lined up ten of them, I'd have a sorry job trying to pick out my two."

"You're describing the average, upper-echelon, middle-European, or Eastern European agent. They don't see enough daylight. They spend a lot of time on the files. They eat too much starch. And the KGB has the best language schools in the world. Crash courses, and they turn out people who can speak the language of the assigned country like a native. Of course, those guys are motivated. If they don't work hard enough learning the language, they end up in Magnitogorsk or some damn place, processing internal travel permits. They're good. Just not very flexible. They're not good at jettisoning one plan in mid-flight and inventing a second one that might work."

"But how could they fit into all this?" Meyer asked.

Max grinned at him. "You want another scenario? The way I read it, somebody goofed badly on something very important. So they sent Igor and Vashily here on a tidy-up mission. Plug the holes. Find out who knows what, report back, and await orders."

"Their presence would imply some importance to this."

Jake laughed, and snapped one of the eight-by-ten glossies with a fingernail. "You bet your ass there's something important going on. The presence of this little sphere proves that. We'll go through the Church of the Apocrypha to locate this Brother Titus and find out if he is coincidence or part of it somehow. I don't have much hope of unwinding anything in Brussels. We've bounced off that wall before. It's very tight over there."

Max stood up and said, "We're very grateful for your cooperation, gentlemen."

"Will you contact us again?" I asked.

"Doubtful."

"How would we get in touch with you?"

"Why should you?" There was some amusement in his steady gaze.

I said, "Who knows? Something else happens that fits in with this, who do we tell?"

Jake said to Max, "If we don't know what's going on, we don't know if they are involved more than they think they are. An identity mixup. Or something observed they shouldn't have seen."

After a moment of thought, Max nodded and wrote a number down and tore it out of his pad. "Memorize this number. Use a phone you can control for a couple of hours. It may take that long for a call-back. Here is what you say. That line will always answer, day and night. The person will say hello. You say, 'Was somebody at this number trying to reach Travis McGee?' They'll say they don't know, but they can check around and find out. Then you say, 'If anyone was, I can be reached at such and such a number.' Then wait. Clear?"

"Perfectly," I said.

Max stood a little taller and said, "You shouldn't have gone out to see Broffski and Slater. The cover story was halfway okay, but frail. What you shouldn't do, either of you or both of you, is push at this thing any more, from any direction. We've satisfied ourselves you can both keep your mouths shut about what you learned here. Finding out the kind of security clearance you had once upon a time, Meyer, helped in that decision. So lay low. Keep down. Keep quiet. In return for that, I promise I'll find some way to let you know when we've tidied up. No, don't leave just yet. I have to make a call."

He made it from a phone in a dispatch case. He grunted and listened, grunted and listened, then said thanks and hung up and slapped the case shut. "No sign of your being followed here. There's no directional bug on your pickup truck, and your home phones on those two boats are not tapped."

"She died a week ago today," I said. "She didn't want to die. She was pushed over the edge. She was pushed off the earth. And you want me to keep down and keep quiet."

Max looked at me with a pitying expression. "If you wanted to thrash around, what could you do? Where could you start? Suppose you knew for sure that the DGI did it."

"What's the DGI?"

"The Cuban secret service. It has been directed and controlled by the KGB for nine years at least. What next? Who do you ask? Who do you go see? And who would know anything anyway? Is whoever killed her still alive? Maybe not. Intelligence operations are compartmentalized. There is only one contact between cells, and few people in any cell. I don't care what you do. Just don't go to the police to complain about an unsolved murder, and don't write your congressman about internal security."

"We can leave now?" Meyer asked.

Max nodded. Jake took a look at the corridor. We left. The day was the same kind of day. But the world was a different kind of world.

8

WE WERE back aboard *The Busted Flush* by four o'clock. My brain seemed to be droning along in neutral. I could not kick it into gear.

Meyer selected a beer. I roamed back and forth with a beaker of Boodles on ice. "I don't want it to be depersonalized," I said. "I want it to be a single person with a single motive. I don't want it to be organizational, a committee decision. You can't get your hands around the throat of a committee. You can't beat the face of an organization against a brick wall."

"Listen to me, Travis. Stop pacing and listen. If she was killed because she discovered something, by pure accident, she should not have known, then it is accidental death. The world is full of secret plans and understandings. A sniper in Lebanon misses and the slug smashes the head of a child a half mile farther away. What can the child's father do? Who does he see? Where does he file his complaint?"

"Somebody aimed at her, Meyer, and didn't miss."

"And your chance of ever finding that somebody is exactly zero."

"Then I'll find who gave the orders."

"Again zero."

"How can you possibly know that?"

"Travis, please sit down. I can't talk to you when you keep walking around behind me. There. That's better. And if you can listen a little, it will be better yet. I live in two worlds, yours and the real world."

"Come on!"

"Just listen. In your world the evil is small scale. It is one on one. It is creature preying on creature. All right, so it can be terrifying. I am not trying to say it is like games in a sandbox under the apple tree. A person can get killed doing what you do, and I think it is a worthwhile way for you to live. In these past few years it has made you a bit morose, but that is only because any kind of repetition leads to a certain staleness of the soul. Too many beds, and too much dying. Greed and love begin to wear the same masks. Gretel gave me high hopes for you. You were emerging from the dolor of repetition. Now you look as if you had been hit on the head with a mallet. In your world, your heart is broken. I want to reach you before you start any kind of move that will break your heart on a larger scale than you can now conceive of. All right?"

"Keep talking."

"When I attend conferences on international monetary affairs, when I go give my little speeches, or go earn a little fee for consultation, I hear of many things. They alarm me. I cannot tell you how much they alarm me. In Iran a little band of schoolteachers dribble gasoline around the circumference of a movie house and light it, incinerating four hundred and thirty people, most of them children. In Guyana nine hundred Americans kill themselves, for reasons as yet unexplained. There are over four billion people in the world, and each day more and more of them are dying in bloody and sickening ways. The pot is beginning to simmer. The little bubbles appear around the edges. Intrigue, interconnected, is multiplying geometrically, helped along by the computer society. Orbiting eyes in the sky scan us all. Poisons abound. The sick birds fall out of the air. Signs and portents, Travis. And here we are in happyland, in a resort town, with the bright sunshine, bright boats, humid young ladies. This is all stage setting. Carnival. Scenario. The real world is out there in a slow dreadful process of change. There is a final agony of millions out there, and one and a quarter million new souls arriving every week. We try to think about it less than we used to. None of it makes any sense, really. But then whatever it is that is out there, it moves into this world in the shape of a tiny sphere of platinum and iridium and deadly poison. Now we have to think about it, but it cannot be personalized. It is all a *thing,* a great plated toad-lizard thing with a rotten breath, squatting back inside the mouth of the cave, infinitely patient."

"So keep on having fun?"

"That's not very responsive."

"Sorry."

"Being an adult means accepting those situations where no action is possible."

"Except joining the Church of the Apocrypha."

"Have you lost your mind?"

"Brother Titus will forgive my sins."

"It's an idiotic idea."

"I have to go out to California anyway, with . . . the ashes."

"When are we leaving?"

I smiled at him and shook my head. "Not this time, Meyer. Part of this trip is trying to get away from myself somehow. I have no delight in what and who I am. Not any more. Not here."

Meyer sat and looked at me for a long moment, the small bright blue eyes intent, the face impassive. "You take yourself wherever you go, Travis."

"A popular truism."

He finished the beer and put it aside. "I'll go get the urn."

"You don't have to bother right now. I can come and get it when I'm ready to leave."

"I might not be there. I'll get it now."

He was back in ten minutes with a cardboard carton, a vise-grip wrench he had borrowed a year ago, and fifteen dollars he claimed he owed me and insisted I take.

And then he was gone. It had not occurred to me that I would hurt Meyer, but there seemed to be no point in going over and apologizing to him. Through me, he had acquired a taste for the salvage business. Now there was nothing left to save but myself. And he couldn't help me there.

I fixed myself another heavy drink and, carrying it along, I went through all the interior spaces of *The Busted Flush*. I remembered all the lovely women. I looked at the huge shower stall, the sybaritic tub, the great broad bed in the master stateroom. I looked at the speakers and turntables, the tape decks and tape racks. Everything had a sweet, sad look. Like a playpen with scattered toys after the child has died.

When the drink was gone, I went down to my hidey-hole in the forward hull and removed all my reserve and took it up to the lounge. Ninety-three hundred-dollar bills. Life savings. Wisely invested, it might bring me almost eighty dollars a month. I sat and planned what I would wear and what I would carry, and mentally distributed my fortune in inconspicuous places.

Then I looked directly at the cardboard carton for the first time. Firmly taped and tied. Ten inches square, twelve inches tall. All the remains of the physical Gretel. It hefted at about the weight of a sizable cantaloupe.

I sat at the little pull-down writing desk again, and I wrote a letter to Meyer:

> I will take this up to the office and give it to Linda and tell her to hold it a few days and then give it to you. By then I will have added the keys to this boat, and to the *Muñequita* and to the car. I will have emptied out the perishables and turned off the compressors and arranged for disconnect on the phone. I am enclosing five hundred in cash—I better make that eight hundred—to take care of expenses around here. I will have put the phone on temporary disconnect and arranged for my mail to come to you. Today is December 18th. If I am going to be able to make it back here, I will get word to you somehow on

or before June 18th. If you don't hear by then, everything here belongs to you. Frank Payne has a will on file to that effect, witnessed and all. I don't really know what is making me act the way I am acting. You would know more about that than I, probably. I have this very strong feeling that I am never coming back here, that this part of my life is ending, or that all of my life is ending. I have been bad company a lot of the time the past few years, going sour somehow. Gretel was the cure for that. I came back to life, but not for long. And this is what the stock market guys call a lower low. I just feel futile and ridiculous. You are the best friend I have ever had. Take care of yourself. Make a point of it. If I don't come back, what you should do is move aboard the *Flush,* peddle your crock boat and the *Muñequita* and the Rolls, and throw a party they will never never forget around here.

I put it in a heavy brown envelope and left it unsealed. It was dark. I took a walk around my weather decks. The night smelled like diesel fuel. A nearby drunk was singing "Jingle Bells," never getting past the sleigh, starting again and again and again. The boulevard hummed and rustled with cars, and there was no sound at all from the sea. A woman laughed, a jet went over, and I went back inside. Somebody working his way into his slip made a small wake, and the *Flush* shifted, sighed, and settled back into stillness.

*   *   *

On the following Saturday morning I found the same man at the Petaluma cemetery, the one Gretel and I had dealt with when we had flown out with John Tuckerman's ashes. He was cultivating and reseeding two parallel curving scars in the soft green turf. He was a broad muscular old man with a bald head and thick black eyebrows. He wore sneakers and crisp khakis. He dropped the tool, dusted his hands, and tilted his head to one side as he looked up at me.

"Weren't you here way last spring? With the Tuckerman girl?"

"With Gretel Howard. Her married name."

"What you got there?"

"Well . . . she died. Gretel died. This is her ashes."

He mopped his face and turned slightly away and looked upward into a tree. He sighed. "Sorry to hear it. Even if it was a sad time for her, bringing her brother's ashes here, it wasn't hard to see you and she were real close, real happy with each other."

"Yes, we were."

"Too bad. Nice size on that girl. Great smile. What did she die from? Automobile? That is what takes most of the young ones."

"Some kind of flu with a high fever and kidney failure."

"I tell people it's the bugs striking back. Those laboratories go after the bugs with powerful new poisons and it stands to reason that the ones that live through it, they get twice as tough and nasty as they ever were before. Of course, John and Gretel's folks, they died premature, but it wasn't sickness. I suppose you want her in the family plot. Dumb-ass question. You wouldn't be here if you didn't."

"Can we go right ahead with it?"

"Don't you remember how it was before? There's got to be the permit, and they've got to have vital statistics for the records, and there's the fee."

"The office is closed."

"I know. They used to stay open Saturday morning, but not lately."

"I've got a copy of the death certificate here, and I've got her birth certificate, marriage certificate, and final decree of divorce. Here, you can have them."

He took them and then tried to give them back to me, saying, "I don't have anything to do with the office part."

"And if the permit hasn't gone up since last time, here's the fifty dollars."

He hesitated and finally took it. "I guess we could do it now and I could give them this stuff Monday. But don't you want any words said? She said the words for her brother."

"As I will for her."

The Tuckerman plot was in that part of the cemetery where the stones were flush with the ground—which, as he had mentioned when I had seen him before, made mowing a lot easier. While he went to get the post-hole digger from his shed, I opened the carton. The urn was shinier than I had expected it to be, and more ornate. It looked like a large gold goblet with a lid.

She had owned a small worn book of the collected poems of Emily Dickinson. She had read two of them over her brother's grave. She had marked the ones she liked best. There were three short ones I wanted to read.

I could just make out the place where the old man had dug the hole before, for John Tuckerman's urn. He chose a new spot and asked me if it was all right. I approved of it and asked him if I could dig.

"Leave the dirt close and neat," he said.

He watched me as I chunked the tool down, lifting the bite of earth in the blades, setting it aside each time, close and neat. Once it was down over a foot, it began to get me in the small of the back. It is an awkward posture, an awkward way to lift.

When it was deep enough, he stopped me. I lifted the urn out of the box and, kneeling, lowered it to the bottom of the hole. I stood up then and read the first two poems, the longer ones. My voice had a harsh and meaningless sound in the stillness, like somebody sawing a board. I said the words I saw on the page without comprehending their meaning. Then I read the one she had read to her dead brother, called "Parting."

> "My life closed twice before its close—
> It yet remains to see
> If Immortality unveil
> A third event to me.
>
> "So huge, so hopeless to conceive
> As these that twice befell.
> Parting is all we know of heaven,
> And all we need of hell."

I bent and dropped the faded blue book down the hole, and then, kneeling, using both hands, I cupped up the dirt and filled the hole and tamped it down, replaced the circle of turf I had cut with the digger, and with the edge of my hand brushed away the loose dirt into the grass roots.

"No marker for her either?" he asked.

"I don't think so. Neither of them had children to come and look for the place." The oblong of marble, level with the earth, reading TUCKERMAN, was enough.

"Those words were like the ones she read that time. Is that some kind of one of these new religions?"

"Sort of."

"I thought so. There's a lot of them these days. I guess having one is better than having none, but it makes you wonder." He looked down toward the office and the road. "Where'd you park?"

"I walked out from the bus station."

"Where are you going? Back to Florida?"

"I haven't decided."

"This town isn't as bad as some. If you need work, maybe I can think of somebody you could go ask. You look sort of down on your luck, mister."

"Thanks. If I come back this way, I'll look you up."

When I looked back from the road he was still watching me. I waved. He waved and turned away, back to his work fixing the scars where somebody had torn up the turf doing funny stunts in an automobile. I dug my duffel bag out of the bushes where I had hidden it and shouldered it with the wide strap over my left shoulder, the bag bumping against my right hip. My poncho was strapped to the duffel bag. I wore work shoes, dark-green twill trousers, a faded old khaki shirt, a brown felt hat, a gray cardigan sweater. I had sandy stubble on my jaws and neck. Before leaving Florida, I'd had my hair clipped down to a Marine basic cut, which could have been a prison cut. I carried in my shirt pocket, for the right occasion, a pair of glasses with gold-colored rims, hardly any correction in the lenses, and one bow fixed with black electrician's tape. I wanted to attract a second look from the average cop, but without stirring enough curiosity for him to want to check me out. But if he did check me out, I had some credentials. I had an expired Florida driver's license with my picture on it, and I had a fragile tattered copy of army discharge papers, and a social security card sandwiched in plastic. They were wrapped in a plastic pouch and were in the compartment in the end of the duffel bag. They all said I was Thomas J. McGraw, address General Delivery, Osprey, Florida, occupation commercial fisherman.

"Well, officer, it was like this. My old lady died and I sold off our stuff and the trailer, and I thought I'd come out here and poke around and see if I could locate our daughter Kathy. She took off six years ago when she was fourteen, and we heard from her two years ago, some postcards from San Francisco, and Petaluma and Ukiah. She said she was joining up with some kind of church. Me, I come here by Greyhound bus."

As I walked, I wrote my autobiography, and the story of my marriage, and my wife's death. I made Peg and Kathy into real people. I made Tom McGraw into a real person. As I walked, I went over and over the imaginary events of my life until I could see them. I outlined my own personality. I was not too quick of wit, and I tended to lose jobs through getting drunk and not showing up. When I worked, I was a hard worker. I was a man of great pride. I did not suffer unkind remarks about my character or my station in life. I was a womanizer when I was in my cups. Peg had been a staunch church-woman. I went with her a couple times a year. I shared most of my political opinions with Archie Bunker. As I walked, I talked to imaginary people, talked as Tom McGraw would talk to them. He was servile when he talked to people in power. He was affable as a dog with his peers. He was nasty to those he considered beneath him. I worked my way into the role.

Long, long ago, I had known an actress. Susan was twenty-four. I was sixteen. She was working in summer theater. I was working in the country hotel where she was staying. She was a lanky lady who cussed, wore pants, and smoked thin little cigars. I found her monstrously exciting. I was worried about myself that year. There had been an episode with a loud chubby girl who, true to locker-room gossip, was willing to put out. But she was so loud that I was less than able. I could almost but not quite count it as the first time. I could lie to others but not to myself, and I had the dread fear Lolly would tell everybody. I was worried about myself.

Though I was a head taller than the actress, she didn't want to be seen with me around town. I would walk out into the country, and she would come along in her borrowed car and we would go up in the hills and park and go walking together. In August, after we had gotten into the habit of making a bed from a blanket and spruce bows, in hidden places, while we were resting from each other, I told her about Lolly and about my fears. She laughed her deep harsh startling laugh and told me that I had less to worry about than anybody she had ever known. It was very comforting.

It was repertory theater, and she had to refresh her memory in a lot of roles. It startled me the way she could turn herself into an entirely different person. We would sit in the shade and I would give her her cues from the playscript, and then we would walk and she would become the character in the play. I had to ask her questions, any questions, and she would respond as that person would have responded. She explained that it was the best way to do it. One had to invent a past that fitted, and memories that fitted. She explained that once you were totally inside a false identity, secure in it, you could handle the unexpected on stage in a way consistent with the character.

And I had used that afterward, many times, and now I was using it again. Susan taught me a lot. Once she got me past the initial shyness, she showed me and told me all the ways I could increase her pleasure while delaying mine. It gave me a wonderful feeling of domination and control to be able to turn that strong, tense, mature female person into gasping, grasping, shuddering incoherence. I was in love with her, of course. I could not stand the thought of the summer ending. I told her I loved her, and I was going to come to New York to be close to her.

I will always remember the way she cupped both hands on my face and looked deeply into my eyes. "Travis, you are a very very sweet boy, and you are going to become one hell of a man. But if I ever find you outside my apartment door, I am going to have the doorman throw you out on your ass. We can end it right now or next week, whichever you choose. But end it we will, boyo, with no loose ends. No letters, no phone calls, no visits. Ever."

And that's how it was.

So now I walked my way deeper into my Tom McGraw role. Trucks whuffed by, with the trailing turbulence tugging at my clothes. Divided highway. Route 101. Looking for the daughter lost. Too many years ago.

This didn't have the bare rolling look of the hills near the sea below San Francisco. There was more water here, rivers and lakes and forest country. I had flown into San Francisco as Travis McGee, taxied to a Holiday Inn near Fisherman's Wharf, and spent a day assembling a wardrobe to go with the new identity I had bought from a reliable source in Miami. The McGee identity fitted into a suitcase. I stored it and paid six months in advance. The storage receipt was the only link, and I didn't want it on me. Small things can be hidden in public places. There was a bank of new storage lockers in the bus station. They were not quite flush against the rear wall. I taped it at shoulder height to the back of the lockers, out of sight. If I could stand up, I could get it back. If I wanted it back.

9

I GAVE up walking when the heel of my right foot began to bother me. The work shoes were too heavy for one who had spent such a chunk of his life barefoot. I wished I had taken a bus.

I found a good place to hitch a ride. I hate to see the damn fools on the highways hitching in the wrong places. It is a waste of energy. You have to be where they can see you a long way off, and where you stand out well against the background. They have to be able to see a lot of highway beyond you, and they have to spot a place where they can pull off. You have to make a gesture at each car, a big sweeping one. You leave the duffel bag at your feet and you take your hat off, and you smile wide enough to show some teeth. An animal will roll onto his back to demonstrate his harmlessness. A man will grin. It is better to trust the animal.

A gaunt old man in a rattle-bang Ford pickup stopped at high noon and picked me up. He wore banker's clothes and a peaked cap that said Oakland Raiders.

"Only going as far as Lake Mendocino, friend," he said.

"Is that past Ukiah?"

"Next door. I can drop you off before I make my turn. Get in." He looked back, waiting for a hole in the traffic, and when one came along, he jumped into it with surprising acceleration.

"Don't know this country, eh?"

"Don't know it at all. This is the first time for me."

"Hunting work?"

"Well, I might have to do some to keep going. But mostly I'm trying to get some kind of trace of my little girl. I think she's out here somewhere."

"There's a lot of young girls out here somewhere. There was a time in the sixties when they'd come drifting up from San Francisco. Communes and farming and all. What they call alternative life-styles. Potheads, mostly. No offense. I'm not saying your girl is one of those. She missing long?"

"Six years."

"Hear anything from her in all that time?"

"One time, and that was four years ago. She'll be twenty now. Peg and me, we married young. Kathy was sixteen when we got those cards from her. They came over a month or so. They never gave an address we could write back to. They were mailed in San Francisco, and then the very last one was from Ukiah. It said she was joining up with some kind of church and we should forget about her forever. You know, when you've got just the one kid, you don't forget like that. It took the heart out of Peg. She died a while back, and after I sold off a little piece of land and the trailer and an old skiff, I thought I might as well use the money trying to find her."

"Friend, this state is chock-full of religions. You can find any kind you are looking for. There's some that'll take you to Guyana and teach you to raise oranges and how to kill yourself quick. They start in the north and go all the way down to the Mexican border, and to my way of thinking, the further south they go, the crazier they get. People are hunting around for something to believe in these days. All the stuff people used to believe in has kind of let them down hard. You'd have to know the name of the religion first, I'd say."

"I learned it by heart. The Church of the Apocrypha."

"I've lived pretty close to Ukiah for ten years, and I can't say I ever heard of it. But I've seen some strange ones drifting around the streets there, selling flowers and candy and wearing white robes."

"I can ask around there, I guess. Big place?"

"No. I'd guess maybe twelve thousand. What kind of work you do?"

"I fish commercial. Net work, mostly. Mullets usually. When they're hard to find, it pays good. When they're easy, it isn't hardly worthwhile going out, you get such small money. What kind of business are you in?"

"Investments."

"Oh." From the way he said it, I knew that was all I was going to learn. He moved the pickup right along, tailgating the people who wouldn't move over into the slow lane.

"Where would be a good place to ask in Ukiah?"

"Maybe the police. Police usually know about the crazies and where they live."

He dropped me off at the Ukiah ramp. The wind felt cool and fresh. I found one gas station that wouldn't let me use the rest room, and another one that would. I shaved off the stubble and put on my wire glasses and looked into the mirror. In the hard fluorescence, my deepwater tan looked yellowish. Deep grooves bracketed my mouth. The gold glasses did not give me a professorial look. I looked like a desert rat with bad eyes.

*   *   *

He was an officer of the law. Not too long ago he had been a fat, florid, hearty man. The balloon was deflating. He had made a couple of new holes in his belt. His color was bad. His chops sagged. He looked me over with a listless competence. And he listened to my story. "Apocrypha. Kind of rings a bell. Short dirty-white robes. Beards. Sister this and Brother that." He dialed a three-digit number and leaned back in his leather chair and began murmuring into the phone, listening for a time while he stared at the ceiling. Then he hung up and took a sheet of yellow paper and drew a crude map.

"Where that outfit was, McGraw, they were over in Lake County. They had a pretty good-sized tract. What you do, you take Twenty East and go over past Upper Lake, maybe two miles, and there's a little road heads off to the east, unpaved but a good surface. You go along that road, mostly uphill, and it winds around and there are little roads heading off it, smaller still, and that encampment is off at the end of one of those. You'll have to ask around."

"Thanks. I appreciate you taking the trouble."

"Afraid it won't help much. Seems they've pulled up and moved off someplace. Might be nobody left there at all."

"It's the only clue I've got."

For the moment he forgot his own woes. "Listen, McGraw. There's thousands of kids took off. A lot of them don't ever show again. It's a sign of the times. What I mean is, don't expect too much. It's a good thing to look around, to satisfy yourself you did all you could. But don't expect too much. Okay?"

"Thanks. I won't. I mean, I'll try not to."

*   *   *

By Sunday noon I had found it. I had spent the night in a small rental trailer under giant evergreens. I had hitched three rides, walked through two monstrous rainstorms, and climbed what seemed to be several mountains.

So now I stood where Gretel and her husband had stood. The signs were large and explicit. Red lettering on white. PRIVATE PROPERTY. NO TRESPASSING. The wire gate she had described blocked the road. Beyond the gate the road curved up and to the right, out of sight behind the trees and brush. There was a lean-to on the right, just beyond the gate. The last people I had asked, the ones who had given me the final directions, had said that they thought there were a few left up at the encampment, but that most of them had gone away. They said that sometimes they saw a van on the road. Black, with a gold cross painted on the sides.

I am Tom McGraw, looking for the traces of a daughter lost. I have a father's bullheaded determination. So I forge ahead. Climb the fence close to the gate, drop the duffel bag, and drop down beside it. Shoulder it and walk up the muddy road.

There was a cathedral of evergreens on either side of the road, standing at parade rest on the slope, the ground silent with needles. The sun was suddenly covered again, and I heard a high soft sigh of rainwind in the pine branches. I trudged up the curve and up a steeper pitch. The stand of trees dwindled, and there were boulders among them big as bungalows. I came out at the top. Far away to the northeast I could see sunlit mountains. I was on an old rocky plateau, quite level, as big as four football fields. It sloped gently down toward valleys and gullies on every side. Off to my right, at the end of the big plateau, was a clutter of small structures. The biggest was a corrugated steel and aluminum building that looked like a prefab warehouse. There were several small cement-block buildings, and several trailers on block foundations. I saw one derelict truck.

There was no sign of life. I wanted to see if the road continued on the other side of the field. I hollered and waited and heard no answer. I walked across and looked. There was no road down the slope. There had been a stand of small trees there, with the biggest about three inches in diameter. They were broken off about two feet above ground level. At first I thought somebody had driven up and down there with a vehicle. Something nagged at memory. I walked down the slope. The damage was not fresh. The wood was splintered and dry. I squatted and found where slugs had creased the bark. Very heavy sustained fire from an automatic weapon would chew them off just like that. Using the bark creases for rough triangulation, I was able to go back up the slope to the approximate area where the weapon had been. I poked around and finally saw a glint of metal in a crack of the rock. I levered it out with a twig. It was a white metal shell casing, center-fire, in a smaller caliber than I would have expected. But it looked as if there was room for a hefty load of propellant. There was an unfamiliar symbol on the end of it, like a figure 4 open at the top, and with an extra horizontal line across the upright.

I tossed it up and caught it and put it in my pocket. A strange exercise for a church group, shooting down a young forest. And then picking up all the shell casings.

I headed toward the buildings, but before I reached them I heard, coming toward me, the sound of a lot of footsteps, running almost in unison. They burst up a slope and onto the plateau about fifty yards away from me. Seven of them in single file, weapons slung, left hands holding the weapons, right arms swinging. I had the impression of great fitness and great effort. They were young. They wore gray-green coveralls, fatigue caps, ammo belts, and backpacks. One of them saw me and yelled something. With no hesitation they stopped and ran back, spreading into combat patrol interval, spinning, falling prone, right at the dropoff line, seven muzzles aimed at me. I shed the duffel bag and held my arms high.

"Hey!" I yelled. "Hey, what's the matter?"

"Down," a voice yelled. "Face down, spread-eagle. Now!"

Once down, I peered up and saw two walking toward me, weapons still ready, while two others were heading for the buildings, running in a crouching zigzag, in the event I had come with friends.

Hands patted me. I was told to shut up. I was told to roll over. One stood over me, muzzle at my forehead, and I suddenly realized she was female. The other, a man with a drooping mustache, did the frisking.

"Now what the hell are you doing here?" he demanded. "How did you get here? What did you do to Nicky?"

"The way I got here, I walked. I didn't see any Nicky."

"You come past the gate?"

"Yes."

"Can't you read? Didn't you see the signs?"

"I saw them. But I had to come up here and talk to somebody about my little girl. She joined up here. Maybe you know her. Kathy McGraw? I'm her daddy, Tom McGraw."

"Oh, for God's sake," the man said. The girl didn't relax her weapon.

"Can I get up?"

"Shut up," the girl said. "What are you going to do, Chuck?"

"What the hell *can* we do? Put him in C Building and wait for Pers to get back."

The girl gasped and said, "Oh, Jesus! Look at what's coming, Chuck."

A huge young blond man was coming across the field, carrying a fair-sized dead buck across his shoulders.

"God damn you, Nicky, why'd you leave the gate?"

He approached and eased the deer to the ground, rolled his shoulders to loosen them. "And this man came in, huh? Oh, great! I ought to kick you loose from your head, fellow."

"You're the one should be kicked, Nicky," the girl said.

"That sucker came right out onto the road and looked at me and ran back in. I shot too fast and missed and gutshot him, and you can't leave an animal go running off like that. I followed him a mile and a half, fast as I could go. What'd you expect you to do, Nena? I killed him, gutted him, and brought him in."

"It isn't what *I* expect you to do," she said. "It's what Brother Persival expects."

"You can get up," Chuck said.

After I stood up, I looked at Nicky. His face was troubled. "Boring damn duty," he said. "Hang around down there eight hours at a time. Nobody ever comes. And then when you leave for a couple minutes, some damn fool climbs the fence."

"He's hunting his daughter. She used to be here," Chuck said.

"What was her name?" Nena asked me. She appeared to be in her early twenties. Olive skin, slender face, very dark eyes. She had that excess of bursting health which gave the whites of the eyes a bluish tint. No makeup. The long dense black lashes were her own.

"Katherine McGraw. She'd be twenty years old by now. Reddish-brown hair and blue eyes and some freckles when she was younger. Maybe they went away."

"Got a picture of her?"

"The best picture we had of her, it was when she was thirteen, and after Peg died, that was my wife, damn if I could find it. I looked all over for that picture. She was a pretty child. She ought to be a good-looking woman. Her ma was."

"You don't know what new name she took?"

"She never said. In those postcards."

"I can't help you. I don't know if anybody can—or wants to, Mr. McGraw. People that join up don't go back to the lives they had before."

"Where did everybody go from here?" I asked.

No answer. They urged me along and shut me up in C Building. It was a cement-block building about ten feet square, with two windows with heavy wire mesh over them. There was a wooden chair, a tree-trunk table, a stained mattress on the floor, and a forty-watt bulb hanging from a cord from the middle of the ceiling. There was a ragged pile of religious comic books, a musty army blanket, a two-quart jug of tepid drinking water, and a bucket to use as a toilet. They had taken my belt, shoelaces, and duffel bag. The door was solidly locked, I heard some bird sounds, and that was all. I wondered if they had all left.

Darkness came, and there was a quick light rain on the corrugated roof of my prison. I heard a distant motor noise and tried to decide if it was coming or going. When the sound did not change, I realized it might be a generator, the engine turning over at an unchanging rpm. So I tried my light bulb again, and it went on. It did not help the decor.

Two of them came and unlocked my door. They had a dazzling-bright gasoline lantern, an automatic weapon at the ready, and a tin bowl full of stew. They were two I had glimpsed before at a distance. One was a sallow blond girl with very little chin, and the other was a young man with an Asian cast to his features.

No harm to object. After all, I was Tom McGraw. "Why are you people pointing guns at me all the time? Damn it, I'm not some kind of criminal. I don't like being locked up like this. Where's my stuff you took away from me? I got my rights. You people are all gun-happy."

"Shut up, Dads," the Oriental said, and they closed the door and locked it.

Even though I had to eat it with a little white plastic spoon, I found the venison stew delicious. And it had been a long time since I had enjoyed the taste of anything. The lack of interest in eating had leaned me down a little over the past weeks.

There was a cook in the camp. Even a slight taste of wine in the stew. Boiled onions, carrots, celery, tomatoes. And a lot of it. After my dinner I read a religious comic book. All about Samson yanking down that temple. Samson looked like Burt Reynolds. Delilah looked like Liz Taylor. The temple looked like the Chase Bank.

After I turned my light off, I stretched out in my clothes on the dingy mattress and covered myself with the musty sheet. And in the darkness, I went over what I knew. I followed Meyer's injunction. Never mix up what you really know with what you think you know. Don't let speculation water down the proven truths. Leap to conclusions only when that is the only way to safety.

People talking outside my door awakened me. I knew it was late. I realized it was just the changing of the guard. I heard the clink of metal and a yawning good night and went back to sleep.

In the morning I was escorted down to a rushing tumbling icy creek by Nicky and the chinless blonde. She carried the weapon. I carried the soil bucket in one hand and held up my trousers with the other. I had asked politely for my belt, and they told me to shut up. They pointed me to the place on the bank where I could wash out the bucket in the fast water. Then I was allowed to go upstream to a place where I could dash some of the icy water into my face. Big Nicky was sullen. The blonde was trying to cheer him. When he answered, I found out her name was Stella. So I had four names out of the group of eight. They marched me back to C Building, again carrying the bucket, now empty, and holding up my trousers. I asked when they expected Mr. Persival, and they told me to shut up.

An hour later I was given cold scrambled eggs and cold toast on a pie tin, with another plastic spoon. They had changed cooks.

At midmorning I saw an interesting tableau from my window. I do not think they realized that I could see it. I had to get my face close to the screen and look slantwise. Two couples. Nena and a young man. Stella and a young man. Out of uniform. Casual clothes. Each carried luggage. Suitcase, or small bedroll or duffel bag. Chuck stood off to one side, watching them closely. He had a whistle in his mouth and what was apparently a stopwatch in his hand. I could not understand the instructions he yelled at them. They walked close and lovingly, laughing and talking together, looking at each other, not at their surroundings. When the whistle blew, they would snatch at the luggage, yank it open, remove an automatic weapon, let the luggage fall to the ground, stand with their backs to each other, leaning against each other, almost, in a little deadly square formation, hold the weapons aiming out in four directions, and revolve slowly.

Then they would repack and do it again. I think I watched fifteen rehearsals. Their time improved noticeably. I guessed that they had it down to just about four seconds before Chuck ended the exercise. Four seconds to change from two couples, lounging along, laughing together, to an engine of destruction.

I disobeyed one of Meyer's rules. I made an assumption or two. I assumed that they planned to put on their little act in a crowded place, like an airport or a shopping plaza, and the guns would be loaded, and people would be blown apart while still caught up in a horror of disbelief.

But why? They worked so very hard at it. They seemed so dedicated and intent. These were bright young people, very fit and disciplined. Playing a strange, strange game.

The noon meal was more venison stew. Still tasty.

The black van arrived in the late afternoon. It passed my window before I could see anyone in it. But I saw the gold cross painted on the side.

At least twenty minutes passed before my door was unlocked. Chuck said, "Strip and pile everything on the floor right in front of the door here. Fold it and pile it. Everything."

"Damn it all, I want to know why I'm—"

"Look. This is an order and it's serious. You want to strip, or be stripped?"

I did as I was told. They backed me into a corner and inspected the room to see if there was anything of mine hidden in it. That search didn't take long. They went off with everything.

It could have been an hour later before anybody came near me. Then it was Mr. Persival himself. A tall stooped figure, shaggy tousled dark hair flecked with gray. Long face and a lantern jaw. Eyes set deep in the bony sockets. The sports clothes looked unlikely on him, as did the big glasses with the slight amber tint, the boldface watch, water resistant to three hundred feet. He was an actor playing a contemporary Lincoln, or a Vermont storekeeper who'd built one store into a chain. He walked with care, the way the ill walk. The girl called Nena slid into the room with her weapon aimed at my chest and moved over to the side to keep Persival out of the line of fire. She was lithe and quick.

"My name is Persival, Mr. McGraw." A deep voice, soft and gentle. An air of total command, total assurance. "My young associates and I would be grateful for some explanation of this."

He held out a big slow hand, and resting on the palm was the cartridge case I had picked up. I spoke without hesitation, blessing the Susan I had known long ago for teaching me how to live a part. "Explanation? I picked that up out there. I never saw one just like it. I put it in my pocket. I mean, if that's the same one."

"I think we will go outside and you will show me where you found it."

"Can I have some clothes?"

"It isn't that chilly yet."

When I hesitated, I saw Nena lower the aiming point from chest to belly. I couldn't read anything in her eyes. She walked behind us. Persival walked just out of arm's reach, off to my left.

"And what were you doing over here?"

"I was looking for somebody so I could ask them about the Church of the Apocrypha, Mr. Persival. I wondered if the road I came up went down this side to more buildings, maybe. Then I saw all those trees down there, the way they were busted off at the same height. I went down and looked at them. I saw trees looking like that after we cleared some people out who were trying to ambush us, but the man on point stopped them in time. It was done some time ago. Weeks ago, probably, from the dead leaves and the dry wood. I saw slug marks on the trunk and I could kind of figure where the weapon must have been. Or weapons. Right over here. So I saw a glint in a crack in the rocks. Here, I think. No, it was this one. Because here is the twig I hooked it out with. It was a kind I never saw before, so I put it in my pocket. And now you've got it."

He nodded at me and smiled in a kindly way. "You were just wandering around here, Mr. McGraw?"

"Looking for somebody to talk to."

He sighed and said, "Yes. Looking for somebody to talk to."

"Then I was walking toward the buildings when the patrol came up onto the flat right over there."

"Why do you call it a patrol?"

"I don't know. People in uniform carrying weapons and ammo, wearing light packs. Not enough for a squad, and they were coming back out of the country. What would you call them?"

"Followers of the true faith."

"Well, I wouldn't know that. I would like to know something about my little girl and how I can find her."

"Let's walk back. It's getting chilly."

"I'd appreciate that," I said. If there is any way to feel more naked than standing out in 60-degree weather as the day is ending, with a girl aiming an automatic weapon at the small of your back, I would not care to hear of it.

On the way back I noticed that he did not walk quite as far out to my left. I could have reached him, if I felt suicidal.

"You were carrying a considerable amount of cash in the double lining of that duffel bag, Mr. McGraw."

"I was hoping you wouldn't look that close."

"We're very careful people. Is it stolen?"

"Hell, no, it's not stolen! Or maybe it is now, hah?"

"Don't become agitated, please. Just tell me where you got it." I told him. He thought it over and nodded. "So you decided to make your funds last as long as possible, so your search would not be hampered by the need to seek employment."

"That's exactly correct."

We went inside. He sat on the straight chair and told the girl to go get my clothes. She hesitated, and he looked stonily at her and said, "Sister?" She scuttled away. She brought the clothing. Persival sent her away. He watched me dress. He said, "You seem to have suffered an extraordinary number of wounds, Mr. McGraw. Are they all service-connected?"

"No, sir, not all. Two are. High on my back on the right side and the shoulder. And here on the left hip."

"How about that huge wound on your right thigh?"

"That was a hunting accident long ago. I went a long time before they found me. It got infected, and I was out of my head and nearly died. Some of this other stuff, I'm in kind of an active line of work. And the guys I work with, when we play we play rough. Beside that, sir, I have a bad temper sometimes. I go out of my head, sort of. I haven't kilt anybody, but I've tried hard."

"You don't seem to have the hands of a commercial fisherman."

I held my hands out and looked at them, backs and fronts. "What do you mean? Oh, you mean like those old boys that go out in the freezing water off of Maine or someplace? They get those big paws like catcher's mitts, and those busted twisted fingers. My daddy had hands like that from working the big nets. It's all nylon now, and you have to wear tough gloves or cut yourself to ribbons. Besides, I haven't been out working the nets for a long time now."

"You seem to be in excellent shape, Mr. McGraw."

"I'm not as good as I'd like to be. You know, the old wind. And the legs give out first. But I've always stayed in pretty good shape. Never had a beer belly."

"And you have had combat experience?"

"As a grunt. I can do the BAR, mortars, flame, mines, whatever. I was in it fourteen months. Got to be a utility infielder."

"Then you must have watched our little . . . patrol with a practiced eye. Would you have any comment?"

"I haven't seen much. They're trained down fine, physically. They move quick and they move well. They carry the weapons at the ready. But all the rest of it? I don't know what they can do. They look good. What are they training up to do anyway?"

"Please sit down there, on the mattress, Mr. McGraw. Make yourself comfortable." He hitched the straight chair closer and leaned over, forearms resting on his knees, long fingers dangling. "I will do you the courtesy of speaking to you with absolute frankness."

"Something happened to my little girl?"

"Please. I wouldn't know about that, nor even how I could find out. I am trying to tell you that if I were to follow my own rules, I would have my young associates take you out into the tall trees and blow your head off."

"Why? Why the hell would you do that?"

"You came stumbling and bumbling in here through an entrance that should have been guarded. The young man responsible will be punished. But I am not taking pity on your innocence and your naïve quest. I am thinking of sparing you only because I believe there is some specific use I can make of you."

"Such as what?"

"Are you in any position to ask me that, right now?"

"I reckon not, if you don't want me to, Mr. Persival."

It was getting so dark I could hardly see his face. I could see a pale reflection of the after-dusk sky in his tinted glasses. He had a strange weight and force about him. Total confidence and a total impartiality.

The distant engine started. The overhead bulb flickered, glowed, brightened. He stood up and stared down at me, then turned on his heel and left, leaving the door open. I walked out and stood with my thumbs hooked in my belt, looking at the faint glow in the western sky, above the sharp tips of the big pines far down the slope. I had the feeling I was being watched, and that it had been set up before Persival paid his call. I yawned and stretched, scratched myself, and slouched back into C Building, wondering if I should have pushed the money question a little harder. Would Tom McGraw have pushed it? Not when faced with the possibility of getting shot in the head.

I wondered when they were going to bring me something to eat, and if it would be the stew again.

Then I heard them all coming. They had flashlights and lanterns. I tightened up, and then heard laughter.

The sallow blonde arrived first, carrying a camp stool and a cooking pot and a flashlight. "We're having a party, Brother Thomas! At *your* house!"

"So come right in, Sister Stella. Come right in," I said.

10

THEY FILLED the room. They brought stools and cushions, a gasoline lantern, food, and wine. Nine of them and one of me. Plastic paper plates and genuine forks. Paper cups and a big container of coffee. Jolly and smiling. I knew Chuck, the patrol leader, and three of his six soldiers—Nena and Stella and the Oriental. I learned that the Oriental was Sammy. The other three were Haris, a slender blond Englishman—the name pronounced to rhyme with police—and Barry, a young black with a shaved head and dusty tan coloring, and Ahman, who looked like a young Turkish pirate. Persival was there, and also Alvor, one I had not seen before. He was chunky, with a broad gray heavy face, colorless eyes and lips, mouse hair, and huge shoulders. I made certain I got all the names right. Alvor had to have been in the van with Persival. Nicky was missing, and I overheard a comment that indicated he was down at the gate as a lookout.

I was sitting on the narrow mattress, leaning back against a cushion, with Nena and Stella on either side of me. I was the center of all attention. When I remarked that it had certainly seemed like a very strange Christmas day, they reacted as if I had said something profound and witty. We had Christmas toasts in a sharp California red. I was being touched by the young women beside me, not in any sensuous way, but with little pats of affection, of liking.

And when the men would squat in front of me to talk directly to me, they would slap me on the side of the leg, give my ankle a squeeze. Wherever I looked there was someone maintaining direct eye contact with me, projecting warm approval. I tucked McGee's suspicions into the back of my mind. Brother Tom McGraw was a lonely man, of lonely habits. So I responded to warmth. And to flattery.

"I knew at once you are a highly intelligent and sensitive man, Mr. Mc-Graw," Persival said. "I could sense that about you. But you seem to feel the need to conceal the real you from the outside world. We are not like that here. We're together."

"In school I never got past—"

"Public education in this country means less than nothing," Sammy said. "From the earliest grades, the children are taught to conform, to be good consumers, to have no interest in their government or the structure of their society. The rebels drop out. The rich get classified as exceptional students and go on to the schools which teach them how to run the world, their world. Never apologize for dropping out, Brother."

The stew was beef this time. I said it was great. Haris, the Englishman, had cooked it. "Whatever there is, we share. Always," he said.

"You're a worker," Nena told me. "You have a skill. You use your skill to feed the people. Even though you are exploited, it's still something to be proud of."

Mr. Persival said, with poetry and force, "We can guess that there have been Christmas nights like this in mountain country all over the world, little groups of determined people, meeting together, all of them willing to give their lives for their beliefs. In the Cuban mountains. In the mountains of Honduras. Mexico, Yugoslavia, Chile, Peru, Rhodesia. Together, sharing, living the great dream."

"What's the dream?" I asked.

"The same as yours, of course," said Persival. "Freedom for all peoples of all colors. An end to imperialist exploitation. To each according to his needs. You are the kind of man who, once committed, would give his life for what he believes."

"I've been known as stubborn. I don't give up easy. But what you were saying there, sir, isn't that kind of Commie?"

He shook his head sadly. "Communist, Socialist, humanist, Christian Democrat, Liberation Army. The tags mean less than nothing, Brother Thomas. We do God's work. We are the militant arm of the Church of the Apocrypha. We are the ones who have been tested. We work for mankind against the exploiters, deceivers, the criminal warmongers. We will win if we have to tear down the entire structure of society. Your daughter believed in the cause or she wouldn't have joined us."

"She wasn't much for destroying things."

"Most of the people in the Church are gentle people. We are the elite. We're pleased with you, Brother Thomas. We may have a mission for you."

It was at that point I began to feel very strange. At first I thought it was because the room was airless, even with the door standing wide open. Colors got brighter. People's faces began to bulge and shrink, bulge and shrink. My tongue thickened. They had popped me with something. It turned the world into fun-house mirrors. And I knew it could give me a better chance of getting my head blown apart. I made my tongue sound thicker than it was. I began to do as much inconspicuous hyperventilation as I could manage. More oxygen never hurt anything. I crawled across to the water jug, sat and upended it and drank heavily, and crawled back. I tipped over my wine by accident and held my glass out for more.

By then we were into recitations of training, with the freedom fighters standing up and declaiming their background.

Nena stood very straight and said in a parade-ground voice, "Basic training at Kochovskaya. Guerrilla training at Simferopol. Selected by World Federation of Democratic Youth in Budapest. Transport arranged by World Federal Trade Unions in Prague."

When she sat down everyone applauded. Ahman stood up and said, "Basic and guerrilla training PLO Camp Three in Jordan and Camp Nine in Lebanon. Graduate, University of Maryland." Applause.

Barry had been trained in Cuba by the DGI and had been a weapons instructor at Baninah near Benghazi in Libya. Chuck had trained at a camp near Al-Ghaidha in South Yemen, along with people from the IRA. Sammy has trained in the U.S. Marine Corps and later in the Cuban training center near Baghdad, where the famous Carlos was an adviser. Persival interrupted to give Carlos's correct name, Ilyich Rameirez Sanchez. Stella had been in the Weather Underground and had trained in their mountain camp in Oregon, and later in Bulgaria.

"How," I said heavily, "how these great people get to go so many crazy places inna worl' anyhow?"

"We selected them, Brother Thomas. We tested them, and we selected them, and we sent them away to be trained and come back to us. We sent them as delegates, most of them, to the World Peace Council meetings in Helsinki, or the World Federation of Democratic Youth in Budapest. You see only a few here. There are scores of them, Brother Thomas. Travel is easily arranged for them. The Church provides the funds, of course. They are pledged to make this a better world. They are saviors of mankind."

I mumbled something unintelligible and slowly toppled over to my left to land with my head in Stella's lap, eyes closed, breathing slowly and heavily. I hoped the show would continue. I wanted to hear more. But my collapse broke it up. They picked up all their gear and the dishes and left, after covering me up and turning out the light. I heard the locking of my door. My head was still thick with whatever it was they had given me. I did some fast pushups in the darkness, and a series of knee bends. My knees creaked and breath came fast. But it helped a little. I slept heavily.

I awakened once before daylight and did not know where I was. It alarmed me. Then I remembered. And I remembered the way Gretel and I had talked about what to do on our first Christmas together. We had decided to take the *Flush* down to the lower end of Biscayne Bay and find a protected anchorage with maximum privacy and swim, and eat, and drink, and exchange Christmas greetings all day long.

No breakfast arrived. I pounded on the door and did some yelling. At about ten o'clock they unlocked the door and shoved Nicky in, with such force that he ran across the room and smacked the cement wall with his palms. He had a purple cheek, with the right eye swollen almost shut.

He sat in the chair and slumped over, staring at the floor.

"What's going on?" I asked him.

"Damn bastards are all uptight. Do it by the book. No variations permitted. According to them, I've fucked up twice in a row, which is twice too many times, but they won't even listen. One lousy weapon. One lousy Czech machine pistol, and I forgot to clean it after it was in the creek. For Chrissake, they've got a whole damn building full of weapons, grenades, plastique, nitro, napalm, and God only knows what else. One rotten pistol." He peered up at me with his good eye. "You fucked up too, eh? Or you wouldn't be locked in."

"I did? I don't know how. I got a little drunk."

"Persival doesn't think you're who you say you are, so they were going to give you some love-buzzing and open you up some, and then try some kind of Pentothal stuff he uses. You must have slipped up. Who the hell are you anyway?"

"Thomas McGraw, dammit! Looking for my girl, dammit! Are you crazy or something? I *like* all your friends. I don't know why they locked me up again. It doesn't make sense."

"You must have slipped up, or you wouldn't be here. That's all I know. Except I know I slipped up once too often. The way I am, when there's no action, I relax. I can't stay all wound up all the time. These characters are gung-ho every minute. Like a bunch of cheerleaders. You *like* them, huh? Because they spent the evening liking you. That's the way it works. Barry, Sammy, and Ahman have had some action. Not much. Chicken-shit operations. Car bombs and burn-downs. In and out, like thieves. I had time in 'Nam, and then Zambia. We were in the hills near Refunsa. The way it worked, the Zambians would cross into Rhodesia and hit and run, and then suck the Rhodesian army units into Zambia, and we'd ambush them. Very tough people. Very tough country. I just can't stand waiting around so long with no action. I get sloppy. Persival says we don't move until maybe summer. Coordinated. You never get to know much. You hear there are fifteen groups and then you hear forty. Who knows? When it comes time, we'll get the word from Sister Elena Marie."

"Who?"

"I forgot you don't know. The boss lady. They send out cassettes. I don't believe in a lot of this stuff, but I believe in her. I believe in her all the way." His voice and face were solemn.

There were questions I wanted to ask, but they were not questions Tom McGraw would have asked.

"Do you think this Sister Elena Marie would know where my little girl is?"

"I don't know. I don't even know if they've got any central records. I don't know where *she* is, even, where she makes the tapes. They say there were like three hundred of them here at one time, and this was a small retreat compared to the others. They moved them out to where they could help raise the money. Everybody has to do that. Your daughter had to do it too. Teams go up and down the streets, hitting every house. Sometimes you say it's for children, and sometimes for foreign missions. You sell stuff. Handicraft stuff. Also candy and artificial flowers and maybe fresh-baked bread. Once you catch on, it isn't hard. Four on our team, we'd raise two hundred, three hundred a day, every day. Ride around in the black vans with the crosses.

Twenty cents' worth of junk candy for two dollars, to help the starving Christian children in Lebanon. You can claim one quarter of what your team raised when you have to stand up in the meeting and shout out what you turned in. They switch the teams around a lot. I'm so big people were always glad I was on their team. It's harder to say no to big people.''

The door opened again. Four of them were there. Ahman and Sammy were in their coveralls, carrying the automatic weapons, left hands clamped on the forestock, right hands around the trigger assembly, long curved clips in place. Persival looked unlikely in an orange-yellow leisure suit and white turtleneck. Stone-faced, no-color, big-shouldered Alvor wore a wrinkled dark business suit, a white shirt with a frayed collar, and a narrow striped tie.

"Come along,'' Persival ordered. The four of them walked a dozen feet behind us. Persival told us where to go. We went to the place where the flats sloped down to the splintered trees, near the spot where I had found the cartridge case.

"Stop there,'' he said. "Move to your right two steps, McGraw. Now both of you turn slowly around and face me.''

My heart gave an extra thump. Ahman and Sammy were aiming the weapons at us. Sammy was holding on Nick, and Ahman on me. Ahman's swarthy face and shiny black eyes revealed nothing. So maybe, when Persival had told somebody to check me out, they had checked more carefully than I had assumed they would, and found that Thomas McGraw had been dead for some time, and never had a daughter.

"What the hell is the matter with you people now?'' I asked. I did not have to fake a definite quaver in my voice.

"You know, each of you, why you are dying today.''

"Chicken shit,'' Nicky said in a husky voice.

"There can be *no* carelessness. *None.* Maximum precautions will be taken to prevent any premature disclosure. There will be no second chance for anyone whose actions could compromise us all. All orders will be obeyed, without question, without argument.''

"Chicken shit,'' Nicky said again.

"Come here, Mr. McGraw,'' Persival said. "Over here. Stop there. Fine. Now turn and face the condemned.'' I was three feet from Persival, but I noted as I turned that Ahman's gun muzzle followed me like an empty steel eye socket.

Persival's voice deepened. "Dear God of wrath and mercy, take unto thy bosom this soldier of our faith and grant him eternal peace. We send him to thee now so that he will not further endanger the holy mission with which thou hast entrusted us, thy faithful soldiers in the army of justice. Amen.''

His hand appeared in front of me, holding a slender automatic pistol with a long barrel. "Take it and shoot him in the head, please,'' Persival said. Same tone of voice as he would have said, "Have some more stew, please.''

And the scenario was suddenly clear. I would shoot Nicky in the head with a blank, and my obedience would remove Persival's lingering suspicion of me, and Nicky would be frightened into being more careful next time. Two birds with one fake stone.

"It's ready to go,'' he said. "Just aim and fire.''

There was no great need to aim. Nicky was perhaps fifteen feet from me.

If you aim a handgun with the same motion you use to point your finger at someone, if the barrel becomes your finger, you can hit a six-inch circle on the other side of the room ninety-nine out of a hundred times.

So I pointed and fired. It made an unimportant snapping sound. A dark spot appeared beside Nicky's nose, on his good cheek. It snapped his head back a little. He made a coughing sound and sagged down onto one knee, then rolled over backward and rolled down the slope. I moved forward to keep him in sight. He came to rest in dead branches, against a splintered trunk, his back to us. One leg jumped and quivered and vibrated for a few seconds and then subsided. He seemed to become visibly smaller.

The life had gone out of him, now and forever. Persival reached around and tugged the weapon out of my hand and moved back away from me. "Turn around slowly," he said. This was not the scenario I had envisioned. I had imagined all of them crowding around me, Nicky included, whacking me on the back, welcoming me to the team.

Instead, Persival was chunking a magazine into the pistol. The slide had remained back after I had fired. So there had been just the one shell in the chamber. This man took no chances. They held weapons on me. Ahman had set his weapon aside and was collapsing an SX-70 Polaroid while Sammy examined the print as it developed. I recalled hearing that tantalizingly familiar sound of the SX-70 a fraction of a second after I had fired and killed Nicky.

They were all curious about me, all waiting for my reaction. I could read a certain righteous satisfaction on their faces. I was fighting nausea and hoping I hadn't turned so gray-green they would suspect how close I was. Nausea, and a tendency of the world around me to fade in and out. Killing is such an ancient taboo. Only freaks ever adjust to killing people they have known and talked to, except when it is to save their own lives. Discipline enables uniformed people to kill unseen strangers. Children can imitate something seen on television, but the aftershock can be deadly. I had killed before, and it has never ceased being a wrenching psychic trauma. As I sought for some reaction which would make me reasonably acceptable to these people, suddenly I lost control of my acquired identity.

I stared at Persival. He was trickery. He was death. He was insane devotion to an incomprehensible cause. He was a shooter of little silver pellets into the necks of the lovely and innocent.

"You dirty, murderous, crazy son of a bitch!" I said in a low and shaky voice.

He raised the reloaded weapon and aimed carefully from eight feet away at a spot on my forehead. I knew where the slug would strike. The spot felt round and icy.

I was convinced I was about to join Nicky. He knew he was going to die, and I could find no better last words than his.

"Chicken shit," I said.

"Any questions, McGraw?"

"There's nothing I want to know that you can answer." I was watching the trigger finger. As soon as I saw pressure whiten it, I was going to dive for his ankles and try to come up with the weapon before Sammy and Ahman could blow me away.

"Any last statement, fisherman?"

"I will state that if you don't make the first shot good, I'll get my hands on you before you can fire that thing again."

He looked at me for a long time, and then slowly lifted the barrel of the weapon until it pointed at the sky.

"I think my first hunch was correct, Brother Thomas. I think we can train you and find a use for you. I think you can become very valuable."

I could feel the tension go out of all of us. Deep exhalations.

He put the weapon away. He turned to Sammy and reached for the picture. After Persival had examined it, he motioned me closer and handed it to me. I was on the right, in fuzzy focus, enough of the left side of my face showing to make me recognizable. The barrel of the pistol was half raised to the perpendicular, the ineradicable habit pattern of people used to firing pistols and revolvers. Nick was near the left margin of the print, in sharp focus. He was going down, but his knee had not yet touched. His head was tilted back from impact, with the tiny death mark visible next to his nose.

Handing it back, I said, "Is this some kind of leverage?"

"It is, Brother Thomas, but not the way you think. Call it a verification of my instinct, useful when I go after permission for what I have in mind."

"I don't know what you mean."

"Ahman, arrange burial. Full roster except, of course, for Barry down on the gate. Have Haris read the service. I am going for a walk with Mr. Mc-Graw."

11

PERSIVAL DID not walk well. He moved slowly and seemed to have trouble with his balance. The sky was turning gray, and the wind was cooler. We walked to the end of the small plateau. He seated himself on the trunk of a large pine which had fallen at the edge of the slope.

He lowered himself carefully. With a wry Lincolnesque smile he said, "I have what the young call bad wheels. I was the guest for a memorable period of time of an amiable old party named Somoza. He had my legs broken."

I sat astride the log about eight feet from him. "This," he said, "is the ancient definition of the best kind of education, the pupil on one end of a log and the teacher on the other."

"What do I—"

He stopped me with a raised hand. "Just let me ramble a bit. Answer me when I ask you a question. You would seem to know small boats and know the sea. And with your background, no one would question your interest in purchasing a certain sort of small boat."

"I don't want to use my search money for a boat."

"You are talking trivia, and when you do, you bore me."

"I came here to find my kid. Maybe that's boring to you, but it's not to me."

"McGraw, you are going to have to learn how to accept discipline."

"Mr. Persival, you can't run me the same way you run those people of yours. I'll answer you when you ask questions, and I'll answer the questions you don't ask. I talk when I please."

He looked me over. He was patently exasperated.

"Brother Thomas, can you swim?"

"Yes."

"I'm glad to hear that. A lot of commercial fishermen can't. Do you know how to use scuba gear?"

"Yes."

"Do you know what a limpet mine is?"

"Yes."

"Can you tell me? I want to be sure you know."

"It's a mine that sticks to what it is going to blow up. It can be magnetic, or covered with stickum. It can have a timer or be blown up by a transmitter."

"Very good! You've worked around explosive charges?"

"Enough to be careful."

"Suppose I gave you the task of fastening a limpet mine to the hull of one of those new tankers which carry frozen liquefied gas. How would you go about it?"

I recalled what he had said about the boat purchase. It was enough of a clue. "In the area where the tanker is, I'd get hold of a commercial fishing boat, small. One-man operation, with an inboard or outboard. I'd dress right for the climate and the place. I'd fish the area, catch fish, sell the catch. I'd keep track of the winds and tides, and when everything was right, I'd have a breakdown and get carried up against the hull of the ship, maybe forward where the flare would hide me from the weather decks. Maybe if I had a little electric outboard let down through the hull, and concealed somehow, I could count on drifting to exactly where I would have to be. The breakdown should be about dusk. I'd place the mine, arm it, then get my breakdown fixed and get out of there."

"Suppose you were stopped and searched by a harbor patrol?"

"I could explain the electric outboard. The limpet would have to look like something else."

"Such as?"

I shrugged. "Maybe a mushroom anchor, threaded so you could unscrew the shank."

I could see that he liked that. "I believe I was right in deciding we can find a use for you, Brother McGraw."

"Not blowing up a ship. I won't do that."

"Whether or not you will do it or won't do it is not the point at issue right now. It would be a considerable time in the future. Things can be worked out, I'm sure."

And I could certainly guess how they'd be worked out. I had been wrong about Nicky. But this was a certainty. The little limpet mine would have a trigger and a timing device and there would be careful instruction on how to set it. But the act of placing it against metal would activate it. I wasn't one of the true believers. I was expendable.

"I don't hold with killing people that never did anything to me. That's terrorism."

"Terrorism? Beware of tag words. General Sherman was a terrorist. The Continental Congress was a terrorist society. How about Pancho Villa, air strikes on cities, the torpedoing of ocean liners? Beware of semantics."

I played dumb. "What do you mean? I've got nothing against the Jews."

"Semantics, Brother, not Semitics. The study of words. In World War Two, the Londoners worshiped their heroic young men who risked heavy flak to drop bombs on Germany and despised the degenerate fiends in human form who flew over, risking heavy flak, to drop bombs on English cities. Begin calls Arafat a terrorist. Begin led a squad which blew up a British hotel, killing scores of people, when he was a young so-called terrorist."

A light rain began to fall, steeply slanted by the increasing wind. Persival got up. "We'll go into all this, Brother Thomas, after you have a chance to hear Sister Elena Marie and think about the message she brings us. Incidentally, you will have been moved by now into one of the travel trailers. T-Six. The green-and-white one. You'll be much more comfortable."

"Is it okay to ask if I can have my money back now?"

"No. It isn't acceptable to ask at this time."

"Do you know when I can ask, Mr. Persival?"

"You will be told. Every effort is being made to locate your daughter. I want you to know that. While you are here, records are being searched."

We were walking back in the light rain, at his pace.

"Is it okay to mention I never had breakfast this morning?"

"You have the run of the place, Brother. Stay up on the flats. Do not head down the hill at any point. I am sure you can locate the kitchen."

A small group was straggling ahead of us toward the buildings. Chuck, Nena, Stella, Sammy, Haris, Ahman, and Alvor, all but Alvor in the short white robes which looked like smocks except for the monk's hoods attached to them. The women and Haris wore the hoods pulled up, and Haris carried a book.

"I see the service is over," Persival said.

"They dig a fast grave."

"It was all prepared," he said. He smiled at me in a fatherly way. He laid his hand on my shoulder. "Actually, Brother, there were two. Just in case."

"In case I couldn't shoot him?"

He took his hand away. "Let's say it was just in case."

*　　*　　*

I checked out my green-and-white travel trailer. It was an old Scottie, sitting on cement blocks. It had recently been cleaned. There were some water droplets on the flat surfaces. There were two folded blankets, no sheets. There was a tiny gas heater, a hand-pumped water supply and a Porta-Potty. My duffel bag was on the foot of the bed. There was no way to lock it. I had the uneasy feeling that Nicky had lived here in this constricted space, had curled his long bulk on the bed that was built across the rear end of the trailer. I kept seeing that Polaroid shot. It was curiously more vivid than what I had actually seen.

I went looking for the kitchen. The steel warehouse building was tightly secured. I came upon Alvor and asked him. He did not answer. He merely pointed. It was the only frame building in the group of structures, about twelve feet by twenty, with unfinished open studding on the inside. There was a kerosene stove, an old kerosene refrigerator, two plank tables on sawhorses, and some unmatched chairs and camp stools. The utensils and plates and cups were on open shelves made of planks and bricks. There was a big blackboard at the other end of the room.

I found butter and eggs, scrambled four eggs, and sat at the plank table and ate them. Barry came in, relieved of guard duty, and smiled at me. "Got everything you need, Brother?"

"This is fine, thanks."

"Want some coffee?"

"Thanks, yes."

He brought it over, as well as a cup for himself, and sat across from me. "Everybody gets tested, one way or other," he said.

"Sure."

"We all liked Nicky, but he was a fuck-off. You can't have your life depending on a fuck-off."

"I reckon so."

"Sorry it had to happen the way it did. Must of made you feel bad."

Barry hadn't been there when I lost my cool. The tone, the eyes in the dark face were innocently sympathetic. But he could have heard about it by now and could be faking to draw me out.

"I was a mite shook up," I said. "But when you come right down to it, I didn't really know him. Or any of you."

"You know me, Brother Thomas. And you know the other brothers and sisters. We your home, man. We all part of the same thing."

"How do you know I'm not like Nicky?"

"All it needs is Brother Persival saying you are part of it. That's all that matters. We all came up through the Church, but that don't mean everybody has to. You got family in the Church, that daughter, right?"

"Wherever she is."

"They looking for her. Don't worry."

"Is there any rule about taking a bath in the creek?"

"None at all. The best bath hole is upstream from the great big rocks, past the little trees. Take a towel off the line if there isn't one in your trailer."

It was a good solid yellow soap, and it worked well enough in ice water. I took my change of clothes with me and washed out the dirty ones, carried them back to the encampment, and hung them on the community line, along with my washed-out, wrung-out towel.

Then Chuck came and got me for lunch. With his drooping mustache, he looked like a Scandinavian travel advertisement. Haris had made some deerburgers, fried with onion. They sat me at the middle of the table, where I could get the full benefit of the love-buzzing, the hush whenever I spoke, the smiles and eye contact and shameless flattery. Yes, they all knew as soon as they saw me that I would be a wonderful addition to the group. Just wonderful. Just what they had been waiting for. Persival and Alvor sat alone at the other table, talking in low voices.

The conversation was slightly strained, and I guessed it was because they felt they should not talk about Nicky, but he was ever-present on the edge of memory. I made a few fruitless efforts to steer the conversation toward politics and violence, but they fielded them deftly and threw to another base.

After cleanup, a screen was set up and a projector wheeled out. I thought I was going to hear a tape by the celebrated Sister Elena Marie, but it was a creaky old black-and-white motion picture about The Long March, with a noisy sound track, a voice-over with a marked British accent, a lot of running, shooting, and gesticulating. They marched across China and up into the hills and caves, while my chin kept dropping onto my chest and I kept waking with a start. It ended with a loud blast of martial music which roused me enough to get up and say good night and go back to my trailer. I couldn't find the light switch and finally gave up and went to bed in the dark.

* * *

I was awakened by the click of the latch on the flimsy door of the trailer, a stealthy and barely audible squeak as it was opened. I wondered if one of the team had decided to correct Persival's decision to keep me alive. I moved in the bunk until I had my shoulders against the wall, until I was braced to move as quickly as I had to.

The generator was silent, the encampment dark. Just enough starlight came through the window above the bunk for me to make out a pale figure moving toward me. It stopped a couple of feet away, and I heard a silky whisper of fabric, caught a faint scent of female, and realized that Nena or Stella was paying me a visit. I guessed I had been asleep for an hour.

She picked up a corner of the blanket and came sliding into the bunk, shuddering with the cold, reaching to embrace me. I faked a great start of surprise.

"It's me, Brother Thomas," she whispered. "It's Stella."

So I was being gifted with the sallow blond lady with the inadequate jaw. "What's going on?"

"Well, whatever you want to go on. Okay?"

"Whose idea is this?"

"What difference would that make?"

"I'd like to know."

"You do a lot of talking, huh?"

I caught her questing hand by the wrist and took it away from me and said, "Is there anything wrong with wanting to know?"

"Look, are you okay? I mean, you make it with women?"

"I like to talk first."

"Jesus Christ!" she said. And then, "I'm sorry. That's blasphemy. But, you know, you are something else."

She turned onto her back, trying to separate herself from me totally, but the bunk was too narrow. Hip rested against hip, shoulder against shoulder.

"All it is," she said patiently, "you're new. Probably they don't want you being restless and wanting to sneak off or anything. So you get food and shelter and, once in a while, a piece of ass. What does it cost? Nothing but time, right?"

"You sound as if you did some hooking."

"I was into it. So?"

"Where was that?"

"So you're another one of those."

"Another what?"

"When I was a hooker, there was always a trick who wanted to know how I got into that line of work."

"Stella, settle down. Where are you going, anyway? Why the hostility? I can ask about you because I'm interested in you, can't I? Is there a house rule against that?"

She took in a deep breath and let it out slowly. "Well, okay. I'm sorry. When I came in here, I was really ready, you know? I don't feel that way very often. But what happens, you want to talk. So I'm losing the edge. It's fading on me. I think I got that ready on account of Nicky dying. Death does it to me in a funny way, I guess. When somebody you know is suddenly dead forever, then I want to get laid. I've heard lots of people are like that. Like in shelters when there's bombing going on. Maybe it goes back to instinct. Like in animals. If people are dying, it's time to make more people and keep the population up. But there was a couple of years there when I couldn't have come no matter what."

"What do you mean by that?"

"If you want talk instead of tail, I'll give you talk. I'm from an absolutely nowhere place. Opportunity, Montana."

"Little west of Butte? South of Anaconda? Flint Creek Range and the South Fork?"

"Hey, you heard of it!" She turned and settled herself more comfortably, fitting the nape of her neck to my arm, one hand resting on my chest.

"Been through there. When did you leave?"

"A long time ago. I don't know who's left there, if anybody."

"Run away?"

"Sort of. With a girl friend. We got in with some rough people in Miami. I got busted for possession, and when I got out, I couldn't find her. A cop put me on the streets, hustling. Then one day he beat me up bad because he thought I was holding out, and I met some people from the Church of the Apocrypha."

"In Miami?"

"You'll find the Church everywhere these days. What I was thinking, I could *use* the Church. They'd take care of me and keep that freak cop away from me. I'd been beaten real bad. What I was then, I was a dumb, selfish, ignorant teenage hooker. What I needed most was some rest from cruising the streets and taking the marks back to that motel room. When I was rested up, I'd take off. But the people in the Church, they knew what I was thinking every minute. They never gave me a minute alone. They loved me. They believed I was precious and they made me think of myself as precious to them. I was a lazy little slut, and they cured me of that. My God, I never worked so hard and so long in my life. It made hooking seem like picnics. Dumb dreary food and not enough sleep ever. Fifteen hours at a stretch, selling stuff to strangers, walking the streets carrying candy and thread and junk, begging money, making quotas. My weight went down to minus nothing. A lot of my hair fell out. I had a scaly rash all the time. I forgot about sex. I stopped menstruating. My tits and my ass like to shrunk away to nothing. And when I was about to believe the life was going to kill me, suddenly I realized I was doing God's work, and that I wanted to drive myself even harder than they were driving me. And once I saw the Light and heard the Word, I started to get better. I ate tons of that sorry food they served at the dorm, and it tasted delicious. And I began to sell more stuff. I *made* people buy it. I turned in big scores every night and slept like a baby. I smiled and sang all the time. The Church had put my head back on straight. For the first time in my life I was *really* part of something. My life had meaning. I worked hard for the Church and for myself, and finally they picked me for a different kind of work."

"This kind? Guns and bombs?"

"It's God's work."

"You said you joined the Weather Underground, didn't you?"

"I didn't join them. It was sort of like cooperative, you know? They bought me a plane ticket out to Portland, and a fellow met me at the airport and drove me practically all day in an old car way down into empty country where they were. I thought I was in pretty good shape, you know? Talk about pooped? I used to get so tired I'd cry. But by three months, I could like run all day, you know? And I felt really alive. Then, when I could move right, they started all the other stuff. Weapons, marksmanship, cover and conceal-ment, grenades, booby traps, reading a compass and maps, and all that. They taught me stuff I never heard of. You know, I could go into the average kitchen anywhere in the States, and in about twenty minutes I could build a bomb you wouldn't believe, just using what's already there."

"I forget where you said you went after that."

"First I went back to Miami, and they took me . . . someplace where I met Sister Elena Marie, and it was the most wonderful thing that ever hap-pened to me. She's fantastic. She knew all about me. She even seemed to know what I was thinking. She told me I was doing very well and I was one of the special ones planned by God for a special purpose. They got me a passport to Amsterdam and I went with a Brother who'd been there before and from there by car to Sofia, and he turned me over to some sort of official who took me out to the camp. It was a lot the same as Oregon, except different weapons and a lot of other stuff I can't talk about. And, well, I got back to Miami, let me see, this is right after Christmas, and so it must have been seven months ago, and so I've been here six months. And maybe it will be six more before we . . . begin."

"Begin?"

"You know. We have to be given our assignments and we have to have a lot of time studying and working and planning so that it will all be automatic. Then we'll just, you know, go do them. It has to be all coordinated in order to work. We all have to be terribly, terribly careful."

"I saw you practicing something, you and Nena, and I think it was Haris and Ahman. Chuck was coaching and timing you."

"Oh, hey, you shouldn't have seen that! Please don't tell anybody, or somebody will get in trouble for not figuring out maybe you could see it. We didn't know what would happen with you, and we thought you would proba-bly be killed. Maybe that's why somebody got careless. But there is always the very small chance you could get away, and if you could make somebody believe you when you told what you saw, then it might make big problems here."

"What were you doing? Your assignments?"

"Oh, no. That's just the Circle of Fire. It's all in the speed, getting ready. Then it's tricky how you set the weapons. You put them on full automatic but you have to learn to give just the quickest little touch. *Bzzzzt, bzzzzt, bzzzzt,* like not more than five or six shots each burst. You touch the trigger when the targets are thick enough in front of you. You keep it at belly level, because that's the way the most damage is done in a crowd."

Yes, indeed, I thought. Get the adults in the belly, the kids in the chest, and the littlies in the head bones.

"Will that be your assignment?"

"Oh, no. That would be a waste of people like us. They say there are people to do that who know how to do just that, and they're willing to do it. I think there's a special place where they train. They don't need as much physical training or training in a lot of different kinds of things. We were just doing it as a kind of training exercise. That's all. So we *can* do it if we have to someday."

"It would be hard to do."

"I know. I know." Her tone was subdued and thoughtful.

I didn't know where to take it from there. I had to assume the trailer was bugged. Yet she would know if it were, and she wasn't sufficiently guarded. She wasn't hesitant in the way people are who know the tape is running.

"It's hard to see the point in doing it at all."

"Doing what?"

"Well, killing innocent people."

"Innocent of what, Brother? If you kill soldiers or police, it doesn't make enough difference. They signed up to take that risk. The people in this country are oppressed and they don't know it, and they don't give a damn. All the rest of the world is involved in a bitter struggle, and here the people are fat, happy, and dumb. The captive press and the television keep telling them they are the best people in the world in the best country in the world. The dirt and pain and sickness and poverty are all covered up. No person has a chance against the capitalist bureaucracy. We've learned that little attacks here and there are meaningless. Like fighting a pillow. They actually think they're free, the fools, even while they are supporting a regime that exports arms all over the world to the other oppressors. We have to make this fat dumb happy public sit up and take notice of the hidden tyranny that is oppressing them. How do we do that?"

Such a lot of it was by rote, repeated from memory in a sentence structure alien to her usual patterns. "How *do* we do it, Sister?"

"We make the oppressors visible to the people by giving them reason to show how cruel and tough they can be. We force them to react. Like Chicago and Kent State, but much much more."

"By going out and killing people?"

"That isn't the purpose, Brother. To kill people. Our civilization has gotten too complicated. It's full of machines and plastics. Brother Persival says it is very sick, and like a sick person, it can't survive if a lot of other things happen to it."

"Such as?"

"Oh, we won't go after things that are really protected, like army places and shipyards and nuclear power plants and government buildings. That's dumb. You can bring everything tumbling down by going after things that would take years to fix. Big gas pipelines and oil pipelines. Bridges and tunnels and big computer places. Refineries and chemical plants and control towers. TV stations and newspaper pressrooms. Blow 'em up and burn 'em down. Targets of opportunity. Anyway, it's all being worked out. And then we'll know what our part of it is. I hope I don't get stuff to do that's too hard. I mean I want to be able to get it done. Then if I get away, okay, and if I don't, okay. But I'd hate to mess up. I hope I don't get a tunnel. I get really itchy going through tunnels. I think of all that water coming down on me."

"How do you do a tunnel?"

"Two people and two vehicles, right? The second one is an old truck. You've got a good big load of explosives, labeled something else. It takes a big blast. The lead car stops and you stop the truck and yank the wire that starts the three-minute timer. Then you run and get in the lead car and get out of there. It's the same for some kinds of bridges. I really don't want to do a tunnel. They make me so nervous I'll do something wrong."

She had turned onto her side, worked her head onto my shoulder. Her arm lay across my chest, her knees against the side of my thigh. She sighed and said, "I didn't have any interest in sex at all until I was in training overseas. Then it started to all come back. It's like that with most of the women who join. I mean the Church becomes the most important love life you have, and it wipes out everything else for a while. Then it's never as important again as it once was to you." She kissed the side of my throat and said, "Enough of all this talking already? You want to make it now?" She snugged the length of her body against me. This was a frightening little engine of destruction, all trained, primed, toughened, waiting only for someone to aim it at a target. Her breath had a faint scent of the deerburger onions. Her hair smelled clean, and her body had a slight coppery odor of perspiration. I remembered noticing at the table that her fingernails were chewed down to the quick.

Poor little assassin. She had gone out into the world with an empty head, and somebody had crammed a single frightful idea into it, dressed up with a lot of important-sounding rhetoric. She couldn't know the frightfulness of the idea because she had nothing by which to measure it. Fifteen to forty groups of from eight to fifteen? From a hundred and twenty to six hundred of them. So take the smallest number, cut it in half, and think about sixty people like this one, armed, mobilized, superbly equipped, and aimed at the pressure points of our culture.

I remembered one of Meyer's concepts about cultural resiliency. In the third world, the village of one thousand can provide itself with what it needs for survival. Smash the cities and half the villages, and the other half keep going. In our world, the village of one thousand has to import water, fuel, food, clothing, medicine, electric power, and entertainment. Smash the cities and all the villages die. And the city itself is frail. It has little nerve-center nodules. Water plant, power transmission lines, telephone switching facilities.

I was beginning to learn the purpose behind Brother Titus, and the reason for all the extraordinary caution.

And if that extraordinary caution carried over to all things, and assuming the trailer was not bugged, then Stella would be asked to give a report about her lovemaking with Brother Thomas.

"Oh, all we did was talk. He asked a lot of questions and we talked, and then after all that, he didn't want to. He said he wasn't gay, but he just didn't feel like it."

She had begun to use her hooker skills, and I had begun to respond to her. After all, what the hell. She was skillful and knowing. To her I was a tumescence of a certain length and girth, differing hardly at all from the many hundreds of others. Emotions need not be involved. I would think only of sensation. It did not have to have anything to do with mind and memory. As I began to switch roles from submission to domination, I told myself I could not, in any circumstances, think about the face and body and love of Gretel Howard.

I sagged back beside Stella and she said, "Hey, what happens?"

"I'm sorry."

"Did something about me put you off, honey?"

"No. It wasn't anything like that."

"What then?"

"I don't know."

"This sure isn't turning out to be one of my better nights."

"I'm sorry."

"Look, I'm not sore. You know what I think it was? It was being conned into shooting Nicky like you did. Something like that, if you're not used to it, can really shake you up inside. And then me coming in here like this when you weren't expecting it. And after all, Brother, you are not some eighteen-year-old guy who can get it off before he's unzipped. These things happen. Don't worry about me. I lost it too. Too much talking."

"I'm sorry."

"Let's just talk. I kind of like talking to you. And maybe we can have a little nap, and after that maybe we'll both be okay again, you know? How about that?"

"All right."

"You sure I didn't spoil it for you somehow?"

"No. You're . . . an attractive woman."

"I'm not much. I've got a pretty good body, compared to most. But I've got this tough yellow skin, and if you look close, one eye points out a little bit, the right one. And the receding jaw. You know, I was saving up for an operation, a fellow that puts some kind of bone from your hip or someplace back here by the corners of your jaw and that pushes it forward, and then they fix your bite. I saw before-and-after pictures. It would really make a big difference. But that's vanity, isn't it? I'll be twenty-six in two months. I used to think about marriage and babies. I think I'd be okay with babies. Better than they were with me, I know. My dad broke two fingers on my left hand once, grabbing me when he lost his temper. They say if you've been abused, you abuse your own. I can't believe that. I'd be okay with kids. But there's no point in even thinking about it now, is there? By this time next year, I'll probably be dead. Like Nicky. He just went a little ahead of the rest of us."

"Are they supposed to be suicide missions?"

"Not really. Everybody is supposed to do their best to get away. And we'll be given a staging area to go to where we can be regrouped and re-equipped and given new assignments. But if a person keeps doing it, how many times can you get away?''

"Everything will be in a state of confusion.''

"You can believe it.''

"But you know who is going to suffer the most, don't you?''

"Sure. The bottom layer of society. The poor and the minorities and the old ones. They won't have the money to take care of themselves when the food and the water and the medicines run out. They won't be able to run. That's when they'll rise up against the state. Then there'll be some kind of burning and killing. That's when the whole thing goes to hell for sure.''

"And who takes charge after that's all over?''

"The Church has plans, Brother. Big plans. You just wait. Big plans.'' Her voice trailed away and her breathing changed and deepened. A woman of her times. Ready to aim the Circle of Fire, belly high. Happy to be caressed, glad to make love. Good with babies, and no good with tunnels.

I had blundered into something extraordinary. A cult that was a cover for a deadly activism. Supported by curious international cooperations. I wished I could talk to Meyer about it. I really had nothing to go on. I knew the temporary location of nine people and a cache of arms and explosives. One out of fifteen or forty of unknown size and location, of unknown target date. Meyer had said, many times, that we run a strange kind of country in the modern world. Customs and Immigration are in a sense token services. Any plausible-looking person can find many ways to come and go unimpeded. Anything that can be flown or floated can be brought in or taken out. We are a wide place in the road in the middle of the world, and they wander through, back and forth, marveling at the lack of restraints. It is, Meyer pointed out, a paradox. The openness which endangers our system is the product of the policy which says that to close our borders and enforce all our rules and back them up with guns would change the system just as completely as any alien force.

I hoped there were enough tough young men like Max and Jake. I hoped somebody had this whole operation taped and wired. I hoped there were long lenses peering through the pine forests, and a lot of career people making little marks on important maps.

*   *   *

Gray daylight was seeping into the trailer when I awakened. She was standing beside the bunk, pulling the long T-shirt down over her head, smoothing it to the contours of her hips with the backs of her hands.

She smiled and leaned and kissed me lightly. "Hey, we slept too long. I got to go on kitchen duty. We'll try it another time?''

"Sure.''

"Listen, don't worry about me saying anything, okay? I mean about you couldn't get it up. You're worried about a lot of things. All this is new to you, right? And your daughter missing and all. Anybody asks me, I'll say we like to screwed ourselves to death.''

"Thanks, Sister.''

"Don't you worry about a thing. Everything is going to be okay for you here. We'll all be looking out for you, Brother Thomas.''

I heard the door close and she was gone. I rolled up in the two scratchy blankets and thought about Gretel in her agony, Gretel on fire. I knew how she would react if I could tell her she had been a victim of some kind of crazy political action cult, of people who wanted to remake the world by tearing it down and starting all over again. Cave people, trying to reinvent penicillin, Zippo lighters, and disco.

It has nothing to do with me, I told Gretel. I never think about stuff like this. It hurts my head. I think about the blue sea and tan ladies and straight gin with lots of ice. I think about how high out of the water a marlin might go, and how much of Meyer's chili I can eat, and how very good piano sounds in the nighttime. I think about swimming until I hurt, running until I wheeze, driving good cars and good boats and good bargains. Sure, I do my little knightlike thing, restoring goodies to the people from whom they were improperly wrested, doing battle with the genuinely evil bastards who prey on the gullible, helpless, and innocent. I was going to keep on doing that from time to time, to support you and me, girl, in the style we like best, if you had consented. I know from nothing about terrorism, funny churches, and exotic murder weapons, like the one they killed you with.

But here I am. In a sense, I was hunting for you.

I have killed one of them in a strange way. And nearly made love to another. I am in it now. I am going to let them run me and see what happens. And I swear before whatever gods there be, including even the one these crazies bow down to, that if they give me the faintest whispery breath of a chance, I am going to blow them all away, every one, without mercy, without hesitation. If I saw a fire starting in a kindergarten, I would throw water on it.

One down and nine to go. This time, my dead love, I am not doing my knightly routine. I have shelved that as inappropriate for the occasion. The old tin-can knight had too many compunctions, scruples, whatevers. For this caper, I am the iceman. I have come here and brought the ice. It is a delivery service. One time only.

12

ON THURSDAY, two days after Christmas, I had my first experience of listening to Sister Elena Marie. It was set up at midafternoon in a small cement-block building the same size as the one where I had been locked up.

Chairs and stools were brought in. The camp generator was cranked up. A Sony color set rested on a low table, with a videotape deck beside it. Blankets were hung to shut out the light from the two windows. There was a feeling of expectancy, a muted excitement. Alvor was the only one missing. Stella sat close beside me.

Persival, almost invisible in the dimness, said, "Let us pray. Our Father, we thank thee for the opportunities which are being given to us. We are humbly grateful to be given a chance to play a part in the great events which will reshape life in this world and the future of humanity. We pray that we will be worthy of your trust in us. Our strength, our resolve, our determination, will all flow from your endless power. Since last we met in this room, one of us has been taken to your kingdom. Forgive our Brother Nicholas for his transgressions, his failure to comprehend the stern disciplines required of your children. There is a new one among us, a Brother Thomas, who came to us in search of his daughter and who has been thinking of remaining with us, adopting our vows, our ways, and our great mission. He is still uncertain, Lord. He is still confused. We are healing his lonely heart. Please give him the understanding of us and our ways so that he may join with us in our resolve, that he may become willing to sacrifice himself if necessary, in your bidding. We are thankful to you for providing this chance to hear, now, our beloved Sister Elena Marie speak your words from her heart. We are together, Lord. We are all as one. We are all united together in your holy cause. Amen.''

Chuck stepped forward and switched the set on, and when it warmed up, he turned on the Betamax with the tape ready to roll.

The head and shoulders of Sister Elena Marie filled the screen. She stood silently, making a strong eye contact with everyone who looked into that screen. She was in color, long warm chestnut hair with golden lights in it. It hung to her shoulders. Oval face, clear features, a look of breeding and composure. Minimal makeup. Eyes of a most unusual shade of blue, almost a lavender blue. Wide eyes, set far apart. Flawless complexion, but with the small signs of age. I guessed her at about thirty-six to thirty-eight. Broad mouth with both lips equally heavy.

There was background music, soft music, an organ doodling with simple chords, as when the crowd has assembled, awaiting a wedding. Or a funeral service.

The music trailed off. She took a step closer to the camera. Just the face filled the screen. It was not a professional production. The camera was evidently stationary. No detail of the shadowy background was visible.

"Brothers and Sisters of the great Church of the Apocrypha," she said. Contralto resonance. Lovely diction. She could have played the Mrs. Miniver part with distinction. "I am looking into your eyes, your special individual eyes, the windows of your soul. I am looking through your eyes, into your heart, into your deepest thoughts. There is nothing you can possibly think that would surprise or dismay me, or make me love you the less. I know of all the dark and evil places that exist in every man and woman, the places we hide from each other and even from ourselves. It is only by joining together we can overwhelm the darkness within and the darkness without."

She paused for several seconds, widening her lovely eyes slightly. I did have the impression that she was looking further inside me than I wanted her to.

"Each one of you has a special place in my heart. I do not love you as a group. One cannot love people en masse, in the abstract. I love you for yourself, for the struggles you have made in the name of goodness and justice and freedom in the world, and for the sacrifices you will make in the future. Though I appear to be talking to everyone in this room, I am talking to you alone. To you!''

Pause. Slow bat of long eyelashes and a half smile, personal and almost sensuous.

"We *are* alone, you know. You and I. Everyone. But we have found something which eases the pain of the essential loneliness of every human. We are together in our purpose. We are all part of one another, forever. In all the endless dying and rebirthing, in all the aeons of time over which we will return here, again and again, we will know and recognize one another, just as we have during this time on earth, and if in some future time it is necessary for all of us to come together again, and save the world and humanity from an epoch of commercial slavery, cruelty, and shameful exploitation, then we will do so, we of the Apocrypha!''

Her voice had risen and strengthened. Though I couldn't decide what she was saying, I found it very stirring. It was flattering somehow to be part of a purpose so great that it overlapped all the thousands of years ahead.

She moved back just a little, then gave a smile of apology. ''Now I must ask you once again for patience. We must proceed with the greatest caution or lose the element of surprise on which we must depend. Our many friends in other nations are helping us, just as they promised. You know that perhaps even better than I. Some small arrangements have been delayed for the sake of greater safety. The transport of incoming supplies is a delicate problem, and it is being solved every day. And every day more of us are being trained. Warehousing, transport, and supply. Everyone is working very very hard on these problems. There is always the danger of penetration of security. Be ever alert. Our technical staff is identifying more pressure points as time goes by. Think of it this way. The longer we have to wait, the greater the blow we can strike. Continue with your training. You are the soldiers of the Lord! You will put him back upon his throne on earth, and you will live all of your days in peace and love and freedom forever.''

She closed her eyes, and the lights that shone upon her face and hair were slowly, slowly dimmed until the screen was dark. The Betamax made a clacking sound, and Chuck leaped to turn it off, then sat again.

Persival said, ''Sister Nena, please give the closing prayer.''

She was behind me. I heard her stand. ''Dear Lord, we thank thee for the privilege of hearing Sister Elena Marie speak your words with her sweet lips. Grant us the patience to endure the waiting, and the skill and the bravery to overcome all odds when at last we march in thy service. Amen.''

She rattled it off so quickly I knew it was rote, and I suspected that I was probably the only one in the room who could not say the usual closing prayer.

Someone pulled the blankets away from the windows, and we were suddenly all squinting in the bright afternoon light. I looked at the television set and the tape deck. They were standard consumer items. But the way they were used was very professional. Very effective. These people seemed exalted by what they had heard. They beamed at each other and touched each other in ways of affection. I did an appropriate amount of beaming and touching. They were holding Sister Elena Marie in their hearts. She had come across to each one of us as an individual. She spoke to aloneness, in warmth and comfort.

I asked Brother Chuck if there were any old tapes I could hear.

''We don't keep any around. We'll show this one again tonight, and everybody will want to hear it again. Then I erase it and put it back in the mailer and send it on back. They dupe the ones for the camps from a master they make at headquarters.''

He looked at me with a telltale intentness. It was the game of which hand holds the marble. I got instantaneous help from my actress friend of long ago. Tom McGraw would ask.

"Where *is* headquarters anyway?"

"Classified," he said, smiling, whacking me on the arm.

"When do we get the next one?"

"There's no schedule. When she has something to say to us, she makes a tape, and they dupe it and send it out. They cost a lot, those tapes, so they get sent back blank to be reduped."

I wandered on out. I filed an item in the back of my mind. Somewhere in America, Betamax tapes were being sent in to a central place. If they were saving money on tape, they wouldn't be wasting it using couriers. If it were my problem, I'd use the mails. And I would have a permanent filler on the first fifteen minutes of each tape. They would be plainly labeled as church property, and they would have some old duck in a backward collar reading a dissertation on the philosophical impact of Martin Luther on political thought in middle Europe. And then the Sister. I would have them sent to a mail drop for courier pickup and delivery to home base. So if I happened to find the mailing address, it would probably give me no help at all.

I sat through it again that evening, and the impact of her was intensified, if anything. She did not fade. She just seemed to get stronger. And it was difficult to shake the illusion that she was looking directly at me. I could not estimate how big a woman she was. There was nothing to compare her to. She was in perfect proportion and could have been three feet tall or seven and a half. Dark-blue velvety dress with lace at the throat. No jewelry.

After it was over, Persival got me aside and said, "I want you working out with the group tomorrow. Any objection?"

"Me? No. No objection. Only, what is being done to locate where my little girl is?"

"They're trying to find her, and when they do, they'll let me know immediately. Report to Brother Chuck at eight sharp. Field exercises."

"Wearing what?"

"Ask him now."

Chuck told me we weren't leaving the land the Church owned, one full section of land, mostly up and down and sideways, so we'd wear fatigues, a light pack, and an ammo belt, and carry a weapon. He and Ahman took me over to supply, after Chuck got the key. The biggest fatigues were a little high in the ankle and short at the wrist. I explained my shoe problem, and they found a pair of size twelve sneakers and some thick nylon-and-wool socks. Ahman threw me the weapon, harder than he had to. The light was bad, just the single bulb going inside the warehouse door, and I didn't grab it close enough to the balance point, so the muzzle end tapped me over the ear, drawing a drop of blood.

"Watch it," I told him.

"Watch out for yourself, Brother," he said.

"What is this thing, anyway?"

"It's an Uzi," Chuck said. "Made in Israel."

"Very small and light. Good weapon?"

Ahman shrugged and said, "You won't be firing it. All you do is carry it.

You'll be glad it's light before the day is over. Some friends picked up a couple of truckloads of these in Lebanon. So we've got some. Makes for nice confusion. Remember what Arafat said after Camp David? He said there hadn't been any terrorism in the United States, and now they had proved themselves ready for some. For a lot, baby. A big lot. So when they bring down some of the Brothers and Sisters with Israeli weapons, they'll wonder what the hell, won't they?''

I carried my issue gear back to T-6. The sneakers felt right with two pairs of the socks. I found the right hole for the belt, filled the canteen, and positioned it at a better place on the belt. Chuck had told me I would be carrying twenty pounds of rock in the backpack, so I made careful adjustment of the straps, bringing the padding to the exact place where the straps hit the tops of my shoulders. Then I inspected the Uzi under the light. It hadn't been built for pretty. It was an ugly, simple, straightforward little weapon. The empty clip snapped into place easily. It had a good balance, and a simple three-way control for safety, single fire, and full automatic. It looked designed for quantity production. I couldn't give it full approval until I had a chance, if ever, to fire it. Then I would learn the cycle of fire and whether it would ride up at full automatic, or whether the gases were diverted just right to make it easy to hold on target. It hung well over the shoulder on its fat little sling and came off the shoulder fast, with your hands falling into the right position. I had heard that since I had been around this kind of hardware they had upped the cycle of fire, upped the muzzle velocity to practically double, and reduced the weight of the projectile. A man could carry a lot more rounds into a firefight, do just as much damage with each hit, and hit oftener.

*   *   *

I was up early and observed the usual routine of the others—that wherever I strolled, somebody was keeping an eye on me. Brother Thomas was an unknown quantity.

When I had been wakeful in the night, I had realized that my assumption that they would mail the tapes had to be wrong. This outfit preferred to take no chances at all. It had to be a hand-delivery system, and so it would do no good at all to try to find a return address.

When I went back to sleep I dreamed of Sister Elena Marie, smiling at me, talking to me. It was very important that I understand what she was saying, but I could only catch a word or phrase here and there, and they were in a foreign language I could not even identify. She was telling me how to get around behind the screen, back to where she was, and she was becoming angry because I couldn't understand what she was telling me. If I could get on the same side of the screen as Sister Elena Marie, then Gretel would be spared. When I yelled at her in rage, it woke me up again.

I ate little because I had a good idea of what they were going to try to do to me. I guessed they could probably run me into the ground. But out of pride I wanted to make them have to stretch to do it.

They had six hundred and forty very rugged acres. It was a bright chilly day, at first. Chuck ran the group with whistle signals. I had to be briefed on those. Most of it was standard operating procedure for patrols. Infiltration, cover and concealment, giving covering fire, without ammo. It involved a lot of running. I had a fifteen-year disadvantage with most of them, and I was carrying eighty more pounds uphill than were the two girls. But they wasted energy in random movements. I husbanded every ounce, made no unnecessary step. I was sweating heavily by late morning, and they all looked dry. They were conditioned.

There were special little moments of humiliation. Once when we had crossed a swollen creek and were going up an abrupt rocky slope on the other side, I got so winded near the top that I was grabbing small trees to yank myself along. As I was doing that, Stella went by me, running uphill on tiptoe, deft as a goat, and turned to give me a smile and a quick wink before leaving me behind, looking uphill at the bounding flex of those hips under the tough denim.

At another time, when I was breathing with my mouth open, gulping air hungrily, I sucked in a large California beetlebug, coughed him out violently, and couldn't stop coughing. But I was damned if I was going to say uncle. I was ready to drop first and be carried in. And I was also ready to cheat. I had weeded my twenty pounds of rock down to about three pounds. It helped.

When I was down to counting the minutes before I would probably pitch forward onto my face, I was saved by misadventure. Sister Nena took a good fast run to clear a creek, jumped well, and landed on a stone that turned as her foot struck it. She fell heavily on gravel, equipment clanking, and moaned as she reached for her right ankle. Her olive complexion was a yellow-white, her eyes squeezed by pain. I was first to reach her, and carefully unlaced the sodden sneaker and eased it off, then peeled the sock down and off her foot.

Chuck knelt beside me, and the others stood around looking down at her. "Busted?" he asked.

I told her to hold on tight, and I slowly manipulated the ankle joint. She sucked air. I made her work it herself. I knew from wide experience it wasn't bad.

"Just a little sprain, I think, but you shouldn't walk on it right away."

Chuck looked around at the slope of the land, the direction of distant peaks. "About a half mile back," he said.

Barry was wearing a macho silk scarf, off-white. Chuck wrapped the ankle tightly and tied it in place. I said I could carry her back. She said she could hobble and hop. She said it was her own damn clumsiness. Barry said he'd carry her. I said he could take over when I got tired. I didn't tell him I was already so tired I wondered if I could make a half mile by myself. Suddenly the sun was covered and the rain began to fall again. Chuck took my pack, hefted it, looked at me with a raised eyebrow, and dumped out the remaining rocks. Two of them. Apple-size. Barry took the weapon. Nena stood up on one foot, with Stella helping her balance. I bent and put my shoulder in her middle and had her lean forward as I stood up with her, my right arm wrapped around her legs just above her knees. She was smallish but solid. The rain refreshed me. It cooled me off. I made pretty good time. A few times I lost my footing on the uneven ground, and when I caught myself it would drive my shoulder into her middle, making her gasp. And each time I apologized, and each time she told me not to bother. Stella walked behind me, telling Nena how soon she would be up and around, which I knew was true. Barry offered twice to take over, but I said I was fine. I made it back in with her and, at Chuck's direction, took her to the trailer she shared with Stella. It was larger and older than mine. I bent over and knelt and perched her on the edge of her bunk, and she thanked me with an unanticipated shyness.

After the noon meal they went out again in the rain, but I was excused.

"We're doing some target work," Chuck explained. "We do it in bad weather when sound doesn't carry well and there's less chance of hikers around the perimeter."

"'I could use some brushup on that."

"You're not cleared for live ammo, Brother."

"Brother Persival is the one who'd clear me?"

"When you're ready."

"What kind of weapon is that?"

He showed it to me but didn't let me handle it. "Pretty good. Better than it looks. It's Russian. Kalashnikov Assault Rifle. It's got a good reach, and it's fast and accurate enough. Of course, for real long-range accuracy, we've got better stuff. Scopes and all. Haris is the best one here at that game. He can hit a pie plate at a thousand meters on a still day."

"Good for Brother Haris."

"Is that being sarcastic or something, Brother?"

"No. I mean it's good shooting."

"Yes, it is." Off he trotted, tootling his whistle.

The camp seemed empty. I knew that Nena was in her quarters. I wandered around, wondering who was watching me. Somebody had to be on the gate. Alvor the silent one, if they hadn't rotated the duty. Persival had to be somewhere.

I thought it out during my aimless stroll in the misty rain. I had not passed any test. I had not proved anything to anybody. So somebody wanted to know how badly I wanted to take off. Would I go down the road or start out cross-country? What would Tom McGraw do? They had all Tom's money, and they were trying to locate his girl. So why not use up a piece of the rainy afternoon calling on the pretty little woman he had carried back to camp? Ask her how she was doing.

I rapped on the door and she called, "Come in?"

"How you doing?"

"Okay, I guess. I was so damn mad at myself. Sister Nena, the gazelle. See how she floats through the air." She was on the bunk. She had been reading.

"What's the book?

She closed it and handed it to me. Worn binding, dog-eared pages. *The Loving Heart* by Sister Elena Marie. "Hasn't anyone given it to you yet?"

"First I ever heard of it."

"You should read it. You should have your own copy. I guess somebody just forgot. It's wonderful. She's a great woman, truly great. I miss seeing her. I used to see her when I was in the regular camps. She used to visit. She still does that sometimes, I think."

"How long ago was that?"

"Five years. More than five. Nearly six."

"Back when you were twelve years old?"

She laughed. "Hardly. I'm twenty-eight."

"You don't look it. Nobody would guess. Were you at more than one of the regular camps?"

"Oh, sure. You get moved around. They don't want you to sink roots anywhere except in the Church. And a lot of us get moved because family has come to try to take us home. When we're already home in the best sense of the word. My mother spent a lot of time and money trying to find me and take me away. But that was a long time ago."

"Where is she now?"

"I wouldn't have the faintest clue, Brother. She is nothing to me. I have no interest in her."

"She's your mother, like I'm Kathy's father."

"That's a biological happenstance, Brother Thomas. I don't think we'll discuss that further. You have no right of approval or disapproval over anything I do or think or am."

"I'm just trying to understand is all."

"Don't try. Just accept. You're not open enough, Brother. You are closed up tight. Sister Elena Marie says there are answers which have to come before the questions."

"Makes no sense to me."

She looked at me with exasperation. "Will you try something with me? Will you let me try to show you something? Will you *really* try to cooperate, by that I mean letting things happen that try to happen?"

"Sure. Try what?"

"Can you sit there, on the floor, and cross your legs Buddha style?"

I sat and managed it, with a certain amount of creaking, saying, "Untangling myself will be something else again."

She smiled and settled down in front of me, not wincing at all as she moved her taped ankle into position, so close that our knees touched. "We take each other's hands like this, so that you are feeling the pulse here, in my left wrist, and I am feeling your pulse in your left wrist. Let the hands and forearms rest like this. Yes, so there's no strain. After a little while, if we are doing it right, our pulse rates will become identical, and quite slow. Like sixty beats per minute. Now you look into my eyes, not in any sharp focus because then you look at one eye or the other. Kind of unfocus a little, so you see them both. Unfocus as if you were looking beyond me. You can feel my pulse? Good. Now what you have to do is take long slow breaths. On each inhalation you say three words very slowly and distinctly inside your head. *We are one.* And you say it silently and in the same rhythm as you exhale. I'll match my breathing to yours, and then it should stay matched without my thinking about it. You say the words until they are meaningless, just sounds, like a mantra. What you have to do is concentrate on looking into my eyes and trying to hear the silent words I am saying. Try to hear my words inside your head and I try to hear yours inside mine. Stay aware of the pulse and the slow breathing. Keep your back straight and your eyes just a little unfocused. And try to kind of . . . *give* yourself to it, and let it happen. Start now. No, wait. I forgot. Don't let any outside thoughts come into your head. If you start to think of anything beside pulse, breathing, looking, listening, and the words, it sets you back. Okay. Go."

So I felt like an idiot. Sitting on the floor of an old trailer, doing some kind of mantra thing with a flaky female terrorist. But I did as directed. When Meyer was into hypnosis, he had me doing some odd things. I was difficult at first, until I realized that it wouldn't hurt me to try to cooperate. Then he could manage it. It delighted him. Going under seemed to make a little roaring sound in my head, reminiscent of the first few seconds before one passes out. I did as I was told, looking into Nena's dark wide eyes, and soon the little roaring sound started, taking me into a different level of consciousness. *We are one.* Quite suddenly I could hear her voice inside my head instead of my own. And I could no longer see the rest of her face with my peripheral vision, only her eyes. The breathing seemed to be becoming much slower. Her pulse was a very slow steady throb against my finger pad. It was all sensation, without thought. Going on and on and on.

I was aware that she had ended it. Her hands were gone from mine. Contact broken. It was like coming slowly up from the bottom of a deep clear pool, seeing the sunlight on the surface above. I gave myself a slow shake, like an old wet dog, and looked at her.

She was flushed, and looking at me oddly.

"What's the matter?" I asked her. "Worked pretty good."

"I know. Better than with most people when it's the first time. I didn't expect that. Knowing your background. Only the most sensitive and imaginative and intelligent people go into *semuanja baik* so quick."

"*Semu*-what?"

"It's an Indonesian phrase. It means everything is all right. Don't worry. Be reassured. Sister Elena Marie says it is synergy. One person plus one person equals more than two persons."

"Were you telling me I'm some kind of dummy?"

"No. It's just very strange you should get so deeply into it the very first time. It was . . . very stirring. And it makes a person feel very sexy."

"I noticed." She was still frowning at me. I felt certain she would report this unexpected facility to Persival and it would rekindle his doubts. I said, quickly, "I used to have this partner I'd go netting with. I used to get these headaches all the time. He said he could hypnotize me out of them, and he tried and tried and tried, and when he was about to give up, I finally went under. It helped a lot. So when you started this *semu*-something, it felt like it did when he was putting me under, so I let myself go."

She stopped frowning and gave a brisk little nod. "Of course. That would be it, wouldn't it? We use it to reinforce the joining together. When people begin to have doubts, when they begin to think they're not strong enough for what the Church demands, then they can do *semuanja baik* and be strengthened and refreshed. When I listen to Sister Elena Marie on the tape, I get sort of the same feeling. Not as intense, but it's there. That farawayness. Brother Persival says it's that quality that made her such a success when she was an evangelist. When she used to broadcast, with a choir of two hundred voices, from the Tabernacle in Biloxi. That was before she founded the Church of the Apocrypha, before she had taken the name Sister Elena Marie."

"What did her name used to be?"

"I wouldn't tell you except she was so well known a lot of people know it. She was Bobbie Jo Annison. She started preaching the gospel when she was sixteen. They got up to over a hundred and fifty stations toward the end, and she took in millions of dollars for good works. But she decided it was not the true faith, and there were too many advisers trying to run things, and the government was after her for taxes and all. And she decided that it was vanity that had taken over for piety, being on the air so much. So she quit and she founded our Church. Maybe it was about nine years ago, or ten. There used to be things in the magazines. Whatever happened to Bobbie Jo Annison? I expect you heard the name before.''

''It sounds kind of familiar, but I was never much for turning on television for anything at all.''

''She is the greatest woman who ever lived.''

''You mean that?''

''I would die for her. I probably will die for her, and be reborn into my own identity in the next incarnation. That's the reward for dying for the Church. Sometimes, after I have prayed a long time, and very hard, suddenly I can hear her voice inside my head saying my words in her voice to the Lord. Sister Stella can make that happen too. It's wonderful when it happens.'' Her face glowed.

''Speaking of Stella, maybe you can tell me the ground rules around here. I don't want to get into trouble.''

''Because she came to your bed? No, there is no objection. It could have been suggested to her. I didn't ask and she didn't tell me. If the two of you slept only with each other, that would be bad.''

''Is that rule in Sister Elena Marie's book?''

''Not in this book. In another of her books there is a chapter about sharing. She says that making love should be a simple function, and not to be given too much importance in this era. She says that when we were all alive in earlier centuries, it was different. We were all faithful to just one person, and it was good and natural and right. And when we come back to earth again, in future centuries, it will probably be like that again. But now, in this world, if we begin to think too much of some other person, it will make us weak in our duty as soldiers in the Army of the Lord. We might forget our own mission in trying to save another person from hurt.''

''Is this sharing okay in the other camps that aren't special? Like when my little girl was here?''

''Oh, no. You have to be celibate your first few years in the Church. You must give up everything for the Church. But we in special training have proved we will not be weakened by sexual pleasure, and if we wish it, it is permitted.''

''As long as you spread it around.''

''Is that some kind of a dirty joke to you?''

''I didn't know any other way to say it, Nena.''

''You must call me Sister Nena, nothing else.''

''How did you come to get selected for this training?''

''Everyone in the Church is watched. Actually they are testing all of us all the time, keeping track of the ones with the strongest faith and the strongest, quickest bodies. When they told me I had been selected for special training, I didn't even know what kind of training it would be. Now I know, and I'll do whatever they ask of me.''

''Like blow up some kindergartens?''

''You really don't understand, do you? The most bloody, savage, awful acts that seem the most pointless, they're the ones that are most productive.

They revolt and shock everyone, and that puts terrible pressure on the central government and local governments to crack down on *all* the people who are nonconformist in any way. When that happens, the resentment makes rebels out of the conformists too, and pretty soon the whole structure crumbles.''

"And you can do these terrible things, Sister Nena?''

"I might be asked to do things that will make me feel sort of sick to my stomach. But I'll be proud of the chance to do them. I'm exalted to think I'll be part of something that's going to change the world. I'm proud of finally finding something in my life that makes sense, Brother Thomas. Has your life *really* made sense to you?''

"Sense? I don't know. I've had a few laughs. I've had some real good days. And some black black ones. Who says things have to make sense?''

"We *want* it to. Every one of us. We don't understand it, and Sister Elena Marie sorts it all out for us.''

"Well, I wish I could go see the lady and let her explain it all to me.''

"You saw the tape. Didn't that help?''

"I guess so. A little bit.''

"Brother Thomas, we are all getting very fond of you, you know. We are enjoying having you with us. Please don't have doubts. Just don't think about it. Be open. And when the time comes, Brother Persival will have a mission for you, and you will want to perform it properly and please us all.''

"Is that a first name or last name? Persival.''

"I really don't know. One of the rules of the Church is that everyone has just one name. And you can pick any part of your first name or last name, or you can make up a name, and then it is yours forever.''

"Don't you get a lot of duplications?''

"Of course. What difference does that make? We don't pay taxes and we're not on social security and there is no payroll.''

"Then it could be tough locating my little girl Kathy.''

"In all the regular camps there must be hundreds of Kathys. People are supposed to forget their last names. So even if they paged her in all the regular camps, she might not answer.''

"The boss lady has two names.''

"Please don't call her that! She is the only person who is allowed to have two names. The only one in the whole Church.''

I had untangled myself, and the feeling was coming back into my legs. She was back on the bed. By the way she moved I could see she no longer had an ankle problem.

"Well, take care of yourself, Sister Nena.''

She smiled at me. "Sure. Sister Stella is very fond of you, did you know that?''

"I thought we were all very fond of each other. Isn't that the house rule?''

She pursed her lips as she stared at me. "Sometimes when you sound sarcastic you are like another person.''

"In what way?''

"I don't really know.''

I changed the subject. "Better stay off that ankle as much as you can.''

"It's okay now. But thanks for carrying me.''

*   *   *

I stepped down out of the trailer and closed the tin door. The misty rain had stopped. I did not see anyone around. I took a bath in the creek and changed to my other set of clothes and washed out the coveralls.

As I scrubbed away, I thought about my very few options. I could stay here and keep my head down and try to get a line on where their headquarters might be located, then try to sneak away somehow and report to that memorized phone number. I could plan and carry out some kind of group ambush, kill every one of them, and then hunt through all their stuff for clues about the rest of the organization. But even if I could see myself executing all these crazies, little girls and all, my ability to do it was questionable. They were trim and tough and wary. Splendid reflexes. I could hang around until my mission, and then defect once I was at sea on the boat I was going to have to buy. By that time things would be popping all over the country, apparently. Sniping, fires, explosions, massacres, and God knows what all.

And once again I saw Gretel's face, the way the fever had wasted her, saw her chest pumping as the machine breathed for her, saw the laugh-lines around her dying eyes.

And I thought then of a provisional plan. Nicky was dead. Maybe they would find out I wasn't what I had pretended to be. If so, the odds might be improved between now and then. Nine to one read better than ten to one . . . a little better. Keep the eyes open. Improvise.

I stood up quickly, turning as I rose, and saw a flicker of movement beyond a big tree a hundred feet away. Suspicion confirmed. Keep an eye on Brother Thomas, but without giving yourself away. And we'll see what he does.

Well, he just hung around and washed himself and some clothes. He spent an hour with Sister Nena. He doesn't seem to want to take off.

That night I got up from the table and went over to where Persival sat with Alvor. I said, "I don't see any good reason why you have to hang onto my money."

"People in the Church have no need of money."

"I'm not in the Church yet."

"Your money is safe."

"You give me a list of the regular camps where my Kathy might be, and I'll go check them out, and then I'll come back here whether I find her or not."

"Would you try to take her away from the camp?"

"No. I just want to see how she looks grown up, and tell her that her ma is dead. That's all. I want to make sure she's alive."

"We're trying to locate her for you."

"You keep telling me that."

"What need would you have for money here? It's safe. Now go back and sit down, Brother. You're doing fine here. Don't spoil it."

"Suppose I decide to leave anyway."

They looked up at me. Brother Alvor had eyes like dry pebbles. Brother Persival said, "Then we'll bury you beside Brother Nicholas and say a prayer over you. And make do without you."

I know the truth when I hear it. I went back to the other table. The others were finishing. They looked at me with curiosity, but asked no questions.

They resumed their conversation. Chuck was being the instructor again.

Topic, thermite pencils. "Remember, they maintain a temperature of twelve hundred degrees Fahrenheit for ten minutes. They aren't like the older ones we had. Those were too complicated. You twist this end one full turn, and that breaks the seal so that the acid starts to eat through the barrier. It will take two hours to eat through, plus or minus ten minutes. Remember, the secret is saturation. A team of four can start at a designated point in the heart of a city, and each head out in a different direction like the spokes of a wheel, on foot. The cover story is the distribution of pamphlets. Each team member can carry and distribute two hundred pencils. You've read the list of preferred types of locations. You walk ten blocks out from the primary target area and then, a half hour later, walk the circumference of an imaginary wheel, building a circle of future fire around the heart of the city. In that way you can trap most of the fire-fighting organizations between the two fires, and also we're told that this dispersion is the most effective way of creating a fire storm."

He was still talking when I walked out.

13

ON SATURDAY, Sunday, and Monday, the last three days of the year, I tried to find out everything I could about the area. I located everyone's quarters and realized there was room for twice as many. Haris told me there had been more travel trailers, and what was now the warehouse had been a bunkhouse, capable of accommodating a hundred and fifty.

The one time I had looked into the warehouse, I had seen, in the light of the small bulb near the door, towering stacks of crates and boxes. It seemed to be much more than these few people could use or carry.

On Monday I learned by accident of one deadly item they were warehousing. It was obvious I had no chance to get in there. I happened upon Ahman out behind the small mess hall, where the grass grew tall and coarse. He was backing away, looking intently at the grass. I did not see what he was looking at for a few moments, and then I saw it, a cylinder about three feet high, three inches in circumference.

"Hard to see it?" he asked. "I've been trying different ways of painting it. The damn things came through all shiny. I striped this one green and brown, vertically. It seems to work the best. Kind of wavy lines, like the grass."

I walked toward it with him. "What is it?"

"It's a little rocket."

"What does it do?"

"It does what rockets do, Brother. It goes *whoosh-bam*."

"Thanks a lot."

He hesitated, then said, "It's on a spike, see? You shove it into the ground at a little slant. You find a good place, a half mile from the end of a runway. Then you pull this top cap off and throw it away. Then you unscrew this little cap down here near the base. Then you push this little switch, and from then on you make no loud noises, Brother. It is an acoustic trigger. A loud noise, like a jet going over low, closes the circuit, and that ignites the propellant and it comes out fast. Little vanes snap open. It's a heat-finder. Little heat-sensitive guidance system. It will pick right up to a thousand meters a second, which is somewhere around two thousand miles an hour. It has a four-mile range and it'll hit the hottest thing it can find, which will be a jet engine, and it's got enough muscle to blow off a wing or a tail, whatever. They come six in a case, labeled kitchen equipment, and we've got ten cases. It's a low-risk operation. The best way is use a telephone company truck. You always see them off on back roads, and you never think twice about it."

"Commercial airports?"

"We certainly couldn't get close enough to military ones even if we wanted to."

"Where are they made?"

"It doesn't say. The instructions come in six languages."

I hoped I did not look as shaken as I felt. If only one out of every six ignited and hit a target, it would be the worst airline disaster of all time. "Ladies and gentlemen, we are on our final approach to San Francisco International Airport. Please put out all cigarettes and make sure your seat belts are fastened and your tray tables are in an upright position. It has been our pleasure serving you, and we hope you will fly . . ." *bam.*

He picked it up gently and, holding it so as not to smear his paint job, carried it off toward the warehouse. I went back into the mess hall. It was my turn on the food detail. I stared at the supplies and couldn't decide what to have. I felt queasy.

I jumped a foot in the air when somebody slapped me on the behind. It was Stella, back from her morning wars, grinning, showing a lot of uneven teeth. And smelling faintly of cordite.

"Hey, you got bad nerves, Brother Tom."

"Looks that way."

"I should come on by tonight and relax you. But, come to think of it, we'll have to make it another time. I'm on the gate midnight to dawn. What's the matter with you? You act down. Is anything wrong?"

"No. Everything is just peachy. Help me figure out what to cook up."

"Get out of the way. Let me see what we've got. Boy, there isn't much. But there's two less for lunch, and Brother Persival and Brother Alvor will be back later on with fresh supplies."

"Who's down on the gate?"

"Brother Sammy, I think."

"Should somebody take something down to him?"

"He can eat after he's relieved."

"I don't even know who runs the duty roster."

"Brother Chuck, mostly. Unless Brother Persival wants something done different. Have you been studying your book?"

"*The Loving Heart?* It sure isn't easy reading."

"You can say that again. You know, there are parts I have to skip every time."

"What I was thinking, if I could read some of it into a tape recorder, one of those little ones I saw, I could learn it faster."

"Oh, I can get you one of those. We've got two in our trailer. And lots of empty tape. Want it right now?"

"Why not?"

She gave me a warm look and a loving smile and went trotting off, leaving her pack, weapon, and belt in the corner of the kitchen area. I moved close enough to it to see that the Uzi clip was full up. They get used to having you around. Good old McGraw. He's getting plenty of exercise, enough food. We've got his money and we're supposed to be hunting for his daughter. Keep an eye on him, of course, but nobody is exactly worried about him.

I had tried to give myself another advantage too. During the field exercises I had tried to keep going when it called for endurance, but I had dogged it when it was something calling for quick. I had blundered around when the order was for silent approach. When we ran the improvised obstacle course, I arranged to finish almost last every time. In unarmed combat, I let the men drop me with a certain amount of fuss and trouble. I was rounding off into top shape, putting on a nice edge. As I clumsied along, I studied each of them to see their flaws. Barry was muscle-bound from too much body building. Haris was very quick but without adequate physical strength. Sammy was too wildly energetic. He didn't plant himself for leverage, and he tried to move in too many directions at once. Ahman was quick and strong and crafty, once he had made up his mind, but he was prone to fatal hesitations. Chuck was the best of them, without a weakness except perhaps a tendency to exhibit more grace than was required, to turn his best profile toward an imaginary camera, to leap a little higher, spin more quickly than the exercise required.

Stella came back with a little cardboard box, silver-colored and battered, and repaired with tape. The Olympus Pearlcorder and accessories were in a jumble inside the box, along with extra tapes and batteries.

"Everybody will have to use one when we get the assignments," she said.

"How?"

"You have to memorize every word of your assignment, and you have to be able to start anywhere, in the middle, toward the end, anywhere. So what you do is read it onto the tape, and then before you go to sleep and when you wake up, you play it and say it right along with yourself, over and over and over. It has to be so much second nature that you don't have to think about it when you go out on an operation. They're very, you know, complete. 'You will get off at the corner of Main and Central. You will walk quickly north on Main on the right-hand side of the street. When you get to the bus stop at the southeast corner of Main and Pearl, you will wait there until precisely fourteen hundred hours. You will turn and enter the General National Bank Building, take the first available elevator, and ride up to the fifteenth floor. You will turn left when you exit the elevator, follow the corridor to the fire door at the end.' And so on. That was only part of a practice operation I did. There were two more pages of orders. By the time I started it, I never had to think of what to do next. I knew. I was like some kind of machine, you know?"

I took the recorder back to T-6 and left it on the bunk and came back and helped her with the meal. Since it was the last day of the year, Persival had canceled all afternoon exercises and given orders for solitary meditation and rest. I acquainted myself with my tape recorder. There was an attachment to screw onto the bottom of it which worked as a voice-actuating device. I tested the sensitivity. I put a tape in and read some of *The Loving Heart*.

"Just as white reflects all colors and black absorbs all colors, the Lord both reflects and absorbs all the thoughts and desires which pass through our mind. When you know that your thoughts are turning negative, that you are losing faith in your own faith, you must become one with a trusted Brother or Sister who loves you, and through that person renew and restore each other to the positive glory of the Church."

I listened to it come back, with little clicks where it had turned off by itself and come back on again at the sound of my voice, sometimes eliminating the first syllable after the pause.

It amused me to think of what Meyer would say about this mishmash. Though perfectly willing to pursue the philosophical concept of the furthest thicket of his mind, he has no patience with imprecision of thought, looseness of expression.

I read the tattered Pearlcorder manual again and pondered where to place the device. Persival and Alvor were the ones I wanted to tap. Alvor had a little square cement house of his own. It resembled him. Persival lived in the most elegant accommodation of all, a fat tan motor home with bulbous rounded corners and six soft but not flat tires. In the evenings he would confer with Chuck or Alvor or both of them in his motor home. It had obsolete Arizona plates and was not readily visible from the broad flat area of the stony plateau.

One side of one tape was good for thirty minutes. Planting the machine was no good if I had no way to retrieve it.

The quality of the light had changed. I opened my door. Snow was falling, big fat flakes, melting as they fell, coming down in ever greater quantity, dimming the sky. As I stood there I heard the van coming. It stopped near the warehouse, and I went out to see if I could help, shoving the recorder into my pocket. There were some small heavy wooden boxes in addition to the supplies they had gone after. Chuck appeared, and as he and Alvor carried the boxes into the warehouse, I was detailed to move the provisions to the kitchen. It took four trips, and when I went back to the van, Brother Persival was standing, grimacing with pain, beside one of the small boxes which had fallen into the snow.

"I shouldn't have tried to carry it," he said. "Would you take it to my quarters, please, Brother Thomas? I'll be along in a few moments."

It was very heavy for the size of it and contained, according to the label, some sort of electronic equipment. The motor home was locked. I rested the box on the step. Just to the left of the door there was a metal grid held in place by simple plastic thumbscrew devices, two of them. I guessed it was to vent heat from the back of the refrigerator. I took out the recorder, set the sensitivity, put it on Automatic Record, undid one thumbscrew, pulled the flimsy metal out a few inches, and shoved the recorder into the small space inside and closed the grid again. It had been an almost instinctive reaction. I did not know how or when I was going to retrieve the recorder. I did not know if it would do me any good. Maybe, if the refrigerator was running, I would merely get thirty minutes of compressor effects. If Stella wanted the recorder back, I would have to say I lost it in the snow or the creek, or somewhere.

Within moments I was wishing I had it back, but Brother Persival came along to open the door. He did not invite me in. He told me to reach in and set the box on the floor. He thanked me, and I went away. I went to a spot where I could see who might be going in and out of the motor home. First Alvor and then Chuck. Then Alvor came out and went to his own place. Chuck stayed inside until it was time to start fixing the evening meal. Celebration. Among the supplies was a batch of barbecued chickens, needing only to be heated up. And there were several half-gallon jugs of Gallo Hearty Burgundy, and ice cream packed in dry ice. End of the year. Hooray for the New Year. Hooray for terrorism, for death and fire and confusion. We were all smiles and fun as we ate. Even Ahman was pleasant to me. Persival and Alvor ate at the big table with the rest of us. The snow was staying on the ground.

With no better plan, I managed a wine drunk. I sang. I kissed the ladies. I was a figure of fun. McGraw, the funny fisherman. Dads, we call him. I whacked Alvor on the back. It was very like whacking the side of his little cement house. And it got just as much reaction.

Suddenly I stopped and stood, weaving back and forth, a hand clapped across my mouth, eyes wide with consternation, cheeks bulging. I plunged to the door and went out into the snow, leaving them laughing.

I made sure I left erratic tracks, but the tracks took me right to the motor home. I had just fastened the thin metal grille back in place when Sammy yelled, "You! Hey! Get away from there! What are you doing?"

I wheeled around and stumbled toward him, arms wide. "Good ol' Brother Sammy. Never knew I was gonna have a Chinese brother."

He tried to elude me, but I embraced him and began a horrible retching cough that panicked him. He struggled free and I fell to my hands and knees and said, "Gotta go home. Help me, old buddy. Can't find old T-Six. Somebody moved it on me."

He helped me up, and I staggered a zigzag course along the direction in which he was leading me. I mumbled thanks and crawled into my trailer. Five minutes later, when I looked out, there was no one in sight. I undressed and got into the bunk under the blankets. The tape had been used up. I rewound it. I used the ivory ear button to listen to it.

It was very indistinct. I experimented with the volume controls, trying to clear it. The voices sounded too much alike. It was Alvor, Persival, and Chuck, talking about people I didn't know. And they were too far from the recorder.

Alvor left the conversation. I could more readily distinguish between Chuck's and Persival's voices.

They both were muffled, but Persival spoke in slower cadence. "—three more here . . . Ireland . . . woman thirty . . . late January . . ."

"—about another vehicle?"

"Later. Maybe at the same time."

Mumble " . . ."

"—tentative approval . . . liked the basic idea. Oil tankers too . . . longer delay . . . arrive tomorrow . . . description of McGraw . . . take a personal look . . . coming up from . . . go back with him . . . you in charge."

And that was all I could get out of the half hour. The rest was all fragmentary, blurred, distorted. I played those parts over and over, trying to get another word or two. Somebody was coming on New Year's Day to take a look at their Mr. McGraw. As a card-carrying pessimist, I could expect nothing good from that. With such a big, careful, patient, rich organization, they would have sent somebody to check out the expired Florida driver's license with my face thereon. Probably sent the license itself. Maybe their Mr. Toomey or Mr. Kline took a look at the license. I had been too tricky. Always keep things simple as possible.

It meant I would have to choose one of my sorry options sooner than I had expected. The most attractive one was to take off in the snowstorm while they thought me drunk. Get to a phone somehow. Call the number memorized at the request of Max and Jake. Hope they would believe me. Hope they would move fast enough.

I dressed warm. Poncho on last. I moved to the door, and just as I got there, it opened and Stella came in out of the snow and ran right into me.

"Hey, where are *you* going?"

"Me? I'm going back to the party."

"That party's over." She grinned. "And now we've got our own private one. You know, there isn't supposed to be this much snow here this time of year, staying on the ground." She gave me a push. "Back to the sack, lover. I got taken off the gate detail, and Nena has some company, so I've got to stay. Here, let me help you get that off, Brother Tommy. Honey, are you too drunk to make it? We'll find out. Don't worry about it. I got lots of ways to help you. Sit down, sweetie. I'll get your shoes off. There. Don't you worry about a thing."

*   *   *

When I saw the first faint pallor of dawn at the window, I made my move. She was asleep on the inside, face to the wall. I had to believe she had been told to stay close to me until tomorrow's visitor could check me out. I got up as quietly as I could and began dressing. Suddenly she rolled over and sat up and said, "Hey? Where you going?"

I held my finger to my lips and shushed her.

"What's going on?" she whispered.

I leaned close as if to whisper in her ear. When she lifted her chin, I popped her on the corner of the jaw with a right that traveled about six inches. In my tension and apprehension, I had hit her harder than was necessary. It bounced her head off the wall behind her and she sprawled face down into the pillow, motionless. I ripped her heavy twill shirt into strips, tied her up securely, poked a wad of shirt material into her mouth, and used the last strip to hold it there, with the knot at the back of her neck.

It was a very still morning, the first day without wind since I had arrived. Welcome to the New Year. The temperature was up, the snow beginning to melt. It made for bad footing. I knew I couldn't risk going too fast. Too many chop blocks in the old days had stretched the knee tendons almost to the point of surgery. I could land on something under the snow that would shift or turn, and from then on I could be caught by a reasonably spry turtle.

My plan was to get down the road as fast as I could, cut off at the last bend, and come up behind the lean-to. I was fifteen yards from the beginning of the road when there was a yell behind me. I turned and saw Barry back near the kitchen building, alone and unarmed. So I began to move a lot faster, hoping for the best. I had made a slippery hundred yards down the hill when I heard three spaced shots behind me and a long screeching blast on Chuck's whistle. I knew that would alert whoever was at the gate, so that plan was shot.

I turned off the road at an angle to the right, hoping to make a wide half circle around the gate and come back onto the public road. I soon realized I wasn't going to give them much trouble. It was very rough country. I couldn't try to brush away my tracks. The snow was too soggy. I couldn't go as fast as they would. They had good knees. I couldn't wait for the damn snow to melt. The only thing I could possibly try would be to make a circle, intercept my own trail, and ambush them. With snowballs, perhaps. And they would realize that this was my only option and would be careful to take the elementary precaution of spacing themselves a hundred feet apart and searching the snow on either side for tracks.

While thinking, I was making as good time as I dared. And I studied the terrain, trying to evolve some kind of plan. There would be at least two, and they would probably be Barry and Chuck, and they would have those little Uzis. I slid down a steep bank into a tumbling brook and scrambled up the rocky ten-foot slope on the other side, picking up a rock a little bigger than a baseball and tucking it into the slit pocket of the poncho, where it proceeded to chunk me on the hip every third step. But it was better than a snowball.

I came to a second, smaller creek. It was shallow enough, so I went downstream, stumbling on the stones, splashing water up to my knees. It dipped downhill abruptly, spilling over the rocks in a miniwaterfall. I had to sit down to negotiate the drop. Around two curves I came upon a place where the racing water had gouged a chunk out of the bank and toppled a big pine across the brook. It had happened many months ago. The pine had wedged itself against two large living trees on the other bank and rested at about a 20-degree angle, crossing the brook fifteen feet above my head.

I stopped and studied it a few moments, then hurried on down the creek and around two more bends, climbing out on the right-hand bank, making no attempt to disguise my exit across the fresh snow. In fact, I purposely went down to my knees and left them a clear handprint to give them confidence. I made a circle back upstream, and when I was away from the rushing water, I stopped and listened. I could hear distant shouts. Then I heard the van and assumed it was going down past the gate, to take up a position on the public road to cut me off if I went that way.

As I neared the fallen tree, I tried to conceal my footsteps as much as possible. I stepped close to the base of trees. I took long slow stretching strides. I crept out along the fat trunk of the fallen tree on my hands and knees, trying to dislodge as little of the snow as possible. The thick dead limbs started at mid-creek, sticking out at right angles from the trunk. I was able to settle myself against two of them, my chest resting on one, my thighs on another, out of sight behind the trunk from anybody coming downstream. By lifting my head I could look upstream. I dislodged a little snow on the trunk so I would not have to lift my head any farther than necessary.

I changed position enough to find a limb I could hook my ankles over. It helped. The position was uncomfortable. I could expect that they, if there were two of them, would both come downstream. It was my logical escape direction. I hoped they would be well spread out. I hoped the one in the lead would not stop and turn around, once past the tree, look back for his friend, and glance upward.

It seemed certain they would come down the creek itself. The terrain was so difficult they would be endlessly slow if they tried to walk beside it, each taking a bank and staying opposite each other. I guessed the temperature had moved up into the high 40s. The woods dripped. Clots of heavy snow fell off the pine boughs. I rehearsed my drop, thinking out each move. There was no time to practice.

It was taking longer than I expected. Suddenly I heard the heavy splashing sound of somebody walking swiftly down the creek. He passed under me. Brother Chuck. He moved well, knees slightly bent, keeping his balance, holding the Uzi in his right hand by the trigger assembly, swinging it to point at one bank and then the other as he swiveled his gaze back and forth. I did not breathe until he was out of sight. I waited for the next one. I hoped there was a next one. Then I heard the screech of Chuck's whistle. Two long blasts, carrying well in the morning stillness, piercing the sounds of the brook, the sounds of dripping from the trees.

So either he would be off and running along my trail, or he would wait there to be sure his number two didn't miss it. I wished I had made it more difficult to see.

Along came the splashing, more rapid than before. I couldn't risk a look. I jacked my feet up onto the limb on which my thighs had rested. I braced myself with my left hand against the limb which had been under my chest. I held my comforting rock in my right hand. When I caught the first glimpse of Chuck's number two emerging from under my tree, I slid my feet off the limb and dropped. I had turned slightly to my right, hoping to land with my feet on the back of his shoulders and pitch him forward into the water. I landed behind him and slammed the rock squarely on top of his skull. I went down, floundering to get up, expecting him to be ready to cut me in half. When I came up gasping, he was face down in fifteen inches of black water, the current slowly turning his feet downstream. I saw the glint of metal and picked the weapon out of the icy water, wondering if it would fire. My right knee would barely support my weight. I shifted the weapon to my left hand, grabbed Barry by the tough clothing at the nape of his neck, and dragged him out of the brook and up the bank to the left.

I had no idea how fast Chuck would be in getting to my tree. I knew he would be thinking as he ran, and as soon as he saw where my trail was going, he would think ambush. When I climbed up on the high bank, he wasn't in sight. Not yet. I looked at Barry. He had an ugly jellied depression half the size of my rock in the crown of his head. But I had no time for Barry. I saw movement. Chuck was coming fast through the trees. Too fast for me to risk jumping up and trying to hobble to shelter. Barry was at the top of the bank, on his back. I sat him up and lay prone behind him. I held him in position with the fabric between his shoulder blades bunched in my left hand. I checked the Uzi. It seemed to be on full automatic. I shoved it forward, under Barry's right arm, and found I could line up the sights.

Chuck disappeared behind the uptilted root structure of the big tree, then came back into view, very tense, crouched, swinging the muzzle from side to side. He looked over and saw his partner sitting on the bank, head on his chest, soaking wet, and I knew his first impulse would be concern, but his second reaction would be to jump back into the cover he had just left. He was quicker than I expected. I caught him in mid-jump and apparently hit him quite high—as he began a back flip before disappearing. I scuttled to my rear and hid behind a tree. When I let go of Barry, the body pitched forward and slid down to the edge of the creek.

I counted up to a reasonable number twice, and then once more for good measure. I circled, went back and crossed the creek above the little waterfall, came around, and finally saw Chuck on his face in the melting snow, his weapon a yard away from his right hand, resting against a rotting stump, as naturally as if he had placed it there.

I moved close enough to have seen him breathing, had he been. I moved in and rolled him over. One high on the right shoulder, two high on the right chest. Probably not instantaneous. He had probably faded away while I was counting.

"The iceman," I said aloud, and the sound of my voice startled me. No need to lose your wits, McGee. No need to talk to yourself in the forest deep. It was a pleasure to be McGee again. McGraw had been a tiresome fellow. Dogged and unresponsive.

I searched them both. I switched weapons. I kept Barry's small pack, Chuck's ammo belt, grenades, intricate wristwatch, whistle cord and whistle, all the clips, both sets of keys, and their combined treasury of forty-two dollars. Though the dead seem to shrink in size, it is hard to get into their pockets. They seem to offer a stolid resistance to personal invasion.

I kept a close watch upstream while robbing my brothers. My knee was coming back. I had progressed from a hobble to a gimp, and from experience I could tell that if I kept moving, it would work itself out the rest of the way.

There was an assumption to be made. Somebody had probably been near enough to the area to hear the distinctive flat drumming of the Uzi in a wasteful burst of about ten. It would be reasonable for them to suppose that Brother Chuck and Brother Barry had come upon Brother Thomas and cut him down in the snow. Since they had been trained in exactly this sort of thing, pursuit and murder, it was not reasonable to suppose the murderee had turned the tables. And I had given them cause to feel a certain professional contempt for the abilities of Brother Thomas. So now they would be waiting for Brother Chuck and Brother Barry to come back out to the road and report. Persival, Alvor, Ahman, Haris, Sammy, Nena, and—if they had found her and untied her—Stella.

Assume somebody on the gate and one person way down the road in the van—or off in the van to pick somebody up. Four left on top of the hill. Five counting Stella. So go in the least likely direction. Back to camp. The hard way. Up the slopes, well away from the road.

By now there was such a confusion of tracks, I doubted they could be easily read. Also, in places where the snowfall on the ground had been light because of the trees, it was melted enough to show the brown carpet of needles.

After a time I came to familiar terrain—where we had been on the exercises, on the training missions. I stopped and listened for a long time and heard nothing. Then I heard five spaced shots well below and behind me, very probably from where I had left the bodies. Five was Brother Chuck's emergency signal on his whistle, taken, no doubt, from the marine emergency signal, five quick ones on the ship's horn.

Probably two down there, one at the gate, one in the van, three on top of the hill, counting Stella. One with, as Persival himself had pointed out, very bad wheels. Alvor, Persival, and perhaps Stella.

All of them were convinced of the absolute correctness of their training, their dedication, their mission. A true zealot can be a fearsome engine of destruction. I worked my way up the slope. The small shattered trees were off to my left. I stretched out and inched forward until I could see all the way down the length of the small plateau. It was seven or eight hundred feet long, three or four hundred wide, with the structures grouped at the far end.

14

As I watched, I heard a motor. It was the van, coming up the hill, approaching rapidly. The road came out onto the plateau a hundred feet to my right. It bounced up over the final ridge so quickly I could not tell if there was one person in it or two.

It rolled to a stop near Persival's motor home and, as Sammy or Ahman got out of it—I couldn't tell which one it was at that distance, close to six hundred feet—Persival and Alvor came out of the motor home. They stood and talked. I could guess that it was excited talk. The newcomer was waving his arms and pointing back the way he had come.

I had the general idea of using the keys to get into the big warehouse building and then making as much all-around hell as I could with whatever I might find there. But my chances of doing that would be improved if I could keep the locals indoors.

There didn't seem to be too much danger in loosing a single shot in their direction. I set my little machine to Single Fire, according to the logo by the small knob. I did not know how much accuracy I could expect. But it did seem a useful idea to make a serious attempt to wing one of them. Alvor struck me as being the most ominous of the three. I aimed as carefully as I could at a spot six inches over his head and squeezed the trigger. The one who was Ahman or Sammy, three feet to Alvor's right, bent over abruptly and fell to the ground. The other two ducked into the motor home. The figure on the ground struggled to get up, then hitched along like a broken bug until he was out of sight around Brother Persival's dwelling. Splendid shooting!

Aim at one, hit another. The slug flew three feet low and three feet to the left. I had had no real expectation of knocking anybody down at that range. The flat little smacking sound of the shot had seemed inadequate and potentially ineffective.

How now? I didn't want to lose my luck. It goes like that, like a giant crap table. One day in a firefight, you never see anybody. You keep falling down, jamming the weapon, drawing fire, and if you do see people, you're convinced you couldn't hit within fifteen feet of them. And a week later, fifty miles away, everything works. The grenade takes a home-team bounce, you spin and shoot from the hip and luck out. You get back and check yourself over and find a hole in your sleeve but none in your arm, and realize you never felt the tug or heard the whispery crack.

We used to call them the John Wayne days. It does not pay to get overconfident, but you have to ride your luck while you have it. Because it can turn on you.

It had all been a long time ago. The scene had a déjà vu quality. I had been here before in another lifetime, and had killed people I hardly knew.

There was another oncoming sound, a roar, and an airplane came in and flew low and slow, checking the plateau. I eased back down the slope. Even though the paint job was yellow and white instead of the more familiar red and white of Bob Vincent's Cessna at Lauderdale, I knew the model. It was an old utility 206, the Super Skywagon, a durable workhorse with a single Continental I0-520A, fixed tricycle gear with fat tires, able to take six people a thousand miles on eighty-four gallons of fuel, if you babied it along at ten thousand feet at a hundred and thirty miles per hour. I saw two heads through the windshield. I could read off the number on the rudder. N8555F. I could remember Bob bragging about being able to get in and out of a five-hundred-foot strip with a light load.

With no perceptible breeze to worry about, the pilot went around again and came in. The wheels touched, and he went bounding and braking, kicking up slush, bouncing on the rocky ground. He came to a stop down near the buildings, and I saw Persival and Alvor on the other side of the plane, hurrying toward it. Alvor had his arm around Persival's waist, apparently supporting most of the frail man's weight as he rushed him to the plane. The prop was still turning. I thought they both got in, but could not be sure. There was a pause, probably for shouted explanations, then the plane swiveled around fast and began accelerating down the field for takeoff. Alvor watched it go, then scuttled back to shelter.

I jumped up and ran out. I had both pack straps over my left shoulder, so I could reach into the pack as it dangled under my arm. I reached in for one of those grenades, pulled the pin, and hurled it, trying to lead the airplane, trying to get the grenade out in front of it. I think the pilot saw it and knew what it was. He swerved and lost a little momentum, then picked it up again. The plane bounced one last time and lifted off the rocky stretch.

If I had to guess what happened, I would say that the pilot decided he had lost just enough speed and lift so that he wasn't going to clear the tops of the pines which grew on the downslope beyond the far end of the plateau. The grenade made a harmless crumping sound and a small cloud of dingy smoke far behind the plane. Perhaps it made the pilot nervous, and he started his turn too soon. He wanted to turn left, toward an opening in the trees. Maybe a gust of wind came along just then. The wing tip touched the ground, and that changed the flight attitude of the aircraft. The tail came up a little. He yanked the wing back up, but the plane went down and almost touched wheels again before he tried to lift it over the pines. At the last minute he tried to slip it through but, in slow motion, he sheared the right wing, thick strut, and right wheel off the machine, and it went plunging through the trees, turning, disappearing, then making a prolonged thudding, grinding sound far down the slope. I waited for the sound of gasoline igniting, but it didn't come. If he had the presence of mind, he would have had time to cut the switch.

Alvor had run out of the motor home. I dropped and rolled over and over and over, hugging my weapon in my arms, over the edge of the plateau and down the slope, hearing the fading banshee scream of a ricochet as I came to a stop.

I did some scuttling of my own, moving to my right toward the road. I heard a shouted order, unexpectedly close. I moved beyond a thick tree and stood up. Ahman, Haris, and Alvor were running toward the spot where I had rolled down the slope. They were spread out, about twenty feet separating them, but they were converging. Alvor was making excellent time. They all had weapons at the ready. I guessed they had come up the road just in time to see Alvor fire at me. I clicked my little piece of machinery to full automatic fire. There was enough snow left on the slope so they could track me. I didn't like the idea of lighting out at a dead run for the buildings, hoping to make it. And I had a very brief moment to do some shooting without being shot at. I put as little of me as possible outside the protection of my tree and sprayed them, as with a garden hose. Ahman, the nearest, went down at once, falling hard, losing his weapon. Haris, beyond him, wavered, staggered, and turned, firing in short bursts in my general direction, firing toward the sound before he spotted me. I got behind my tree, snapped a new clip into the weapon, leaned out again, and found Haris shockingly close, lurching like a drunk but firing as he came. A very ballsy performance for a thin man with at least one slug in him. My burst took him squarely in the chest, hammering him back up the few feet of slope and onto the flat, where he fell backward, dead before he could comprehend that finality. A far more authoritative projectile chunked into my tree, and I could imagine that Alvor had one of the assault rifles. I looked around the other side of my tree, a very quick look indeed, but time enough to see Alvor running like a fullback toward the buildings, cutting, feinting, fooling the tacklers. I was moving out to take a chance at him with a long high burst when I saw movement out of the corner of my eye and fired at it immediately, with no pause for conscious thought. Ahman had retrieved his weapon and had been bringing it to bear on me, with every good chance of sending me to join Haris. The burst took him in the higher shoulder, and out of momentary panic I kept the weapon on him, rolling him over and over, a ragged bundle spraying blood and tissue.

A lot of it was luck. A lot of it was having a John Wayne day. But some of it was that old training which eliminates the last hesitation. Death comes while you are struggling with your application or lack of application of the Judeo-Christian ethic. While you work out the equation which says, If I don't kill him, he will kill me, so even if I have been taught not to kill, this is an exception—while you are working that out, he is blowing chunks of bone out of your skull. The quick and the dead is an ancient allusion. They were quick and I was quick and lucky. There was some cunning involved, of course. Being able to see how I might use that tree over the water. Coming back here instead of heading off at a full run. Remembering to scuttle far away from the place where I had rolled out of sight off the plateau. Using Barry as a shield, to shock Chuck momentarily into inaction. So they were gone. Chuck and Barry. The almost-forgotten Nicky. And Persival and the two who had arrived in the plane—probably all dead, from the sound of the impact. Now Haris and Ahman too, leaving only Alvor and the two women. A veritable massacre. A bloodbath. Butchery. I kept the horror bottled away. There would be time to examine that later on. Right now there was the high-riding pleasure of doing some difficult thing far better than you expected to be able to do it. I had been as slow and clumsy as I dared during the exercises. How many of them had died with a feeling of disbelief, frustration, anger? With the ghastly toothy grin of the skull-head of death looking over my shoulder, I was intensely alive. I was alive in every thready little nerve fiber, every capillary. I was tuned to quickness, the world all sharp edges around me, my ears hearing every small sound in the world.

Push the luck. Keep pushing. But the women? I somehow did not think I could open fire from ambush on them, as I had on the others. Had I been as hesitant about the others, I would now be as dead as they were.

I moved along to the head of the road, discarding the nearly empty clip, mounting another. I wanted to be in better position to kill the Dodge van if Alvor should decide to hop in and make a run for the gate. I could guess that he was reasonably certain there was more than one of me. He'd heard the report to Persival about the killing of Chuck and Barry. And he knew the airplane had gone down. Ahman and Haris lay on the thin wet skin of the last of the snow. Rivulets of water ran off the plateau.

I moved across the head of the road and took shelter on the other side. I tried to sort out the people, guess at their assignments. If Ahman and Haris had gone looking for Chuck and Barry, then Sammy was the one I had knocked down with the single slug meant for Alvor. And if they had left somebody on the gate, it would have to be Nena. It was possible Stella was still tied up, that nobody had looked for her in T-6. It was possible that Sammy was waiting for me, armed. Make it four to one, two of them women. But no special advantage to me there—they were as quick and well-trained and toughened as the men had been.

I heard a sudden motion, a slipping sound, then a heavy thud and a grunt, and then a woman said, venomously, "Sonnabitch!" I moved farther back. Sister Nena—I recognized her voice—had been coming up the road and had slipped and fallen. My luck was holding. Water was running down the road through slush and mud. She was watching her footing, but she held the weapon at the ready as she rounded the final bend. I could have shot her then. I held on her and thought of the savage slaughter of the innocent she was quite willing to undertake. I thought of the connection between her and the silvery little sphere which had been used to slay my woman.

I dug a grenade out of the pack. I did not pull the pin. I lobbed it with a slow sidearm so that it would arch over her head and fall on the roadside beyond her. The moment it was in the air, I was on my feet, weapon on the ground. The grenade hit and she spun toward the sound, and I charged her. She heard me coming, but she was caught for a frozen moment in a dilemma of choice. Run from the grenade or turn and cut me down. She ran several steps down the road, tumbled and rolled in expert fashion, and ended up in the prone firing position, getting off one wild shot before I kicked the Uzi out of her hands to turn in the air and land in the shallow wet ditch. I grabbed her and she came up, popping me under the chin with her head so hard the world was full of stars and lights. I turned and took a hard kick on the thigh that could have disabled me. Then she tripped me, somehow, and got loose and went scrambling away, running in a strange fashion on her hands and her feet with her rump high in the air. She had registered that the ring was still affixed to the grenade, and she went after it instead of the Uzi. I tried too fast a start and slipped and went down again. She snatched up the grenade, standing and turning as she did so, yanking the pin, releasing the handle. I saw her lips moving as she counted. Her face was screwed up by the intensity of thought, like a child with a puzzle.

I couldn't get to her. She was moving backward quite rapidly, up the hill. She held her arm back, ready to throw. Whichever way I went, she would lead me, and she was nearing her count. I feinted one way to draw the throw and ran the other way. Just as she tried to throw it underhand, both feet went out from under her and she sat down hard in the slush. She had thrown it and I couldn't see it anywhere. She had a dazed look. I saw it suddenly, coming down. The fall had made her throw it straight up in the air. It hit behind her and bounced off stone, almost as high as her head, before it went off. I weaved my way over to the other ditch, crossed it, and held onto a small tree. It was a good time for Alvor to have happened along, had he only known it. I found my weapon and picked it up, checked it out. I wondered if I was going to be sick. I knew I was not going to look at what was left of Sister Nena. Not now.

How much luck remained to me? I had needed it more with Nena than with any of the others. Her timing had been perfect. A very accurate count. She was planning on an air burst right in my face.

I had the feeling that this had been a warning to me. This is the way They had used up the very last of my luck. All at once. Good-bye, John Wayne. I went around the side of the plateau, around the end, through very difficult country, staying well below the level of the plateau, moving as quietly as I could. Chuck's complicated wristwatch said it was ten o'clock. I had thought it was at least three in the afternoon. I had lived through more bad hours than the watch would admit. Cover and concealment. The day was overcast, and the misty rain began. I had muddied my face. I worked my way up the slope behind the warehouse, walking my forearms along, digging with the toes, watching everything, listening to the dripping eaves, the rain, the silence. It seemed strange to me that I had never heard any birds up here. There should be birds.

Now what would I do if I were old Alvor—Brother Alvor with the broad meaty shoulders, the square gray face? Why, I would set up in a good place. I would set up on a high place. I would, by God, set up on a roof, not necessarily the highest roof around, but one where I could lie doggo, and then pop up suddenly and blow the fisherman to fishbait bits. I looked around very carefully. I backed down the slope and came up in a new place and looked around some more.

Finally I had an idea where I might find him. Persival's motor home had one of those ladders that go up to a depression on top that forms a luggage receptacle, with a little chrome fence around it for the tie-downs. It was a handy place for Alvor. He could have climbed the ladder out of sight of the road area. Yes, it would be a very wise choice. But how to check it out and remain alive? I moved again, back down the slope and up again to where I could come out behind one of the little cement-block structures, out of his sight *if* he were on top of the motor home. I was beginning to get very ragged in the nerve department. I was certain my luck was gone, and so it took just about all I had to stand up and move in close to the wall of the little building. I leaned against it, feeling sweat run out of an armpit and tickle my ribs as it ran down. My hands were shaky. Sammy was waiting in one direction to blow me apart, Stella in another, and Alvor on the high ground. End of the saga. Twilight of the great John Wayne day.

I did not want to leave the shelter of my nice solid little building. It can get to be like when you were a kid, standing on a high place. Wait too long and you can't jump.

Check the weapon. Breathe deeply. Where had all that zest gone? Who stole the gusto? It went when somebody blew the head off Sister Nena.

One way to go at it. I put an eye around the corner of the building. The motor home was right there, about forty feet away. A hide of very thin alloy with an enamel coating. If he was elsewhere, I would be taking the risk of letting him know I was close. But that was acceptable.

I leaned against the building, aimed, let it go on full automatic, cartridge cases dancing away, slugs smacking into the metal, punching holes, making creases in the roundness, making a lot of metallic banging, screech of ricochets, quackety roar of the very rapid cycle of fire. There was an answering roar and something leaped off the roof, out of the depression, and down on the other side of the incongruous vehicle. Have fun on the road. Drive me to Yellowstone. Plug in the water, the electric, and the phone, and adjust the TV aerial.

I had to make my run. But I had a spot right in the middle of my back, right where Sammy or Stella was going to drive it home. I had used the next-to-the-last clip to drive Alvor off the roof, and I put in the last clip when I went hunting him. The silence after all that great rackety clatter was astonishing. I braced my back against the motor home, snapping my head from side to side, wondering if he were already running out across the plateau.

I eased myself down and looked under the vehicle. No feet. I stood up—and felt a faint movement of the whole vehicle, not unlike the slight movement of a heavy boat when somebody steps aboard. Okay, so he had eased the door open and gone in. It moved again. So he was creeping around in there. And might have a shot out of the right window at a steep enough angle to knock off a piece of my head or shoulder. I dropped again and eased under Brother Persival's house. It was a close fit, but I pulled myself slowly, on my back, over to the other side. Now he was in there, peering out the windows, trying to spot me. And I had no idea what in hell I was going to do. All I knew was that I was in a spot where he couldn't see me.

I felt more movement, heard a creak. And then, twenty inches from my head, a muddy shoe came down, stealthily. And the second one as he stepped out of the vehicle. I was dragging the Uzi along by the muzzle, still hot from the long burst, and I knew I had not the time nor the room to pull it to position, aim, and fire it. He stood there, and I reached out and snatched his ankles and pulled them out from under him and tried to snake myself out from under that thing in the same motion. I was halfway out when he kicked me loose. He tried to bring the barrel of his rifle down to bear on me, but I got inside the arc of the muzzle and swarmed onto him, hitting him once in the face. He bucked me off and rolled over and over, but I had hold of the rifle and tore it away from him. I tried to turn it on him, but he came inside the arc just as I had done and butted me up against the side of the vehicle. He was a very powerful man, and a very quick man. I saw the gleam of metal, dropped the rifle, and went for his wrist. We rolled over and over, and I could see that from somewhere he had come up with a stubby, broad-bladed, evil-looking knife. I hate a knife. Then I was on my back and his weight was on me, and with all his strength he was slowly forcing the blade down, bending my arms in the process. I got my feet under me and bucked him off over my head. I snatched his rifle by the barrel and swung the stock at him as he was rolling to his feet. It took him squarely in his thick throat.

His eyes bulged. His face began to change color. He was kneeling, both hands at his throat, tearing the shirt collar away. I could see his chest heaving with the effort to get air through the smashed passageway. His face darkened and his wide eyes saw nothing any more. He sat back on his haunches, then rolled onto his side in the mud, still pulling at his shirt. There was one long rippling, quivering, muscle-jerking spasm, and then he was still. I retrieved the Uzi from under the motor home and stood, listening and listening.

Not luck this time. The strength and the speed of utter, demoralized panic. The extra adrenaline that came from the horror, the terror, of knives.

I went looking, very cautiously, for Sammy. I found him inside the motor home. He sat on the floor, leaning against a pillow. His eyes were half-open. On impulse I closed them with my thumb. The belly and groin and thighs of his coveralls were dark and heavy with blood, the color turning from dark red to chocolate. Evidently one of my slugs had clipped a major artery.

I went to T-6. Somebody had taken the gag out of Stella's mouth and freed her hands and ankles. She was on her back, the edge of the blanket across her waist. She breathed quickly and shallowly. The breathing stopped after every half-dozen or so breaths, and she would be still for perhaps thirty seconds before taking a deep gasping throat-rattling inhalation. I touched the pulse in her throat. It was light and fast. In the dingy light I bent closely and eased her eyelids up. The black pupil of the left one was twice the size of the one of the right eye. I knew the signs. Sister Stella was dying. It is called cerebral hemorrhage.

I looked down at her, and saw her die. Poor sallow little dishwater blonde, a hustler recruited for more serious duty. She had pleasured Brother Thomas. McGee had never touched her. McGee could not remember ever touching her . . . in that direction lies a tantalizingly attractive kind of madness. To become two people means that one need take no responsibility for the other. The pleasant release of guilt or tension can widen the gap between the two.

I covered her to the chin and went out into the blowing mist. There had been ten of them, and two more in the incoming aircraft, and now there were none. I was glad the wind had started again. It was far better than the silence. I shed the belt. I had lost the pack under the motor home. I slung the Uzi over my shoulder. It was comfortable to carry. I went looking for the airplane.

It had gone much farther down the slope than I had supposed. The engine and pieces of the cowling were jammed into a rocky bank. The tail section was up in a tree. The fuselage was in two large parts and dozens of ragged pieces. Seats and bits of plastic and wiring were scattered over a broad area. There was a stink of fuel.

One of them had apparently gone into the rocky bank, as had the engine. He lay bent in wrong directions, missing an arm, and it was impossible to discover what he had looked like. There was a faded tattoo of a blue-and-red eagle on his right wrist, almost obscured by curly blond hair. The eagle held a little scroll in its claws. It said "Charlene."

Another was on his face, and he was draped over a boulder, spread-eagled, hip pockets high. He looked almost normal until I noticed how totally flat his chest was. From back to front he seemed to be about four inches thick. He had huge pale hands. I wanted to see his face, but I didn't care to roll him off his boulder. I sat on my heels, put a hand under his cold chin, and lifted. He had no visible eyelashes or eyebrows. His fine blond hair was cropped short. One small gray eye was open, the other almost closed. A conspiratorial wink. A little mouth, a delicate little nose, and a face pitted and scarred by the acne of his youth.

"And how are you, Brother Titus?" I asked him.

Middling, he seemed to say. Just middling.

"Help!" I dropped Brother Titus's head and scrambled back, tripped, and sat down. "Help me!"

I moved over to the larger part of the wrecked fuselage. Brother Persival lay on his back, on what had been the side wall and windows. The gas stink was stronger.

I made certain his hands were empty before I knelt. He frowned up at me. "McGraw? McGraw, don't touch me. I think my spine is smashed. I can't move my arms and legs."

"Makes quite a problem."

"Get some of the others and rig a litter. If you roll me carefully, you can slide me out of here."

"There aren't any others."

He closed his eyes, then opened them again. "Brother Haris has had some medical training."

"There aren't any others."

"They . . . they ran?" Incredulity.

"They're dead."

After long thoughtful moments he moistened his lips and said, "Then you're a bird dog. You brought a team in."

"No. I'm alone."

"I don't understand. *You* killed them all? How, for God's sake? All those brave young people. Some of our very best. So many thousands of hours and dollars in training them."

"I had a lot of luck. And of course I had some practical experience in their line of work. And motivation. Let's not forget motivation, Brother."

"Who *are* you?"

"I'm not Brother Thomas, the commercial fisherman."

"That had become evident. It was checked out. I got word about that yesterday. Who are you?"

"Just your average idle Florida beach bum. Name of McGee. Travis McGee. Salvage consultant." I grinned idiotically at him and stuck my hand out. But of course he couldn't take it. He had closed his eyes. I waited a long time before I touched him on the cheek. "Brother Persival?"

He looked at me. Impatience. "Yes, yes. What is it?"

"Your group killed my woman, in Florida. They went out of their way to give her a death that looked like illness."

"Why would we do that?"

"She had been here a long time ago, looking for her husband's kid sister, and she had seen Titus. Then she saw him again in Fort Lauderdale, negotiating to buy land for some Belgians, and recognized him. They shot a little sphere into the back of her neck and she died."

The look of puzzlement faded. His eyes closed again as he talked. "I don't know about it, of course. But I can see why it could have happened. There are strict rules about security. The friends who are helping us are ruthless about eliminating any link between the religious mission and the political mission. It is perfect cover. I knew we had access to that . . . particular method, but I didn't know it had been used. It was supposed to be undetectable. Odd. Odd. They help the same sort of groups . . . everywhere." He opened his eyes and said, "You came here because of her? Just because of her?"

"Just because of her."

"Strange. To undo so very much. So easily."

The next time I touched him, he didn't respond. His sleep looked comfortable enough, in the circumstances.

"Just because of her," I told him again. But he was beyond all movement, all reply, all understanding.

15

I WORKED hard all the rest of that first day of the New Year. I found a bale of coarse blankets in the warehouse. I found some nylon rope and a sharp knife.

The idea, after I went down and made sure the gate was closed and locked, was to recover the farthest bodies first. Chuck and Barry. I took the van down to where I had left the road. It took me longer to find them than I had expected. All the snow was long gone. Spread the blanket. Roll body onto blanket. Tie twice around. Grab corner of blanket near the head and drag back to van. Lift in. Go get the other one. Lift in. Drive up sloppy road to warehouse. Unlock, lift bodies out, drag them inside one at a time. Drag them to place beyond narrow aisle where it widened out again. Side by side near far wall. Neat.

Next, Brother Titus, Brother Persival, and the faceless nameless one-armed third man. Very difficult pulling them up the steep slope. Three in a row. Went and got van. Two into the back, one into the side door. Unlock warehouse, unload, drag them through, one at a time. Five in a row. Neat. But no arm! Went back and looked. Looked everywhere. Finally realized that for some time as I was searching, I had been making a small strange whimpering sound. I put my hand over my mouth and stopped it.

Two out there in the flat. Ahman and Haris. Dragged them one at a time all the way. Easier than lifting, loading, unloading. Seven in a row. But one arm missing. Not as neat as I wanted it to be.

Nena next. Not neat at all. Could not stand the thought of poking around, looking for missing bits. Then Stella. Nine. Easy to drag. Alvor was difficult and bulky to drag. Messy getting Sammy onto the blanket, but okay after that. Eleven of them. Why not twelve? I stood there and counted them, pointing at each one, saying the name. Eleven!

I had missed somebody. Somebody was out there. I counted them over and over, and I was beginning to make that noise again. And then I remembered the twelfth. Nicky. Executed by me. Buried by his comrades.

Not much of the fading daylight came in. I sat on a crate purporting to contain electronic equipment. Eleven silent ones. I felt a strange affection for them. They were so docile. This was my own tiny little Jonestown. We had shared together the final climactic emotional experience. Did dark shadows move within the fading electrical charges of the emptied minds? Did the final instant record on continuous replay, over and over, each playing dimmer?

I got up and felt my way out and locked them in, safe for the night. They'd had a very bad day, but they were safe for the night. Luck had run against them. John Wayne had deserted them.

I found two big flashlights, camp lanterns. I did not want to fool with the generator. I didn't want to listen to it. I went down to the creek with soap and towels, aimed the lanterns, and bathed and scrubbed in the black slide of ice water. I dressed in fresh coveralls, went to a trailer where nobody lived and where nobody had died, and rolled up in three blankets—rolled onto my clenched fist to ease the hollowness of my empty belly—and slept twelve hours without dreaming, without waking, without, as far as I could tell, moving at all.

In the morning I was able to eat. Then I went collecting. I looked for books, notebooks, tape decks, tapes, letters, documents, money, identification. Brother Persival had the team's petty cash in a lockbox in the bottom of his hanging locker. Almost thirty-six thousand. It all fitted reasonably well into the double lining of my old duffel bag. I remembered the airplane and went back to the wreck and hunted until I found the flight log. It was damp with evaporating gasoline but legible. Dates, engine hours, destinations—some in the clear, some in code. Passengers and freight carried. Clear and coded. Fuel consumption. Estimated payloads. Maybe somebody could decipher where it had been and thus find some of the rest of these little warrens of Brothers and Sisters waiting to be bloodied. I found the flight log, but not the arm. I walked farther afield, looking for it. I studied the trees, looking up at the crotches and crevices. No arm. Not one. Anywhere.

There were very few documents. It was as if they had been ordered to keep nothing personal. Everything I found fitted into one large suitcase from Alvor's cement house. It was black metal, like those carried by immigrants in old movies.

I had washed out the van. It had not been in bad shape. The blankets had saved it. I put my duffel bag in the van. I put the suitcase in the van. In one of the travel trailers I had found a big shiny old-fashioned alarm clock. I took it into the warehouse. I did not go all the way through to where the bodies were. I tested the alarm. It was very loud. I had located one case of six rockets. I set the alarm for five hours in the future, which would make it six in the evening. I uncapped six rockets, aimed them into different parts of the storage piles, jammed them in firmly. I took off the little acoustic caps. Just turn the switches and tiptoe out. I looked and thought, then screwed the acoustic caps back on and put the rockets back in the case, walked out and threw the alarm clock as far as I could, relocked the warehouse, and left.

I drove down to the gate, unlocked it, drove out, locked it behind me. The morning had been muggy. The afternoon was colder. I drove a black van with big gold crosses on the side. I tried to look pious and preoccupied. The second day of a brand-new year. I tried to hurry, but every time I looked at the speedometer, I was back down to thirty miles an hour. It seemed fast enough.

I found a big gas station near Ukiah. I got change from the office and placed the call to the memorized number.

It rang three times and a hushed voice, male, said, "Hello."

"Was someone . . . was someone at this number trying to reach Travis McGee?"

"I can try to find out for you."

"If you find out they were, I can be reached at this number." I read it off the pay phone.

"If they were trying to reach you, they'll call back."

I had parked the van next to the phone booth. I sat where I could hear the ring. At four o'clock the man came out from the station. "Are you okay?"

"I'm waiting for a call."

"All this time?"

"I'm waiting for a call."

He looked me over carefully. "You sure you're all right?"

"I'm fine. I'm fine."

After that he would come out of the building about every fifteen minutes and stare over at me.

At 6:10 P.M. the phone rang. I moved quickly and shut myself in the booth.

"Hello?"

"McGee?"

"Yes. Are you Max or Jake?"

"Neither. But I know what went on."

"Can you prove that?"

"If you can think of a way, maybe I can."

"I was with a friend. He stayed outside. We used a code."

"Hold on. I saw that in here somewhere. Here it is. The word 'hat.' To mean a weapon. Bring your hat."

"Okay. I think somebody better get here. I think they better get here fast. I keep kind of slipping off, in a funny way."

"Where are you?"

"Near Ukiah, near an off ramp, near a Shell station. Ukiah, California."

"Because you call, we should come?"

"I hope you're recording this, pal. Because I don't feel like going over it if you don't believe it. Brother Titus is dead. And Brother Persival and ten more of them. They're in a warehouse up in the hills. The warehouse is full of weapons, ammo, incendiaries, plastique, grenades, rockets. They were terrorists who trained all over the world and they—"

"Hold it! Can you see a motel anywhere near you?"

I looked around. "Talmadge Lodge."

"You have cash?"

"Enough."

"Go there and check in. And wait."

"I'll use the name Thomas McGraw. How long will I have to wait?"

"I'd guess until six tomorrow morning. Or seven. I want to get the two you met back in on this thing. They're . . . pretty far away."

*   *   *

There were nine of them, in three nondescript cars, and they did not want to waste any time sitting around chatting. They seemed to be under intense strain. I was in the lead car with Jake at the wheel, pointing out the way. Max leaned over from the back seat. "Why the hell did you come out here?"

"Why not?"

"People like you can screw everything up."

"So why didn't you get out here first?"

"It was way down the list. We'd have gotten around to it. We're understaffed. Jesus Christ, McGee, each one of us is doing the work of three men. The government solution to a problem is throw money at it. So what do you do when you can't really mention the problem?"

"Why the big rush? Everything is still there."

Jake said, "We've gotten to too many places right after the moving men have cleaned it out."

I thought I had missed one turn, but I hadn't. I unlocked the gate, swung it open, and got back in. The three cars went barreling up the narrow steep road, sliding on the greasy turns. All the structures were there. The silence was there. I pointed out the building.

I unlocked the door for them and stepped back out of the way and let them go in. I went back and leaned on a car. In five minutes two of them came out, looking a little green. Max was one of them. After they breathed in some fresh air they went back in. Ten minutes later Max came out, another man following him with a notebook.

"—and I want unmarked trucks up here, with secure drivers. The biggest that can make that last hill and the curves. They'll take the long way around from here to Fort Bragg to go into classified storage. Our people will look at the stuff there to see if there's anything new and different. Got that?"

"Got it."

"I want to sneak a helicopter in here big enough to fly out with eleven bodies. They should bring body bags and some graves registration people. Secure people, of course."

"Got it."

"I want them taken to Home Town fastest. I want a priority on those pix and prints they're taking in there. They should be about ready to give them to you, and then you can take off. Who's got that black tin suitcase?"

"It's in the trunk of Red's car."

"They'll fly back with us to Home Town, and when you're setting the other stuff up, make sure they get good people on E. and A. Take them off other stuff if necessary. Now read back, just the highlights."

"Mmm. Unmarked trucks, secure drivers, classified storage at Bragg. Bodies out on helicopter. Body bags and graves registration people, direct to Home Town. Priority on the pix and prints, and I take them in. Take black suitcase out with me . . . no, that goes with you. What I do is get Evaluation and Analysis primed to go when it gets there."

That was all. He went back into the warehouse. Max motioned to me, and we strolled across the flats. I told him I would show him where the airplane went in.

"So many of them," he said. "Jesus!"

"I know."

"Are you all right?"

"I don't know what the hell it is. Like some kind of combat fatigue. Look at my hand shake. It was a long time ago, and it all came back at once."

"You went kind of crazy?"

"No. Not like that. I was—pretty calm, actually. I mean you go along and you figure the odds of doing this and the odds against doing that, and whatever you do, you make it sudden and final."

"You say three were in the Cessna? So you waxed eight of them."

"Nine. There's one buried over a week ago. Nicky. They gave me the gun and told me to shoot him and I did. That was what started all the rest of it. Like letting some kind of bad spell out of the bottle. I thought it was a fake execution, so I fired and killed him."

We got to the slope and looked down to where we could see bits of the airplane. "I got all the records out of there I could find," I said. "And I looked everywhere for that goddamn missing arm. I looked high and low. I can't imagine how it hid itself so damn well." My voice was getting high and thin, but I couldn't seem to stop. "Somehow we've got to find that damn arm!"

"Hey," he said. "Hey, fellow. Take it easy, huh?" He turned me around and headed me back toward the cars. "I'll have some of my guys go down there and find it."

We walked in silence.

"How'd you get them all?"

I used as few words as possible.

He gave me a strange sidelong look. I've seen people at the zoo look at the big cats that way, as if they are wondering if the creature could bang right through those bars if he felt like it.

"You're going to have to come back for debriefing."

"Debrief somebody who was never briefed?"

"It's just a word we use, McGee. I think they'll go at you for a week or more. It won't be bad. You'll get good food and rest. The motivation people will want to know just about every word those people spoke to you."

"The one they should talk to is Sister Elena Marie. She used to be Bobbie Jo Annison, the evangelist."

"We know. We'd like to talk to her for a long long time. And the people who pull her strings, and write her words. We think she's on an island off the south coast of Cuba. Maybe there'll be a lead in those papers. You shouldn't have gathered them up for us."

"I did that when I was going to blow the whole place to rubble, buildings, people, and all. I was saving the papers for you and Jake. I collected all the money. I think I was saving that for myself. Some of it is mine, about nine thousand. Some twenty-seven thousand is theirs."

"I can't understand why they didn't kill you out of hand. That's their style. That's their standard program. No infiltration. No way to do it."

"I was looking for my daughter."

"Daughter?"

"I'm sorry. I'm past making much sense."

"We'll leave here soon. It's a strain on you, having to stay here."

"Can we stop in San Francisco? I left my ID there, and my clothes."

"Of course. You're not under detention."

"For murder?"

"For self-defense. We'll let the record read there was a jurisdictional squabble and they fought among themselves. Look, you should be getting a medal, McGee. But what you are going to get is some very serious and earnest advice about keeping your mouth shut forever. I think you cut down their firepower and manpower some. If the documents give us a lead to other camps, we can cut it down some more. But the summer timetable is probably still on. They can't keep their tigers waiting forever. And they have to have something to show the folks helping them from overseas. No matter how much security we lay on, they are going to create one hell of a series of bloody messes from border to border and coast to coast. A lot of sweet dumb innocent people are going to get ripped up. Headlines, speeches, doom, the end of our way of life, and so on. Terrorism is going to pay us one big fat bloody visit, McGee. But it will only be a visit. They underestimate our national resilience. Aroused by that kind of savagery, we can become a very tough kind of people. You are a pretty good example of that."

"My luck was running, and I let it run."

"They were supposed to be their best, huh? Educated abroad. Honed fine. During the debriefing, you'll have to go into infinite detail about the training, what you saw of it."

"Everything I can remember."

"They'll want to go into hypnotic drugs to make sure they pull everything out."

"I'm in no position to object."

He stopped walking and turned to face me. "And when it is over and they turn you loose, all the information stops, then and there. You never get any more from us, and nobody ever gets any of what you have from you."

"Except Meyer."

"Nobody!"

"Except Meyer."

"I am serious, dammit!"

"Me too. So you better not turn me loose. There is no way on earth that I can keep from telling him every damn detail of every damn day I spent here. Can't you remember the clearance he used to have? You checked it out. Remember?"

"Oh, hell, yes. Okay. Meyer. And only Meyer."

Two of them came out and spoke to Max in low voices. He came over to me and said, "Take your last look around. And hope they never find out who did their people in."

"I think they know."

"If I was sure they know, I would set up a whole new identity for you, from plastic surgery to colored contact lenses."

"I wouldn't accept it anyway."

"You don't care if they come after you?"

"Frankly, not a hell of a lot, Max. Not a hell of a lot."

In a little while we headed down out of the hills. Jake told me that when everything had been taken out, they were going to truck a couple of bulldozers up there and knock everything flat and push it off the edge. I said that would be nice. They said we would stay overnight in San Francisco, so I could rest up a little, and fly out in the morning. I said that would be nice. They said that maybe the money problem could be resolved in my favor. Like a kind of unofficial reward. Like, maybe, a bounty. I said that would be nice. So they stopped talking to me. I looked out the car window at the tall evergreens and wondered why all the birds had left this part of the world. Jake turned the wipers on, smearing the small sad rain. I think they were glad to stop trying to relate to me. They felt uneasy about me, about being close to me in a small car. I think they felt not exactly certain of what I might do next. And I knew they would not have felt better about it if I had told them I didn't have the faintest notion, either, of what I might do next, today, tomorrow, or ever.

epilogue

WE HAD found a little cove around behind the Berry Islands, and with the small chop slapping us in the transom, I had bumped twice getting over the bar into the still water. But that was at low tide, and the charts for that day in late June said it was unusually low, so no sweat about getting out, getting that absolute jewel of a cruiser out of there.

It was named *Odalisque III,* and it was the splendid playtoy of Lady Vivian Stanley-Tucker of St. Kitts. It was a fifty-three-foot Magnum Maltese Flybridge cruiser, built in North Miami Beach. Twin turbocharged diesels cruised it at an honest thirty miles an hour. Paneling, radar, recording fathometer, air conditioning, ice-maker, tub and shower, huge master stateroom, double autopilot system, stereo music, wine locker, microwave oven, live wells, loran, pile carpeting. I knew it would knock close to a half million without extras, and it was the third time her husband had given her a boat for her birthday.

"The other two were huuuuuge!" she had said. "Great vulgar monsters. Had to have a crew aboard at all times. Now this one is cozy, what? Intimate, you might say. The old boy was playing the gold market and got pinched a bit. Apologized for the smaller boat."

I was over on the beach and had found a sandbar that was supporting more than its share of clams. Lady Vivian and I had been out about two weeks, provisions were running a little short, and soon we would have to decide whether to put in to Nassau or run on over to Miami. I was putting the clams in a string bag. The sun felt needle-hot on my bare back. I was turning saddle brown, and Lady Vivian had turned to a very lovely reddish gold, except for the sunburned tip of her nose.

The deep chord of the air horns made me look out toward the *Odalisque*. Shave and a haircut, two bits. Then she came out onto the bow, a tiny golden figure in a white bikini, and motioned me to come aboard.

I hung the string bag around my neck, swam out through the warm crystal-clear water, and came up the boarding ladder.

"Good nap?"

"Splendid! And I felt absolutely marvelous until, like the dutiful person I am, I turned on the thingajiggy at call time, as usual, and damn me if the old bustard wasn't trying to get me. Baaaaad news, sweet McGeeee. I have to fly on down. His damned awful sister had decided to come out for a visit, and he thinks it would look most odd if I'm not there to greet the old party. So what I told him, I would go on into Nassau tomorrow and fly from there, and find some dear friend who'll take the *Odalisque* on over to Lauderdale. Who might that dear friend be?"

"Give me a hint."

"Damn, I was having such a lovely time. And we're getting so horribly healthy. All this popping into bed must be awfully good for one."

Though tiny in the distance, she was substantial up close, a green-eyed, toffee-haired woman just barely on the sunny side of forty, if you could believe her. She gave the healthy impression of someone about to burst out of her clothes, and in fact was willing so to do when the provocation was sufficiently explicit. She had very fine-textured skin, gentle as cream, and her body temperature seemed to run permanently at about four degrees above normal. In bed she was like a stove. She radiated both heat and need.

I put the clams away for later, washed up, and then mixed us a pair of the sour rum drinks she doted on. We sat out on the afterdeck under the tarp I had rigged for shade.

We touched glasses, and as she sipped, she smiled with her eyes.

"So, there will be another cruise at least," she said.

"As long as I can last."

"You are a dear man. I see no sign of faltering, as yet."

"I sneak megadoses of vitamins, Viv."

"You are the only person in this whole wide world I have ever allowed to call me Viv. Why do I like it when you say it?"

"Because you are helplessly in love with me."

That got a hoot of laughter, her great bawdy laugh of derision. "You know, dearest McGeeee, I would feel a great deal better if I'd been able to pin you down about really helping us."

"I don't think I could do any good."

"Utter nonsense! You could do it easily, probably. It was my money, you know, not Sir Charles's. From my Uncle Merriman. His people made it in the War of the Roses, or some bloody thing like that, selling slop to both sides, I imagine. After death duties, not very much came down to me, as you can imagine. But it was *comforting*. You would know. You wake in the night and think of something that you might want, and you know you can *buy* it. It was truly a magnificent necklace. For forty thousand pounds, it had to be. And somehow, between appraisals, that wretched little animal switched it on us and now pretends to know nothing about it, and there is nothing we can do. Should you get it back for us, dear heart, we shall auction it at Christies and give you half the gavel price. Your customary arrangement, isn't it?"

"When I work, it is. I work when I need money. Otherwise I am retired. Like now."

"Ha! Living off my involuntary generosity? Last night the only possible roll to escape a double gammon was that incredible six four you rolled. Dear, I am really terribly serious about the necklace. Would you try? For me? For jolly old Viv?"

"Why not? I'll need the one he substituted, probably. I'll try to work something out."

"*Bless* you!"

And the great warm tide of her pleasure and her gratitude took us down into the cool humming, buzzing grotto of the *Odalisque* below decks, into the deep bunk—leaving behind us on the carpeting a hasty trail of bikini top, swim trunks, and bikini bottom—where, with the accompaniment of her giggles and sighs and little instructional signals, we played our favorite game of winding up that luxurious engine of a body of hers to such an aching pitch that a single slight touch, carefully planned, pushed her over the edge. After that, as always, she went into lazy yawning, smiles, a gentle kiss, and her deep deep sleep.

I picked up the discarded clothing, put on my trunks, and quietly fixed an oversized old-fashioned glass full of ice and Boodles. Sipping size. I went topside to the fly bridge, lounged on the padded bench in the fading heat of the late afternoon sun.

I remembered how it had been when I had come back home to Bahia Mar, to *The Busted Flush*, in mid-February, after the teams of skilled interrogators had pulled every last scrap of information, no matter how trivial or unrelated, out of the stubborn tangle in the back of my mind. It took me a week to tell Meyer all of it, at my own pace, quitting whenever I came up against something that needed more thought before I could talk about it willingly.

Meyer had been patient and understanding and, best of all, willing to believe what I still considered unbelievable.

"Travis, did you get any clue at all about whether they can stop the other teams?"

"I saw Max and Jake one more time, a few days before they let me come home. They let me ask some questions. They didn't answer a lot of them.

They'd acted quickly enough to terminate a few of the training centers, but the rest of them moved out in time. At best it will push the target date further into the future. Maybe it will begin to happen a year from now.''

"What about that Brussels thing?''

"A dead end. It was probably going to be one of their restaging areas, for retraining and re-equipping the survivors of the early strikes.''

"And Gretel had the bad luck to see Titus. That was why they . . . did away with her?''

"He was the link between the Church of the Apocrypha and the terrorist arm. They had a fat file on him, but not as an important wheel in the Church. Now the Church has gone underground. That cripples the financing. They probably overreacted. If they had just given up the land purchase, forfeited the payment, it would have been enough. What could Gretel have done, other than tell Ladwigg she had recognized his visitor? Overkill. Paranoia. Maybe just an urge to test a new deadly toy.''

"Who did kill her?''

"Nobody seems to know. Or care very much. It wasn't anything particularly personal, killing her or Ladwigg. It was just a case of trying to tidy up a security lapse.''

"Will you be told anything more?''

" 'There's no need ever to contact me again,' Jake said.''

"Are you sure you're all right?'' Meyer asked earnestly.

"I don't know how I am. Or exactly who I am.''

"Remember when I talked about the new barbarism last December? About the toad-lizard thing with the rotten breath, squatting in its cave? You met it, Travis. You felt the lizard breath. It is man's primal urge to decimate himself down to numbers which can exist on a wornout planet. It is man's self-hatred. The god of the lemmings, and of the poisonous creatures which can die of their own venom. It takes time to back away from that, Travis. Time.''

It had taken most of the five months to finish the job of sorting myself out. Meyer had put me on the right track. I didn't know what he had meant when he said to me, "Not one of us ever grows up to be what he intended to be. Not one of us fulfills his own expectations, Travis. We are all our own children, in that sense. At some point, somewhere, we have to stop making demands.''

There was no great moment of my saying, "Aha!'' or "Eureka!'' It just slowly came clear, like the mist rising on a mountain morning. There was a black, deep, dreadful ravine separating me from all my previous days. Over there on the other side were the pathetic and innocent little figures of world-that-once-was. McGee and his chums. McGee and Gretel. McGee and his toys and visions.

I could not approach the edge of that ravine and look down. Far far below were the bodies of the dead.

And here I was, on this side. This side was today. This side was the crystal taste of icy gin, the brute weight of tropic sun, the tiny beads of sweat on my forearm, the lovely lines of the Magnum Maltese, those white popcorn gulls way out there, afloat after feeding, Viv's glad little cries of love, the way the stars would shine tonight, the way the clams would taste, the way we would fit together as we slept.

I tasted all the tastes of today and felt in me a rising joy that this could be true. I had raised myself up from many madnesses to be exactly what I am. It had become too constant a pain to try endlessly to be what I thought I should become.

I thought I saw movement over toward the shallows, sixty feet away, where water danced in sunlight. I looked in the drawer and took out the Polaroid glasses and put them on. Yes, there were some bonefish tailing across the grass, feeding. I went down and changed the rig on the little Orvis spinner, knifed open a clam for bait, sneaked out near the transom and was barely able to drop the clam far enough ahead of them so as not to spook them.

For a little while I thought they would feed right on by, but then came the soft mouthy movement. I counted to three and gave him a quick little hit, and he took off, screaming the reel, hissing the line. There is an almost indescribable elegance about the first run of a big bonefish. Big meaning anything from five pounds to ten. No flap, no wobble, just incredibly smooth acceleration. He circled from the port quarter around the stern about a hundred feet from the boat, and around to starboard. I had no hope of turning him. I managed to pass the rod around the aerial and outrigger without losing him, but I could not manage to get up the ladderway to the bridge fast enough to clear the line, and he broke loose. I laughed at myself, and I wished the fish good luck and long life. His acids would dissolve the hook within days. He would have something to tell the others. How he outwitted monsters.

I stowed the rod and went back up to the gin. The sun was moving down toward the horizon, losing some of its sting. Viv came climbing up to the fly bridge, glass in hand. She was wearing a short beach robe with big red polkadots. She kissed me. She smelled of her French soap, and tasted of her mint toothpaste. She put her drink down, combed her hands back through her hair and stretched on tiptoe, then sat down, sipped her drink, and smiled at me.

No need for words. Her eyes were wishing me luck and long life. I had outwitted monsters.

Free Fall in Crimson

❖

For Dorothy again

I had so often in the past seen dumb domestic animals in Africa so aware of the secret intent of the people who had bred and reared them and earned their trust that they could hardly walk, knowing they were being led to a distant place of slaughter.

LAURENS VAN DER POST
The Night of the New Moon

He will wonder whether he should have told these young, handsome and clever people the few truths that sing in his bones.

These are:

(1) *Nobody can ever get too much approval.*
(2) *No matter how much you want or need,* they, *whoever* they *are, don't want to let you get away with* it, *whatever* it *is.*
(3) *Sometimes you get away with it.*

JOHN LEONARD
Private Lives in the Imperial City

1

WE TALKED past midnight, sat in the deck chairs on the sun deck of the *Busted Flush* with the starry April sky overhead, talked quietly, and listened to the night. Creak and sigh of hulls, slap of small waves against pilings, muted motor noises of the fans and generators and pumps aboard the work boats and the play toys.

"I don't really know how the law works," Ron Esterland said. "But I would think that if you arranged someone's death, even if he were dying already, you shouldn't inherit."

"Where do you come in?" Meyer asked.

Esterland took a long time answering. "All right. If some money came to me, I wouldn't turn it down. Maybe to that extent I've grown up a little. But I can get along without it. Years ago I would have turned down anything my father wanted to give me or leave me. If, Travis, as a result of your efforts, anything *does* come to me, the deal is that you get half. But the chance is so remote, I pay expenses."

I got up and stretched, went to the rail, and did some push-offs against it and some deep knee bends. The night was chill for April, and after my heavy morning workout, sitting so long had made me stiffen up.

I turned and asked Ron to straighten out the chronology of the Esterland wives for me. "I guess it is confusing," he said. "My mother, Connie, was wife number one. She died when I was eleven. Dad married Judy Prisco when I was twelve. She was a dancer. They had no children. They were divorced in six months. It was quick and ugly, and she accepted a sizable settlement. When I was thirteen he married Josephine Laurant, the actress. She and I got along well. I was sent away to school when I was sixteen. Romola, their daughter, was almost three then. I never really went home again. There were some big scenes. My father didn't like to be crossed by anybody, for any reason. He and Josie got a legal separation after ten years of marriage. Romola was nine. A nice little kid. Josie went out to the West Coast to live. It was what they called a friendly separation."

"When did they find out your father had cancer?" I asked.

"A little over three years ago. He spent the first few months liquidating his holdings. That is, when he got out of the hospital after the exploratory, and when the radiology and the chemotherapy didn't leave him too debilitated. Then he began to feel better. He had a remission. That's when he moved down here to Fort Lauderdale and bought the motor sailer and moved aboard with the woman who had been working for him for several years. Anne Renzetti. As part of putting his affairs in order, he made a new will. As I remember, his previous one left me ten dollars. So he could mention my name, I guess. The new will set up some bequests for Josie and Anne and left the bulk of the estate to Romola. Then there was a paragraph about what should happen if Romola predeceased him, which nobody really expected her to do at that time. If that happened, then the money she would have gotten would go to the setting up of an Esterland Foundation, to make grants for research into neutralizing dangerous chemical wastes before disposal by industry. He thought that's where he got his cancer, from working with plastics and reagents, chemicals of all kinds. That portion of the will, that contingency portion, left me a hundred thousand dollars. Which of course I didn't get. But it was nice to know my stock had risen that much in his estimation."

"And then Romola had her accident?" Meyer asked.

"Yes. Two years ago next month. May tenth. There was a severe skull fracture, and she never came out of the anesthetic. She was plugged into a life-support system. The brain waves were increasingly flat. Josie kept trying to believe there was hope. She died finally on August tenth. She had turned twenty. But by then my father was dead. He was beaten to death near Citrus City on the twenty-fourth of July. So Romola was his heir."

"How much did the girl inherit?" Meyer asked.

"Three and a half million after taxes, but then of course when Josie inherited from Romola, the government took a large slice. A little more than a million dollars."

I went back and sat down. Ronald Esterland sighed audibly. He was a blond man, going bald at thirty-four, with big hands and thick shoulders, a bland face, a good smile.

"I think what is bothering me," Meyer said, "and Travis too, is why you waited a year and a half to look into this whole thing."

"I can't give a good answer to that. I'm sorry. I was in London, and I had a chance to exhibit in the Sloane Gallery. I had enough work on hand for about half the space they were ready to let me have. And it was a chance to work in some bigger pieces. I kept telling myself I didn't care what had happened to my father. He was a brutal man. He said brutal things. He tried to destroy the people around him. And somebody had the good judgment to beat him to death. I worked like hell, and I filled the good spaces in that gallery. The show was a success. The reviews were better than any of my group expected. Eight paintings were sold at the opening, and by the end of the first week there were only four left unsold, and three of those were huge. I went back one afternoon. Very few people there. I roamed the show, seeing all the little red stars they stuck on the paintings to indicate they were sold. I had a feeling of pride and satisfaction, but at the same time I felt a kind of desolation. A kind of bleakness. I realized then that my father had been dead a year and I hadn't really understood what it meant to me. A lot of my motivation had been to *show* him that I had value, that I was valued by the world, and so I was worthy of his love and his respect. He had never shown me love or respect. I know how deeply I had wanted those things. I had wanted to make him come around. And I couldn't. He was gone. He had somehow escaped, and I felt frustrated. When the show came down, I closed the studio and moved back to New York. Back home. I found that I could work, after a fashion, but not as well as I wanted to work. I kept thinking about my father and Romola and the ugly fact of the murder of a dying man. So I came down here because this is where he had lived, aboard his boat, for the months before he died. That's how come I ran into Sarah Issom. I hadn't seen her for years, since I lived in Greenwich Village. She's doing damned fine work, and she said you bought one of her paintings.''

"A little seascape. An aerial view. Lots of blue in it. I am a junky for blue.''

"She has a lot of skill. She told me you did a favor for her a few years ago, and you might be the one to do a favor for me.''

"I'm not a private detective.''

"You said that before. I know.''

"I have no official standing. I don't want to get into anything where I attract too much attention from the law, because I have no status. They don't like people meddling. They don't like amateurs.''

"I've put ten thousand dollars aside for expenses.''

"I want to think about it,'' I told him. "I'll be in touch one way or the other.''

So we shook hands around and he went down the ladderway and back to the stern and down the little gangway to the dock. I heard his heels on the cement as I watched him walk off, passing under the dock lights, his long shadow moving and changing with each light.

I went back and sat by Meyer.

"So?'' he said.

"So. So I know now that I can't make it doing odd jobs here and there, and if I want to make it, I will have to seek honest work, like in Rob Brown's Boat Yard. Or with Acme Diving and Salvage. Or working for a yacht broker. Travis McGee, your friendly boat salesman. With a salary, bonuses, and a retirement plan.''

"And,'' said Meyer, "on your days off you can sit around here on the houseboat and whine and whinny about how jaded life has become.''

I stared over at him in the darkness. "I have been doing that quite a lot, haven't I?''

"Not more than I can stand. But enough.''

"What can I tell you? I swam for three hours yesterday, some of it as hard as I could go. I woke up this morning feeling great. Absolutely great. Busting with energy. Know something? I *want* to get involved in the life and times of Esterland and son. I want to go out and con the people. I want to have to bust a couple of heads here and there and have somebody try to bust mine for me. Why should I feel a little bit guilty about feeling like that, Meyer?''

"Maybe you got so you were enjoying the ennui.''

"The what?''

"Ennui, you illiterate. That is the restless need for some kind of action without having the outlet for any action at all. It is like *weltschmerz*.''

"Which, as you have so often told me, is homesickness for a place you have never seen. I miss Gretel, Meyer. God, how I miss her! But she is dead and gone, and the stars are bright and the night wind blows, and the universe is slowly unfolding, revealing its wonders. What was your impression of Ellis Esterland?''

"I did spend a couple of evenings with him. And Miss Renzetti. Not actually out of choice. He wanted to pick my brain, and I his. He wanted to know some of the banking practices in Grand Cayman, and I wanted to know which plastics companies were going to lead the pack in the future, based on new discoveries. What was he like? He tried to give the impression of being bluff and hearty and homespun. But he was a shrewd and subtle man. A good watcher. A good listener. I had no idea he was as sick as they say he was because that had to be—let me think back—two years ago in May, two months before he died.''

"What happened to his lady? Do you know?''

"Anne Renzetti? She stood up to him pretty well. I think he had a habit of bullying his women. I heard that she's over in Naples, Florida, working in a resort hotel. Mmmm. Eden Beach! Correct.''

"She was in the will?''

"I don't know, but I would think she was. She had been an employee. When he sold out his plastics company years ago, he set himself up as a management consultant, specializing in chemical and plastics companies, and from what he said I think he must have had a staff of a dozen or so. The offices were in Stamford, Connecticut. When he got sick he sold out and kept the Renzetti woman as a private secretary to help him put his affairs in order. After he was killed, the executor let her live aboard the boat until it was sold.''

I went back to the rail, snuffed the night. No traffic sounds. No surf sounds. Fifty boats away a night woman gave a maniacal cry of laughter, as abrupt and meaningless as the honk of a night-flying bird. I did not trust the rising sense of anticipation I felt. I had tried to fit myself to somberness, to a life of reserve. I had located a couple of boats for people, for a finder's fee. I had ferried a couple of big ones—a Hatteras over to Mobile, a Pacemaker up to Maryland—and flown back. I'd done some work for one of the brokers, putting bargain boats through their paces for people who wanted to believe how easy it was before making the down payment.

I told myself I had lived in a house of many rooms, but there had been a fire, and it was all charred to hell except for a small attic bedroom. A bed, a chair, a table, and a window. And if anybody wanted to take a shot, I would happily stand in the window.

But you can't cut your life back like some kind of ornamental shrub. I couldn't put the old white horse out to pasture, hock the tin armor, stand the lance in a corner of the barn. For a little while, yes. For the healing time.

It was more than economics. I could tell myself I needed the money. And I did. More than the money, I needed the sense of being myself, full size, undwarfed by my disasters.

I turned to Meyer and said, "I think I could find something where the chance of some kind of recovery would be better.''

"Maybe.''

"Ron Esterland is a little paranoid about the whole situation. He's got a hang-up about his father. He isn't thinking clearly.''

"Probably he isn't.''

"I don't see what Anne Renzetti would be able to tell me that would be any help at all."

"Neither do I."

"Want to ride over to Naples with me?"

"I would enjoy that. Yes."

"Thanks for talking me into it, Meyer."

"For a little while I didn't think I could do it."

2

MEYER WAITED in my old blue Rolls pickup while I talked money and time with Ron Esterland. Then in midmorning on a fine April Saturday, I drove over to Alligator Alley and we went humming westward past the wetlands, the scrub palmetto, the dwarf cypress. Traffic was heavy. Each year the gringos stay down longer. Each year too many of them come down to stay forever. Once the entire state becomes asphalt, high rises, malls, highway, fast food, and littered beaches, they will probably still keep coming.

The computer in one of the basements inside Meyer's skull predicts an eventual Florida population of thirty-two million folk, and by that time it will level off because it will not be any more desirable to live in Florida than it is to live in Rhode Island or West Virginia.

"What can you remember about Ellis Esterland's murder?" I asked Meyer. He walked back into his computer room and checked out the right floppy disc and played it back for me.

"On a very hot day Esterland drove up to Citrus City, in River County. That is about a hundred and twenty miles from Fort Lauderdale. Miss Renzetti offered to drive him, but he said he would go alone. She said he was feeling much better that month, even though he was depressed by his daughter's condition. He did not tell Miss Renzetti why he was going to Citrus City. And nobody ever found out. He was driving a dark gray Lincoln Continental. He had lunch alone at the Palmer Hotel, in the center of the city, and sat in the lobby for a time reading the *Wall Street Journal*. No one noticed his departure. Apparently he drove his car back over to the Florida Turnpike and stopped at a rest area six miles south of the interchange for Citrus City. A trucker found the body and reported it on CB radio. He was face down on the floor in front of the rear seat with his legs doubled under him. His wallet was on the front seat. His money was gone. Miss Renzetti said he probably had about two hundred dollars with him. He had been severely beaten. Blood beside the car and spattered against it indicated that he had probably been tossed into the back after the beating. Skull fractures, jaw fracture, broken facial bones, broken ribs. Nobody saw anything. No witness ever came forth. There were no clues."

"I think I was out of town at the time."

"You were. It was an overnight sensation. DYING MILLIONAIRE SLAIN. KILLED IN HIGHWAY ASSAULT. But it soon became yesterday's news. Oh, as

I remember there was a second little flurry when the terms of his will became known. GIRL IN COMA INHERITS FORTUNE. That sort of thing. I think the headlines called him the Plastics King."

"And if you had to guess?"

"Ellis Esterland was a very abrasive man. He was cordially disliked by a great many people. I think that if he felt unwell, he would have stopped where they found him. And if anyone had tried to talk to him, he would probably have said something ugly to them. I would guess there was only one person involved."

"Why do you say that?"

"The money was taken, but not the expensive car. It was a new car. If two people had arrived in one vehicle, one of them could have taken the car. If there was only one person, their identity could have been traced through the vehicle they would have left behind."

"Meyer, there is a difference between logic and implausibility."

"I've never noticed that logic needs be plausible."

He retreated into silence. I knew that he was back there in one of his thinking rooms, working things out. Staring into the fire. Patting the cat.

I noticed a marsh hawk on a dead branch and pointed it out. *"Circus cyaneus hudsonius,"* Meyer said. I turned and stared at him. He coughed and said, "Sorry about that. It's a twitch. Like hiccups. Compulsive classification. I try not to do it. Can't help observations. Such as what you do when you get annoyed. You go ten miles an hour faster."

I dropped the speed back where it belonged.

We got off the Alley and took 858 into downtown Naples and out to the beach, turned right, and drove along hotel row until we came to the Eden Beach. I drove the long curve of sleek asphalt past the portico and on over into their parking area. A man tending the plantings stopped and stared slack-jawed at the Rolls pickup. It has that effect. The conversion was done clumsily during the Great Depression. Four fat women in shorts were on the big putting green, grimly improving their game. Through big-leafed tropic growth I could see the blue slosh of the swimming pool, and I heard somebody body-smack into it off the rumbling board. I saw a slice of Gulf horizon, complete with distant schooner. We went up three broad white steps and through a revolving door into the cool shadows of the lobby. A very pretty lady behind the reception desk smiled at us, frowned at her watch, picked up a phone, punched out two numbers, then spoke in a low voice.

"She'll be right out," the nice lady said.

"What kind of work does she do here?"

"Oh, she's our manager! She's the *boss*."

Anne Renzetti appeared a few minutes later, looking unlike a boss. I had forgotten what a vivid little woman she was. Black black hair, dark eyes, black brows, a slash of red mouth. She wore a beige suit, white crisp shirt, green silk scarf knotted at her throat, very high heels. She walked trimly, swiftly, toward us, giving Meyer a smile of genuine pleasure at seeing him again, holding her cheek up for a kiss, favoring me with a quick handshake and a dubious look.

"McGee?" I said. "Travis McGee?"

"I think I remember you. . . . Meyer, how *are* you? You look absolutely wonderful. Gentlemen, perhaps you will join me for a drink? I was getting ready to leave. Marie? I'll be at my place if anything comes up."

We followed her out the west doors, through the pool area past a thatched outdoor beach bar, and down to the farthest cabana. It was on pilings six feet high. We went up the stairs to a shallow porch with a broad overhang. A nice breeze was coming off the Gulf. The tubular chairs were comfortable. We approved her suggestion of vodka and grapefruit juice, and she declined any help. When she came back with the drinks on a small tray, she had changed to white shorts and a pink gauze top.

Meyer said, "Congratulations on your exalted position, Anne."

She made a face. "It was sort of an accident, actually. First, I was secretary to Mr. Luddwick and then the company moved him to Hawaii, to a bigger hotel. His replacement was driving from Baltimore, and he got into a really bad accident. He was alone and fell asleep and went off the road. They thought he might be laid up for six weeks to two months, and they asked me if I could carry on alone here—with a small raise in pay, of course. I said sure. They had to pin the man's broken hip, and he got an infection, and finally, when he was ready to report, somebody had the good sense to look at the results for the three months I had been running it, and they decided they shouldn't change a thing. I owe getting the top job to Ellis Esterland."

"You do?" Meyer said, astonished.

"I cover every inch of this place at least once a month. I know what every employee is doing and what they are supposed to be doing. I know where every penny of expense goes. I listen personally to every gripe. Ellis taught me that there are people who try to look as if they are doing a good and thorough job, and then there are the people who actually damn well do it, for its own sake. I'm proud of myself, damn it. And I *love* being the boss. I really love it! Everything you do in life is worth infinite care and infinite effort, Ellis said. He said that in a half-ass world the real achiever is king. He used to make me do things over if I made the tiniest mistake. He used to make me cry. But, wow, I really owe him."

"Nice-looking place," I said.

"Why have you looked me up?" she asked.

Meyer left it up to me. "We were talking with Ronald Esterland yesterday night in Lauderdale, Miss Renzetti."

"With Ron! You were? How is he? What is he doing?"

"Fine, apparently. He had a big show of his work in London and he sold most of it. He is beginning to get a lot of attention."

"I'm so *glad!* You know, I thought Ellis had really gutted him. I really thought Ron would never amount to anything. His father thought Ron's ambition to be a painter was absurd. He thought it was a cop-out, an excuse for not working. I tried in little ways to get Ellis to get in touch with Ron. But he wouldn't. I felt . . . maternal about Ron, which is strange because he's a little older than I am. I think Josie felt that way, or feels that way, about him too, and though she is older than he is, she certainly isn't old enough to be his mother. It really crushed Josie, losing Romola the way she did. . . . What does Ron have to do with your looking me up?"

"His attitude toward his father has mellowed, Miss Renzetti."

"Please call me Anne."

"Thank you, Anne. Ron realized that he lost some of the fun of success because his father wasn't alive to see it happen."

"Ellis would have been totally astonished. He used to say to people, 'I've got a middle-aged son living abroad making funny daubs on canvas, trying to live in the wrong century.' "

"He isn't satisfied with the story of his father's death."

"Who is? They never found out a thing. Not a single thing. And it happened in such a public place. It doesn't seem possible they couldn't find out *something*."

"So I'm poking around."

"Are you some sort of police officer?"

Meyer answered, "No, he's just a private citizen. But he's had a lot of luck finding things for people, answering questions people have had. You can trust him, Anne."

"With what? I don't know anything I haven't told the police long ago. It wasn't too pleasant, you know. I was a single woman living aboard a fancy boat with a rich old dying man. They were less than polite. They wanted to know what boyfriends I had on the side. They wanted to know, if Ellis was so sick, why I hadn't driven him up there. Was he getting a divorce from Josephine? Did I plan to marry him if he got a divorce? Had we quarreled before he drove up there? Finally I had enough and I told them I wasn't answering any more questions. They tried to bully me, but I had been bullied by one of the world's greatest, so it didn't work. Look, tell Ron I'm so glad he's making it. And tell him I feel quite certain Ellis would have come around and been proud of him too. Will you do that?"

"Of course we will," Meyer said. "Did Ellis go off on trips like that often, without telling you why?"

"Never! Here's all I know about that trip. He was feeling better. He'd been—regaining lost ground for a month. He had picked up some of the weight he had lost, and his color was better. He was talking about being strong enough to fly out to Los Angeles to see Romola and talk to Josie and the doctors. He wanted to see Romola, but at the same time he dreaded it. He had talked to the doctors on the phone. They said there was no hope at all for her. It was a terrible thing for him. I think he really loved Romola. I don't think there was ever any other person in his life he had loved. Not me. Not anyone. So, okay, when I came back from shopping on Monday, the day before he was killed, he was talking on the phone. Mostly he was just saying 'Okay, okay, okay.' I had the feeling it was a long-distance call. They checked the phone records afterward, and if it was long distance, it wasn't an outgoing call. He seemed thoughtful that afternoon and evening, and before we went to bed he told me he was going up to Citrus City the next day. He said he would go alone. He wouldn't tell me why he was going. He told me to stop asking questions."

"Do you have any idea why he didn't want to tell you?"

"It wasn't like him not to. Not that he was so very open with me. It was just that he didn't care what I knew about him. I wasn't in any position to disapprove of anything he might do. I don't know why I didn't walk out. It just didn't occur to me that I could. Does that make any sense? I was in a cage with the door open, and I never even noticed the door. Now here is the only dumb guess I could come up with. He had a scientific mind. He started as a research chemist, you know. The one thing he hated above all else was doing something ridiculous and being found out. He knew how sick he was. We told each other that the remission was holding, and maybe he had licked the cancer. But he knew better than that. It had metastasized before it was first diagnosed. Chemotherapy had knocked it down for a little while, long enough for him to recover from most of the effects of the therapy, but when the remission ended, the next series of chemotherapy treatments would, if they suppressed the cancer at all, knock him back further than the previous set. And the pain would be back too. The only thing I can think of that would make him keep a secret from me was the idea I might ridicule him. Hope can be a dreadful thing, I guess. If he was going off to track down some sort of a quack cure, I don't think he would have told me."

"Is there some kind of miracle cure available in Citrus City?"

"I never tried to find out. But I would think that if there was, the police up there would have checked to see if he made contact, once they knew of his condition."

Meyer cleared his throat and looked uncomfortable. We looked at him and he said, "There's always the remote possibility that he didn't tell you because he thought you would try any means of stopping him if you knew."

"Knew what?"

"That he knew exactly what was in store for him with what was left of his life, and he had been arranging to get himself killed."

She stared at him wide-eyed. "No," she said firmly. "No, Meyer. Not Ellis. Not like that. This might sound sick, but I think he was enjoying the battle too much. He was a very gutsy man. All man. Cancer was challenging him. It pushed and he pushed back. He would delay taking pain pills, and keep track of how bad the pain was. No. To him it would have been like some kind of dirty surrender. He was building himself up to give it another battle."

"Suggestion withdrawn," Meyer said.

"Would it have had anything to do with Romola?" I asked.

"If that was so, he would have told me."

"Could he have been going to buy a present of some kind?"

"He wasn't much for presents and surprises. On my birthdays he would give me money to go out and shop for myself."

"Was there any clue as to what he was going to do in what he picked to wear?" I asked.

"Not really. He wore gray slacks and a pale blue knit sports shirt with short sleeves. He took a seersucker jacket along to wear if he was in very cold air conditioning. I think he wore it in that hotel, from what the police said. But he wasn't wearing it when he . . . when they killed him."

She hitched her chair forward and hooked her bare heels over the porch railing. Her legs were well-formed and slender. The skin, moderately tan, looked flawless as plastic.

"I've been over it ten thousand times. It seems so pointless, dying like that. I wouldn't admit it to myself at the time, but I did later: I was relieved. I'd been bracing myself to go all the way with him. Through all the pain. Caring for him when he became helpless. I was getting myself charged up to really do a job. But at the same time I dreaded it. Which is natural. He didn't love me. He sort of *liked* me. I had good lines and I was obedient, like a show dog. And I sort of loved him.

"There can be a habit of love, I think. You justify the way you are living by telling yourself that love leaves you no other choice. And so you are into love. Women stay with dreadful men. You see it all the time. You wonder why. You know they are wasting their lives. You know they are worth far more than what they have. But they stay on and on. They grow old staying on and on. They say it is love so often to themselves, it does become love. I can't understand the Anne Renzetti I was then. I look back and I don't understand her at all. We're all lots of people, I guess. We become different people in response to different times and places, different duties. Maybe in a lifetime we become a very limited bunch of people when, in fact, we could become many many more—if life moved us around more.

"Well, it moved me here and I know who I am now, and I will stay with this life for as long as I can. I never even suspected who I might really be. If it hadn't been for that new manager falling asleep at the wheel, I might never have known about this Anne. You can't miss what you don't know, can you? Maybe that's why we all have that funny little streak of sadness from time to time. We are missing something and don't even know what it is, or whether it will ever be revealed to us."

Meyer looked approvingly at her. "When you know who you really are, you fit more comfortably into your skin. You give less of a damn what kind of impression you make on people. My friend McGee here has never been at all certain of his identity."

She gave me a quick, tilt-eyed, searching glance. It had an unexpected impact. "Thinking of himself as some kind of rebel?" she asked.

"Something like that," Meyer agreed. "A reluctance to expend emotion, and a necessity to experience it. Cool and hot. Hard and soft. Rattling around in his life, bouncing off the walls."

"Would it make you two any more comfortable if I went for a walk?" I asked. "Then you can really dig into my psyche. Meyer, for God's sake, what kind of friendship and loyalty are you showing me?"

"Sorry," he said. "I keep thinking of Anne as an old friend of both of us. As a matter of fact, we only really talked one time, didn't we?"

"For a couple of hours one night, aboard the *Caper,* after Ellis went to bed. But it made me feel as if I'd always known you. All the way back to childhood."

"The way he can do that," I said, "could have made him one of the world's greatest con men. But he has scruples. And they get in the way of the con."

"So you are sort of a team of con men, conning me?" she asked.

"Let's say we share your interest in finding out more about how Ellis Esterland died," I told her.

"Perhaps I haven't got a hell of a lot of real interest left? No. That's unfair. He was an important part of my life. I worked for him for six years. I can say I never really understood the man."

"Did any of his wives?" I asked her.

"I don't know about the first one, Ron's mother. Her name was Connie, and I've heard she was a real beauty. I've never seen a picture of her. Ellis didn't keep pictures of people around. Of course Judy Prisco and Josie Laurant were—are—both handsome. He liked to be seen in the company of women who make heads turn. I would suspect I was low on the list. But in the right light I've had my moments. Whenever we went out together he would look me over first. Very critical of the color and design of clothes, the shape of a hairdo, the right jewelry. The marriage to Judy ended very quickly. And she did very well; she walked away with a bundle. Of course, at his death, he was still married to Josie, even though they were legally separated. Maybe she understood him, I don't really know. I like her."

"You've met her?" Meyer asked.

"Oh, yes. When Ellis went downhill so fast, in the beginning, she flew out. I don't really know if it was genuine concern or a feeling of obligation. He was sending her almost five thousand a month as support. She spent a lot of time with him during the ten days she was in Stamford. She and I talked a lot, after visitng hours were over. That was after the exploratory. We were wary with each other at first. You can understand that. After all, she was still married to him, and I was the quote other woman close quote. She's an unusual person. She's very emotional. I don't think she knows what she's going to do or say next. And I will tell you, she at that time was just about the best-looking mother of a twenty-year-old I have ever seen. Wow. Fantastic. And she used to be such a marvelous actress."

"She gave it up?" I asked.

"Or it gave her up. Ellis talked about it a few times. Too much temperament. Or temper. Too hard to handle."

"Have you seen her since?" I asked.

"No. But we talked, after Romola was hurt. She would call me up and we would talk. It seemed to help her to talk to me. It seemed to settle her down. She'd be practically hysterical when she would place the call."

"Did Ellis know how bad off he was?" Meyer asked. "Did the doctors level with him?"

"Oh, yes. They had to. He was quick to detect any kind of evasion. It was almost impossible to lie to him. He had an excellent specialist. Dr. Prescott Mullen. Prescott flew down several times to check him over when we were living on the *Caper*. We became very good friends, actually. He's a fine man." There had been a subtle stress on the qualifying word "very." "As a matter of fact," she continued, "I'm expecting him here tomorrow, to stay for a week. He said on the phone he's been working too hard and needs a break."

"I wonder if he could add anything," Meyer said.

"Like what?" Anne asked.

"Well, if Esterland was facing a very untidy end, a highly unpleasant finale to his life, he might not have told you, Anne. I still wonder about his arranging his own death. Was there insurance?"

"Yes. Quite a large policy. But it would have been good even if he had killed himself with a gun. He'd had it a long time."

"You knew his personal financial affairs?"

"I was his secretary, Meyer. I kept the books, balanced the checkbooks, dealt with the brokers and the lawyers. That was my job. There was a lot to do because he changed his legal residence to Florida and established new banking and trust department connections in Fort Lauderdale. The bank and I were co-executors of his will, so I got a fee for that as well as the money he left me. I can see you both wondering. Was it very much? I'll tell you. It was twenty thousand dollars. It fooled me. I guessed it would be lots or nothing. I thought it would be nothing because I wasn't in the will. It was a codicil he'd added a month before he was killed. But to repeat myself, Ellis would never never arrange his own death.''

"The point Ron was making," I told her, "was that anybody who arranged the death of a dying man shouldn't inherit. So what we are talking about is the way Josephine Laurant Esterland inherited the bulk of the estate.''

It startled her. She swung her feet down from the railing and turned to face me more directly. "Ron is thinking that? It seems sort of sick. I mean, it seems so . . . cumbersome. A public place like that. Witnesses. So much could go wrong. I see what he means, of course: that if Romola died in that coma, which she so apparently was going to do and finally did, then Josie would get only a small bequest. The support stopped when Ellis died. We— Ellis and I—we were taking it for granted that he was going to outlive his daughter. And we were talking about the foundation. And he had appointments with the lawyers and trust people and his CPA to work out the final details. He died before he could keep those final appointments. He hadn't really put much thought into the foundation until Romola had that terrible accident. And we knew she probably would die. And yes, it did make a difference of an awful lot of money to Josie to have Romola outlive her dad. Josie would make such a terrible conspirator. She babbles. She can't keep secrets.''

"Are you in touch with her?" I asked.

"I think I owe her a letter. We've been tapering off. After all, Ellis was all we had in common, and memories of Ellis aren't enough to keep a friendship going. In her last letter she said she was going back to work, that it wasn't really a very good part, but she was looking forward to it, to working again.''

She sighed, looking downward into her glass. I liked the line of cheek and jaw, the gentle look of the long dark lashes, the breasts small under rosy gauze, the pronounced convexity of the top of the thigh. Except for small lines at the corners of her eyes, a puffiness under her chin, the years had left her unmarked. She checked the glasses, took them in to fix another drink.

When she came back out, she said, "I can understand why Ron is suspicious and upset. But I think it just happened. I don't think anybody planned it. What will you do next?''

"Go to Citrus City and see if the River County sheriff has anything at all," I said.

"If he had anything, wouldn't he have arrested somebody?''

"You have to have some pretty solid facts before you arrest anybody. He might have some suspicions he'd talk about.''

"Let me buy you gentlemen some lunch, one of Eden Beach's great luncheon taste treats.''

"Why should you buy us lunch?" Meyer asked.

She patted his arm. "Promotion and advertising, dear Meyer. I have a nice expense account all my own and I hardly ever get a chance to use it. So humor me.''

3

In the early afternoon I turned off Route 41 onto 846 and drove the small empty roads over past Corkscrew, Immokalee, Devil's Garden. The tourists were booming down the big roads, white-knuckled in the traffic, waiting for the warning signals from their Fuzzbusters, staring out at endless strips of junk stores, cypress knees, plaster herons, and instant greasy chicken. We rumbled gently along through the wild country, watching the birds, the dangle of Spanish moss, the old ranch houses set way back under the shade trees, the broad placid faces of the Brahma cattle.

I went up 27 past Sebring, Avon Park, and Frostproof, went over 630 through Indian Lake Estates, and came up on Citrus City from the west. The groves marched over the rolling land, neat as Prussians. Some rain guns were circling, the mist blowing across the ranks of trees.

We agreed on a motel west of the city limits at about six o'clock. Low white frame structure with a central office and restaurant portion looking like a piece of Mount Vernon. About five cars were lined up in front of their thirty units.

There was a thin, middle-aged, weather-worn woman behind the desk. She had tooth trouble and held her mouth funny when she talked, and quite often put her hand in front of her mouth, the gesture of a child hiding laughter.

Once we had signed in and paid in advance, I said to her, "Say, is Dave Banks still sheriff?"

She stared at me. "Lordie, no! Dave's dead six year anyway. Guess you *have* been gone a time. The sherf we got now, he's new last election. Milford Hampton. They call him Fish, but not to his face, on account he looks kind of like a fish, his mouth and the way his eyes are set. Maybe you heard of the family. His granddaddy had the big Star Bar ranch north of town. Still in the family, what's left of it after they sold off some for groves and some for town houses."

"I think I heard the name."

"He's trying to do a job, but this place is getting rougher every year. I don't know what's doing it. Floaters and drifters. Boozing and knifing folks. Used to be quiet and pretty and nice. Now a lady wouldn't want to go into town of a Saturday night at all. The good stores, they're all out in the Groveway Mall. Look, you men want a good honest dinner at an honest price, we're serving from six to eight thirty. Tonight is ribs and chicken."

*   *   *

The River County sheriff's office and jail were in a white modern building diagonally across the street from the ornate yellow turrets and minarets of the old county courthouse. County cars and patrol cars were parked in a wire enclosure beside the building. When we went in, I could hear the flat mechanical tone of voice of the female dispatcher somewhere out of sight. A fat girl in a pale blue uniform with arm patch sat behind a green desk, typing with two fingers.

She glared at us and said, "You want something?"

"Sure do," I said, "but if I asked you for it, you'd probably bust me alongside the head."

569

"Oh, *you!*" she said, with a chubby simper. "Who you wanna see?"

"Whoever is still assigned to the Ellis Esterland killing."

"Esterland. Esterland. Oh, the rich millionaire guy. That was a *long* time ago. Look, what we got around here, we got Sunday evening, which is supposed to be a big rest from Saturday night, but tonight it isn't, you know what I mean? I got to finish this dang thang. It has to go in. Couldn't you come back tomorrow, fellas?"

"Would it be assigned to anybody in particular?"

"I wouldn't rightly know myself. My guess is, it would just be an open file, you know. And in the monthly meeting, the sheriff, he goes over the open files with the officers, to kind of remind them to keep their eyes open and keep asking questions even when they're checking out other stuff. You fellas from another jurisdiction?"

At that moment a sallow man in baggy yellow slacks and a Polynesian shirt came out of one office, heading for another, a stack of papers in his hand.

"Oh, Barney! Look, can maybe you help these fellas? They want to know who's still working on that rich millionaire that got beat to death at that rest stop over on the turnpike a long time ago."

He stopped and stared at us, a slow and careful appraisal, and then managed to herd both of us over into a corner away from the girl typing. He smelled tartly of old sweat.

"My name is Odum," he said.

"Meyer. And Mr. McGee," Meyer said. There was no hand extended.

"What would be your interest in that case? We're shorthanded here at the best of times. No time for book writers, newspaper people, or those who're just damn nosey."

As I hesitated, hunting the right approach, Meyer stepped in. With a flourish, he handed Odum one of his cards. I knew it was meaningless. But it is a thick card on cream-colored stock with raised lettering. There are a lot of initials after his name, all earned. In the bottom left corner is his adopted designation: Certified Guarantor. He had conducted some field surveys of his own and had weeded his options down to these two words. They sounded official and had the flavor of money and personal authority. People treat a Certified Guarantor with respect. If they asked what it meant, he told them in such a way that respect was increased.

"Mr. McGee is assisting me, sir," Meyer said. "The Esterland estate is a phased estate, in that certain incumbrances and stipulations have to fall into place in a time frame that takes heed of certain aspects of taxation on properties coexistent with the residual portions. So I'm sure you understand that just as a formality, sir, we have to go through the motions of testifying and certifying that yes, we did indeed proceed to Citrus City and review the status of the open case of murder and report back to the administrators and adjudicators, so that things can move ahead and not be tied up in jurisdictional red tape. Please believe me when I tell you that in return for your cooperation, we will take a minimum of time from busy officers of the law."

Odum's eyes looked slightly glazed. He shook himself like a damp dog and said, "You want to just . . . check out where we are on that thing?"

"On a totally confidential basis, of course."

"Sure. I realize that. Fine. Well, I guess Rick Tate, Deputy Rick Tate, would be the one who'd have it all clearest in mind. Where's Rick, Zelda?"

She stopped typing. "Rick? Oh, he's went up to Eustis with Debbie on account of her mom is bad off again. He'll be back on tomorrow on the four to midnight."

"You can get hold of him tomorrow," Odum said. "He'll come in about three thirty, around there. I won't be here."

"If we could have some kind of informal authorization?" Meyer asked. "Maybe you could just write it on the back of the card I gave you."

He went over to a corner of Zelda's desk and wrote on the card, *Rick, you can go ahead and tell these men everything we got to date on Esterland, which isn't much anyway. Barner Odum.*

When we walked back out into the warm evening, I said, "Certified Guarantor! You could write political speeches."

"Let me see. You are a Salvage Consultant. Anne called us a couple of con men. From now until tomorrow what do we do?"

"We can check out the Palmer Hotel. Where Esterland was last seen alive. You did nicely with Barney Odum, friend."

"Yes. I know."

Most of the old hotels in the central cities of Florida, in the cities of less than a hundred thousand, have gone downhill, decaying with the neighborhoods. Some of them have turned into office buildings, or parking lots, or low-cost storage bins for elderly indigents.

Though the neighborhood had evidently decayed, the Palmer was a pleasant surprise. A clean roomy lobby, pleasant lighting, trim and tidy ladies behind the desk and the newsstand. Walnut and polished brass.

The dark bar off the lobby was called The Office. Prism spots gleamed down on the bald pate of the bearded bartender, on shining glassware, on good brands on the back bar, on the padded bar rim, on black Naugahyde stools with brass nailheads. A young couple off in a corner held hands across the small table.

The bartender said, "Gentlemen," and put coasters in front of us. I ordered Boodles over ice with a twist, and Meyer selected a white wine. After serving us he moved off to that precise distance good bartenders maintain: far enough to give us privacy if we wanted it, close enough to join in should we speak to him.

"Good-looking place," I said to him.

"Thank you, sir."

"Do much business?"

"Not much on weekends. Big noon and cocktail-time business during the week."

"This is a very generous shot of gin."

"Thank you, sir. This is not really a commercial place, I mean in the sense that there is a lot of cost control. It's owned by National Citrus Associates. The cooperatives and some of the big growers maintain suites here. There's a lot of convention and meeting business, a lot of businessmen from overseas, a lot of government people, state and federal. It's something like a club. The number of available rooms is quite limited."

Meyer said, "A friend of ours from Fort Lauderdale had lunch here the day he was killed at a rest stop over on the turnpike. A year and nine months ago. Ellis Esterland."

"A tragic thing," the bartender said. "Beaten to death and robbed. There is so much mindless violence in the world. I've been here five years, and I can see the difference in just that short time. Mr. Esterland had a drink here at the bar before he went to the grill room for his lunch. He sat right where you are sitting, sir. He had a very dry vodka Gibson, straight up, and soon after he left there was an order for another one from the grill room. Of course, I did not know his name at that time. They showed me his Florida driver's license, the police did, and I recognized the little color photograph as the man who was in here."

"What did they ask you about him?" I asked.

He shrugged. "If we had any conversation beyond his ordering his drink, and I said we didn't. I had a dozen customers at the bar, and I was quite busy. I had no chance to notice him, really, to guess at his state of mind. That's what they asked. Was he nervous? Was he elated? I just couldn't help them at all. From his manner I judged him to be a businessman of some importance, used to good service. He spoke to no one else, and no one joined him. They questioned his waitress and the people at the desk and the girl at the newsstand. I don't think they learned anything useful. At least they've never arrested anyone."

"It's puzzling," I said. "Why would a man pull into a rest stop on the turnpike after he had been driving only six miles?"

"Car trouble?" the bartender said.

"He had a new Lincoln Continental with just over two thousand miles on it," Meyer said.

"Perhaps he felt unwell," the bartender said. "He didn't look like a really healthy person. His color was bad."

Three new customers arrived, laughing and hearty, dressed like Dallas businessmen, ranch hats and stitched boots. Juice moguls, maybe. They called the bartender Harry, and he greeted them by name. Two bourbons and a scotch.

We had a second drink and then went to the dining room for better than adequate steaks, green salad, and baked potatoes, served efficiently by a glum heavy woman who knew nothing about anybody who'd been a customer over a year ago, because she had not been there a year.

Back at the motel, Meyer went to bed with a book called *Contrary Investment Strategy*. I told him to be sure to let me know how it came out. I tried to think about Esterland's misfortune, but my mind kept veering into trivia, to a memory of the fine matte finish on the slender Renzetti legs, and the tiny beads of sweat along her forehead at the dark hairline as she sat in silhouette against the white glare of beach. Meyer, in bright yellow pajamas, frowned into his strategy book.

I slipped away into nightmare. I was running after a comedy airplane. Gretel was the pilot, very dashing in her Red Baron helmet, goggles, white silk scarf, white smile as she turned to look back at me. The little biplane bounded over the lumps in the broad pasture. I was trying to warn her. If she took off, she would fly into the trees. She couldn't hear me because of the noise of the engine. She thought I was making jokes, chasing her. I could not catch her. The engine sound grew louder and the tail skid lifted and she took off toward the pines.

As I ran, still yelling, I saw her tilt the plane to try to slide through a gap in the trees, saw the wings come off, heard the long grinding, sliding, clattering crash into the stones. I climbed down the slope. The whole gully was cluttered with large pieces of airplane, but strangely old, stained by time and weather, grass growing up through rents in the aluminum. I couldn't understand. I kept hunting for her. I flipped over what seemed to be a small piece of wing, big as the top of a card table, and there was a skull in the skull-sized stones, helmet in place, the goggle lenses starred by old fractures, a bundle of soiled gray silk bunched under the bones of the jaw.

Meyer shook me out of it, and I came up gasping, sweat-soaked.

"Okay?" he asked.

"Thanks."

"A lot of moaning and twitching going on."

I wiped my face on a corner of the sheet. "Gretel again. She doesn't seem to want to stay dead."

He went back over to his bed and covered himself and picked up his book. He looked over at me, thoughtful and concerned.

"How is the book coming?" I asked.

"The bad guys are winning, I think."

"Sometimes they do. Sometimes you can't tell the bad guys unless you buy a program at the door."

And when my heart slowed back to normal, I was able to go back to sleep.

* * *

At breakfast Meyer said, "I'd hoped to be back by early evening. In fact I would very much like to be back."

It took me a few moments to understand the urgency. Then I remembered that Aggie Sloane was due in on her big Trumpy again, called the *Byline*. Aggie, an ex-news hen who had married a publisher and assumed the management of the chain of papers when he died, had first come to Meyer as the friend of a friend, with a delicate international money problem. Their friendship had blossomed during and after Meyer's deft solution to her problem.

Though Meyer loves to look upon the lively young beach girls and is often surrounded by little chittering platoons of them, running errands for him and laughing at his wise jokes, when it comes to any kind of personal involvement, Meyer feels most at ease with—and is usually attracted to—mature capable independent women, the sort who run magazines, newspapers, art galleries, travel agencies, and branch banks. For them, Meyer is a sometime interlude, reassuring, undemanding, supportive, and gentle. They return, refreshed, to their spheres of combat. They are women who take great good care of themselves and are not inclined toward any permanent attachment. Meyer smiles a lot.

Aggie Sloane makes an annual pilgrimage. She flies down and boards her big Trumpy in Miami, cruises up to Lauderdale to pick up Meyer, and takes him along on the one-week vacation she allows herself every spring.

"Aggie arrives today?"

"I suppose there'd be pretty good air service back."

"Would you mind driving Miss Agnes?"

"Not at all. Of course, when I drive that thing, I always feel as if I'm hurrying to catch up with the antique classic car parade. But why?"

"I think a nice inconspicuous rental would be more useful somehow. And —I might go back to Naples and have a chat with that doctor."

"Just for the hell of it?"

"I'll give your regards to Anne."

"I think she might be too involved with that doctor to hear much of what you say. She had that look when she brought him up."

"I didn't notice."

"I think you'd better get back in the habit of noticing everything, Travis. That trait has kept you alive up until now."

"I've noticed one thing I should mention. Whenever you feel a bit guilty about anything, you give these little stern warnings to people, usually me."

His bright blue eyes looked quite fierce for a few moments. Then he smiled. "All right. The guilt isn't about Aggie, of course. It's about leaving you alone with this Esterland thing."

"I managed everything alone for quite a few years, professor."

"Always happy to leave you to your own resources. The things you get into make me highly nervous."

"I didn't mean that the way it sounded. Give my love and admiration to the lady Sloane. I might be back late tomorrow or the day after. But you won't be there, will you?"

His smile spread wide under the potato nose, wide and fatuous and tenderly reminiscent. "With any luck, I won't."

4

RICK TATE was a lean, dusty, bitter-looking man with eyes deep set under shaggy brows, narrow nose, heavy jaw—a slow, lazy-moving man who looked competent in his pale blue cotton, black leather, and departmental hardware. I guessed his age at forty.

He took the card and held it by one corner, looking at it with suspicion and distaste as he read it. "Says men," he said.

"My boss had to get back."

"Why you got to know this stuff?"

"My boss explained it to Barney Odum. It's a legal and tax thing."

He slammed the door of his gray steel locker and twirled the combination dial. We went out the back door into the lot and stood in the shade of the building waiting for the cars to come back in from their shifts. There were only three out, he told me.

"Look," he said, "instead of your riding around with me, the best way is I give you the file so you read it and then we talk, but I don't damn well know you at all, McGee, and I don't feel right about not being with anybody when they are reading a file I put together."

"Dave Banks could have told you I was all right."

He shoved his hat back off his forehead and stared at me. "Hell, I married Dave's middle girl."

"That would be Debbie?"

"Sure would."

"How's Mrs. Banks these days?"

"Not good. Not good at all. She's up in Eustis, living with her sister. We was up to see her yesterday. Looking terrible. It cut Debbie all up to see her mom looking so poorly. What she's got is kidney trouble, and they put her on a machine up there once a week. They drive her over to Orlando. Costly."

"Social Security paying for it? With the Medicare?"

"They pay shit. They pay eighty percent of what it used to cost to have it done eight years ago. With the four kids, we can't help out as much as Debbie thinks we should. The oldest girl, Debbie's sister Karen, lives in Atlanta, and she sends what she can. Now they say she should have it twice a week instead of once, and that's how come she looks so bad. I don't see how the hell we're going to swing it. I really don't."

"I'm sorry to hear about it."

"Well, come on in and I'll get you the file, and you can set and go through it in one of the interrogation rooms. Then when you get done with it, take it back to Records and ask them to ask Dispatch to tell me to come in and pick you up."

.   *   *   *

The file was thick. There was a sheaf of glossy black-and-white photographs of the body still in the car, and the body on the stretcher. Closeups of left profile, right profile, and full face. Sickening brutality. To hit a man once that hard is brutal. To keep hitting him is sickness.

Fingerprinting got nothing, as usual. There were lab reports on blood samples. Trace of alcohol. Contents of stomach. Decedent had eaten approximately two hours before death, give or take a half hour. There was a long technical report on the physical findings dictated during the autopsy procedure. Cause of death was massive trauma to the brain causing a pressure from internal bleeding that suppressed the functions of breathing and heartbeat. Five broken ribs, all on the left side, indicating a right-handed assailant. Incisions from operations noted. Decedent had multiple areas of evident malignancy affecting the liver, spleen, lymph glands, and soft tissue areas, adjudged terminal.

All the local newspaper coverage had been Xeroxed and put in the file. The *Citrus Banner* had given it a pretty good play. The rest of the file was taken up with signed statements, depositions, and reports made by the officers assigned. Rick Tate had signed most of the reports.

I read the reports and interviews and statements with care and I made notes of the things I had not known before.

———"I would guess he sat there in the chair in the lobby for nearly three quarters of an hour, reading that newspaper. I did notice that every little once in a while he would look at his watch, as if he was waiting for somebody or had to be somewhere at a certain time. I didn't see him leave. I guess I was busy when he left."

———"It was one hot day in July, and I remember I was hoping it would rain some. But it didn't. That Lincoln car was parked right out in the sun all closed up tight and locked, and I saw the man come from the hotel, shucking his coat off as he walked. I was just standing in the store, over here by the window, looking out, wishing somebody would come the hell in and buy something. He was parked in that space second from the corner. The second meter. And I saw the red flag was up in the meter, but they don't check it real careful in the summertime like they do in the tourist season. He unlocked the driver's side and he pushed on something in there, and all those windows all went down like at once, and I thought how handy that was. He threw his coat into the back, and he got in and started it up, but he yanked his hands back when he touched that wheel. So he got out again and stood around, and I guess what he was doing was letting the air conditioning cool it off in there for him. I'm always watching people, trying to figure out what they are doing and why they do it. Pretty soon he got in and all those four windows came sliding up, nice as you please, and then he turned out of the parking place and headed east on Central. I guess from what I read, he went all the way out Central to where it becomes Seven Sixty-five and takes you right to the interchange. Got on it and went six mile south to get beat to death. Wouldn't have had an inkling any nasty thing was going to happen to him. Comes to dying, money don't help you a damn."

——"What I do when I start getting the nods, I pull off soon as I can, make sure I'm locked in good, and I climb into the bunk behind the seat and set this little alarm for twenty minutes and put on my sleep mask and put everything out of my mind. Then when I wake up I get out of the cab and walk around for ten minutes or so to get the blood stirred up, and I'm good for another five or six hours. So yes, I noticed, or half noticed, that Continental when I first stopped. It was parked a hundred feet in front of me, angled in toward those logs they've got that mark the edge. I remember wondering what kind of gas mileage they get on those things now with that automatic shift-overdrive deal. There was a big orange moving van parked behind me. I had passed him and pulled into a parking area ahead of him. I think there was maybe a camper van pulled in way beyond the Continental. So I corked off and the alarm went off and I climbed down out of the cab and stretched and started walking around. The Continental was still there, and it seemed strange because that sun was coming down hot, and it wasn't in any shade. I couldn't see anybody in it. First I thought maybe somebody had gone off sick into the bushes. They don't do much business at that rest area. There's no shade where you have to park, and no crapper. There are bushes and trees between it and the turnpike so it's quieter than most, a good place to nap. I walked on over to it and looked in and seen him on the floor in the back, kind of kneeling and slumped, blood on the side of his face and neck. I ran back to my rig and got onto Channel 9 and told my story and waited until the patrol car came screaming in."

——"He ordered a drink and I went out to the bar and Harry made it right away and I took it back. He was very careful about what he wanted to eat. A green salad with our creamy Italian dressing, and the baby lamb chops, asparagus, boiled potatoes, iced tea, no dessert. It's not hard to remember about yesterday, because we had a slow day. And he was the kind of man you remember. How do we make our house dressing, and exactly how big are the lamb chops, and is it canned or fresh asparagus. Like I said, he was very careful and serious about ordering. It came to six something and he left me a dollar tip along with the dime and some pennies that was in his change. He seemed, you know, cold. Knew what he wanted and was used to getting it. He certainly didn't look like any happy kind of person. He wasn't somebody you'd kid around with when you're taking their order or anything. He was real tan, but he didn't have good color under the tan. Yellowish, kinda. What I keep thinking, he wasn't the sort of person you hit. Not for any reason at all. I know that doesn't make sense, but I can't help it. I just can't imagine somebody hitting that man in the face. It's a terrible thing to happen. But lots of terrible things are happening everywhere, I guess. Why is everybody getting so angry?''

————"I'd say he pulled up to the pump about eleven thirty or quarter to noon. You can see from the ticket he took six and four-tenths gallons of unleaded, which come to eight sixty-four. I did his windshield and he asked me was there a good place to eat and I told him the fast food places were further along, and he said he meant a real good place and I told him to go on into town to the Palmer Hotel, that I couldn't afford to eat there but it was supposed to be the best. I said it got awards every year for being good. He showed me a bug smear on the windshield I'd missed. Then he signed, and I gave him back his card and his copy, and away he went.''

*　　*　　*

When I'd finished the whole file, I took it back to Records. Dispatch called Rick Tate, and he told them to tell me he would pick me up out in front of the building in five or six minutes. It was almost six thirty. He came ghosting up to the curb and I got in. Daylight was dying, and I had heard distant booms of thunder as I waited.

"Like the file?" he asked.

"You sort of took it right out to a dead end."

"What do you make of it, McGee?"

"He got a long-distance call in Fort Lauderdale, aboard his motor sailer, telling him to meet somebody at that specific rest stop on the turnpike six miles southbound out of Citrus City, at a specific time. It was important to him to be there, and he either decided to be alone or it was requested that he be alone. It had to be in reference to something important to him: his illness, his money, his dying child, or the woman he was living with. So he drove on up in plenty of time, got gas, found a good place to eat, waited in the lobby out of the heat until it was time to go to the appointment. He kept it and they killed him."

"Anything else?"

"It isn't as bad a place for a killing as I thought. I'm going down the road and take a look at it tomorrow. Apparently, it is screened from the highway traffic. And it is not a high-use facility, especially in the heat of a late July afternoon. A planned killing taking place there would look unplanned, I think. Kind of coincidental. Spur-of-the-moment. And no problem getting away clean, back into traffic."

"Any more?"

"Not much. Vague stuff. Somebody had to decide on the place. Why up here, all this way from Lauderdale? Did they come and scout it out first? Or is it just a kind of cleverness—that when a well-to-do traveler is killed far from home, it always sounds like a coincidental killing, a robbery with assault. Kill a man close to home and the choices are broader."

"Ever a lawman?"

"Not quite."

"I put it together pretty much the same. Except the appointment and the killing could be two different people. If he was early, he could have been killed, and then when the person who called him showed up, they took one look and took off like a rabbit. A few years back in Florida and Georgia we had an M.O. of somebody sneaking up on sleeping truck drivers, shooting them in the head with a twenty-two long-rifle hollow-point, and taking whatever money they had. A long-haul trucker tends to carry a fair piece of cash for emergencies, especially an independent owner. As I remember there were eight or ten incidents. Never solved. They just all of a sudden stopped. My guess is that whoever was working it got picked up for something else. Maybe he's in Raiford and it'll start again when he gets out. He had the truckers real jumpy all over the area, believe me."

"I remember reading about that."

He started up and cruised toward the center of the city, moving up and down the side streets, looking at the dark warehouses and old apartment buildings as he talked.

"That murderous little bastard had to have some kind of transportation. We gave a lot of thought to that. A report came back from south Georgia, where he killed a driver in a rest stop on Interstate Seventy-five, just up past Valdosta, that a driver turning in had seen a motorsickle taking off like a scalded bat, and the rider didn't hit the lights until he was back out onto the interstate. The way they think he worked it, he'd sneak in and trundle his machine back into the bushes and hide and keep watch on the night traffic in and out of the rest stop. He might have to wait two or three nights until he got the right setup, a single driver in a truck, the truck parked well away from any others, and enough waiting time to be sure the driver was sacked out. But the killings stopped soon after that, before they could set anything up to try to trap him."

"What are you getting at, Rick?"

"That old M.O. that never got proved out stuck in my mind, and I woke up before dawn the day after the Esterland killing and went on out there and looked around back in the bushes. You won't find this in the file because I didn't put it in the file. We were getting the July rains. The ground was pretty soft. I poked around until I found where somebody had run a real heavy machine back through the bushes and made a half circle and brought it back to the place where it had been driven in. Okay, so it was a brute. It made a deep track, so I'd guess about a five-hundred-pound bike, and where the tread was clear in one place in the mud I saw that funny Y pattern of that rear K-One-twelve of a set of ContiTwins, like those BMW Nine-seventy-two cc come through with. You pay six or seven thousand for one of those, for just the barebones machine. I would like to think no biker had anything to do with it."

He parked in shadows and turned toward me.

"Listen, we got a group of nice people here. Maybe close to thirty couples in our club. The C. C. Roamers. Me and Debbie, we got a Suzuki GS-550-ET I bought used. We don't get a chance to go as much as we used to, but we still go when we can. We take tours. Guys and their wives or girl friends. There's real estate salesmen, and a dentist and his wife, store managers, computer programmers, a couple of builders, a guy in the landscaping business. People like that. It's great. We lay out a tour so we can take the back roads, ride along there in the wind. Have a picnic in a nice grove. You can hear the birds and all, those engines are so quieted down these days. I like it. So does Debbie. A lot. We've got our own special matching jackets and insignia. But the outlaw clubs give the whole thing a bad name. Like those damn Bandidos out west, and those Fantasies down in south Florida. Some of their officers are into every dirty thing going. Maybe, like they say, most of the troops are pretty much okay, just blue-collar guys from body shops and so on, who like to go roaring around with their women and drink a lot of beer and get tattooed and let all their hair grow and scare the civilians. Little recreation clubs like ours draw a lot of flack, McGee. And when there is biker violence, it reflects on us too, and people look at you funny and make smart remarks. That's why I hope whoever was on that machine, he just pulled off to adjust something, or get out of the sun, or eat his lunch, or some damn thing. But he could have been an outlaw biker riding alone, and he could have run short of cash money, and so he hid there behind the bushes waiting for somebody to stop who looked worth robbing."

"And if that's how it was?"

"He's away clean. No ID, no witnesses. I couldn't even get a mold of the tire track. The rain washed it out before I could get back with the kit."

"What do you really think?"

"I've got the gut feeling that whoever was on that machine beat Esterland to death. How long would it take him, a man powerful enough to hit that hard? You saw the autopsy report. They guessed he was hit six or seven times. Pull him out of the driver's seat, brace him against the car, bang him six times, open the rear door and tumble him in, and slam the door. Fifteen seconds? Twenty seconds? Take the wallet, take out the cash, toss the wallet into the car. Walk back into the brush, crank up, and roll away. Forty seconds?"

"Was it the person he had the appointment with?"

"I've got no gut feeling about that at all. Maybe yes, maybe no. When you try to figure out the odds on whether a man setting up a secret meet is going to get killed by somebody else who just happened to be there, you can tend to say it had to be the one he was meeting. On the other hand, it could be just another one of those damn coincidences that screw up the work I do forty times a year.

"I appreciate your cooperation. And when you see Mrs. Banks, you give her my best wishes."

"I surely will. Dallas McGee? Is that right?"

"Not quite. Travis. Tell her it's been ten or twelve years. I was at their house for supper. With them and those three pretty daughters."

"My Debbie was the middle one. Here, I'll drop you on back at your car. Seems like a quiet night around here, thank the good Lord. I better knock wood. Soon as I say quiet, those grove workers start sticking knives in each other. Or rolling their pickups over and over, dogs and shotguns flying every whichaway."

He drove me back to the jail. We shook hands. He went off down the dark streets, a man alone in a county car on an overcast evening, waiting for somebody to do some damn fool thing to himself or to somebody else, wondering as he made his patrol, if he was going to have to peddle the Suzuki to be able to help out with his mother-in-law's new schedule of dialysis.

5

I CHECKED out of the motel after breakfast and headed southwest in my little dark blue rental Dodge, a Mitsubishi, I think, with a VW engine and almost enough legroom. I took it over to Interstate 4 and made the mistake of staying on 4 all the way to the outskirts of Tampa before turning south on 301.

It had been a couple of years since I had driven that route, and I found all north-south highways clogged full of snorting, stinking, growling traffic, the trucks tailgating, the cowboys whipping around from lane to lane, and the Midwest geriatrics chugging slowly down the fast lanes, deaf to all honkings. Bradenton, Sarasota, Venice, Punta Gorda, Fort Myers—all the same. Smoggy vistas and chrome glitterings down the long alleyway between the fast food outlets, the sprawl of motels, car dealerships, shell factories, strip shopping centers, gas stations, and gigantic signboards. It is all that bustling steaming growth that turns the state tackier each year. Newcomers don't mind at all, because they think it has always been like this. But in two years, they all want to slam the door, pull up the ladder, and close the state off. Once in a great while, like once every fifty miles, I even got a look at a tiny slice of the Gulf of Mexico, way off to the right. And remembered bringing the *Flush* down this coast with Gretel aboard. And wished I could cry as easily as a child does.

I had phoned ahead to the Eden Beach, and they had a second-floor single for me, with the windows facing inland. After I put the duffelbag in the room, I went over to the lobby to find Anne Renzetti.

I saw her coming diagonally across the lobby, walking very swiftly, her expression anxious and intent. Today she wore an elegant little dress: a cotton dress in an unusual shade of orange coral, which fitted her so beautifully it underlined the lovely fashioning of hips, sweep of waist, straightness of her back and shoulders. The color was good for her too. A small lady, luxuriantly alive.

"Hey, Anne," I said.

She came to a quick stop and stared at me, an instant of puzzlement and then recognition. "Oh, hello there. Mr. McGraw."

"McGee. Travis McGee."

She was looking beyond me. "Yes, of course. I'm so sorry. Travis McGee. Is Meyer with you?"

"He had to get back."

She started to sidle away. "You will have to excuse me. I really have to—"

"I was hoping you would introduce me to Dr. Mullen. I want to ask him about Ellis Esterland's condition at the time he—"

Even the sound of his name made her glow. It seemed almost to take her breath away. Her smile was lovely. "That's why I'm so busy at the moment. He didn't get in yesterday. He's due any minute. I just checked the room I set aside for him, and the damned shower keeps dripping and dripping. Excuse me just a moment, please."

I followed her to the desk. She told Marie about the leak, and Marie picked up the phone to get the maintenance man on it. Anne turned back to me and looked beyond me toward the entrance. Her smile went wider, and she flushed under her tan and slipped past me, quick and cute as a safety blitz. She half ran toward the entrance, arms outstretched, and I heard her glad cry of welcome.

The man was in his middle thirties, with a russet mustache, blow-dried hair, tinted glasses with little gold rims. He had a likable look about him. Strong irregular features, a good grin. And he wasn't very big. He was a dandy match for Anne Renzetti. Five foot two fits pretty well with five foot seven. He put his hands on Anne's shoulders, kissed her on the cheek, and then with a gesture very much like a magician's best trick, he reached behind him and pulled a large glowing blonde. She topped the good doctor by an inch or two. They both wore the same jack-o'-lantern toothy grin, and over the lobby sounds I heard a portion of his introduction of her: ". . . my wife, Marcie Jean . . ."

Anne's shoulders did not slump. I'll give her that much. And I think her smile stayed pretty much in place, because she was still wearing it when she turned around and came back, leading them toward the desk. I sensed that this was no time to ask for an introduction to the doctor and his bride. Anne kept smiling while the doctor registered. She pointed out the location of his room on a chart. A bellhop went with them to cart their luggage through the gardens to their room.

The two girls behind the desk had arranged to disappear. They recognized the storm warnings. Anne leaned back against the counter, her arms crossed, staring at me and through me, a glare that pierced me through and through, at chest level.

"Honeymoon!" she said in a half whisper. "Big dumb blond dumpling comes out of nowhere and nails him. And I put two bottles of chilled champagne up there in the room. Shit! Hope the shower never stops dripping."

"Pretty hard to stop a good drip in a shower."

She slowly came back to here-and-now and focused on me. She tilted her head a little bit to one side and looked me over with great care. She moistened her lips and swallowed. "What did you say your damn name is? McGee? You are a sizable son of a bitch, aren't you?"

"Wouldn't try to deny it."

She looked at me. She was all a-hum with ready. She was up to the splash rails with electric ready. Everything was working: all the blood and juices from eyeballs to polished toenails.

"You better comfort me with apples, fella. Or is it roses? And stay me with flagons, whatever that means. Always wondered. And for God's sake you better be discreet or it'll undermine any authority I have left around here."

"Appointing me an instrument of revenge?"

"Do you particularly mind?"

"I'm thinking it over."

"Thanks a lot! Take your time. Take four more seconds, damn it."

"Three. Two. One. Bingo."

"My place," she said. "Nineish."

"Try to remember my name."

She tried to smile but the smile turned upside down, the underlip poked out, the eyes filled, and she spun and darted away toward her office, the proud straight back finally curving in defeat.

*   *   *

I was on time, after wondering all the rest of the day whether to show up or not. It made me feel ridiculously girlish. Despite all the new freedoms everybody claims they have, I still feel strange when I am the aggressee. One wants to blush and simper. I was dubious about my own rationalization. She seemed a nice person, and her morale had taken one hell of a scruffing when the Doc had walked in with his surprise bride. What would be the further damage if even the casual semi-stranger didn't want her as a gift?

Anyway, it seemed to me that after a day of thinking about it, she would have cooled on the whole idea. It had been an abrupt self-destructive impulse that had made her proposition me so directly. She might not even be at her cabana on stilts. And if she was there, and if she said she had reconsidered and it was a dumb idea and all, then it would be time for both of us to disengage gracefully.

She was there. A thread of light shone out under her cabana door. When I knocked the light went out, and she came out onto the dark porch, shaded from the starlight, carrying two glasses and the ice bucket, and a towel with which to twist out the champagne cork. She wore dark slacks and a white turtleneck against the night breeze off the Gulf. She said, in too merry a voice, "Champagne for you too, pal, so you shouldn't feel everything is a total loss."

"Second thoughts, eh?"

"Definitely. I don't know what the hell I was thinking of. I mean I do know what I was thinking of, and it wasn't my very best idea. I was wondering a little while ago, what if you arrived all eager and steamy? Would she or wouldn't she?"

"You'll never know. I guessed you'd have second thoughts."

"Thank you. Any friend of Meyer is a friend of mine. Meyer has pretty good taste in friends. Open that good stuff."

I unwound the wire and stood the glasses on the rail, where the starlit sand beyond gave enough light for me to fill them properly. Poured. We clinked glasses.

"To all the dumb dreams that never happen," she said. "And the dumb women who dream them."

"To all the dumb dreams that shouldn't happen, and don't," I said.

She sipped. "You are probably right. Ellis was dying. Prescott Mullen was an authority figure. He was comforting. When you lean on strength, I think you can get to read too much into it."

"I thought you seemed very very happy with your job here."

"Oh, I am! I wouldn't *think* of giving it up. He was going to come down and go into practice here. Another segment of the dumb dream."

We drank, chairs close together. Silences were comfortable. I told her portions of my life, listened to parts of hers. We had some weepy chapters and some glad ones. About five minutes after she had snugged her hand into mine, I leaned over into her chair and kissed lips ripe and hot as country plums, and when that was over she got up, tugged at my wrist, and said in a small voice, "I think I have been talked into it somehow."

* * *

We lay sprawled in the soft peach glow of a pink towel draped around the shade of her bedside lamp, sated and peaceful and somnolent. Big wooden blades of a ceiling fan turned slowly overhead, and I could smell the sea. A passel of marsh frogs were all yelling *gronk* in a garden pond, voices in contrapuntal chorus.

She propped herself on an elbow and ran her fingertips along the six-inch seam of scar tissue along my right side, halfway between armpit and waist.

"How many wars did you say you were in?"

"Only one, and that wasn't done there. That was an angry fellow with a sharp knife, and if I could have had it stitched right away, there wouldn't be hardly any scar."

"You should put out a pocket guidebook."

"Some day I'll arrange a guided tour. Meyer says there isn't enough unblemished hide left to make a decent lampshade."

"Are you accident-prone, darling?"

"I guess you could say that. I am prone to be where accidents are prone to happen."

"Why do you want to ask Prescott about Ellis?"

"I haven't really got anything specific to go on. It's what I do, the way I go about things. If I can get enough people talking, sooner or later something comes up that might fit with something somebody else has said. Sometimes it takes longer than other times, and sometimes it doesn't happen at all. Like finding out last night that whoever beat Esterland to death might have been a motorcyclist, a biker."

"Why would you think that? I don't understand."

So I went through it for her, editing it just enough to take out things that were obviously meaningless. Her arm got tired and she snugged her face into the corner of my throat, her breath warm against my chest. I slowly stroked her smooth and splendid back as I talked, all the way from coccyx to nape and back again.

When I finished, she said, "Well, I guess it is interesting, but I don't see what a motorcycle would have to do with anything, really. The only person I ever met who knew anything at all about motorcycles is Josie's weird friend Peter Kesner."

It startled me. "He rides them?"

"Oh, no! He's what they call out there a genius. He's a double hyphenate."

"A what?"

"No, darling, it is not some form of perversion. He made a couple of motion pictures where he was the writer-director-producer. He made them years ago on a very small budget, and they were what is called sleepers. They made a lot of money, considering what they cost. Maybe you heard of them. One was called *Chopper Heaven* and the other was *Bike Park Ramble*. It was all a kind of realism, you know. He used real tough bike people and hand-held cameras. And they were sort of tragic movies. The critics raved. I saw one of them, I can't really remember which. It was too loud and there were too many people getting hurt.''

She sat straight up and combed her dark hair back with her fingers and smiled down at me.

"Dear, I'm getting chilled. Can you reach the fan switch?'' I turned it off. She reached down and got the end of the sheet and pulled it up over us when she stretched out again.

"You said Kesner is Josephine's weird friend.''

"He came to Stamford with her when Ellis was in the hospital the first time. That's when I met him. He's big, maybe about your size, and from what I could gather from Josie, he's been on every kind of pill and powder and shot ever invented. He was treating Josie like dirt, and she didn't seem to mind a bit. It's hard to carry on a conversation with him. I can't describe it. It's just . . . frustrating. And he's weird-acting. Really weird.''

She kicked at something, then ducked under the sheet and came up with her discarded briefs. She held them to the light and said, "One of my romantic little plans for the good doctor.'' They were white, with a regular pattern of bright red hearts the size of dimes.

"Glad he didn't get a chance to appreciate them.''

"You didn't appreciate them. I got shuffled out of them too quickly.''

"Protesting all the way?''

"Well—not really. Did you notice how fat her face is?''

"What?''

"The bride. A fat face and piggy little eyes.''

"I didn't particularly notice because I was watching you, Annie. I lay there in my trundle bed in the Groveway Motel last night and thought about your pretty legs hiked up on that porch railing until I had to get up and take a cold shower. And then I came dashing down here in my domesticated Mitsubishi. Meyer had told me you had eyes for the doctor, but I didn't want to believe it.''

"Come *on!* Really?''

"Cross my heart. Hope to spit.''

"You know, that makes me feel a lot better about this whole—uh—happenstance.''

"I've really enjoyed happenstancing with you, Miz Renzetti.''

"Always before I felt squeamish about big tall men.''

"And little dark women have not exactly figured large in my erotic fantasies, kid.''

"They might from now on?''

"Front and center.''

"You said enjoyed?''

"I did.''

"Past tense?''

"My dear lady, it is quarter past three in the morning.''

"So?''

"My ramparts are breached, my legions scattered, my empire burned to the ground, my fleet at the bottom of the sea. And you would—''

"Hush,'' she said softly.

And so in time the impossible became at first probable and finally inevitable. As before, I found that through her response she led us into the way she most enjoyed. She was not, as I would have guessed, one of the twitchy ones with tricky, swiveling, kinky little tricks and games, contortionist experimentations. What she wanted, and got, was to be settled into the unlauded missionary position, legs well braced, arms hanging on tight, and there exercise a deep, strong, steady, elliptical rhythm.

*   *   *

She lay sweat-drenched and spent, small face bloated and blurred, mouth puffed and smiling. "There!" she said. She pulled my mouth down for a sisterly kiss. "Everybody to his own bed, darling. Be sneaky, huh?"

By the time I was dressed she was snoring softly. I pulled the sheet and the thin blanket over her and turned off the light. When I went out the door, I made certain it locked behind me. I walked out to the edge of the water, where the small waves lisped and slapped against the sand. A seabird flapped up, honking, startling me.

The hours before dawn are when the spirits are supposed to be lowest. That is when most hospital deaths occur. That is when the labored breathing stops, with a final rattle in the throat. I tried to heap ashes on my head. McGee, your handy neighborhood stud. Always on call. Will provide references. I tried to summon up a smidgin of postcoital depression. But all I could tell about myself, in spite of all introspection, was that I felt content. I felt happy, satisfied, relaxed—with an overlay of a kind of sweet sadness, the feeling you get when you look at a picture of yourself taken with someone long gone on a faraway shore long ago.

6

THE DINING room at Eden Beach had a wing like a small greenhouse, with an opaque roof. Broad-leafed plants in big cement pots provided the illusion of privacy for each table.

I arrived for brunch at one thirty, and while I was still examining the menu, a pair of unordered Bloody Marys arrived, complete with celery stalks for stirring. A few moments later the lady herself arrived and slid into the chair across from me. She looked shy and a bit worn. Her lips were puffy and there were bruised patches under her eyes.

We looked at each other in that moment which has to set the style for the whole relationship. I had guessed that perhaps we would have a bawdy little chat about how we had missed arranging a nooner, and how exhausted the male might be, and how badly lamed the female.

But from the look in her eyes I knew that was not the way to go, and knew that I would have relished that kind of talk as little as she. So I hoisted the glass. "To us."

"To us," she said, and we touched glasses. The drink was spice-hot and delicious.

"It's going to be kind of difficult and awkward, keeping control of my staff, Travis. I really want us to be very very discreet, very careful. This job does mean an awful lot to me."

I smiled at her and said, "You are implying, of course, that these fun and games are going to continue."

She flushed and said, "Don't you want to? I thought we were—"

"Hey! I was afraid you might have second thoughts. Remember, I was sent into the game as a substitute for the doctor."

"That's not fair!" she said angrily. I kept smiling. Anger faded. She laughed. "Well, maybe that was the way it started. Okay. Let's say I got lucky."

"We both got lucky. It has to happen like that sometimes."

She reached and touched my hand, her eyes glowing, then looked and saw a waitress coming and yanked her hand back.

"Look," she said in her business voice, "I have to finish this and run. I really do. I am getting some kind of a short count in supplies, and as it isn't my people, it has to be the wholesaler, and I had him hold the next truck. I have to go down there with my bookkeeper and prove to him he's got thieves in his warehouse. I talked to Prescott Mullen this morning—by the way, he looked kind of shrunken and uninteresting—and gave him your name and told him you were checking out how Ellis got killed and said you'd find him sometime today."

"Thank you."

"We always put a sprig of mint in the half grapefruit. All the time Prescott was talking to me, Marcie Jean stood there smiling, with a piece of mint leaf stuck on her front tooth."

"I've thought it over and decided she does have a fat face."

She patted my hand. "Thank you, dear. You know the old joke about the ideal wife?"

"Deaf and dumb and owns a liquor store?"

"Right. Well, you've got an old lady now that runs a hotel, and she's entitled to put dear friends on the cuff, so you better count on coming across the state at pretty regular intervals, hear?"

She got up, touched a fingertip to my lips, and hurried away.

*   *   *

I found Dr. Prescott Mullen on the beach, sitting in a sling chair under a big blue and white umbrella. The bride was face down in the shade beside him, a towel over her head, her legs and back pinked by fresh sunburn. Her new rings winked in reflected sunlight. I introduced myself and he told me to pull another chair over, but I sat on my heels, half facing him.

"I'm just doing a favor for a friend," I told him. "Ron Esterland is suspicious of the timing. If Ellis had outlived his daughter, a lot of money would have moved in a different direction."

"Some of it to him?" the doctor asked.

"Yes. But I don't think that's the primary motive."

"So what is?"

"Anxiety. Guilt. A sense of loss. He's sorry they didn't get along, and he's sorry his father didn't live to see him make it as a painter."

Prescott Mullen looked thoughtful. "I suppose in some sense it would be an easier murder to justify than if the man was healthy. How many months was he robbed of? If I had to guess, I'd say six at the outside. And the last six weeks would probably not have been what you'd call living."

"What was his attitude toward his illness?"

"He seemed to think of it as a challenge. To him the cancer was an entity, an enemy, a thing that had invaded him and plotted against his life. I was no fan of Ellis Esterland. He was a highly competitive organism. I used to wonder how Anne could put up with him, why she didn't just walk out."

"When did you last see Esterland?"

"Mid-June. About five weeks before he was killed. He looked better than I expected him to look. But he was in pain. He wouldn't admit it. I know he was in great pain."

"How could you tell?"

"Observation. You see a lot of pain, you know what it looks like. Sudden sweats. Quick little intakes of breath. A sudden pallor. I think he could probably handle more pain than most, just out of arrogance and pride. He was a stubborn old man. I knew there would be more coming, and it might get to the point where he couldn't handle it. I tried to get him to admit the pain, and I tried to tell him it would get worse. He told me not to worry about it. He said he was fine. I remember giving him a little lecture about the psychology of pain."

"Would he have arranged to get himself killed rather than admit he was hurting?"

He shook his head slowly. "No, I can't see Esterland in that role. I gave him a lecture about the effects of the hallucinogens on pain. We know now that cannabis can quell the nausea some people feel during chemotherapy and radiology. Cannabis and hashish and LSD have an interesting effect on the subjective experiencing of pain. Intense and continuing pain seems to the patient to be a part of him, something swelling and burning inside of him, taking him over. The hallucinogens have the odd effect of making the pain seem aside and apart from the patient. The pain may be just as intense, but it is, subjectively, off to one side. Pain creates a terrible and consuming anxiety, on some very deep level of the brain. Pain is nature's warning that something is terribly wrong. If anxiety is quelled by any hallucinogen, then pain, though still as intense, becomes less frightening and consuming. That may be the answer. I thought Ellis was fighting the pain relievers because they would dull his wits, dull his perceptions of the world. He wanted to stay just a little brighter than anybody else he knew. I urged him to find a private source for hallucinogens and experiment with them. I explained that it would leave his mind unimpaired but would enable him to handle pain better. I told him that it was the best way for him to get any enjoyment out of the time he had left."

"Did you tell him how long he had left?"

"I told him my guess. That was our relationship from the start. Total candor."

"Maybe the pain got worse and he took your advice and went up there to make a buy. That's why he didn't take Anne or tell her why he was going."

"And somebody cheated him and killed him? Possible. I can tell you that if he did buy something, he would take it secretly, and if it helped, he would never have told Anne or me. It would have been his private solution. It would leave his macho image unimpaired."

"Lovely guy."

"Prince of a fellow," Mullen said, grinning. "McGee, I like your reconstruction. It seems to fit what I read about the circumstances of his death. The news accounts implied he was keeping some kind of appointment at a highway rest stop."

"Did you recommend any particular substance?"

"I think I told him that hashish would be easiest to manage, and probably reasonably available in the Miami area."

"Everything you ever heard of is available in Dade County. But he couldn't get much with two hundred dollars."

"That's all he had?"

"Anne gave out that figure, and she kept the accounts."

"I have the feeling that Ellis Esterland could put his hands on money in one form or another without Anne knowing about it."

"Okay, suppose he was carrying five thousand dollars. If Anne had known that and reported it, the local authorities would have been thinking about a buy that went wrong. There could have been contacts they could have developed. In his condition, at that point in the progression of the disease, how much pain do you think he should have been feeling?"

He thought it over. "Enough to send me running for the needle, whimpering all the way."

The big bride rolled over, clawing the towel off her head, looking blankly and stupidly at the two of us. One nipple showed above the edge of her white bikini top. Prescott Mullen, smiling, reached down and tugged the fabric up to cover her. A few tendrils of russet hair curled out from under the bikini bottom.

"Whassa time, sweetie?" she asked in a small sweet voice.

"Three fifteen, lambikin. This is Travis McGee. My wife, Marcie Jean Mullen."

"Oh, hi," she said. She prodded her pink thigh with an index finger as she sat up, watching how long the white mark lasted. "Honeybun, I better get the hell off the beach. I think the sun kind of reflects in under the umbrella from the sand and sun and stuff." She stood up, yawned, swayed, and then lost her balance when she bent to pick up her towel. She yawned again. "Marcie Jean Mullen. Still sounds strange, huh?" She beamed sleepily at me. "Used to be Marcie Jean Sensabaugh. Hated every minute of it. Be a rotten world if you had to keep the name you were born with." She picked up her canvas bag and looked inside. "I got a key, honeybun. See ya in the room."

"Pretty lady," I said when she was out of earshot. "Congratulations."

"Thanks. She's a great girl. Absolutely perfect disposition. No neuroses. Healthy as the Green Bay Packers. And an absolutely fantastic pelvic structure. She was a delivery-room nurse."

"That's interesting."

"We've talked it over. We want as many kids as we can have. She's twenty-three and I'm thirty-six, and as near as we can tell, she's two months pregnant right now. We agreed not to get married until we were sure we could have kids. I don't want her to have them too close together. It wears a woman out too much. They should be two years apart. Okay, she'll be twenty-four when our first one is born. Her mother had her last baby when she was forty-four. So, with a two-year spacing, we could have nine or ten. Of course, her mother had one set of twins."

"It's nice to see people get their lives all worked out."

"I always wanted a big family. It was a case of finding the right girl before I got too old to enjoy the kids. As it is, if we stay on schedule, the last kid won't get out of college until I'm about seventy-eight."

"That's cutting it pretty close, doctor."

"I guess it is. But I come of long-lived stock. Both of my grandfathers and one of my grandmothers are still living. Late seventies and early eighties."

"It's something to look forward to, all right."

"I think of it as a very precious responsibility. It's really the only immortality we have. Did you ever think of that?"

"I guess I think of it all the time."

"Are you married?"

"No."

"Then you better find a healthy woman right away, Mr. McGee. Or you won't be young enough to enjoy your kids."

I stood up and shook hands with him. "Thanks a lot. That's probably a very good idea. Nice to have had this chat with you, doctor."

"If I can be of any help, please call on me. Funny thing. Ellis was dying and I didn't particularly like the man, but it made me furious that somebody had the gall to kill him. My patient!"

*   *   *

That night in Annie's cabana, she had thrown a pale green towel over the lampshade. It gave the room an underwater look.

The fan overhead made a small ticking sound. The waves were louder. A mockingbird tried silvery improvisations. She was saying, "And so, of course, Sam couldn't believe that any of his people were stealing. It had to be my people. He acted as if he was doing me a big favor, checking that big order item by item. But then the discrepancies began to show up. Short cases, opened and resealed. And his face sagged and his voice got tired. I felt so sorry for him. All his people have been with him for years and years, and he has been so good to them. And it did look as if one person couldn't have done it. It had to be two working together. I got credits on the other shortages we had picked up. He was really depressed when we left. I found myself wishing I wasn't a boss. But not for long. Not for long. You talked with Dr. Mullen, I hear."

"Had a nice chat. Have you got a fantastic pelvic structure?"

"My God! I don't know. You mean for babies. Well, I'd have a little problem, I guess. I always heard I would. My mother had two Cesarian deliveries. Why?"

"Would you be prepared to watch your final child graduate from college when you are sixty-five?"

"Hell, no! He can carry his diploma home to his poor old mom. What *is* this about, darling?"

So I told her the conversation with Prescott Mullen. At first she was incredulous. Was I sure he wasn't joshing? When I convinced her that he was totally serious, deadly serious, in fact, she went into something close to hysteria. That then subsided into a giggling fit, and that turned into hiccups.

"Poor big old brood mare—*hic*—can hear him saying—*hic*—roll over, Marcie Jean—*hic*—time to start number six—*hic*. And I wanted to get myself into a deal like *that?*—*hic*. Oh, God."

I poured her more wine, and she sat on the edge of the bed to drink it out of the far side of the glass, holding it in two hands like a child. There was a pale narrow stripe across her back matching the pallor of her buttocks.

She lay back again, saying, "All gone. Thanks."

"Were you there when he gave Ellis the argument about maybe he should try hash or LSD for pain?"

"Oh, yes. The last time he saw him. In June."

"Did you know Ellis was in pain?"

"I didn't know how much. He'd get up in the night and go up on deck. Sometimes he would get up from a meal and go walking. His face would twist. But he wouldn't let it twist if he knew you were watching. Prescott told me Ellis was probably in a lot of pain. After Prescott had gone back north, I tried to get Ellis to do what he had suggested. But he got angry with me. He wouldn't listen. He said he wasn't going to baby himself. He said he was not going to turn into a junky at the very end of his life. He said it was demeaning."

"After talking it over, both Dr. Mullen and I have the feeling he went up there to Citrus City to make a buy. We think that was what the long-distance phone call was about."

"But wouldn't it take more money than he had?"

"What makes you think he had only two hundred dollars, more or less?"

"But I took checks to the bank! I knew what we had and what we needed. I paid the bills. I made the deposits."

"Let me ask it another way, Annie."

"I've never let anybody else in my life call me Annie except you."

"After he was killed, it was up to you to go through everything on the boat. You and the man from the bank. Tell me this. Did you come across anything —anything at all—which led you to believe that maybe there were some money matters you didn't know about?"

"How did you know about *that?*"

"Know about what?"

"The Krugerrands. Those big gold coins from South Africa, guaranteed one ounce of pure gold in each one."

"I didn't know about them at all. I just had the idea that he was the kind of man who would have to keep secrets from everybody, even you."

"There were ten of them. Worth, I don't know, five or six hundred dollars each at that point. There was no clue as to when or where he got them, or at what price. They were way in the back of the hanging locker, in the pocket of one of his old tweed jackets that he never wore any more. When I lifted it out, it was so fantastically heavy. It made me *so* damn mad, him hiding something like that, like some sneaky little kid. But what has that got to do with anything, dear?"

"Where there were ten, there could have been twenty, or forty. The ten you found were worth from five to six thousand dollars. What if he took half of what he had stashed?"

"Could be. Yes. Yes, damn it! *Damn* him."

"So I'll go on from there, assuming he left half of them home and took half for the buy. And see what I can turn up. And I will look into the question of bikers, hard core."

"How?"

"I have a contact who has good reason to trust me."

"Who?"

"I am very glad you don't mind me calling you Annie."

"I see. Okay. When are you leaving, dearest?"

"Midmorning, I guess."

She dipped a finger in her remaining half inch of Moselle and drew a slow circle on my chest. "Hmmm," she said.

"Hmmm what?"

"I guess everybody has heard that ancient joke about how do porcupines make love."

"Very very carefully," I said.

She reached and set her empty glass aside. Her eyes danced. "So?"

I gathered her in. "Let me know if it gets to be not careful enough."

7

WHEN I arrived back in Lauderdale the next morning at eleven o'clock I turned the little car in at the airport and taxied back to Bahia Mar. After I dumped the laundry in the hamper aboard the *Flush,* showered, and changed to a fresh white knit shirt and khaki slacks, I checked the houseboat over to see if the phone was dead, or the batteries, or the freezer. I was hungry, and I decided I'd go over to the Beef 'n' It for their big sirloin—decided to walk over, as the miles in the little car had made me feel cramped. I fixed a Boodles on ice in one of the heavier old-fashioned glasses and carried it up to the sun deck to stand and survey what I could see of the yacht-basin world.

I looked over toward the ships'-supplies place and was surprised to see the familiar lines and colors of Aggie Sloane's big Trumpy. I locked up and walked down there, glass in hand. There was a mild fresh breeze off the Atlantic that fluttered the canopy over the little topside area where Meyer and Aggie were hunched over a backgammon board.

I hailed them, and Aggie invited me aboard. I went up and took a chair and said, "Go ahead. I don't want to interrupt the game."

She said, "It might just be over. Meyer, take a look at this." She picked up the big doubling cube from her side of the board and plunked it down on his side. The number on top was 16.

Meyer studied the board for a long time. He wore a sour expression. He sighed. "Too slim," he said. "No, thanks. Travis, if I take the double, she just might close her board on this roll."

"Class tells," said Aggie, marking the score pad.

"Aggie," I said, "you look fantastic."

In her husky baritone she said, "Just because I had a few more tucks taken in this sagging flesh? Just because I got back down to one thirty? Just because I do one solid hour of disco every morning, starko, behind locked doors? Just because my hair is longer, and this is the best tint I've had in years, and my new contacts are this nice lavender color, and I'm off the booze, and after three years of shame I've been able to get back to bikinis? Thank you, darling McGee. I think I do look rather fantastic, comparatively speaking. I went through all this hell as a special present for good old Meyer.''

"Good old Meyer appreciates it, dear lady,'' he said. "It all fills me with awe. But I think you did it for the sake of your own morale.''

"Why is he so often right?'' she asked me.

"Because he is Meyer. It's a character flaw. What are you doing here anyway?''

She looked exasperated. "We are waiting for some kind of a turbo-seal whatsit that has to be flown down from Racine. It blew yesterday. Made a noise like a gigantic fart. My dear little captain will not proceed without it. Some sort of fetish, no doubt. It is going to shorten our little cruise, maybe down to no cruise at all. But what the hell. Lovely place here. Not a trace of mal de mer. Of course, it does work out a bit more pricey than a hotel suite. But the two dear little papers I added to the chain last year are churning out money you wouldn't believe. It's almost vulgar what you can make these days out of a monopoly morning paper in a city of forty thousand people, after you really get into automation and electronics and all.''

"Jay Gould would have loved her,'' Meyer said.

"Foo,'' she said. "My taste would have run more to Diamond Jim Brady. Or John Ringling.''

"How did you make out?'' Meyer asked me.

"The doctor arrived,'' I said. "With a new bride. Blond. With a fantastic pelvis.''

Meyer looked startled and then amused. "Not according to Anne's plan at all. So you were the catcher in the awry.''

"Please!'' Aggie said. "Not when I'm thinking of eating. I'll go down and make sure they are fixing enough for three.''

"I can't stay, Aggie. Really.''

"Nonsense, dear boy. I would really resent it if you left. Today we are eating Greek. With the feta cheese, the moussaka, the grape leaves, and all. And they always fix tons, so there'll be enough for them too.''

She went off belowdecks. I said, "That has really turned into some kind of special lady.''

"Always was, had you but the eyes. How is Anne?''

"Recovering from the shock. She really runs one of the better places around. Anyway, I can give you a very quick rundown of the facts and hunches so far. Ellis was hurting badly, refused to admit it. The doctor tried to talk him into one of the hallucinogens to moderate pain. Good chance pain was getting worse. Ellis set up some kind of contact. They called back with a time and place for the meet. He went up there with a batch of Krugerrands to pay for his hash or fix or whatever. Traces found of a heavy motorcycle in the shrubbery. Possibility that the vendor, confronted with an elderly fellow, decided to keep the product and the money both. Or perhaps it was a scam from the beginning. Come to the place alone, Dads. Or no sale. Knowing there would be no sale anyway. Oh, one more thing, which may or may not fit: Josie's boyfriend, since the separation, is one Peter Kesner, weird cinematic genius who made two motorcycle movies on small budgets and got a big reputation. I mention it only because motorcycles have started cropping up. I thought I might go see my friend Blaylock about people who peddle from their bikes. I mean, if it's a common practice or what. I can see the advantages. Narcs can stake out street corners, but they can't stake out the countryside."

"Why so far upstate?" Meyer asked.

"That's a question for Blaylock. It might be a territorial thing."

Aggie came back up and said it would be twenty minutes. We fixed another drink from the little rolling bar. It was nice under the awning, watching the pedestrian traffic, laughing at bad puns. We went below and ate in the alcove off the main lounge, served there by a very skilled Cuban lad. A slightly resinous wine went beautifully with the mountains of Greek groceries. I left in good season, full of resolve. But once I was aboard my houseboat, my knees began to buckle. I nearly dislocated my jaw yawning. I stripped down and fell into my gigantic bed.

The rattlesnake buzz of the bedside phone awakened me and I groped for the phone in the dark, wondering how it had gotten to be night.

"Uh?" I said.

"Well, hi! Were you asleep?"

"Certainly was. What time is it?"

"Little after nine. Missed you, love."

"Me too."

"Wondered if you made it back okay. Tell you the truth, I found time for a little nap today myself."

"Good for you."

"I know you will be as upset as I am to know that the bride picked up another dreadful sunburn this morning and is in bed with chills. And terrible little runny blisters all over her big meaty thighs."

"You are a mean one, aren't you?"

"Not really. I feel sorry for both of them. As a doctor, he should have seen what was happening to her and gotten her out of the sun."

"Interrupted honeymoon."

"I had a drink with him before dinner. She was sleeping, finally. I really looked at him and listened to him. You know, he is a very good-natured, sweet, earnest, solemn, dull little fellow. He chuckles a lot, but he hasn't any sense of humor. He laughs in the wrong places. Really, he's a *very* good doctor. Practically any cancer clinic in the world, you go in and mention Dr. Prescott Mullen . . . Travis, I just don't know how there got to be such a difference between what I thought he was and what he really is."

"Myths. Meyer says we build our own myths. We live in the flatlands and the myths are our mountains, so we build them to change the contours of our lives, to make them more interesting."

"I haven't had such a dull life so far. I invested some of my very good years in Ellis, of course."

"Right now is your very best year, maybe."

"I see what Meyer means about myths. I mean you take some bored little suburban wife who plays bridge at the club every Thursday, she can dream that she and her tall brown tennis pro have something going, something unannounced, that they can never dare admit to each other. And that's her myth. If she tries to carry it to the point of its actually happening, it will blow up in her face.''

"Like that, I guess.''

"And right across the front of her, just above the cleavage, she's got a lot more of those runny little blisters. Hey, Travis?''

"What?''

"I didn't call you up to talk about the blisters on the doctor's bride. I had something profound to say. About us. Now it sounds trivial, I guess. The point is, I don't really want to think about us, about you and me, in the way I thought I would always have to think about somebody I was falling in love with.''

"Love, Annie?''

"Let me just barge ahead and leave explanations until later, okay? Being in love has been to me a case of being up to here in plans. Whatever you might think, I wasn't being some kind of opportunist with Ellis. He was a very autocratic man, and he was very very experienced as far as women are concerned. I was dumb about him, and it is still sort of blank in my mind the way he hustled me into bed that first time. Then a person says, Oh, hell, whatever harm is done is done, and you get hung for a sheep as high as for being hung as a lamb. I think it goes like that. And I got to love him. He was a dear man in lots of little ways nobody knew about because he kept himself so much to himself. But let me tell you that anybody who had the wives he had certainly wasn't an unattractive man. I hope you are following all this. Anyhow, with love came plans. I worked it all out. Some day he would divorce Josie and marry me, and do it soon enough so I could have a child with him, and the child would make him a warmer person to be with. Then came the news about the cancer, and so that plan was shot to hell. Right? So there was another plan. I would nurse him and care for him and he would live a long time, and the sickness would purify him. It would burn away the nasty. Then he was killed and I was really down. But I put my life back together, and I am a very fulfilled woman, businesswise. Now here I am falling in love, and I don't find myself planning anything about us, and that makes me wonder if it is love, really. All I think about is that maybe our lives are like the end of some long period of planning. I am here and you are there, and we are going to see each other now and again until we are too old and rickety to make it across Florida. But I know I am falling in love because I think of you and I turn hollow inside, and the world kind of veers. You know? Like it goes a little bit sideways for an instant. Hey, I wanted to tell you all this as if it was something important. And when I stop talking to you, I don't want you to feel any kind of obligation to say anything about love. Men hate being pinned to the wall like that. If you feel it, someday you'll say it, and that will be okay. And if you don't ever feel it, that will be okay too, as long as you don't ever try to fake it.''

"Listen, I—''

"Don't say anything, dear. I can talk enough for two. Any time. Anywhere. So go back to sleep. Good night.'' *Click.*

I reached and put the phone back. We had been hooked together for a time by General Tel, and the softness of her voice in my ear in the darkness had recreated for me a world long forgotten, when I had stretched out on the leather couch in the hallway, phone on my juvenile chest, and while the family was in the next room listening to the radio, to Fred Allen or Amos and Andy, I was linked to the erotic, heart-stopping magic of leggy Margaret who, at fourteen, kissed with her eyes wide wide open.

I remembered the previous night when, with her head resting on my chest, Anne had stared off into some thoughtful distance. I could look down and see the black lashes move when she blinked. I could see a tiny slice of the gelatinous eyeball. You can repeat a word over and over until it means nothing, until it becomes just a strange sound. You can do the same thing looking at a familiar object until you see it in an entirely different way. Here was a strange wet globe, a shifting moving thing of fluids and membranes and nerves, tucked into muscle that could move it this way and that, that could shutter its lid to remove any dust, to moisten the surface of it. It had looked at me and relayed images of me into the gray suet of the brain behind that eye, where they would remain, instantly available whenever she remembered me. I stroked the dark hair. The wet eye blinked again. The dreaming thoughts behind it were unfathomable. I could never truly reach them, hers or anyone's. And mine would always be as opaque to others.

The phone rang again and she said, "I was so darn busy exposing my beautiful soul, Travis, I forgot to tell you another thing I called about."

"Such as?"

"I talked with Prescott about the drugs for Ellis. He told me that after he got back to Stamford he had a call from Josie. She knew he had flown down to check Ellis over, and she called to find out how he was. He told her what he thought Ellis's life expectancy was, and it depressed her. He knew that Josie still had a certain amount of influence with Ellis, so he told her to tell Ellis that there was really no point in being so damned brave about his pain and to encourage him to make a connection and buy something. I think she must have tried to do that, because in early July he had several calls from her, and they all made him cross. Crosser than usual. He just didn't like people meddling in his life."

"But it was okay if he meddled in theirs."

"Exactly. That's just how he was. You know, you are really very good at sizing up people. It makes me nervous, in a way."

"Exactly how?"

"Well . . . anybody who is really good at reading people can be very good at finding the areas where they are vulnerable and then taking advantage of that vulnerability. You know what I mean."

"I will have to get Meyer to explain me to you."

"Can't you do that yourself?"

"Not as well as he can. According to him I take all emotional relationships much too seriously."

"It is very nice for a person to be taken seriously."

"I had this same conversation with a girl named Margaret before you were born. She was fourteen. She wanted to be taken seriously."

"And did you?"

"To the point where I couldn't eat and I walked into the sides of buildings."

"I'm jealous of her. And so, good night again, my love."

Once again she hung up quickly, before I could equivocate.

Meyer says that if I could, for once and all, stop my puritanical ditherings about emotional responsibility, I would be a far happier and less interesting man. In childhood I was taught that every pleasure has its price. As an adult I learned that the reprehensible and dreadful sin is to hurt someone purposely, for no valid reason except the pleasure of hurting. Gretel, in her wisdom about me, said one night, "You are never entirely *here*. Do you know that? You are always a little way down the road. You are always fretting about consequences instead of giving yourself up totally to the present moment."

Add those ingredients together and stir well, and you can come up with a lasting case of psychological impotence. Meyer said to me, "You spend too much time in the wings, watching your performance onstage, aching to rewrite your own lines, your own destiny."

"And just what the hell is my destiny?"

I can never forget his strange smile. "It is a classic destiny. The knight of the windmills. The man rolling the stone up the mountain. The endlessness of effort, Travis, so that the effort becomes the goal."

Right, in a sense. But Meyer is not all that infallible. There are times. Annie had been totally *now*. An immersion. So vital and hungry I had no need to be the man in the wings. I turned on the handy projector in the back of my head and ran through a box of slides, of still shots of her in the underwater green of the towel over the bed lamp, when she was biting into her lip and her eyes were wide and thoughtful, and she was shiny with the mists of effort. Being the neurotic that Meyer believes I am has the advantage of giving me a far narrower focus of pleasure than if I did not truly give a damn. The *now* is that unexpected, unanticipated place where the mind and the body and the emotions all meet in a proper season, destroying identity, leaving only an intensity of pleasure that celebrates all parts of that triad: body, mind, and spirit.

It is the difference maybe between gourmet and gourmand. In a world of fast food chains, the gourmet seldom eats well. But this again is too much of a celebration of sensitivity: "Oh, my God, look at how vulnerable and sensitive I am!" Which becomes a pose. And turns one into that kind of gourmet who looks for sauces instead of meat.

The only suitable attitude toward oneself and the world is the awareness of pathetic, slapstick comedy. You go staggering around the big top and they keep hitting you with bladders, stuffing you into funny little cars with eighteen other clowns, pursuing you with ducks. I ride around the sawdust trail in my own clown suit, from L. L. Bean's end-of-season sale: marked-down armor, wrong size helmet, swaybacked steed, mended lance, and rusty sword. And sometimes with milady's scarf tied to the helmet, whoever milady might be at the time of trial.

Meyer has pointed out that condition, that contradiction, which afflicts everyone who thinks at all: The more you strive to be sensible and serious and meaningful, the less chance you have of becoming so. The primary objective is to laugh.

8

FRIDAY MORNING I drove the Rolls pickup up past Deerfield Beach, turned inland on 887, and after nine miles of nothing much, I came to Ted Blaylock's Oasis, looking not much shabbier than the last time I had seen it.

The long rambling frame structure paralleled the highway, obviously built a piece at a time over a long period. Most of it had a galvanized roof. The sign out at the edge of the right-of-way had been assembled in the same manner, one piece at a time. THE BIKER-BAR. Happy Hours 3 to 7. *Customizing—Trikes, Shovels, and Hogs.* Chili and Dogs. *Service on Carbs, Brakes, Tires, Spokes, Tanks, Frames, and Springers.* Tank art. Body Art. *Paraphernalia.*

I could look right through the open shed structure at one end, and it looked as though Ted had put up some more cabins out back. Men were working in the cement-floor shed, and I heard the high whine of metal being ground down. One portion had a display window with decals of trade names pasted on it and racks of shiny chrome accessories visible between the decals, next to some motorcycles in rank, new and shiny bright. There were some dusty motorcycles parked in front of the center part, in no particular pattern, along with a couple of big brutish pickups, on top of their oversized tires, and a rack with a few bicycles. As I got out of the car, somebody dropped a wrench and it rang like a bell as it bounced off the floor.

I went in through the screen door and it slapped shut behind me. Ceiling fans were whirring overhead. The combination bar and lunch counter stretched across the back of the room, with a dozen stools bolted to the floor in front of it. There were a half dozen wooden tables, each big enough for four chairs. There were new posters behind the bar, big bright gaudy ones, showing semi-clad young ladies who, according to their expressions, were having orgasmic relationships with the motorcycles over which they had draped themselves. Another poster showed a cop beating on a biker's skull and had the bid red legend ABATE.

Three of the brotherhood were on barstools, all big, all fat, all bearded. They wore sleeveless tank tops, denim vests with lots of snaps and pockets and zippers, ragged jeans, boots, a jungle of blue tattooing on their big bare arms, and wide leather wristlets, studded on the outside of the wrists with sharp metal points. Their vests were covered with bright patches and faded patches, celebrating various runs, meets, and faraway clubs. Their helmets were on a table behind them. All three heads were going thin on top but had long locks down almost to the shoulders.

They stopped talking and gave me the look. It is supposed to instill instant caution, if not terror. The girl behind the counter gave me a different kind of look, empty as glass. She was apparently part Seminole, thin as sticks, wearing white jogging shorts with red trim and a tight cotton T-shirt with, between the widespread banty-egg lumps of little breasts, the initials F.T.W.

I said to her, "Ted around?"

"Busy."

"You want to tell him McGee wants to see him?"

"When he's through in there, okay?"

"Coffee, then. No cream." I took the end stool, and the mighty threesome lost interest in me and went back to their conversation.

"Well, what that dumb fucker did, he put in that time pulling out what he had and fittin' in them Gary Bang pistons and that Weber carb and all, and when he got it all done, that shovel wasn't worth shit. Man, he couldn't hardly get out of his own way. We come down from Okeechobee first light Sunday, rammin' it all the way, heads all messed up from that shit Scooter was mixing with ether, Whisker and me racing flat out. I come in maybe fifteen seconds behind Whisker and we could have took naps before Stoney come farting in. After all that work on it, he was so fuckin' mad, he jumped off'n it and just let it fall. And then he run around it and kicked it in the saddle, screaming at it, and he was still so mad he run over to a tree and swung on it and cracked his middle knuckle and got a hand that swole up like a ball. We like to had a fit laughing. That old boy just ain't handy, and that's all there is to it."

"Hey," said the one in the middle, "we got to move it, you guys. See you around, Mits."

"Sure thing, Potsie. Have a nice day, guys."

They worked their helmets on as they walked out, swung aboard, and started their engines, and after some deep *garoong-garoong-garoong* revvings they went droning and popping out onto the empty highway, turning toward the west, riding three abreast.

Mits gave me sly slanty glances as she cleaned the counter where they had been. I said, "Wouldn't hurt to just let him know."

"You selling anything?"

"I'm an old friend."

She shrugged and went out. She was back quickly. "Hey, you can go in. He asked her and she said it was okay you could watch."

"Watch what?"

"He's into body art, and this one is kinda pukey, but it's what she wants, I guess. Go on through to the second room there."

When I opened the door and went in and shut it behind me, Ted looked up from his work and said our traditional greeting. "Hi, sarge."

"How you, lieutenant?"

"Come see what you think of this."

He had his wheelchair rolled up close to a cot which was elevated on four concrete blocks. A doughy broad-faced young girl lay on the cot. Her denim shorts were on a nearby chair. She wore a yellow T-shirt, and she was naked from the waist down. Ted had his tray of needles and dyes close at hand. There was a broad strip of masking tape placed to keep her big dark bush of pubic hair pulled down out of the way so that he could start his design right at the hair roots. It was almost done. It was a pattern of three mushrooms, growing up that white-as-lard lower belly, chubby romanticized mushrooms, the kind under which would squat a Disney elf. There was a book open nearby with a color drawing of three mushrooms growing in a cluster. Ted had simplified the drawing somewhat.

He went to work. The girl compressed her lips and closed her eyes. The needle machine buzzed. The window air conditioner rattled and thumped. She snorted and her belly muscles quivered.

"It's wearing off again," she said. "Jesus!"

"Almost through. Hang on."

It took about five minutes more. The buzzing stopped. He caught a corner of the tape and ripped it free.

"Ouch! Goddamn it, that hurt!"

"Stop being such a baby, Lissa. Go look at yourself."

She swung her legs off the couch and slipped down to the floor and walked over to a narrow wall mirror. She had a white hippo rump, a bushel of meat jiggling and flexing as she walked. She stared at herself and giggled and said, "Wow. This's gonna blast ol' Ray right out of his skull."

"I can believe it," Ted said.

She came walking back and picked up her shorts. Before she put them on she gave me a speculative look and said, "Whaddaya think?"

"Well, I'd say it's unusual."

"You bet your ass it's unusual. And I got your word of sacred honor, right, Ted? Nobody else gets the same thing?"

"Not from me, they don't. Even if they get down on their knees and beg."

She put her shorts on and fastened the snaps.

He said, "Here, I forgot. Rub this into the design now and when you go to bed and in the morning. It's an antiseptic cream. For three or four days. Don't forget. No, go in the can and do it, hon. I'm a little tired of looking at you."

She shrugged and left, slinging her big plastic purse over her plump shoulder.

When the door shut, Ted said, "Play your cards right, Trav, and you could cut a piece of that." He rolled himself over to the sink with his tray of equipment.

" 'Mirror, mirror, on the wall. Who's the fairest one of all?' I think I'd be overcome by all that gentle beauty. You know, you're pretty good at that, Blaylock."

"Necessity is the mother of income. Tattooing is very very big lately. You should see my dragons and snakes. The mushrooms took a little over an hour. For eighty bucks. I've got one crazy broad for a customer, I've put over a thousand dollars' worth of dye under her hide. Very strange stuff. No anesthetic cream for her. The thing for her is that the pain of the needle is a turn-on. It's all a marine motif. Dolphins and pirates and old ships, mermaids, things like that. I wish you could see her. Unlike dumpy little Lissa, she's got a hell of a nice bod. Too nice for what she's having done to it."

I sat down beside his desk, and when he came rolling over I got a better look at him. He was even thinner than before. His color was bad and his thinning hair looked dead.

"You feeling all right?" I asked.

"Not too damn wonderful. Like they told me in the beginning, I'm severed so high up, I got what they called a limited life expectancy."

"Where's Big Bess?"

"Well, there was a very very flashy Colombiano pistolero came in, and he really took to her, she being about twice his height and weight, and she was tired of waiting on a paraplegic crip, so now he has her stashed down in the Hotel Mutiny there, eating chocolates and watching the soaps, while he is out around town gunning down the competition. But I've got Mits, my little Indian, and she is a wonder. She's quicker and better and a lot cleaner than Bess. And my God, that little bod is strong. She can pick me right up and walk with me. Loyal as hell. I wonder why I put up with Bess for so long. Or she with me."

"Business going okay?"

"Real well. I really like this body-art work."

"You draw pretty pictures."

"That was what I was going to be, several thousand years ago. I had two years at Parsons." I knew we were both thinking of what had come after that. Basic training, OCS, battlefield promotion, and finally a morning of hard cold rain and incoming mortar fire when I had helped carry the litter down the hill and prop it in the weapons carrier.

"In the VA hospital," he said, "I did a lot of sketches of the guys. I wanted to try to be a commercial artist—not enough mobility to make it. Then this came along. I studied up, mail-ordered the gear, started practicing on my friends. It's a gas. Want one on the arm? Eagle? Anchor? Hi, Mom? Semper Fidelis? F.T.W?"

"No, thanks a lot. I always figure a tattooed man either got so sloppy drunk he didn't know what was happening, or he needed to have a tattoo to look at to reassure himself he was manly. That F.T.W. is what's on the T-shirt out there, on Mits. What is it?"

"It's been around awhile, Trav. It's the outlaw biker's creed. It stands for Fuck the World."

"Oh."

"Something special on your mind?"

"I shouldn't come out here and ask for favors."

"This is the second time in . . . what is it? . . . Anyway, lots of years. I just hope to hell there's something I *can* do."

I leaned back and rested the heel of one boat shoe on the corner of his desk. "What I need to know is how much the bike clubs are into the drug traffic."

He closed his eyes for a moment. It accentuated the death look of the long bones of his skull. "So far, the question is too loose. The answer is too complicated."

"Ramble a little."

"Well, take the Fantasies. The insignia is the black fist and the yellow lightning, with a red circle around it. With the local affiliated clubs they could maybe put five to six hundred machines on the road, as against the two thousand the Bandidos could mount out west. Now most of these guys are factory workers and warehousemen and mechanics and such. They have meets and shows, smoke pot, wear the sincere raggedy garments and heavy boots, get tattooed, sport a lot of chains and medals, grow big bushy beards, zoom around on weekends with their so-called foxy ladies hanging on behind, drink a lot of beer, smoke a lot of pot, blow coke. What they have, Trav, is a kind of brotherhood hang-up. Anybody is in trouble, they all help. They look a hell of a lot nastier than they are. It's a charade. You get hard with them, they'll stomp you flat into the ground. But if there's no provocation, they have nothing to prove.

"Now as to trafficking in drugs, the story is a little different. There are the club officers, with what the law calls no visible means of support. The officers are the link between the troops and the drug importers and distributors, the money washers, the mafia accountants. Now say we take some group leader captain, call him Mother Machree, and he gets hold of one of the troops, Tom Baloney, and he tells Tom that when he gets off work at the body shop he is to go to the corner of First and Main and sit idling his engine and somebody will hand him a package, and he's to run it up to such and such a corner in Hialeah, weaving around through the back streets, shaking any tail, and get there at seven on the nose and hand it to the woman in the red dress who asks him how many miles he gets to the gallon in that thing he's riding."

"What's the payoff to Baloney?"

"That's one of the points I want to make. He gets the knowledge that he has been full of brotherhood and loyalty, and he knows that Mother Machree will toss five hundred bucks into the pot for the next beer bust. But the troops are getting restless. They know that maybe Mother got six thou for setting up that foolproof run, and there's the feeling around that maybe the officers are getting too far into the business. Some of them have taken to wearing the corporation garments, blow-dry hairstyles, limos with Cuban drivers. Too much separation between the officers and the troops. That is the kind of bitching I hear. They are being used, and they know it."

"Do any of the troops do any retailing on their own?"

"It could happen, but I don't think it would be a big thing. It really wouldn't go with the image they try to project. It would have to be a situation where there was a heavy cash-flow problem, a man out of work. Or maybe a favor for a friend."

"Suppose a man in Lauderdale got a call that somebody would meet him at such and such a time way up the line, over a hundred miles away. And when he went up there to buy, the man who called him wasted him, and though there were no witnesses, maybe the machine the biker was using was identified as to make."

"Recently or way back?"

"Two years in July."

"That's very heavy action, Sergeant McGee. What kind of machine?"

I dug the piece of paper out of my shirt pocket. "The man who saw the track says it was the rear K-One-twelve of a set of ContiTwins, deep enough to indicate a quarter-ton machine, so he guessed a BMW Nine-seventy-two."

"Pretty reasonable guess. But it could have been an HD, or a Gold Wing Honda, or a Kawasaki KZ series, or a big Laverda or Moto Guzzi, or a GS series Suzuki, or an XS series Yamaha. All burly machines. Big fast bastards. But sweet and smooth. You almost can't stress them. And they could all wear ContiTwins. Where did it happen?"

"Up near Citrus City, on the turnpike. A Man named Esterland who was dying of cancer."

"I think I remember news on the tube about that. Sure. But there wasn't any mention of drugs or bikes."

"Not enough to go on, so it didn't get in."

"Where do you come in, Trav?"

"A little favor for the guy's son. Ron Esterland. By the way, he's an artist too. Had a big sellout show in London."

"Hey, I know the name. Didn't make the connection. Saw some color plates of his work in *Art International*. Pretty much okay."

"So what should I do next?"

"I don't understand why the buy should have been set up so far out in the boonies. But I can tell you that any one of those kinds of horses I named would be owned by somebody known to the brotherhood. Up by Citrus City and from there on up, it's a different turf. Up there you've got the Corsairs. But there's a lot of interclub contact, when bikers from both clubs go to out-of-state rallies and rendezvous. I think that maybe, if it was nearly two years ago, it's become part of the legend."

"How so?"

"Trav, these people go back to a kind of tribal society. Myths and legends. Whoever was involved would keep his mouth shut and make his woman keep her mouth shut. But after a long time there's not much heat involved. Maybe his woman has switched riders. With lots of beer and grass and encampments in the night, the word gets out. A little here and a little there, and it gets built up into something a lot wilder and more romantic than it was. Do you understand?"

"Sure. I think so."

"If you can find a legend that seems to fit and then unravel it all the way back to the way things really were, you can maybe—just maybe—come up with a name. And even that won't mean much. It'll be a biker name: Skootch or Grunge or BugBoy. And there's turnover among the troops. Some get into heavy action and get put away. Some of them, when the fox gets pregnant, decide to pack up and get out."

"Can you find out if there's a legend about Esterland?"

"I can listen. I can poke around a little but not much, because it makes these people nervous. I get along fine because I carry good merchandise, and my people do good work, and the prices are right, and the law has never learned a thing out here. And if you learn anything from me about that little party . . ."

"You don't need to say it. Now, something else. A couple of biker movies a few years ago. *Chopper Heaven. Bike Park Ramble.*"

"Saw them when they came on the cable. What do you want? Some kind of critique?"

"Whatever."

"The outlaw bikers came off meaner and nastier than they are as far as tearing up civilians is concerned. And they came off a little more clean and pure than they are the way they act within the group. Enough stimulation, and they can get into gang-bang situations. And if anybody finks to the law, man or woman, they can be a long slow time dying in the piney woods. Technically there were very few mistakes. A lot less than usual. I understand they used outlaw bikers as technical advisers. The sound track was too loud. And those pack leaders were just a little bit too evil to be real. They came out close together, those two movies, at least five years ago. Probably seven years ago. The straight clubs are still bitching about those movies because they think the civilians can't tell the difference between outlaw and straight. I see they still run them on syndication, late at night. Why do you ask?"

"Ted, I'm just rummaging around in this thing, kicking stones, shaking the bushes. The fellow who wrote and produced and directed those two movies stood to maybe get hold of a lot of money due to the killing of Esterland."

"How could that be, for God's sake?"

"Esterland's daughter was dying, in a coma. No chance of recovery. If Esterland survived her, most of the money would go to a foundation. If he died first, the daughter would get it; and then it went to the mother, who was still legally married to Esterland, on the death of her daughter a couple of weeks later. And that movie person, Peter Kesner, is or was close to Mrs. Esterland."

"Way way out there on the end of a long stick, pal."

"For two and a half mil, net, you can think up some very strange things. People will take a lot of pains over that kind of money."

"Did Kesner need money that bad?"

"I'll probably go out there and see what's going on. I haven't really decided. I'm on expenses, but I don't want to waste my friend's money."

"I heard over the grapevine you'd tapped out, Trav."

"In what way?"

"The quiet life. The straight life. Peddling boats or some damn thing. Heard you got scuffed up and turned into a nine-to-five person. When I heard it, I said there was no way. I said you were too used to conning the world, knocking heads, saving maidens. I said that you could lose an arm and a foot and an ear, but when they rang the bell, you'd still slide down the pole and hop onto the truck."

"Meyer said the same thing, but in a slightly different way."

"How is that old egghead?"

"As hairy and belovèd as ever. He's being entertained by a chain of small newpapers."

"That's nice."

"You'll be in touch?"

"I get even a whisper, I'll give you a call. Look, send Mits on in with a Doctor Pepper. Thanks."

I went out and found her rinsing glasses and told her what Ted wanted. She nodded and I said, "He doesn't look too great."

She straightened up and turned to face me. "He isn't too great. That's for sure. These last weeks, he's been going down. It makes me nervous."

"Can you get him looked at?"

"I've tried. You better goddam believe it."

"I believe it. He is a strange and special guy."

"I know."

"He's very fond of you, Mits."

"I know that too."

"Look, here's my number. Any real bad turn, you can phone me and I'll be out here with a doctor."

"You can't get a doctor to make a house call."

"How much would you like to bet?"

The shiny black eyes looked me over, and suddenly the impassive brown face broke into a big smile that wrinkled the nose and squeezed the eyes almost shut. "No bet. Thanks."

When I went out, there were two large bikers staring into the front of my pickup. They had opened it up.

"Something I can do for you?"

They turned to stare at me. Whiskers and hair and hard little eyes, like professional villain wrestlers.

"That's a Merc you got in there, right?"

"Close. It's a big Lincoln."

"Custom heads?"

I edged past them and closed the hood. "Yes, and some other goodies."

"What'll it do?"

"Absolutely no idea."

"Too chicken to take it all the way?"

"Not exactly. The needle sits against the pin at one twenty."

"Why do you keep the outside looking like shit?"

"I wasn't aware that it did."

One looked at the other and said in a higher voice, "He wasn't aware that it did. Look, you use it to run something? Is that why it looks cruddy?"

"Right now, I run myself home. Okay?"

The near one grabbed me by the arm and pulled me back as I started to step onto the running board. "Maybe you're not through answering questions, Ace."

It made me feel tired. I took his hand off my arm. "Friend, it has been nice having our little chat here. I do not want any childish hassling. Nobody has to prove anything. Okay?"

The screen door opened and Ted came wheeling out onto the concrete walk. He said, "Hey, Mike. Hey, Knucks. What's happening?"

"You know this guy?"

"I know him. So?"

"Do you know he's got a smart mouth and a funny-looking truck?"

"My sincere recommendation, Knucks, would be don't mess with him."

"Don't mess with Ace here? You kidding? This cat is over the hill."

I looked at Ted, wondering why he was setting me up. I said, "What are you trying to do?"

He shrugged. "It's been dull around here, sarge. And good old Knucks here has a nasty habit of trying to grope Mits every time she walks by."

With an inward sigh I moved a few inches farther out of range. I'd been working out faithfully of late, and was right at two-oh-five, which is a very good weight for my six foot four. I look as if I would go about one eighty. The big advantage I had over these too-lardy fellows was a great deal of quick. Quick is what counts. Without the quick, they get to hit you in the face, and that is both demeaning and discouraging. Also, it hurts a lot. The secondary advantage is, or course, quite a few years of scrabbling around, learning that the healthiest attitude is to inflict maximum pain in minimum time.

And the way to create an opening is to create rage. I smiled at them.

"Knucks? Ah, *you* are Knucks. You better recheck your tendency to grope the ladies. You look faggoty to me, pal."

He came roaring and swinging, big roundhouse right and left blows, too smart to be a headhunter. At least not yet. He wanted to cave my ribs in first. I trotted about twenty feet backward, just out of range, and when I estimated he had picked up enough speed to compensate for the heft of him, I clapped both hands on his right wrist, rolled backwards, got my feet into his belly just as he was tumbling over me, and gave him a very brisk hoist, while still clinging to the wrist. He whomped the dust like a sack of sand dropped off the top of a building. As I released him, rolled to the side, and came up, I guessed from the sound of impact that good old Knucks was out of the game.

I focused on Mike, coming at me at a half run, right fist cocked. I had time to decide whether to go under it, inside it, or outside it. Outside seemed best, but he waited so long I had to do a Muhammed Ali lean to get my face the final inch out of the way. I felt the breeze of it. He ran on by and was just starting to turn when I heel-stomped him in the back of the knee. He went down and came up, fighting for balance, arms spread wide. I hopped very close, braced my right heel, and pivoted so as to put my hips, back, shoulder, and arm into a very short straight right that went wrist deep into the bulge a few inches above his very fancy brass belt buckle.

He lay down in a fetal position and began throwing up. Knucks was sitting up cradling his right arm. His face was all screwed up like a schoolyard child trying desperately not to cry. His arm came out of the shoulder at a slightly unusual angle.

Ted said, "You're not getting older. You're getting better."

"They might not take kindly to all this, later on."

"You heard me advise them not to mess with you."

"They are fat and they are slow. Not exactly a proud victory."

"And they are not legitimate members of any club, Trav. Anybody moves against me, and the Fantasies take care of it. Right, Knucks?"

"Jesus, Ted! Jesus Christ! I can't stand it. Help me, somebody."

By then the mechanics had moved in. They gave me quick looks in which wonder and disbelief were mingled. Mike was moaning to himself and trying to sit up. They were being given all necessary assistance, so I waved to Ted and Mits and got into Miss Agnes and drove off eastward toward the coast, wondering if this would become one of the ongoing legends and be distorted out of all relation with reality. Showdown at the Oasis. Fat and slow and dumb. Dumb was the most serious sin. Without the dumb additive, they would not have charged, would not have tried to hit. They would have waited, circled, grabbed, and given me a very bad day. Pale-eyed stranger whips over five hundred pounds of angry meat in a shade over fourteen seconds. It had worked very very well, better than I had any right to expect. So I should not get carried away and come on fearless with the next couple of bikers, who might very well be just as quick and just as able. Or might feel more comfortable with knife or gun or piece of pipe.

What I did not want, most of all, was to become some kind of symbol of challenge, so that their buddies would look me up to take a chop and try their luck. I wanted no part of any OK Corral syndrome. I had long outgrown that kind of testicular lunacy. People who become legends in their own time usually have very little time left.

9

ON SATURDAY morning I saw that the *Byline* was gone and knew Meyer would have a shortened cruise rather than none at all. I had some ideas to throw at him. He always seems to know which ones to field and which ones to let roll on out to the warning track. I took a swim, took a beach walk, and intercepted a Frisbee with the back of my head, an incident that seemed to strike horror into a group of fourteen-year-old ladies. I gave it back, into the wind, with all the wrist flick I could put on it, and by great good fortune it stood still after it reached them. They stared at it, and one of them reached out and picked it out of the air.

So it made a game. Three of them on one side, one of me on the other. It is a great game for running, stretching, and leaping. Usually in any group of teens, one out of three will give promise of growing up into a dog. But not one of these. Comely maidens all, and very competitive. They whirred that championship plastic at me with sincere attempts to whack my head off with it. They were practicing catching the Frisbee behind their back and under a leg, and I served up floaters to give them a sense of achievement. Their brown leaping bodies and half-formed breasts and hips instilled in me such a wistful lechery, I wondered if it might be best if I turned myself in. They could put me away where I'd do no harm.

The game broke up. We had never exchanged a name. They went trotting into the sea, and I went walking back to Bahia Mar. After my shower, I got out the battered old looseleaf address book and sat in the lounge in my robe, turning pages, looking for the right California connection. And in the L's I found Walter Lowery, both his business phone in San Francisco and his home phone in San Mateo. I brought the phone on the long cord over to the curved yellow couch, swung my feet up and tried the San Mateo number, got a recorded announcement, got a different number from information and entered it in my book, and tried it.

"Hello?" said a cautious female voice.

"Marty?"

"No. This is Ginny. Who is this?"

"My God, you sound all grown up, Gin. This is T. McGee, your honorary uncle in Florida. Your father around?"

"Hi! I'll get him. Hold on."

After a long minute he came on and said, "Obviously, sir, you are an impostor pretending to be a friend I used to have."

"Time flies, friends flee, temperance fuggit. Look, maybe I'm coming out there."

"People usually know whether they are coming out or not."

"Then let's say I will be out. *When* is not certain. I am out of touch. You still have the office in Los Angeles?"

"Yes, we do."

"Is Lysa Dean still a client?"

"Let's say she doesn't have as many legal problems as she used to. But yes. We're still on a retainer arrangement."

"And you do remember recommending me to her?"

"Indeed I do. Let's say she was very satisfied with your performance professionally, and furious as hell at you about something else, which she never explained."

"I get the impression she's doing a lot of game shows."

"Indeed she is. At very good rates. She's in demand because she is really quick and often very funny, which is rare out here with most actresses. And she gets some cameo roles now and again."

"She gave me the impression—back when I knew her—of knowing everything about everybody out there."

"Gossip is a hobby with Lee."

"Did she ever marry that forty million dollars from Hawaii?"

I heard him sigh. "She came close, buddy. Really close. He was on the verge of getting his annulment through the Vatican when his wife came down with leukemia. So what could he do? He settled a nice little bundle on Lee, and they kept up the relationship, and he died of a heart attack last year. His wife is still living."

"Lee live in the same place?"

"Same house. Beverly Hills. She redecorates it every twenty or thirty minutes." I read him the address out of my book and he confirmed it.

"Have you got her unlisted number?"

"Before we go into that, Travis, if she feels toward you like I think she feels toward you, you won't get past hello. Secondly, it is quarter to ten out here, and she won't even lift the edge of her sleep mask or take out an earplug until noon."

"So I'll call her at four o'clock my time. And I will never tell her where I got the number. And I will try to keep her from hanging up on me."

"I'll give you the number if you tell me what you did to make her so furious."

I thought it over. It certainly wasn't in the kiss-and-tell category. "Well, Walter, our business was finished. She had the photographs and the negatives back. I was at her place to pick up the money I had coming, by agreement. She started worming around on my lap starting to shuck herself out of her tight knit pants, and I suddenly wanted no part of her. So I gave her a big push and she went flying back and landed on her fanny on a white furry rug and rode it backward all the way across the room. I told her I would take the short count on the money but I would like to skip the thankful bang, as it would mean very little to me and less than nothing to her. So I left, dodging elephants from her little collection. And she knew a lot of ten- and twelve-letter words. Knew them real loud."

"Mother of Moses in the morning," he said in an awed hushed voice. "I doubt there's three idiots in the world have turned that down. Maybe there's only one. And you think she won't hang up?"

"Time has passed, Walter. Woman's curiosity. Maybe she has a little feeling of disbelief. Maybe it didn't really happen that way."

"Can I ask you why you want to talk to her?"

"To get a line on some other people out there."

He waited and when I didn't go into it any further, he said, "If they've had any connection at all to the Industry, Lysa Dean will know when and where they got every traffic ticket."

I wrote down the number he gave me, and then we chatted a little while about old times, old places, old friends. He said it wasn't the same out there, wasn't as much fun. The money had gotten too heavy. You get a budget over twenty million dollars, a lot of the fun goes out of moviemaking. But people were getting in trouble as often as before, and he was kept busy. He said Ginny had grown into a truly beautiful girl, and if she ever tried to get into the Industry, he would shave her head, bind her feet, and have all her teeth extracted. Marty got on to tell me how much they both missed me, and why not come out once in a while, and I said that from now on I would.

That is one of the great troubles, I thought, after I hung up. The people you have great empathy with are never conveniently located nearby. Many are, but the rest are scattered far and wide. You see them too seldom. But you can always pick up right where you left off. You know who they are. They know who you are. No reintroductions required.

I took the robe off and worked with the weights until I needed another shower. Had a drink, fixed a light lunch, went to bed and set the alarm for four.

When it awakened me, I looked in the address book and checked out her new number and dialed it. I had made some notes beside her name. Little things she had told me, accidentally or on purpose. I looked at the notes as the phone rang.

A woman's voice answered by repeating the last four digits of the number, on a rising intonation of question, "Three three five five?" She had a subtly Japanese way of handling the consonants.

"Lysa Dean, please."

"I will see if she is in at the moment. May I say who is calling?"

"Tell her I have a message from Walter Lowery's office."

"You may give me the message, sir."

"My instruction is to give it to her personally."

"Just a moment, please."

I sat listening to the electronic humming.

"Who are you?" demanded Lysa Dean. "What the hell does Walter want told me on a Saturday? That I'm being audited again? I already for Christsake know that." The throaty, furry, flexible voice had a steely ring behind the fur.

"I scampered out of your life in a hail of elephants, love."

"What?"

"This is Lee Schontz, isn't it? From Dayton, Ohio. Would it have been 1610 Madison Street? Was daddy a fireman? Do you photograph well in the buff, love?"

"Could it be . . . No! McGee? Is this you, McGee, you rotten dirty son of a bitch?"

"Lee, it's so damn wonderful to hear your voice."

"Let me sit down. Jesus! You got me out of the shower. What the hell do you mean, calling me? What a nerve! Where did you get this number? I had it changed two weeks ago. Did you get it from Walter? I'll tear him to ribbons!"

"I wouldn't put a friend on a spot like that. I got your number from another source. You remember how resourceful I am, don't you?"

"Look, let me go get a robe on and take this in the bedroom." Several minutes passed. She came back on, a half octave lower. "Now I'm comfy. Are you in Florida, dear?"

"Aren't you going to hang up on me?"

"No, dear. I shouldn't be angry at you. You did me a great favor, actually. You made me take a good close look at Lysa Dean. And I wasn't too enchanted with what I saw. I saw myself through your eyes. And I felt cheap. Yes, cheap. I thought that anything Lysa did was acceptable because it was Lysa doing it. But it wasn't, was it?"

"How much of that is bullshit, Lee?"

"Practically all of it, Travis. Nobody else ever made me that mad. I steamed for months."

"But you got over it."

"Hell, yes. My dearest hope would be that you have thought about me for years and years and you want to come out here and pick up on what you turned down a long time ago. I would lead you on, baby, and then I would cut you right the hell off at the pockets. Or nearby."

"Wouldn't blame you a bit."

The voice softened. "You know what really hurt me? What really really hurt me? The way you said that making love with you would mean less than nothing to me. You were wrong, dear. Wrong, wrong, wrong. I was *infatuated* with you. And it would have meant a great great deal to me. I was going to prove to you how much it meant. Oh, hell. This sounds like bullshit too, doesn't it? I guess it is."

"Heard about your bad luck with Mr. X in Hawaii. Sorry it had to come out that way."

"Thanks, dear. Louie was an okay person all the way. He couldn't leave Muriel once she got sick. It would have poisoned our marriage, building it on that kind of luck. But he was very good to me. I've sort of forgotten what the wolf looks like."

"I ran into you twice on game shows, when I was spinning the dial. You were in a little box up in the air, looking very very good."

"I'm keeping well, they tell me. I can't exactly pass for twenty. Or even twenty-seven. No mere slip of a girl. Can't get away with the cutesy stuff any more. Elfin old me. I work because I like it, dear. Are you still slipping about, doing shifty things for people?"

"It's a living. Salvage consultant."

"Boy, you sure salvaged me that time. I'm forever grateful."

"How's Dana Holtzer?"

"Great. Her husband finally died. She's Dana Maguire, and she's still making babies. She found out she's good at it. Four, and one in the oven. Darling kids."

"Say hi for me when you see her. I want to know something about a couple of people you probably know. I guess I want to know everything you might know about them."

"Who?"

"Josie Laurant Esterland and Peter Kesner."

"That's what they mean when they talk about a bucket of worms. Look, are you in town? Could you come over here?"

"I'm in Florida."

"Oh, heck, I thought you could come over and maybe we could level with each other, and I'd cancel my tennis date and we'd sort of mess around a little and get reacquainted. With no cutting off at pockets or anywhere else. Afternoons are fun. Look, it will cost you a hell of a phone bill if you listen to all of this."

"Let me ask a couple of questions, and then maybe I'll come listen in person."

"Okay."

"Are they together?"

"God only knows. That is what is called a volatile relationship. They are somewhere in Indiana or one of those states there in the middle, making a disaster movie."

"A disaster movie?"

"A financial disaster. That's what they call those around here lately. Disaster movies. Never never work in something your boyfriend is directing. Romance ends."

"What kind of a movie is it? What about?"

"It is rumored to be about balloons."

"Balloons?"

"You know. Little baskets hang under them, and they have gas burners, and they are all pretty colors, and you go sailing away over the pretty farmland, saying oh and ah. Hot-air balloons."

"It's an independent production?"

"Like practically everything else except for comic-book stuff like the Empire series at Fox. And it is pretty well established here, among those who like to snigger, that Josie is helping bankroll it. I hear they had a long long struggle with script, and finally Peter rewrote it himself, poor lamb. Then they scrounged some bank money and some money from the distributor and went out on location a few weeks ago. And they've had rotten weather. They are together in the balloon picture, but elsewhere, as in the sack, I don't know. Hey, you better come out here, McGee. I'm getting such a nice little rush out of just talking to you. Really. You're filed under Unfinished Business."

"I don't know. Bits and pieces have to come together. I'm like an old blue tick hound, running back and forth at the edge of the swamp, nose in the air, wondering if there's a trail worth following and kind of hating the idea of going into the mud and the snakes and the gators."

"Goodness, how quaint! How picturesque! I hope that when you are trotting back and forth with your tongue hanging out, you'll get downwind of me. I'll be sending out a message."

"What's happening to ladies? What's happened to buttons and bows, and shy sidelong smiles, and demure blushes?"

"You must be some kind of old-time chauvinist. What's the matter? We alarm you?"

"Sort of, I guess."

"When you were solving my little problem were you thinking of it in terms of swamp and snakes?"

"I think so. Walk into the back of anybody's skull, be they born-again, big mullah, or resident of the death house, and you'll come to the edge of a swamp that stretches as far as the eye can see. It's part of the human condition."

"How cynical!"

"Not really. Meyer says that knowing it is there is half the battle. Beware of those turkeys who really believe they are absolutely pure, decent, honest, God-fearing, hard-working, patriotic Americans. They'll slip a rusty blade into your belly, look upward, and proclaim it God's will. They'll believe they've done it for your own salvation."

"Then you have no need to beware of me, my dear. I am impure, indecent, dishonest, lazy, and permanently randy. You can trust me all the way. I've got a swamp you wouldn't hardly believe."

I thanked her for her help and broke off with cheery goodbyes. I had not known how she would react to me. I had inflicted such a deep wound in her pride, it was probably still draining. There she was at that time, Lysa Dean, a genuine celebrity, a sex symbol, a box-office draw, mobbed wherever she went, star player in the erotic fantasies of a million men she would never meet, and when, out of gratitude, out of affection, she tried to bestow upon a nobody from Fort Lauderdale a warm morsel of all her international magic, giving him a memory that would make him vibrate for the rest of his life, the dreary ungrateful damn fool had turned it down. And, given the insecurity of the aging actress, I could guess that the rejection haunted her in the bleak hours of the night when the sleeping pill had worn off. She wanted to get her hands on me, and there were two ways she could go. She could either build me up to an overpowering urgency and turn it all off, or she could really devote herself to proving what a hell of a deal I, in my ignorance, had turned down. Prudence said to stay the hell away from her. I remembered her slanted green eyes, very handsome, and merciless as a questing cat.

10

AT NOON on Sunday Annie phoned me and told me she had just had a full hour of good sun right out in front of her cabana, had come in and had her shower, and was stretched out on the bed under the fan, letting the moving air dry her off and thinking of me.

"Cut it out, Annie!"

"Saturday morning I got word that they're going to let me have the extra wing I've been asking for. Twenty more rooms over on the other side, two-story. The architect is coming down."

"That's nice."

"We've been out of balance here. When we're full, we have more bar and dining room and kitchen capacity than we're using. I hate to encourage a lot of outside business coming in, just to eat and drink. Sooner or later that creates problems. If we make it with our guests, it's more like a club. If it could possibly be done by December, I can really show them one hell of a season next year. Already we are reserved almost full for the first quarter. Are you interested at all in this kind of stuff? I have nobody else to brag to."

"Of course I'm interested, Annie."

"I bet. It's exciting to me. It is kind of like farming. I mean you have a nice harvest of tourists coming up, and all of a sudden you get a tornado, or a red tide, or a big oil spill, or the country goes on gas rationing. So it's always a little bit nervous. Or a hurricane will come and wash us away. We're pretty exposed here."

"Sooner or later one will. Just hope it's later."

"Very cheery."

"Any chance of you ever getting away, Annie? Like for a week or two. A little boat ride to no place in particular?"

"Not anytime real soon. I fired my assistant manager. He kept telling me how wonderful I am and slicing me up whenever I turned my back. Caught him at it. I've got a new guy now. And I think he is going to work out. He hasn't had a lot of experience, but he knows food and liquor service and he gets along with the guests and the employees. It looks as if by maybe some-time in July I could give him a trial run, by going where he can't ask me questions. Is July okay?"

"Great. Maybe I'll bring the *Flush* around and pick you up over there and we'll flip a coin for which direction we go. North or south."

"Beautiful. I wouldn't want to stay on a boat too long. I spent too much time on the *Caper* with Ellis. There's no place to put anything, and no real privacy. It was like the walls were closing in."

"The bulkheads."

"The walls, honey. Walls and floors. Kitchen and bathroom. Upstairs, downstairs. Inside and outside. Ellis was so damn picky about being seaman-like, I decided after he died that the whole thing is a crock. I lived aboard until it got sold, and I called everything by the civilian name for it, and it made me sort of happy."

"I want to ask you something else. You told me Josie called Ellis a couple of times. Several times, I believe you said. Early in July. At that time she must have been terribly concerned and depressed about the condition of her daughter, Romola."

"Oh, she was. Of course."

"You said that the phone calls from her made him cross."

"I see what you mean. I knew that they weren't about Romola or any change in her condition, because he always told me things like that. And news of his daughter would make him either very depressed or very jubilant. Not cross. That's why I think she must have been urging him to buy some-thing for pain, the way Prescott had asked her to do."

"Josie was willing to do that in spite of her major worry?"

"Look, she couldn't do anything about her major worry. There was Romola all hooked up to a life-support system that was even breathing for her, all tubes and wires and things, and nothing to do but wait. She didn't die, legally, until August tenth. I would guess that Josie was very restless. She'd welcome anything that diverted her from her worry. I would guess that she wanted Ellis to come back to her and stay with her. Maybe she brought that up too. And that was what made him cross. He always told me she was a very nice woman, and absolutely impossible to live with."

"I might be going out there."

"What for?"

"Josie Laurant has been financing a motion picture project for Peter Kesner. She's acting in it, I think."

"Oh, God, that's terrible!"

It was a lot more reaction than I had expected. "Terrible?"

"I should have told you. Ellis, through his banking connections, arranged a personal report on Peter Kesner. An absolutely, totally unreliable person. A disaster area. He had the discipline to make those two little films that got rave reviews and made a lot of money, but it went to his head and he blew the whole thing. They gave him a big-budget film to produce and direct, and he went way over budget and it turned out to be a dog. They gave him a chance to do a little picture, like his early two, and it was so completely bad they never released it at all. By then his money was gone, of course. Tax judgments, the whole thing. It was clear that Josie was supporting him. I remember when Ellis dictated a three-page single-spaced letter to her, telling her to have as little to do with Peter as possible and saying why. Knowing Josie, I knew she'd turn it over to Kesner. I told Ellis I thought that would happen, and he said he wouldn't mind if she did. There was nothing actionable in the letter. It was all fact. He said maybe it would give Kesner a better look at himself. When I typed it I softened it a little bit, but he caught it and marked up the original and had me type it all over again. What this really means, I guess, is that the money Josie got from Romola's estate is down the drain, or soon will be."

"Ellis didn't put any strings on it?"

"He talked about it, but he never got around to doing it. He talked about setting it up as an annuity for Romola, but then when we were both certain Romola was going to die before he did, he put all his attention into refining that foundation concept of his. Which never got used."

"Important question: Would Kesner know the terms of the will?"

She thought for a moment. "I would certainly think so. Josie knew, long before we moved down here from Stamford, that Romola would get the bulk of it, and if Romola died first it would go to a foundation. Yes, she asked me and I told her about it. I think she was wondering what would happen to her support, to that fifty thousand a year, and I didn't blame her for wondering. I told her I thought she would get a hundred thousand and that would be the end of it. Yes, I told her that's what she would get. And anything Josie knows, Josie tells anybody she happens to find sitting next to her at the table."

"And so Kesner was vitally interested." There was a long long silence. "You still there?"

"Yes, I'm here. I had a kind of ugly thought."

"Such as?"

"You remember how Romola got hurt?"

"Nobody ever told me. I assumed it was a highway accident."

"It was a bicycle accident, yes. She was way over by Thousand Oaks, twenty tough miles from home. There were witnesses. She was going along pretty fast on a ten-speed. A dog rushed her and she tried to dodge, but she hit the dog and went over the handlebars and fractured her skull on some curbing. What she was doing out there was a big mystery. Josie thought she was in class in UCLA. It turned out—I don't really know how they discovered it—she was using a little house out there owned by a woman who was temporarily in London, doing a screenplay over there for a British company. The neighbors had seen Romola coming and going for a couple of months. They said she rode the bike a lot. Oh, I remember how they found the house. Romola's little car was there, some kind of an MG. And with her car keys in her pocket she had a key to the little house. There was evidence she had been staying there for some time. She had moved some of her things from the Beverly Hills house to the little house, without Josie noticing. She had not been in classes since early February. She was an exceptionally beautiful girl. I saw her just once, when she was fourteen, and she was breathtaking. The extraordinary secrecy was very strange. It was a place of assignation, apparently. But there wasn't any real urge to find out who because she was in such critical condition."

"And the ugly idea?"

"Maybe it's too ugly. Peter Kesner knew that Ellis had terminal cancer. And he knew that Josie would get a lump-sum settlement that wouldn't be enough to support him for very long. And he knew Romola would inherit. He was perfectly capable of seducing Romola. And that would have made her very very careful to keep it a secret from her mother. I'll bet you a dime that lady screenwriter is an old pal of Peter's. It was the screenwriter's bike, by the way."

"Yes, that is an ugly idea. And if the fall had killed her outright, then when Ellis died of his problem, the foundation would have gotten the money."

"But she hung on. And suddenly Peter realizes that if Ellis should die before Romola, he will still be in clover. Or even better off than before. He can finance another chance at moviemaking, possibly. But, Travis, it is one long long shot, isn't it, to try to connect Peter Kesner with something that happened so long ago near Citrus City?"

"Very long."

"I didn't call you up to talk about that!"

"What did you have in mind?"

"Do you want five hundred guesses?"

"I give up."

"That's sort of what I had in mind."

"Once I get onto the Alley it is only eighty-four miles. But aren't you a working woman on weekends?"

"All I have to do from now on is take one of my famous walks through the bar area and the dining room between seven and nine, check a couple of empty rooms at random, and take the totals off the register tapes. A grand total of—call it forty minutes. And as soon as I hang up I am going to have a nice nap, and then I am going to put little dabs of scent here and there. Park at the far right end of the lot and take the path down past that fountain with the stone benches, and you'll come out right behind my place, and the rear door will be unlocked. Welcome, darling."

And she hung up before I could change the plan in any way.

* * *

I stayed in her place with her Sunday night, in the queen-size bed under the fan, with a yellow towel over the lampshade and with a pretty good surf thudding onto the beach in a steady rhythm all night long.

We knew a lot more about each other, the things that quickened and the things that delayed. She was joyfully diligently sensuous. She just purely enjoyed the living hell out of it. She was a kid, and bed was the big candy store, and she had the keys to every cabinet.

At one point, resting, she said, "Look, do you mind about me and Ellis?"

"In what way?"

"Him being so much older. I'm younger than his son. Did I tell you that already?"

"I think so. So what?"

"You take a younger woman who moves in with a well-to-do old man, it looks as if she's going where the money is. I don't give a damn what most people think, but I want you to know that it wasn't like that. It really wasn't. Two years before he got sick we went down to a meeting in New York when there was an industry-wide convention. He always picked me when there was work he wanted done just right. By then I was almost over a rotten affair with the man I had wanted to marry until I learned he had a boyfriend on the side. Ellis landed a huge consultant contract at the convention, and we had wine in his suite—I lived across the hall—and he managed to hustle me into bed somehow. I told him I had to quit. I wasn't going to be a sleep-in secretary to anybody. He said if I had to quit, I had to quit. Okay. The next day I quit, and he said the fair thing to do was to stay on until he could find somebody just as competent. Later he said that inasmuch as I was quitting anyway, and as long as we had been to bed together once, it would be stupid not to continue while he looked for a new girl. I felt a little bit crawly about him being so old. But it turned out to be all right. Then on account of the chemotherapy and the radiation, he all of a sudden couldn't. He was sorry and I was sorry, but, as I told you before, I had a moral and emotional commitment to him. He was mean, but he never cheated me. He never lied to me. And he was always pleased when I looked nice, so it was fun to dress up for him. And because I never did really quit the job when I said I would, I felt I owed him. And I had to believe it was a kind of love that kept me with him. Hey! Are you asleep?"

"No. Heard every word. Understand the whole thing."

"And now what do you think you are doing?"

"In the immortal words of Burt Reynolds, something has come up."

"Which, all things considered, love, is very very flattering."

"I know."

* * *

By twenty minutes after dawn I was on my way back across the peninsula, yawning and singing, beating time with the heel of my hand on the steering wheel. Roll me over, in the clover. . . . With 'is 'ead tooked underneath 'is arm, 'e 'aunts the bluiddy tower. . . . Never let a sailor put his hand above your kneeeee. . . . And other tender love songs and ballads of the years gone by.

When I awakened in my own bed at noon, I put a call through to Ted Blaylock. Mits answered in a small uncertain voice. He had lost consciousness Saturday evening and had been rushed to Broward Memorial. His condition was not good. She had just come from there. She was going back in the late afternoon.

"What is it?"

"Kidneys. That's what he's been afraid of. You saw how kind of yellowish he looked."

"I noticed, yes. Can I get to see him?"

"He wants to see you. He told me how to get you by phone, but I didn't even try on account of I don't want to do anything to tire him out. Anyway, I don't think they'll let you in. I told them I'm his wife."

"Does he have something to tell me?"

"I think so."

"Get him to tell you, then. I don't want to tire him. You can tell me. You got a ride in?"

"One of the guys is taking me and waiting."

"What room is he in?"

"Why?"

"So I'll know where to wait for you when you come out."

"I can only be with him like five minutes. I guess if you want to come meet me, five o'clock would be okay. Across from the main entrance."

I got there at four thirty. I looked around the area and I found a big silver and black Harley Davidson parked in the shade, a thin brown Indian-looking fellow standing by it, smoking, leaning against a tree.

"You bring Mits in?" I asked him.

"You McGee?"

"Right."

"She told me you'd be around. I'm Cal. I'm her cousin. She's really nuts about that Blaylock. You the one messed up Knucks and Mike?"

"They kept pushing me."

"They're like that. Be a long time before they do any more pushing. You tore up Knucks's shoulder pretty good. And Mike is in the hospital, this one right here, for observation on account of something might be busted inside. He can't keep food down. A lot of people are glad they got wiped out. They get too much kicks out of beating on people."

"I have the idea those two are dumb enough and ugly enough to take another try at me when they feel up to it, but not with the bare hands."

He nodded. "Sure. That would be the way they go. But they been given the word you're under the protection of the Fantasies."

I looked at his rear mudguard and saw the emblem. "That's nice. I really appreciate it. That pair doesn't fill me with terror, but I don't like having to look around behind me all the time. Why the favor?"

"You did the Fantasies a favor, okay? Knucks had been told about groping Mits. He was told not to do it. It was like some kind of a joke to him. Mits is my first cousin, so she's in like an affiliate. Fantasy Foxes, under our protection. Like the Oasis is under our protection because Blaylock has been a true friend to the club. So some people were going to get around to Knucks and maybe break his hand or something. But you worked him over. So if you want, you can wear the pin. There's one for associates, without the red circle around it.''

The keen dark eyes stared at me, and I knew I was on very delicate and dangerous ground. Ridicule is unforgivable. But I had the feeling I'd been transported back to one of the schoolyards of my youth, where if you belonged to the right group, the big kids wouldn't beat you up and take your lunch money.

''I'd be very honored to have the pin and wear it, Cal.''

The tension went out of his shoulders. ''I'll see you get one. What my squad captain did, he checked you out with Blaylock, and he got a good reading. Hey, here she comes. I guess things aren't so great.''

Mits came slowly toward us. Though she was expressionless, tears were running down her brown cheeks. She was in jeans and a blue work shirt, both too big for her. Her helmet was slung on the machine, next to Cal's.

She acknowledged my presence with a nod, went to Cal, held his forearm in her two hands, and rested her forehead against his shoulder for a moment. ''In't gonna make it,'' she said in a muffled voice. ''Din't hardly know me at first. Then he came back, like from far off, like from being dead.''

She took a deep breath and let it out, and then turned to me and said, ''Other things are going bad. Inside. Like he knew they would sooner or later. But, damn it, this is sooner. It isn't fair.''

''Can we get going now?'' Cal asked.

''I can see him another five minutes at six o'clock. I think I better stay here.''

''Maybe I can get back. I don't know, Mits. I'll have to get off work.''

''I'll stick around and run her home, Cal.''

She looked at me dubiously. ''Sure you wouldn't be too much put out?''

''Sure.''

Cal handed her her helmet, swung aboard, cranked up, and went droning out of the shade and into the road and away.

She looked around and saw a bus bench in the shade and headed toward it. I followed her. She took cigarettes out of her shoulder bag, offered me one which I refused, and then lit up, sucked the smoke deep, huffed it out to be pulled away by the late-afternoon breeze.

''They said I should expect him to die tonight or tomorrow.''

''Soon.''

''Everything has gone bad. They say he had to be in pain for a long time, saying nothing about it. I knew he hurt. He'd make a sniffy sound if I lifted him wrong. How old do you think I am?''

The question startled me. ''Nineteen? Twenty?''

''Hah! I'm twenty-eight, man. Half Seminole. A skinny Seminole, you can't tell the age. With the fat ones you can tell. Okay, except for my little brothers when I was growing up, nobody in my whole life has ever really needed me except Ted. I mean *really*. He turned that place into home for me. So now what? I have to make some kind of plans, get some kind of work. But I can't even think about it.''

''Don't try. There'll be time to think about it.''

"McGee? What was he like when he was young?"

"I knew him in the service."

"That's what I mean."

"He was a good officer. He didn't showboat and draw fire. When stupid orders came down, he'd drag his feet until they were out of date. He tried to make sure everybody got shelter and rations and transport. He didn't mind the kind of goofing off that didn't matter, but if anybody didn't do their job when it did matter, he'd chew them out good. He was an okay officer, and he was down in a little ravine helping a medic slide a wounded man onto a litter when he got a mortar fragment in the back, right through the spinal cord."

"Did he ever laugh, joke, smile?"

"As much as anybody."

"Did he have a girl?"

"I don't recall hearing anything about her if he did."

"It's been a lot of work taking care of him. It makes a long day and into the night seven days a week."

"Must have been very hard."

"I would have done it if it was twice as hard. Oh, I asked him if there was something I should tell you. It doesn't make sense to me. I hope it does to you. His mind seemed to be kind of wandering. Here is exactly what he said: 'Tell Sarge there is a legend about how Dirty Bob and the Senator made it all the way in fifty hours flat out, popping Dexamyls, and then faded away.' Mean anything?"

"Not right off."

"I think his head has gone all weird. I held his hand. It was like ice."

"Say it again?"

" 'There is a legend about how Dirty Bob and the Senator made it all the way in fifty hours flat out, popping Dexamyls, and then faded away.' He made me say it twice too."

I found that interesting. It meant the message was significant in the shape and form it was told.

"Could those be biker names, Mits?"

"Oh, sure. I've heard about Dirty Bob, but I don't know where or when. And when they take a long hard ride, they do it on uppers and coffee. Night and day, they really go. And it's safer there's two at night, riding side by side, with the two headlights showing, the two taillights in back."

"Fifty hours would be how many miles?"

"All the way acrosst. I knew a cat went from Toronto to Mexico City without sleep. A while back, there was kind of a thing about setting records. But it's dumb. People got killed. You can lose your best troops that way." She picked up my wrist and looked at my watch. "I think I'll head back in there. I'll stay as long as they let me. You sure you don't mind?"

"You go ahead. I'll wait. Good luck."

"There isn't any more of that left. But thanks."

She came back at ten after six, dry-eyed. "Look, you want to take off, it's okay. They're going to let me set with him. They got curtains around the bed. He doesn't know me any more, or know anything, I guess. But everybody has to be somewhere, and I might as well be here."

"You going to get anything to eat?"

"I couldn't eat."

I gave her my number again. "You call me when you want to leave. It will take me fifteen or twenty minutes to get here. Is that all right?"

"I hate to have you doing this for me."

"If I didn't want to, I wouldn't."

There was a nod and a fleeting smile and she turned and went back to the hospital.

* * *

The phone woke me a little after three in the morning. She was waiting by the bench where we had sat. She climbed up into the Rolls, chunked the door shut, and said, "He died at a quarter to three. He stopped breathing and then tried to kind of rise up and fell back with his eyes half shut and his mouth open. I got his stuff here in my bag they took from him. The watch and ring and wallet and keys."

"I'm sorry, Mits."

"F.T.W."

"What? Oh. Right."

"I signed a couple of things there. I signed them Marilyn O. Blaylock. They didn't ask for any ID. I always liked the name Marilyn. I think what they do, maybe, they get to collect from the VA somehow."

"Probably. Did he have any living relatives?"

"I never heard of any at all."

"What will happen to the place out there?" I asked as I started up, heading north.

"He said he had it all worked out, but he never said how. His lawyer has the papers on it, he said. Man name of Grudd up in West Palm."

We rode in silence. She sighed heavily. "Oh, God, somebody's got to go through all his stuff and decide what should happen to it."

"Maybe Mr. Grudd has instructions. Better contact him first."

"First thing."

"Hungry?"

"Like some kind of wolf."

So I pulled into 24 HOUR CHICKEN and she ate one of the big breast baskets all by herself, with fries and a chocolate shake. I told her I was going to be given a kind of associate-type pin that put me under the protection of the Fantasies, that Cal was going to get it for me.

She studied me for long moments as she sucked up the shake, cheeks hollowed by the effort. "What could save your life and save your ass, you shouldn't try to be funny about, okay?"

"I wasn't trying to be funny."

"There isn't anything funny about that Knucks. He is genuine through and through crazy. Someday they are going to put him away."

"Cal is going to get the badge to me. I've been voted in."

"I know. Because it got the message to Knucks about not messing with me any more. At least I hope it did. I hate being grabbed like that. And he's so rough, he hurts a lot."

"Have you got people close by?"

"Not close by. They're all down near Monroe Station on the Trail. Lots of brothers. When this thing is settled, I might go down there awhile, sew up some tourist skirts, get a good rest, go frogging."

"It would probably be good for you."

"What the hell would you know bout what's good for me?"

"Excuse me all to hell, lady."

She came sliding over and put her hand on my arm."Oh, Jesus, I'm sorry. I didn't mean it. Look, I'm hurting and I want to hurt back, but I shouldn't be hurting you."

"Forget it. No harm done."

She had nothing to say the rest of the way. She got out with helmet and shoulder bag and thanked me. I waited until she got the door unlocked and turned and waved.

By the time I had tucked Miss Agnes away and biked from the garage back to the *Flush,* there was a faint pallor across the eastern sky, close to the horizon line. I chained the bike up and went walking on the empty beach, not too healthy a night activity of late. Some of the jackals cruise our area from time to time, and have shot an innocent man in the head, raped a woman on the beach, cut a man up while removing his wallet and watch. Subhuman freaks, looking for laughs.

I stashed my sandals where I could find them, rolled up the pants legs, walked the water line. The sea thumped in and slid up the sand, pale suds in starlight.

I walked and thought about the lieutenant. I could never feel easy about his gratitude toward me. If I hadn't helped carry him down the hill in the rain, somebody else would have. And maybe he would have been better off not being carried at all, being left there. But he didn't think so. I had run into him again by accident, fifteen years after he was wounded. It had been up to him to recognize me. He was fifty pounds lighter and a hundred years older than I remembered.

Okay. Okay. Okay. But, by God, it seemed that an awful lot of people were into dying. The "in" thing this year, apparently. No chance for practice. You had to do it right the first and only time you got to do it. And you were never quite certain when your chance was coming. Stay braced at all times.

11

THE *BYLINE* did not come hulking into the marina until midmorning on Thursday the twenty-third. Meyer and Aggie were standing up in the bow. I went along with the yacht, keeping up easily at a walking pace. They both looked several shades darker and very content.

"Lovely cruise," Aggie called. "Just lovely."

I helped with the lines and went aboard when the crew had rigged the gangway. They greeted me. I kissed Aggie on the cheek and asked them how far they had been.

"Just up to Jupiter Inlet," Meyer said. "We anchored in a very secluded cove. And we had a nice time. And then we came back."

"I admire the way you seafarers put up with the rigors of the deep dark ocean blue."

"Don't be snide, darling," Aggie said. "No one needs to be bounced about on a lot of angry ugly waves in order to enjoy a cruise. Don't you agree, Meyer dear?"

"Aggie, I always agree with everything you say."

"Mary time?" she asked. "Below or up here? It *does* seem nice up here, don't you think, Travis? Raul, *tres marías piquantes, por favor.*"

She sorted herself out on a sun chaise on the upper deck, crossing her long tanned elegant ageless gleaming legs, arching her magnificent back just a little, tossing that rich ruff of hair back, favoring me with a slow and sardonic wink. It was, not invitation. It was confirming our mutual approval of the effort that had made the tight pink bikini feasible, with only the smallest roll around the middle. She was a big rich glorious engine, and a very smart tough lady who, a bit belatedly, had come into her own in every way and was enjoying every moment of it.

"Aggie is flying out from here at one o'clock," Meyer said, "instead of cruising back to Miami."

"I was going to be a day late," she said, "but after two phone calls, I learned better. One of the media monsters is nibbling at my poor little string of papers, salivating. Wants to stick us in with all their magazines and television stations and bulk carriers and tampon factories and give me a fat consultant contract."

Meyer spread his hands apart and said, "Aggie, it depends on what you want. If you take the cash, put it in tax-frees after paying capital-gains taxes, you could have over half a mil a year with very small tax to pay on it. You could spend a lot more time aboard this vessel."

"What I want, dear man, is to run my world better than anybody ever ran it before, or will again. A business person, making business moves all day."

"So you shouldn't sell."

"I seem to have a business I can't sell," I said.

They both stared at me and Aggie Sloane said, "*You* have a business? How quaint, dear boy! Of what sort?"

The drinks arrived, and I took a swallow before I turned to Meyer. "You heard me talk about Ted Blaylock."

"Yes, of course. The crippled lieutenant."

"He died Monday night."

"Sorry to hear it."

"An attorney named Daviss Grudd, two s's, two d's, phoned me and told me about it Tuesday afternoon. That whole enterprise of his, Ted Blaylock's Oasis, Inc., was in a closely held corporation. Very closely held. One hundred shares of stock outstanding. So he left fifty to me and he left fifty to a skinny little half-Seminole woman named Millicent Waterhawk, called Mits, one of the famous Fantasy Foxes. And I can't sell that damn stock or give it away until there has been an appraisal of the vlaue of the whole damn thing, and God only knows how long that is going to take. Grudd says the thing has got to keep operating or the value of the shares left to Miss Waterhawk will go down, and Grudd said that there is a note in his office to me from Blaylock, saying that it was the only way he could think of to protect Mits's interest and he was sure I would make sure she didn't get a tossing."

I jumped up so quickly I splashed some of my drink on the back of my hand. In a higher than normal voice, I said, "I don't *like* this! My God, when it got so you couldn't rent a car or check into a good hotel without a credit card, I had to sign up. I had to have a bank account to get the credit cards. I keep getting into more and more computers all the time. Boat papers, city taxes, bank records, credit records, IRS, army records, census records, phone company records. . . . God damn it, I feel like I'm getting more and more entangled. Like walking down a dark corridor into cobweb after cobweb. I didn't sign up for this kind of lousy regimentation! I don't want to be a damn shareholder, owner, manager, or what the hell ever. I'm getting smothered."

They were both staring at me. "There, there," said Aggie. "Poor baby." She turned to Meyer. "Poor baby doesn't comprehend the modern way of guaranteeing anonymity and privacy, does he?"

"Tell him, dear," Meyer said, looking fatuous.

"Sit down, Travis. The computer age, my rebellious friend, is strangling on its own data. As the government and industry and the financial institutions buy and lease more and more lovely computers, generation after generation of them, they have to fill them, they have to use lots and lots of programs, lots of softwear to utilize capacity. How am I doing, Meyer?"

"Very nicely."

"Meyer taught me this. What you should do from now on, Travis, is to make sure you get into as many computers as possible. Lots of tiny bank accounts, lots of credit cards, lots of memberships. Have your attorney set up some partnerships and little corporations and get you some additional tax numbers. Move bits of money around often. Buy and sell odd lots of this and that. Feed all the information you can into all their computers."

"And spend my life keeping track of what the hell I'm doing?"

"Who said anything about keeping track? If you can get so complicated you confuse yourself, imagine how confused the poor computers are going to be."

"Is she putting me on, Meyer?"

"She's giving you good advice. If you try to hide, you are easy to find. You are leaving only one trail in the jungle, and the hounds can follow that one. Leave forty trails, crossing and recrossing. The computers are strangling on data. The courts are strangling on caseload. Billions of pieces of paper are floating around each month, clogging the inputs, confusing the outputs. A nice little old lady in Duluth had twelve post office boxes under twelve different names, and had twelve social security cards and numbers, and drew checks on all twelve for eight years before they caught up with her. And they wouldn't have, if she hadn't signed the wrong name on the wrong check five years ago. The government seeks restitution. She says she lost it all at bingo. Think of it this way, Travis. With each new computer that goes into service, your identity becomes more and more diffuse and unreal. Right now today, if every man, woman, and child were put to work ten hours a day reading computer printouts, just scanning the alphabetical and numerical output of the printers, they could cover about one third of what is being produced. Recycling of computer printout paper is a giant industry. We're all sinking into the oblivion of profusion, and one day soon we will all be gone, with no way to trace us."

Aggie began to giggle and gasp. "Millicent Waterhawk," she said in a strangled voice. "Your business partner."

"What's so damn funny?" I asked.

Meyer started laughing, and pretty soon I had to join in. It was such a dreadful blow to my self-image that it took me a while to see any humor in it. But there was a lot, I guess.

*   *   *

The funeral service was on Friday noon in the little Everglades settlement of Bonahatchee. There was a better turnout of the Fantasies than Mits had expected. She was obviously pleased that almost a hundred and fifty machines had assembled at the Oasis and had rumbled at slow funeral pace to Snead's Funeral Home in Bonahatchee and, subsequent to the eulogy and service, had followed the hearse out to where the flowers covered the raw dirt mound of the pre-dug grave.

All the brothers and sisters wore black arm bands. After the graveside service things began to break up, and they milled around for a time, talking to people they hadn't seen since the last biker funeral, then peeled off in twos and threes, roaring past the two state trooper cars which had apparently been summoned just in case, no doubt by nervous residents of the town, unstrung by the bearded, burly, helmeted visions which made such a powerful and flatulent sound as they moved through the town slowly in columns of four.

Daviss Grudd came over and introduced himself after the service. Mits had pointed him out to me and said he rode a 900cc Suzuki with a new Windjammer fairing for touring. She had to explain what she meant. He was a smallish man with big shoulders and a big drooping mustache and a voice like something in the bottom of a barrel. I introduced him to Meyer. He followed us back to the Oasis, which was closed for the day. He brought in the portfolio he took out of a saddlebag, and the four of us sat at one of the tables in front of the bar.

"Meyer," I explained, "is my adviser in business matters."

Mits said, "I can't believe I'm gonna *own* half this place. I never owned anything in my life."

"The cash situation is pretty good," Grudd said. "What you've got to have here is management. Ted, for all his kidding around, was a good manager. It has always looked messy around here, but it does turn a dollar."

"I wouldn't want to manage it even if I could," I said quickly.

"Who kept the books?" Meyer asked.

"Ted did," Mits answered. "They're in his desk drawer. You want them?" Grudd nodded, and she went and brought them back. Checkbook, journal, ledger, inventory sheets, payroll, withholding, state sales tax, ad valorem tax records.

"I've got the corporate books, minute book, and so on."

Meyer flipped pages, ran his thumbnail down columns of figures, went backwards through the checkbook. Then he said, "I can make a couple of preliminary judgments."

"Hey, I like how he talks," Mits said.

"Pay a good manager what he would be worth, a manager who can get along with and attract the kind of trade the place caters to, and there'll be damn little left over for dividends. If there is anything left over, it should go into replacing equipment and maintaining the buildings. At first glance I see a very clean debt situation. There are nine acres of land with a seven-hundred-foot frontage on a not-very-busy terciary road. Land value, twenty-five to thirty thousand. Liquor inventory, fifteen hundred. Motorcycle and parts inventory, about ten thousand to twelve thousand at cost. Liquor license, how much?''

"Maybe twenty thousand if we can move it somewhere else," Grudd said.

"Shop equipment and tools, say five thousand. Let me see, that would come to about sixty-five to sixty-eight thousand. My advice would be to liquidate.''

Mits glared at him. "Now I don't like the way you talk. No damn way do we liquidate. No way!''

I don't know whether or not he was going to try to talk her into it. Two big machines came in, popping and grumbling. Mits jumped up and looked out and said, "Hey, it's Preach and Magoo.''

"Top officers of the Fantasies," Grudd explained. "Let 'em in, Mits.''

Preach was tall and thin and wore a gray jump suit with a lot of silver coin buttons. He had long blond hair and a long thin blond beard. Except for the little gold wire glasses he was wearing, he looked like folk art depicting Jesus. Magoo was five and a half feet high, and about four broad, none of it fat. If he could have straightened his bandy legs, he would have been a lot closer to six feet. His arms were long, large, sinewy, and bare, with a pale blue tracery of dragons, fu dogs, and Chinese gardens under the tan. His head was half again normal size, with a brute shelf of acromegalic jaw. The expression was at once merry and sardonic, happy and skeptical.

Preach put his hands on Mits's shoulders and looked down into her small brown face with warmth and compassion. "Mits, Mits, Mits," he said. "A bad thing, eh? Couldn't make it in time, kid. We're sorry. We were in Baja when we heard. Flew back.''

"I wondered," she said. "It's okay. You know Daviss Grudd. This is Mr. Meyer and this here is Travis McGee.''

"Preach," he said, and stuck his hand out to me, ignoring Meyer. His hand was thin and cool, the handshake slack. I saw his eyes flick down to take in the metal badge Cal had slipped to me, and I saw a trace of amusement. "McGee, meet Magoo." His was a hot beefy grasp. "Heard about you," Preach said. He turned to Grudd. "What did Teddy do with it?''

"Half and half. Mits and McGee. An even split.''

"Interesting," Preach said.

Mits broke in. "Mr. Meyer thinks we ought to sell if off.''

Preach studied Meyer. "What would give you thoughts like that, book man?''

Meyer smiled at him. "Common sense. Blaylock didn't draw salary. And he slacked off on maintenance and repair. Some of the cycle inventory has been around a long time. Once you start paying a manager and picking the place up, there won't be enough left over.''

"Whose friend is he?" Preach asked Grudd.

"He's with me," I said.

Preach wheeled around and studied me again. "You tell your friend Meyer that management will be provided.''

"He says management will be provided, Meyer," I said.

"Are you being a little bit smartass, McGee?" Preach asked.

"Just enough so you'd notice."

"I notice you," he said. "Grudd, you folks deal the cards or something. I'm going walking with the McGiggle twins here."

We went out in back where the cabins were, the brush tangled around them. Magoo's big arms hung down to his knees. He hopped up and sat on the trunk of an ancient red Mustang convertible, top long gone, rusting in the grass, dreaming of hot moonlight nights in the sixties. Preach leaned against a cabin, arms crossed, smiling at me, the Jesus eyes blue and mild. I perched my rump on the edge of a concrete birdbath with seashells stuck into the top of it in a design.

"What's your action?" Preach asked.

"Favors for friends, when I have to. This and that."

"Big old bastard, aren't you?" It didn't need an answer. He continued, "It doesn't take too much to handle a pair of fat dummies. Maybe there's a couple more fat dummies you could bust for me. I mean not just as a favor. Cash in hand."

"No, thanks."

"What if you've got no choice?"

"What does that mean?"

"That means that if you don't want to do me a favor, Magoo here and some of his friends will do me a favor of breaking your elbows. It's known to sting a little."

I smiled at him and shook my head. "If you give the orders, friend, tell them to kill me. You'll sleep better."

"You think so?"

"Whatever gets broken will mend, one way or another. And I would not come back at you from the front, Preach. Something would fall on your head, maybe. Or something you picked up might blow up. Or you could be in a room that catches fire and the door is locked. If I came at you from the front, I might not get you. And I would want to be absolutely sure. So, as far as taking orders are concerned, do you want me to tell you what you can go do in your helmet?"

He pushed himself away from the cabin, stretched and winced, and said to Magoo, "We better do more riding, you know that?"

"I know it," he said. "The last fifty miles my ass was getting sore. I mean, how much chance do we get lately?"

Preach studied me. "Testing, testing. Blaylock told me about you one time. Said you don't push. Neither do I, so I understand you. I've got an idea or two about this place. But I want to know something. Are you fixing to make any moves on Mits?"

"No."

"What ideas have you got about this place?"

"Once the legal estate thing is settled, I want to see how quick I can unload my half in any way I can unload it."

"How are your civil rights, McGee?"

"I don't know what you mean."

"I mean if you are a convicted felon, I can get you a pardon so you can vote again."

"That's nice, but I'm clean."

"That's nice because you should keep owning half. It could be a nice thing for you."

"In what way?"

"You won't have to come anywhere near it. You won't know anything about it. You won't know that we'll have some nice little pads built back here, and a lake dug, and an airstrip, and a meeting room put in, like a little convention center. And the whole place will be wired so a rat can't sneak in without turning on the red lights. Somebody will bring you what you have to sign, on corporation things. You and Mits will sign a management contract with somebody. I don't know who yet. The books will show a loss, you'll get dividends in cash you won't have to report. They could be nice dividends."

"Mits gets the same deal?"

"Maybe. Maybe not. Why should you care?"

"I care."

He moved toward me and put his hand out. "We can get along." We shook hands again. "You handle a bike?"

"Not for a few years. But I can if I have to."

"Why were you out here the other day, McGee?"

In the next ten silent seconds I shuffled through all my choices, all the ways I could go. "I was hoping Blaylock could give me some kind of a lead on a biker who beat a sick old man to death near Citrus City nearly two years ago."

"There's been a lot of that going around. I would be very disappointed in you if this has anything to do with law enforcement."

"It has to do with the old man's son taking a screwing in the will."

"No law?"

"I'm helping out. A favor for a friend. My line of work."

"Blaylock help any?"

"He came up with two names. Biker names. Dirty Bob and the Senator."

Preach turned to Magoo and said, "Anybody like that in the Corsairs you ever heard of?"

"God's sake, Preach, ever since that goddam movie there been Dirty Bobs sprang up all over the place."

"That's where I heard it!" Preach said. "That movie, that *Chopper Heaven*. The name they called the boss biker was Dirty Bob."

"And," said Magoo, "they called his buddy the Senator. Can't remember what their names were, their real names."

"That pair was supposed to have ridden all the way from California in fifty hours, without sleep, using uppers," I said.

"Then hell," said Preach, "maybe what you're looking for is the same two that was in those movies. The originals. I heard they were both Hell's Angels out there. Or Bandidos. I forget which. Dumb damn moving pictures. Any club goes around ripping up the civilians like in that movie, the smokeys would stake out the highway and shotgun those fuckers right out of their saddles." He gave me the broadest smile I had yet seen and said, "There's quieter ways of ripping off the civilians."

As we entered the room where the others were, Preach hung a long thin hand on my shoulder. "We're getting along just fine," he said to Mits and

Grudd. They both looked relieved. "McGeek here decided he might just keep on owning this garden spot. Mits, you keep hanging in."

"Sure thing, Preach."

"Gruddy baby, I will be in touch anon."

"Fine."

"Come on, Magoo. Put your sore ass back to work."

They went booming back out onto the highway, kicking up pebbles, riding hard and fast.

Grudd said in an uncertain voice, "He's . . . a very unusual man."

"What does he do, actually?" Meyer asked.

"Don't ask. I don't really know. He's got an office in Miami. Karma Imports. He's got some kind of leasing business."

I said to Mits, "He wants to make a lot of improvements here, bring in a manager."

"Anything he wants to do suits me fine," she said. "Shall we just . . . open up here and keep going?"

Grudd nodded. "Probably best. He'll move quick, I think. Mits, you go through all Ted's personal stuff, will you? Sort out the giveaway, and the stuff that has value, and the stuff you have questions about. Keep a list. I'll be back Monday. No, make that Tuesday. I have to be in court on Monday."

We all had to be leaving. Mits walked out with us. She said, "This is going to be one rotten weekend, guys. There was a squeak in the left wheel on his chair. I oiled it three times but it didn't go away. I'm going to be hearing that squeak coming up behind me. . . . Thanks for everything, guys, okay?"

In the old blue Rolls on the way back to Bahia Mar, I told Meyer about my talk with Preach. "I don't think I want any under-the-table dividends from an operation I have to stay away from."

"What will he be doing out there?"

"God knows. Home industry, maybe. A little pharmaceutical plant. Smugglers' haven. Wholesale distribution point. National headquarters for the outlaw bikers."

"Grudd is frightened of the man. Through and through."

"I got what I wanted from him. The back trail is very tricky, very old and cold, but if it leads where I think it is going to lead, it goes right back to Peter Kesner. Back to Josephine Esterland. Now I want to see those biker movies."

After I was alone aboard the *Flush* I could not account for my feeling of unrest, uneasiness. It had begun the instant Preach had put his hand on my shoulder. It had not been friendship or affection. It had been a symbol of possession. He and Magoo had walked me out into the weeds, raped me in some kind of deft and indescribable way, and walked me back in, announcing that I had enjoyed it. I wondered if I had been blowing smoke when I told him I would go after him if they busted me up. Testing, testing. Was pride enough? Maybe I'd spent too much of myself in too many hospitals over the years. Did Preach think I meant it when I said it? If I wasn't really certain I meant it, then I would try to be careful to keep my elbows intact. It is the new warning system. They hold it on a concrete block, one man on the wrist, his feet braced against the block, and they give the elbow a smack with an eight-pound sledge, crushing the joint. If they do them both, you end up being unable to feed yourself. The Italians do kneecaps; the dopers do elbows.

I looked in my little book and tried the Miami number for Matty Lamarr. It was five after five. They said he was retired and living in Guadalajara. They gave me an extension number for Lieutenant Goodbread. He was on another phone. Yes, I would hold.

"Goodbread," he said. The voice gave me a vivid recall of that big face, with its useful look of vapid stupidity.

"McGee in Lauderdale."

"McGee? McGee. Oh, sure, the smartass that kept me out of trouble that time with the great big rich important general. You kill somebody?"

"Not recently. But I met a biker today who seems to be trying to put some kind of arm on me. He's boss man of a biker club, the Fantasies. And he operates down in your area, maybe even legitimately. People call him Preach."

"Under that arm could not be such a great place to be, McGee. There are some people around who want harm to come to him, enough to gun down anybody in the area. His name is Amos Wilson. He owns Karma Imports. Many arrests, no convictions at all. He has access to lots of bail. I thought he was pulling out of the biker scene."

"What is he?"

"Believe me, I can't nail it down. It's easy to say what he *might* be into. He might be big in imported medicinals. Or he might be importing people from unpopular countries. Witnesses disappear. The feds tend to forget things. He isn't in any known pattern."

"What would he want with a big tract of land out in the boonies, with lots of security, an airstrip, and so on?"

"This is just a guess, friend, What I *really* think is that he and his animal pal, name of Magoo, they run a service business for people who are into untidy lines of work. Those people need transport, security, communications, and muscle. I think he is once removed from the action, and it is a smarter and safer place to be than out front where we are aiming at them."

"Will you nail him for anything?"

"I used to say that sooner or later we get everybody. But nowadays, that is hopeful bullshit. We don't. We're short on money and troops. There are too many groups on the hustle. Nobody is in charge any more. People like Preach, they jump in there, right in the confusion, develop a reputation, and take their fees to the bank in wheelbarrows, and sometimes they own the bank. I really envy Matty down there in Mexico. I told him to save room for me."

"Thanks for the time and the information."

"What have I told you? You ask me about a very smart one with a lot of moves. Times keep changing. Every month a better way to bring in the hash, the grass, and the coke. Every month people getting mashed flat by the competition, or sent out swimming with weights on, or crashing tired airplanes in empty areas zoned for tract houses, where only the roads are in. Preach runs an advisory and investment service, maybe. With a place to go when you're too hot. Maybe he settles disputes between A and B and can arrange with C to get D killed. What I would say is unlikely is that he is out front on any of it. He can lay back and take a percentage of what nine groups are bringing in, and do better than any one of them in the long haul. I hear rumors he is buying old office buildings, little tacky ones, and fixing them up and renting them pretty good. But, like I said, I would stay way clear if I were you. There are people who'd like him dead, him and Magoo both. It's always good to stay out of a target area."

"Thank you very much, lieutenant."

"Some day I'll need a favor from you, McGee. I'm just building up my equity."

12

SATURDAY I visited my neighborhood travel agency, put the houseboat in shape to leave it for a time, had a long phone talk with Annie Renzetti and another with Lysa Dean. Sunday morning in Miami I boarded the L-1011 nonstop to Los Angeles, sitting up there in first with the politicians, the airline deadheads, and the rich rucksacky dopers. There is more legroom, the drinks are free, and the food is better. Also, somebody else was paying. I had the double seat to myself.

I was aware of the flight attendant giving me sidelong speculative glances as she roved the aisles. She was a pouter-pigeon blonde with a long hollow-cheeked face which looked as if it had been designed for a more elegant body.

Finally when she brought me a drink she said, "Excuse me, Mr. McGee, but I feel almost certain I know you from somewhere."

"Maybe from another trip?"

She looked dubious. She frowned and held a finger against her chin. They like to identify and classify all their first-class passengers. Tinker, tailor, soldier, sailor . . . .She couldn't figure the stretch denim slacks, knit shirt, white sailcloth jacket with the big pockets and snaps, boat shoes.

When I did not volunteer more information, she went on to the next drinker, probably convinced that I was just another doper, running Jamaican hash to the Coast. I sipped and looked down through scattered cloud cover and saw the west coast of Florida slip back under us, six miles down. We'd had our life-jacket demonstration. I've never been able to imagine a planeload of average passengers getting those things out from under the seats and trying to get into them while the airplane is settling down toward the sea with, as Tom Wolfe commented, about the same glide angle as a set of car keys.

Had drinks, ate a mighty tough little steak for lunch, got into LA before lunch their time, found my reserved Hertz waiting, studied the simplified Hertz map and found my way through traffic to Coldwater Canyon Drive, found the proper turnoff on the second try, and stopped outside the pink wall, with the front of the little Fiesta two feet from the big iron gate.

An Oriental looked inquiringly at me through the bars of the gate. "McGee," I called out.

"You Messer McGee, hah?"

"Messer McGee, pal. Miss Dean expects me."

"I know, I know," he said and swung the gates wide, showing a lot of gold in his Korean smile. "Drive by," he said. "Park anyplace. Miss Dean in the pool, hah?"

The plantings were more luxuriant than I remembered. They'd had a few years to grow. Her big pink wall was due for repainting. I remembered Dana telling me that a Mexican architect had done the house for Lysa and her third husband, in a style that could be called Cuernavaca Aztec. I walked around to the poolside. It was quiet and green in here behind the wall, and the city out there was brassy, smelly gold, vibrating in sun, heat, and traffic, already into midsummer on only the twenty-sixth of April. When I went around the corner of the house, the world opened up, and I could see the cheeze-pizza structures of the city under the yellow haze, far beyond the pink wall that crossed the lower perimeter of her garden. She was swimming a slow length of her big rectangular pool, using a very tidy crawl, with no rolling or wallowing, sliding through the water with the greased ease of a seal in an amusement park. She saw me and angled over to the ladder and climbed out. She was wearing a pink bathing cap and an eggshell tank suit of a fabric so thin that, sopping wet, it fit her like skin, showing the dark areolas around the nipples and the dark pubic smudge. She yanked her cap off and shook her blond bleached hair out as she came smiling toward me. She stood on tiptoe and gave me a quick light kiss on the corner of the mouth, flavored with peppermint and chlorine. She tossed the pink cap into a chair, picked up a giant yellow towel, and began using it.

"Well!" she said. "How about you? You look fantastic."

"We're both fantastic."

"Look, I have to work on me. I have to think about me all day every day. Diet, exercise, massage, skin care, hair care, yoga."

"Whatever you're doing, it works."

I followed her over to a marble table, out of the sun. And after a slender Korean maid brought a Perrier for her and a rum and juice for me, Lee went into the house and came out ten minutes later with her hair brushed to gleaming. She was wearing lipstick and a little tennis dress.

"I really hated you, McGee."

"It wasn't a really great time for either of us."

"These are better years, amigo. I was very hot back then, getting lots of scripts to choose from, spoiled rotten. Also I was trying for the world boffing championship. The all-American boffer. Anything that came within reach. And I seldom missed. As I did with you. Anyway, my psychiatrist pulled me out of that swamp. What I decided about you, McGee, was that if you were some sort of funny-looking little guy with pop eyes and no chin and a dumpy little body, you wouldn't have turned me down. You wouldn't be turning anybody down. You would take what you could get and be grateful. So, my friend, your reluctance wasn't based on character. It was based on appearance. And that puts us both in the same line of work."

"Actors?"

"Get used to it. We're out front. I don't need to work, dear, but I keep right on scuffling. I don't want anybody to ever say to me, 'Hey, didn't you used to be Lysa Dean?' You do your share of posing, both for yourself and other people."

"You're smarter than I remember."

"Maybe I started thinking with my head instead of my butt."

"Looks good on you."

"And you are here to talk about Josie Laurant and Peter Kesner."

"I think I'm going to go at this a different way than I planned at first, Lee."

"Meaning?"

"I was going to keep the bad part of this to myself and con you along a little, here and there. But I find you just enough different to let me drop the whole bundle in front of you."

"Go ahead."

"Before I do, let me tell you one thing. Aside from the people whose help I had to have, I have never mentioned one word about your problem with the photographs and the blackmail."

She nodded. "I know. I expected the worst after you walked out. I thought maybe you were justifying your own actions to come. Like hanging onto a set of prints and doing an interview for *Penthouse*. I held my breath for a year. You get used to backstabbing in this business. Finally I decided you were straight, and I thank you for it."

"It would be nice if you would keep all this just as quiet."

I liked the fact there was no instant promise. She thought it over, frowning. "Well, okay. It'll be hard for me, but okay."

"You know anything about Ellis Esterland?"

"Just that he was a rich plastics tycoon, and he and Josie had the daughter with the strange name who died as a result of a bad accident. Rondola? Romola! Josie must have lived with her husband for ten years. They never did get divorced. A legal separation, though. They lived in the New York area and she did some theater work, not much, and then came back out here after the separation. Didn't he die a couple of years ago, in some strange way?"

"He was beaten to death. He had terminal cancer at the time. No arrests, no clues. He and his ex-secretary were living on a boat in Fort Lauderdale at the time. He drove inland alone and was killed. The reason for his trip is not known."

"I heard that Josie inherited a pretty good slug of money when Romola died. And that the money was from her father's estate." She tilted her head, took off her dark glasses, and looked at me with those vivid slanted green eyes. "Josie was involved with his death?"

"I don't know. Here is how it looks right now. It looks as though Josie, through her friendship with Anne Renzetti, the secretary, knew everything there was to know about Esterland's financial setup, his will and so on. And whatever Josie knew, Peter Kesner knew. Josie was supporting Kesner. When it became evident that Romola was a hopeless case, and if she died first Esterland's money would go to a foundation, it was in Kesner's interest to make sure Esterland died first. A problem in elementary mathematics. A couple of million is better than a hundred thousand, and worth taking some risks for."

"Josie, no. Forget Josie. Peter, yes. But how would he work it?"

"Very very carefully. He has contacts among outlaw bikers based on those two movies he made several years ago."

"For low budget, they were very good."

"Though I can't prove it and probably nobody ever will be able to, I think those two bikers who were in one or both of those movies rode all the way across the country, set up a meet with Esterland, and beat him to death. In the movie or movies they were called Dirty Bob and the Senator."

"I remember. Very tough people. Authentic tough, you know. You can always tell authentic tough from acting tough. Bogart was acting tough, but he was also a very tough-minded man on the inside. Nothing scared him, ever. Those bikers sort of scared me a little."

"Would they kill people?"

"If the price was right, yes."

"How do I find out what their real names are?"

"You find out from me, right now. Be right back." She went in and came out five minutes later with a thick, well-thumbed, paperback book. "My bible," she said. "The basic poop on five thousand motion pictures. All the statistics." She checked the index, found the right page. "Here we are: *Chopper Heaven*. The part of Dirty Bob was played by one Desmin Grizzel. My God, can that be a real name? It probably is. And the Senator by one Curley Hanner. Let me check that other one. What was the name of it?"

"*Bike Park Ramble,* I think."

"Sounds right. Yes, here it is. Same fellows. It was a sort of Son of *Chopper Heaven* and not quite as successful."

"Any way I could get to see the movies? Just one would do. Either one."

"I can call around the neighborhood. People are getting big collections of movies on videotape, the home-television kind and the three-quarter-inch commercial. I can show either one. I get tapes from the shows I'm on."

"If it wouldn't be too much trouble."

"Why am I doing you favors anyway? Okay. After lunch?"

"Had it on the airplane."

"It'll just be a salad. Choke it down. Or the Snow Princess will snap a gusset."

She led me on into the terrazzo silence I remembered, where there was dark paneling transplanted from ancient churches and portraits in oil of the owner. There were white throw rugs, and sparse white furniture, and a large wall cabinet of glass and mirrors containing a collection of owls in pottery and crystal, in jade, wood, ivory, bone and silver.

I stopped to admire them. "Used to be elephants," I said.

"They're in the bedroom."

She led me to an alcove off the dining area where there was a window table for two overlooking the pool, the long slope of the garden, and the city beyond. The Korean maid brought the salad in a big wooden bowl, fresh spinach, with cheese and mushrooms, some bits of bacon, a dressing of vinegar and oil with an aftertaste of garlic. Tall nubbly glasses full of iced tea with mint.

In Lee's casual conversation, in her expression, in her tone of voice, in the way she held herself, she seemed to be making an offer of herself, to be advertising her accessibility. And because any actress is such a mannered thing, such an arbitrary construction, I could not tell whether she was merely being her habitual self or inviting mischief.

"Who occupies the secretarial suite these days?"

"There's not as much to do, of course. Not like it used to be. A darling young man comes in and works in there three days a week. The letters and cards keep coming, thank God. A lot of it from those late late late late shows, the pictures I made at the time they were filming *Birth of a Nation*. I had my eighteenth birthday on location. I was aching to look at least twenty. Can you imagine?"

She smiled at me over the rim of the iced-tea glass, green eyes as frosty as the glass.

It took her three phone calls to locate a home videotape of *Chopper Heaven*. A boy on a bicycle delivered it. Her little projection area was an alcove off the bedroom. Two double chaises faced the oversized screen on which the television image was projected. The set and projector were between the two double chaises. The sound came out of two speakers, one on either side of the screen. There was no window in the alcove. Daylight filtered in through the drawn draperies in the bedroom.

I watched the eighty-minute show with total attention. Peter Kesner was given the writing credit, directing credit, producing credit. The sound track was old-fashioned hard rock. And loud. Hand-held cameras, grainy film, unadjusted color values from scene to scene. But it moved. It was saying that this biker world was quick, brutal, and curiously indifferent to its own brutality, almost unaware of it. The characters seemed to want things very badly and, when they got them, discarded them. The dialogue was primitive but had an authentic ring. The bikers' girls were sullen and slutty. After death and bombings, Dirty Bob and the Senator rode off down the highway toward the dawn, bawling a dirty song in their hoarse untrained voices, over the rumble of the two big machines.

She got up and turned it off and pushed the rewind key. "Interesting," she said. "It doesn't hold up. At the time it was more daring than it is now. It cost a million and a half and grossed maybe fifteen to twenty."

"Would Kesner have made a lot of money?"

"Darling! This is the Industry! The really creative people are the accountants. A big studio got over half the profit, after setting breakeven at about three times the cost, taking twenty-five percent of budget as an overhead charge, and taking thirty percent of income as a distribution charge, plus rental fees, and prime interest on what they advanced. If he made a million, including fees for his services, I'd be surprised. Peter lives *very* well. I'm surprised Josie could afford him. Anyway I remembered the picture as being better. Some of *my* old ones seem to be much *better* then I remembered. Odd, isn't it?"

"Did you ever meet those two? Grizzel and Hanner?"

"On a talk show several years ago. They were a disaster. They came stoned to the eyeballs. Big noisy smelly fellows, thrashing around and saying things that had to be beeped off the air, thinking they were hilarious, apparently. One of them grabbed me by the behind and actually left big dingy fingermarks on my yellow skirt. I told him if he touched me again, I'd cut his heart out and fry it. I meant it and he knew I meant it. I didn't know their names. They were just Dirty Bob and the Senator."

I knew I would recognize them if I saw them again anywhere. Dirty Bob, a.k.a. Desmin Grizzel, had a full black beard and a moon face with high cheekbones and such narrow eyes it gave him an Asiatic look, like a Mongol warlord. The full beard was a fringe beard, growing thick around the perimeter but not very lush around the mouth. It looked to me as if he had done his own tricks in the motion picture. If so, he was very quick and spry for a man of his considerable bulk.

The Senator, a.k.a. Curley Hanner, had a long narrow face, a long narrow nose, a tight little slot of a mouth. His eyes were so close together it gave him a half-mad, half-comedic look. His little slot mouth turned into a crazy little V when he smiled. On the right side of his forehead there was a deep, sickening crevasse, as though he had stove it in on the corner of something. Black thinning hair, and a black thin mustache that hung below his chin, like an oldtime gunfighter. Throughout the movie they had both worn thin red sweat bands just above the eyebrows. They were ham actors and could have spoiled the picture if the director had let them.

"Where did Kesner find that pair?"

"No idea, Travis. The story was that he'd auditioned some very hard-case types from the Bandidos and Hell's Angels, picked a half dozen, and then let them fight it out for the two parts. But that was probably some studio flack's idea of exciting copy. I heard that Kesner got a motorcycle and went riding with one of the outlaw clubs, and that's where he got the idea for the picture and found the people to play in it. You saw how many there were altogether. Fifteen or twenty."

"And Kesner is on location now?"

"Out in farm country somewhere. With Josie. Making a balloon picture. Hot-air balloons."

"How do I find out where they are?"

"You have me, dear. Girl guide to the wonders of the Industry. Let me phone. You stay put." She gave me a pretty good rap on the skull with her knuckles when she went behind the chaise. She went to the bedroom phone, sat small on the side of her big bed, her back to me, as she hunched over her phone list. I got up and roamed over to a wall rack which seemed to hold scores of videotapes. It was too dark to read the titles. There was a little gallery light over the rack and I pulled the chain. The titles were visible. They ranged from X to XXX. With a very few R-rated here and there. I could hear her on the phone. There was a shallow drawer under the middle shelf of the rack, and on nosey impulse I pulled it open. And there was the little white Prelude 3 System massager, fitted with what I believe is called the Come Again tip. Beside it a small vial of lubricant. I slid the drawer shut and went back to the chaise, then remembered the light, went and turned it off, and stretched out again.

Scenario for a lonely lady. With frequent insomnia. Slip in here from the bedroom, put on a dirty tape with the sound turned low or off, and surrender to the throbbing hum of electrical ecstasy.

No obligation for dull conversation before or after. No awkward emotional entanglements. No jealousies. No involvements. Just an interwoven pattern of as many climaxes as she cared to endure, and then turn off all the machinery and go back to bed, to a sleep like death itself. The modern female, making out with no help from any male. I had never felt more superfluous—which in itself is a comment.

She came back in and sat on my chaise near my knees, facing me. "Well, I know where they are, almost. In Iowa, at a place called Rosedale Station. It's northwest of Des Moines and southwest of Fort Dodge, somewhere off U.S. Route Thirty. What you have to do is fly to Des Moines and get a car there, and it would be maybe sixty miles."

"Now I have to come up with an approach."

"What do you mean?"

"Nobody there in Rosedale Station, neither Josie nor Kesner nor those two bikers—if they're there—would have any idea who I am or what I want. And I can't exactly go up to Josephine Laurant and say, 'Honey, your stepson Ron hired me to find out who beat old Ellis to death.' What I am talking about is some kind of a cover story. People making motion pictures keep a good guard up to keep the local hams and autograph hounds away. I can't exactly start cold and ingratiate myself."

"What is it you want to do when you get there?"

"I don't know. Mill around. Make friends. Trade secrets back and forth. Beat heads. Lie a lot. I don't know. I improvise. If you have made some good guesses about something that happened in the past, you can usually stick the pry bar into the right crack. If nothing much happens, you know you guessed wrong."

She tilted her pretty head and studied me. "Who should you be? I'll have to think about that. Let me see. You should have some authority of some kind, so they'll have to be nice to you."

"I know nothing about their line of work. Or about hot-air balloons."

"Hush. I'm thinking." With doubled fist she struck me gently on the knee, again and again. Lips pursed, eyes almost closed. "Got it!" she cried.

"I give up. Who am I?"

"It so happens I own a nice little piece of Take Five Productions, sweetie. And some of their nice letterhead. We do daytime game shows. So let's go to the darling secretary's office and compose a letter."

> Mr. Peter Kesner
> President, Major Productions
> On location
> Rosedale Station, Iowa
>
> Dear Peter,
>
> This will introduce Travis McGee, one of the consultants on our new and exciting project for prime-time television, tentatively titled THE REAL STUFF.
>
> As you may or may not know, I have an ownership interest in Take Five Productions, and I have had the privilege of being in on the planning phase of this new program scheduled for next fall on ABC.
>
> It is our intent—and I know you will keep this confidential—to go behind the scenes of the entertainment industry, not only in America but around the world.
>
> From backstage ballet to the back lot of the carnival, to big band rehearsals, to animal training, to moviemaking. We will

go for action and pictorial values, and we have no intention of skimping on the budget. Some very excited sponsors are waiting in the wings to see what we come up with as a pilot for the show.

In discussions here, it occurred to us that the picture you are making, about hot-air balloons and the people who fly in them, out there in the lovely springtime in the heartland of America, might make a very vivid episode in our projected series THE REAL STUFF.

I hope I am not imposing in asking you to give Mr. McGee the run of the sets and to answer his questions. I am certain he will be considerate. Should we want to use clips from your rushes, I can assure you the compensation will not disappoint you.

I wish you all manner of luck with your picture. And please say hi to darling Josie for me.

Affectionately,

Lysa Dean

She read through it again and signed *Lee* with a flourish, a swooping curlicue thing that went back under her name and crossed itself in a figure eight stretched out on its side.

"Such utter crap!" she said. "But you know, it is just ridiculous enough to appeal to that freak. Especially the hint about money. Can you carry it off, do you think?"

"Provided you tell me the kind of questions I should be asking."

She did not hear me. She was staring into the middle distance. Finally she said, "You know, it really might make a program. I'm going to take it up with Sam."

13

I GOT into Des Moines late on Monday night, stayed over in a motel near the airport, and drove to Rosedale Station on Tuesday morning, the twenty-eighth of April. I drove through soft gray rain, the wipers thudding back and forth in slow steady rhythm. The flat fields and the hedgerows and the ditches beyond the shoulder of the highway were green, the bright new green of springtime.

My road atlas said that Rosedale Station had 2,812 people. It had a railroad track, grain elevators, a central school, a dozen churches, a dozen gas stations, a new downtown shopping mall, a couple of fast food outlets, a lot of white houses and big trees, and a very few traffic lights.

I drove around in the rain until I came upon a brick and frame structure called THE ROSEDALE LODGE. FINE FOOD. It had its own gravel parking area to the right of the entrance. I pulled the rental Buick into a slot and trotted under the dripping trees, up onto the veranda, and into the front entrance hall.

There was a tall thin old lady behind the oak registration desk. I asked her if there was a vacancy.

"You with that movie bunch?"

"I'm not *with* them. But I have some business to transact with them."

"Then you're with them, the way I see it. I've got a single. It's fifty dollars a night. In advance. Food is extra."

"Is Mr. Kesner staying here?"

"Yes."

"Is he in now?"

"I wouldn't know and I won't ask."

"Is something wrong?"

"Nothing is wrong with the people around here. Do you want the room or don't you?"

"I'll take it for the night. Why are you being so rude?"

"Let's say it's catching."

She slapped my key down: Room 39. I paid and signed in, using the Burbank address of Take Five Productions.

"Third floor, all the way to the back on the left," she said.

"Would it be against your house rules to tell me Kesner's room number?"

"Twenty-five and -six," she said, and turned away.

"Pretty good room rate," I said.

"When you people go back where you belong, it will come on back down to normal."

"Welcome to Rosedale Station. Nice little town."

"Used to be," she said, and went into the switchboard alcove, pulled an old-fashioned plug, and let it snap down into its recess.

I took my duffelbag on up to 39. There was a big tree outside my single small window. Through the leaves I could see a neighboring lumberyard. My wallpaper was a design of crossed ropes and little old sailing ships, in brown, gray, and blue. My single bed was hammocked in the middle. The toilet and shower shared a three-by-six closet. The sink was in the bedroom, beside the shower-room door. There was an oval mirror over it. I had to stoop to look at myself. The backing was coming off, so that my image was fragmented. The spit-colored eyes looked back at me with more calm than I felt. I did not look like your ordinary consultant-type person. I looked more as if I worked with a sledge out in the sunshine, turning big rocks into little rocks. I took my shirt off and scratched my chest and thought about the tragicomic inconsistencies of the emotional life of McGee. A repressed libertine. A puritanical wastrel. A lot of names rolled around in my skull. Old ones: Puss and Glory and Pidge and Heidi and Skeeter and Cindy and Cathy. New ones: Gretel and Annie and Lysa.

Ah, the eternal compulsion to leap into a marvelous stew of boobs and butt, hungry lips and melting eyes, rolling hips and tangled hair. But I had to pause before the leap, like some kind of shy farm girl interrogating the traveling salesman after they have dug their nest in the side of a haystack: Wait, Walter! Is this for real?

Lysa was the peach which had hung long on the tree, gone from green to ripe to overripe, bursting with the juices that had that winelike tang of early fermentation. She had made all the moves she knew, and she knew a lot of moves. But I had bicycled around the ring, keeping her off with a long cautious left jab, avoiding the corners, slipping, rolling, tying her up. I had wanted her so badly I had felt as if I was carrying paving blocks around in the bottom of my belly. But of course, it wasn't for real, and it wasn't forever. I had the sap's record of spurning her once before, and apparently I was out to win the world title for sapistry.

And here I was on a rainy day in a sorry little room in a country hotel, a long long way from that lady of Sunday evening, that queen of the game shows who had wanted merely a jolly cluster of bangs in the night, topped off with steaks and a swim and a farewell bang for luck. But I had left her to the tireless throb of her Prelude 3 System and the technicolor stimulation of her blue movies.

Maybe what I was saying to myself by sidestepping a quantum bang was that I wanted but one lady at a time. Regardless of what Annie's reaction would have been, it would not have been anything I would have wanted to tell her. That did not improve my image. I wanted the free ride and I wanted to be paid in my own coin—meaningfulness or sacrament, or some kind of spiritual dedication—something that would give Hefner the hiccups. What gave me pause was the thought that for a fellow of my hesitations, I had sure cut myself a wide swath through a wall of female flesh, dragging my canoe behind me. Cheap apologist is the phrase that comes to mind.

I put on a fresh shirt and went down the stairs and found rooms 25 and 26. I could hear murmurous voices in there, which stopped when I knocked. A tall, strong, dark-haired young girl with a glassy look in her wide eyes opened the door and said, "Yeh?" She was wearing a very faded purple T-shirt with a drawing of Miss Piggy on the front of it and, as near as I could judge, nothing else.

"Peter Kesner in, please?"

"Whaddaya want with him?"

"I've got a letter here for him."

She whipped it out of my hand, said, "Stick aroun'," and closed the door smartly. I waited at least five minutes until she opened the door and beckoned me in with a motion of her head, a lift of her shoulder.

Peter Kesner was sitting on an unmade bed, folding the letter into a paper airplane. "How is that old bag, Lee Dean, holding up?" he asked.

I didn't answer because my attention was riveted on Purple Piggy. She was putting one foot carefully in front of the other as though walking an invisible tightrope. She made a right-angle corner and went six feet, made a right angle in the other direction, and walked until she came to a low solid oak table against the wall that apparently was intended for use as a luggage rack. She swiveled onto it and assumed the lotus position. She rested her head back against the wall and closed her eyes, her hands, palm upward, resting on her thighs, which looked uncommonly meaty and heavy for the rest of her.

"Don't mind Freaky Jean," Kesner said. "She's having one of her ninety-degree square-corner days." He glided the airplane toward her, and it hit the wall beside her and fell to the bench.

"What's she on?"

"She is into Qs. Like they were popcorn. How's Lee? I haven't seen her in a year. She's a money head. Pieces of this and pieces of that, and she puts them together nice. She's going to own as much of California as Bob Hope."

"She looks fine. She looks great."

He yawned and picked up a bound mimeographed script and riffled the pages. "I shouldn't tell you this because maybe you can come up with some pesos which we sure God need, but I think this thing is becoming a turkey. I should never have farmed out the script. Should have done it all myself. When you start with a piece of shit, no matter which way you turn it, form it, shape it, revise it, you end up with the same piece of shit. But the pictorials are great, when they happen. Jesus Christ, we are either getting rain or we are getting winds over nine miles an hour. And over nine, those balloon-club freaks won't fire them up. Can you imagine? And if the weatherman says a front is fifty miles away and moving in on us at fifteen miles an hour, they won't even take the gondolas out of the trucks. And if we get an absolutely beautiful day, say five-mile-an-hour wind, bright sun, warm and pretty, they will fly in the early morning or the late afternoon. And that is all, period, fini. Everything by FAA regulations, and they have saddled us with a resident FAA spook to make sure about getting every i dotted and t crossed. What we are doing here, McGee, is running too fast through the money and too slow through the film. And pretty soon I am going to have to take *Free Fall* back to LA, do the studio shots, and try to fake the rest from what we've gotten so far."

I swiveled a straight chair and sat there astride, arms crossed on the back of it, staring at him with an attentive questioning look, waiting for more. He wore jogging shorts and ragged blue canvas shoes. I guessed his age at fifty. Once upon a time he had been in shape. He had long ropy muscles, blurred by fat. He had dead-white skin and a lot of curly black hair on his body, even on the tops of his shoulders and down the backs of the shoulder blades. His face and forearms and the top of his bald head were deap tan. His trimmed beard was speckled with white hairs. He wore two heavy gold chains around his neck, one with some kind of a tooth hanging from it, and a thick gold chain around his wrist. His eyes were deep-set, and he wore Ben Franklin half glasses with little gold rims.

"I admire your early work, Mr. Kesner."

"Make it Peter, please. What have you seen, Travis?"

"*Chopper Heaven,* of course. And *Bike Park Ramble.* Very significant contributions to popular culture, Peter. I was very impressed with the quality of the performance you got out of those amateur actors, Grizzel and Hanner particularly."

He beamed at me. "It was long years ago, Travis. When I was young and hungry. They were existentialist films, both of them, tied into the significance of the immediate moment. Desmin Grizzel is still with me, by the way. He's working on this picture. Not in front of the camera. He's sort of a personal gofer. The Senator, Curley Hanner, is dead, of course."

"Dead? I didn't know that."

"It was covered in the trades and on the wire services. Accidental death. A year ago. He was coming down the coast road, working out a new machine, a Moto Guzzi Le Mans One Thousand. They were just north of Point Sur, really winding it up, very early in the morning. Desmin estimates a hundred and twenty-five to thirty miles an hour. The Senator was out front by fifty or sixty yards when without warning he ran into a cloud of sea gulls, just as he was starting to lean into a curve to the left. Dirty Bob thinks one of them took him right in the face shield. He straightened out and went out over the edge. Low tide and it was three hundred feet down to a shale beach. That was his fourth crackup and his last. Over two thousand bikers came to his funeral, some of them all the way from across the country. There was TV news coverage. Where were you?"

"I have to travel outside the country often."

"Consultant. That's the way to go. What do you want to see? What do you want to know?"

"Is everybody staying here in this hotel?"

"God, no! We'd be out of money already. We leased some pasture five miles north of town when we first got here. Nearly everybody else is out there, with the mobile units, vans, house trailers, campers, pickup trucks, and so on, sitting out the rain, bitching, gambling, freaking out. Oh, we were real big when we came to town. We were going to put Rosedale Station on the map. They were all smiles. But, you know, the crew likes a little fun, and there are some townie girls who've learned how fun-loving they are, and there are some townie dudes who got broken up in little arguments about this and that. Now things are very cool, and they talk about us from the pulpits. And overcharge us."

"I've got an eighteen-dollar room upstairs for fifty dollars."

"And the old bat behind the desk was happy to see you?"

"Not exactly."

"Okay, for Lee's bad idea for a program, what are you looking for?"

"Behind the scenes, how problems are solved. What goes wrong with the balloon scenes until you get it right."

"We are up to here in what goes wrong. We can show you lots of that, McGee. One trouble, we're down to eight balloon teams now. The rest of them got sick of waiting around and took off. We had thirty teams here at one time. Freaky Jean here, she dropped out of one of the teams that took off. Right, Jeanie? Hey, you! Jeanie!"

She opened her eyes slowly and took long seconds to focus. "Wha?"

"Where'd the buddies on your team go?"

"Wha?"

"Forget it. Look, I got some more script work here. Afterwards, I can take you out and introduce you to the kids. About noon or a little after. So kill some time and I'll get back to you. If you want, pal, you can take Jeanie here along with you. She's a real workout."

"Not right now, thanks."

"Feel free, any time. Courtesy of the house."

"Thanks. What's the theme of the picture?"

His face changed, and he looked demented. "The free flight in the hot-air balloon is the symbol of the yearning for freedom, like any dream of flying.

We see the life-worn female, trying to reenter the freedom of her youth, seeking it in blue skies, searching and yearning, but the dream of flying contains implicit within it the dream of falling. Age is a falling away, a manner of dying.''

''Oh.''

''Gallantry in the face of disaster will underline the symbols of her life, the young lover deserting her, her child dying, the man who wants to take her on this last splendid voyage.''

''Lysa Dean said that Josephine Laurant is starring in the picture.''

The demented look vanished and the odd face scowled. ''She will by God win awards with this role if she will for Christ's sake keep saying the lines the way they are written, not the way she thinks they should have been written.''

''She's an investor?''

He stared at me. ''Why do you ask?''

''Lysa said there was a rumor around.''

''There are always rumors around. Yes, we are both investors, friend. We are both betting our asses and all we own in this world on a fine artistic venture which will, because of its message, be a commercial success. I know how to combine those two elements. I bombed out on two films because they wouldn't let me go my own way. They controlled me. They turned those two films sour. Now it's like the old days. Complete artistic control, casting control, direction, production, writing, everything. Because we staked everything, the two of us, the distributor and the banks came into the picture for nine mil, and wished upon me a godawful little ferret-faced money man to watch every cent spent, checking every scene against the story boards, setting limits on the number of takes, cutting down the camera angles on both units. So all my wonderful control doesn't mean shit. And it keeps raining. Look, let me get to work here.''

So I left, taking with me the memory of Freaky Jean's placid young freckled face, of the dazed mind riding atop the ripe maturity of the animal body.

At a little before one o'clock I rode out to the rented pasture in Kesner's rented car. He was a ragged driver, accelerating too soon, braking too late, wandering over the center line, talking with his hands. The rain was dwindling. Sunshine was predicted for afternoon. Kesner was full of optimism.

The thirty or so vehicles were parked in random order under a long roadside row of big maples. The pastureland had been trampled into mud paths that followed the traffic pattern. They had wangled a hookup to the power line, and the wires led down to a temporary meter on a pole. There were camera booms and camera trucks standing in the drizzle, their vital parts shrouded in plastic. There were lights shining through the windows of some of the trailers. People wandered around in rain gear. Kesner led me to the cook tent, to a large helping of excellent beef stew on a paper plate, served with a big tin spoon and a cup of india-ink coffee. He settled for just the coffee and a banana.

He introduced me as ''A television person who can maybe set us up for some exposure on a network show, so be nice to him.''

I couldn't retain the names. They came too fast. Chief cameraman, second unit director, script girl, lighting technician, some actors, some balloon people. Everybody seemed very cordial. And then Dirty Bob came in, in a shiny orange jump suit with water droplets on the shoulders and chest. Unmistakable bland moon face, the fringe of beard now flecked with gray, the small Mongolian eyes, slitted and slanted.

"Hey, Desmin. Meet one of your fans. This is Travis McGee."

I stood up and shook hands with him. His hand was thick, dry, warm, and so slack it felt lifeless. As Kesner explained why I was there, Desmin Grizzel stared out at me through those little blueberry eyes set back behind the squinty lids. And I looked back at him. There was something going on behind those eyes. He was perhaps adding something up, something he had heard, measuring me in all the ways I didn't fit the present role. Or maybe it was some primitive awareness of a special danger.

I sat down, and he sat down with us.

Kesner said, "I gave Kitty the changes for the pink sheets. Did they get that goddam duplicator fixed?"

"Early this morning. She's caught up on back stuff."

"What's with Josie?"

"She come in here for lunch today. Now she's doing backgammon with Tiger in her trailer."

"What about the fellow from Joya's balloon?"

"It turned out it was pneumonia, and they run him on down to Des Moines in Jake's wagon."

"Jesus Christ! It's clearing and I want to do number eighty-one. Jesus Christ, is he in that one?"

"No. I checked it out with Kitty. No scene, no lines, nothing. That's why I didn't call in."

"How did the special project go after I left last night?"

"Mercer thinks it's pretty much okay. He just doesn't like the Mickey Mouse equipment and no chance to make cuts."

"Where's the girl?"

"Linda's looking after her."

"Good·thinking. McGee, if you're through, I'll go introduce you to Josie. Dez, what you do is get people going on makeup and have Kitty get the pages distributed for number eighty-one, and get those balloon crews ready to go out there to the takeoff area soon as the sun comes out."

I followed Kesner through the mud to Josie's big dressing-room trailer, stepping with care. She let us in, and he kissed her on the cheek and said, 'We'll be able to roll this afternoon. Here's what we'll be doing, if we stay lucky."

When he introduced me, she gave a vacant nod and began skimming through the script pages. I found it hard to believe she was as old as she had to be. A small woman, dainty, dark, fragile, with a lot of energy and vitality in her expression, in the way she moved.

She moved her lips as she turned the pages. Suddenly she threw her head back, dashing the dark hair away from her forehead. She threw the pages at Kesner's face.

"I told you! I will *not* do that. I will not!"

"Not do what?"

"I will not go up in that goddam wicker basket!"

"And I told you fifty times, damn it, that you *will* go up to eight feet off the ground. The damn balloon will be anchored! I want you up there with Tyler for your scene, the big one. The lines that are going to break hearts." He picked up the pages. "Look. Right here. Where it's marked. That's where we take you out of the basket and put Linda in. We back off for a low angle and get Linda when she jumps out of the basket into the net. Then it goes on up and we pick up the fall after they throw out the dummy, and all the rest is process. Eight feet in the air, for God's sake."

"I don't like the height. It could get away somehow. It would kill me. It would stop my heart. No."

"I'm telling you, there will be three ropes this big around tied to that basket and tied to three trucks on the ground."

"The propane will blow up."

"It is safe! Absolutely safe! I know what I am doing."

She switched emotions instantaneously, from indignation and fury to cool sardonic query. Posture, expression, voice quality—all changed.

"Do you now, darling? Do you really know what you are doing? Do you really understand the extra risks you're running?"

"What would you rather have me do, mouse? Wind it all down or try to keep it going?" It seemed to me that he gave her some look of warning, some sign to be careful.

After a moment of hesitation, she said, "It makes me nervous."

"You don't have to know anything about it. Or even think about it. Okay? Maybe you don't even have to think about being in the basket way up there in the air, eight feet. Maybe Linda would be better all the way through. Go back and do your scenes over with her. Her skin tones are better by daylight."

"You son of a bitch! She's a stuntwoman. She's no actress."

"Listen! You were run out of the industry because nobody could trust you not to fuck up and spoil scenes and cost big money. For God's sake, it's *your* money you're wasting!"

"So I'll waste it if I want to!"

"I'll use Linda for the whole thing. I need a picture in the can more than I need your famous face, lady."

She hesitated. "Three real strong ropes?"

"Big ropes. This big around."

"I better start to get ready."

I followed him back out into the mud and along the row of vehicles to a yellow four-wheel-drive Subaru parked next to a big cargo trailer and a small house trailer. A woman sat in the doorway of the house trailer, mending the toe of a red wool sock. She wore bib overalls over a beige turtleneck. She looked lean and husky, with big shoulders and a plain, intelligent face, red-brown hair combed back and tied.

"Hey, Joya," Kesner said. "This here is Travis McGee, who is a consultant, and he'll get us some prime-time exposure for free, if we're lucky. Joya is the boss lady of the balloons we got left."

She had a muscular handshake, a direct, crinkled smile, a pleasantly rusty voice.

Kesner said, "I'd like to get them off the ground in maybe two hours. The weather looks okay."

"The forecast looks good," she said.

He drew in the dirt with a stick. "The wind is going to keep coming out of the southwest. Did I say wind? The breeze. Five knots and fairly steady, they tell me. So right here we do a tethered scene with Josie in the number-one balloon. Then we get her out, then Linda jumps into the net, then you balloon people take it up, and I want about five hundred feet on it when the dummy gets tossed out. We'll cut from Linda jumping to the free fall at five hundred feet. Now when we take the low angle on the dummy coming out, I want to see balloons up there, not placed so they'll get in the way of the cameras. I want enough of them in the scene so in the editing, we can go back to where we had them all going nice that day, remember?"

"Sure."

"So the closer together and the closer to the number-one balloon, the better. So what you do is establish the placement and the order of takeoff, and when you get the gear spread out, I'll set up the camera stations. Okay?"

"Fine."

"I want to put Simmy with a camera in the number-three balloon, so that better be the one to come off last, so he can get wide-angle stuff of the other balloons and the fall. I want him back in the basket and low, so the other cameras don't pick him up."

"Upwind, then, about two hundred feet from number one, with a simultaneous takeoff, and Red has such a nice touch on that burner, he can hold it anywhere you say in relation to number one."

"I'd say a little higher, but not so high the envelope gets in the way of his camera angle. With the set of the wind, he should get the kind of landscape we want to show below number one. Joya, please, honey, it has to go right the first time."

"Do everything I can."

"Sorry to hear about Walter."

"He'll be okay. We thought it was some sort of flu, and then he began to have trouble breathing. They've got him on oxygen and full of antibiotics."

"Leaves you shorthanded."

"We were already shorthanded. There's just me, Ed, and Dave."

"So here is your new man. Travis McGee. Consultants are supposed to be able to do anything. Give him the speedy balloonist course. Okay with you, McGee?"

"Fine with me."

There was something in her quick glance which I could not identify. It seemed like some kind of recognition. It gave me the strange feeling that she knew I was an impostor, here for some private purpose. It made me wonder if I had seen the woman before, known her in some other context. But I am good about faces, and I knew she was a stranger. I knew I had not misinterpreted some kind of flirtatious awareness. It gave me a feeling of strangeness, wariness, distrust. Proceed with caution. She either knew something about me she had no right to know, or she was making some kind of very poor guess about me. In the glance, in her body language, in her voice, there was the sense of a secret shared, a private conspiracy.

THE MIST was gone, the sky brightening, and the encampment came alive, with people trotting back and forth from chore to chore, engines grinding as they moved vehicles into position.

Joya told me where to wait for her, and after she had organized the positions and told people the timing she came back to me.

"McGee, I hope you are a quick listener, because I don't have much time. Stop me any time you have a question, any time anything is unclear, okay? We like to fly in the early morning before the thermals begin to kick up, but this should be a similar situation. The air is cool enough to give a nice lift. We've got a nice launch site here. The direction of the breeze will hold, and the first thing in the way is that line of trees at least a half mile off."

A truck pulled up to us, and two men hopped out and started to wrestle the wicker basket out of the back. Joya introduced them. I helped them with the basket. They lifted a big canvas sack out of the basket, set it on the ground, and began pulling the seventy feet of canopy out of it. It was very brightly patterned in wide vertical yellow and green stripes.

"It's ripstop nylon," Joya said. "We stow it into the bag in accordion folds, inspect it when we fold it in, inspect again when we spread it out. We check the deflation port and the maneuvering vent."

"Whoa."

"The maneuvering vent is a slit on the side, up beyond the equator, ten or twelve feet long. You pull a cord and let hot air out to descend. When you are just about on the ground, you pull the red line for the deflation port, and that opens the top of the balloon and collapses it. It has a Velcro seal. They are checking the numbered gores and the vertical and horizontal load tapes. As owners, we're authorized to fix little melt holes with patches. And the places where damn fools walk on the canopy. Bigger damage has to have FAA-authorized repair."

When they had the big bright envelope spread out, downwind, Joya and the two men brought the propane tanks from the truck and slipped them into the stowage cylinders in the corners of the basket. They bolted together the support frame for the burners, hooked up the fuel lines from the ten-gallon tanks to the burners, then tilted the basket onto its side with the frame and burners toward the spread-out envelope.

At the other locations Joya had selected, the teams were doing the same things, getting set for a coordinated launch. They seemed to be trim and attractive people in their late twenties and early thirties. There was an earnestness about them, a cooperative efficiency, that reminded me of the sailing crowd, of preparations for a regatta. About half of them were women.

As the men were hooking the load cables to the tie blocks, Joya showed me the small instrument panel and explained it to me: variometer for rate of ascent and descent, pyrometer for temperature up in the crown of the balloon, compass—which she said was not very meaningful because there was no way to steer once you were aloft. There were gauges on the top of each propane tank. She showed me the sparker used to ignite the propane and to reignite it quickly should the flame go out. There was a small hand-held CB radio strapped to the side of the basket, which she said they used for contact with the chase vehicle.

She showed me the red line for deflation and the line to the maneuvering vent. She ran through a checklist with her ground crew and then turned to me, shrugged, and said, "Now we wait until it's time to inflate. Nothing else we can do at the moment, Mr. McGee."

When I asked her how that was arranged, she said we could walk over and watch them at the number-one balloon. They brought out a power-operated fan, and two crew members held the mouth of the balloon wide open as the fan blew air into it. One crew member held a line fastened to the crown of the balloon and kept watch to see that it didn't roll in any kind of side wind that would twist the steel cables at the mouth. When the balloon seemed about three quarters inflated, they started the burner, and it made a monstrous ripping, roaring sound as it gouted flame into the open mouth of the balloon.

She leaned close to me to holler over the burner sound, "Flying, you use over twelve gallons of propane an hour, enough to heat ten houses. George is working the blast valve. See. Now there's a little lift."

The roaring stopped. The balloon lifted free of the ground and slowly swung up, righting the basket as it did so, and another man climbed into the basket. The basket was tethered to a truck and to a smaller vehicle. George pulled on the blast valve, giving it a three-second shot of flame up into the balloon, waited, and then did it again.

"Short blasts are the way to do it," Joya explained. "You don't get any reaction for maybe fifteen or twenty seconds, and then you get the lifting effect of the new heat."

She took me closer to where we could look up into the balloon. It was blue and white and crimson, segmented like an orange, and there was enough daylight coming through the fabric to dim the long blue flame of the burners. The sun broke through. Kesner was walking around, arguing, waving his arms. Josie Laurant arrived, leading her small entourage, and Kesner picked her up and put her in the basket. I couldn't hear what she was saying, but she was visibly angry. They brought the camera boom close and wanted the area cleared. I went back to the number-two balloon with Joya.

There was no diminution in my awareness of her special attitude toward me. She carried on a second conversation at a nonverbal level. She was telling me that she and I had some sort of arrangement. And, in addition, she was curious about me. It seemed an unemotional curiosity, speculative and slightly anxious, expressed by the quick sidelong glances, the set of the mouth.

The number-one balloon lifted to the limit of its tether. The breeze kept it canted toward the northeast. Kesner yelled through his bullhorn. They seemed to be having trouble over there, doing the scene in between blasts of the burner needed to keep the balloon aloft at the end of the tethers.

"You want to take this flight with me, Mr. McGee?"

"I don't know anything about it. I wouldn't be in the way?"

"I like the extra weight. Dave was going to come along. Let me ask him."

She went over to the truck and in a little while she came back with leather gloves and a helmet. "He says sure. See if these are okay. If you lose balance or something, you might touch the burner or the coils that preheat the propane. Helmet is standard for landings. They can get rough. The thing is to face the direction of flight, hang on, and don't leave the basket. That's important. Without your weight it could take right off again and get in trouble. Look, do you want to try it or not?"

"I'd like to try it, but not very much."

She studied me and smiled. "That's an honest reaction. This should be a routine flight. What do people call you?"

"Travis. Or McGee. Or whatever, Joya."

"Joya Murphy-Wheeler. With a hyphen, Travis. Mostly what you have to do is keep out of my way, which isn't easy, and admire the view."

We killed time for an hour, and finally they took Josie down to ground level and let her out, and put another propane tank aboard and another smallish dark-haired woman dressed like Josie.

"That's the stunt woman," Joya said. "Linda." She said the name the way she might say "snake."

They took the number-one balloon back up again to twenty feet above the ground. Linda held the burner support, straddled the side of the basket. The man with her, who had been in the long scene with Josie, grabbed for her and missed as she toppled over the side. She fell neatly into the safety net, bounced up, clasped her hands over her head, duck-walked to the edge of the net, grasped it, and swung down. George stood up out of his concealment in the basket and hit the blast valve for a few seconds. The balloon sagged down anyway, and the crew grabbed the edge of the basket. The actor climbed out and then was told to climb back in. The dummy was brought aboard and stowed. After a small conference, Linda climbed aboard too, and Kesner yelled through his bullhorn, "Joya, get your people ready to go."

It took about thirty minutes to get all seven balloons inflated. They seemed to come growing up out of the field like a crop of huge poisonous puffballs. The gas blasts were almost constant. Joya had arranged the signals. When number one took off, number three followed almost immediately, staying near it, gaining a little height on it. Joya's crew people, Dave and Ed, held the basket down and made bad jokes about what I might expect of the flight.

"Weight off!" Joya ordered. They removed their hands. We had positive buoyancy, and she blasted for eight or ten seconds. A little while after the blast ended, we began to lift more rapidly, following the first two in their mated ascent.

"I'll have to try to stay close, for the sake of the cameras, but then we'll peel off."

"I thought you said you couldn't steer these things."

"You'll see." She worked the blaster valve, ripping the silence with that startling bray, a snorting sound that shot the blue flame high into the envelope. Without that noise, there was a strange silence. We were moving with the wind, so there was no wind sound. I heard the other balloons blasting in short staccato sequences, then heard the wicker of the basket creak as she rested her hip against the edge. The ground had dropped away. Behind us I could see the pattern of vehicles, of the muddy paths, the trailers and trucks.

"There!" Joya said.

I looked where she pointed and saw the lifelike dummy ejected from the number-one balloon, about seventy feet above us and ahead of us. I heard the rattle of the clothing as the dummy fell, turning slowly. It seemed to pause and then pick up a terrible speed as it dwindled below us to smack into the tough pastureland.

We held position for a little while until Joya said, "I think they have enough." She pulled the line to the maneuvering vent and bent to watch the variometer scale, explaining that we were too high to use visual reference points to indicate altitude. She let us sag downward until it seemed to me that our descent accelerated. At just that point she began feeding it short intermittent blasts. The harsh sound startled me each time until I learned to watch her gloved hand on the lever.

The others were far ahead of us, much higher and leaving us well behind. "Higher wind speeds aloft," she explained. "They'll be coming down soon, to fly close to the ground. That's when it's best. You'll see."

She gave all her attention to stabilizing the balloon at the height she wanted, explaining that as we came down we were pushing cooler air up into the envelope, thus decreasing lift. She leveled it out at about twenty feet above the ground. The breeze carried us along at I would guess ten miles an hour. Now and again she would pull the blast lever for a short sequence of that ungodly racket, and in a little while I began to comprehend the rhythm of it. If there was a tree line ahead she would give a two-second blast which, thirty seconds later, would lift us up over the trees.

We moved in silence, looking at the flat rich country. We heard the birdsongs, heard a chain saw in a woodlot, heard horses whinny. Children ran and waved at us. We crossed small country roads and once saw our reflection in a farm pond.

"What do you think?" she asked.

"There aren't any words," I said. There weren't. In incredible silence between her infrequent short blasts for control, we moved across the afternoon land, steady as a cathedral, moving through the land scents, barn scents, the summery sounds. It was a sensation unlike anything else in the world. It was a placid excitement, with the quality of an extended dream.

We beamed at each other, sharing pleasure. It made her strong plain face quite lovely. It was the instant of becoming friends.

At last she bumped it up to two hundred feet, where her exquisite coordination was not as imperative. We used the wrench to cut an almost empty tank out of the line and tie in another full one. She explained that we had wasted gas by using the maneuvering vent to drop us down, but she had wanted to get down quickly and get away from the others. From our altitude I scanned the horizon and could see but two of the others, little round pieces of hard candy way off to the west of us. "Divergent winds at different altitudes," she explained.

She perched a hip on the edge of the basket again, one hand overhead on the blast lever. She glanced at the control panel, then looked at me with the questing look she had concealed before.

"Travis, I can't add anything to what I told them on the phone."

Moment of decision. The proper thing to do would be to express all the confusion I felt, to take her off the hook, to correct her misapprehension. But there was a flavor of conspiracy, and I did not want to sidestep anything that might become of use to me. Apparently she and I were having a clandestine meeting, hanging up there in a wicker basket under a seventy-foot bulge of rainbow nylon, moving northeasterly across middle America.

I took my time with the response, knowing it was make or break. "They said they felt it would be better if I got it from you, rather than secondhand from them."

"I thought they were taping it. There was that little beep every few seconds."

"Listening to a tape and listening directly to a person are two quite different experiences, Joya. So if you don't mind . . ."

She shrugged, sighed. She pointed out a small deer, bounding toward a woodlot. And then she told me the story.

They had been going to leave when a lot of the others left. But she had been concerned about what happened to her friend, Jean Norman, who was staying at the hotel with Kesner. There was a large trailer at the far end of the leased pastureland, fixed up like a bedroom set. There the withered little technician named Mercer used a video camera setup with a videorecorder, and with Dirty Bob and Jean and Linda, who was gay, they made cassettes, masters, which were flown to Las Vegas, where a distributor paid three thousand apiece for them and could then duplicate a thousand copies a day, title them, package them, and send them out. They kept Jeanie on pills and paid so little attention to her that she heard more than they realized. She signed releases every time, and they gave her a little money every time. Lately they had been bringing local girls into the action, making them think it was going to be some sort of screen test. The girls got some false reassurance from the presence of Linda and Jeanie, but the fake rape turned out to be real rape, and the screams were real as well. With enough Valium in them to quiet them down, they would take the money later on and sign the release and never dare reveal what had actually happened, hoping only that no collector in Rosedale Station ever bought one of those X tapes and recognized his neighbor's daughter or granddaughter in the jolly tattooed clutch of Desmin Grizzel.

"I haven't got any proof at all," she said. "I shouldn't have gotten involved. But I think it is rotten. And they should pay somehow for what they did to Jeanie, if for nothing else. She told me bits and pieces when she was sort of lucid. And I put it together. I don't think Josie Laurant knows about it. I like her. Kesner and Dirty Bob are monsters. Like I told your people on the phone, we're cutting out. Dave is driving the chase car and Ed is driving the truck with all our gear. I don't even want to take you back to where we left from. It's going to get very dangerous around there. The people around there hate the movie people and us too. If any one of those girls talks about what happened to her, it could start a shooting war. It's almost a shooting war now. One balloon came in with three rifle-bullet holes right through it, but little holes won't bring a balloon down. From now on it's up to you people."

"How did you know I was the one?"

"They said somebody would be here today, somebody with a cover story, to look around and decide whether it is worth further investigation." She looked up into the envelope and down at the variometer dial, gave a five- or six-second blast, frowned at me, and said, "Anyway, you *look* like the sort of person I expected them to send. What will you do?"

"Try to nail down the violations. Interstate transportation of obscene materials. There's a corrupt organizations statute that might fit."

"Will they go to prison for a long time?"

"Probably not."

"One of those girls was fifteen."

"If she would testify against them, it would be a big help. Lots of nice charges there, with the locals in the driver's seat."

"She probably wouldn't ever testify."

"Well, we're very grateful for the help of any citizen."

"You're welcome. I've got to get back anyway. I've taken too much time off work. I'm from Ottumwa. All four of us are. We're shares on the balloon. It's a Cameron. We've got about four thousand total in it. We really wanted to see it flying in a movie. But I don't think there'll be any movie. I tried to read that script. It doesn't make any sense at all. I think Peter Kesner is crazy."

"What do you work at?"

"Oh, I'm a systems analyst, and I do some computer programming. It's kind of a slack time right now, so they let me off work. I think we better come down, and I think I see a good place. And there's the search car." She pointed it out to me, the Subaru with a yellow and green target painted on the roof, running along a road that paralleled our course.

She took the CB out of the straps, extended the aerial, and spoke into it. "Breaker Thirty-eight, this is Joytime, calling Little Sue. Come in, Little Sue."

"Little Sue sees you, Joytime."

"Take your second left and go in about two hundred yards, and that should be about right, Little Sue."

"Got you. See you there."

She made a face at me as she packed the CB away. "Not what you'd call good radio discipline. But it gets the job done."

She turned her attention to the descent, checking the stowage of loose equipment, checking on helmets, reading the surface wind, telling me where to stand and what to hold on to. She worked the maneuvering port line, bringing us down at a steady angle, clear of any obstructions. We passed the parked Subaru, twenty feet in front of it and a few feet higher than its roof. Ground speed seemed to increase. At the instant the bottom of the basket bumped the earth, she yanked the red line to empty the envelope and turned the fuel tank valve off. We bumped along for perhaps a dozen feet and stopped.

She scrambled to keep any part of the nylon skirt from touching the hot burner. Dave, round, redheaded, and heavily freckled, came trotting up, saying, "Great work, Joya. Real nice. You like it, Mr. McGee?"

"It's fantastic."

A pack of farm children arrived on bicycles and hung back at a shy distance until Dave and Joya gave them chores. She bled off the fuel pressure, and then we emptied the envelope by holding the mouth closed and squeezing the air out toward the apex. Dave disconnected the pyrometer, and we packed the envelope in the bag, inspecting it as it was accordion-folded in. Everything fitted on or in the Subaru. As I helped fold, lift, and carry, I wrestled with my conscience and with my liking for guile. Guile won. So I was not going to walk her a little way down the road and confess. I walked her a little way down the road and asked for the name of the fifteen-year-old, knowing what a useful lever I might make of it.

"Karen," she said. "Thatcher? Or Fletcher? Hatcher! That's it. Karen Hatcher. Blond. With some baby fat."

"Thank you for the balloon ride, Joya."

"It was a good private place to talk. I . . . I'll be watching the newspapers. I hope you smash them flat. I really do."

So we said goodbye to the farm kids, and Dave made a rendezvous with the truck, let Joya off there, and we moved the basket and the rest of the gear into the truck. Then Dave drove me back to Rosedale Station. The last of the breeze was gone. The late afternoon was utterly still.

There was no one behind the desk at the Rosedale Lodge. I was tall enough to bend over the counter and lift my key out of the box. I went up the stairs, walked silently down the corridor to rooms 25 and 26, listened at both doors, and heard no sound. I went up the next flight to my fifty-dollar room and sat on the edge of my narrow sagging bed.

There could not, I realized, be any clean resolution of this whole thing. Ellis Esterland had been killed twenty-one months ago. And what he had been killed for was long since down the drain, flushed down by an erratic and talented middle-aged woman, misled by her parasitic friend, Peter Kesner. Circumstances changed for the folks in the black hats, just as they did for the white hats. And the gray. Their universe continued to unfold. The Senator flew over the cliff with a sea gull in his face. Up until now I had not been able to feel any particular personal imperative at work. Annie Renzetti had dropped delightfully and unexpectedly into my arms, but possessing her did not act as a spur to action, to learning what really did happen to Esterland.

In my blundering about, with my dull uncomprehending smile, my earnest clumsiness, I had inherited half a motorcycle haven and tattoo parlor. And now I had joined the FBI, or the equivalent. I had begun to feel a little bit like Sellers in his immortal *Being There*. I felt no urge to enrich either Ron Esterland or myself. And no urge to punish Josie Laurant any more than she was going to be punished by the gods of stupidity at some time in that future which was getting ready to crash down on her. I was a fake consultant in the employ of Lysa Dean, queen of the game shows. I represented, to Kesner, a chance for free promotion of a motion picture that would probably never be shown in the unlikely event it was ever completed.

I had zigged and zagged until, finally, I had completely confused myself. I had spent some of Ron's money and had myself a nice balloon ride, and I wished heartily that Meyer would happen along, listen, and tell me what to do next.

At least, now, there was a sense of personal involvement. The misdeeds of the vague past seemed unlikely. What is the penalty for killing a dying man? But I had seen Freaky Jean, Joya's ex-friend, and I could visualize blond Karen in her baby fat as, under the lights of the improvised little studio, she came to the horrid and ultimate realization that the creature of her nightmares, Dirty Bob himself, was going to jam that incredible ugliness right up into her while the women watched and the wizened little man came closer with the camera and the hi-fi rock masked her yelps and hollers, her pleas for mercy.

The fracture line was, of course, somewhere between Peter Kesner and Desmin Grizzel. And I could improvise a pry bar of sorts. Perhaps there was another vulnerable area between Josie and Kesner, labeled Romola. Daughter lost and gone. Twenty months gone.

Time to try to close the store.

15

I DROVE my rental Buick back to the pasture five miles out of town. Kesner's car was there. Clouds were bulging up to interfere with the last of the sunlight. There was the usual amount of milling about, but there appeared to be fewer vehicles.

After asking three people where I could find Kesner, I finally located him in Josie's trailer. She was not there. He let me in, went back to the couch where his drink was, and continued his conversation with a thick-bodied man of about fifty who sat bolt upright in a chair and had no drink at hand.

"What's your name again?" Kesner asked him.

"Forgan."

"Forgan, this is Travis McGee. He is here as a consultant for Take Five Productions. He is representing one of the owners, the famous actress Lysa Dean. I ask you, Forgan, would they be interested in doing a network feature on this operation here if we were some kind of scumbag ripoff?"

Forgan gave me a single brief glance, his brown eyes as still and dull and dead as the glass orbs in a stuffed bear.

"I want to talk to a woman named Jean Norman," he said.

"I told you, they're *looking* for her. They're *looking* for her. Jesus!"

"Where's Mrs. Murphy-Wheeler?"

"Forgan, why do you keep asking me the same shit over and over? I told you before, she was on flight today. We did one of the big scenes. They're coming back in now, one at a time. Eight balloons." I saw Kesner stiffen with sudden realization. "Hey, you flew with her, McGee! She back?"

"That's what I'm supposed to tell you, Peter. They were all packed up to take off after the flight, so they wouldn't have to come back here. She has to get back to work, she said. Back in Ottumwa."

He smacked his fist into his palm. "Goddamn! That makes three who broke away today. Those bastards have got me down to five balloons. They're trying to kill me. They've been getting free chow, free propane, and a hundred bucks a day per balloon. What do they want?"

"So Mrs. Murphy-Wheeler isn't returning here?" Forgan asked.

I could see interesting complications if he got to Joya and she told him about me. But I couldn't see anything I could do about it. This man Forgan was official. He had all the rich warm charm of a tax collector. Or of J. Edgar Hoover.

"I told you before, Forgan. Feel free. You and your skinny buddy. Poke around. Ask anybody anything. But get it over with, because this is a working set and we got work to do, and delay costs money."

I tried to look at Peter Kesner out of Forgan's eyes. The bald tan head, long white ropy body, big flat dirty white feet, lots of dangling gold jewelry, graying chest hair poking out of the pink Gucci shirt, crotch-tight blue jeans, faded, frayed, threadbare, half glasses perched halfway down his generous nose, thick fingers saffroned by the ever-present cigarette. Forgan would second a motion of no confidence.

Forgan stood up slowly and turned toward the door. He stopped and gave me a long official look, memorizing me. Apparently I failed to meet his standards too.

At the door he turned back toward Kesner and said, "Besides this Grizzel clown, how many more people you got working here with records?"

"I wouldn't have any idea. Most of them are hired by my office in Burbank. They have the personnel records there. Major Productions. They're in the book. The production people here on location are all trade union people, guild people. The payroll is killing me."

Forgan stared into space. "I never go to movies," he said softly, and went out and pulled the door shut. The trailer moved a little on its springs as his weight left the step.

Peter Kesner sprawled on the couch, leaned his head back, sighed, took off his little glasses, and pinched the bridge of his nose.

"Sit down, McGee. Sit down and relax. How was it?"

"The flight? A great experience. I appreciate your making it possible."

"I went up with Joya once, and with Mercer, and we took a hell of a lot of footage of going across country in a good breeze at about zero altitude. That lady was scraping the gondola on the tops of the cows and chickens. Like a fun ride at the park as a kid. What I can't understand, why would Joya turn me in on some kind of weird rap about making dirty tapes? She say anything to you?"

I handled that one with care. "Just that she was worried about what was happening to Jeanie Norman."

He hit his forehead with the heal of his hand. "Shit, yes! Sure. They used to be friends. Old Freaky Jean. God only knows what Jeanie thinks is happening around here. She's around the bend, way around. If anybody hooked her, Linda did. Linda has good sources, and she likes big brunettes. It's easy to see how Joya might get the wrong idea from things Jean might tell her. There's videotape equipment around, portable recorders, and Jap cameras. The kids fool with it. It's a professional tool, the way a photographer will use a test shot on Polaroid film before going ahead with the real stuff. A bit player can improvise a death scene or whatever, erase the tape, and try again. You can look at the scene in living color the minute you've finished it. They probably got Jeanie involved with some of their horsing around, and she got the wrong impression, or Joya got the wrong impression of what Jeanie was trying to tell her. I can't afford all this hassling!"

He got up and paced the small area, walking back and forth behind my chair, appearing and reappearing in the mirror over the couch.

"I've got special things to say, McGee. I have special visions to reveal to the world. I can compose scenes within scenes, dialogue behind dialogue. When realities are composed in a certain way, a scene becomes referrent to a Jungian sybmolism, and millions of people will be moved and disturbed in a way they cannot understand."

He came around in front of me to stand looking down at me.

"There is such a thing as an artistic imperative. Genius demands the communicative medium. It's my mission to change the world in a way you can't even comprehend, McGee. And I will sacrifice anything at all to that mission. Right in the midst of the bad dialogue in this turkey script I am working with, I can project an instant of magic so precious I will lie, cheat, steal, kill, torture, in order to have the chance to do it. I am beyond any law, any concept of morality, McGee, because I have this gift which has to come out. I have to use everything and everyone around me, for my own ends. A little bureaucratic turd like Forgan can't comprehend the necessity of the mission. The mission is bigger than all of us. So I do what I have to do. When the money gets thin, I have to make more somehow, to keep this project alive. Do you understand that?"

"Not exactly. Maybe I do."

"I can always tell when the chance is there," he said, his voice animated, his expression full of excitement. "I get a big rush, a really stupendous flowing feeling, and I can see all the symbols and relationships as if a fog lifted. I can then move the camera just so much, change the lighting a little bit more, get the people in a different postural relationship to each other. And it doesn't matter what they say. The symbols are speaking and the words mean nothing. This is my chance to do it perfectly and change the world!"

"Now I understand," I said.

He reached and clapped me on the shoulder. "Good! Good! Right from the start I had the feeling you could catch on, Travis. You have sensitivity. Your inputs are open. Desmin thinks you're some kind of fake. It got me worried, and I called Lee Dean and she vouched for you. Are you sore at me for checking you out?"

"Not at all, Peter. Not at all."

The windows had darkened. He turned on two lamps and stretched out on the couch again. There was the sound of a key in the door and Josephine Laurant came in, wearing a white safari suit, with a leopard band holding her hair back and a white silk scarf knotted at her throat.

She nodded at me and said to Kesner, "It's raining again, hon."

"Jesus jumping H. Christ!" he yelled. "What are they trying to *do* to me?"

She knelt on the couch beside him and patted his cheek. "It's all going to be all right."

He pushed her arm away roughly, got up, and walked out without a word. She looked at me and managed a weak smile. "Peter gets very tense when he's working. There's been a lot of rain."

"So I've heard."

"It will really help us if Take Five will give us some advance publicity."

"When is it going to be released?"

"That isn't firm yet. There's an awful lot of editing and dubbing to do yet. Peter always does the film editing personally. It's an art, you know."

"I guess you both have a lot of reasons for wanting it to succeed."

She tilted her head. Her eyes looked old. "Exactly what do you mean by that, Mr. McGee?"

"I guess I meant that you've both invested money in it. And you've been sidelined for quite a long time. And Peter bombed out on his last two tries. I mean it must be very important to both—"

"I don't need that. I don't need any part of it. I didn't ask you in here. Get the hell out! Move!"

She had snatched up a heavy glass ashtray. I moved. I walked through light rain to the cook tent. Desmin Grizzel sat at a corner table for four with Jean Norman. He and I stared at each other until he beckoned me over. I sat across from Jean, with Dirty Bob on my right. He had been in the rain. The corona of gray-black beard was matted. He smelled like an old wet dog. Jean was in dirty white pants and a yellow top. She was hunched low over her plate, eating her stew with her hands. Her mouth was smeared, and gravy ran up her wrists.

"Hearty eater, ain't she?"

"Did Forgan get to talk to her?"

He took his unlit cigar out of the corner of his mouth and stared at me. "What would you know about that?"

"Only what Peter told me. Joya phoned the FBI about you people here making porno tapes before she took off for good."

"Peter told you that?"

"I was there in Josie's dressing room with him when he was talking to Forgan."

"Oh. Nobody here knows anything about any tapes. Jeanie here didn't know a thing, did you?" She ignored him. He pinched the flesh of her upper arm. She winced and looked at him. "You didn't know a thing, did you?"

Her expression was one of intense alarm. "No, Dez. Nothing at all. Nothing."

"Keep eating, princess."

She dipped down again, her chin inches from the pile of stew.

Grizzel smiled at me. He popped a kitchen match with a thumbnail and lit his sodden third of a cigar. There was a curious flavor of latent energy about him. I felt as if I were sitting next to one of the big jungle cats, and neither it nor I had any good idea of what it might do next.

I said, "Peter was giving me some ideas about his work."

"So?"

"I couldn't make a lot of sense out of what he was telling me."

"Why should you?"

"Frankly, it sounded spacey. It sounded unwrapped."

He studied the end of his cigar. "I think you should keep your mouth shut."

"I just meant that if there isn't going to be any motion picture, I'm wasting my time here."

"Peter Kesner turned me into somebody, pal. From dirt nothing to somebody. I've got a beach house, pal. I've got great machines, and a Mercedes convertible, a batch of bonds, and a lawyer working on getting me a pardon on a felony I did once. I owe him."

"You can see the reason for my concern."

"It isn't scheduled to rain tomorrow. We'll get going early, with the flying, and we'll wrap up the last location shots, and we'll go back home, and he'll put it all together. It'll be great. So don't sweat it, Ace."

He stood up, slowly, heavily, inspected the red end of his cigar again, took another drag on it, then leaned and hissed it into the little pile of stew remaining on Jeanie's plate and walked out.

She sat there staring at the upright butt in glum confusion and then stared at me. "Am I gonna be with you?" she asked. "I thought I was gonna be with Dez."

The little dark-haired stunt woman came striding in, directly to the table, directly to Jeanie, ignoring me. She was wearing boots, jeans, a red shirt, a suede vest. She clucked in dismay, scooped up the dirty plate, and went off to scrape it into the garbage can over near the coffee machine. She came back with a damp towel and sat beside Jeanie. Jeanie tilted her face up, eyes closed, as Linda mopped her clean. Jeanie's face was immature, with a spray of freckles across the unemphatic nose, dark soot of lashes lying against the cheek. Linda swabbed the girl's hands and wrists clean, gave her a little pat on the shoulder, a little kiss on the forehead, and took the towel back to the counter. She came back and sat where Desmin had been, braced her chin on broad brown little fists, and looked at me with flinty eyes.

"You want pieces of this turkey for some kind of television?"

"Just to show how things like this are done."

Her laugh was abrupt and humorless. "Things like this are not done like this, fellow. I have busted fifteen bones in this line of work, which comes out to one a year since my first stunt where I fell off a cliff onto the roof of a stagecoach. I know good from bad. These people here are nuts. Peter, Josie, Mercer, Tyler, all of them. The money is almost gone and they keep making up new story lines. Peter calls it free association. How did you get mixed up in this?"

"Lysa Dean sent me here, for Take Five Productions."

"Now there is one hard-case lady. I doubled for her three times. No. Four. Drove a convertible into a culvert. Red wig. Broke my collarbone when the safety belt snapped. Can't remember the name of the film. It was very big at the time. When she was very big. She has—like they say—carved out a new career."

"Linnnnda?"

"Shut up, sweetie, We're talking. I saw you go up with Joya. How'd you like it?"

"Very very much. Not like I thought it would be."

"Me too. I hear Joya cut out, after turning us in for something she made up. She and I never got along at all. She'll be lucky Peter don't send Dirty Bob down to Ottumwa to slap her loose from her shoes."

"Something about tapes, wasn't it? Videotapes?"

"This is no kindergarten, and the people Kesner brought here are not churchgoers. When you have toys around, people will play with them. When you have candy around, people will eat it. If Joya didn't like it, she could have left any time. She didn't have to try to make trouble. She didn't, as it turned out. The two they sent here looked around and took off. If they were after like controlled substances, it might have been something else."

"Linnnnda?"

"Hush, baby. You could get to fly again tomorrow, or at least help out with the ground crews, because we're shorthanded again. Make it out here early, like practically dawn." She leaned toward Jeanie and snuffed at her and frowned and said, "You smell musty, sweetie. Linda's going to take you in to the Lodge and give you a nice hot bath." She got up and pulled Jeanie to her feet and led her out, looking back to wave and smile at me.

The babble of conversation and the clatter of spoons in the coffee cups died for a few moments as they left and then picked up again. There was a smell of burning grease, and a drifting odor of garbage. I went back through the night to my car and drove back to town. I stopped at the BurgerBoy microphone, put in my order, and drove around to the window. A plump girl gave me the paper bag and took my money. I drove over to a parking slot, turned off the lights, and let the radio seek out a strong signal.

It was an FM station in Ames, Iowa. When it began on the local news, I was reaching to turn it off when the announcer said, "The two teenagers who died in a one-car accident this evening on State Road One Seventy-five just west of Stafford have been identified as Karen Hatcher, fifteen, and James Revere, seventeen, both of Rosedale Station. The vehicle, a late-model pickup truck, was headed east at a high rate of speed when it failed to make a curve five miles west of Stafford, traveled two hundred feet in the ditch, and then became airborne for another hundred and ninety feet, ending upright in a field. Both passengers received multiple injuries. The Revere boy was pronounced dead at the scene, and Karen Hatcher died while en route to the hospital. . . . Legislators today issued a statement that the anticipated bond issue will not be validated—"

I punched it off. I felt a little curl of visceral dread which slowly, slowly faded away.

It was, I told myself, no part of my ball game. If a plump little girl had gotten herself into more emotional trauma than she and her boyfriend could handle without spilling themselves all over an evening landscape, that was too bad. And this year three hundred and eighty-six thousand people would die as the result of lung damage and heart damage from cigarettes. And that was too bad too. Death and despair and misery were all unfortunate. There were a lot of Peter Kesners and Desmin Grizzels and Lindas and Jeanies and Josephines at large in the world, and my only function was to use some of Ron Esterland's money from his paintings to ease his curiosity about the death of his father. And get back as soon as possible to the pliant pleasures of my executive hotel-manager woman. And figure out what to do with my motorcycle business.

Lecturing oneself does not cure the megrims. It does not create the indifference one seeks.

When I parked and went into the Lodge, the old dragon was behind the desk. She said, "You'll have to be out of Thirty-nine by tomorrow morning."

"How about the others?"

"They've been told. All the rooms are reserved. All you people have to be out."

"If that's the way you want it."

"That's the way I want it. That's the way the town wants it. The best thing you can all do is get out of town and stay out, all of you. It might be the healthiest thing you can do.''

"Like the Old West, huh? Don't let the sun set on yuh, stranger?''

"Nobody is in any mood for jokes tonight.''

"Anything to do with the Hatcher girl?''

She froze for a moment. "I bet you'd even joke about that too. Jamie was my sister's only grandson. You people are vile. You are wicked. You are an abomination in the eyes of the Lord God. Drugs and rapine and fornication and a bunch of *prev*erts!''

"Now wait a minute!''

"I don't have to wait on you, mister.''

And there was nothing else to say, because there was no one to say it to. She had ducked out of sight back somewhere behind the counter. It is possible to feel the guilt that is assessed only by association. Maybe each one of us has enough leftover unspecified guilt so that it is always available in case of need.

I plodded up the creaking staircase, through a smell of dust and carpet cleaner, belching an echo of BurgerBoy onions. Before I reached the second floor I heard the yelling and the thumping. The noise was coming from 25. There was a thud, a grunt, a curse, a heartbreaking moan of anguish. I tried the knob. It was locked. I backed off, raised my leg, and stamped my heel against the door just above the knob. It ripped the bolt out of the old wood and swung open just in time to reveal Peter Kesner, in his underwear shorts, holding Josie Laurant against the wall, his left hand at her throat, while he landed a big swinging blow against her left thigh with his balled fist. They both stared at me, Josie through streaming tears.

After only slight hesitation, he went back to the task at hand. His splayed left hand held her flat against the wall. She tried to writhe her hips and legs out of the way, but he kept on thumping her with those big swings.

I took three steps and caught his wrist as he wound up to swing again. "Hey! Enough already, Peter!''

16

THIS IS a private domestic argument, McGee!'' Kesner yelled. When he took his hand away from her throat, she sagged to the floor. She was wearing a pale yellow terry robe, floor length, with a big white plastic zipper from throat to hem. Her face was bloated and streaked.

"It's too noisy to keep private,'' I said.

He came at me, grunting and swinging. He looked insane. He swung at my head, and I had time to get my fists up by my ears, elbows sharply bent and angled toward him. He was very slow, but those fists were hard and he swung them with all his might. I can move very quickly, and so, as soon as I had read his timing, I was able to let him waste his punches by getting my elbows and forearms in the way of his wrists. His little gold glasses fell off. It was my earnest ambition to pick the right moment, step quickly inside, and chop-chop—left in the gullet and a right hand deep into the soft white gut. But I realized how badly he was wheezing and gasping. The blows were softening. His mouth was sagging open. He was in that peak of physical conditioning which would cause him to get winded by changing his socks. So I let him flail away, and when he took an exceptionally hard, high swing at my head, I ducked below it. He went all the way around, got his legs tangled, and went thumping down like the dummy tossed from aloft.

As he lay there on his face, Josephine Laurant Esterland came crawling over to him on her hands and knees. She raised her fist and popped him in the back of the skull. She shrieked and sat, hugging her fist in her lap, rocking back and forth.

"Had enough?" Kesner asked me in a breathless, hollow voice.

"I give up," I said. The room door was ajar. I went over and closed it. I rolled Peter over, sat him up, helped him to his feet, and walked him over to the bed. He sat there, and I flexed my arms to relieve some of the pain and the numbness where he had hit muscle and bone.

Josie stood up slowly and carefully. She said, in loyal explanation, "He never marks me. I never show my thighs onscreen. They're too short and fat. He never marks me." She turned and glared at him. "Every cent? Every damn cent gone? What happened to the budget? What happened to that mealy little accountant person?"

"Shut up, Josie."

"That means the house is gone too, you son of a bitch. You can't finish without money. You're not half through the story boards. Jesus Christ! It *finishes* me! Don't you care?"

"Shut up and get out of here."

"You are unbelievably mean and cruel. I'll be lame for days. You impoverish me and then you beat me when I object."

"Leave!" he yelled, pointing to the connecting door.

She hobbled to it, head high, slammed it behind her.

"You shouldn't break in on a domestic discussion, McGee."

I straddled a chair, facing him. "How much did you have to pay Dirty Bob?"

"What do you mean? He's on salary."

"Oh, I don't mean for what he's doing now. I mean for the long ride when he and the Senator went over to Citrus City and beat Esterland to death, so he wouldn't outlive his daughter and leave all that good money to his foundation. I'd think he could bleed you forever for something like that."

He peered at me. "Friend, you've got to be covered with needle marks."

"Anne Renzetti knew the terms of the will, and she told Josie. Ellis had terminal cancer, and Romola was going to get all the money, and the support would stop, and Josie wouldn't be able to support you any more. That's when you went after Romola and set up the hideaway where you two could be together."

He looked toward the closed door and back at me. "Lower your damn voice, you idiot! Who are you? I think Dez was right about you. What do you want?"

"Then she had the bike accident, and when you knew she was really going to die, you explained to good old buddy Dez how nice it would be for everybody if the old man went first. Then the money would come to the daughter, and on her death to Josie, and you would be able to stay in the trough.''

"Not so damn loud!''

"If you were doing the talking, you could keep your voice down.''

"I see what you mean. All right. About Esterland, it just happened to work out lucky for me. I don't know who killed him. You have Dez all wrong too. I wouldn't say there wasn't a time when he might kill somebody, but that's all behind him. He's a good citizen. Who are you anyway?''

"A consultant, like Lysa's letter says. Two birds with one stone. Ron Esterland told me if I ever ran into you, I should ask about his dad, about you arranging to get him killed.''

"Friend of his?''

"And of Anne Renzetti. They both think you arranged it, Peter.''

"You're getting loud again!''

"Because you're not saying anything interesting.''

"All right, all right. That's a very high-strung lady beyond that door there.'' He lowered his voice even further. "Don't say anything else about Romola, please. It's a terrible guilt load for me. I had a wonderful father-daughter relationship with that lovely child. She was the one who decided it had to turn into something else. Neither of us could stand the thought of hurting Josie. I found us a pad. It wasn't against the law, McGee. I know just how I'm going to handle it in my autobiography. Tender, gentle, sensitive. Two people caught up in forbidden sexual obsession, secret meetings spiced with guilt and shame. Honest to God, when she ran over that dog and fractured her skull, I thought it was God's judgment on both of us. I'll never forget her. Never. She had the most beautiful damn body I've ever seen on any woman.''

"That's very touching, Peter.''

"So get off me about that other.''

"What if Grizzel and Hanner decided on their own to do you a little favor? What if it could be practically proven?''

"Proven?'' He studied me, his expression wary and dubious. "Look, I may have done some bitching about the situation, and I suppose somebody could have grabbed that ball and run with it. Would that be my fault? What kind of proven?''

"Not airtight. Ron says his dad went to Citrus City to make a buy of an illegal substance, to relieve his pain, intending to pay with Krugerrands. I don't know the details, but it has something to do with tracing those gold pieces to Hanner or Grizzel or you.''

"Not to me! Jesus! No way can that be true.''

"There's a rumor around that Grizzel killed Hanner.''

"You show up here pretending to be a big fan of my work, and then you hit me with all this shit. Anybody can hear rumors. I heard a rumor too. I heard he had a woman a while back who caught Dez's eye, and Dez was always able to take Curley's women away from him. Then she is supposed to have said something to Dez that she should not have known unless Curley had talked a lot more than he should have, about something involving the two of them. And then Dez waited until the right time. Maybe while he was waiting for the right moment, Curley ran into the sea gulls.''

"Have you thought of writing for pictures?"

"McGee, I hate a smartass, especially when he takes shots at my work. Nothing about this conversation is important. I'll tell you what *is* important. I am going to finish this picture. There's enough left to do the final flight scene early tomorrow. With the footage I've got, there are a lot of directions I can go in. I can use voiceover to pull it together plotwise. There are scenes in the can that really sing. On Movieola, no score, they sing. They've got my imprint. A hundred years from now, kiddo, people will be going to see *Free Fall* in the basements of museums, to see the unmistakable mark of Peter Kesner. The dynamics of each scene, unfolding, the people working in a kind of magic rhythmic counterpoint in their relationships to one another, and with the cuts underlining the tempo of the score. We fold up shop here tomorrow and head home, and in eight or ten weeks, eighty-hour weeks, I'll put it together. *That's* what's important, not you coming here bugging me with this Esterland bullshit. What's with this Ron? He didn't make the will?"

"I heard on the radio that Karen Hatcher is dead in a one-car accident. She was fifteen."

"She—Who did you say?"

"Come off it, Peter. Joya was right, wasn't she?"

He looked thoughtful. He got up and went over and picked his glasses up off the floor, put them on, nodded, and said, "She was right and she was also wrong. I wanted to know as little as possible about it. Josie knows nothing about it. I happened to know about that one, is all. She was well over fifteen. You could tell from the tits and the rug. This is depressing me. And my arms are sore. Look at the bruises coming up. I'm going to take a line to shape up. I can spare one if you want."

"No, thanks. You go ahead."

He went over to the bureau and put a careful pinch of white powder from a jeweled case onto the smooth bottom of an overturned dinner plate. He chopped it fine with a single-edged blade and scraped it into a thin line, bent down to it, and snuffed it up a soda straw, moving the straw along the line as he took the long slow inhalation, pressing his other nostril shut. It was quick and deft. Not a single motion lost.

He straightened, flexed his arms, worked his shoulders, slapped himself on the belly, and turned and smiled warmly at me. "You did con me, you son of a bitch. You know that, don't you?"

"Two birds with one stone. The Take Five situation is legitimate."

"I know. I checked with Lysa. Tell you what, you bring her to the lab in Burbank in about two weeks, and I'll show you a sequence that will knock your ass right off. That lady in there, let me tell you, that lady in there is giving one hell of a performance. She's hard to handle, but she's a classic talent. Bergman, with a whiff of Taylor. When they are very very good in bed, it shows on the screen. It shimmers under all the lines they say. You see it in the backs of their eyes."

"The Hatcher girl and her boyfriend were both killed."

"Do you realize how much you're boring me?"

"There could be some very real trouble about that, if anybody knows she starred in one of your dirty tapes, Peter."

"Screw her and screw this town. We'll be out of here by lunch. We've only got one of the big location rigs left. And what we do, we have to do it right the first time."

He sat back on the bed.

"What you can do, you can do me a favor by being out there real bright and early. We're down to five balloons and we're short on ground crew to handle them. I've got that Tyler sequence to shoot, where the balloon comes wobbling down with him stretched out dead in the basket, and all frosty from being so high he froze to death. Mercer invented some kind of crystal stuff he can spray him with. I wanted to have the other balloons settling down too, like the way animals gather around a wounded member of the herd, but you can't control the damned things that way, so the way we work it tomorrow, we have them take off from a close formation and then later I'll splice it in to run backward, so it will look like they are coming in, gathering from far off. I wanted it to be a big scene, but with only five balloons left, what can you do? I think I can work in some of the stuff when we had thirty of them taking off, and some bits of that could be run backward too. Will you be out there to help out? Listen, I would really really appreciate it, McGee."

What was there to say? There was no way to tell him what he was, even had I been entirely certain. I had the feeling that neither my vision of him nor his image of himself was particularly close to reality.

I said yes and went up the stairs to my overpriced room. Choice was still open. I could get up in a couple of hours and take off for Des Moines. Or I could go out there in the morning and help out and see what was happening.

I had as much as I was ever going to get out of Peter Kesner. I was personally convinced that Dez had taken Curley along and taken care of that little matter for Kesner, as a favor. Bravado. Help out your friends. It would probably be enough to satisfy Ron Esterland. He had performed the filial duty. Time to head home.

Yet on the very edge of sleep I realized that I was going out there in the morning on the slender chance that I could get some sort of confirmation out of Desmin Grizzel. It was a narrow chance and a big risk to try to trick him into some sort of partial confirmation. He might well want to throw me to the sea gulls, off some inconceivable cliff in the flatness of Iowa.

And also, of course, there was the slender chance I might get to ride in the gondola again, and that would give me a chance to find out if the second ride could possibly be as elegant and hypnotic as the first, moving in that sweet silence across the scents, the folds, the textures of the soft green April country.

17

WITH THE oncoming sunrise a broad gold bank along the eastern horizon, the area was coming awake. There was a smell of coffee, truck engines starting, balloonists breaking out the bags, baskets, tanks, spreading the big colorful envelopes downwind, ready for inflation. I was pressed into service on number five as a member of the ground crew, taking the place of a member of that team who had broken his hand landing the previous day. He had a cast and a sling, and he trotted along a half step behind me, telling me over and over everything I was supposed to do. He was very fussy, and he had a high nervous voice.

"The envelope bag has to be stowed on board, stowed in the basket. Fold it up. No, not like *that*. Open it up again. Bring in the sides and fold them flat onto the bottom. Start on that side, and fold the whole thing over. Now fold it again. See. Now put it in the basket. Not *underfoot*. Shove it behind that brace. Right there. Now we have to check the connecting pins and rings. And then the sparker. And then the safety line. If you always check everything twice or three times, Mr. McGee, you will not have those accidents which arise out of carelessness."

The sun appeared and the balloon colors turned vivid as the warmth struck us. Kesner, in feverish energy, was moving camera positions back and forth with orders over his portable horn. Linda and Tyler, fresh from makeup, were sitting on folding chairs, waiting.

"Blow them up! Blow them up, you people!" Kesner brayed.

"He means inflate," said my interpreter. "Put those gloves back on. And fasten the buckle on your helmet, please."

They positioned me out beyond the crown of the balloon, holding a line that was fastened to it, with instructions to counter any movement during inflation if it should show a tendency to roll in any side wind. Rolling would entangle the cables at the mouth and damage the burners.

By the time the sun was up above the horizon, all five balloons were upright, fully inflated, swaying in the morning breeze, estimated at five knots, coming out of the northwest. Number five was vertically striped in broad alternating segments of crimson and light blue.

I was put to work picking up the tools and equipment used during inflation, along with the inflator, and stowing them in the box in the big rugged pickup used by this team. It became clear to me that I was not going to get another ride. They were all waiting for the takeoff signal. The tether rope had been untied from the pickup truck bumper. Linda came over and vaulted briskly into the basket. The pilot was a lean man with a deeply grooved face, an outdoor squint. He looked like a cowboy in a cigarette ad. One of the team was on one side of the basket, holding the rim, and I was on the other. Every time the pilot gave the blast handle a twitch, I could feel the sense of life and lift in the basket long seconds later.

The balloons were in a pentagon formation, about a hundred and fifty feet apart. Kesner decided he did not like that. He had one walked to the middle of the area and ordered enough deflation so it would look tired and flabby. He had the other four walked in closer, so that the flabby one was in the middle of the hollow square.

The breeze was freshening slightly, and at that point a caravan of perhaps twenty pickups and vans came roaring down the road. The lead pickup turned directly into the big field, smashing aside the barricade of two-by-fours. They came closer, spread out, came to spinning, skidding stops, and fifty or so young men came piling out. They wore jeans and T-shirts, and they carried tire irons, ball bats, and short lengths of two-by-four. They came toward us in a dead, silent run, and there was no mistaking the dedication and the intent. There was going to be no measured appraisal of guilt or innocence. We were all—balloonists and grips, cameramen and drivers, script girls and lighting experts—going to take a physical beating that would maim and might even kill. This was a mob. They had whipped themselves up. The fact that they looked young, clean-cut, and middle-American did not alter their deadliness.

In the silence of their rush toward us, I heard the prolonged ripping, roaring sound of the burners on one of the balloons. Everyone seemed to realize at the same moment that this was the best chance of escape. "Peter!" Linda screamed. "Peter! Here!" He came on a wild scrambling run, and as she began the long continuous blast of heat into the bag, he dived over the wicker rim, hitting the pilot with his shoulder. The pilot bent forward over the rim, and Peter snatched his ankles and tumbled him out. I swarmed over the rim as it began to lift. The other ground crew member let go. It moved with a painful slowness. Two beefy blond young men came running after us, too late. We lifted just out of reach. Something pinged off the round side of one of the propane tanks and went screeing off in ricochet.

We lifted more rapidly. I looked at the pyrometer and saw it moving close to the red line, and I knocked Linda's hand off the blast valve.

"What are you doing!"

"Melt the top of this open, and we'll drop."

She understood and watched the gauge with me. It went on up right to the edge of the red and then began to fade back. The inclinometer needle held steady. I guessed we were at about eight hundred feet. I looked back and down and could see the knots of people, flailing away and struggling and falling. Two other balloons were airborne, both at a lower altitude, one ahead of us and one behind us. The flabby one was half deflated on the ground. People were fighting close to the basket of the other one, and it seemed to be deflating. Bodies lay silent in the grass. The cook tent was aflame, as was Josie's trailer-dressing room. As I watched, three of them caught up with a running man and beat him to the ground and kept on beating him.

"They've gone crazy!" Linda said. "Look! There's two cop cars. They're parked down the road there. They're not going to even try to stop it!"

"You people didn't make many friends."

"We brought a lot of money into this hick town," she said. "What the hell has happened to everybody?"

"I can guess. I think the little Hatcher girl told her best girl friend what you wonderful moviemakers did to her, and after the two kids were killed in that accident, the girl friend decided she didn't have to keep quiet any more. She didn't have to keep her word."

"Oh." She turned on Kesner. He was sitting with his back against the wicker, his arms wrapped around his upraised knees, his face quite blank. "I told you that girl was too damned young."

"I didn't ask for a driver's license. She said nineteen." He pulled himself up. He looked back and saw the fires, pallid in morning sunlight. "They don't know what they're doing," he said. "They don't know what they're destroying."

"Hey, we're coming down!" she said.

"We better try to fly low," I said. "Take a look."

The pickups and vans were streaming away from the pastureland, taking the roads that led southeast, that followed our drifting pattern.

"Why don't we go high?" Kesner asked.

"Because these things won't go all that high. The higher you go, the less efficient they are and the more gas they use up. And we'd stay in clear sight even at ten thousand feet, and they could follow us until we come down. If we go low enough, maybe we can lose them."

When we were at fifty feet and descending ever more rapidly, she opened the valve. It continued to sink. The basket brushed the top of low bushes. A red barn was rushing toward us. Kesner pointed at it and screamed. The lift finally took effect, and we rose above the crest of the barn roof, missed the silo, and then, because of the long blast, went right on up to five hundred feet.

"Short blasts, dammit," I said. "You have to use short blasts."

"Run it yourself!" she said.

And so I did, badly at first. The response always came so late, it was difficult to time. When I had the hang of it, I gained some altitude, found the wrench, and changed to fresh tanks. I could see chase cars a mile away on a parallel road, kicking up dust. I took it back down, and soon we came to a big agribusiness installation, a line of tractors, in offset pattern, working a giant expanse. They waved to us.

It was Kesner who pointed out the balloon that was spoiling our strategy. It was above us, in a fresher breeze than ours, well behind us and gaining on us. It was pumpkin and green, with bands of white. The chase cars could follow him easily. I took us up to where we could yell at him to fly low, as we were.

Linda recognized him first. "Hey, it's Dirty Bob. All alone! Wouldn't he be alone, though?" She yelled at him. "If you fly lower, they might lose you. Hey! Fly low, Dez. Low!"

He ignored us. I worked our balloon back down again. He was even with us for a time and then moved a little ahead and a little farther off, to the left of our line of drift.

I kept glancing at him too often. I didn't see the power lines in time. The big ones, the high structural towers, the spiderweb look of the thick cables swooping from tower to tower. Even with a constant blast I did not think we could lift over them.

"Get ready to land!" I said.

"No!" Kesner yelled. "I saw them following us, right over there, past those trees."

"We've got to come down right now!"

I yanked on the line that opened the maneuvering port just as Linda sprang and opened the blast valve. We were too high to risk opening the deflation port at the top by pulling the red line. I jumped at Linda to pry her hand free, but she was too wiry and strong. We started to lift, and I made the almost mortal decision that we were as low as were going to get. So I went over the side, hung, kicked free, and dropped, facing the direction of flight.

If I had to swear on all the books, I would say it was a forty-five-foot drop, at ten to twelve miles an hour. I went down toward the cultivated brown-dark earth. I dropped, pinwheeling my arms for balance, trying to remember everything I knew about falling, relaxing, rolling. The laws of motion state that a body falls at forty feet per second, but it did seem one long long second. One doesn't get much practice at stepping off the roof of four-story buildings.

I landed on the balls of my feet, inclining slightly forward, and as I hit I hugged my chest, tucked my chin down, and turned my right shoulder forward and down. I felt the right knee go, and the forward momentum took me into a shoulder roll. I went over and right back up onto my feet, where I didn't especially want to be, and then tried to take some big running steps to stay there. But the knee bugged out, and my body got ahead of my legs, and I took a long diving fall onto my belly that huffed the wind out of me and chopped my teeth into the dirt of a corn row.

I pushed myself up, gagging for air, spitting dirt, and saw the balloon angling up toward the wires. Relieved of my weight all of a sudden, it had taken a good upward surge. But it was still going toward the power lines. In retrospect I decided that the upward bounce had not been lost on Peter Kesner. The racket of the gas blast stopped abruptly, and an instant later a figure came tumbling down, falling away from the basket. She had, I would say, seventy feet to fall. She was a tough little woman, athletic and nervy. I learned later that she had done some sky diving, and I think that she spread-eagled her arms and legs in an attempt to stop the tumbling caused by her being thrown out of the basket by Kesner. Maybe the tumbling would have stopped it if she'd had more falling room. A lot more room. She made a single lazy turn and landed at a head-down angle that snapped her neck a microsecond before the heavy thud of her body into the soil.

Kesner was higher. The blast was ripping away, jacking that long blue flame up into the envelope. He was going to make it over the power lines. From my angle of sight he was already clear when the basket and cables struck the power lines. There was a stunning crack, loud as an antitank gun, a condensed flash of blue lightning, and then a big orange ball as the propane tanks blew up. The orange and crimson ball melted the striped crimson and blue envelope almost instantly, and a stream of debris came tumbling down in free fall, one morsel of it the flame-shrouded mannikin which had been Peter Kesner, landing under the power lines, thumping down beside the shredded and blackened basket with an impact that blew the flames out and left him smoking for a moment before the flames began again.

Beyond the lines, high and off to the left, the pumpkin and green balloon floated in the breeze, moving away from me. Outlined against the blue sky beyond, I could see the silhouette of Desmin Grizzel from the waist up, standing there in the hard weave of the wicker basket, looking back down at us, motionless and intent. I stood up, favoring the right leg. I was dazed, and I was sickened by the pale and dying dance of flame on Kesner's body and the small silence of Linda. Out of some vague impulse I raised an arm to Desmin Grizzel as he dwindled against the morning sky and saw him wave in response.

I heard the hard whine of the engines of the chase cars and looked for a place to hide. I could not run to the distant row of trees. I hobbled over closer to Linda's body, stretched out face down, dug with two paws like a dog, wormed myself against the soil, lay with my face wedged into the breathing hole. As a final act of guile, I pulled the wallet out of my pocket and pushed it down into the dirt at the bottom of the hole under my face. The earth smelled rich and moist.

They came running, feet thudding, breathing hard.

"Oh, Jesus! Oh, Jesus! Look at that one, Ted!"

There was a coughing sound, a gagging sound, and then a gush, coughing, and another voice saying weakly, "I'm sorry, guys. It was the smell."

I took a deep slow breath and held it. Somebody put a foot against my hip and shoved. "Maybe this one's alive." I felt hands poking at my pockets.

The hands went away. A deeper voice said, in exasperation, "What are you doing, Benny?"

"Nothing."

"Get your hands off her."

"She's got something here on a chain around her neck."

"I said get away from her!"

"Okay, okay, okay. What's the matter with you?"

"Ted, come over here. Look, guys. I think we ought to go back to town and split and keep our mouths shut."

"What about that balloon still in the air?"

"There'll be guys after it. This thing got out of hand. Right? Everybody got too excited. I saw Wicker kill a little old guy. I saw him do it on purpose. Nobody agreed to anything like that. Nobody said anything about setting fires. I saw Davis go down, and it looked as if he was hurt bad. There was a lot of blood on his face. Here we got two more dead people and one maybe dying. It got too big. There'll be television guys and newspaper guys from Des Moines all over the place."

"You remember what we all agreed, Len. It was for Karen and Jamie. It was in their memory. These are evil people."

" 'Justice is mine, saith the Lord.' I think we ought to cut out right now, guys."

They seemed to reach an agreement. When I heard voices again, they were too far away for me to hear what they said. I knew the explosion wouldn't have gone unnoticed. Others would be arriving. I retrieved the wallet. Somebody had scooped dirt onto Kesner and put out his fire. I brushed dirt off me as I walked out of the big field. The knee had popped back in, leaving the tendons stretched and sore, okay for limited and careful use. When I reached the tree line, I found that they were planted alongside a narrow asphalt road. I looked back and saw a glinting of vehicles back near the power lines and some tiny figures moving about in the field.

There was no traffic. I walked and rested, walked and rested, and finally reached a crossroad. Bagley and Perry were off to the east, Coon Rapids and Manning off to the west. A rumpled old man with a harelip and a lot of opinions about the mess in Washington gave me a ride to another crossroads, where a very fat woman in a van upholstered in sheepskin gave me a ride through Rosedale Station and on out to the location. When she stopped, the cops tried to wave her on, but I got out. She drove on. A young officer said, "This area is closed."

I pointed out my rental Buick and showed him the keys. He took the keys and made certain they worked. He wanted to see the rental agreement, and I took it out of the glove compartment. Then he asked for identification.

"What's going on here anyway, officer?"

"All hell has been going on here. How come your car is here and you weren't?"

"I left it here last night when I rode into town with someone else. I meant to come back and get it, but I didn't get around to it."

"Where did you stay last night?"

"The Rosedale Lodge."

"Are you with this movie company?"

"No way," I said, and from the back compartment of the wallet I slid the folded machine copy of Lysa Dean's letter to Kesner. He read it carefully, his lips moving. He was broad and young and plump, and he had high color in his cheeks, a thick chestnut mustache.

"That Lysa Dean, she is a really quick-witty person," he said. "She's been around. When I was maybe fourteen, I had a terrible case of the hots for her. And, you know, she still looks damned good. What's she really like, McGee?"

"She's a very shy and retiring person, officer. All that sex-pot front is just an act."

He sighed and said, "You'd never know it," and gave me back the letter. "I'm sorry you told me that."

"What *did* go on here?"

"Were you going to use some of the balloon stuff on the TV?"

"I'm going to recommend against it. Was there a fire here?"

We stood and looked out across the field. A lot of the trucks and private cars were gone. There were two television news teams at work, interviewing people out on the field, taking shots of the bright empty envelope on the ground, the overturned basket.

"What they were doing here, on the sly, Mr. McGee, they were making dirty videotapes, conning some of the young people around here to appear on those tapes, paying them for it, making them sign releases. It didn't all come out until one of the young girls they made perform for them got killed yesterday, and her girl friend broke down and told what had been going on. This is a Christian, God-fearing community, Mr. McGee, and a big bunch of the friends of Karen Hatcher came out here early this morning to bust everybody up. And they pretty much did. We've got twelve high-school seniors locked up, and three in the hospital, and warrants for the rest of them. There were two dead right here on the field, two of the movie crew, and another that will probably die. A lot of expensive equipment was destroyed and burned, and from what we can find out, a lot of the movie film was burned up too. A report came in a while back that two or three more got killed running into high-tension lines way southeast of here. Some of them got away in time in balloons, apparently. It's just one of those things that happen. It's a godawful mess. It's hard to say who's to blame in a thing like this. It really is. One of the ones in jail is my kid brother."

"Sorry to hear that."

"Billy would never in this world set out to kill anybody. His dog fell out of the loft one time and broke his back. Dad said it was Billy's responsibility to shoot Old Boomer. He plain couldn't do it. It wasn't in him. Of course, he was only twelve. I had to do it for him."

"It all got out of hand, probably," I said.

"That's exactly it, mister. That's exactly it. They don't want people who don't belong here hanging around here, okay?"

"Okay."

"Oh, wait a second. If you know anything about that sideline of making those tapes, maybe they'd want to talk to you some."

"Officer, I got here yesterday morning. All I've seen are balloons."

He nodded. "Okay. You can take off."

18

THE WORLD turned further toward summer. Vennerman scheduled my knee in May, and by early June I was walking at a reasonable pace, but only for a mile at a time, and I worked with the weight Velcroed around my ankle every evening—swing the leg up straight and hold it, and let it down very slowly.

In mid-June there were a few unusual days when Florida became almost too hot to touch. Annie Renzetti came over from Naples, and while she was there, making lists of what she'd bring on the promised cruise aboard the *Busted Flush*, Ron Esterland came to town for our long-delayed accounting. He had been out in Seattle making additions and changes in a big show of his paintings which were about to go on the museum circuit, all of them on loan from museums and collectors.

Meyer came over in the morning and got his big pot of Italian meat sauce started, checked it out at noon, and came back at drinking time, toting a sufficient amount of Bardolino.

It made a very good group. Ron and Annie were obviously fond of each other. He said to her at one point, "You were maybe the luckiest thing that ever happened to that crusty old bastard."

She said, "I'll always owe him. He taught me to do my work as perfectly as I was capable of doing it, and to think about better and easier ways of doing the chores as I was doing them—not to take my mind off them and drift. He used to say—"

"I know," Ron said. "He used to say ditchdiggers are the ones who can design the best shovels."

After we were all bloated with more pasta than anyone had intended to eat, I went and got my expense sheet and presented it to Ron Esterland.

His eyebrows went up. "This is all?"

"I tried. First-class air fare. Car rentals. Steaks. It just didn't last long enough."

"When I saw Josie last week I didn't see any point in telling her you were looking into the old man's death as a favor to me."

"How did she seem?" Annie asked.

"Okay. She misses Peter terribly. She told me there had been some vicious gossip about Peter and Romola, but neither of them had been capable of betraying her that way. She was very busy. She and somebody from one of the agencies were working out a lecture schedule for her and going over her materials.''

."Lectures!'' Annie exclaimed. ''Josephine Laurant?''

''It seems that Peter is becoming a cult fiture,'' Ron said.

Meyer went to his old cruiser, the *John Maynard Keynes,* came back with a clipping he had taken from a small literary journal, and read it to us, with feeling.

'' 'Perhaps it is too early to attempt an appraisal of the lasting value of the contributions of Peter Gerard Kesner to the art of the cinema. At the heart of the pathetically small body of work he leaves us are the two gritty little epics about the outlaw bikers, vital, sardonic, earthy, using experimental cuts and angles that soon became clichés overused by the directors of far less solid action films. The hard-driving scores, the daring uses of silence, the existential interrelationships of victims and predators gave us all that odd twist of déjà vu which is our response to a contrived reality which, through art, seems more real than life itself.'

''More?'' Meyer asked.

''Don't stop now,'' said Annie.

'' 'In the two big-budget films which he directed, and which failed commercially, we see only infrequent flashes of his brilliance, of his unmistakable signature on scenes noted otherwise only for their banality of plot and situation. The truth of Kesner, the artist, was stifled by the cumbersome considerations of the money men, the little minds who believe that if a film is not an imitation of a successful film then it cannot possibly be a success.

'' 'We can but dream of what a triumph *Free Fall* would have been had it not been destroyed in that tragic confrontation in the heartland of Iowa. Those who were privileged to see the rushes say that it was Kesner at his peak of power and conviction, dealing with mature themes in a mature manner, in a rhapsody of form and motion. A lot of footage survived, and we understand that it is being assembled as merely a collection of sequences of visuals, of flight and color, with score by Anthony Allen and narration by Kesner's great and good friend, Josephine Laurant, who will, during her narration, deliver one of the scenes written for her by Kesner. The people behind this project, who include of course the backers of *Free Fall,* whose losses were recouped by the usual production insurance, hope to enter this memorial to the great art of Peter Gerard Kesner in the Film Festival at Cannes.' ''

''Wow!'' Annie said. ''Was he that good? Was I dumb about him?''

Meyer smiled and folded the clipping away. ''My dear, you have put your finger on the artistic conundrum we all struggle with. How, in these days of intensive communication on all levels, can you tell talent from bullshit? Everybody is as good, and as bad, as anybody wants to think they are.''

Ron said, ''Josie is taking the film on the road, doing the university circuit, adding remarks and a question-and-answer period. Expenses plus fifteen hundred dollars a shot. Which comes, of course, from federal grants to higher education. She says she owes it to Peter's memory.''

''I don't think that movie would ever have been released,'' I said.

''The legend now is that it would have been an epic,'' Meyer said. ''And there are all the funny little sidebar bits of immortality too. They've updated and released that old book ghost-written for Linda Harrigan, *Stunts and Tricks: The Autobiography of a Stuntwoman in Hollywood.* And then, of course, there is that girl from that team of balloonists, the one from Shenandoah. What was her name, Travis?"

"Diana Fossi. I never met her. She's the one who got smashed across the base of the spine with a tire iron. They've named one of the events in the big international meet for her. The Diana Fossi Cross-Country Marathon. She'll be there in her wheelchair, to present the cup to the winning team."

"What happened to the boys who did all that?" Ron asked.

"Nothing much," I told him. "Except for the death of Mercer, the cameraman, they couldn't pin down who did what to who. They indicted a boy named Wicker for that. They haven't tried him yet, but I think he'll get a term in prison. They've negotiated probation for the others. And one town boy died weeks later of brain damage he received during the fracas, which tended to make it a little easier to get the others off."

I remembered my knee treatment and went and got the weighted canvas anklet and sat on the couch beside Annie. Meyer said, "What is interesting, at least to me, is the production of myth and legend. Look at that situation, for example. Hundreds of professional news people, law officers, investigators descended on that little city. It was a story that had everything. Dramatic deaths of celebrities, a pornography ring, a murderous riot, innocence corrupted. From what you told me, Travis, I gathered that in his scrambling around for funds to keep going, Kesner came up with a sideline. Using a trailer studio and Mercer, Linda, Jean Norman, Desmin Grizzel, and local young people, he was making pornographic video cassettes and Linda Harrigan was flying them over to Las Vegas and peddling them for cash on the line."

"That was the picture Joya Murphy-Wheeler, the balloon lady, gave me, information she'd gotten from Jean Norman, who apparently wasn't as totally zonked out all the time as the others thought. It turned out that Linda had Jeanie on Quaaludes, hash, Dexedrine, and Valium, which should have turned her brain to porridge."

"What happened to her?" Annie asked. "To Jeanie?"

"I have to backtrack," I said, "to tell you how I know. Driving to Des Moines that afternoon, I knew I had to square things with Joya. So I kept on going, on down to Ottumwa, looked her up, found her, and confessed I'd faked her out and that the real, the genuine, the true blue F B and I would no doubt track her down, probably in the person of one Forgan. She was one of the maddest women I've ever seen. She was furious. She had heard some of the news on her lunch hour. She knew there'd been trouble but didn't know how much. Yes, she'd heard of the death of Karen Hatcher and her boyfriend, and I told her how that had been the incident that ignited the whole thing. She had been shocked to hear that Kesner and Linda Harrigan were dead. She was fascinated by the story of my final balloon trip, and she shuddered when I told her what happened when the gondola hit the power lines. Finally she halfway understood what my mission had been, and why I had let her believe I was something I wasn't. We parted friends. I phoned her from here in May, the day before I went in for the knee operation, and she said that she had never been contacted at all, probably because the people she had implicated in her phone call as being the ringleaders were either dead or missing: Kesner, Harrigan, Mercer, and Grizzel. She understood that Jean Norman had been institutionalized in Omaha, near her home. Through her contacts in the balloonist groups, she had heard that they had taken several statements from her to be used in prosecuting Desmin Grizzel, and they were confident that she was making a good enough recovery so that she would be able to testify against him in court."

"And here is the legend," Meyer said, "growing to full flower. Unbeknownst to the cinematic genius, Peter Kesner, his creature—Dirty Bob—had corrupted Mercer and the stunt lady. And the stunt lady had recruited Jean Norman. They used a portable set after hours, when Kesner and Josie and Tyler were not on location, made the tapes, and peddled them through Linda's contacts. And the word is out that the distributors of the porno tapes, under the X-Lips label, had Grizzel killed in order to save them a lot of time and trouble and possible legal action. Grizzel, with monumental idiocy, did not hide his face when he performed on those tapes. He enjoyed being on camera. Miss Norman is also identifiable, I understand. Miss Harrigan wore a silver mask. And the amateur talents they recruited in Rosedale Station are of course identifiable. So the chain of evidence is clear enough. By the way, having a recognizable Dirty Bob play the heavy made the tapes more valuable and more salable. The prosecution has picked up over a dozen of the tapes made there in Rosedale Station. The distributor, in a single public statement made before the lawyers muzzled him, claimed the tapes were acquired from an intermediary, a third party, who had represented them as being simulated rapes, which is apparently very big with what they call the hard-core audience. A very dirty business indeed. The victims contributed to their own disasters by being hungry for the glamorous life, an appetite that made them vulnerable. And then, like victims the world over, they helped rope new victims because that made them feel their own humiliation was diluted thereby."

Annie said, "My God, Meyer, where do you *get* all this stuff?"

"He buys those strange newspapers they sell at checkout counters," I told her.

"Only to recheck my grasp on reality," he said. "Reality tells me that Desmin Grizzel is alive and well."

Ron frowned. "But wouldn't they have a reason to have him killed?"

"What for?" Meyer asked. "They act as corporate entities. Incoming cash is distributed. If problems arise, collapse the corporation and move to the next floor and start a new one. It is a lot cheaper and safer and easier than arranging a murder. Pornography is all mob-connected, of course. If somebody consistently pirated the product, I suppose they would arrange a little demonstration of how unhealthy that sort of thing is. But Grizzel is a celebrity. Somewhere in the world tonight those two early motion pictures are playing, probably in three or four countries, with the Japanese or Italian or Arabic or Portuguese dubbed in. A known face is a very risky kill, as those who did away with Jimmy Hoffa would agree. From everything I have read about Desmin Grizzel, I think he is a survivor. Some children found that downed balloon in the woods, three days later, miles south of Interstate Eighty."

Ron frowned and said, "Back to topic one, Travis. Did Grizzel kill my father?"

"My gut feeling is that he did. Alone or with Curley Hanner. No strong evidence. Just little bits and pieces. Kesner aimed them at Ellis Esterland. Maybe indirectly. Maybe he just said that things would be fine if only Esterland died before Romola. We'll never know what hook they used to get Esterland up to Citrus City alone. Probably to buy something from someone for the pain. He didn't want to admit to Annie here that it was getting too bad to endure any longer. Once the murder was done, Grizzel owned a slightly larger share of Kesner. And so did Hanner. All I got out of Kesner was that hint about how maybe Grizzel had gotten rid of him. Or maybe it was the sea gulls."

"So," said Ron, "can we assume that Dirty Bob, the California biker, has disappeared back into the roaring stream of camaraderie, the helmeted knights of the road, protectors of their own?"

"Not very damn likely," I said. "He hasn't got a face you'd call forgettable. That moon face with the corona fringe of beard and the big high cheekbones and the little Mongolian eyes. He became the role model for too many imitation hard-case types."

Meyer said, "Let's consider the problem from his point of view. It might be constructive. Travis, he told you he had a beach house, motorcycles, a convertible Mercedes, a portfolio of bonds, and an attorney working on a pardon for an earlier felony. Suddenly he is on the run, and his toys are gone. But is the offense serious enough, from his point of view, to keep him on the run? Can't he hide behind Kesner and say he was following orders? Travis, after your confrontation, or whatever you want to call it, with Kesner at the Lodge, wouldn't he have had time to talk to Grizzel the next morning?"

"Of course."

"And if Grizzel had been exploiting his relationship to Kesner, using it in every way he could think of to benefit himself, and if Kesner wanted to pry him loose a little, what would he say?"

I thought it over. "I think he'd tell Grizzel that the killing of Esterland hadn't been so clean after all. That I was looking into it, and that I was curious about how Hanner had died,"

"And then," Meyer said, "he was on the scene when you disposed of Kesner. His meal ticket. His hero. The man who made him a celebrity."

"But I didn't!"

"How would he know that? You dropped, the woman dropped, and Kesner went up into the power lines. And then you waved at him."

"Look. There's just a vague suspicion that he killed Esterland."

"How does he know how vague it is? How does he know he didn't make some kind of terrible mistake, that somebody wasn't watching?"

"Somebody *was* watching," Annie said. "Curley Hanner."

In the silence I began exercising the knee again. They all watched in mild autohypnosis. "He'd change his appearance," Ron suggested.

"Heavy eyebrows?" Meyer asked.

"Very. Big and black and bushy, speckled with gray. Why?"

"If he shaved his head, beard, and eyebrows, the eyes might still look familiar to people. Mirrored sunglasses could cure that. And if he changed his mode of dress completely—"

"Hide forever?" Annie asked.

"Possibly. Or maybe long enough to take care of the problem of the Norman girl. And then find you, Travis, and see what you know or don't know. Or maybe not even bother to ask."

"Oh, fine! And just how would he find me?"

"Through Lysa Dean, of course."

I stopped flexing the knee. Annie looked out at the dark night and hunched her shoulders slightly. Ron frowned at the floor.

Meyer said with hearty cheer, "We're just playing games. The ancient and honorable game of what-if."

Long after they had gone, Annie Renzetti made me turn on the light and try once again to reach Lysa Dean on the bedside phone. She nestled close to me and we both listened to the sound of ringing. I let it ring fifteen times and then hung up.

"But it doesn't make any sense," Annie said. "Those people have answering services. They have to."

"Maybe not on the private, private line. When friends call long distance, if there is no answer, she's out. It saves toll charges."

"Do you believe that?"

I reached and turned the light out. "Certainly."

"If you really did, you wouldn't sound so overconfident. Was Meyer trying to scare us?"

"He likes to make guesses about people. He's pretty good at it, but he'd be the first to tell you he strikes out a lot."

"You've known Lysa Dean a long time?"

"I helped her out of a jam a long time ago."

"Did you sleep with her when you went out there in April? That's not a jealous question, really. I don't have any claims on you. You're free to do whatever you want. You know that. I just wondered. It's such a dumb question, you don't even have to answer it. I mean, the years go by and she just seems to get lovelier."

"No, I didn't."

"Did you want to?"

"The possibility did occur to me."

"Could you have?"

"I wouldn't even want to guess."

"You know, you don't have to lie. Not with me."

"I know that, Annie love."

"Could you just hold me a little bit tighter?"

"My pleasure."

"I have the feeling something is going wrong in the world, something involving us in some terrible way."

"Nothing bad will happen."

"Why did her phone keep ringing and ringing? You said she has a live-in staff."

"It probably doesn't ring in their quarters. It's her special private line. Go to sleep, Annie."

"I'll try."

"Think about your hotel. Count the silver."

"One, two, three, four, five . . ."

"Silently."

"Oh."

19

THAT WAS Sunday night, of course, the twenty-first day of June. On Monday morning Annie showered and dressed early because she had to get back to her hotel chores. She stirred me awake and then went to the galley to fix the waffles and sausage. While doing so, she turned on the tiny Sony machine she had given me: AM, FM, cassette tape, and a fierce sharp little black-and-white screen. She turned the television to *Good Morning, America,* and in a few moments she came running in to get me. I was just shouldering into a robe and heard only the last part of the news item.

I tried CBS and NBC and, minutes later, got the item in its entirety—or at least the entirety granted it by those blithe morning people who twinkle and sparkle as they speak of horrors beyond belief.

"Mystery surrounds the disappearance from the drug rehabilitation center of Jean Norman, the voluptuous brunette balloonist whose testimony was crucial in the indictment of Desmin Grizzel, a.k.a. Dirty Bob, still at large after the Iowa riot on the location of *Free Fall,* where porno videotapes were being made while Kesner's lost epic was in production. She had been given the freedom of the grounds and was due to be released in the custody of her parents in another two weeks. When her parents visited her yesterday, she could not be found. Police joined in the search. Another patient saw her at approximately two P.M., talking across a low stone wall to a tall man. A fresh smear of blood on the edge of the stone at that location proved to be of the same type as Miss Norman's. The patient could not identify pictures of Grizzel as being the man she had seen by the wall."

"Meyer is a witch," Annie said. "Call Lysa Dean."

"It's four thirty in the morning out there. Later."

"Okay. Later, but then will you please call me and tell me if you talked to her?"

"I promise."

"Would you like your waffle black or charred? Don't look so abused, Trav. There's more batter. That one was supposed to be mine. I'll start yours when you come out of the shower."

*   *   *

I tried Lysa at three that afternoon, and she answered on the second ring.

"Hi. It's me. McGee."

"You damn thankless *bastard!* Did you forget I got you that 'in' with Peter Kesner? I didn't know if you got killed or buried, or you sailed off in a balloon, or what. Where the hell are you?"

"Fort Lauderdale."

"Were you in Iowa when it hit the fan?"

"I was indeed. It got a lot of coverage in the press. I didn't think you'd need a play-by-play from me. I'm grateful you thought up the idea that got me through the door."

"You weren't as grateful at the time as I wanted you to be."

"I thought I thanked you very nicely."

"Sure."

"Let me tell you why I called. Have you got a minute?"

"Three, maybe four."

"All right, then. Dirty Bob is still at large. It looks as if he got to that girl who was going to testify against him and took her off somewhere. Without going into details, he has, or thinks he has, some very pressing reasons to find me and beat the top of my head in."

"I'd even help him."

"The only way he can trace me is through you. He saw that letter from you. I think he holed up for a while, and now he is moving again. He might pay you a visit."

"So?"

"He might ask questions in a very ugly way, Lee."

"I am not afraid of that big dreary ass-grabbing motorcycle bum, darling. I have no reason to love you, or even like you, but also I have no reason to hand out information about you, so don't fret. Momma won't let big bad bully come after poor wittle McGee baby."

"Dammit, Lee, think about it. He killed Ellis Esterland, and he killed Curly Hanner, and he has probably killed Jean Norman."

"Oh," she said in a smaller voice.

"I called you because it's my fault you're in the line of fire. I'm sorry. I didn't think far enough ahead." I have lost some very great ladies because I was too slow, too stupid, and too careless. This time I was giving warning. "Can you go away for a while?"

"I'm better off here. I've got the Korean couple and a damned good security alarm system. I'll be careful."

"If he shows up, tell him where to find me. I'd like to see him again."

"You sure of that?"

"It would be a lot easier than losing you."

She started laughing, and when I finally got her to explain what was so funny, she said, "Sweetie, you can't really lose something you've never really had."

"Tell whoever patrols that area to check you out oftener than usual. Tell them you had a nut call."

"This *is* a nut call. I wouldn't be lying."

"Take me seriously, will you?"

"Honey, I've tried that twice already, and it didn't work," and still laughing, she hung up.

I phoned Annie at the Eden Beach immediately and held while they ran her down.

"Yes? Anne Renzetti speaking."

"Just hung up after a talk with Lysa."

"Wow! I'm always so glad when one of those bad feelings doesn't work out. Will she go away? I could hide her out here—well—until somebody recognized her, which would be in about eleven minutes. Bad idea. It would be fun to get to know her. I feel as if I already do know her."

"She was impressed. She's going to be careful."

"Good. I'm glad."

I locked up and wandered down the dock to Meyer's cruiser. He wasn't aboard. Then I saw him coming, evidently from the beach, trudging along, smiling to himself.

"Back a winner?" I asked.

"Oh, good afternoon! A winner? In a sense, yes. There was a gaggle of lanky young pubescent lassies on the beach, one of the early invasions of summer, all of them from Dayton, Ohio, all of them earnest, sunburnt, and inquisitive. They were huddled around a beached sea slug, decrying its exceptional ugliness, and I took a hand in the discussion, told them its life pattern, defensive equipment, normal habitat, natural enemies, and so on. And I discovered to my great pleasure that this batch was literate! They had read books. Actual books. They had all read *Lives of a Cell* and are willing to read for the rest of their lives. They'd all been exposed to the same teacher in the public school system there, and he must be a fellow of great conviction. In a nation floundering in functional illiteracy, sinking into the pre-chewed pulp of television, it heartens me to know that here and there are little groups of younguns who know what an original idea tastes like, who know that the written word is the only possible vehicle for transmitting a complex concept from mind to mind, who constantly flex the muscles in their heads and make them stronger. They will run the world one day, Travis. And they won't have to go about breaking plate glass and skulls and burning automobiles to express themselves, to air their frustrations. Nor will these children be victimized by the blurry nonsense of the so-called social sciences. The muscular mind is a cutting tool, and contemporary education seeks to take the edge off it."

"As you have said before."

"What? Sorry about that. Lecture Eighty-six C."

"Did you hear about the Norman girl in Omaha?"

We settled into deep canvas chairs in the cockpit of the *John Maynard Keynes*. "I heard on the noon news," he said, and got up and unlocked the hatch to belowdecks, went down, and came back with two icy bottles of Dos Equis, drank deeply from his, wiped his mouth on the back of a heavy and hairy hand, and said, "The body will turn up, perhaps, sooner or later."

"Lysa Dean is okay. I talked to her a little while ago. Alerted her. I think she'll keep her guard up. I told her that if he gets to her, to tell him where to find me."

In a little while I noticed how motionless he was, how he was staring into the distance. When a lady stalked by wearing a string bikini, a big pink straw hat, and high-heeled white sandals, Meyer didn't even give her the glance she had earned. She went off into the dazzle of white hot afternoon.

Finally he stirred, sighed, finished his beer. "There is certain standard information about Desmin Grizzel. Rasied in Riverside, California, out on the edge of the desert, a one-parent family, with the children divided among foster homes when the mother was killed in a midnight brawl in a parking lot. Desmin went from foster home to reformatory to penitentiary, emerged into the close fellowship of the outlaw biker. A passable mechanic. A brawler. A skilled rider. And so there he was, riding toward his very limited destiny, when Peter Kesner came into his life and told Grizzel, Hanner, and their associates he wanted to use them in a motion picture. Probably they thought it some kind of joke. They became Dirty Bob and the Senator, lived the parts, made production suggestions, and so forth and so forth. It's all in the fan magazines. So they became celebrities, cult heroes to a limited segment of America. Two movies. And the consequent talk shows, endorsements, public appearances at biker meets, races, and rallies. And some bit parts in TV series and B movies.

"Desmin Gizzel read the press releases about how, by accident, his life had been changed. He had been pulled up out of the great swamp of common folk and placed on a hilltop, where he vowed that he had seen the light, that he would never return to the wicked ways of his prior life. This is always a popular theme. I think that Desmin Grizzel began to enjoy security, if not respectability. He was closing in on forty. He had done a dirty little chore for Kesner, and he had worked Kesner for as much of Josie's money as he could grab, put it into the security of a beach house, vehicles, bonds, and the lawyer working on his pardon.

"He had made it possible for Kesner to get seed money for the new motion picture project. He had bunted his old friend Hanner over a cliff, removing an irritant and a possible danger. He was Kesner's gofer, taking orders perhaps slightly demeaning for a man who had once been a star in his own right. Then, in the matter of the tapes, he had a chance to indulge simultaneously his yearning to be on camera and also his sadistic appetites, apparently not realizing the danger involved in not hiding his identity.

"And it all went to hell. He saw Kesner die and saw you survive. He hid out somewhere, somehow, for nearly two months. Wanted. Pictured in all post offices. Federal indictment and local indictments in Iowa. Now what is his concept of his future? There is no possible way he can fit himself back into any area of security and respectability. No way at all. The myth of redemption is shattered. The fans of past years are gone. The onetime outlaw biker is once again an outlaw. Back to his origins. Society raised him up and then smacked him down, leaving him no out. He's not the sort of creature who'd turn himself in. He's a predatory animal. Big, heavy, nimble, and cruel. The fact he was tamed for a little while makes him more dangerous. He's on the move because he has somehow acquired a safe identity that gives him mobility. I would say that he probably thinks of himself in some strongly dramatic context, as a betrayed man who will take out the betrayers before the pack brings him down. The betrayers are the Norman girl, Joya Murphy-Wheeler, Lysa Dean, you, and possibly some others. He can take a lot of pleasure in the hunt, sharpened and sweetened by the knowledge that these are the last acts of his life."

"Meyer, you can't climb inside his skull."

"I know that. I can try to come close."

"He could be into a lot of heavy things that could addle his wits. He could just be thrashing around."

"True."

"But I might as well try to reach Joya."

"It shouldn't hurt," he said.

*   *   *

I couldn't find the number I had written down for her. I got it from information and then waited until she would be likely to be home from work. I went over what I wanted to tell her. She had seemed very forthright and direct. I remembered how she smiled when I finally experienced that strange pleasure of the balloon journey at low altitude across the land.

The voice that answered was frail and tentative. "Hello?"

"Is Joya there?"

"No. Who is calling?"

"This is Travis McGee. In Florida."

"Were you a friend?" The past tense froze my heart.

"Who are you?"

"Alpha. I'm her sister. What was it you wanted with her, Mr. McGee?"

"Is it possible to speak to her?" I knew instinctively how dumb that question was.

"No, sir. It is not possible. We had the services for her yesterday. She is . . . she has passed on."

"What happened to her?"

"You aren't another newspaper person, are you?"

"No. I went ballooning with your sister."

"She was crazy about that. She loved it. She always said it was worth it, but I couldn't see it. That's another thing I got to sell of hers, I guess, her share in that stupid balloon."

"You're the executor?"

"Sort of. She was divorced a long time ago and there weren't any children. She came back here to stay at the home place all alone. I mean I've got a husband and children and a life of my own. I told Joya that she shouldn't live here alone. It's on just a farm road, you know. Like two trucks a day go by."

"What happened to her?"

"Well, it happened last Thursday, the eighteenth. What she always did, except when the weather was bad, she'd get up and put on her running clothes and take a long hard run and come back and shower and eat breakfast and go to work. She kept herself in wonderful shape. Bruno always ran with her. He's part Airedale, and practically human. They never have found Bruno. When she didn't show up at work and didn't phone in, finally a girl friend of hers that works there phoned me, and I phoned Alan at the store, and we drove out there, and I used my keys to get in. The burner was turned low under the coffeepot and it had boiled dry. The clothes she planned to wear to work were laid out on the bed. By then it was noon. Well, by late afternoon there must have been fifty people hunting for her, and they found her body finally in tall grass a quarter mile from the house. She had been beaten. Her poor face was a mess. Somebody had raped her and then knotted one of the pant legs of the jogging suit around her neck, very tight. The grass was all matted, like animals had been fighting there. Practically everybody in the whole area has been questioned about whether they saw strangers around. Whoever it was, they had a long time to get out of the area. It seems like such a terrible waste. I'm almost glad Momma died last year so she wasn't alive to know what happened to Joya.''

"Are there any suspects?''

"I don't know. I don't think so. After the funeral yesterday, we—Alan and me—we talked to a fellow Alan went to school with. He has something to do with the law. He said it could have something to do with all that trouble over at Rosedale Station, but of course Joya left there before anything happened. Everybody thinks it was just some bum, some vagrant, some kind of drifter. There's so much crazy violence around these days. Well . . . I'm here trying to pack up her things. What is your name again? McGee. Oh, God, I was about to say that I'd tell Joya you called. I've got to hang up now. I'm going to cry again.''

*   *   *

I talked to Meyer again in the evening, aboard my houseboat.

I explained to him my reservations about the professionalism of one Forgan. "From the conversation I had with Kesner after Forgan left, I know that Forgan told Kesner that Mrs. Murphy-Wheeler had put in a complaint about their making the dirty tapes on location. A citizen who complains to the authorities should be protected, unless he or she is willing to make sworn statements.''

"Maybe she was. Or maybe Mr. Forgan didn't take it all that seriously. Maybe he thought he was dealing with somebody who'd been released or fired, trying to get even.''

"Okay. But I was the idiot who told Grizzel about it when I sat with him and with Jean Norman later.''

"If you hadn't mentioned it to him, certainly Kesner would have, Travis. And probably long before you saw Grizzel. Kesner would have wanted to warn him about Forgan and his partner looking around the area. You pick up imaginary guilt the way serge picks up lint.''

"Joya was a very able and happy lady. She was outraged about how they had turned Jean Norman around. She wanted people punished. And I think it got her killed.''

"But you didn't get her killed.''

"Okay, Meyer. All right. I didn't.''

The midnight news told us that the nude battered body of Jean Norman had been taken out of the Missouri River by a police launch after having been reported by a tug captain. It said that authorities believed there was a possible connection between the murder of Miss Norman on Sunday night and the brutal rape murder of Mrs. Murphy-Wheeler near Ottumwa the previous Thursday morning. Law enforcement units all over the Midwest were on the alert for any information as to the whereabouts of Desmin Grizzel. Bikers in nine states were being stopped and interrogated.

"And that is the one way he would not travel,'' Meyer said.

"I don't see how he can risk any kind of traveling, not with that well-known face.''

"He's found something that works,'' Meyer said. "Think about Jean Norman. Would she have walked over to a wall to talk across it to Desmin Grizzel? To talk to something out of her nightmares? I'll bet she had no idea until he grabbed her and yanked her across and took her into the bushes. Would Joya, dressed for running, let Grizzel catch up with her?''

"He can't disguise his dimensions. He's the size of an offensive guard. Six two, two sixty or seventy, great big gut."

After I thought about it a while, I phoned Lysa Dean. It was a little after ten in the evening her time.

"You again?" she said. "Look, I've got guests."

"I can hear them. I won't take up much time, okay?"

"What is it?"

"Dirty Bob managed to get very close to two people who had every reason to be very wary of him."

"The woman in Omaha and the one in Iowa?"

"You've been keeping track. Good. I'm trying not to be boring about this, Lee. I don't know if there's any chance of him coming after you. I don't know if he wants to get to me that much. I don't know how much risk he's willing to accept, how crazy he is. But you know the dimensions of him."

"Big big old boy."

"Just don't put any trust at all in any stranger who comes in that size, man or woman. He can disguise everything but his size."

"I shall consider myself warned."

"I could come out there. A live-in guard."

"Well, you do tempt me, but no, thanks."

20

THE THURSDAY newspapers carried diagrams of the floor plan of the Lysa Dean house, with those Germanic-looking crosses newspapers use to indicate where bodies are found.

A person or persons unknown had snapped the gardener's neck and flung him into the pool. The slender Korean woman who had served us the salad and tea had been chopped across the nape of the neck with a kitchen cleaver wielded with such force it was clear that she had been dead before her body hit the kitchen floor. Lysa Dean had evidently been caught a few feet from the panic button of her alarm system, in the corner of her bedroom near the bed.

It had happened, as near as could be judged, at eleven in the morning on Wednesday, the twenty-fourth. Miss Dean had not been on call that day. The dotted line showed that the intruder had been admitted to the grounds by the gardener, through the front gate. He, or they, had killed the gardener near the rear entrance to the kitchen area. He or they had then slain the maid, who had been fixing Miss Dean's breakfast of tomato juice, dry toast, and tea, and gone through the house of find Miss Dean just leaving her dressing room. There she had been chased, caught, taken to her custom bed, and brutalized. Broken fingers, chipped teeth, and bruises, which were said to have happened at least an hour before death, indicated that she had been kept alive for a considerable amount of time before she was finally smothered by being jammed face down into her pillows.

There were the inevitable references to the Manson murders, to which they bore no resemblance at all. There was editorial comment in the newspapers and on television about drugs, terrorism, pornography, the ineffectuality of the law, the vulnerability of prominent persons, the decay of morality, the decline of values.

Sidebar stories detailed her long career in cinema and television, her marriages and divorces, her awards, her life-style. Others gathered comment from people she had worked with and worked for.

"It is a sad and sickening loss. I hope whoever did this terrible thing will be brought to justice."

"She had a lively style, a quick and earthy wit. Television will be the poorer for her loss."

"Lysa Dean was an unashamedly sensuous woman who very much enjoyed her life and enjoyed being Lysa Dean."

"Everybody I know is out buying more locks and chains and alarm systems. You wouldn't believe the panic that has hit this town. It's like we're back to the Charlie Manson days all over again."

An editorial expressed bafflement at how any suspicious person or persons could have avoided detection by any of the public and private patrols. But it did say that it was a lot easier to invade the area during broad daylight than at night. Deliveries were made during the daylight hours, and unlike some of the newer secure communitites, there was no central checkpoint through which all traffic had to pass.

I had a feeling of loss, but in some strange way it was diluted by the many faces of Lysa Dean. There was so much artifice involved, so much playing of games, so much posing, I could not identify the single specific person who was gone. And indeed it was that bewildering variety which had made me uncharacteristically less than eager to bed her down both times she had made her availability unmistakable. There is a curious reluctance to play that ultimate game with a composite of strangers, with all the faces of one particular Eve. She was lively, fun to be with, but I did not know her. Perhaps the closest I had come to comprehending the real Lysa Dean was when I had been in her little projection room and seen her collection of X-rated tapes and her little drawer containing the massager. Maybe at the very heart of her there was an icy and unbelievable loneliness.

*   *   *

I looked up the number for Ted Blaylock's Oasis. Mits answered.

"Who? Wait a sec, I got to shut the door there's so much noise out back . . . Okay. Who'd you say? . . . Oh, McGee! Hey, how is it going?"

"How is it going with you?"

"Pretty much okay, I guess. I tell you, it is very damn noisy here, with a lot of big yellow machines churning around out in back."

"What are they doing?"

"Lots of things at once. A fence and a wall and an airstrip and some kind of generator plant. They don't tell me anything hardly. We're getting a lot of business from those guys working here, though, and the motorsickle business is holding up okay. Did you get your dividend? No? I got mine Monday. Five hundred cash, and then there was a check for salary on account of I'm sort of being a manager while they're looking for one. Somebody will probably bring you your dividend. Preach told me, he said, 'Don't declare it, kid. It's for spending.' ''

"I want to know how I can get hold of Preach. I tried the number for Karma Imports in Miami and they told me they never heard of anybody named Preach or anybody named Amos Wilson. Then I tried Daviss Grudd and he said that he never gets in touch with Preach; Preach is the one who makes contact."

"Well . . . I have this number to call in case some kind of county or state inspectors show up out here asking lots of questions. If it wasn't any emergency, he might get sore at me."

"It's an emergency, Mits. Really."

Though reluctant, she gave me the number.

It was a Miami number. I phoned, a man answered, I asked for Preach, and he came on the line.

"I met you out at Blaylock's," I said. "You and the fellow with you talked to me out by the cabins in back."

"How far are you from a pay phone, timewise?"

"Ten minutes."

"Go look at the number, come back and phone this number, and give the pay phone number to whoever answers. Then get back there and expect a call at half past on the button. What time you got?"

"Eleven before three."

"You're two minutes fast." *Click.*

I did as instructed and went back to the pay phone affixed to a marine wall in its plastic shell.

It rang on schedule. "McGee here," I said.

"My hard-nose hero buddy. You better be very entertaining, because I am taking time off from something worth more money than you'll ever make in your life. Also, McGiggle, I am going to have somebody bouncing some little Indian piece off some walls for giving out a number."

"I conned her out of it, Preach. Don't be hard on her."

"So what is this emergency situation you have to take me out of a meeting?"

"Remember we talked about Dirty Bob and the Senator."

"They have come up in the news now and then. The Senator crashed."

"With, I think, some help. On the right kind of road, with no traffic in sight, all Dirty Bob would have to do is lean into the Senator, give him a little shoulder."

"That cat's right name was in the paper. Desmin Grizzel."

"I convinced myself he's the one that beat the old man to death. I told you about that."

"What has that got to do with the price of anything?"

"Chalk up also one pot-head girl named Jean Norman, one balloonist-type lady named Joya, and one movie-queen quiz-show-type person named Lysa Dean, along with her Korean servants."

"Busy old bastard, ain't he? They *think* he totaled the movie lady. If he did, I take it on the unkindly side. I always thought I might get a chance to get so famous I could run out there and boff that lady a couple dozen times. But again, pal, so what?''

"It's a reasonable assumption he is going to come to Lauderdale and take care of me next.''

"If he does, I suppose I will read about that in the papers too.''

"You and Magoo are supposed to be the top brass of the Fantasies. You remember the pin I was wearing that day? Doesn't that give me the right to call upon the brotherhood for assistance? I am a genuine affiliated, associated sort of member.''

"I am giving up all that motorcycle shit and that one-for-all-and-all-for-one shit and that childish brotherhood shit. If you need protection, call the cops.''

"You are probably a little less interested in doing business with the cops than I am. But not a hell of a lot less, Preach. I don't need that kind of exposure. I need some people as near like Grizzel as I can get. Fight fire with fire.''

"Forget it. Solve your own problems.''

"When I tried to get hold of you, I tried Daviss Grudd. He couldn't help me. But he did say that within a short time I'll be a half owner of that business out there, and I'll be able to do anything with my stock that I want.''

"If you've got any idea of trying to push me around, I'd better tell you we're willing and able and ready to do your elbows any time. You'll have to hire somebody to pick your nose.''

"Who said anything about pushing you around? I really don't need any part of any motorcycle emporium and tattoo parlor, Preach.''

"Even if it spins off five hundred tax-free a month?''

"I thought I might sign my interest over to the Gold Coast League of Retired Executives with the stipulation that they can't sell that half interest. If they try, they have to give it back to me.''

"What kind of an outfit is that?''

"Just what it says. Retired executives from big industry who have banded together to run small businesses and do consulting work. They know all about corporations and overhead and voting rights and all that stuff. They run things as a hobby.''

"Jesus Christ, dozens of old silver-tips crawling all over the place? That's a rotten idea.''

"Not so. They'd turn it into a real profit out there.''

He was silent for a time. "I certainly wouldn't want my brothers in the Fantasies to think I had turned down a legitimate plea for help from a genuine affiliated associated kind of member.''

"And on the other hand, Mits might like to own the whole place.''

"I think we can always get along, McGee. We're so much alike.''

"What I want are two very hard people, one little wiry one and one big one with muscles. A couple of years back I would have tried to hero this thing myself. But with this one, I want to be totally sure.''

"Should they be carrying?''

"If licensed, okay. If not, I can supply.''

"One more time, friend. I had you checked out after our talk. You came on so hard-nose, it got my curiosity up. So I know where you live and how you live, and it is more small-time than I would have guessed. Okay, I can send you a couple of the best. So this Dismal Gristle comes calling and has a sudden heart attack. Whether or not cops move in at that point is something I need to know before I pick the two people.''

"I will go over it with them, and if they think it can be handled so quietly there will be no police, then they stay and help. Otherwise, they're free to go.''

"Fair enough. You want an inconspicuous arrival.''

"And soon. Slip F-Eighteen.''

"The old houseboat with the sunken tub. I know.''

*　　*　　*

"This isn't like you,'' Meyer said, after I explained it.

"I know. What I had last year was enough incredible luck to last me the rest of my life. So I am counting on not having any at all, or having it turn up all bad. Look, I have sat at table with this cat. He is something impressive.''

"Like Boone Waxwell?''

"Yes. Except bigger and stronger and quicker and, I think, even more warped in the head than Waxwell was. There is a kind of surface plausibility about him that Waxwell didn't have. More shrewd, I think. Look, I went over it. They have a police guard on Josephine Laurant on the far-off chance he might have her on his crazy list. I talked Annie Renzetti into hiding out with good friends and not leaving word at the hotel where she went, just in case he might know about her from talking to Kesner. I thought of being bait and using you as backup, but I just don't have the confidence that I could protect myself and you too.''

"You think I would be just standing there maybe?''

"Don't get sore. A man who can do the unthinkable without a half-second hesitation has a lead over you and me. And more over you than over me. Don't think of it as a criticism. Nine out of ten adult males would find it impossible, thank God, to shove a knife into the belly of a fellow human, even if their own life seemed in danger.''

"You're setting him up to kill him?''

"If I have to. If I can't take him, I want somebody there who will, because I do not want him loose in the world.''

*　　*　　*

My assistants arrived just after dusk, an hour after Meyer had gone back to his cruiser. I checked them out before I opened up.

"Preach sent us,'' the small one said. "I'm Gavin. This here is Donnie.''

"How did you come?''

"Car. Parked way down and walked in.''

After I had closed the lounge draperies, I turned on more lights and took a better look at them. Gavin was pallid, sandy, compact as a jockey or a good flyweight. There was a flavor of Australia in his diction. He was in his thirties. His blond sideburns came down to the corners of his mouth. He wore a white guayabera, dark red slacks, Mexican sandals. Donnie was younger, tall, lazy-looking, with dark hair modeled in a wave across his forehead, with a heavy drooping mustache. He wore a work shirt, khaki shorts, and running shoes. His legs, though very tanned, looked thick and soft.

"You know what this is about?''

"Somebody wants to blow you away, Preach said. You want us to make sure it doesn't happen," Gavin said.

"Are you people armed?"

"Donnie's got nothing. I got a knife." He wore it between his shoulder blades, with the blade up for grasping, for a quick grasp and quicker throw, with a full snap of the arm. It's a French fashion, deadly when the man has years of practice.

I watched them handle the handguns I gave them. I gave Gavin the Airweight Bodyguard from the bedside holster, and gave Donnie the Colt Diamondback from the medicine cabinet hidey-hole. They checked the weapons with reassuring aplomb, spinning the cylinders, dry firing, then loading. I took the nine-millimeter automatic pistol for myself, the staggered box magazine holding the full fourteen rounds.

Then I showed them what I had in mind. I made them practice the routine over and over until they could get into their hiding places quickly enough to suit me.

There is a full-length mirror affixed to the bulkhead at the end of the short corridor between the two state-rooms. Quite a while ago I had a master carpenter move the bulkhead out a few inches and make a stowage locker on the other side shallower. The two-way glass mirror is hinged on one side, held in place by a catch which can be released by shoving a wire brad into an almost invisible hole in the right side of the mirror frame. A man can step in, pull the mirror door shut, fasten it with a simple turn block. As it is only twelve inches deep, he cannot turn around. He has to step backward, and he can watch the corridor from there. Donnie fit the space with little to spare. Gavin fit reasonably well in the stowage locker in the lounge, the one with the upholstered top used for extra seating. I had emptied it out before their arrival. There was a small hole near the floor which gave him limited vision and better hearing.

"I want to make sure I understand," Gavin said. "We're backup. We're insurance. If there's big action, we bust out and take him if we have to. Or if things start to go sour for you, the code word is Preach?"

"If I have to use it, I'll yell it, and I'll be moving fast by then."

"What does this dude look like? Is there just one?"

"You've probably seen him in movies. He played the part of Dirty Bob."

Donnie spoke up in his slow deep voice. "He's nothing but a movie actor, isn't he?"

"Outlaw biker first."

"And he's been killing women," Gavin said. "I read about it. He's a bloody big sod, that one. Is he really mean?"

"Yes."

"What does he want with you, McGee?"

"He blames me for the death of a friend, the man who put him in the movies. I don't think he needs much reason. I think he is probably certifiably insane."

"When do you think he'll show up?"

"Yesterday he was in Los Angeles. He was there looking for my address. He's had thirty or more hours to get here."

"People know his face, don't they?" Donnie said.

"One time that I know about, he and his friend came across the country on motorcycles in fifty hours."

"Good time," Gavin said, "but it beats you to death."

"If it turns out that there is any way to take him alive, I'd like that."

"To give to the law?"

"Yes."

"Okay, if you keep us out of it," Donnie said. "We'll keep it in mind. But it looks safer if we kill him. How long do we go before you decide he isn't coming?"

"Until Sunday night?"

"Preach didn't tie any strings on it," Gavin said. "So it's whatever you say, mister."

"You've been . . . uh . . . involved in this sort of thing before?" I asked.

"Better you shouldn't ask," Gavin said with a sandy little smile. "We eat here, I suppose?"

"I put provisions aboard. And liquor."

"Donnie and me, we don't drink except after a job is over. Look, I didn't mean to turn you off about what you asked. I'll tell you this much. For what you've got in mind, you won't find any better south of Atlanta. Okay?"

"Glad to know it."

"You live aboard here all the time?" Gavin asked. "What do you do for a living? You retired?"

I smiled at him. "Better you shouldn't ask."

"Anyway, Preach must owe you a big one. I'm not asking. Okay? I was just making a remark."

21

THE SLIGHTEST pressure on the mat where people come aboard the *Flush* from the dock at the stern, where the hinged rail is flipped over and latched, rings the small warning bell—a solemn *bong,* like a discreet telephone in an advertising office.

It sounded in the early afternoon on Friday, on a day that seemed hotter than all the rest, hot enough to bring the water in the yacht basin to a slow boil, bubble the varnish on the play toys, make the metalwork too hot to touch. The sky hung low in a thick white glare. The air conditioning groaned away, eating my purse. Through the narrow gaps in the draperies I could see the tourists on the docks, milling around in slow motion, straining for a good time.

At the *bong,* I was in the galley, looking at the labels on the canned goods. Gavin and Donnie were in the lounge. They slipped quickly, quietly, neatly away to their assigned places.

The pistol was tucked into my belt, under the oversized yellow shirt, slanted on the left side, grip toward the right, handy for grasping. There are many schools, going back to the flintlock dueling-pistol days when it was thought advisable to present one's body in profile to the opponent, the right side—the side without the heart in it—nearer the opponent. The gunslinger school had its own mythology. I had long since worked it out to my own satisfaction. It was the shortest travel distance for my right hand, and as I pulled it free, I could pivot into a full-faced squat, weapon held in two hands, aiming it for full instinctive spray, like a man putting out a fire at gut height.

I touched it through the shirt to be certain it was properly positioned, went to the rear entrance to the lounge, thumbed the curtains aside, and saw Meyer's solid and reliable face a few inches beyond the door.

I unlocked the door, and just as I swung it open, the delayed warning hit me. There had been something wrong about Meyer. I backed away and he came in, moving in such a slow and uncertain way, it was as if he had forgotten how to walk. He wore a dull apologetic smile, and all the bright hot light had gone out of his little blue eyes.

The old man was right behind him, bent over, nodding, muttering to Meyer. A wattled old man with a naked polished skull, a soiled blue long-sleeved shirt, dark greasy pants, sneakers.

He urged Meyer in, slammed the door behind them with a flip of his elbow, and then, as he straightened to full height, he pushed Meyer roughly ahead of him. Meyer stumbled and nearly went down. I saw the weapon revealed, the one he had been holding against Meyer's back, four short ugly barrels of a large-caliber derringer. Grizzel stepped over to me and said, "Pull the front of that pretty yellow shirt up, Ace. Slow and easy."

With the four barrels aimed at my face, I didn't feel as if I even dared breathe. He lifted the pistol out of my belt with his left hand, squatted, and placed it on the floor, and with the edge of his foot he scuffed it into a corner without looking at it.

I glanced at Meyer. There was going to be no help there. It happens sometimes. I think it is the deep unwavering conviction that life is about to end. It is an ultimate fear, immobilizing, squalid. It crowds everything else out of the mind. There is no room for hope, no chance of being saved. I have seen it happen to some very good men, and most of them did indeed die badly and soon, and the ones who did not die were seldom the same again. Were a man to awaken from sound sleep to the dry-gourd rattle of a diamondback coiled on his chest, head big as a fist, forked tongue flickering, he would go into that dreadful numbness of the ultimate fright.

"You've changed," I said in a dry-mouthed voice.

"Sit on the floor!" Grizzel said to Meyer. Meyer sat so quickly and obediently he made a thick thudding sound. Grizzel kept his eyes on me. "Down a hundred pounds. Tried to hold at one ninety, but it wouldn't stop. Something in here, eating on me, Ace. Like fire and knives, all the time. That old fart trying to buy hash for his misery, I put him out of it, and now I got it myself. We got to find some nice quiet way to do you, Ace. Right in the middle of all these boats and folks. Maybe your best buddy in all the world can give me a little help with you."

"Why me?" I asked.

His eyes were the same. Nothing else. "Why not you? You and Joya fucked up the world for Peter K and yours truly. With Freaky Jean's help.

All my life you smartass people have been on top. It's my final sworn duty to bring you down, every one of you I can get to, and I have got to a lot so far."

"Including the Senator?"

"No time for confession hour. Wish I had time to tell you about the snuff job on that movie-queen pal of yours. Would have made a great tape, Ace." He motioned toward his crotch with his free hand. "Old King Henry here hasn't lost an ounce, and he can go as good as he ever did. Should have seen Jeanie's eyes too, when she saw who the hell it was she was talking to, who this skinny old man all bent over, with the whiny voice and limp, who he really was. Strong kid. Fought nice. That's when it's best, when you got a fighter."

"You get around pretty good, pretty quick."

"Stall, stall, stall. I don't think I'm going to get any help from your dearest closest buddy here, which is what everybody calls him. Peed his pants. I travel nice, Ace. Good luggage, good clothes, first class all the way. Money came mostly from country stores, where by the time you bust the second finger on them, they tell you what shelf the money is hid on, and it is more than you can imagine. Tried a bike, but the bones of my ass are too close to the surface. These are my working clothes, Ace. Harmless old saggy fart, shuffling around. Lots of wrinkles from the weight dropping off so fast."

His glance flicked away from me and back again, over and over, so quickly it gave me no chance at all. He was looking the interior over. "What I want you should do, Ace, is let yourself down very very slow and easy. Thaaaaat's it. Hitch a little bit more toward me. Now lay back nice and slow. Good boy."

He sidled into the galley, moving with the speed of an angular bug, and emerged instantly with one of my steak knives in his left hand. "You won't hardly feel this at all, Ace,"

He moved cautiously toward me. Beyond him I saw the padded cover of the stowage locker lift silently, and I saw Gavin stand up, right hand high, holding the throwing knife. I think Grizzel saw a reflection of the movement out of the corner of his eye in one of the lounge ports. And he was quick. My God, he was quick! He swiveled and fired, and the slam of the shot in that enclosed space was deafening. Gavin's grunt of effort came simultaneously with the shot. There was a silvery glint in the air, and Grizzel dropped with an eerie bony thud. He dropped loose, agawk, open eyes almost immediately dusty, without further breath or quiver, wearing the braided leather grip of the throwing knife in the crenelated socket of his throat, under the loose jowls. The slug had taken Gavin in the center of the chest, banged him back against the bulkhead, and from there he had rebounded to fall face down, heart shredded, toes still hooked over the edge of the locker.

Donnie squatted beside him and laid his fingers on Gavin's throat. "Goddamn," he whispered. "Oh, goddamn, goddamn, goddamn."

I could hear no running outside, no shouts of query, or noises of excitement. The muffled explosion had passed unnoticed.

Donnie placed my Colt carefully on the coffee table. He said, "Just hold tight, huh. I'll come back with the word."

Meyer and I were alone with the bodies. He looked up at me with the querulous expression of a child who cannot understand why it has been so punished. Tears ran down his face.

I helped him up and he looked down at Grizzel's corpse and walked woodenly to the head and closed the door quietly behind him. I heard the water running.

Donnie returned in a half hour. His eyes looked pink and irritated. In his slow and heavy voice he said, "What will happen, it will be a cleaning truck, maybe in three quarters of an hour, and the security will let them in here for a pickup, right? This carpeting is shot. Better you shouldn't try to get it cleaned. They will take it up and roll them up in it at the same time and horse them out to the truck, and you can forget it from then on. Any stains came through, they're your problem. Preach don't want no contact from you."

"What will they do with them?"

"Usually it's construction foundations where they go." He straightened and sighed. "Me, I got to tell his girl he had to go back home to Sydney, Australia, on a family emergency."

epilogue

ON AN August afternoon I worked the *Busted Flush* into a bayou ringed with mangrove down near the mouth of the Snake River, below Naples. There, like a mother spider, I began building my web of lines, finding good holding ground for anchors, tying off other lines to the sturdiest mangroves, and making allowance for big tides.

A medium hurricane named Carl was due to bash Cuba by midnight, on a course that would carry its diminished muscle up through the Straits of Yucatán. We would get some of the fringe of it, and if it curved back toward the Florida west coast, we might get a hell of a lot more of it than we wanted.

We had plenty of fresh water, fuel, and provisions, and Annie was excited and stimulated by the idea of sitting it out. The afternoon was hazy white, with high tendrils of unusual-looking clouds and some burly rain clouds out over the Gulf.

After she had helped me do everything I felt we could do to assure our safety, we went up onto the sun deck and sat under the canopy at the topside controls in the big captain's chairs where we could watch the weather.

Out of nowhere she said, "I still feel pretty strange about you getting yourself associated with people like that Preach."

"Who is associated?"

"How about through that Indian person, that Mits?"

"She owns the whole ball game now."

"But doesn't she give you money?"

"She tries hard."

"Doesn't it come from some kind of rotten source, like drugs?"

"Probably. Indirectly."

"Am I boring you?"

I turned and grinned at her. "Not most of the time."

"It's just that I want to be—"

"Respectable?"

"That's not the right word. It's not as stuffy a word as that."

"Independent?"

"Closer."

"That is something I have always been, Annie, and always will be. I steer through a pretty crowded track, and once in a while I brush up against a Preach, who wants to tame me by breaking my elbows, or a Dirty Bob, who wants to punish me by killing my friends. Okay, I have a lot of moves. Earnest apology. Happy sapistry. A good straight left hand when needed. They nearly had me quelled, kid. That was before all this with Esterland."

"Will you tell me all about it sometime?"

"Probably. They had the lid almost hammered down on me. But I couldn't take a life that flat. You know. Things have to move. Like, I lied to you about not being able to run away from the storm. We probably could have. But this is a better way."

"I know we could have. I checked the charts."

"I have a lot of trouble with bright women."

"You couldn't stand any other kind." She hesitated biting her lip "After the storm, are we going to hurry back to Lauderdale?"

"If you can call anything this crock can do hurrying."

"I think about Meyer."

"So do I. Look, he has to be alone for a time. Maybe it is long enough by now. I hope so. He failed his image of himself because I think he fashioned that image a little too closely to his image of me. I am more of a physical person than Meyer. He has too much imagination. That's what helps people break themselves. He didn't expect it. He's been in tighter spots. This time he saw something in the crazed, dying, evil eyes of that man. He saw his death there, and it sucked the heart right out of him. And he's ashamed, though he shouldn't be."

"Have you told him he shouldn't be?"

"Of course. I told him it can happen to anyone at any time, and I tried to tell him it had happened to me too. It almost did, once. But not quite. And I couldn't lie well enough to convince him."

"What will happen?"

"He'll want to get into something rough. He'll look for a chance to try to recover his self-respect. And it might be a very close play indeed to try to keep him from getting himself killed. He seeks that absolution, the end of shame. And that is a primitive reaction. Whatever it is, I am going to have to help hunt for the situation, and I am going to have to see that he gets away with whatever foolish move he makes."

"Then he'll be okay again?"

"Practically. Not quite. Because he knows it can happen."

A breeze came skitting into the bayou, silvering the black water. She lifted her face to it. "Hey! Feel that!" It faded away, and a mosquito sang into my ear. "Will we get a lot of wind?"

"Maybe."

"Will it turn into a constant shrieking like they say?"

"Maybe. But it is a roaring kind of shriek. Deeper than plain old shrieking."

"Could we maybe, while it's roaring or whatever, make love?"

"I will certainly see if I can arrange it, Annie. I will put some thought to it. I really will."